Eclipse

The Girl Who Saved the World

George Phillies

ISBN-13: 9781730762154

CONTENTS

ACKNOWLEDGEMENTS

For their comments on earlier drafts of the book, I must thank
Dani Zweig, Jean Lamb, Starshadow,
Jefferson Swycaffer, Cedar Sanderson,
and all the other good folks at the Worcester Writers Group.
Their suggestions were very helpful;
the remaining faults in the book are mine.
I must specifically thank Chris Nuttall for leading me
to cover artist Brad Fraunfelter.

Prologue

Meet Eclipse.

She's twelve. She's hardworking, bright, self-reliant, good with tools, vigorously physically fit, tough as nails, still young enough to disguise herself as a boy. She's also a persona: She flies, reads minds, and is not afraid of necessary violence.

She had a bit of a problem with her mom. Her mom threw her out of the house. Then Mom blew up the house and disappeared

Now she's procured the Holy Namestone, the Key to Paradise. And everyone in the world will be happy to kill her to get their hands on it.

Meet Trisha.

She's not quite a year older than Eclipse. She's friendly, considerate, really good in school, athletic, does more than her share around the house. She's also a persona. She has superspeed…an hour of housework in a minute. She flies, including from here to the next galaxy in an hour.

She also has a bit of a problem with her parents. They always treat her with complete contempt, totally grounded her, and won't say why.

Her brother and sister are personas, too. Year-younger sister Janie is a budding world chess and go champion. She also reads minds, sees distant events, and can kill with a glance. Her twin brother Brian is incredibly good with tools, builds fantastic models from scratch, has a nearly unbreakable force field, and summons plasma beams that cut battleships in half.

Eclipse is Volume 1 of the This Shining Sea series. Volume 2, Airy Castles All Ablaze, will be a major rewrite of my much older novel This Shining Sea. There will be a Volume 3, Of Breaking Waves, because Eclipse still needs to save Spindrift from having died.

Flashforward

The Invisible Fortress
Evening

I woke up at half past dark. To put it mildly, I hurt. If there were any places where I didn't hurt, I couldn't find them. Most girls of my twelve years, hurting this much, would have laid there crying for their mommies. For me, of course, crying for help where anyone could hear me would be worse than useless. It would get me killed. Yes, I was doing mind control on myself. My pain nerves screamed their agony, but thanks to mind control I only heard them as distant murmurs. Mind control meant I could sleep. I still knew I hurt. A lot. 'Hurt a lot' was still infinitely better than the alternative, which involved being seriously dead.

I wondered confusedly what had happened. I was lying in bed, not in my normal sleeping position. The room was dark. For minutes I was too dazed to think clearly. I peered over my bedsheet and quilt …I was in my own bedroom. Beyond the glass wall separating me from my balcony, the silent stars glittered in a cloudless night sky. If I waited long enough, I'd see the stars sink one by one into the pitch-black hills of the coastal range. The shadows on the wall were my collection of Captain Infinity Atomic Soaker pistols, ultrasoakers, except the one pistol that very definitely did not project water.

Suddenly I remembered. Atlanticea. It was the most wonderful memory in the world…or would have been if I didn't hurt so much. I'd threaded the Maze, the Maze that defeated Julius Caesar and Jackie Fisher and Spearthrower Owl and the French Imperial Guard. I'd reached the Tomb and matched wits with the Martyr himself. He'd given me that palm-size sphere of crystalline sky, the Namestone, the Key to the Earthly Paradise. No one else in history had ever come close to capturing it. I'd done it! The Namestone was the birthday present I'd given to myself, a couple months late for my twelfth birthday. It was almost as good a birthday present as my two ponies. Snapdragon and Daffodil are better. I gave them to me, too.

On the bright side, when I grabbed the Namestone my chances of living another six hours moved up from zero. Death…That's the penalty for not solving the Maze. On the less bright side, when I grabbed the Namestone my reward was a big list of people who want to kill me.

Thanks to the Maze, I am seriously wrecked up. Credit for some wrecking up goes to the League of Nations, and to a Lord of Eternity. They'd both made a maximum effort to kill me, just to get their hands on the Namestone. They almost succeeded. Almost, not quite, but 'almost' only counts in horseshoes, and with hand grenades.

No matter how tired I felt, I called very slightly on my gifts. The null links to my pets were quiet. Two ponies slumbered in their barn. Two cats cuddled together dreamily in the loft above. Anything else was very small, or very far away. Perception? The only thing I worried about was the Namestone. There it was in my den, almost impossible for me to find behind its quarter inch of impervium shielding. And I knew exactly where to look. No one else would ever find it. The Namestone. I have it. Not the League of Nations. Not the Lords of Eternity. Me. Eclipse! I have the Namestone. In my home! It's mine, all mine!

The healing matrix was fixing me, but…oh right, healing matrix. I should have remembered that already. I said I'm a bit dazed, didn't I? I summoned the glyph for Medico, its associated rules engine. Nothing in violet. Nothing was killing me despite the matrix. Of course, the matrix is supposed to drag me conscious if I am dying, and it hadn't. Nothing blue, long-term near-death threat. Red warnings? Let's see. Three broken ribs, stitched by telekinesis. That's why I was on my back, the lousy sleeping position Medico told me to use. My right shoulder? Nothing broken, but bits of force field are holding things where they belong while the matrix forces repairs. Internal bleeding from high-impact collisions? Cured. Gold - a black eye, a few bone bruises, but I've been here before, just not so many ways at the same time. Green – slices, scrapes, abrasions -- my skin is being returned to perfection as I lie here. My face was cleaned up by the Namestone before I faced the Martyr, but the rest of me was my problem. My healing matrix is fixing everything, way faster than I'd heal naturally. I still need a couple weeks to recover.

Home! That's the keyword. I'm home and safe. I dropped my mind out-of-body. Astral projection is decidedly not my strongest gift, but I can pull it off. If I am very careful. Actually, the preset didn't give me any choice. Some time back I did mind control on myself, so that whenever I was in a serious fight, escaped, and got back home safe, I would go out-of-body, whether I wanted to or not. If someone planted mind controls on me, I probably break them when I leave my body behind. I stepped out from my body. The preset grabbed my gifts and ran a scan, fast as thought, to see what trojans might be lurking in my mind-space. Yes, the scan runs at the speed of thought, but it has a lot of mind to scan. Meanwhile, I hovered above my body, looking into my momentarily sightless silver-gray eyes and platinum-white eyelashes, listening to me breathe, ever so slowly.

Done. Control of my mind returned to me. There is a way to break the mind control, if things go wrong, but everything went the way it was supposed to. Mum had been careful about showing me exactly how to arrange that preset, because seven ways from Sunday doing mind control on yourself is dangerous. I dropped my mind back into my body, wiggled fingers and toes, and blinked twice. Everything worked.

Gifts? Just before I left Atlanticea I'd pushed my gifts way deep, much deeper than I'd expected to need them, driving my shields toward their ultimate limits. Now I shouldn't even consider calling any of my gifts. Not flight. Not teleportation. Not any of the neat ways I can seriously wreck things. Not force field – yes, there's a low-level screen tacking my ribs together. I could go way deep into my gifts right now, if I absolutely had to, but if I did, I'm going to hurt myself.

My memories took me back to Atlanticea. The Martyr gave me the Namestone. I climbed the Outer Stairs, out of the Maze into the waking world. Ahead of me, wisps of cloud were incandescent white against a cerulean sky. I was sufficiently wrecked up that climbing those stairs was incredibly demanding. After each step, I half-felt ready to quit. Before I did the Maze, I had zerolined all of my gifts, flat as possible. Under the rules, while in the Maze, any gift I called, the Maze could call at three times the power. That was its rule. Curiously, three times zero is zero. I did not give the Maze any advantages.

While I climbed the stairs, I desperately tried to re-open my power levels. I could barely touch The Sky. After a moment of terror, The Sky opened. With The Sky powering my gifts, my force field would stop a determined punch. I could fly somewhat faster than I could walk. With an effort that left me dizzy and gasping for breath I managed to reach down to The Breaking Wave. With The Breaking Wave powering my gifts, I could fly faster than most sports cars. I am not embarrassed to say that the first gift that I called was mind control, to suppress pain. Just before I sliced the last fellow open from guggle to zatch, he gut-punched me. Hard. After my next step I managed to find life support. With broken ribs, it hurt to breathe. Once I didn't need to breathe, I could focus. I remembered to summon the Medico rules engine. It would have been truly stupid to bleed to death after I got my hands on the Namestone. Medico reported that I was not dying, not even close. Mayhaps the Namestone would have protected me until I finished climbing the Outer Stairs. I didn't count on it.

I kept reaching for more power levels, further and further down. They came more and more easily. The Sea of Grass, The Temple, The Sun, and The Matrix opened up. Each time I reached a deeper level, my access to my higher, weaker levels broadened. Now, with the Sky powering my force fields, I was probably bullet proof. OK, I did not forget to call my shields. I might have a reception committee, someone who thought it was easier to steal the Namestone from me than from the Maze. Before I reached the top of the Stairs, I was sort of back to normal. I could touch all the power levels I can usually reach. I just couldn't tap them for very much. Not yet. Not without taking a lot more damage. I could go way deep into my gifts if I had to. I hoped I didn't.

At the top of the Outer Stairs I had company. Waiting for me were Valkyria, the super-heavy combatant of the League of Nations Elite Strike Team, and the Screaming Skull, himself. Alas, they weren't fighting each other, so I couldn't smile once, duck twice, and flee their island paradise.

"Where is she, little girl? Where is the bearer of the Holy Namestone? I'm here to take it for the League!" That was Valkyria, shouting at me. Valkyria? Six feet tall, impervium-plated battle armor, heavy duty body field, not to mention a flaming sword that was mostly a special effect shrouding a pointblank range plasma attack. Yes, there is also an endarium blade inside the flames. Her explosive throwing katana remained in its scabbard, over her back where her other arm could reach it. There is a tradition of people in plate mail being idiots. At the moment Valkyria was living up to the tradition. Her long blonde hair fluttered in the ocean breeze. Bad form. Mum always said Valkyria should wear her hair short or mound it under a helmet, failing which someone would grab it and spin her head over heels into the ground.

I suppose I shouldn't've been surprised. For thousands of years the Namestone has been the Key to Heaven, the artifact that will transform the World into the Millennial Kingdom. All you needed to do in order to use the Key was to get your hands on it. That was easier said than done. To take the Namestone, you had to solve the Maze. Vast numbers of people have tried and failed, with fatal consequences for them. The League of Nations has passed decree after decree claiming the Namestone for themselves, just so soon as someone else does their work for them and removes it from the Maze. Now I had the Namestone, so they wanted it. I'd removed it from the Maze, so they were going to give me a chance to hand it over voluntarily. Their idea of 'voluntary' is a bit strained.

Valkyria must have thought I'd be intimidated when she shouted at me. Sorry, but I just did the Maze. Next to the solid shadows, Valkyria did not impress. I was a bit miffed. OK, she does have three-quarters of a foot on me, but 'little girl' is not the nicest imaginable greeting. True or not, 'Little girl' is rude. Valkyria should have been less threatening. After all, I was carrying the most powerful artifact in the world. I still needed a few minutes before I could teleport out. I had to play for time.

I did a crash drop, calling all the power I could find. Crash drops into bottom levels are seriously bad for the health. For a moment, Medico flashed blue-shading-toward-violet warning glyphs at me. I was approaching killing myself by overloading. I shoved all the power I could find into my shields. I really wanted to teleport away. Teleport is a lifesaving gift, as good a gift as flight, but teleporting far enough to avoid a chase needed a lot of power, more than I could call just yet. Yes, I could have switched power from shields to teleport, and jumped out. The moment I shifted the power out of my shields, they would have faded, enough that I'd surely have been toast before I could disappear.

"I'm twenty feet in front of you," I answered. After it was too late, it occurred to me to answer 'she's twenty feet behind me, but I have to leave before she can come up here'. Oh, well. I never expected that question.

"Aren't you … isn't the real Bearer taller?" Valkyria asked. She sounded confused.

I glowered. OK, I'm not into my teen growth spurt yet, an event I don't yet see how to avoid, though I'm looking, but it's not as if I didn't pass five feet last year. "I am tall," I answered. That's when I ran out of patience. Valkyria hadn't even been civil to me. She might at least have congratulated me on walking the Maze. If she wanted to insult me, there's no reason I couldn't return the favor. "Wait!" I continued. "Who are you? Isn't the real Valkyria a bit less pudgy? I mean, how do they manage to squeeze you into that armor?" Her nostrils flared. I guess she's sensitive about her weight.

"You!" Valkyria shouted. "Inform the Bearer. She must hand the Holy Namestone over to League of Nations. At once! As fast as possible! Immediately! That is a direct order! From The League of Nations!" I could hear her Prussian mindset without reading her mind. Unless something had gone very wrong, the whole world had watched me do the Maze. Valkyria should have recognized me.

"I am the Bearer. If you wanted the Namestone, you should have walked the Maze first and taken it," I answered. I called my gifts as fast as possible, reinforcing my shields, but when you start at absolute zero this takes a while. I confess I was getting a bit nervous that the Screaming Skull was standing there, politely not saying anything. No, we haven't met, but when your mother is a persona, you tend to inherit bits of her gift fine structure, enough that he'd eventually figure out whose daughter I am. That would for sure not be good.

"Give it to me! Now! The League has decreed: The Namestone is the property of the world," she demanded.

"Give it to you? You and which army?" I asked. I yawned. That was an act. I should have been more polite. In my own defense, I was thoroughly exhausted, not to mention I'd taken major body damage during the hand-to-hand combat segments. I expected congratulations, not threats. After all, people have been trying to thread the Lesser Maze for three thousand years, with no success. I'd done it. Old English proverb: Battles are events between inadequate opportunities for rest. I wasn't resting. I was powering up my gifts as fast as possible. It was even money whether I'd power up fast enough to escape, or whether I beat the Maze and lost to my welcoming committee. Some people my age would have been terrified. I was too busy, not to mention too tired, to be frightened.

"This one?" She waved her fingers. What had to be the whole League of Nations Elite Strike Force teleported in at her back. There were several dozen of them, not that I counted them carefully. Mind you, I don't know who most of them are, other than really tackily dressed, not at all like my highly stylish and tasteful garb, but the Strike Force is respectably powerful. The Strike Force began to spread, left and right.

"That's far enough," I announced. They kept spreading.

It's a very special gesture with hand and wrist. My palm ends up facing skyward, the Namestone a cerulean flame a few inches above, Namestone's tuneless tune being heard distantly in every ear. Yes, I did remember to cue my body aura, not to mention my personal theme music, a bold brass opening folding into the richer tones of the flugelhorn. No, I can still call on Namestone's power even if I can't move. Nor do I need the music or aura to call on all my gifts. My aura actually is the same blue as the Namestone's glow. My platinum blonde hair and pale gray garb look really well with it.

"Behold the Holy Namestone. Come no closer or face my wrath." Mum taught me how to sound truly pompous. To my surprise, it worked. Europalord did not quite fall on his fat face when he tripped over his own feet. Of course, he is a drain, so personal combat training is not quite the issue it is with his team-mates. His task is to sit there and suck power out of his opponents, incidentally shoving it all into his personal force field. "The Namestone is mine," I reminded them.

"You're defying the League!" Valkyria shouted. "International law specifies: The League of Nations owns the Namestone. Hand it over, you stupid girl!" In retrospect, she might have done better if she'd been a bit more tactful. She could hardly have done worse.

"You know the Maze Rule: Namestone belongs to he who takes it. I took it," I said.

"No, it belongs to the League!" she screamed.

"You keep repeating that same wrong statement. I just told you: I took it. It's mine! Are you deaf, or just stupid? Or maybe both; you're for sure stupid." I answered. By now I was in a really sour mood. I wanted to go home and go to bed. And, very soon, I would have broadened my call on enough levels of power to do just that. I could feel teleport blocks in place around me, meaning I was going to need a lot of power to smash them into little pieces. No, I do not feel guilty about what would happen to the people and machines creating those blocks when I did the smashing. Meanwhile, Valkyria is said to be short-tempered. People who are busy losing their tempers for sure aren't thinking clearly, a positive outcome for me. Well, a positive outcome, except I was in the process of losing my own temper.

"The Namestone is too dangerous for mortals," the Screaming Skull announced. "Give it to me, or it is you who will face my wrath."

"You're supposed to be an improvement over her, fatso?" I snapped. I could have been more polite to the Screaming Skull, but exhaustion makes me impatient. Besides, the Skull is a (whole bunch of words Mum would not like to hear me use) egomaniac with delusions of adequacy. Unfortunately, the

Skull is also really good at telling people to drop dead, and having it happen. I did not quite use any of those words Mum did not like, though I was tempted. Insulting him might cause him to think even less than he usually does, assuming that is possible.

"Team! The Namestone is indestructible! Kill her!" Valkyria shouted. Oh, dear, I thought, not to mention several other words Mum would not have approved of my using, Valkyria is even more short-tempered than rumored. She could readily have drawn out this conversation for some time yet, say until I felt comfortable about teleporting away. No such luck. Valkyria tossed her explosive throwing katana. Her katana's explosion packs the power density of a starcore weapon. Her team launched a totally bizarre mixture of high power attacks. Not one of her team-mates seemed to notice that if they killed me I would drop the Namestone, which would then roll back down the Stairs into the Maze, there to be returned to the Martyr. Mayhaps Valkyria counted on the explosion from her throwing sword to blast the Namestone free.

I'd forgotten the Screaming Skull, even though I had just told him off. Over-focus is very dangerous in combat, but at this point I was outnumbered close to twenty to one. I'd paid too much attention to Valkyria, and paid no attention to the Skull, even after he threatened me. He used the moment to launch his most deadly attack, the Shower of Total Death. Being attacked by the League of Nations Elite Team was bad news, but the Skull is a Lord of Eternity. His attack? It works on people, it works on a tree, and now I'll see if it works on me. I've actually never been positive my second level shields do anything. It's not as if there are a lot of second level attacks wandering around to test them against

My scramble for more and more power levels worked. Barely. My shields did everything needed. Then Valkyria's katana hit me. Of course, I've seen starcore energy densities before, real ones, and my shields worked just fine that time, too. It's just I was very tired, the gifts being used against me were incredibly powerful, and I had to go truly deep to hold my defenses against all of them at the same time. I didn't quite fall over, but the world was getting a bit gray. Medico flashed a warning, blue shading farther into violet. My reception committee was coming too close to killing me through my own shields, assuming I didn't kill myself first with the crash drop I had just made. For half an instant, the Skull looked surprised. He could tell: I was not drawing on the Namestone. He'd tried to kill me, and my personal defenses were good enough to stop his (several other words that would not meet with Mum's approval) attack in its tracks.

I really wanted to grab Valkyria's broadsword. Using it to give her a straighter backbone sounded really appealing. Kicking her face also sounded attractive. Alas, if I continued to fight, they got to do the same. Besides, she was wearing armor. Here and now was not a favorable battlefield. I did not give them a second chance. I was down through enough levels to hold all my shields, keep slack, shatter the teleport blocks, and teleport. I flicked my wrist back. Namestone vanished. I smashed the blocks and teleported out, far far away, all the way to the Dark Side of the Moon, then a half dozen fast jumps, one triple cycle loop, and finally a pause in case someone was following me. I'd ended someplace that looks like it could be my base. It isn't, but it looks really basey. Base-like? Basious? OK, it looks like a high-power persona base.

Pursuers who could track my teleports, a truly rare gift, would see I had stopped moving and charge after me. I hadn't hurt any of them yet, but if someone followed my jumps they'd learn how good I am at wrecking things. That's very good at wrecking things. Wrecking pursuers, in particular. I waited until the teleport traces faded away. There were no pursuers. Fortunately, teleport traces do not fade by becoming ever fainter, so you don't have to wonder if someone with really, really good tracking gifts can follow you. Teleport traces chug along and then stop dead, gone forever. A few more jumps brought me to the second-floor study in my very own house. I don't remember what I did next. I must have dropped the Namestone into its hiding place, stripped off my garb, and fallen into bed, because here I am, lying under my quilt, looking up at the stars.

One of the times when I woke up, the healing matrix prompted me to ramp down my mind control, so the matrix could tell exactly where I'd been injured. I overdid it. I cut the mind control off. Pain swallowed me. I burst into sobs and uncontrollable tears. The healing matrix kept me from going into shock. After a few minutes I remembered I could ramp control back up. By then I was soaked in sweat.

That brought me to the here and now. I was incredibly thirsty. Stomach said a solid meal was in order. I rolled out of bed, every muscle complaining. The floor was beautifully finished silken-smooth hardwood, chill beneath my bare feet. I padded to my bathroom for a glass of water. I was more than a bit cold, but water was definitely the first priority. I remembered to check the bathroom scale. I'd lost weight. A fair piece of weight, remembering that I'm all of five-foot-three and muscular-slim in bare feet.

A night light threw a feeble shadow up the stairs. I dropped into my down bathrobe, shoulder and ribs protesting at the motion, and headed to the kitchen. Down bathrobe? I'd left the heat pump at low, keeping the house temperature in the mid-50s, enough to keep the pipes from freezing.

Yes, I have some neat photographs of the Pluto ruins, taken with me and camera inside my body field, but right now my gifts were very definitely turned off. The robe kept me warm, or I'd be cold indeed. Climbing down the stairs was painful. I held firmly to the railing, taking some of the weight off my knees. Besides hand-to-hand combat, the Maze set other physical and mental challenges, enough to push me to all my limits. Mum had taught me to be thoughtful and physically vigorous, but endurance and weight training only take you so far.

The oven clock said my half past dark was in fact just one hour past sunset. The oven light was more than enough, especially when I knew exactly where everything was stashed. Sunset? I must have slept the day around. No, I'd woken up once and again for a glass of water.

I'd had the foresight to cook in advance. Cold chicken fresh off the bone, soda biscuits with unsalted butter, stir-fry curried vegetables warmed in the microwave, more chicken and soda biscuits, milk, sliced plum tomatoes, and finally rum raisin ice cream with chocolate fudge crumbles did just fine.

Soon I was going to go back to sleep. The healing matrix said not-quite-dawn as my drift from slumber moment. Was there anything I really had to do first? The very slightest bit of telepathy, no matter how dizzy it left me, confirmed ponies and barn-cats were all safe. I already knew that, but I wasn't thinking clearly enough to realize I'd checked once that my pets were well. The ponies would want currycombing tomorrow. Dishes were rinsed and in the dishwasher. Counters were bare. I dragged myself up my stairs.

My garb? It was in the closet, absolutely clean, not a stitch out of place. Clean? After what happened to me? That must have been the Namestone, insisting that the Bearer always looks perfect. In fact, when I met Valkyria, my garb had been immaculate, down to the flawless drape of my cape. I'd remembered to flare the cape so the video audience could see my sigil, the moon occulting the sun.

Namestone? Safe in its hidey-hole. Anything else? Rules engines, your opinions? The usual warning is that you can carry one rules engine 'Marksman on how to shoot', or if you're really good a second 'Medico on how to use your healing matrix', but if you try carrying four rules engines you go bats. Mum taught me how to break that limit. I'm a working demonstration. I have like fifty of them floating around, actually not inside my head where they'd cause problems, all being called at once. My rules engines all had something they wanted to tell me, but mostly they cancelled. The ones on buying and running a house were pretty calm. The emergency priority flag rose above 'Psychist – going bats for fun and profit'. The Lesser Maze was too much for almost anyone. I was building up pressure again about Mum.

Everything I now had, I'd earned for myself. From Mum, the Maze, and aftermath I'd learned the most important lesson there can be: Never trust anyone. Not ever! Not anyone! For a moment bitter tears overwhelmed me. I washed my face, noticed I was getting cold from standing in bare feet, and went to bed. Curled up under my quilt, I drifted off, to sleep, perchance to dream.

Flashback

Kniaz Kang's Shanghai Marco Polo
North Cosmopolis, Washington

The sign in the parking lot announced:
Kniaz Kang's Shanghai Marco Polo.
Featuring the finest in Chinese, Italian, and Russian Cuisines.
Invented Here -- General Tso's Pizza!
Invented Here -- Il Professore's Dessert Pizza!

It was 7:30 in the morning. The sun barely glowed over the North Cosmopolis horizon, even at a restaurant atop a hill. Inside, Kniaz Kang himself -- a man who was not a prince and whose name was not actually Kang -- supervised the morning help in readying his restaurant for another day. The front rooms were filled with his regulars, early risers, and high school students from the Atomic Tech branch across the street, all enjoying his superb breakfasts. After all, hash, egg rolls, borscht, and pizza are in large part based on chopping many things very finely, a skill that his employees denied was a gift. Kang turned to considering his customers and their wants.

In the morning he served high school students, and some of their teachers, though not in the same room. The isolated corner window was always reserved for the Gang of Three or So. Teranike did not discuss being what Kang knew she was, namely a Polarian from Otherearth stranded when her Empress closed the WorldGate. Teranike had taken a room upstairs, did heavy physical work for the restaurant with no complaint or sign of fatigue, and did not emphasize what she had in her suitcases. She happily ate whatever was set in front of her, but who could fault her love of General Tso's pizza, not to mention Il Professore's dessert pizza--double fudge. After all, those were the house specialties.

Dorothy Elizabeth Schumacher was North Cosmopolis's best-known open persona. She had not planned to be open. However, when the assassin from the League of Terran Justice walked up to the front entrance of her private high school, screamed "Down with Private Education", and started shooting up student automobiles, Dorothy had done what any persona should. She put up her force field, ran directly in front of the agent thus taking some dozens of rounds square in the chest, and flying -- literally -- tackled the loon into a wall. Hard. She was unhurt. The loon ended in a prison hospital. Dorothy confessed to being the known public persona Silk, until then most noted for having rescued dogs, small children, and a moose from various not-quite-frozen ponds.

It was not until last year, early December, that the Greater Cosmopolis Seance and Channeling Society put Dorothy on the national news. The Society had decided to channel the greatest motion picture actor in the history of Oregon. They expected to speak to Stanford Smith, who twenty centuries ago had made more than two hundred westerns and gone on to be Grand Tradesmaster of All Sarnath. The Society's survivors were not quite clear on what had gone wrong. They obtained a physical materialization, not the expected disembodied voice. The materialization was a two hundred yard tall reptile with radioactive flame breath. It waddled majestically toward the outskirts of North Cosmopolis, incinerating everything in its path. The first three persona teams that tried to stop it were flattened.

Silk appeared on the scene. Only if you looked very carefully, Kang recalled, would you observe that she was now wearing a force field bracer. Any number of people noticed that she was armed not with her usual Ruggels 0.60 pistol but with a Krell disruptor. The flame breath had no effect on her. Her first shot took down the creature, who reverted into the Society's Occult Master. Asked why she hadn't mentioned having the extremely rare and powerful Krell weapon, she said that she hadn't had it. The now very ex-boyfriend had lent it to her. He had it back. They'd agreed, when they broke up, that they would forget each other. An unnamed mentalist had ensured that she had no remaining memories of him. The boyfriend was not the ex who had, for a while, shared breakfast with her. No one knew who he was.

The usual third at her table was the seventh-grade boy who, if pressed, announced he was Silk's heroic side-kick Jim, he who protected her from truly dangerous villains. Jim had his trusty slingshot for that. He confessed that he never carried his slingshot. Someone could get hurt. Today Jim was missing in action.

Kang had gone no further in reviewing his customers and what new dishes he could inveigle them into trying when the doors slammed inward. Running through them at top speed was Kang's number-two man, Wang the Imperturbable.

"Lord Kang! Lord Kang!" Wang shouted in Mandarin. "The Sun! The Sun! It rises with a central eclipse!"

Kang tapped the computer screen above his chopping block. 'Central Eclipse' had an unfortunate implication, at least if you wished that people did not try that insanely dangerous stunt that always killed them, and sometimes killed large numbers of their minions. Headlines scrolled across the screen. There was much news, but the astral omen was not yet reported. He tapped the screen again. The All-Continent News Network was usually fast off the start. There was the ACNN "Special News Bulletin" warning. The text alternated every few seconds between orange lettering on a blue field and violet lettering on a yellow field, colors reserved for the most serious emergencies.

A half dozen split-screens came up. There was the sun, blinding white, a black disc covering its middle. As Kang watched the disc grew wider and wider. In a few minutes the central eclipse would block all sight of the sun everywhere on earth. Voices from different video bands spoke. "First seen ten minutes ago in London... Observers in Athens heard celestial trumpets... Moscow reports the sky has turned imperial purple... We now join PNN reporter Vera Durand. Where are you, Vera?"

"This is Vera Durand with the Persona News Network." Her voice was sharp and clear. Behind her were jagged rocks and a smooth marble terrace. Centered on the terrace was a staircase, leading down. "I am now broadcasting from Atlanticea. The dull roar you hear behind me are breaking waves. Once again, Atlanticea has been raised from the ocean by the power of the Holy Namestone. Not one hour ago, a figure appeared above the entrance to the Lesser Maze. She announced she was challenging for possession of the Namestone. The island promptly rose to greet her – yes, the Martyr has indicated that the challenger is a 'person of the female persuasion'. She has already entered the Maze. All-band video broadcasting of the contest by the Namestone itself will begin momentarily."

"Vera, who is the challenger?" ACNN lead announcer Richard Markovian asked.

"We don't know, Richard," Durand answered calmly. "The Martyr only revealed her gender. I caught a glimpse of her. We have this very short take." Across the video screen flashed a figure. From behind, the figure was pale-haired and pale-skinned, seemingly short, and boyish in her build. "There were rumors that the League of Nations Elite Strike Team was going to try, soon, to recover the Namestone, but the solitary figure who entered the Maze is not a League Operative. The Namestone translocated me here before she entered. I had no interview with her. I don't know why the Maze deemed her qualified to challenge."

Kang returned to his chopping, the thump of his cleaver pausing only when he gave instructions to his assistants. "Benito, just keep making pizza shells. We're going to have a huge business today. Nikolai, that cabbage was a bit mature; steam it an extra ten minutes. Wang, lower the sports video screens. Almost everyone will want to watch. Oh, there's the announcement, Governor Molnar is cancelling public school sessions; 'After all, the kids will be paying absolutely no attention'. Schools stay open so children have a place to be if parents are working. Charles, put that announcement 'All Public Schools No Classes Today' up on the Big Sign."

There was a gentle tap on the counter. Kang looked over his cash register.

Dorothy Schumacher smiled back at him.

"You looked distracted," she said. "Is something wrong? Three takeout giant caramel chip cookies, please?"

"Ah, Miss Schumacher. The usual breakfast, the usual extra. You haven't heard? Some woman is trying to do the Maze. You didn't know in advance?" Kang asked. "Or will you be the next challenger?" She was a fine young woman, he thought, one who uses her gifts well and precisely.

"Me?" Dorothy giggled. "Challenge the Maze for the Namestone? Thanks, but I like being alive. I just have a few gifts. If I flew to Atlantis, the Martyr wouldn't give me the time of day. You want gossip about the challenger, ask the people who take your private classes." Kang lectured several evenings a week, she knew, on the hidden energies that underlay all gifts. His large classes appeared on video screens across America. He also gave entirely private classes to select students, many of whom were on their national persona teams, and some of whom were said to be wanted by members of those persona teams. Registration lists for private classes were well-kept secrets. "Atomic Tech might have no classes. Then I'm going to Tech's library to study. As always, breakfast was excellent."

"Miss Schumacher, you are a woman of iron will," Kang continued. "There hasn't been a real challenge since that chess player, 50 years ago. You aren't going to watch?"

"Kniaz Kang, whoever it is," Dorothy said, "she is going to be degraded, hideously wounded, shredded, and in the end beaten to death and blown to pieces. Unless the solid shadows eat her. I couldn't stand to watch. I'm not afraid of doing something dangerous, if it's gift-true, but watching someone die—I can't face that."

"I can't, either," Kang answered. "Which is why I am not facing a video screen, and why there is no sound behind this counter. The contest will be over this afternoon, if not sooner. At three o'clock there will be bright sunlight everywhere in the world as the Maze marks its newest prey. Then I can watch the news again."

The sports screens now showed the Namestone's video broadcast of the challenger, someplace in the Maze. The view was always from behind. The challenger's hair hid under a stocking cap, with strands of yellow gold peaking from underneath. She wore a long-sleeved blouse and long trousers tucked into her boots. Her garb was an off-white, tight enough to show solid shoulders, a tight waist, and wider hips. Her face was never seen. Very briefly, she had passed by a wall whose stone blocks had a historically-known height. The challenger was close to six feet tall. Kang was puzzled. This woman did not look like the challenger Durand's cameraman had filmed. She was too tall. Her hair was too yellow. Her build was not so boyish. Were there two challengers? Or had the Maze somehow tricked the cameraman? The Maze was notorious for doing such things.

~~~~~
~~~~~

Early afternoon. Kang stood in his restaurant, intervening as need be to maintain the flow of food and drink to his customers. He'd opened both kitchens, called in all the cooks and part-timers, but keeping ahead of the take-out and delivery crowd had been a struggle. All that time, he never looked at a video screen. Someplace out in the Atlantic, someone was about to die, horribly, pursuing a hopeless quest older than history. Kang couldn't hide from his windows, though, windows that were brighter when the defenders of the Maze did well, dimmer when the challenger advanced. The same was true all around the world.

Suddenly all went black outside. He couldn't resist glancing at the news feed. "Bangkok - sky is pitch black. Rio de Janeiro - the sun just went out. Imperial Vienna - only street lights illuminate the Ringstrasse. This is Vera Durand on Atlantis. It's a planetary total eclipse. Not three minutes ago, the challenger was losing in hand-to-hand combat. She was grappled and unable to break free. Suddenly everything went dark."

"Vera," Richard Markovian said, "The Maze must have won. Where is the Sun?"

"Here on Atlantis, even the stars have gone dark." Durand's cameraman panned across the terrace. "You see me because my trusty cameraman has his own lamp. Wait, I'm getting video from the Maze again."

Kang stared at the screen, unable to help himself. All activity in the kitchen ground to a stop. The screens showed a long, grey marble corridor, illumined by two rows of unblinking cressets, flames that burned without pause or flicker. A figure could be seen limping away from the camera, whatever the Maze used for cameras, toward an open door. Who was it? What was going on? By now the Maze must have killed the challenger, but that was surely the challenger, if barely on her feet. Kang held his breath.

The figure crossed the threshold. Instantly, the room beyond was flooded with sunlight, sunlight visible nowhere else in the world. The point of view shifted.

The challenger stood in the Tomb of the Martyr, the final resting place of the man who had brought the Namestone to Earth. There was the Martyr himself, lying in state atop his sarcophagus, hands crossed, his corpse unchanged over the thousands of years he had waited. Above his fingers floated a glowing sphere of crystalline sky, the brightest of royal blues. He held the Namestone, The Artifact That Grants Every Wish, The Key to Paradise.

The challenger walked slowly across the polished stone floor. She was indeed a woman, Kang decided, very slim, but decidedly not boyish in her build. Her garb was torn and stained with blood. She'd lost the stocking cap in a fight. Sweat plastered her hair to her scalp. When she approached the Martyr, stains and rends in her garb's fabric disappeared. Her hair fluffed out, revealing short, perfectly cut golden curls. Down from the ceiling floated a pale grey cape. It folded over her shoulders, draping perfectly, its fall extending almost to her ankles. She reached down and tugged at the cloth. The cape flared, revealing a sigil, a solid circle overlapping a sun in glory. Kang had a near-perfect photographic memory. The challenger's sigil, indeed any sigil including even a part of Lord of Eternity Solara's sun-in-glory sigil, he had never seen.

She reached the Martyr. "I am here," she announced. Her voice, Kang thought, was an upper soprano, its tones brilliantly clear. "I have read *The Copper Book of Harvest Stars* and obeyed its mandates. I'm here for the Namestone."

"Are you here to take the Holy Namestone, the Key to Paradise?" The voice came from everywhere and nowhere.

"I am here to ask you for the Namestone, if I'm worthy. So speaks the *Copper Book*," she answered.

"Speak your name," the voice commanded.

"Eclipse is my persona. I am glory herself."

"Then reach out, Eclipse, and take the Namestone."

Eclipse cleared her throat. Someday, Kang thought, her children will cower in terror at that sound. The restaurant was dead silent. Every conversation had stopped. Diners sat, forks paused in mid-air, staring at the video screens.

"Then reach out, Eclipse, and I will give you the Namestone," the Martyr announced.

Eclipse leaned forward. The Namestone rolled from the space above the Martyr's hands into Eclipse's. The Martyr lay back, his hands now clasped together.

Cheers from the restaurant audience were deafening. Even the oldest patrons would not have watched Jackie Fisher and the combined Grand Fleets being sunk, the last time a serious effort had been made to recover the stone, but most had seen that defeat from period motion pictures. The chess player who fifty years ago had won three games, then quit while ahead three to zero, was viewed as exhibiting another of his fabled eccentricities. For this day, mankind had waited thousands of years.

Beyond the Sarcophagus were stairs leading up. Eclipse began a slow climb out of the Maze.

The sky outside the restaurant burst into bright daylight. Video split screens showed the same all around the world. From a total planetary eclipse, now there was total planetary daylight.

"This is Vera Durand on Atlantis." Durand spoke without hesitation. "It's suddenly full daylight again. It's bright, the sky is blue from horizon to horizon, but there is no sun in the sky. I'm standing on a ledge close to the Grand Exit, waiting for Eclipse to appear. I'll do my best to get an interview."

A slight popping noise came in the distance. Twenty feet in front of the stairs, a tall, blonde woman wearing plate mail and holding a flaming sword now stood. "Richard," Durand said, "that's unmistakably Valkyria, lead persona of the League of Nations Peace Enforcers. I must be surrounded by her invisible teammates. Valkyria? Would you care to tell the audience how you feel at this historic moment?"

Valkyria ignored Durand. Her eyes remained fixed on the stairs, where Eclipse was about to appear. Kang wondered what Valkyria was thinking, but her helmet hid her face. There came the faintest sound of tearing cloth. Standing twenty feet to the side of the stairs was a short, solidly-built man dressed entirely in black: Black boots, black trousers and belt, black shirt and vest, and broad-brimmed, floppy, solid-black straw hat. His face was locked in a deep frown.

"Now a Lord of Eternity is here. That's the Screaming Skull himself," Vera said, not that any of her viewers did not already know.

A figure came up the stairs from the Tomb. Her hair was as golden as Valkyria's. From the new camera angle, there could be absolutely no doubt that the figure was a tall young woman. The Namestone was not to be seen. Kang felt momentarily puzzled. Was this the person he had watched enter the Maze? The body builds were discordant. Momentary surprise crossed Valkyria's face.

"Miss Eclipse," Durand started, "what are your plans for…"

"Be still, Durand. There is important business." The Screaming Skull's voice was as chill as a tomb. His face was as impassive as the stone wall behind him. Durand found herself frozen in place, unable to move or speak.

"Where is she, little girl?" Valkyria snapped. "Where is the bearer of the Holy Namestone?" Kang stared sharply at the video. How was it that Valkyria didn't know Eclipse's name? For that matter, how was it that Valkyria couldn't recognize the bearer? And why was Valkyria saying 'little girl'?

"I'm about twenty feet in front of you," Eclipse answered calmly.

"Aren't you … isn't the real Bearer a bit taller?" Valkyria asked. Kang felt increasing confusion. The bearer appeared to be Valkyria's height, that being close to six feet.

"I am tall. Wait! Isn't the real Valkyria a bit less … pudgy?" Eclipse responded. Valkyria's nostrils flared. There was nothing, Kang thought, like a friendly, considerate opening to potentially delicate negotiations. "I mean, how do you keep fitting into that armor?"

"You!" Valkyria shouted. "Inform the Bearer. She is to turn the Holy Namestone over to League of Nations Supreme Chancellor Lars Holmgren. Immediately! That is a direct order!"

"I am the Bearer. If you wanted the Namestone, you should have walked the Maze before I did, and taken it," Eclipse answered.

"Give it to me! Now! The League has decreed: The Namestone is the property of the world," Valkyria screamed.

"Give it to you? You and which army?" Eclipse said indifferently.

"This one." Valkyria waved her fingers. Most of the League of Nations Elite Strike Force appeared at her back. Kang recognized a fair number of them as former special-class students. Disruptra and Madmind wore the same orange and violet garb, colors reversed from one set of garb to the other, the first shredding mentalic screens and the second attacking with insane nightmares. Plasmona, Electra, Lord Roentgen, Eks, and Enn had, respectively, a plasma torch, lightning bolts, coherent X-ray blasts, quark beams, and high-energy neutrons as attacks, all in power ranges that would swiftly turn a city to a pillar of fire. The folks in League paisley with copper-green trim were mentalists; he didn't know any of them. Europalord and his team of drains wore identical green uniforms with sigil and trim of yellow, 12-armed sun crosses.

It was a safe bet that the League teleport block team was parked someplace safe in Europe. They would be targeting Eclipse through Valkyria's eyes. The area they could cover from a distance was small, but that should be perfectly adequate for this situation. They had the limit, Kang considered, that the strength of a teleport block team was the strength of its strongest member. If the strongest member failed, the next strongest member would still be blocking. A team of weak blockers could still wear out a strong teleporter by a process of exhaustion. That was one of Kang's standard classroom demonstrations. The Strike Force began to fan out, left and right, moving toward Eclipse.

"That's far enough," Eclipse announced. The Strike Force kept advancing.

Eclipse gestured, ending with one hand facing skyward. The Namestone appeared, its cerulean fire burning a few inches above her palm. The Namestone's eldritch tune was faintly audible. Eclipse brought up her own body aura, a color not different from the Namestone's, and what sounded to be her own theme music, a mixture of brass and sweet woodwinds clearly audible in Durand's microphone.

"Behold the Holy Namestone. Come no closer, or face my gifts." Someone, Kang thought, had given Eclipse superb training in rhetoric. "The Namestone is mine. I took it. I keep it," she said.

"You defy the League! International law specifies: The League of Nations owns the Namestone. Hand it over!" Valkyria screamed.

"You know the Maze Rule: Namestone belongs to he who takes it. I took it," Eclipse answered calmly.

"No, it belongs to the League!" Valkyria shouted.

"You keep repeating that same wrong statement. I just told you: I took it. It's mine! Are you deaf, or just stupid? Or maybe both; you're for sure stupid." Eclipse's response dripped with contempt.

"The Namestone is too dangerous for mortals," the Screaming Skull announced. "Eclipse! Give me the Namestone, or face my wrath."

"And you're supposed to be an improvement, fathead?" Eclipse asked.

Kang's eyebrows rose. Few indeed were the people who would gratuitously insult a Lord of Eternity, no matter that the Screaming Skull was widely known to be one of the dimmest bulbs among the Lords.

"Team! The Namestone is indestructible! Kill her!" Valkyria drew her explosive throwing katana. That weapon, Kang thought, packs the power of a star-core bomb, liquid-density plasma at 20 million degrees, albeit plasma that disappears after spreading a few yards. Valkyria threw the katana at Eclipse. The Screaming Skull gestured. Black hail fell around the Namestone-Bearer. Flashes of unbearably bright light marked the rest of the League Elite Team launching their attacks. Something, Kang decided, was protecting Durand and the island, both of which would otherwise have been obliterated by the energies being unleashed. The camera's electronic filters were shielding it from burnout, but made it impossible for Kang to identify the attacks being used.

Eclipse simple stood there, her shields unwavering under attack after attack. Finally the throwing katana struck. Eclipse was swallowed in an impossibly bright sphere of incandescent plasma.

The sphere vanished. Eclipse was still there. So was the Namestone. She flicked her wrist. The Namestone vanished. Eclipse stepped into a royal blue waterfall, unseen bells tolling, leaving behind a vacant flight of marble stairs. Teleport, Kang thought, the waterfall and bells are the signifiers of her teleport. And someplace in Europe, a team of teleport blockers are somewhere between having splitting headaches and becoming rapidly-expanding clouds of incandescent gas.

Kang pondered what he had just seen. He had never heard of this Eclipse person, which was at least unusual, given her power. She'd done the unbelievable, walking the Maze and taking the Namestone. The League of Nations Strike Team was perhaps the most powerful group of mortal personas in the world. Valkyria's throwing sword created the temperature found at the core of the sun. The Screaming Skull was a Lord of Eternity, a group of immortals whose powers almost defied human comprehension. They had all attacked, and this Eclipse person's shields had not fallen to pieces. Then she teleported from the battlefield, presumably by breaking the grip of the League's teleport blockers. Efficient shields demanded much less power than most personas would believe possible, but the defenses Eclipse had deployed against the Europeans and the Screaming Skull were still remarkable.

CHAPTER THREE

The Invisible Fortress
Morning

The Healing Matrix had promised: I would wake before sunrise. Indeed, here it was, not yet seven in the morning, the sky still dark, the first hint of dawn's early light mayhaps visible in the east, and I was awake. I still hurt a lot. I was also ravenously hungry. The Healing Matrix had done more in two days than normal healing would do in two weeks, but it demanded calories. You can call on gifts instead of eating, if you have the right gifts, but that's not a good idea for a girl my age. Not eating is an especially bad idea if you are doing high-intensity healing, which I am. You really want solid food to replace all the chemical bits and pieces you are consuming. Mum was emphatic about that, not that I wouldn't want her cooking. Now I have to put up with mine.

My bedroom's full-length mirrors, complete with all-angle view so I could check the fall of my cape, confirmed that my cuts and abrasions were gone, gone as though they had never been. The Namestone had cleared up my face for the video, but the rest of me was healing more naturally. The mirrors also showed I was looking a bit thinner than I usually do. I am girlishly slim. I weigh more than people think…muscle does that…but I don't have that many pounds that I can afford to lose. Getting rid of possible scars thanks to high-grade healing is still good. Yes, there are guys who think a few strategically placed scars make them attractive to women. I am not a guy, thank you. And I am very much not convinced that scars, not to mention irregular shaving and under-bathing, make guys attractive.

I dutifully spent fifteen minutes doing stretches and bends under the healing matrix's guidance. The deep bruises would take a while to heal. Exercise, however painful, speeds the process. I had my mind control ramped well up so I did not exactly feel the pain, but there was surely a lot of it. At the end, I very much enjoyed a long, hot shower.

The time to start wearing my boy clothing had arrived. Most people see what they expect to see. I dressed as a boy, in boys' cotton corduroys, properly lined and not at all tight, not girls' somewhat tighter blue jeans.

Actually, I like the boys' long-sleeve loose hunting shirts. They are heavy, soft-cotton jacquard weaves, warm, all with pretty polychrome patterns. They have nice big pockets, not to mention elbow patches. Moose-skin slippers. Hair combed with a part. Cue the slight crackle in my voice. Anyone who met me would see and hear a boy. I may not be able to do that in three years, but I can do it now.

Soon I would have to start dyeing my hair again. By now there were probably ten million personas, not to mention most of the world's billion people, all looking for me. Almost none of them qualified as threats, but I want peace and quiet, not a shootout every time I stop at a grocery store. Disguise is how I make that happen. Notwithstanding Twain's famous story, almost no one will look at a girl and think 'this could be a boy in disguise', let alone the other way around. And when I dress to go shopping, no one will look at the dowdy old woman in heavy coat, three pounds of pearl necklaces, pale blue hair, and a heavy veil from her fifty-years-since-stylish hat, and think they are looking at me. This morning I could go outside wearing a woven cap. No one would be around to recognize my hair color.

Meanwhile, my kitchen waited. Water started heating for tea. Pear and raisin compote went into the microwave. Milk and orange juice went to the table. A steak went onto the electric grill, to be followed in due time by two slices of soda bread. The slow part of this was the steak -- I like mine close to well-done. That's why it's called well-done, after all, because it has been done well rather than so poorly it is still bleeding. The breakfast room has a small video; I cued up Eagle News-News for Adults. They are sometimes a bit heavy on financial coverage, but focus on real news, not celebrity scandals. I was shocked, truly shocked to find they were talking about the Namestone and the mystery persona who walked off with it. There was great enthusiasm for the earthly wonders that would soon be bestowed upon the people of the world by the bearer. A brief excursion covered other news notes. Alliances between the thirteen Great Powers drift slowly in time. After the 1908 Summer War, no one wants another World War. National persona teams are rough on small, breakable objects, like forests and cities. Even the Prussian Kaiser builds museums on the horrors of war.

The South American strangeness received extended coverage. "Invisible sky octopus" made no sense, but -- and my attention was drawn sharply toward the video. Supposedly an Argentine village of 500 people had been destroyed overnight. There were almost no survivors. Kudos, however, to the little boy who grabbed his family's camera, pointed it up as he ran, and snapped image after image. Most of his family was safe, He had taken really strange pictures. A creature, a cross between a jellyfish and a squid, floating in the sky. Tentacles. Claws. Teeth. But the tentacles and claws and teeth weren't attached to each other, and moved in wrong ways. A pair of images clicked in my memories. Those weren't pictures of a standard quadridimensional object, but it was something like that. Someone might be able to figure out the shape. I leave that to folks who have copies of all the picture files, lots of computer support, and some smart math people. I like math, but unscrambling those pictures is way above what I know how to do. Yet.

The smell from the electric grill reminded me that I do know how to cook, and my steak was approaching ready. Setting the table left-handed was inconvenient, but my right arm was staying below shoulder-level for the next few days. Hot water went into the tea pot. This was surely an Earl Gray morning. One thing I did not feel was sleepy. After all, I'd been asleep almost continuously for a couple of days.

The orange juice was beautifully sweet. Butter and currant jam did fine on the toasted soda bread. I remembered to pace myself on eating. As the pangs of hunger faded, I started considering my to-do list for the next week. "Heal" was at the top of the list. "Dye hair" might need to wait until tomorrow. Eyelashes are a nuisance. The Namestone was safe in its jar. I wasn't going near it until I was completely recovered. Until then it lurked behind a quarter-inch of impervium. People looking for signs of my using it would be sorely disappointed. Or mayhaps they'd find signs, even though the signs didn't exist. My new bookcases were ready for mounting. I'd finished painting them before I left. Eventually I would have to do barn work, a real nuisance while one-armed. Not today. The healing matrix was emphatic on that.

My ponies had to wait on being ridden. Tomorrow I would curry-comb them and check their hooves. We have soft soil, and I do not ride on roads. Not having to worry about horseshoes greatly simplifies my life. The ponies still want to feel appreciated. A few apples and some maple sugar would help. I'd like to ride, but my ribs need to recover first. The barn cats had their automatic feeder, and good shelter for their nest. I should pop the cat door behind the kitchen open. Occasionally the cats do like to visit. They do not get to walk on my back while I'm sleeping, not until I'm way better. There was still reading to do, and lessons to finish. I can't say I'm behind, relative to my grade level, not hardly, and I am tougher on myself than Mum was. I still have lots of reading I could do.

Now the League of Nations Supreme Chancellor was on the video. He threw three kinds of fit. He was outraged. I didn't do what he said I should. There was now a price on my head, with contributions from some of the Great Powers. I listened carefully to that one. Austria-Hungary was prominent for its complete absence from the list of contributors. So were the Satsuma Daimyo and the American Republic.

League artists had created drawings and paintings of me. The video signals from Atlantis actually showed me as a blur. People saw sharp images of me because the Namestone created illusions of what I look like, illusions seen on every video screen in the world. The news showed the drawings. They made my hair gold-blonde. I'm square-jawed, not pointy-tulip jawed. The garb looked impractical. It was way too tight to let you move easily.

Lots of girls, ten years older than I am, would happily kill to have the silhouettes in the drawings. I'm much happier to be me. How did the artists go that far wrong? Possibly Namestone showed them someone who was not me. That would explain why Valkyria was so confused. She was looking for a hot babe, minimally dressed, in her mid-20s. She found me instead. Not hot. Not babe. Not vaguely mid-20s. Perfectly decently dressed.

Holmgren introduced his number-two man, the head of the League Peace Police. Mum had said this Dreikirch fellow was a Nationalist-Capitalist, someone barely fit to live. His rant was even worse than Holmgren's. Today the League would have an emergency meeting to talk about me. I could tell. I wasn't going to get their cheers and congratulations for solving the Maze.

I changed channels to the Persona News Network—All Personas, All the Time. My satellite feed went into a distributor box. From the outside, the mythical people who live here were perpetually viewing a dozen channels, giving outsiders no chance to see which channels I actually watch. The Persona Network was discussing various plans to capture me, once I was found. I'd've been happier if they didn't have a half-way accurate estimate of how much power I'd used to make my last getaway. They kept talking about the network's big program, this evening, all about ways to kill Eclipse and capture the Namestone, at which moment the Earth would become Paradise. I set the video's recorder to be sure to capture that program. I am not much interested in people saying how great I am. I am extremely interested in people who think they have newer and better ways to kill me.

I cleaned up after breakfast, and decided that it was time for another nap. I was alert, but physically exhausted. When I woke the sun was beyond the zenith, I felt much better, and I really wanted something to eat again.

Two roast chicken sandwiches, all grain bread, plenty of lettuce, just a bit of butter, and more of the curried vegetables did quite nicely. I postponed the ice cream and fudge crumbles until later. Water came to a boil while I was cleaning up. Some parents would have been scandalized that I was brewing coffee, worse, cocoa-tinged coffee. I really am a persona, not easily poisoned. Coffee makes me a bit sharper while I am reading, but all the alkaloids burn off fairly quickly, leaving me ready to drop into sound sleep. Besides, I really am too young for chocolate to have its alleged effect. I suppose if I always ate like this I would worry a bit about my figure, but that is one of my gifts. I may eat, but I remain leanly athletic.

After lunch it was clearly time for my next book. I could start studying again. I decided to read a history. For some reason, Mum did not entirely approve my reading historicals. I agree that most books on history are pretty pointless. Here are these great men and women and their heroic deeds that you can copy. Here is a record of past ages and their mistakes, leading upward to the present when we do everything right. If you don't like moral histories, there are historical mysteries. Historical mystery books tend to be completely crazy. Yes, it is hard to understand how the eight different civilizations of ancient Washington, 2000 years ago, could clearly have coexisted along the Columbia River, had advanced science, technology, mathematics, and art, yet failed to notice each other. Even if they weren't all there at exactly the same time, whichever came later might in their historic records occasionally have noted ruins of the past. No such luck. Massachusetts is even more confusing. There are 12 or 15, I tend to forget, different ancient advanced civilizations whose traces may be found near Massachusetts Bay. Most of them left at least some reasonably detailed historical records. Seven left observations on the moons of Jupiter and Saturn and Uranus, observations that make no sense. They had the moons in wrong places. You'd think they couldn't see the sky. There was a mystery here, one in which most people seem to be remarkably uninterested. The few people who are interested in ancient civilizations write totally crazy things. They talk about world civilizations of 50,000 years ago, before Homo sapiens evolved, with a remarkable collection of nonsense as allegedly serious evidence.

Finally I curled up with a book, a very thick history of the Grand Tradesmasters of All Sarnath, many of whom were real characters, to put it mildly. Stanford Smith was by far the most pleasant and sensible of the lot. He had made a vast number of westerns, films whose location is in dispute between Utah and Mongolia, and the esoteric, substantially incomprehensible motion picture Casablanca, which is still said to be one of the greatest films made in the last several thousand years. The history listed some of the books that attempt to interpret a scene at the end of the film, in which the Inspector throws a bottle of water into a trash can. The scene is so brilliant that no one can understand it. Smith was the sort of person you would like as an older friend, if he hadn't died a couple thousand years ago.

All good books come to an end. *Live Forever and Own All the Money* was no exception. I looked up. It was well after dark outside. OK, it's January. Dark happens early. My mocha pot was empty. I'd really gotten lost in the book, especially toward the end when Grand Tradesmasters were alcoholics, child molesters, lunatics, and monetary reformers, concentrating hard enough that I didn't think about my pain. I still hurt, a lot. At the end, I'd had to take getting gut-punched. Hard. Things were still uncomfortable down there. Before I started reading I'd remembered to pull up a quilt, so I hadn't gotten cold. My gifts will protect me from cold, but only when I'm calling them.

A shame so many Tradesmasters were lunatics. For a few moments my memories carried me back to a book I'd read last year, a book on another lunatic, the not-American Ambassador. One fine day, there had appeared in Vienna a man claiming to be the American Ambassador, which he was not. He had an impressive set of papers saying he was the Ambassador not for the American Republic but for a "United States of America", a country founded in 1776, not 0017, and not to the Empire of the Hapsburgs but to a "Republic of Austria". The parallel universe crackpots had a field day. Telepathic examination, as a start to curing his delusions, found that he had a full set of wrong memories going back to being a little boy, all memories of a world that does not exist. Particularly alarming were his very detailed memories of 'the first flight to the moon', a flight allegedly carried out within the last few decades using, Goddess spare us, a chemical-fueled rocket. The alarm was that he remembered lots of details of the rocket—it had been a boyhood fixation—and careful engineering analysis of this complete bit of absurdity showed that the rocket would have worked, if it hadn't blown up first. He refused to believe in personas or gifts, even when someone hovered in front of him. He claimed that his "United States" was part of the world's first technical civilization, that there are no ancient steel and concrete ruins, that writing is not older than homo sapiens, and that Massachusetts had been settled from of all places Britain, in 1600, that being only 20 centuries too late and from the wrong direction. In short, he was stark raving mad.

He also spoke neither Modern English nor Ancient English. His 'Standard Edited English' was close to real English, but he would say 'perhaps' not 'mayhaps', 'Ayup' not 'OK', and would split infinitives as the correct way to talk. More peculiarly, part of his mind was not there. He would talk about how his country was governed, and every so often his thoughts would vanish. Moments later he would be talking again, but there would be mysterious gaps in his logic, as though he could think and say things, but no one else could be aware of them. He was under very close observation when he suddenly disappeared, every atom in his body vanishing at the same moment.

I needed more food, but the healing matrix said first I needed some rigorous stretch and bend exercises, my partly-healed ribs protesting where force fields kept them clamped absolutely rigidly together. Then I got to eat. Cooking is a big time sink, there being only one of me, but I actually can cook, so some of my lentil, spinach, and kielbasa stew moved from freezer to microwave, followed by shredded lettuce, slivered carrots, and a few artichokes onto a big salad plate. Lemon juice, a scoop of chickpeas and chopped onions marinated in Roman salad dressing, and a sprinkle of parmesan cheese followed. After dinner I'd take a short nap, and then chemistry and astronomy. I'd cleaned the house thoroughly before I left. It could wait a few more days.

OK, be honest with myself. The short nap was another nine hours. I lay down on my bed, pulled the quilt up to my shoulders, and when I awoke it was well closer to dawn than dusk. Yes, when I need to I can really draw deeply on my gifts. Afterward I pay a price, and not a small one, either. Mayhaps someday, when I grow up, the price will be smaller. But right now I'm only me, I only have the gifts that I have, and I'm paying the price for drawing deeply on them. On the positive side, I always liked getting up early enough to watch the sun rise. After nine hours of deep sleep, I really was awake again. I'd be happy to say the stretches and bends weren't as uncomfortable as yesterday, except they were worse.

Chapter Four

The Wells Residence
Arbalest Street
Medford, Massachusetts
Evening

For the Wells family, dinner approached completion. Wind from the blizzard rattled tree branches and whistled through their house's ornate eves. All the blinds in the breakfast room were pulled, covering three walls of glass with bright-white honeycomb fabric. A brass and crystal chandelier hanging from the high ceiling gave brilliant light. The fourth wall opened onto a large, modern kitchen filled with cooking gadgets: bread maker, ice cream maker, coffee grinder, six burner gas stove,...only the classic nickel-plated drip coffee pot referred to an earlier century.

"That was really good Indian pudding, mom," Janie Wells said, pushing pitch-black falls of hair back from her ears. Thanking Mom was always safe, she thought, so long as you gave brother Brian credit for whatever he cooked. His cooking was superb, as good as Mom's. Janie's much-taller year-older sister Jessamine Trishaset nodded enthusiastic agreement, her curly red hair bobbing as she nodded.

"Thank you," Abigail Wells said. Three children had left her with a slightly stocky build. Her still-raspberry-blonde hair was tied into a bob. "My recipe, but Brian did all the work. And grades? It being that day for you seventh and eighth-graders?"

"A's," Trisha said. "Mostly A-pluses. Except Gym. C-minus. OK, I have to be really careful not to give away I'm a bit faster than some other kids."

"I suppose faster than sound does qualify as a bit faster." Patrick Wells frowned. Trisha sank into her chair. She knew what that frown meant. She was supposed to setting an example for Brian and Janie. Missing an A-plus in two courses meant for sure Dad would be having some private words with her.

"Even better that you have not betrayed that you have gifts," Patrick announced. Janie and Brian grimaced, just for an instant. "And it's good of Sunssword to go flying with you." Trisha's father took off his glasses, and waved them in one hand. His black hair, lined with occasional bits of silver, matched the metallic silver frame of his spectacles. "Your mystery patron supplied you, all three of you, with garb that does hide who you are. Or would have, if you two hadn't given things away." He pointed at his twin children.

"Da-aad," Brian complained, not quite seriously. "The other choice was getting stomped flat by those giant robots. It could have appeared anywhere in Massachusetts, and Emperor Roxbury just had to appear right in front of my school. Besides, I got A-plusses on everything. Even if I'm not quite up in course levels with Trisha."

"That was algebra we were both studying, wasn't it, Brian?" Trisha asked.

Janie wondered if Dad was playing dumb, or if he was teasing. He could hardly not know that Trisha did all the sewing, though it was her games winnings that paid for the fabric, and...Janie allowed that Trisha's top flight speed was indeed faster than...sound.

"To answer your question?" Janie shrugged. "I got straight As on my exams, well, mayhaps not A-pluses like Brian." She tried to hide her annoyance that Brian had better grades. Again. That was so annoying. It wasn't unreasonable, she allowed. "Brian puts more time into schoolwork. But I'm studying something far more important. Games!"

"And you are doing just fine, Janie," Patrick said. "You're the youngest person on the National Junior Team, and you got that draw last Fall against Kurchatov. Your grades are hardly suffering. Don't worry about them." Trisha sank even farther into her chair. Janie's grades were worse than hers, on easier courses, but Dad was saying nice things about Janie, would be saying really bad things about her work when he got the chance, and all the while she was stuck doing almost all the housework for all three of them, except when Brian wanted to cook.

"Except Romeo and Juliet makes absolutely no sense at all," Janie said. "I just wrote down what I memorized from those other crazy books. You were right, Dad. Finding those other books helped a lot, no matter how stupid they were, when I needed to write crazy stuff on my exams. But if I had crossed out half the 'not's in my sentences, what I wrote would have made exactly as much sense. The teacher said it was lots of extra books, not just one, and I could name them, so I got my A. How did you do it, Brian? How did you pull an A-plus in that course? We read the same extra books."

"Oh," Brian said, "I added stuff about 'the unbearable agony of separation'. Whatever nonsense that is. I lifted it from Trisha's romance novel *Pirate Lord of the Aztecan Gulf*." Janie rolled her eyes. Brian was reading romance novels? Yuck! But it had been a pirate novel, and his last model had been a pirate ship, so it wasn't totally stupid.

"I only have one pirate novel!" Trisha interrupted. "It's a reading assignment. For my genre fiction requirement! It's unbearably awful. It's even worse than that Regency romance. And I still don't understand what 'uninherit' is or why it's so terrible. I even asked the teacher after class, not that it helped." Trisha hoped that Dad believed her. If he thought she was reading romance novels because she liked them, he would be down on her like three tons of bricks.

"Disinherit," Patrick corrected. "But that happened right here on this street." His three children had his full attention. "Marjorie Blake was your first babysitter, Trisha, though you might not remember her. She was just finishing High School. She had a boyfriend. They agreed to get married. He was totally unsuitable, and didn't ask her father's permission before asking her to marry him. Her parents were furious. When Marjorie and boyfriend posted the banns in preparation for getting married, her parents disinherited her. That means she had to move out of the house and never return. Also, she was legally removed from Doctor Blake's will; she will inherit nothing when he dies."

"Oh, yes, thank you, Daddy," Trisha gushed. "that makes complete sense in the Regency novel, except my teacher said my novel had to do with the Heinlein Act, which made no sense, not that I'm sure what the Heinlein Act is."

Abigail rolled her eyes. "The Heinlein Act is that Navy monstrosity. But you knew Heinlein, didn't you, dear?" she asked Patrick.

"Indeed I did," Patrick answered. "He was a fine Navy Admiral who'd won three skirmishes, officially with pirates, and retired with combat injuries. He wanted to become a writer, but needed to support his family, so he'd read law. A few years later, along came this young lady, about the age of you three, and about as bright, who wanted Heinlein to use bad wording in a California state law to divorce her parents. Her name is under seal; her initials were P.W. Her parents, it later turned out, were truly terrible people. Her case reached the Supreme Court. Heinlein won his case. Congress codified, the Heinlein Act, rules letting adult-competent children divorce truly bad parents. Heinlein then took up writing, full-time, and made a fortune."

"Sorry your novel was so terrible, Trisha," a chastened Brian said. "But, you see, that novel was good for something. You made the sacrifice, you read it, we all learned something from Dad, and it got me an A+."

"You talked about, yuck, romance novels?" Janie asked. "That's gross! What do they have to do with that stupid play about Italians going into suspended animation? You think I can get an A+ if I insert something intelligent instead? I could talk about Chess or City of Steel or outward influence on my next English exam. Yes, outward influence. Those crazy dueling families in Romeo and Juliet do things to get spread-out advantage far away. That's outward influence, just like in stones. And at the end of Hamlet everyone is in zugzwang, and they all move anyhow, littering the stage with bodies. That's what I should have said, they're all in zugzwang, and then for sure I would have had my A+." Janie decided not to notice her parents shaking their heads.

"I lucked out," Brian said. "I guessed Romeo and Juliet had something to do with romance novels. I can't tell what. I wasn't really sure. But, Dad, why is fiction called 'genre fiction'? Why not just 'fiction'?"

Patrick looked at his wife. "Yes, I think they are old enough," he said. "We've had those discussions, after all."

"Very well." Abigail looked to have bitten into a particularly bitter lemon.

"There is also 'literary fiction'," Patrick said. "Most people don't like it, so while real, meaning genre, fiction gets the Nobel Prize for Literature, 'literary fiction' readers have their own awards, such as the Joyce and Hemingway Prizes. Joyce was famous for slapping together incomprehensible strings of words and claiming they were novels. He was quite mad. The 'literary novel' you will all be stuck reading, in twelfth grade, is Hawthorne's *The Scarlet Letter*. It's a truly disgusting work, in which a young woman becomes a fallen roundheel and ends up bearing a child, when she is not married. Instead of having the child taken away to be raised by decent people, as would happen in the real world, she is allowed to keep the child, and matters go downhill from there."

"Yuck!" Janie said. Her brother nodded in agreement.

"I have to read that?" Trisha tried to remember alternatives to taking twelfth grade. Dad had mentioned that Rogers Tech did not care if students had a high school diploma or not. That sounded helpful.

"What if I try inserting some of the instructions from one of your model ships..." Janie's voice trailed off.

<*Miss Wells?*> The interruption was mentalic. The telepathic voice came with the image of a short woman wearing the pale cream with copper-green trim uniform of a FedCorps mentalist. Her black hair had a widow's peak matching Janie's.

< *I'm having dinner,*> Janie answered telepathically. <*Can't interrupt. Dad would kill me. You have to wait an hour!*> This was weird, she thought. She never had strangers call her, but this woman was the fourth today. The other three had got her RadioBell number somehow and called by voice. Two were at least gamesmen, but that Vera Durand had been incredibly insistent, not to mention so arrogant she just assumed Janie knew who she was. Janie checked her mental shields again, carefully, just like Sunssword had taught her. You had to be really careless to take damage through a telepathic link, but it could be done. It would not be done to her, she told herself. Who was the woman? Not a senior gamesman she knew personally. Then she recognized: The woman was Krystal North, Captain-General of FedCorps, the American Persona League, and she had other people with her.

<*This is the Washington, Federal District, and it's important!*> Krystal North said. Her annoyance showed through the mentalic link.

<*This is Massachusetts, where America was founded,*> Janie answered. <*We've been here two thousand years. The world waits for Massachusetts.*> Janie heard the echoes of another mind, someone older than Grandpa, chuckling at the exchange.

<Speaker of the House Ming wants to speak to your Dad,> North said. That remark came with another image, the Speaker in his scarlet robes and cape. *<You're in danger of being kidnapped. Again.>*

<My apologies for interrupting,> Speaker Ming's voice came though the link. *<There's a major national issue here. I need to ask you about City of Steel, and your move against Kurchatov.>*

"Jane Caroline," her father announced firmly, "We know you are a telepath, and so are some of your friends, but having them interrupt dinner with telepathy is as rude as answering a RadioBell while we are eating." Patrick Augustus Wells almost never raised his voice, but his tone was completely clear to all three of his children.

<I'll ask,> Janie said. *<But Dad is going to kill me.>*

"Daddy, that isn't a friend," Janie said. Her father raised his eyebrows. "Well, she's friendly. You met her. That's Krystal North, herself. You know, Krystal North, lead of the American Persona League. She was here two years ago. When Trisha and I got kidnapped. She wants me to forward a mentalic call to you, Daddy. The Speaker wants to talk to you. I had to get across: We're having dinner. He has to wait. She said they're in the Federal District. I said back we're in Massachusetts, and that's better. Two thousand years ago, Massachusetts created the American Republic. She was a bit stubborn. But I was more stubborn."

"Speaker?" Patrick asked.

"Speaker of the House," Janie said. "Speaker Ming. The top guy in Washington. He was polite about asking if he could interrupt dinner. He said it was important. I said I'd have to ask," Janie answered. She decided not to mention that through her Krystal North, Speaker Ming, and whoever else was at the other end were still hearing the conversation. Her parents already had those looks on their faces.

"What is going on?" Janie's mother asked fearfully. Abigail Wells wished her children had been less involved in persona events, even if none of them had been their fault. "Have you been doing the persona thing again? Blowing up more robots? And not telling us?"

"No!" Janie realized that she was at the edge of getting into really deep trouble, for something that was not her fault. "No, Mommy. And the robots last December were trying to kill Brian and me and our whole class. I didn't do anything. Speaker Ming wants to ask me about City of Steel. He needs your and Daddy's permission to talk to me."

"I suppose you should be honored," Patrick Wells said. "I didn't even know the Speaker plays City."

"It's one particular move," Janie answered. "The one Eclipse used to beat the Maze. It's the move I pulled on Kurchatov, only hers was better. I was saving that variant for the National, and… Now Eclipse used it first!" Janie pounded a delicate fist on the kitchen table. It was unbelievably terrible. Her move had been used, and not by her. Now it would be the Eclipse Gambit, not Jane's First Gambit! Nothing could be worse than that! "No one knew about that move. No one." She pounded her fist again, then looked momentarily thoughtful. She hadn't told anyone, had she?

"Dear, dinner or not, the Speaker is a very busy man," Patrick said. Hopefully, he thought, my daughter did not insult the First Citizen of the Republic too much. "You should forward what he has to say. And you two bite your tongues." Patrick glared at his other two children. Brian nodded vigorously. Trisha sagged back in her chair.

"OK," Janie said. Suddenly the entire Wells family saw, standing directly in front of each of them, a short woman wearing a cream tunic and trousers. Standing to her right was an elderly gentleman, balding, silver-haired, smiling, eyes sparkling, dressed in the scarlet robes, high-collared cape, and multipointed hat assigned by law to the Speaker of the House.

"My apologies," Speaker Ming said, "for having intruded, and I hope that young Janie here is not in any trouble as a result of my intrusion, but the hour seemed late enough to be after dinner, though I see I was mistaken, and the urgency of my interruption is indeed great. In any event, the issue is that the Bearer of the Namestone played City of Steel against the Lesser Maze and used a novel move, rather a move that was novel until it was traced back to Miss Wells here. I gather that the Bearer actually played a variation on Miss Wells' original move. There is great interest in what light Miss Wells can shed on this circumstance. I would like to ask her about this. My own position, which I have been heard to say repeatedly by the press, is that the Bearer–this Eclipse person--took the Namestone fair and square, so she now owns it."

"Janie knows how to reach me once you decide on an answer," Krystal North added, "but time is of the essence. From the number of hits on the web pages of *City of Steel Review*, in particular the pages corresponding to Janie's games, a large number of other people seem to have figured out the same thing we did."

"I get a champion, don't I?" Janie asked. Sunssword had explained all about champions, something 'you need to know'. "Someone who makes sure no one takes advantage of me?" Speaker Ming nodded in agreement. "OK, I know exactly who to ask. Who's questioning me? If Dad and Mom agree?"

"The North American champion," Krystal North said. "The Visitor. That's Kurchatov and Hornpiper. Speaker Ming. Mayhaps the Supreme Gamesman. I'll provide mentalic support, to keep people honest. We're ready in an hour. However, it's up to you to agree or not."

Janie caught Krystal North's nod and broke the link. "Daddy, mommy," Janie said, "I could hear what was behind her thoughts. She thinks something bad probably happens to me very soon now. Tonight, even. Unless I agree. I get to ask a friend to our house. Someone to protect me. When they question me. Daddy knows Professor Lafayette. That's a good choice of champion."

"Not your coach?" Abigail Wells asked. "Lafayette? Who is he?"

"Champion?" Brian asked. Janie glowered. Brian had listened to Sunssword explain about champions. Janie reminded herself that Brian was a boy, so he wasn't supposed to pay attention to things that he didn't care about, even when they were important. And he hadn't cared about champions. Boys! She thought.

"She," Patrick corrected. "Morgana Lafayette. Works at Rogers Tech. In biochemistry. She showed up at the back door, right after Janie and Trisha were kidnapped." Abigail looked perplexed. "Human female, tall, gold-blonde, blue eyes, not nearly as pretty as you are, dear." Abigail broke into giggles. Patrick was describing the persona Sunssword, but using her private persona name, the name Abigail had never heard.

"But, Janie, why didn't you just say Sunssword?" Abigail asked.

"Sunssword doesn't want her public persona to be tied to me," Janie said, "She's real careful where she coaches us. We have a coach. No one knows it's Sunssword. We never name her public persona. I thought you knew who she was, Mom. But Daddy knows Professor Lafayette. They both work at RTI. No one is surprised to see Professor Lafayette being my champion."

"In particular," Abigail said, "Sunssword never told me who else she was, and has that garb that doesn't let you see most of her face. And you were polite to Sunssword, not telling me who her private persona was." Sunssword, Abigail considered, had done mentalic checks that Janie and Trisha had not been hurt when they were kidnapped. Now Sunssword was coaching the three Wells children on using their gifts.

"Besides being a persona," Patrick said, "Morgana Lafayette is also one of the country's leading biochemists. She gave up trying to keep her public persona a deep secret. She's a member of Stars Over Boston. Or was, anyhow. They had another stupid argument about theology. OK, opinions on the Speaker's request?"

"I think we'd better," Abigail said. "If it makes Janie safer."

Trisha shrugged. "Sunssword is a nice person. We go flying sometimes. But I've only met her public persona. To me she's Sunssword, just not wearing garb. She taught me cloud-diving. In fact, Janie, you knew she was Lafayette, but you never told me. That's you being gifttrue."

"Bragging rights!" Brian announced. "Grandmasters come to Medford to learn City of Steel from my sister. The guys will never top this. Not even if they get home runs off the Boston Doves' lead pitcher."

"I think we agree," Patrick said. "My Federal research support is about to be reviewed. Having Speaker Ming remember me favorably is desirable. Unless Janie has really strong objections."

"Just so they don't ask me about my other variants on that move." She paused, thinking. "No, I can tell them about the variants. And champion," Janie explained, "means a government persona shows up to talk. You get your own persona to watch your back."

"Yes, they would be asking Janie about City of Steel, wouldn't they,"

Patrick said. "Having said that, these people are my guests in my house, so you will treat them politely." He stared at his son. Brian nodded vigorously. "Janie, I'll phone Morgana. It's simpler."

A few minutes later, there came a knock at the back door. "Lafayette is here!" The speaker's voice was a rich alto. "You called, Professor Wells?"

Patrick stepped through the vestibule and opened the door. "I did indeed, Morgana." Patrick stood aside to admit the tall young woman. She wore a baggy royal-blue sweater and loose blue jeans, but seemed unbothered by the blinding snow, gale-force winds, and below-zero weather. Nor had snow lodged in her hair or clothing. Patrick turned to his family. "I believe you all know Professor Morgana Lafayette under one name or another."

Morgana took Patrick's hand, just for a moment. "I'm not in garb, so Morgana is good." She glanced at Patrick's children as she swept around the table. "Have you three been staying out of trouble?" Patrick decided not to notice his twin children looking furtively at each other. For Abigail Wells, Morgana had a firm hug. "It's been way too long," Morgana said. "We should really get together to talk. Soon. I can always be free at lunch."

"There's more Indian pudding if you'd like some," Trisha announced.

"You have to ask? Please? I know about your mom's cooking. Or is it yours? However, we have almost no time," Morgana said. "I know it's not polite, but, Janie, please give me a fast update mind-to-mind of what they all know." The two women stared at each other for a few moments.

"That was just what you've all heard," Morgana said. "OK, have you folks ever had a champion before? It's like having an attorney. What mostly matters is that at the end Krystal North wants mentalic contact with Janie, to confirm that what Janie said is true. That's, well, it's not dangerous, but while that is going on Janie would be relatively open to someone trying to tamper with her mind. I'm here to stop that. Also, Krystal is well behaved, but sometimes you find persona who try to shout or bludgeon people into submission. Worse, our friends across the waters have some very different opinions about good manners. Some idiot from over there might try to kidnap Janie and interrogate her about her hypothetical contacts with the Bearer. That's forcibly interrogate. I'm very definitely here to stop that."

"What's the issue?" Patrick asked. "Janie, you didn't have time to tell us everything."

"They think I know who has the Namestone," Janie answered. "Or I have the clue! The clue tells them who has the Namestone. It's all in that City of Steel move. The one I was going to spring at Nationals. But Eclipse used it first! I hate her!" Once again a delicate fist pounded on the breakfast room table. "Eclipse is the most terrible person in the world. No. She's the most terrible person in the Universe. She's more terrible than the Silver General and the Lords of Death, put together! She used my move, and she used it first. Speaker Ming, when I was speaking to him before you heard him, said 'If your parents will consent to having you questioned by the American

Persona League, we can say that you have been questioned, everything that could be learned from you has been learned, and therefore you should be left alone.' " Janie decided that photographic memory actually did have other uses besides studying games, like remembering exactly what other people said, even if the people in question were only politicians, so they were way less important than Players.

"Did you ever tell anyone about the move?" Morgana asked. "That's what they want to know."

"I never used it in a match," Janie said. "I was saving it for National. Now Eclipse used it! I have friends my age who come over to play Steel. We try all sorts of moves, but we don't record."

"Actually, these days it was mostly one friend," Abigail said. "Joe Cartwright is a very polite young man, OK, boy, he being slightly older than you, Janie. You said he was a good player."

"He got a lot better," Janie said. "And he's only a bit older than me." She turned at her brother. "Don't say it, Brian." Her tone of voice held a touch of steel.

"I wasn't going to say he's your boyfriend," Brian rushed out. Janie briefly considered, enthusiastically, violently unpleasant things she could do to her twin brother. "Honest! You think I want you and Trisha to kill me, just because I deserve it?" Brian asked. "Besides, he's not. Your boyfriend, I mean. And I wasn't going to say the other thing you told me, either."

"Brian!" Janie and Trisha did not quite shout at their brother.

"Oops!" Brian managed.

"And this would be, Brian Arthur?" Patrick asked ominously.

"Joe asked me not to bring it up, Dad," Janie said. "Because it didn't matter. Besides, I knew that you knew already. He's the guy who saved Trisha and me. When we were kidnapped. Except I was sure you and mom knew already."

"He's the young man who saved you?" Abigail said. "He is an extremely polite, well-brought-up boy. It's very nice of you, Janie, to reward him by playing City of Steel with him. Especially, she thought, very nice by comparison with some of the other things girls sometimes did to thank young men who risked their lives to save a young lady.

"And you, Trisha?" Abigail asked. "Did you tell Joe about Janie's move?"

"No. Joe and I, all we did was go cloud-diving a couple of times. Cloud-diving!" Her parents gave her a very odd look. Trisha blushed deeply. "Nothing else! We for sure didn't play City of Steel! I hardly play the game at all. I couldn't give Janie's move away if I wanted to. I don't even know what the move is." But, she thought, I'm going to be blamed for giving it away, no matter what.

"Complication planet!" Morgana said. "And we're way short of time."

"What's wrong?" Janie asked. "Joe can't have the Namestone. He's a boy! The Bearer is a girl. The Bearer looks like you, Professor Lafayette, not him. Well, sort of like you, if you wore slightly tighter clothing. Then you'd look like her. Joe's mom is too tall to be the bearer. Joe doesn't have any brothers or sisters. He told me. Besides, I'm not even sure I played that move against him." Janie was baffled. Joe couldn't possibly have anything to do with the Namestone.

"Slightly tighter?" Morgana rolled her eyes. "As in 'spray-painted on'? Except I'm quite sure the real Eclipse doesn't look like the paintings. Valkyria didn't recognize her. The wanted posters give the bearer my height or Valkyria's -- five-ten or so -- but the real Eclipse is I'd guess five and a couple-four inches, mayhaps not quite your height, Trisha. No matter. The complication…let's save that for later. Where does this Joe live? How do you phone him? Who are his parents? If Janie might've played this move against him, they're going to want to question him next."

"I've only met him twice," Patrick said. "Dear, it must be in your Rolodex."

"I thought you knew, Patrick," Abigail answered. "Janie, you must have visited his house."

"Ummh, er, no." Janie shook her head. "I have the good City playing set. The big board, the extra-large heavy unit counters, the nice table in the sun room. He teleports, remember? He could live anywhere. But that's odd. I never thought to ask. I always get Bell numbers and interlink IDs from new friends, first thing. I just never thought of it." How did I forget? Janie asked herself. It was really annoying, especially if Dad and Mom decided to blame her for forgetting. Every so often they did blame her, if only after they were done blaming Trisha for everything.

"We talked a few times," Trisha said. "He was very nice and polite. I figured you had his address and everything, Janie. But we only went flying after you two played your moves out."

"Let's save this for a bit," Morgana said. "But there's something a bit odd…later! OK, tonight they'll teleport in. Your driveway would be good, except there's two feet of snow on it."

"I can try snow-blowing," Patrick announced.

"I'll take care of it," Trisha said. She faded into a blur of motion headed for the basement stairs.

"Just a moment," Janie said. "I have to find Krystal again, tell her we're good for 8 P.M."

"And there's a blizzard, so they need their winter clothing," Abigail added.

"They want to bring the Supreme Gamesman," Janie finally said. "He's visiting from Russia. I agreed. I've never met him! It's beyond belief! Mom, you need to get some photos of the four of us standing over my game table! Please?" Abigail went to fetch her camera.

Trisha reappeared from nowhere, leaning against a kitchen cabinet. "I shoveled the driveway, Dad," she announced.

"In two minutes?" Patrick grumbled. "What if the neighbors saw you?"

"Two minutes. Superspeed. You can hardly see the house next door, and the Goosedotrs are in Florida. You can't see the street lights. Besides," Trisha added, "I stayed invisible the whole time, and inside the snow cloud I raised."

"Invisible?" Patrick asked.

"Like this," Trisha said. She vanished from sight. Her voice came from the same part of the room as before, but nothing was to be seen. "I'm right here but you can't see me. Well, maybe you can, Professor. I was going to tell you all what I just found as a gift, but these other things came up." Trisha reappeared.

"Shoveled?" Abigail asked. "The entire driveway? Not 'flew the snow onto the lawn'?"

"Shoveled. As in 'I'd like to take a shower and change my clothes', that being really a lot of shoveling I just did. And not 'flown'. I'd for sure accidentally pick up the concrete."

"Trisha," Brian asked, "That was the last of the Indian pudding, but may I heat some of my apple pie up for you? And warm milk? For when you come down here again."

"Please?" Trisha answered. "That was really a lot of snow."

"You could've asked for help," Patrick reminded. Sometimes, he thought, his older daughter had no sense at all. Actually, most of the time she had no sense at all. Janie was a Junior Gamesmistress, Brian made these fantastic models, but Trisha never did anything, no matter how often he tried to improve her thinking. Music? Despite her mother's aspirations, Trisha's singing at best often hit a real note.

"Don't work too hard, Trisha" Abigail said. "You could hurt yourself." Janie realized that no one else caught Trisha tensing when Trisha heard what Mom said. Mom kept saying things that put Trisha down, and Trisha kept being hurt more and more and retreating farther and farther into herself. Trisha's feelings really hurt when her parents put her down like that, but there was no way, Janie realized, to help her. More and more often, Mom reduced Trisha to tears saying things like that, tears that only Trisha's superspeed let her hide.

"Mo-om! You guys were all busy," Trisha answered, diffusing her mom's criticism. "And it's really fluffy snow. I'll be back down in a bit." She vanished in a blur.

"Folks," Morgana said, "The clock is ticking, and I can readily tell Jessamine Trishaset is just fine. Your Indian pudding was excellent, Brian, especially since I skipped dinner. And lunch. There was a major NIH grant due, but it's done."

"I think there's an extra slice of my pie left," Brian said, "and the vanilla ice cream I made yesterday. Trisha will want some, too."

"I can't just..." Morgana began to protest.

"You will have a real dinner, Morgana," Abigail interrupted, "and we should have you over more often, now that I know who you are. My family has been scrupulous about respecting your privacy, as in knowing that you and Sunssword are one person, and not telling me. Though looking at the clock, dinner is after this meeting. While you three are doing your homework." The last sentence was directed at her children.

"Already done," Brian said. "I was going to work on my new model. I'm making real progress." His current project, the ship-of-the-line George Washington, had 1200 pieces, most requiring modest woodworking prior to assembly.

"Me, too," Janie added. "Grades night. Not much homework. But my new stones book is on thickness." I'm not making enough progress in playing stones, she thought. I keep losing. I have to work harder.

"Thank you," Morgana answered. "No, really. Dinner would be great. But we're running short on time. Let's see where I am. Janie, you played that move against Kurchatov. You have not, if I heard right, ever used the Eclipse move in match play. You were saving it for the Nationals. Right? You have friends your own age over for play. Are any of them any good?"

"Does everyone have to call it the Eclipse move?" Janie shook her head. The whole thing was terrible. That was her move. Eclipse was getting the credit. Killing Eclipse was too good for her. Unless she could throw Eclipse into the Sun. Slowly. "Not really. We play. They get better. Joe improved the most. He always remembered his mistakes. He didn't make them twice. Sometimes I play Territories on-line. Anonymously. Universe of Warfare site doesn't allow personal information. They don't know who I am." They just know, she thought, that I thoroughly thrashed them.

"There was this communications gap on who Joe is. Except he teleports. And flies. And has combat skills. He was a friend your age. Am I right so far?" Morgana asked.

"Completely," Janie answered.

"Did you ever talk about him rescuing you?" Morgana asked. <*You two weren't carrying on, Janie, were you? I know you're way young for that, but it matters legally, so I have to ask. If you were, you can't be questioned about him.*> The telepathic question went unheard by the rest of the Wells family.

<*No! Absolutely not!*> Janie tried unsuccessfully not to sound offended. That idea was beyond totally gross! It was sick! What did people think she was! "We kept in touch, after he rescued us. He and I could reach each other mentalically. I never needed to phone. We'd agree on good times for him to show up. Mom and Dad said it was all right. Didn't you, Dad?" Janie asked. He nodded. She had asked, she told herself, and Dad had seemed to understand her question. "Sometimes we all played base ball nines together. A few times, Brian needed extra players for his team. Trisha was always catcher. She insisted. And never managed to hit the ball."

Trisha, now dressed in a scarlet red pantsuit, cuffs and collar ornately trimmed and stitched in orange flames, reappeared and sagged bonelessly into her chair. "I might've hit the ball out of the park by accident," she said.

"Absolutely," Patrick answered. "Joe was a good person. I'd have liked to have met him. Actually, I did meet him. He was very polite. But you somehow forgot to mention who he was, Janie. He did save you two, and I gather he took a pistol or knife or something away from one of those scoundrels, the people Stars Over Boston flattened. Fortunately, you shouted for help, and he managed to avoid getting hurt."

"He's a great guy. He even helped us move the firewood into the garage," Brian said. "And once he made this unbelievable catch and throw to win a nines game for us. He throws like a girl, a girl who plays hardball all the time."

"Last November," Trisha added. "The delivery guy just dumped the wood in the driveway."

"Last time we hire him," Abigail said.

"So we three got to carry it into the garage," Janie said. "No gifts allowed. The neighbors would've seen them."

"But Joe showed up and helped. He said he owed Janie for playing City of Steel with him," Trisha explained. "He helped a lot. Of course, he's my height, or almost, but really strong. Not gift-strong--you can tell--but strong. Strong as I am."

"Afterward on that?" Morgana said. "OK, there is a rule here, which is why you need a champion, Janie. Joe is clearly not Eclipse. Wrong height. Wrong hair color. And he's a boy. And you're not sure you even played the new move against him."

"We talked about my move," Janie said. "I was really proud of it. We talked about some other variations. And why they weren't so good. That's what I thought then. We might have talked about the special move. But it was a bunch of friends doing things. Or him and me playing City of Steel."

"May I confirm, mind-to-mind, that each of you does not know where Joe lives or has any of his contact addresses?" Heads nodded. "Just focus on that statement. Good. He has shielded the line between his public and private personae. That's an absolute legal wall, like someone asking my private persona, Professor Lafayette, who my public persona is, not that it's much of a secret at this point."

"Everything is good?" Abigail asked.

"We talk afterward," Morgana said. "However, the clock is approaching eight. The simplest approach is that you open the garage door, I'll be framed in the light, and Janie will be right next to me. You two, Abigail and Patrick, will be a few feet behind us. Then we come upstairs. Are people good with that, it being your house?"

"Unless we want to use the front door?" Patrick asked.

"Big snowdrift, dad," Trisha said. "I think I can get it in time, but it's more snow than the whole driveway."

"Skip the front door," Patrick answered. As usual, Trisha never showed any sense, say the sense of asking for help.

"Trisha and I will get out your good City board," Brian announced.

"That's very thoughtful of you to do that, Brian," Patrick answered.

"We'd better get our coats on," Abigail said. "That includes you, Patrick. Do you want to borrow a coat, Morgana? We may be standing there for a while."

"That's very kind of you. I'm quite weatherproof, thanks. Actually, I'm going to leave my sweater here. I may need to move quickly," she answered. She draped her sweater over the back of a chair. She wore underneath a white silk blouse. An intricately-worked gold necklace centered a single huge blood-red stone on her chest.

Coats were donned. The Wells family stood in the family garage. "Three of eight," Abigail said, "Time to open the door." Panels creaked and groaned as the door rotated up and over. Snow and bitterly freezing air rushed in from the street.

Precisely at eight in the evening, Krystal North and her four companions appeared in the driveway. Janie waved to Grandmaster Kurchatov, who waved back. Morgana Lafayette pressed her hands together and bowed slightly to Krystal North. North recoiled a half-step.

"For the purpose of this conversation," Morgana announced coldly, "I am Professor Morgana Cysgodol Lafayette, Rogers' Technological Institution. I am the Wells family's persona champion. I am here to ensure that Miss Wells, confronted with a persona, is not placed at a disadvantage during a valid lawful process, and that there is adherence to the privacy codes. That goes for your remote watchers, too, Gamesman Kamensky."

"I am Krystal North, Captain-General of the American Persona League," a shaken North said to Lafayette. "My companions are here to ask Miss Wells about her new City of Steel move, hopefully to prevent possible unfortunate outcomes. I am here as the American persona champion, to validate the conversation, subject to the privacy codes. You will recognize Speaker Ming. I believe Janie knows Grandmasters Kurchatov and Hornpiper, and may recognize Supreme Gamesman Alexander Vladimirovich Kamensky. Given our balmy New England weather, mayhaps we might move inside?"

Chapter Five

The Wells Residence
Arbalest Street
Medford, Massachusetts
Late Evening

The Wells family again sat around their dinner table, Morgana between Janie and her mother.

"You were really great, Janie," Brian said. "You went through the bad variations, and sort of skipped the good ones, except Eclipse's. And the three Grandmasters just stood there nodding."

"Speaker Ming stayed awake," Patrick said, "An art in itself."

"He plays," Janie said. "Whenever he asked about the board, he asked the right questions." Janie decided that the Speaker was really a nice person. After all, he had said good things about her command of the game. She yawned. She'd had three grandmasters grilling her about her move, for two hours, sometimes interrupting each other, sometimes interrupting her before she could get an answer out. It had been exhausting, but she'd learned so much from their questions, so much about how to think about game positions. With real luck, she'd fed them the subtly bad variations on her move.

"He is a gentleman," Patrick said, "so of course he plays the Five Games." Unlike, he thought, my oldest daughter, whose skills at the Five Games are non-existent. She may be good in school, but in her development of personal excellence she is hopeless, gifts not counting toward excellence.

"You two were very thoughtful," Morgana said to Brian and Trisha, "to prepare tea for everyone. In nothing flat. I assume the caramel-frosted hazelnut cookies were Brian's again?"

Brian nodded. "I made them last Sunday and was saving them," he answered. "Well, I was saving the ones Janie and I hadn't eaten yet. Trisha, I told you that you were perfectly welcome to have more of them. Especially after you did all that shoveling. That's why I made so many of them. I knew we'd have snow shoveling."

"Professor Lafayette," Janie said, "You were hiding it really well, but you looked nervous."

"Just a bit," Morgana answered. "The Americans were fine, but Kamensky had the Russian Imperial Elite Strike Command at the far end of his leash. If he'd decided that Joe is Eclipse, which to me sounds massively idiotic, he might have had his people try to kidnap Janie to extract details from her."

"No!" Abigail said. "My little girl?"

I'm not little any more, Janie thought. I'm twelve. Well, barely twelve, but twelve. And the Russian who puts a hand on me is dead.

"I said try," Morgana answered. "Janie was safe. You were all safe. The Tsarists? Unless things went massively bad, after they finished discussing good manners with me they were toast. Burnt toast. Two out of three safe isn't bad, is it? OK, I was more worried about the neighborhood. But there are two things I need to do here, and then I really need to go home and make dinner."

"You are having dinner here," Abigail ordered. "We owe you much more than that. What do you need to do?"

"For the first I need your agreement," Morgana said. "The first is called a null link. It's not mentalic, exactly. But if anything happens to any of you, I know something is wrong and exactly where to find you. It's very slight editing of your subconscious, like crossloading an app onto a RadioBell. Oh, when I'm done, you won't remember that I did it. Except you, Janie, you know your own mind too clearly. You will remember. You will also not remind anyone that they have one. It's a safety precaution. Agreed?" Patrick, Abigail, Trisha, and Janie nodded. Brian grimaced but finally mouthed agreement. "This just takes a moment."

"Now," Morgana continued, "the two things I need to do," she winked at Janie, who smiled back, "are to find out if there's a reason none of you know where Joe lives, and if so, what the reason is. Each of you, try to remember to ask Joe for his phone number the next time you see him." Her eyebrows wrinkled. "That was very interesting, but not the way I expected. I can go to the next step, unless you want to drop it." Janie needed a few moments to realize what had just happened. Morgana had planted null links in her parents and her siblings, and in her mind, too. None of them remembered it. She hadn't felt a thing when her link was implanted. She could tell it was there, but it had just appeared, as if by magic. It was very good, that Morgana was so skillful, and very bad, that her own mindscreens were so completely worthless.

"What was interesting?" Patrick asked.

"I just asked you a certain question. You don't remember me asking. You can't think about the topic. You can think about related things, though maybe only with me sitting here, but not the question you just thought about. Even you, Janie, and you have solid mentalic defenses. You each had your minds changed, so soon as I asked the question, but the mind changing was not done with mentalics," Morgana said. "That's why your mentalic screens didn't trigger, Janie, what was done was not mentalic. And some of my wards, ones that normally never do anything, were poked, not gently."

"Is it dangerous?" Abigail asked.

"In this world, nothing is safe," Morgana answered. "Someone placed a geas on you and your house. That's all of you. Having a geas like that in your house is almost certainly dangerous. Yes, geas, a stable fourth-order construct. It controls what you think, about a narrow range of topics, inobtrusively. Leaving it there, now that you know it exists, even though you can't remember what the topics are, is probably even more dangerous. To remove it, I need a blank sheet of paper on a clean table."

"Got it," Trisha announced. The suddenly clean table had a large sheet of blank paper on it.

"Three of you will see nothing." Morgana pressed the paper flat. "Abigail, Patrick mentioned that your grandmother on the O'Rigamy side had the second sight, so you may see a blue haze. Janie, you will see clearly what I am doing, but you should absolutely not, not even if it's life and death, try anything like this, not until you know exactly what you are doing. Clear? And the rest of you, don't interrupt."

"Yes, ma'am," Janie managed. A boy would try something just because he was told not to. She was not a boy, she told herself. If she was told not to do something, because it was way too dangerous, she wouldn't give in to temptation. Well, not Brian. He was almost sensible enough to be a girl. *<Can you teach me how to do…whatever it is? Or at least how to protect myself?>* Only Morgana heard her question.

<Yes. But not soon. Sorry. Unless you want to give up games. Talk later,> Morgana answered.

<Ulp? Later.> Janie answered. Give up games? That was unthinkable, undenkbar, nevoobrazimy…and she realized that studying German and Russian, so she could read their games literature, had suddenly started to work.

"Good." Morgana touched the paper. "Nin amner Morgoth." To Janie's eyes, a point of blue light appeared on the page. Morgana tapped the paper again. "Nin amner Calirath." Another point of light appeared. Morgana continued her chant. When she touched the fifth point, the light from the points flowed out, forming a star etched into the paper, surrounded by circles within which burned words in a script Janie did not recognize. To Janie's eyes, the letters seemed to move, curling into and out of the page like tiny earthworms. "Now, all of you, try to remember that you want to ask Joe about his home address. Good. Wait." Morgana gestured above the circle, her fingers making an intricate cat's cradle that wove in and out. Janie saw what her siblings did not, bands of light and lines of text connecting Morgana's fingers. The lights vanished. The circle faded away, to Janie's ears like the tuning fork that, once struck, fades and fades but never quite stops. "All done," Morgana announced, slumping back in her chair.

"What were you doing?" Brian asked. "Are you all right?"

"That," Morgana announced, "was a fourth order attack in use. Until I erased it. It made sure that anyone in this house would not think that Joe had a home address or interlink ID, let alone wonder what they were. Usually you would just think someone else knew the answer, so you didn't have to ask. The geas also made sure that no one would think it was interesting that the Joe here was the same as the Joe who rescued Janie and Trisha. The attack followed Joe around, within a mile or two, so no one else would wonder." She leaned back farther in her chair. "I'm all right, but it was very solidly embedded."

"Who could do that?" Brian said, not quite making it sound like a question. "Are you sure you're all right?"

Morgana threw up her hands. "At a guess, Joe's mom. But I don't know who she is. 'Cartwright' is not a persona I can name. Almost no personas can do things like this. I don't remember that any of the ones who can have children. And thank you for asking, Brian. Mayhaps another cookie, please? That was more than a bit tiring." Brian handed her three cookies, the first of which rapidly disappeared.

"You much look as though you need dinner," Patrick announced, "and you three young ones need to give us a private conversation. Your grades from Morgana, remember?"

"Yes, sir," Brian answered. "Forward to modeling." The three children headed upstairs.

"And now, Morgana," Abigail said, "we are going to hear our children's grades on your coaching them with their gifts, and you are going to get a reasonably solid dinner. And tell us about the specialist support you arranged for Trisha. Dinner was not meant as a suggestion. Young people like you are too careless about eating properly at the right hours." Abigail turned to the sideboard and began bringing dishes back to the table.

Morgana looked at the ceiling. "Patrick, you really didn't tell your dear wife what you know about me through the tenure committee, did you? I know you promised, and I understand that you Americans are very strict in respecting the privacy of private personas, but under the circumstances…" He really had not told his wife, she thought, and that bit of New England propriety was about to create an interesting conversation.

"Young lady, that is we Americans," Abigail said, "since Patrick did mention that you were an Englishwoman but had taken American citizenship, just like several of my ancestors did, five and seven centuries ago. Yes, Patrick has completely respected the privacy of your private persona, enough so that I knew there was a Professor Morgana Lafayette, and I knew there was a public persona Sunssword, but I had never met you, the Professor, to know that you were Sunssword. And now you have half of a roast chicken, shoe peg corn, sliced potatoes with sautéed onions and sour cream, and what is left of the tossed salad with Roquefort dressing. Oh, yes, several croissants with butter. Brian was too busy with his cooking to snatch any of my chocolate fudge, which is just as well as chocolate would have gotten him into all sorts of difficulty. Now I can sit down and hear what is going on."

"I hope you don't mind if I eat while we're talking," Morgana said. "There are ways to cheat on eating, in an emergency. Your cooking, from the smell, is absolutely superb, far better than the alternative. My cooking has never poisoned anyone. Well, not recently. At least, not accidentally. In any event, to use a line almost as old as I am, the kids are just fine. The worst problem was that Janie has an extremely rigid and accurate sense of gifttruth, at the level that leaves people paralyzed with fear that they have done something wrong. She got over the fear. Fortunately, she got over the fear before The Emperor Roxbury's robots showed up at her school, because she had to do something violent to deal with them. She did. She's absolutely fine." And in a few moments I get to explain just how she overcame her fear.

"I was more worried about Trisha. Flying faster than sound could be dangerous. What if she accidentally left the Earth's atmosphere? I told Patrick that she needed specialist coaching, but he assured me that everything was in good hands," Abigail said.

"Ummh, I think we all agreed that so long as she was not doing anything dangerous, I would be trusted with my professional judgement on coaching her," Morgana said. I talked it over with Patrick, she thought; I'm sure he understood what that statement meant. And Trisha actually is too cowed by her parents to talk to them about how wonderfully good a flier she actually is. I should have leaned harder on her, so I could find out what she'd told her mom and dad. "So I was the specialist." Morgana paused. Abigail stared at her. Trisha hadn't told her that.

"You're the specialist?" Abigail asked. "But, then, I inherited grandmother O'Rigamy's second sight. I saw what you had on the table, Morgana. You are no mere hedge witch, are you? That was a full ritual casting."

"I think I'd better go back a step, Abigail, since you have absolutely no idea about my other public personas," Morgana said. Abigail nodded. And I dodged the question, Morgana thought.

"I try not to tell people this," Morgana said. "The tenure committee agreed to a memory shield block, meaning that if anyone tried to read their minds about this, the block would use up the memory before the shield was worn through. They could remember what I told them, but no one else could extract the information from them. I'd rather you agreed to the same, it being much for your own safety." Abigail nodded. There were a few moments of silence.

"First, notwithstanding that half of the grad students and post-docs in my and several other departments have what is supposed to be a secret betting pool on which of them will be the first to seduce me, the woman who is obviously the youngest female Professor at RTI, I am not a young woman. My persona name is not Sunsword, the Boston Post notwithstanding. It is Sun's Sword, because I was, once upon a time, the Golden Warrior, the

Living Sword of the Sun Goddess Amaterasu. That was the title; if there is such a Goddess, we have not met. That was in the court of the Japanese Emperor, when I was living in the Nipponese capital, which at the time was Heian-Kyo. Their capital has since moved.. I'm not at all offended that you thought I might not be up to coaching your children, since you had no idea who I am."

"You're how old?" Abigail asked. "Before we go farther, how is it that I've ended up with you sitting in my kitchen? It would be like discovering that you're Solara in disguise. I'm not complaining. I'm truly grateful for what you do for my children, but the coincidences seem strained."

"Why am I here?" Morgana responded. "Far before you reach my actual age, you realize that you want to live in Athens. The most civilized, cultured, sensible place there is. In the Tenth Century, that was Heian-Kyo. At another time, Byzantium, Baghdad, and Cordoba were mayhaps more civilized, but less welcoming to women. Once upon a time, it was the Leviorkianu Domain, and others it was Marik-on-the-Sea or Gaia Atlanticea or Sarnath. And now it is Cambridge, the American Athens."

"Second," Morgana continued, "we really need to talk more about what it means that Trisha and Brian and Janie are all really first line personas. It's not just they have a few gifts. Yes, Brian can ignore machine gun fire. Janie can read minds. Trisha can fly really, really fast. We'll get back to that in a moment." Morgana paused to finish part of another croissant. This was going to be more difficult than she had hoped. She hadn't realized quite how carefully Patrick and Abigail supervised their children, or how little they respected their own children's judgement, poor Trisha's in particular. No wonder Trisha was short on self-confidence.

"They're all in good health." Morgana tried to sound reassuring. "They may catch the flu, but they recover in a few hours. They are almost certainly immune to chocolate...but their friends aren't. Janie and Brian, in very different ways, can focus very deeply on what they're doing. That's why Janie has her Highly Respected by the Lords of the Hexagon, and Brian's models sell for enough to pay for his hobby, the extra books he buys Janie, and Trisha's sewing supplies and books and extra athletic equipment. Trisha is a physical fitness fanatic, except...really, please stop telling her she'll hurt herself if she works too hard. Please? She won't, not to mention she'll recover in a bit if she totally overdoes things. Your feedback is confusing her." Actually, Morgana thought, it's hurting her very deeply, but she'll never say a word about it, and I can't be telling her parents that.

"That's just what mothers say," Abigail countered. This was going to be a mess, Morgana thought. Trisha is taking her mom literally, and I am not going to be able to explain to Abigail what that means when she talks at Trisha. Nor can I tell Trisha not to listen to her mom.

"Absolutely," Morgana said. "The two feet of snow and plow curl she removed from your drive...she wasn't vaguely close to her muscle and bone limits. For her, that was just a healthy bit of exercise. She knows it. Please keep in mind that superspeed passes normally for her. She actually had to shovel your driveway of two feet of heavy snow, one scoop at a time. And catch her breath when she needed to." Hopefully, Morgana thought, I have made a dent in the problem. I can't very well tell Abigail that she is absurdly condescending in ways that are hurting Trisha. "However, there is also the third thing."

"Third?" Patrick asked. To Morgana's eyes, Patrick looked deeply thoughtful. She had no idea what influence he had on his wife, who seemed to be the source of the issues Trisha was facing.

"Trisha does fly faster than sound," Morgana said. "Faster than light indeed being faster than sound. And all three kids have full deep space gifts, so flying to the moon or wherever is not an issue."

"Faster than light?" Abigail asked. "That means that in a few minutes Trisha could be millions of miles from Earth, and get lost. We go to the supermarket, and she gets lost, can't remember where we parked the car."

"Has Trisha actually flown very far at high speed?" Patrick asked. "I'd hate to think she tried flying to the Moon and ran out of steam part way there."

"We were going to discuss this," Morgana said, "because she had this really neat photograph she wanted to show you, admittedly taken with one of my cameras, of the Milky Way galaxy. The picture is from well to the Galactic South, so you can see all the spiral arms. That's about 600,000 light years out from the Galactic center, which she covered in under half an hour, notwithstanding the need for acceleration and deceleration and being careful not to fly through anything large and solid along the way. Oh yes, she has the safe form of superspeed, so she isn't getting any older if she spends a couple of subjective hours shoveling the driveway, the way she just did." Morgana pulled a bitstick from her blouse pocket.

"Socket under the table," Patrick said. "The screen comes down from the ceiling when in use." The three waited a few moments. Up on the screen came an image, a huge photograph of a galaxy, multiple spiral arms all clearly visible.

"Furthermore," Morgana continued, "Trisha, Jessamine Trishaset, has true deep space navigation. She cannot get lost, up to local hazards that she can fly away from, anywhere in our universe. She knows exactly where home is. And her other gifts would let her make that flight, all the way across the universe, though she might want a nap at the end." Abigail swallowed deeply.

"That's our galaxy?" Abigail asked. "My specialty was computational astrophysics, not observational astronomy."

"That's ours," Morgana answered. "Trisha took it. She did want me along, half to kibitz on camera setup, half because…she could do it by herself, it's perfectly safe, but she doesn't trust herself." Mostly because people don't trust her, Morgana thought, and people keep telling her that she has bad judgement and will hurt herself if she tries anything challenging. "We did a timed flying run. Trisha is undoubtedly the fastest persona in the world, including any of the Lords of Eternity."

"To finish the grades," Morgana continued, "Brian has a first rate set of screens, not to mention several plasma attacks that did a fine job on Emperor Roxbury's robots. If he were a grownup, he'd be welcome in Stars Over Boston, though it would be a waste of his time. His model building is a gift, but a very rare one. He'll probably develop other gifts as he goes on, but he's the type that develops a few things deeply rather than many things broadly. Janie is an absolutely first-rate mentalist. Besides telepathy and screening, she is one of the few personas I know who can read machine minds. Very recently, she developed a mentalic attack, something that will kill people. I emphasize that she has a very well developed sense of gifttruth, so she is safe with the gift in question, but if she is driven to the point that she decides that she has to kill someone, they will be very dead very quickly indeed.

"Brian and Janie between them have an additional gift, mayhaps because they're almost identical twins, because the random sort of chromosomes for fraternal twins managed to give them almost the same set of chromosomes, though obviously not quite the same, namely they can trade their gifts. They did. It was Janie using shields and plasma torch who took down the last of Emperor Roxbury's robots. As we've said, Trisha has ultrafast flight, deep space navigation, life support, meaning she can breathe for the people she's carrying through space, this invisibility which she just mentioned, and telescopic vision. On a clear night, especially if she goes above the atmosphere, she views a fair number of stars as having obvious discs. And planets. Questions?"

"I did say," Abigail said, "that we should respect my children's privacy so long as they were not going to get into any trouble or do anything dangerous. From what you're saying, my twins are safer with their gifts than they would've been without. What am I missing?"

"There was the issue I learned about yesterday, which is alarming but not dangerous," Morgana answered, "and there is the issue I learned about tonight, which may be dangerous. The alarming but not dangerous issue is that on rare occasion the Wizard of Mars invites people for tea. Those people are very well advised to go. That's totally safe for the people involved, as opposed to visiting the Wizard of Mars and playing trade questions. Trading questions with the Wizard of Mars rates up there with flying to the center of the sun… as a suicidal act. For reasons I do not know and am not about to fly to Mars to ask, the Wizard of Mars has been inviting Trisha and Janie and sometimes Brian for tea. He asked that they not tell anyone, because it would be dangerous to the whole world, and they fortunately had the wisdom to honor his wishes. The last time they visited, he said that they could tell their sensei, and I could tell you. So far as I can tell, he has been asking them completely innocent questions, and telling them educational stories. I think he's why Janie got over her issue with gifttruth. I would strongly urge you to rely on the Wizard of Mars having good intentions. He always has. Also, the warning 'dangerous to the world' should be taken extremely seriously. If someone had given the Lords of Eternity that warning, they would've had conniptions."

"Brian is selling his models?" Patrick said. "He never mentioned. He only talks about fixing things. Wait! My taxes!"

"I checked," Morgana said. "Harry Truman's Lemonade Stand exemption. It's strictly Brian's work…he might get audited, but there's no tax." Patrick, she thought, is a truly self-centered person, someone entirely worried about how his children's actions might reflect badly on him, and not at all on what might happen to them. Most heads of state would sell their families into slavery for an invitation from the Wizard, and he is brushing it off in favor of his income tax being paid correctly.

"If you say the Wizard is safe for Janie and Brian," Abigail said, "I believe you. I don't think anything is safe for Trisha."

"Why am I having dinner here?" Morgana asked. "That returns us to the issue I learned about tonight." Trisha's parents seem to think, Morgana thought, that their smartest and most sensible child is a complete idiot. There's no way to fix that. "Joe. Janie mentioned she had a regular playing partner of that name, which is perfectly reasonable at her age. It's a very common name. I didn't connect with the persona who saved her a few years ago. I don't think the geas -- the one I just removed -- would have misled me. I'm very good at spotting geases that try to bother me.

"However, the Joe who plays Janie seems to have been very careful to make sure that I never met him. After all, I'm the only person other than your daughters who knows what Joe-the-Public-Persona who saved your daughters looks like. I'm significantly impressed if this Joe, whoever he is, is actually as strong physically as Trisha, given that neither of them have strength as a gift…and Trisha would know if Joe had that gift. Two years ago, no one else got a good look at him. However, I would've innocently assumed that if Janie had run into the fellow who saved her, she would've talked about it. She did, except for not saying that they were the same person. Do Janie or Trisha ever talk about what happened to them, two years ago?"

Morgana kept trying to fit the puzzle pieces together in her mind. They refused to cooperate. Janie had this remarkable City of Steel innovation. She had this boy who had saved her, a boy with remarkably potent gifts. Someone was casting geases. Hopefully that someone was not Joe. The thought of a child who thought he understood fourth level work was seriously alarming.

Patrick and Abigail looked at each other. "We told both of them," Patrick said, "that if they ever want to talk about it they may. If they want someone else to talk to, we can arrange that. They both said they were entirely comfortable talking with you. What I didn't expect, though maybe I should've, is that Brian wanted to be sure he understood what his sisters went through. Janie shared mind to mind with Brian what she remembered. They all said that Joe's mom did something, so that they remember what happened, but they don't remember being frightened, and they are not frightened when they think about it. Or did you help with that?"

"I would've done that for them," Morgana said, "but Joe's mom did it first. She did a very good job of it." Morgana looked down at the table. "Actually, she did a truly fine job of it, and I can't imagine who she is, either. I could've taken care of their minds if they needed it. Goddess only knows I've had enough practice healing people with after-combat mental distress. What I meant to ask about was not those horrifying few hours, but the physical details of the persona combat."

Abigail shook her head. "Trisha was out cold almost the whole time, and Janie said she didn't see much except occasionally things got bright. She was busy shouting for help. She did pull Trisha over the edge of a sand dune."

"Janie shouting for help is how I got involved," Morgana answered. "If the two of them hadn't been persona, the kidnappers would've ignored them. If Janie hadn't been so good at mentalics back then, the kidnappers might have gotten away with it. Unless Joe stopped them. One of the kidnappers had a very strong mentalic screen, strong enough that Janie had to be really loud to be heard outside. Fortunately, we heard her. But when I met Janie and Trisha I could tell they were very deeply gifted, and needed a practiced hand guiding them. That was me."

"In any event," Morgana continued, pausing once and again for more chicken, "there was press coverage of Joe saving Trisha and Janie. The press made it sound like the villains teleported out to Sand Crab Island. In the middle, Joe somehow separated them from their pistol, following which Stars Over Boston came to the rescue. Then Joe got your daughters back to you. The miscreants must've been seriously injured while resisting arrest, because they all died that evening. None of that is false, but there are some minor details left out." Morgana paused to finish off another croissant.

"Janie described Joe teleporting them, first to someplace in northern Canada and then to Frog Pond Park," Abigail said. "They were both worried about Joe, because when they left him he was shivering."

"Chills are common if you go way too deep into your gifts," Morgana explained. "And I mean way too deep, not just a bit too deep. That's not surprising, given what he did. Fortunately, he or they moved the whole thing to Sand Crab Island. That combat was not a couple of guys wrestling over possession of a knife. Joe was the good-guy side of the deepest level persona combat in New England since Crittenden's War. Joe is in the power range where he could easily level a city block of brownstones with one plasma blast, which is truly unusual for a boy his age. The people on the other side were probably about as good. The pistol that did not quite take down Joe's shields was indubitably a Krell disruptor pistol. It's a starcore weapon. If the villains had fired it at Boston, they would have torched everything on the ocean side of Beacon Hill with one shot. Assuredly it hit Joe's shields, and his shields did not go down. Joe won by himself. On the way out, he grabbed the pistol and a Krell shield bracer from one of the miscreants. The miscreant was dead at the time. Joe killed him. Joe seems to have no compunctions about killing people. Stars Over Boston got there after everything was over. I am morally certain. Joe teleported out with your daughters because he saw me appear.

"Then, afterward, something broke into Castle Island Prison, put the guards to sleep without their noticing anything, hid its presence from the three members of Stars Over Boston who were also guarding the place, and exfoliated the memories of the surviving villains, incidentally killing them. The villains were very deeply tranquilized and being given medical care. Mighty Mind was going to search their memories, but was waiting for the needed court order. Something else did not wait. You may have heard about the ring of perverts in our country's southern neighbors, the ones who were kidnapping persona children and torturing them to death? The people captured in Boston were their strike team. The same night that the prisoners died, something appeared above the perverts' main base, smashed down a very high power set of force fields, killed the personas defending the place, and rescued a bunch of children. The political aftermath, when the detailed records were made public, is still reverberating. People have heard the parts, but not connected the dots."

"Is Janie safe near Joe?" Abigail asked. "Isn't it dangerous to have personas that powerful wandering around in their vicinity? I'm not counting you, of course."

"The only time I've seen Joe use his powers, that from a distance, he was protecting Trisha and Janie at what I hope he realized was a considerable risk to his own life. Trisha and Janie have nothing to worry about, so far as I can tell. Joe took a big chance to fight that crew. I'm not sure whether or not he knew he was taking a chance. He may have thought he would just stomp the people attacking Trisha and Janie into the ground. If they'd been ungifteds, he would have. I want to speak to him. With that sort of power, unless you have good training, your slight errors can get large numbers of people killed. Including you, if you make a big enough mistake. Also, someone put a geas on your house. I find that bothersome. There aren't a lot of people who can do that, and none that I can name appear to have a motive."

The wind gusted, hard enough that the shutters rattled. "However, I am keeping you up late," Morgana continued, "I still have a paper to write, and I've given your children their grades. They are all Excellent. Your meal was most appreciated. So far as I can tell, you five are not in any particular danger. I should be on my way." Morgana stood, hugged Abigail, and took Patrick's hand. "Next time, I should bring some of my cooking. I have, after all, had a few years to figure out how to recognize boiling water."

"Thank you for everything, Morgana" Abigail said. "You're sure you don't want to borrow a coat for the flight back? And you do get a box of my cookies. And some of the fudge."

"I'm not planning on flying," Morgana said, "but I would love some of the cookies, and some of the fudge." Abigail, Morgana thought, really doesn't recognize that I'm entirely weatherproof. She waited moments for the box.

"Thank you for backing up Janie, Morgana," Patrick said. "Matters could have been much worse. However, the Tenure Committee really does look at publications."

"Yes, Professor Wells. Publish or join the glorious dead. Patrick, call at once if Janie disappears. She won't. And if she does, I should know instantaneously. Krystal North had the fear of the Goddess put into her. So did the Tsarists. It was a delight to have dinner with you, and your children are excellent students. With that I must bid adieu." Her figure became transparent and vanished from sight.

~~~~~

Great Dome of the Capital
Washington, Federal District
Late evening

The atmosphere under the Great Dome was even frostier than the Cambridge blizzard. Speaker Ming, three Gamesmasters, and Krystal North stood in a circle.

"The notion that this slip of a girl can come up with such a move is absurd," Supreme Gamesman Kamensky announced. "She must have backers, backers she failed to divulge. That's lying to this inquiry, and grounds for more rigorous interrogation. Under the Tsar, she would be removed to the tender graces of the Okhrana until she revealed who her backers are. This could still be arranged."

Grandmaster Kurchatov's face stiffened. "Fortunately, Kamensky, this is a civilized country. Such things do not happen here."

"Alexander Vladimirovich," Krystal repeated, "Cambridge is in the American Republic, so such an outcome does not arise." Kamensky and his crew appeared to think that they were the lords of the Earth, entitled to do whatever they wanted. She hoped she could talk some sense into them.

"Miss North. Really. I would not dream of violating your quaint local customs," Kamensky answered unctuously. "Though Miss Wells' second, that charming college professor a third my age, would hardly have been a serious threat to my escorts."

"Alexander Vladimirovich," Krystal said, "That young lady, as you put it, is a first-line combat persona. I can name three times she had a serious brawl with a Lord of Eternity. She came out on top all three times. In case you haven't noticed, the Tsar's Persona Corps has no one who can stand up against an Eternal, one on one, for more than a few seconds. If your unseen Russian Imperial Elite Strike Command had tried what you suggested, Count Supreme Gamesman Kamensky, they would have been reduced to ashes. It
~~~~~

was painfully obvious that Professor Lafayette could tell where your team would be appearing, to the inch, and was ready to eliminate your precious national team as they arrived. That's before my League rode to the rescue. That's Janie's rescue. Professor Lafayette needed no rescue. Indeed, my League's major task on arrival would have been to sweep up the ashes. If you'd been a co-conspirator, we would be sweeping up your ashes, too. With modest luck, the Federal Senate would later have agreed that you had acted on your own, not on behalf of your government, in which case America would not be ending this month by going to war with the Tsar. I hope I have made this point adequately clear."

Kamensky turned on Speaker Ming. "I must protest these idle American threats."

"Supreme Gamesman Kamensky," Ming answered. "Miss North was simply clarifying the political situation for you. I believe she is in error on only one point. In my opinion, if the Russian Army invaded Boston and tried to kidnap and torture a little girl, it would have been absolutely impossible to convince the People and Senate of the Republic that you had been acting on your own. We would then have had a full-scale war without limits."

"In that case," Kamensky announced, "I prefer to return home. Security!" Kamensky vanished. Krystal felt a flood of relief. If Kamensky had tried kidnapping Jane Caroline, matters would have become extremely unfortunate extremely quickly.

"Interesting company the little girl keeps," Kurchatov said. "I suppose Miss Wells must have come up with her new move for herself. Though those variations she proposed all looked flawed."

"Victor," Grandmaster Hornpiper said, "I had had the same thought, but then decided that if I were in her predicament I would have been delighted to tell you about many variations on my move…the bad variations. In her position, if I'd been asked about chess openings, I would have talked at length about the Horns of Hattin opening, or mayhaps the Glorious Shield of Sarnath."

"You're mean, Honarius," Ming said, not at all seriously. "Surely this sweet little girl would not pull such an underhanded trick?"

"This sweet little girl," Kurchatov said, "forced me to offer a tie when we played, a tie she gleefully accepted. She had good chances of winning, too, but preferred the certainty of a draw. That put her ranking up very considerably. She is highly underhanded."

"Good for her," Ming said. "She embodies the highest aspects of the American gaming spirit." The two Grandmasters nodded affirmatively.

"Gentlemen," Krystal said, "I am happy to have both of you teleported home, it being late indeed, but I need to have a watch put on the Wells residence and on all three children. And their parents. Baron Kamensky might be smart enough to back off, but some of his backers are decidedly less cautious." All we need, she thought, is a war with Russia, on top of whatever outcome the Namestone and its bearer create. "Mister Speaker, I fear we need to have a short private conversation. Please?" Ming nodded.

~~~~~

Speaker Ming's office looked out at the Washington monument and the Aqua Potomociae. The Jefferson Monument rose in the distance. Tapestries lining the walls, carefully reproduced stitch by stitch from the originals, showed the founders of the Republic. Two thousand years ago the founders had arrived in Massachusetts Bay, fleeing the Pacific Northwest and the ruins of Leaviork. The globe-spanning empire of the Leviorkianu had ceased to exist. In the course of an afternoon Solara had laid it waste, leaving behind only the desolate remains of its crystal towers.

Speaker Ming gestured at her and one of his deeply-padded arm chairs. "Tea?" he asked. "Or something much stronger? Krystal, I have known you for two decades, and that is the closest I have ever seen in you to sheer terror. Whatever is wrong? You had the entire National team ready to cover your back if Kamensky had tried something foolish. The Wells family seemed to be nice people, whose deaths in this case would have been a cause celebre, something tragic, something you would have worked heroically to avoid, but that did not seem to be the issue." Krystal pointed at the tea pot. He poured two cups of his special blend. "It's by now cool enough to drink immediately."

North waited for her hands to stop shaking, sniffed the bouquet, sipped, and set the cup back in the saucer. "Mister Speaker, there are certain national secrets that I bear on account of my office. Only rarely does my office reveal them. This particular one was given to Speaker Adams as King George's fleet approached, to Speaker Seward at the start of Crittenden's War, but was not discussed by my predecessor with Speaker Roosevelt during the 1908 Summer War."

"I see," Speaker Ming said. "Or mayhaps I do not see. I trust your judgement whether to tell me."

"Actually, Mister Speaker, the difficulty is that you did see, though for some reason you did not notice what was under your nose," Krystal said. "You are a very observant man. Mayhaps you couldn't see it. There are ways of doing that. Professor Morgana Lafayette. Her necklace was, unmistakably, the Orb of Merlin. Supposedly the bearer only reveals it if its use is likely to be imminent. The not-at-all young lady wearing it also calls herself by a three-word respelling of the name she currently uses."

Speaker Ming paled. "As found in a certain Constitutional Amendment?" Krystal nodded. "These are indeed very deep waters." The Speaker shook his head. "However, I did not see the ashes falling from the sky, nor hear the shrieking of the damned souls. I am not complaining that Lafayette's other persona did not manifest itself. Do you think Miss Wells knows who her champion actually is?"

"Unlikely," Krystal answered. "The middle name Lafayette claimed. It's a
~~~~~

literary reference to a famous novel of a previous cycle, a novel cycle that every child then read in school. It means 'the one in the shadow'."

"She looks like a happy young woman, not like…her manifestation," Ming said.

"Hopefully she will stay that way," Krystal answered. "If she actually became annoyed with the Tsar, tens of millions of his subjects would perish."

Chapter Six

Secure Chamber Alpha
The Palace of Peace
Geneva, Switzerland

League Chancellor Lars Holmgren tapped his walnut gavel twice on its black elm sounding block. "Good morning! Gentlemen? Ladies? I know it has been a very long few days. May we have order, please? This meeting of the League of Nations Special Peace Executive is now in session, Legate Hong taking any needed notes. Thank you, Legate Hong. I believe we have all reviewed the recordings of Wednesday's events. I have circulated an agenda. Under the non-emergency rules, we begin by naming ourselves."

"For the American Republic, Ambassador Thaddeus Buncombe." Buncombe, wearing a classic pinstripe three-piece suit with broad red, white, and blue vertical-striped tie, leaned back in his chair. Now, he thought, there would be the representatives of the foreign kings and princes, and their pompously useless titles.

Buncombe looked around the room. The Peace Executive sat at a horseshoe-shaped white marble table, with Holmgren in the middle and Buncombe at the heel of the horseshoe's right branch. A thin layer of synthetic diamond formed the table's surface, ensuring that the table was in little danger of being scratched. The walls and floor were the same brilliant white marble, carved and inlaid with what the European founders of the League viewed as scenes showing the triumph of civilization. To Buncombe's eyes, those scenes mostly represented Europeans trampling other parts of the world under foot. Curiously, images of King George the Mad attempting to trample America were conspicuous for their absence.

"For Austria-Hungary, Count Karl-Michael Ferencz." Buncombe nodded respectfully at Ferencz. Emperor Joseph III had spent forty years requiring that his representatives be highly competent. The Count might have a title, but he had surely earned his post.

"For the Brazilian Empire, Ambassadrix Amanda Rafaela Mascarenhas da Silva." The speaker was a woman in her early sixties, hair a deep black, her blouse, vest, and long dress a brilliant royal blue fringed in gold. Buncombe smiled warmly at her. She was one of the truly thoughtful people on the

Peace Executive.

"For the Queen-Empress Victoria, the Third of her Name, Lord Reginald Featherstonehaugh." The current Featherstonehaugh, Buncombe considered, was considerably less arrogant than his father, who Americans could readily imagine as one of the crown officials who cheered on King George III, George the Mad, as he launched the 1774 British invasion of the American Republic.

"For the Celestial Republic of the Han, Prince Shi Fang." Shi looked politely around the room, the blank look on his face masking his inner thoughts.

"Speaking for the Emperor of All France, Napoleon the Sixth, I am Imperial Grand Marshall Bernard-Christian Davout." Davout wore the polychrome uniform of a modern French Field Marshal. It was possible, Buncombe thought, that some color had been omitted from his ensemble, but if so it was by oversight. For all his military decorations, Davout's military experience was quite limited. Davout's own conquests were more focused on the boudoir, and over the years had included several of his fellow Ambassadors, though despite his best efforts not Amanda Rafaela.

"For His Aweful and Terrible Majesty, the Almighty Supreme Warlord of All the Germans, Kaiser Friedrich the Fourth and Greatest, I am Markgraf Heinrich Moeller." All the Germans, Buncombe thought to himself, if one forgot the Austro-Hungarians, the Swiss, the Bavarians, and the residents of the French Rhineland. In the proliferation of pompous imperial titles, though, Prussians had no peers. The Prussians were perpetually inventing new honorifics for their Kaiser, mayhaps as a break from scheming to recover the mythical past borders to which they thought they were entitled, these being all the places where German had at one time been spoken. Their schemes had as their primary effect solidifying the anti-Prussian alliance that included all of their neighbors.

"The Speaker for the First Speaker of the Mexica and the Inca." Lord Smoking Frog leaned back in his chair. His feather cloak rustled as it wrapped around the polished wood.

"For the Osmanli padislahari, the Emperor, may his wisdom increase forever, has sent me, his Grand Vizier, Suleiman Pasha." So that's who he is, Buncombe thought, a fellow I have never met. And Suleiman Pasha normally stays out of sight, so the Emperor gets all the credit for Suleiman's good ideas, and Suleiman avoids all blame for his own bad ideas. Why is he here, then?

"Ambassador Fateh Singh of the Sikh Empire, Speaker for all South Asian states." Singh's cloth-of-gold coat appeared to Buncombe to be wasteful, not to mention cold. Similar criticisms might be made of most of the other foreigners, few of whom had adopted the simple, frugal, not to mention comfortable style affected by American diplomats. Singh, however, was a man one could speak with privately, and have some confidence that he was not saying whatever he thought you wanted to hear.

"I am Saigo Shigetoshi, Legate of the Satsuma Daimyo." Buncombe nodded politely at Shigetoshi. Relations between the America Republic and their Pacific neighbor had always been friendly, each side recognizing that any other attitude was pointless. Shigetoshi's seven layers of polychrome kimono, besides being gorgeously colorful, were both warm and comfortable.

"Legate Hong Sangui of Manjukuo." Hong carefully turned away from Buncombe. Relations across the Bering Straits had been frigid since the Manjukuoans discovered that their failure to contest the ownership of Alaska had given away huge gold and mineral deposits. Of course, Buncombe considered, the Empire had been so little interested in Alaska and places beyond that they had retained a Russian to explore them.

"For Peter, Emperor of all the Russias, Princess Elizaveta Petrovna Romanoff." The oldest daughter of Tsar Peter VI wore classical Russian court dress, complete with a tiara. Romanoff's coat and blouse and trousers were brilliant scarlet spackled with silvery lace and trim. The platinum alloy highlighted her long hair, faded by the decades from raven-black to pure white. At sixty, she preserved the slim figure she had had at twenty, a figure that distracted male viewers from her sharp wit and sharper memory. The figure, Buncombe thought, was undoubtedly in fair part a consequence of her wearing at all times a substantial tonnage of silk and precious metals. All times, of course, except those in which the tonnage was being removed by any of several of the other Ambassadors or good friends, since she adhered to the traditional European standard 'who cares who has a slice of the cake, once the cake has been cut?'

"Colonel-General Wilhelm Christian von und zu Dreikirch, League Secret Political Police." Dreikirch snapped to attention and clicked his heels. Dreikirch was a good Prussian, who affected all the Prussian mannerisms down to kissing the air over a woman's hand. He was certainly not partial to the desires of Kaiser Friedrich, much to the Kaiser's frustration. After all, there was a regulation against Dreikirch doing that.

"League Elite Persona Brigade, Brigade Leader Valkyria." The tall, blue-eyed woman now wore a mid-calf-length flame-orange dress rather than her more familiar battle armor. The loose sleeves of the blouse failed to hide her substantial muscles. Unlike many folks in plate mail, Buncombe reminded himself, Valkyria was not stupid, just vigorously rules-oriented. In some ways, rules-oriented could be worse.

"League Chancellor Lars Holmgren." Unfortunately, Buncombe considered, the Chancellor was unlikely to consume too much from his pocket flasks, no matter how amusing the consequences would be.

Where was this meeting going, Buncombe wondered? The Ambassadors had met often enough that most of them, most of the time, did not feel obliged to insult each other. Positions of the Great Powers on ownership of the Namestone were hardly state secrets, at least among the powers that believed that the Namestone existed. The Celestial Republic of Prince Shi was by no means convinced that there actually was a Namestone. After all, if the Namestone existed, the Martyr would undoubtedly have given it to the Perfect Man, the Emperor of the Middle Kingdom, Lord of All the Earth, when the Martyr first arrived on Earth three millennia ago, and he had not done so. The IncoAztecan Speaker for the First Speaker doubtless agreed with the Celestial Republic's Ambassador, except of course that the Martyr would undoubtedly have given the Namestone to the First Speaker, the Living Sun.

Holmgren directed his attention to the chief of the League Secret Political Police, who looked bedraggled. Dreikirch had been awake most of the time for four days, ever since the universal solar eclipse began. "General von und zu Dreikirch, is there any progress to report? I know there is also an agenda, but first things first." Buncombe considered Dreikirch's dress uniform, which was as gaudy as the uniforms worn by the majordomos of not-quite-first-line New York hotels and the Admirals of some minor-country navies, the ones whose ships might or might not float if they were taken out of dry dock. The New Hampshire State Guard used the same color scheme, minus ten pounds of gold braid and jingling medals, for its winter camouflage uniforms.

"We are pursuing every lead," Dreikirch answered, his bushy grey mustache all aquiver. "There has been an extremely thorough search for persona fitting Eclipse's description. Every one of our files has been carefully examined. Inquiries were made by Interpol to the police forces of every nation. The garb we saw on video is registered with Niederhof's on the Vienna Ringstrasse, but as you know absolutely no one has ever penetrated Niederhof's security arrangements to see the persona behind the garb. Tomorrow their lead window display will be replicas of Eclipse's three garbs -- yes, she has three of them -- and 'Niederhof, supplier of fine garb to Eclipse, the Glorious Bearer of the Holy Namestone' will be their selling point. I infer that the customer paid in gold thalers that were promptly melted down and reminted, so there is no DNA trace.

"Other than that, there is no record whatsoever. My staff agrees that Eclipse is a woman, not too advanced in years, likely late twenties, and rigorously trained. Who is behind her? There must have been a huge support team, but they remain in the shadows. There was a fuss because the Bearer used a move first revealed by that American girl, Jane Wells. Wells was interrogated at length by two grandmasters and the Supreme Gamesman himself. They found no indication that she was the source of this Eclipse's move. I have no more to report." Dreikirch, Buncombe noted, carefully skipped over the issue that the Russians had been prepared to kidnap Wells, but the Americans were protecting her. From Hornpiper's video recording of the interview, there was something very strange about Wells' persona champion, something not in the coded reports Buncombe had been sent. Surely Krystal North, she who had faced two dozen IncoAztecan Sun

Knights by herself, and slaughtered them like rabbits, could not be afraid of this wisp of a college professor?

"Ah, yes," Holmgren said, "the Agenda. As we are now in Regular Order, there is a Speaking Stone, and an order of speaking. The first issue is the complaint, actually, complaints, about the League Strike Force and its actions on Atlanticea. The speaking order is the order in which I received complaints, followed by standard order. Several of you have made emphatically clear that you object to treating these issues in closed session, so we are not closed. We begin with traditional short opening remarks and then turn to substantive issues. Ambassador Moeller, I believe you speak first."

Buncombe braced himself. Once again, Moeller would be about to prove that Prussians were perfect masters of bloviated loquacity. Moeller straightened his tie. "The Supreme Warlord of All the Germans is most concerned with the lack of properly aggressive action by the League Elite Persona Brigade. The moment that the Bearer refused to hand over the Namestone, the Bearer should have been summarily executed, without giving her any warning or further argument. League resolutions, binding on every person in the world, make clear that it is entirely and most strictly forbidden for any private person to retain custody of the Namestone. Equally, League Resolutions, binding on every person in the world, make clear that it is entirely and most strictly forbidden for any private person to dispute the right of the League to take possession of the Holy Namestone for the benefit of all humanity. After all, once the Namestone is in the hands of its proper owner, the Millennial Kingdom will soon arrive. Every city around the world will be as clean and orderly as good Prussian Cities. Magnificent forests will crown every mountain and hill. The delights of nature will invigorate the pure-blooded people of every nation."

Buncombe pulled from one of the desk drawers at his side a small glass pyramid and set it on the table in front of him. You won't, he thought, make those claims without a vigorous objection. On the other hand, those claims were even more impressive in the original German, which you do not know that I can read. In fairness, who ever heard of an American who could read or speak a foreign language? Most Americans viewed studying foreign languages to be among the enumerated unnatural acts, for all that many of their fellowAmericans actually did so. Buncombe nodded politely when Featherstonehaugh put a similar pyramid on his section of the desk.

"However, the Bearer was not summarily executed." Moeller pounded the table. "It is therefore the irrefutable opinion of the Supreme Warlord that the leadership of the Elite Brigade should be replaced, the Brigade being given new, competent, and therefore of course necessarily Prussian leadership." Valkyria's face stiffened. Several more pyramids appeared on desks. And why, Buncombe wondered, was Moeller bothering with such a proposal, which no one in their right mind except a Prussian would accept?

"We are further particularly concerned that large numbers of persons around the world watched this Eclipse persona while she defied the entire League and thus the collective wisdom of all mankind," Moeller continued. "The notion that single individuals are entitled to disobey, no, even to question the directives of their superiors is entirely and most rigorously unacceptable. That position must be categorically rejected by this Executive and by extension by all civilized people. Failure to reject this notion will leads to riots, disorders, strikes, disobedient children, anarchism, independent thinking, and support for the League of Terran Justice, an intolerable state of affairs that must be put down like the mad dog that it is.

"Finally," Moeller said, "the Invincible Supreme Warlord of all the Germans notes that League Resolutions make it explicitly clear that it is the separate and overriding duty of every Great Power to make every effort to arrest and capture the Bearer and obtain for the benefit of the League of Nations and thus all humanity the Key to Paradise, the Holy Namestone. Accordingly, the Supreme Warlord has ordered and directed that the German Elite Persona Team is to move immediately to wherever in the world the Bearer is found, there to incapacitate her and take control of the Namestone. In the name of the League of Nations, of course, exactly as the League has already voted and directed. There is of course always a hazard in operations of this type that other parties will suffer minor injuries or that there will be some trivial incidental damage to property. Such costs are appropriately born by the country in which the damage takes place, because if that country had acted in an effective and rapid manner, the Bearer would have been captured before the German Elite Persona Team could have deployed to the scene to take command of the Namestone for the benefit of all humanity." Additional pyramids appeared on various desks. Moeller glanced at Holmgren, who indicated that the IncoAztecan Ambassador was to speak next.

"I speak for the Living Sun. I bring you greetings from the One World, the Six Regions, and the Land of the Obsidian Hummingbird." Lord Smoking Frog, Buncombe considered, never actually spoke his own name. In his home country, for him to speak his own name might have been an impolite way of reminding people that the Empire of the Mexica and the Inca was in fair part run by the Maya. Unfortunately, while the Incans had supplied the governmental structure, and the Mayans had long provided the backbone of the Civil Service, it was the Aztecans whose military and theological leadership had become paramount. "The First Speaker, the Living Sun, notes that the Bearer did not immediately comply with the direct and explicit orders of Brigade Leader Valkyria. The First Speaker, the Living Sun, is most concerned that Miss Eclipse's depraved behavior will serve as an ill example for the piously faithful and diligently industrious workers and peasants of the One World," Lord Smoking Frog paused in his remarks. "Those people are all fine citizens of our glorious Empire, but like all people other than the Living Sun Himself they are at risk of being led astray by malevolent foreign interests. This risk must be eliminated as rapidly and diligently as possible.

"Furthermore, the Assembly of the Tlatoani and the Council of the Realm are united in insisting that in the face of a League Resolution this Eclipse person owed instant obedience to Commandant Valkyria. That is the way it is in all well-ruled countries. Those who lead direct. Those who follow obey without question, hesitation, or thought. When Eclipse was seen not to obey, she set the example that disobedience can ever be a valid option, which of course it is not. At the first moment that she refused to obey, she should have been struck dead. Better, of course, she should have been rendered unconscious, separated from the Namestone, and then she should have been tortured to death. Slowly. Her agony and death would have sent a clear message on the virtue and correctness of that unthinking obedience that is the true strength of all civilized lands. Therefore, we believe a Special Commission should immediately be appointed to deal with the most important of all questions, namely choosing for Miss Eclipse the most painful and terrifying possible form of execution, following which her still-beating heart should be offered up to Huitzilopochtli. Also, to avoid a repetition of her escape, command of the League Elite Persona Brigade should immediately be transferred to the Perfect Warrior, The First Speaker, the Living Sun of the Inca and the Azteca.

"Finally, the First Speaker, the Living Sun, is most emphatic that the Namestone must be recovered as soon as possible and used to bring Heaven to Earth. Under the Namestone's watchful gaze, every man will seek his proper place. Every man will be obedient to his betters. Accordingly, the First Speaker has ordered that His Jaguar Knights be immediately ready to attack the Bearer, no matter where on earth she is found. The Jaguar Knights are well-equipped with teleporters and high power combatants, so there can be no doubt that the Bearer will be overwhelmed by their attack. We are in complete agreement with the Supreme German Warlord that while there is a possibility of incidental or collateral damage, such damage must be recognized as a heroic sacrifice on the part of those suffering the damage, for which of course they do not need to be compensated. In saying this, we do not deny the privilege of the ruler of any of the Great Powers or the other powers to compensate his citizens for any damage they may suffer while being associated with the heroic act of capturing the Namestone." Buncombe noted that several of his fellow ambassadors were looking significantly askance at the remarks of the Speaker for the First Speaker. The Speaking Stone was passed to the next ambassador.

Grand Vizier Suleiman Pasha looked around the room. "The Emperor of the Ottomans, Defender of the Faithful, Protector of the Three Holy Places, may his piety and virtue redound to the heavens, has taken note of the failure of the League Strike Team to procure the Namestone. On one hand, it is entirely sad that there was no capture. With the Namestone's power, every desert would blossom. Every city's buildings would be carved from the purest of white marble, its windows encrusted with gold and precious gems. On the other hand, the Emperor, may his wisdom increase forever, recalls that this body discussed at great length the protocols to be used if someone other than us managed to thread the Maze and recover the Namestone. His Imperial Wisdom believes that the League Strike Team did in fact execute the plan that we all agreed upon. The Leaders of the Corps of Janissaries have advised the Emperor: It is unfortunate that the agreed-upon plan was not successful, but that is the nature of plans. They do not always work. The Emperor therefore does not believe that it would be particularly appropriate at this time to transfer command of the League Strike Team from its current command staff to the Commandery of the Worshipful Hosts of the Virtuous and Faithful for Monotheism and Pious Struggle, as the Ambassador of the German Warlord has so wisely suggested."

To Buncombe's eyes, Moeller looked dumbfounded. "In particular," Suleiman Pasha continued, "there might be some confusion arising from the issue that the League Team includes both men and women, the women not serving as camp followers and bed warmers, contrary to any reasonable arrangement within a military force." Buncombe noted that the women in the room were all striving not to break into laughter. Fortunately, they had heard this line before from the usual Ottoman Ambassador. "Also, in all our planning we made no allowance for the possibility that a Lord of Eternity would be present. Even less allowance was made for the possibility that an Eternal would seek to intervene in the recovery of the Holy Namestone. Our plans were therefore less than complete. We are saddened but not alarmed that they were unsuccessful." If the Ottomans sent their Prime Minister, Buncombe thought, they are taking matters much more seriously than I might have expected. For better or worse, that replacement can't happen to me, it being illegal for Congressmen to travel outside the American Republic.

"Having said that, the Protector of the Three Holy Places has at his beck and call what is undoubtedly the most powerful group of personas in the entire world. There is therefore no need for foreign groups to enter the Lands of Peace in pursuit of the Namestone. Such an entry would provoke unfortunate consequences for the intruders, for which the Defender of the Faithful could not possibly take responsibility." Buncombe brought to mind several ancient American adages involving the slow train wreck. It seemed more than a bit likely that several foreign powers would be perfectly happy to have their persona teams invade the territory of other foreign powers, with what would be claimed to be the best of intentions, do astonishing amounts of collateral damage to key industrial facilities, and then leave. The net result, he suspected, would not be entirely favorable for world peace or local property values, even before the Bearer resisted the persona teams trying to capture her.

"Finally, his Wisdom the Emperor notes the great likelihood, given that the Bearer identified Eclipse as having the highest possible state of moral purity, that this Eclipse person is to be numbered among the ranks of the

Faithful, in which case it will always be appropriate for Hosts of the Faithful to come to her aid if she is attacked." Oh, fantastic, Buncombe thought, now we get a religious war, too, with people showing up on both sides relative to the Bearer. He watched as several ambassadors placed ruby-glass pyramids on the table. Those were the *threat of war* pyramids. He contemplated an image of the persona hosts of the thirteen great powers all converging on the same location with contradictory objectives. The Grand Vizier passed the Speaking Stone to Legate Hong.

"Already the Great Khan, the Emperor of Manjukuo and All Mongolia, from the center of the world to the Polar Sea, has issued the most fundamental of all orders: 'Men and women of the Horde! To your horses!' " Hong wore pale yellow court robes, embroidered left and right with a pair of five toed dragons, showing a close tie to the Imperial family. A large scarlet fire sigil sewn on each forearm of the robes indicated his performance on the Imperial Examinations. He had finished in the highest rank. The lower ranks test memorization, Buncombe reminded himself, but the highest ranks were based on puzzle solving. Hong hid a top-notch mind behind his refused shoulder. Legate Hong raised his voice. "All the personas and all the soldiers of all Manjukuo are immediately ready to advance against the Bearer, no matter where she is found, so soon as she is located. There is no doubt but that she will be overwhelmed and her stolen artifact recovered for all the people of the world. Soon the thoughts of every man and woman will be purified, every villain will confess each of his sins and be given a proper penance, the steppes will be lush with grass, and every child will have his own bow, arrows, sword, and riding horse."

Buncombe steeled himself for the bloviations of the remaining ambassadors. The Russians would undoubtedly interpret the Prussian remarks as a threat of war. The Prussians would feel threatened by the Ottomans. The French and the Austro-Hungarians would speak of welcoming the Bearer into their midst, and using tactful means to persuade the bearer to use the Namestone as the League requested. It seemed unlikely that either Ferencz or Davout would be able to explain the concept 'tact' to most of their fellow ambassadors. Buncombe realized that while he was collecting his thoughts the Speaking Stone had moved several more times, so the Sikh Ambassador was speaking.

"Finally," Ambassador Singh said, "I have been asked to bring word from the Tibetan Lamanate. While the Dalai Lama is temporarily absent awaiting reincarnation, the Sera Lama has extended an open invitation to this Miss Eclipse to visit Tibet to meditate with him on the hazard that the Holy Namestone creates for her soul, for surely a device that grants all worldly desires will distract us all from tranquil meditation. Indeed, the Sera Lama counsels us all that we should abandon our interest in the purely worldly temptations offered by the Namestone, in favor of the celestial awards resulting from renouncing all worldly goods. Once he receives the Holy

Namestone, he will convert us all to his supernally wise philosophy."

The Speaking Stone eventually reached the American Ambassador. "Mind you," Buncombe said, "I would be remiss in my duties as Ambassador of the American Republic if I did not note that most of our citizens have a complete lack of sympathy for the League's assertion that it has a claim on the Namestone. The American position for centuries has been that the Namestone belongs to he who took it. I agree that many Americans would also have preferred that Miss Eclipse simply joined the extremely long list of people who bet their lives against the Namestone and lost. We do not wish Miss Eclipse ill for performing her heroic deed, but the Namestone was better left in the Tomb in the hands of the Martyr." Several of Buncombe's colleagues glared in his direction. "Of course, it was two Americans who, separately, entered the Maze and were the only challengers ever to survive. They both quit while they were ahead." Some of Buncombe's colleagues turned beet red. Four appeared to be struggling to avoid breaking into laughter at his tweaking of the lion's tail. The English and Prussians had lost the core of their navies in Jackie Fisher's attempt. The English 'world chess champion', close to two centuries back, had declined to emulate his American challenger. First the Englishman had dodged the challenger, when the challenger had visited England. Then the challenger had entered the Maze, won all his games, and dared the Englishman to duplicate his feat. The Englishman had not attempted to do so.

"In any event," Buncombe continued, "my Republic's frugal Congress may well take its own good time about authorizing any part of our very limited incomes to be spent in Miss Eclipse's pursuit, assuming that our Congress in its wisdom does not decide that she is the proper owner. We are a poor and thrifty nation and have better uses for our meager resources. In particular, we use them to better ourselves, not to seek out some magic gewgaw which will allegedly spare us the need to work." Buncombe silently congratulated himself on saying his final few sentences with a straight face. It was painfully obvious that the American Republic was by a very considerable margin the wealthiest country in the world.

"Last but most important, America is a sovereign nation. Foreign attacks on our citizens and residents, including in particular attacks on the hypothetical Miss Eclipse if she is an American, would be acts of war and will be treated as such. We have no intent of sending our armed forces abroad in pursuit of will-o'-the-wisps. We will, however, consider favorably requests for assistance from countries in the Americas. Furthermore, President Daniel Oliver Webster has indicated that if the Governor-General of any of the Canadian Dominions requests emergency aid, then, so long as the Queen-Empress and her Ministers do not object, arrangements might mayhaps be made. After all, if your neighbor's house is on fire, you break out the hoses first, and consider your minor historical disagreements with your neighbor after the fire is extinguished." From the looks on various faces, Buncombe had indeed set several foxes loose in neighboring chicken coops. American foreign policy had for many centuries been based on noninvolvement in foreign affairs. Protecting southern neighbors from the IncoAztecan Empire was viewed as a domestic matter, given the series of wars that had been fought between America and the Aztecans. And now, Buncombe thought, he had announced a minor change in American foreign policy. Buncombe handed the Speaking Stone to Ambassador Featherstonehaugh.

"Curiously,' Featherstonehaugh said, "the position of Queen Victoria, the Third of Her Name, and Her Ministers is in many respects similar to that of the American Republic. I realize this circumstance may sound surprising to some. In particular, Her Majesty's government is unenthused with the notion that foreigners are entitled to appear in our country uninvited with the intent of using our lochs and rills to fight a war. Her Majesty and Her Government must categorically and absolutely refuse to be responsible for the consequences to the invaders and their nations if such an event were to occur. While I could go on at greater length, I am in the common position of Final Opening Speaker, namely I believe that we might all find it useful to consult with our governments about your preliminary remarks, some of which were not quite what official positions would have led us to expect. Naturally, we are all gentlemen and ladies, so we do not employ spies," the room burst into giggles, "so none of us had any non-official knowledge before the meeting of what was about to be said. If any of you are curious, my actual prepared introductory remarks are in the meeting packet. I will be happy to meet privately with any of you who have questions on my instructions. I therefore propose a pleasant recess."

"Does anyone else want to be heard on this matter?" Holmgren asked.

"Manjukuo pledges one hundred tons of gold to the persons who locate and catch Eclipse, and gain for us the Namestone," Manjukuoan Legate Hong Sangui interrupted. Holmgren smiled and applauded. His audience might need a little while to realize that this interruption was pre-rehearsed.

"In that case," Holmgren continued, "I propose that we recess until after dinner, so that we may receive instructions. I see several objection pyramids on the table. Those might mayhaps be the first order of business this evening. Is there objection to a recess? Hearing none, we are recessed." Holmgren wished he had not seen Buncombe and Featherstonehaugh exchange knowing glances. What might that unlikely duo be planning? A lack of world peace would be a disaster, and that lack might appear rather quickly. He took another deep sip from one of his vest flasks. This meeting had gone no farther than preliminary remarks, and already the latent hostilities between the Great Powers were coming to the surface.

Chapter Seven

The Invisible Fortress
Morning

I'd be even more delighted to say that on the fourth day I was fully recovered. Not hardly. Not with the amount of damage I'd taken. The healing matrix was doing all it could, including prodding me to eat more, a request I was happy to honor. At least all my teeth were in the right places. Regrowing teeth is really unpleasant. However, it was day four after I left the Maze, so all my bruises were vigorously reminding me of their existence. That's what day four is like, the time of maximum discomfort. The matrix changes how fast you heal, but some things remain the same. I felt like I had a really bad case of flu, something I only know about because I can read other people's minds.

I was sore, stiff despite morning exercises, and half-inclined to go back to sleep. The worst part of being uncomfortable was that I could do very little about it. Mind control on yourself is fine for averting severe pain, but awareness of all the discomfort is tied into the healing process. It's part of how the healing matrix knows what needs fixing. The ungifted trick of aspirin and warm tea does not help. After all, having a good set of gifts does mean you are mostly immune to being poisoned. I assume Mum was teasing when she told me not to try breathing nerve gas just to show that I could. I know perfectly well that I can, but see no reason to take a chance on it, if I don't have to. Immunity to poisons, though, also means that drugs like codeine don't work on me, so minor aches and pains are something I have to live with. The chemicals in coffee are kind of at the edge. Like I said, it's a while until I discover if chocolate matches the fairy tales about it, or if I'm immune to that, too.

Breakfast was things that are not much work to cook. I dropped frozen waffles into the toaster, heavy cream into the mixer, and pear compote into the microwave. My stock of orange juice had a while to go before I had to reconstitute from frozen. I finally remembered to turn on the video, and then very much wished I hadn't. There was the League Peace Executive in its secure chamber. The ambassadors weren't screaming at each other, which made their words all the more frightening. Half the Great Powers were promising to send personae to attack me, as soon as I was found, no matter where in the world I was at the time. In particular, no matter if I were found inside the territory of another Great Power. The other Great Powers were saying that if the personae of another Power showed up to attack me, in their territory, they would come to their territory's defense. Its vigorous and violent defense. To his credit, the Japanese—no, Satsuma Daimyo—ambassador pointed out that if someone attacked me I might get annoyed and shoot back. Satsuma viewed the likely outcome at that point to be disadvantageous, at least to the neighboring planetary hemisphere. Discussion went downhill from there. I'd assumed that people would be grateful that I had recovered the Namestone. They were certainly all confident that it would end hunger and poverty, cure all disease, give every family its own palace, smite every corrupt politician, and eliminate disobedience among children. Instead, they were preparing to start wars over me. An argument about which approach should be used to execute me, the Aztecan god-feeding ceremony being discussed at some length as a closer, was a tiny bit dismaying. I am perfectly happy to believe that priests of Huitzilopochtli can flay someone alive without killing them, preparatory to frying them and then cutting their still-beating heart out, but I don't need them to prove it by doing it to me.

I finished my breakfast, strongly considered putting more pear-raisin compote in the microwave, and decided that I should check on my cats and horses first. I did that yesterday, mentalically. I could tell from their minds that everything was fine. Everything, of course, except they missed having seen me. I rinsed everything and dropped the dishes into the dishwasher.

I felt awful, but Medico said I should stop whining, that exercise would be good for me. At the back closet I changed into my barn-cleaning clothes. Bending over to slip on my heavy outdoor socks and sneakers reminded me of some of my bruises. It reminded me a lot. However, I wore black sneakers. No girl in America would be caught dead in black sneakers. White sneakers? That was totally the opposite. Sometimes I don't quite understand that sort of thinking. Actually, almost all the time I don't understand that sort of thinking. I slipped into my heavy, loose windbreaker, my right arm complaining loudly even though I was very careful, and dropped into a paper bag four apples, two big chunks of maple sugar, and some cat treats. It was cold enough I could pull up the hood on the windbreaker without looking suspicious. That was enough to hide my hair.

The barn was two hundred yards, well downhill, from my house. I did it at a slow walk. The realtor had apologized profusely to the person he thought was my mother for the bad layout. He was actually speaking to me. Fortunately, I'm in a state where lawyers never got involved in conveyancing. When it came time for everyone to sign the papers, the title insurance people confirmed the past owner had signed, they thought they witnessed my mother signing, and we were done. I signed. I paid for it, after all. Putting down cash in advance, a good chunk in silver cartwheels and gold thalers, makes people agreeable, especially when you offer a bit more than the asking price. Not too much more, not enough to make anyone suspicious, just enough that you could say "I really want your house. And I wouldn't dream of interrupting your vacation on Pago Pago. The embassy can witness your signing, and the people here can witness mine." Everyone was happy, especially after I paid the closing costs.

There had been a time, right after mum threw me out of the house, when I was panicked about where I would get money. Fortunately I already had another persona. Pointelisme flew, teleported, was very good at long-range telepathy, had extremely solid force fields, and was very good with tools, just like me. After all, she is me. Close-in solar observatories run into technical problems, but very few persona are comfortable flying into the solar corona to fix them. It gets a bit warm there. The people who hired me could tell I was completely comfortable with viewing the sun from a million miles away. I did not mention that I was completely comfortable because three months ago Mum and I had flown to the core of the sun just to see what was there. I got to use ultravision to look at the solar deep structures. Yes, I get a real headache afterward, but I can use ultravision. Notwithstanding the dozen past human technical civilizations that have studied them, people really do not understand what the deep structures of the solar core are, other than that they are highly regular, huge, not made of chemical matter, and gradually change in time.

A reasonable solar observatory costs five billion dollars to construct, another billion dollars to get into low solar orbit even with persona help, and tends to break down. The people who hired me were delighted to pay a large sum of money in cash, provide me with the tools, and walk me through everything I would need to do. Pointelisme's garb is opaque everywhere, not to mention not formfitting. They had no idea who she is. Everything worked almost perfectly, except half the bolts in the real observatory were seriously stuck. It is truly helpful that telekinesis can amplify the torque your screwdriver is applying, in a way which absolutely for sure will not damage the head of the screw. I switched out bad modules for good modules, looked carefully at everything to see if anything else was going wrong – rather I looked carefully and the three people watching through my eyes via telepathy checked if anything else was going wrong – and came back to earth. I now have in my subbasement an extremely large amount of cold cash. Cartwheels and gold thalers are so much better than bank transfers or paper money. If you are careful to heat treat them, there is absolutely no way they can be traced, which is why vast numbers of people insist on using them.

Once I had a decent amount of money, I went to Idaho and took advantage of the Heinlein Act. The Federal Heinlein Act lets you prove you can take care of yourself, and are therefore an adult. It's very different from the court-authorized emancipated minor status, meaning you are still a minor but no longer belong to your parents, which requires revealing who you and your mother are. There are a set of competency tests. You pay off the state, not cheap, with money you can prove that you earned. The process is highly anonymized. I marched through it and acquired my Heinlein certificate, just in case someone complained that I am too young to own a house.

It was a perfectly respectable walk out to the barn, and would've been considerably more of a walk if we had had a half-foot of snow. I say 'barn' but the lower level is a three-and-a-half-sided shelter, while the top level is enclosed. The land is low enough that I do not get snow very often, rarely more than half a foot, and besides snow shoveling is superb exercise. Snow does mean that the horses prefer that I feed them. Today I spotted my Appaloosas in the lower pasture, grazing. That pasture was planted in oats and had gone to seed in the fall, so they would have had plenty to eat, even if there had been a foot of snow on the ground.

The horses had all the feed that they might want. Was that safe? There are perfectly adequate numbers of claims, a few thousand years old, that if you leave a horse with a big pile of barley it will eat itself to death. Modern horse breeders think horses are not that stupid. After all, horses are as smart as dogs, if not as smart as cats.

I decided not to call the horses while I mucked out the barn. Some work was needed. The weather had been bad enough that the horses had taken shelter for a day or so. Medico said 'emphatic yes' on the work as exercise; exercise kept various bad things from happening where I had deep bruises. Every so often, I simply had to stop until the pain receded. Cleaning was a real chore, even with the robot manure spreader, because I really had to lift everything close to one-armed. Spreading hay afterward was also not a great deal of fun. Yes, telekinesis would've made it a whole lot easier, but I don't use my gifts at home if I can possibly avoid it. The gift you do not call cannot be detected. My doing mind control on myself, suppressing the pain so I could sleep, was not supposed to be detectable.

Toward the end I had a feline audience. The two barn cats had noticed that I was back and were watching from a safe distance while I went about my work. After all, Bluebell and Columbine were quite certain that once I was done cleaning up the barn I would give them treats, scratch their stomachs, and comb their fur. I did go up the stairs to the perch where they had their nest. There was a considerable pile of straw, clear signs that they had found this, that, and the other thing to line it inside, and at the far end of the perch a neat stack of tails where various rodents had contributed to feline diets. The automatic cat feeder appeared to be working just fine. Its storage hopper was good for another couple of weeks, by which time I wouldn't mind hauling a 30 pound sack of cat food from the house. I have fixed the feeder once, and can fix it again, but working with tools is going to be a chore until my shoulder heals.

The cats like regular warm lunches. Careful examination of the tails indicated that they were probably spending most of their time hunting in the fields and bringing dinner home. I sat with my legs over the edge of the perch, dropped a cat treat on each side, and waited for not very long. Soon I had a large cat leaned up on each side of me, both of them rubbing their heads against my arms as they waited for me to give them more treats or better yet a good combing. That went on for a solid 20 minutes, at the end of which I was out of treats, the curry comb had been cleaned several times, and they were both purring loudly.

At the sound of horse's hooves, I clambered back down the stairs. Usually I would just lean forward and rotate one-handed off the ledge. It was only seven feet, enough so I'd barely flex my knees when I landed. Not today, thank you; I was too beaten up. A horse's lips nuzzled my hair. I pivoted happily. "Oh, Daffodil, you've really missed me, haven't you?" A second Appaloosa came into the barn. "You, too, Snapdragon." The horses really loved being hugged, especially at the same time, but my right arm was not going to cooperate. Not today.

I produced from my bag a pair of MacIntosh apples, and dropped them toward the newly-cleaned barn floor. The ponies greedily gobbled them up, and repeated when I gave them another pair of apples. I did hold the maple sugar in my hands, carefully. Daffodil and Snapdragon waited patiently for their combing. They also got a careful check of their hooves. There were no stones, no signs of other issues. Vigorous scratches behind their ears were clearly appreciated. "You want me to ride you, don't you?" I asked. "I'm really sorry, but you're both going to have to wait."

What else needed doing? A slow walk around the house and barn, slow being the fastest I could manage, showed no weather damage, no sign of people trying to force entry, no mark of anything else unusual. Keeping an eye open for approaching cars, I walked out to the mailbox, slipped open the rear door of the hopper, and pulled out everything that had been delivered in the past week. The nice thing about a hopper type mailbox is that the postman drops things in the front end, but has no way to tell how often the mail is being picked up. What did I find? Newsmagazines. Advertising. Three new bank statements. All of my bills are on automatic payment, so as few people as possible ever see one of my checks. I realized I'd been out dealing with the barn and the cats and the ponies for several hours now. I don't usually need nearly that long, but until arm and ribs recovered I was going to be slow.

I left my barn cleaning shoes in the box at the back door, hung my barn cleaning clothes in the back closet, dropped all the mail on my desk, and went to my room to shower and change. I'm sure if anyone else had been around they would've agreed I had a distinct smell of horse. The hot water felt very good over various bruises and strains.

My target today was one of Mum's forbidden books. Yes, I was feeling really out of it. I'd put off reading any of those books while I prepared for the Maze. I might not get much out of them, but I was not going to wait any longer. *Liouville's Butterflies* makes remarkable claims about historic time. I'm not sure why Mum didn't want me to read it. I curled up in my comfortable chair, my feet on the large hassock, with a pot of mocha, pitcher of milk and vacuum mug at my side, pulled up a quilt, and began reading. The front part of the book was fairly simple. I could even understand it. There were computer pictures of how atoms move in air. They show -- I noticed that the book skipped the proof -- if you make tiny changes now, in not very long what happens is hugely different. If you do time travel – I did not just tell you whether I can travel in time or not – go back not very far at all, and make very small changes, when you return to now the world may be totally different. The famous story is the fellow who traveled in time to just before the maiasaurs started their march to intelligence, smelled a flower by shooing away a butterfly, and when he returned to the present there had never been a dinosauric civilization. Most small changes have tiny effects, but some are different.

Liouville was a French mathematician. The fellow after him was an American, Gibbs. What they showed, the part I had to struggle to understand even slightly, is that the past is as big as the future. No, let's be honest. I really did not understand almost any of the math parts. For what they needed to prove, they used calculus. I think. I'm not terrified of a single derivative, at least if someone else is taking it. I even know sort of what they are. Kind of. Mayhaps. Well, I asked Mum what they are, and she told me.

No, I'm not one of these people who have infinite math genius, but Mum always said I was way ahead in math. That's way ahead, even though I actually have to learn the stuff, not have Mum pass it to me mind-to-mind. Things you learn mind-to-mind you aren't creative with, not easily, so I'll have to work really hard to write great love poems in Atlanticean. I'm heartbroken, truly heartbroken. Mum did pass me lots of things not quite mind-to-mind, but she was mostly interested in helping me learn how to use my gifts effectively. She thought using gifts was way more important than math, or science, or money technology. I could learn those the usual way at my usual speed. OK, my usual speed is not slow.

In any event, Gibbs wrote down a whole forest of derivatives in a big square. Down on my study pad went 'Hamiltonian', 'Jacobian', 'determinant', 'permutation', and a bunch of other words I don't know. I suspected there were a lot of parts I did not know yet, even before I got to the forest of derivatives. When I reached the derivative forest I took a break for caramel ice cream and chocolate fudge crumbles…a lot of fudge crumbles. Still, I was reading a forbidden book, and I have all the time in the world, if I'm careful, to learn it. All the time in the world? When I do high-power healing, I age backwards. Balancing that so I never get older? Just think: Do it right, lose six months of age. Do it wrong? Lose your life before you can heal. That's not a safe future.

The original Gibbs proof about the past and the future was two short paragraphs of which I could make neither head nor tail. The book spent 30 pages breaking the Gibbs proof up into small parts. Each part was supposed to be easy to follow. The fellow who wrote the thirty pages is said to be the greatest science writer since Amizov, Amizov being the muse of clear science writing. Except when I talked about muses with Mum, for Terpsichore Mum had an image of this statue, but for Amizov she remembered fondly this old guy with funny whiskers. I even understood two of the parts that he wrote. It's just that after you had followed all the small parts you had come a very long way, and you wondered if you had really come all that far or if the wool had been pulled over your eyes.

I skipped to the end. The Forward said it was OK to skip like that. There was an image, translating the forest of derivatives into a simple picture. The picture I understood. I think. The picture is a line of pawns on a huge chessboard. The pawns represent whole worlds where history starts out slightly differently. They start out next to each other, farther away sideways being more different. By the time you get well sideways across the chessboard, history is completely different. The start points are ancient time. The simple view of history is that the pawns all move forward one space at the time, always staying in their own file. Worlds that start very similar to ours end up very similar to ours. Worlds that start out very different end up being very different. The butterflies show that every so often a pawn takes off sideways, so two pawns that start next to each other do not end up that way. The pawn next to ours marches off sideways and ends up halfway across the board. That's maiasaurs not becoming intelligent.

You might think that would simply leave a gap in the file next to ours. No, there are as many files at the start of history as there are at the end. What Liouville and Gibbs showed, and someday I will understand that part of the book, is that every file was full at the start of time, so when we reach the present every file must still be full, one pawn per file. If the pawn next to us took off and ended up way across the board, there must be another pawn that started off someplace way across the board and ended up at our shoulders. I thought the mirror imaging looked pretty obvious. We're not someplace special on that chessboard. If some of our nearby-at-start pawns end up someplace else, pawns from someplace else must end up nearby, because if they didn't we would be at someplace unusual, someplace pawns from far away could not reach. Lots of people get extremely upset with the idea that world history could've started off completely different from ours, but when we get to the present the two worlds are almost the same. *Liouville's Butterflies*, the forbidden book, is the famous proof that some histories converge. Most of the book is the arguments about what Liouville's result means. If you were a parallel timeline believer, the "United States of America" Ambassador was proof that you were right.

My den had a very comfortable sofa, and I had a warm blanket. At some point, several cups of mocha later, I drifted off to sleep for half the afternoon, waking when I was ravenously hungry. Grilled steak, salad, and rice mixed with artichoke hearts and pine nuts simmered in chicken broth did quite nicely. The healing matrix insisted I break out more ice cream. It was burning through calories like mad to do repairs, and I had to eat enough to catch up.

Uncomfortable or not, I made a list of all the things I had to start doing. Living by yourself is a real chore. Schoolwork. Housework. Home improvement. Exercise. Okay, serious exercise waits until my ribs and shoulder finish reassembling. At some point, after I am completely recovered, I need to work up my nerve enough to deal with the Namestone. I had done the Maze, and now I had second thoughts about the next step. I really do have to finish healing. Yes, the Namestone was perfectly safe, sealed behind a quarter inch of impervium, but in the end I have to deal with it. That's I get to deal with it, not it gets to deal with me. The latter is a real danger. The Namestone corrupts its users. That's a design feature. First, I have to recover from several hand to hand fights, gifts carefully suppressed, followed by the League Elite Strike Team and the Screaming Skull vigorously trying to kill me.

It wasn't that late in the day, the sun not yet approaching the winter horizon, and Medico spoke up for more moderate physical activity. I walked back and forth between the work shed and the family room, on each trip carrying a single bookshelf, painted two weeks ago, the enamel now being cleanly cured. Carrying a shelf under each arm was just out until my shoulder finished healing, and mounting the shelves one-armed would be tedious, but I could at least get the shelves into the right room. A solid hour took care of that chore.

Finally, it was time for real studying. Chemistry and astronomy were on the list for tonight. I felt terrible, but when I focused deeply on what I was reading, the pain faded. Chemistry and astronomy are fun. Up on the screen came my chemistry reading. A side panel reminded me about the classes I was neglecting. The answer appeared to be all the science, math, rhetoric, everything except the topics I had crammed to prepare myself for the Maze. The good part: If I'd gone to a public school and taken a three month vacation every year, I'd be incredibly far behind where I am now. And I'd be taking courses like 'Genre Fiction'. The bad part: Studying is something you tend to forget how to do, and I hadn't been doing it in a while. I would be slow for a few days yet, and then there would be serious catch-up. Nonetheless, I took a while to settle down, and then forgot how uncomfortable I was, in favor reading about the periodic table of the normal elements, and the electron orbits that made the periodic table the way it is. After an hour and a half Medico interrupted. It was my still-early bed-time. I did what it told me to do, and went to bed. OK I went to bed after fifteen minutes of peeking at the lessons on astronomy, these being the extended chapters on archeological explorations of the planets, moons, asteroids, and Kuiper bodies, most of which made no sense. Yes, I have flown to some of the ruins myself, and I can't explain them either. Oh, a simpler riddle. Who or what is 'Kuiper'? The name appears in historical records of several past civilizations, with no explanation.

Chapter Eight

The Great Chamber of Wisdom
The House That Is Forever

Around a gold-inlaid teak table waited the Lords of Eternity. An empty chair was reserved for Solara's daughter Corinne, she who lies sleeping until her death may die. Prince Mong-ku sat at the table's head. It was one of those centuries, he thought. As had been true for far longer than normal mortals suspected, it was again his turn to maintain civility. Of the dozen Lords at the table today, only the Screaming Skull wore formal garb. Solara had donned a white silk tabard. Starsmasher was in another of his seemingly infinite supply of vest-and-cardigan sweater combinations. Plasmatrix, she who was indeed Plasmatrix-The-Desolation-Of-The-Goddess, was for a change wearing real clothing, not her usual strategically-placed bits of incandescent plasma, plasma carefully locked behind force screens so it would not burn down whichever building she approached. If the Prince's ruby and bronze silk robe and layered garments underneath somewhat resembled garb, it was that his breakfast hour was slowly approaching. To him a housecoat seemed highly appropriate, given the hour in his normal time zone.

"Having managed to sleep through the whole thing," Prince Mong-ku observed querulously, "it is nonetheless my duty to describe the situation that required summoning this meeting. Why shouldn't I have slept through it? After all, surely no one in their right mind expected this unknown nonentity to solve the Maze. It's absurd. Nonetheless, this Eclipse person managed to walk the paths of the Maze, beat down every obstacle, and remembered that she wanted the Martyr to give her the expletive-deleted Namestone. Then she just stood there while the Europa Elite Team hit her with dear me, a truly great deal, not to mention that one of us expressed his disapproval of her continued life."

"Worse," the Screaming Skull said, "after I expressed my extreme disapproval of her basal metabolism, she was still standing, seemingly unharmed. And now she has disappeared without a trace." Meaning, Mong-Ku thought, the Screaming Skull will spend the next century, unless he kills Eclipse first, inflicting on us his annoyance that she declined to die.

"Berndt," Prince Mong-ku addressed Starsmasher, "don't our files show anything? After all, the whole world only has a billion people, of whom mayhaps five or so million are personas of any significance. Surely a list of the personas with her gifts -- starting with starcore class force fields and second order shields -- ought to be limited." My dear colleagues, the Prince thought, are supposed to be contributing part of their efforts to completing the Great Plan. For once, I have a path to make them give the Plan the attention It is owed. Besides, Berndt is one of the really intelligent people here. He may have a solution.

"The new Bearer is clearly none of the Eclipses whose persona names are widely known," Starsmasher answered calmly. "Actually, there are a good twenty of them, of whom ten are astronomers, space travellers and teleporters who can move satellite telescopes to useful locations. Not one is a young woman. Nor is any a shapeshifter who could disguise themselves as a young woman. Having said that, you are the persona you choose to be. Someone could have assumed this Eclipse persona, garb and all, just for a day."

"We can rule that one out." Solara shook her head. "Niederhof's has revealed that Eclipse is a long-time regular customer. She's one of the 'reduced rate if you let us display replicas of your garb when you become famous' people. In a few days, replicas of all of her garbs will be on display."

"Speaking of useless information," the Screaming Skull commented.

"That fact actually signifies," Plasmatrix said.

"How?" Starsmasher asked. "For reasons we all know, absolutely no one can penetrate Nieferhof's security. Niederhof might know who she is, but he will not talk. And boasting that he made her garb is good for his business."

"She paid cash," Solara answered. "Gold coins, melted down at once. That I got from one of my European friends." Featherstonehaugh, she considered, was in his tastes remarkably like his great-grandfather, if slightly taller and stronger. But in this century the Silver General had fortunately disappeared from sight.

"Ah," Prince Mong-ku answered, his face wrinkled with smiles. Now, he thought, he would get to explain the obvious. What game was Starsmasher playing? He surely saw the issue. "Niederhof does not make that offer to the hoi polloi. It would reduce his profits. And, obviously, he did not make that deal after she did the Maze: She already had the garb. No, whoever she is, Niederhof knew in advance that she might be a person of adequate importance, even though she was completely unknown at the time."

"Niederhof is a clever fellow, not a clairvoyant," the Screaming Skull objected. "He would have needed evidence that she might become important. What could that possibly have been?"

"Eclipse. Not well known." Plasmatrix ticked choices off on her fingers, hoping as she did that her fellows would see her reasoning. "Not a known protégé. Actually, except screens and teleportation, not a lot of power that we have seen. Teleporters aren't quite a dime a dozen, especially ones who risk the Dark Side of the Moon in one jump." Mong-ku nodded politely. For all her eccentric taste in garb, Plasmatrix had a real brain and did not hesitate to use it.

"That, by the way, is where she lost me," Dark Shadow said. "What's left?"

"Rare and subtle gifts," Prince Mong-ku said. "She did have second-order screens, good ones. Few indeed are the people outside the room with those. Her rhetoric was trained, not something engifted." He paused. "Oh, of course. If one of us showed up at Niederhof's and announced 'This is my daughter Eclipse, would you please put together quality garb for her', the daughter would be granted the special rate. There was promise of greatness, not because Niederhof is impressed by a mere Emperor or Lord of Eternity, but because we can engift our progeny with all our powers. Did one of us do that?"

"I think I would remember having had a child recently," Plasmatrix said. She sent a smile toward Mong-Ku, who returned the smile. She had made clear to him and to Starsmasher that she would like a child by each of them, one century or another; they had not accepted the invitation yet. "There's something about it you don't forget. I think I'd know if anyone else here had had a child recently. How many persona are so good that their kids will get the Niederhof special treatment?"

"I'll do a search on that," Starsmasher said. "Gifts mostly are not inherited. Go down the list of current elite-class persona. You've never heard of their parents, let alone their children. Promise only works with those of us who can engift our descendants."

"Mayhaps she's a construct," the Screaming Skull said. "They're hard to kill. Could the League of Terran Justice have done this?"

"Eclipse was clearly a persona," Plasmatrix said, "Someone with at least a few first-rate gifts. The League builds combat androids. Mayhaps even smart androids. Controlled engifting is our monopoly."

"Not quite," Starsmasher reminded. "For starters, our dear friend the Silver General engifts people." Solara grated her teeth. She had never forgiven the Silver General for seducing Featherstonehaugh's great-grandfather away from her.

"Returning to topic," Prince Mong-ku asked. "Whoever has her hands on the Namestone may be able to use it to engift people. What if the Terran Justice people start cranking out agents who are high-level personas?"

"The *Copper Book* speaks to that," Starsmasher answered. "The Namestone lends gifts, but does not give them away. We could face one persona as powerful as the Namestone itself, but that's it."

"The Namestone is a foamspace tap," Solara said. "But it has an aperture, one whose size we know. Even without the Ambihelicon, some of us in a pinch could match it. Therefore, it is an annoyance, not something that can prevent the Great Plan from being brought to fruition."

"Solara, Starsmasher," Plasmatrix said, "I know you are very fond of your

Namestone Standard Model. But there are still these little gaps in your reasoning." Solara rolled her eyes. "First, the *Copper Book* may be fibbing about Namestone's gifts. The Book says 'these are the gifts' not 'these are the only gifts'. Second, this Eclipse person, whoever she is, may be able to use her own gifts to drive the Namestone. She's obviously not a complete weakling. That would make the Namestone far more powerful. Third, and I only finished the translation a century ago, the *Goetica Arcana Stella Magnus* clearly states that the Knights found occult ties between the Namestone and the Solar Deep Structures, ties implying that the Namestone's gifts are vastly greater than you propose."

"I read your translations," Solara said dismissively. "At those power levels, the bearer will fry herself toot sweet."

"The Namestone, yes," the Screaming Skull said. "It would be a useful tool for us. But Eclipse? When she escaped Atlantis, it was too soon for her to have the Namestone's power. She used her own gifts to survive and escape. She is no weakling. Mayhaps she can't use Namestone's full power yet, but she may still wreak havoc. On the great chess board, it seems there is a new formidable piece. It must be found and destroyed."

"We should," Starsmasher agreed, "except for the minor detail of finding her. Assuming it is actually a her and not a cleverly disguised him. The resources of most of the League, though less than that guiding genius Dreikirch thinks, are behind this search. Surely it will eventually succeed? My resources are devoted to this issue, though I have another so-to-speak problem. Have any of you been following the screaming and raving between the Argentine and Brazil over the giant sky octopus?"

"Giant sky octopi?" Prince Mong-ku asked. He perched his chin on his long fingers. "Did I sleep through those, too? I have been elsewise occupied, casting the runes for the return of the three whose names are not to be spoken. They are indeed drawing closer, but not yet so close that I can forecast their arrivals."

"Do tell," Plasmatrix said. "I've been busy with other matters, too."

Starsmasher forced a smile. His fellow Lords of Eternity, he thought, were undoubtedly the most powerful personae in the world, not to mention having access to technologies and libraries undreamt of by normal men, but sometimes they were a bit distracted from reality.

"I've seen press reports," Colonel Pi said. Starsmasher bit his tongue. Colonel Pi was the House's leading scientific researcher. He resented meetings as events that took him away from his important tasks, notably advancing the security of The House That Is Forever. If he were also perpetually trying to gain a deeper understanding of gifts and their mechanisms, one could either say that he knew more than anyone else, or that he had made almost no progress. "The photographs are very strange indeed. Shall I try reassembling them?"

"Reassemble?" Plasmatrix asked. "Aren't honest photographs good enough, well, up to image enhancement?"

"The images don't make sense," Starsmasher explained. "Solid bodies can't do those things, and holograms can't bite holes in buildings. The concern is that the Argentines claim the octopi are some Brazilian construct. The countries are drifting toward war."

"We are too close to the next polar conjunction," Prince Mong-Ku responded. "The runes are very clear. We cannot afford to have a major commotion ongoing when one of those who are not to be named returns! I have already ramped up the SkyVoice, up to the point that truly sensitive sorts may lose their minds, to keep this cycle on the proper track."

"The Argentines are not alone," Starsmasher said. "They have solid American backing. After two millennia of isolationism, the American Republic is emerging from its tortoise shell, not at the most helpful possible moment. The Brazilians have Portuguese and hence English backing, and the IncoAztecan Empire may well see an opportunity to improve its northern and southeastern borders, so soon as the Americans appear to have entangled themselves in a foreign altercation over the Namestone. Not to mention, of course, that the Great Powers are threatening war over the Namestone."

"How convenient," Plasmatrix said. She sounded unconvinced.

"I glanced at the photos," Colonel Pi said. His beard ruffled the uppermost corners of his laboratory coat. The garment was royal blue, with rows of arcane symbols stitched into every seam. His seal, the variant pi character in dark blue on a light blue circle, was emblazoned on his lapels. "If they are real, the object -- sky octopus or whatever -- is clearly at least quintidimensional. That's assuming that the images are not a clever fake."

"If you want fake evidence to start a war," Solara asked, "why fake evidence of something completely crazy? Why not fake evidence of the other side's Persona Corps conducting atrocities?"

"See?" Plasmatrix shrugged dismissively. "The evidence has been planned to be so crazy that people conclude that the photographs must be real, because no one would fake something so ridiculous."

Prince Mong-Ku buried his face in his hands. "Plasmatrix? You have another one of those espionage schemes, one in which absolutely anything might be true and facts lose all meaning? Yes, I know you solve these puzzles. Still!"

"There are also the combat troops that appear with the sky octopi," Starsmasher said. "They appear to have very strange gifts, ones that do not match gifts that we routinely distribute to the transient people. Indeed, some of the reported gifts don't resemble anything that I can identify."

Prince Mong-Ku tried to be patient. In any event, he thought, the three who are not to be named had to be dealt with before the next Polar Conjunction, which was not so many millennia away. Obliterating and replacing world civilization, as would need to be done thrice, could not be done overnight. There was still enough time to complete the Great Plan, but there was not much time to waste. "Colonel Pi might usefully try to reassemble the images of the sky octopus, and someone might stand ready to be teleported to the scene of the next event, to capture a few of the perpetrators, so that they may be invited to explain their misdeeds. Are we good with this?" Heads nodded. "Is there anything else on our plate? Anything that can't wait until the next regular meeting?" Heads shook. "In that case, I believe that we have reached my breakfast time, so we must be adjourned."

Chapter Nine

The Lafayette Laboratory
Compere Biological Sciences Building
Rogers Technological Institution
Early afternoon

"Pardon me?" The voice at the door to Allison Moreland's lab came from a short young woman with raven-black hair and widow's peak, conservatively dressed in gray vest over white blouse and grey trousers.

"Yes?" Moreland answered. Moreland was short, solidly built, her sparkling blue eyes being flanked above by dark hair pulled into ponytail, and below by a long white lab coat that yielded to blue jeans and sneakers before reaching the floor. "May I help you?"

"Sorry to bother you, but I'm trying to find Professor Lafayette's office, and the map says here." The speaker waved an RTI map printout.

"She's in class. She should be out of teaching in a bit," Alison answered. "The map is wrong. The office is down the hall. Oh, I'm Allison Moreland, the senior post-doc. Is there something I can help you with?"

"I'm Krystal North," the woman in the door answered. "Yes, that Krystal North. I need to talk to her about something she did." Moreland smiled politely. Krystal North not in garb looked very little like the same woman dressed as a combat persona. When you saw Krystal in combat garb, you tended to remember North incinerating The Mad Mind with a purely mentalic attack.

"Professor Wells and daughter?" Allison asked. "Professor Lafayette told me about it, in case anyone showed up looking for her, not that it wasn't in the morning Boston Post."

"The Post?" Krystal asked, sounding a bit crestfallen.

"With pictures," Allison answered. "Of you and your Grandmaster friends and Speaker Ming outside their home. The snow if not the wind had briefly died down, and one of the neighbors had come back to Boston to check on his house. He took some photos as you left. We need to wait for Morgana; I'm sure she didn't tell me everything. Would you like some tea? Fresh-brewed, in the group office, of course, not in this lab."

"That would be very kind of you. I've been running so much I missed breakfast," Krystal answered.

"There are scones," Allison answered. "I baked them myself, packed with raisins and hazelnut flour, and caramel icing. I try to keep things on hand, just in case we have another, ummh, distinguished visitor."

"Distinguished visitor? Me?" Krystal asked. "I'm just a civil servant."

"You. Distinguished. Also, this Department has six Nobel Laureates, fourteen members of the National Academy, a Fields Medalist that Course 18 keeps trying to steal from us, not to mention on occasion a visiting Lord of Eternity. So I keep refreshments available, except when Dr. Ashton has baked his chocolate brownies. Well, there is a little baked brownie with white chocolate chips under the chocolate orange mocha icing," Allison said, "so they are brownies." She led Krystal down the corridor.

The group office had comfortable chairs, a large central table, desks facing the sweeping windows, a massive video screen covering most of one wall, and at the far end of the room a refrigerator, microwave, coffee and tea service, and what was clearly a covered tray piled high with scones. Standing with her back to the doorway was Morgana Lafayette, making final adjustments to the coffee brewer.

"Allison, Krystal, good morning. I got out of class early," Morgana announced, not turning around to see who was behind her, "and I'm just loading up the Jamaica Blue Mountain, fresh-ground. But it's good to see you, Krystal, even if I have to disengage my hands from the machinery before I can face you to say hello. Just a second." She extracted herself from the brewing system and turned to her guests. "Krystal, it really is good to see you under conditions where nothing unpleasant is likely to happen. I see despite the cover of blizzard we managed to get ourselves in the newspapers. Fortunately, being someone's champion is a matter of public record, so there won't be a lot of Nosy Parkers asking questions about who I am. Well, someone might wonder why I was Janie's champion, but there's a good cover story that is even true."

"Blue Mountain?" Allison asked. "Isn't that a tad expensive?" Like $200 a pound? she thought.

"I wouldn't make a habit of it," Morgana said, "but I did notice Krystal arriving at the Institution teleport stages and figured I should have things ready for an honored friend and guest. Allison, I hate to do this, but the shared project group meeting is in five minutes in 26-850 and you are the only person other than me who actually understands what we are about to do. As I have a guest, I get to ask you to run the meeting. I believe this was the occasion on which were going to tell everyone what we are actually doing, since as far as I can tell none of them have quite figured it out."

"Yes, Ma'am." Allison bowed her way out of the office.

"A project so secret that the people working on it don't know what it is?" Krystal asked. "That sounds really clever. What could it be? Not that I'm prying if it's a real secret."

"It's my gift to humanity," Morgana said, "on which all the pieces are well known, so I will claim no credit for doing it. The publications will report exactly what each person did as part of the effort. We're curing sickle-cell anemia. Not a bone marrow transplant scheme, the full genetic alteration scheme so that neither the sufferers nor their descendants will have the condition. But all the parts are entirely well-established; only the full cure is new. And don't worry about keeping it a secret. The group all knew that we had this as a general project. They just didn't realize it was happening now, not in ten years. Even if I told them not to talk, the research group would leak like a sieve, given what we're doing."

"Won't the League of Terran Justice complain?" Krystal asked. "They have this idea about inherited genes being sacred."

"Anyone who cures a genetic disease, except that your kids still inherit it, is a moral pervert," Morgana answered, "the sort of person I will happily feed to a Star Demon. Slowly. Contemplate what happened when Atlanticea sank. Atlanticeans had genetic cures, assumed that kids could always be cured the same way as their parents, so they didn't need to adjust the germ lines, and when the continent went under… there were a lot of young people, generation after generation thereafter, who died in ghastly ways, notably collagen failure shortly after having children."

"The League sometimes gets rough," Krystal noted, "like their campaign against private schools."

"The League's lead assassin got taken out by a tenth-grader in Washington," Morgana said. "Silk, who by the way is under-rated as a persona -- had a decent force field, and a willingness to fly into a wall. Hard. Why the villain was sent to assassinate student automobiles is beyond me. But I did have a big boss of theirs in my office. He came to threaten me. That was the first time, in a very long time, that I did a manifestation. I promised him exactly what I would do to his organization if they bothered me. I also showed him memories from post-Atlanticea. He saw my point."

"Should I ask how your cure works?" Krystal asked.

"I would bore you with details, Krystal, even though you are surely up to understanding all of them, so mayhaps we should grab three or four scones and some large mugs of coffee and advance to my office. Whatever you want to talk about, the office is totally secure against spying."

~~~~~

Professor Lafayette's office was the traditional 15' by 20' that the Rogers Institution assigned to its more junior faculty. Lafayette had decorated her office entirely in white, from gleaming white vinyl tile flooring to shelves and curtains and a white computer server box. The one concession to color was a circular carpet woven in an intricate scarlet, white, and black pattern. Krystal North carefully stepped around the carpet. It might be harmless, she thought, but it looked remarkably like a high-power third-order schema. She hadn't spotted them, but surely Morgana had arranged defenses in depth to shield
~~~~~

this room.

"It's always a delight to see you again," Morgana said.

"More so when it's not a surprise," Krystal agreed. "I confess that I very much did not expect to see you when the garage door opened. Miss Wells is anything but a political innocent."

"Janie is a very nice person," Morgana said. "And it can hardly be a secret that she has a few gifts, since she plays matches while behind a double Overton cage, guaranteeing she is not using mentalics to spy on opponents, not to mention that she was almost kidnapped by the Perversion Circle two years ago. Fortunately, her dad knows me, so she proposed 'Professor Lafayette' as her second. However, I am reasonably certain she does not know who all else I am. Assuredly, none of the Wells family recognized my necklace."

"She has some idea who you are?" Krystal asked. "My main concern is that I have put overwatches on each member of the Wells family, in case Baron Kamensky and his friends decide that Janie should be relocated to the hands of the Okhrana, no matter what the Tsar said. I don't want them to get in the way of anything you might do, or tell the Wells family things that they should not know."

"The Wells family knows what is an open secret, namely I am the persona Sunssword," Morgana continued. "I installed several security precautions that should not get in the way of yours, both to protect each member of the Wells family and also to protect their home. I hope you warned Kamensky about how dangerous I am, this being international politics level?" Krystal nodded. "As it is tactically relevant, your people should realize that the two younger Wells children are not harmless. Brian is at least as dangerous as any member of Stars Over Boston, other than myself. Fortunately he has an extremely placid approach to life. If anything, he will not do something violent until it is a bit late. You should emphatically warn your intervention team, should they be needed, that they should not get between Janie and her targets, unless they are absolutely sure she knows they are going to be there and has time to react."

"Why not?" Krystal asked.

"She will feel very guilty about any of your people that she accidentally kills," Morgana answered. "Even if I assure her afterwards that she has bettered the species. She is extremely gift-true, but she is very definitely not harmless in a combat situation."

"Our people do all have mentalic defenses," Krystal said.

"The effect will be a little less dramatic than what you did to The Mad Mind," Morgana said. "She won't put enough power into someone's mentalic shields to heat their body to incandescent plasma. However, if people teleport into her line of fire, they will probably become deceased very quickly, screens or no. She certainly has not had enough combat training to pull a blow under combat conditions."

"I'll keep that in mind. And these are truly fine scones," Krystal said. "But how do you know about Janie and Brian's gifts?"

"After Janie was almost kidnapped, I took up tutoring her and her sister." Morgana nibbled at her scone. "Her brother came along with her. The three are very good, very gifttrue, but their power levels are so high they could damage things they were trying to protect."

"Thank you for protecting the local real estate," Krystal said. "It's always problematic when children that young have high-power gifts. Mentioning high-power, these scones. They're excellent!"

"I'll tell Allison you want the recipe," Morgana said "She'll be delighted. But now I have a riddle for you. Did one of your people, mayhaps two years back, put a geas on the Wells house?"

"I can't imagine why anyone would have done that. They were not of interest, once the kidnapping was solved, until very recently. Not that I have many people who can geas anything," Krystal answered.

"This was a top-chord fourth level schema, mayhaps touching fifth. It was a considerable nuisance to remove," Morgana said.

"I see." Krystal bit her tongue. The number of people who could place or remove a fourth-level construct was vanishingly small. "What did it do?"

"Nothing that made sense." Morgana took a deep sip of her coffee. "Janie had a City of Steel playing partner, a guy about her age, a boy named 'Joe'. The geas meant that you weren't going to be very interested in exactly who he was, where he came from, how to contact him, or where else you might have met him. Janie knew who he was, but didn't bother to tell her parents she had met him earlier. He was very interested in becoming a better City player, no matter how unpleasant the intermediate losses were. Playing Janie, the losses were extremely unpleasant."

"When did she meet him earlier?" Krystal asked.

"Joe was the young man who rescued Janie and sister from the Perversion Circle, two years ago," Morgana answered. "When I learned that, I did ask Janie the key question, legally speaking, the one that determines if I can legally ask her about him? Yes, I asked mentalically, so as not to annoy her parents. Some parents would be annoyed that I asked. Some would have become absurdly annoyed if the answer had been 'yes'. In any event, he and Janie are not carrying on with each other."

"Oh, good. She's awfully young for that. Can you imagine the legal complications if they had been? She wouldn't be available as a witness, and couldn't give any information about how to find him, and life gets complicated from there. Is his private persona private? What do his parents think of all this?" Krystal asked. After a moment, she made the connection. "If we don't know who he is, how can we warn his parents, or protect him from Kamensky and friends?"

Morgana wished that truly young personas were not involved. That situation could readily become distinctly ugly. The modern world was not the distant past that only she remembered. Even if Janie and Joe were ungifted, they were almost certainly too young to carry on with each other. Strong personas like Janie and Joe matured later than ungifted children did. They'd have to be two or three years older than they were now before they'd be at all interested in the possibility, and older than that before the associated hazards were significant.

"There is a minor detail that now mayhaps matters. Two years back, on Castle Island, Joe made off with a Krell disruptor pistol. That's the pistol that shot him, square into his shields, without his shields going down. He was ten or eleven at the time," Morgana answered.

"A ten-year-old with a Krell pistol?" Krystal's question was purely rhetorical. "Why not a strategic transmutation bomb, too? Hopefully he realizes it is not a toy? And how did his shields not go down?"

"I don't know who his parents are," Morgana answered. "I don't know where he lives. The geas ensured that. It wouldn't have blocked me, but I never met Joe to ask. I don't know what he did with the pistol, the matching force field bracer, or why he was so interested in playing Janie. Extremely strong shields covers a great deal of uninformative ground. Asking him your questions requires that he shows up again to play Janie, which he has not done in several weeks. In fact, not since Eclipse made off with the Namestone. Hmm. I wonder if Joe knows Eclipse. That would explain how she found out about the move. If you count, someone planted that geas. This kid has shields more or less as good as yours, except he was ten at the time. Also, after Joe rescued Janie, something marched through the Castle Island Jail, exfoliated the kidnappers' minds, and neutralized the Perversion Circle. That something does not appear to have been Joe. The seriously fuzzy image says the person was close to six feet tall. There are some first rate personas moving near the Wells family, without leaving enough of a trace that I can identify them."

"On the bright side," Krystal said, "Joe has had that thing for the better part of two years now, and I haven't heard about any large urban areas getting flattened by accident. Wait a moment. The giant reptile in Washington last year. It was taken out by that teenager, a girl with a Krell disruptor and a force field bracer. She for sure could not disguise herself as a ten year old boy. Not then, not a year earlier. Except she said she had a boyfriend. And they'd done memory deletion to forget each other." Krystal took another bite out of her scone.

"Silk. That girl was Silk," Morgana said. "Protégé of Kniaz Kang. She's the one who took out the League assassin, too. She goes to school across the street from his restaurant. But she's…just a moment." Morgana held up her right hand and gestured with her fingers. Then she frowned.

"Something wrong?" Krystal asked.

"I have tracers on all five Wells family members," Morgana said. "Something just happened to Jessamine Trishaset. She's conscious, in school, not frightened, not using her gifts. Her mood just switched to catastrophic foreboding." Morgana gestured again. "She is walking down a corridor, between classes. There is no obvious threat. Her brother is walking the other way, away from her."

"Teenagers," Krystal said. "I wore the wrong sweater to school. My reputation is ruined forever."

"True. Also a difficult family situation. Her sister is a Highly Esteemed. Her brother builds astounding models. Trisha is way above grade level, does huge amounts of housework, is a fitness fanatic, sews her own clothing, and her parents simply do not notice. They didn't even say anything to her after I told them how fast a flier she is." Morgana shook her head. "It's tearing the poor kid apart."

"Is she that fast?" Krystal asked.

"I won't break confidentiality." Morgana shook her head. "She is deep space fast."

"I shouldn't have asked," Krystal said. "All this, and we may have a war on our hands. 'May' is too optimistic. The first question is whether the IncoAztecans will wait for an Eclipse sighting as an excuse to invade, will fake an Eclipse sighting as an excuse to invade, or will simply lie and claim there was an Eclipse sighting. Then there are the Brazilians and the Argentines. I have not heard anything about a Lemurian rising to take advantage of the situation, but that's certainly a possibility. At least last Fall their invasion of China was met with a unified world response. I certainly couldn't promise that would happen now. However, you've answered my key question, it is 2 P.M. sharp, and this afternoon I have another 24 hours of work to complete today. At least."

"Understood," Morgana answered. "You must go. You should take a sabbatical and become a faculty member someplace. Afterward you could say how little work you have, now that you are back from being a professor. Please do keep the scones you haven't finished yet."

Chapter Ten

Corridor Nine
Benjamin Franklin Technical Junior High School
Joseph Henry Boulevard
Medford, Massachusetts

Brian Wells stared down the corridor. He absolutely had to talk to Trisha to warn her, and this was the only time in the day that their paths crossed. Except half the time she took the other corridor and the second set of stairs. There she was. He hurried toward her. He had to tell her what he'd heard, and then not be late for his class.

Trisha saw Brian pointing at her, smiled, and stopped. "I've got a class," she said.

"Me, too. Urgent," Brian said. "I dashed back to get my homework this morning. I heard mom and dad talking. Mom is totally hacked off you went cloud diving with Joe. Totally and completely. She even raised her voice." Trisha folded in on herself. "Dad was just as angry. 'She's a complete disgrace to the family' was his line. He said he'd put a stop to that. And if you didn't he'd ground you, no flying or anything, for a year." Trisha almost burst into tears. "Sorry, but forewarned is prepared. Got to run." Trisha, ashen-faced, trudged off to her Genre Fiction Class.

~~~~~

The Wells Residence
Arbalest Street
Medford, Massachusetts

"Hello! I'm home," Trisha called, hoping there would be no answer.

"Good afternoon, Trisha," Abigail called from her first floor office. "Didn't you have singing today? Did anything else happen?"

"Music is tomorrow, Mom. Tomorrow I'm here at a quarter past five. Someone, I forget, thought I knew something about this Joe fellow. I don't. He always was here to play City with Janie. I certainly wasn't going to mention stacking all the firewood."

"You didn't tell people about cloud diving, did you?" Abigail asked grimly.

"Mom! Give away I'm a persona. N. O. No. Besides, that was last Fall, a
~~~~~

long time ago," she answered. "I'd almost forgotten about it." You would have been happy to do it more often, she thought, but he was too busy with some project.

"But whenever he was here, you would sit talking with him," Abigail continued.

"Mother," Trisha said, "he was a guest in our house, so I was polite, just the way you taught me. He'd always be here on time, Janie's chess class always lets out late, and you not me said he should come inside, not sit on the front porch in the cold, so I talked with him rather than leaving him alone until Janie got back, even though he was a boy and so he didn't know much and was really dull even if I had to laugh at his jokes." Actually, she thought, he knew a great deal, so it was like talking to another girl. "And then Janie would show up and they'd break out her game board." They were always funny jokes, Tricia thought. And he was ahead of me in math. All that time I waste singing to keep mom happy got me there. "Are there any chores that need doing? I'll get the dishes and furniture polished soon as I change out of my school clothes, but I have a lot of homework."

"You never went cloud diving again?" Abigail asked.

"That was last Fall, mom. Twice," Trisha said. "Morgana wanted me to practice, and I found someone to practice with, the way Morgana asked, just like Brian and his base ball nines team and Janie and all her game opponents. But then he was too busy."

"But you asked Janie if she'd seen him. Several times," Abigail said.

"I was being polite," Trisha said. Just like I'm being polite now, no matter I want to go to my room. Why is she quizzing me? "Janie really liked him as an opponent because he remembered everything from their back games and kept improving so that when she last saw him she really had to work to beat him, and he never complained, which boys like to do because they don't like to lose; so are there any other chores that need doing?"

"Promise me you won't go cloud diving with him again." Abigail said.

"How can I, mom? He's disappeared." She spread her hands in confusion.

"Jessamine Trishaset, I asked you a question!" Abigail snapped.

No, Trisha thought, you didn't. But it doesn't matter. No, I will not ask why. You'll only get angrier. Besides, it doesn't matter, and I don't care what the answer is. "Yes, mother, I promise I won't go cloud diving with him again." The advantage of super speed, she thought, is that you can wait until you calm down, enough you don't say something stupid, and no one else can tell. Just concentrate on none of this mattering. "Are there any other chores that need doing?"

"Your father was going to put his tool chest in order. He'll need a week," Abigail said.

"On it," Trisha answered. She trudged up the stairs. It was a fine house, she thought. Mom and Dad had their second floor bedroom wing. Janie had the second floor rear, the new extension, built like a rock to support her books. Brian had second floor front and lots of space for model stuff, with his heavy machine tools in the basement, and she had third floor front for her bedroom and the tower room directly above for studying. Third floor back and sides were family and guest rooms.

The tower room was the conceit of a former owner of the house. It sat high above the street, with wide glass panels on all four walls and magnificent views down toward Cambridge. Its ceiling was painted the palest of cocoas. Hanging from the ceiling's apex was a black wrought-iron chandelier. More light from the room came from the line of fluorescent lights hiding behind valances along the ceiling's perimeter. The walls, where they were not glass, were walnut; the floor was white-bleached maple. Brian had helped Trisha build bookshelves on three of the sides. Two sides had rows of shelving and then a wide sill that held two dozen potted plants, violets and Christmas cactus. At the outside of each sill was a grate letting the perimeter radiators heat the room. One side was a long, wide window seat on which she could lie down. Under the window seat was a two-layer storage compartment, and under that was a secret compartment, and inside the secret compartment was a second secret compartment. A third secret compartment went into the wall. It was small, but good for money and jewelry. It would have been good for jewelry, she thought, if she'd ever had any. The last side was a desk with a big writing surface and a computer. The desk faced north, so she never had the sun in her eyes while she was studying. If she went up to the tower, no one ever, ever bothered her, so she could study in complete peace and quiet.

Trisha slipped out of her school clothing, into her chore clothing, summoned her gifts and flew down the stairs. Extreme care meant that she made not a sound while emptying the dishwasher, oiling all the living room furniture, and dry-mopping the living room floor. Then she dropped down to the basement. There were masses of tools, not in their right places in the tool chests. That was easy to fix, even taking the time to oil all the metal parts. All sorts of nuts and bolts and nails were in a big pile, with neat ranks of empty sorting trays behind them. She focused, calling deeply on her gifts. Sorting everything, cleaning the now-exposed workbench, floor, and everything else, seemed to go on forever. An hour had gone by, real time. Her hands hurt from all the work she'd done. She realized she'd cleaned up some of Brian's modelling power tools. She'd have to apologize to him. He was sensitive about that. It was time to go upstairs and bury herself in her books. She almost made it as far as the kitchen.

"Trisha," Abigail called. "Where were you? I went up to your room, and you weren't there."

"I was in the basement, mom" she answered. What was the question? After all, she was coming up the stairs. "I cleaned up Dad's workbench for him, like you asked me to, sorted everything, and cleaned the place up. And now I need a bath. I smell of machine oil. And then I need to start studying."

"You understand why I made you promise no cloud-diving, don't you?" Abigail asked.

"Yes, mother," Trisha answered.

"Why?" Abigail snapped.

"Because you said so, mother," Trisha answered.

"No, the better reason," she said.

"Mother, that's the best possible reason," Trisha answered. "You asked me to."

"Go to your room! Go to your room, and don't come down until I tell you to!" Abigail shouted.

"Yes, mother," Trisha answered. She couldn't remember the last time mom had screamed at her. She headed up the stairs, keeping the tears inside until she'd reached her room and started filling the bathtub. The noise hid her crying. She'd been very patient for very long, but finally she'd reached her limits. No matter what she did, her parents talked her down. She'd need a shower first, to get all the dirt out of her hair, but then a soak would help. Her hands ached.

~~~~

The Tower Room
The Wells Residence
Medford, Massachusetts
Late Evening

Trisha looked up from her homework. She'd heard the door knob of her bedroom turn. She listened carefully. Those were Dad's footsteps, coming across her beautiful maple floor and up the stairs to her tower. He hardly ever came up here. She made herself concentrate on her homework. Proving the quadratic formula required a bit of work. Proving the cubic formula was a chore, but it was a homework problem in the book.

"Jessamine Trishaset!" Dad's voice boomed from the top of the stairs.

"Oh, hi, Dad. I didn't hear you," she said, looking over her shoulder. She stood. And I didn't hear his voice before now, she thought.

"Jessamine Trishaset, you were not at dinner," he said sternly.

"Mom told me to go to my room until she called me. She hasn't, so I'm here," she answered. "By the way, I cleaned up your work bench and got everything sorted."

"Stop changing the topic!" he growled.

"Yes, dad." I did all that work, she thought, and he doesn't even care.

"You understand why your mother is upset?" Patrick Wells asked.

"No, I don't. What's wrong?" Trisha decided after it was too late that she had given the wrong answer, not that there was a right answer.

"Of course you do!" He balled his fists. "You are to stay in your rooms until breakfast tomorrow, appear at breakfast, go to school, and until I say
~~~~

otherwise you will be in your room, at meals, at school, or in transit."

"Yes, dad," she answered. "Chores?"

"You will also do all your chores, whatever your mother says," Patrick answered.

"Yes, dad," Trisha said.

"And remember, I love you and we are doing this for your own good," he said.

I will not say anything, she thought. I know he wants me to say that I love him, too, but I will not say that.

"Don't you have something to say?" he finally asked.

"I have homework to do," Trisha answered coldly. Patrick stamped down the stairs, slamming her bedroom door behind him. After a while she realized she had been staring at the stairway, waiting for her hands to stop shaking, for a good ten minutes.

Sunssword had been very clear about super speed. Trisha knew that she could turn down her gifts much of the way, lie down and sleep for nine hours, and only that number of minutes would have passed. But she wouldn't get more than nine minutes older. So long as she was very quiet, that was an extra nine hours of reading or studying every night. She hadn't done it before, not more than a couple times for completing term papers, but the online classes would let her do it. She could wing her way at lightspeed through all her courses, finish high school, and she'd be entitled to leave. The school handbook said so. Sunssword had also warned her not to try studying at superspeed, not until she'd had her gifts considerably longer, because it wouldn't work right, which was a nuisance. After tonight, leaving couldn't happen soon enough.

~~~~

The Tower Room
The Wells Residence
Medford, Massachusetts
3:15 AM

Trisha stretched and yawned. She'd had her nine hours of sleep, compressed into as many minutes, but it was still strange to be reading at this hour. The blinds were all pulled. They were metalized honeycomb, light-opaque; no one could tell that she was here. And if dad or mom came to check on her, she would turn invisible, fly downstairs, and be in bed before they finished opening her bedroom door. She was already in her light if frilly nightgown. The house heat was way down. Her gifts meant she was aware the temperature was in the low 60s, without her feeling cold. The screen on her computer was flat white, giving more than enough light for reading, at least with her vision. Being confined to her room created a problem for exercise. There was an after-school fitness club; she could switch out of music into that.
~~~~

<?> The question was telepathy, but it didn't sound like Janie. That was a bit alarming. Janie and Brian had really solid mindscreens. She had next to nothing.

"Yes?" she whispered. <*Does this work?*>

<*OK. Brian here.*>

<*What? How?*> she asked.

<*Dad and Mom announced we can't talk to you, except over a meal with them there listening. And Janie was ordered not to use mentalics to talk to you. So we switched powers, just for a few moments. No one told us not to. We had to wait until Dad and Mom are both asleep.*> Brian explained.

<*What is going on? What did I do?*> Trisha said.

<*They won't tell us. It's something to do with Joe and cloud-diving,*> Brian said. <*And Dad is waiting for Joe to show up. He's really mad at Joe. No. He said he's going to kill Joe, and I'm sure he was not joking.*>

<*Wait. Please tell Janie I'm sure Joe and I never talked about City of Steel. I barely know the rules, and for sure don't understand why her move mattered, even when she explained it,*> Trisha said. She shifted in her seat.

<*OK. She says, she never thought you told him anything. And if you did, you didn't know it was important, so she forgives you,*> Brian answered.

<*Good. Please thank her for me.*> This was all so strange, Trisha thought.

<*Are you still awake? You're sitting.*> Brian said. <*It's real late.*>

<*I got nine hours of sleep. In nine minutes. Super speed does that.*> Her stomach growled. She had missed dinner. <*Absolutely positively don't tell mom or dad! So I'm reading. It doesn't matter. No matter what I do, I don't even get thanked. I only get blamed. I even cleaned up Dad's workbench for him, and all he said was 'Don't change the topic.' That reminds me; I vacuumed a few of your power tools, not that they really needed it. I know you don't like that, but I was a bit tired and got absent-minded. I'm sorry.*>

<*Thank you,*> Brian said. <*You really didn't need to. You already do almost all the housework. I should do more, but mom will complain that you aren't doing it. We'd help you, but we don't understand either. At dinner mom and dad were both angry, and spent the whole time lecturing us. And wouldn't let us ask any questions. What they said, it made no sense. It was all about the family's good name and reputation,*> Brian said.

<*Tomorrow. She's asleep now. Ask Professor Lafayette. She might have an answer.*> Trisha wished that was true, not that it mattered. Nothing really mattered any more, except getting out of here.

<*We're here. But trading powers is a strain,*> Brian said.

<*Then put them back. And go back to sleep. You sleep in real time. I don't have to. It was really great of you to do this. Wait! Tell Janie she doesn't know that Joe and I didn't talk about her move. We can't have mom and dad figure out we're talking to each other.*>

<*She says: Thanks for reminding her,*> Brian said.

<*I love you, Brian. You, too, Janie. Good night,*> Trisha said.

<*We love you, too,*> Brian answered. The mentalic link vanished.

Chapter Eleven

Secure Chamber Alpha
The Palace of Peace
Geneva, Switzerland
Early Evening

Holmgren stood at the head of the table, waiting for the ambassadors of the Great Powers to be seated. They had arrived. Now all they had to do was to take their places. He leaned into his chair and tapped his gavel once. "Our recess is over. We are again in session. I hope you all had pleasant lunches and dinners. The ambassadors who placed objection markers at our last meeting have each told me that they insist on raising their objections before we advance to Brigade Leader Valkyria and her report on the events at the Maze. I therefore recognize Ambassador Buncombe."

"Mr. Chancellor," Buncombe said, "during the earlier part of the meeting this morning several ambassadors indicated that it was the intent or position of their government that in the hypothetical case that the Bearer was found, within a country other than their own, their governments would be entitled to send persona teams or even military units to the location of the Bearer to seize the Namestone. For example, if the Bearer were to be found in scenic Buffalo, North York, Buffalonians might find themselves visited by the persona teams and armed hosts of a series of countries I will not embarrass by naming." Buncombe had not incidentally named one of America's wealthiest and most significant industrial cities.

"The President and Speaker of the American Republic are in complete agreement that such a visitation into the American Republic, made without the invitation of the American Republic, which assuredly will not be forthcoming, would be viewed as a declaration of war. The American Persona League would be ordered to the scene to dispose of the invaders. Furthermore, Speaker Ming has called upon the Governors of the seventy states to place in readiness their Persona State Guards to advance to the assistance of the American Persona League. The American team is under direct and explicit orders from the President that such an invasion is to be put down without quarter being offered, unless the invaders immediately and without offering resistance surrender themselves.

"In addition, the American Republic would view it to be an act of war for any foreign power to insert their persona teams into the territory of any of the Canadian Dominions, unless Her Majesty's government had invited them, in which case the situation would be taken under advisement. As an exception, any effort of the IncoAztecan government to insert its persona teams or armed hordes into the territory of any other country in the Americas will be taken to be a declaration of war on the American Republic, a declaration against which the American Republic will respond in full and without limit. I believe that Ambassador Featherstonehaugh is the next to speak, and I yield to him." Buncombe wondered how long would be needed for other powers to deduce that the Republic had discussed his anticipated remarks with Her Britannic Majesty and her Ministers. Some ambassadors, he considered, would doubtless need to have it explained to them, slowly and in words of few syllables.

"On behalf of Her Majesty's government," Featherstonehaugh responded, "I will say that we are grateful for the offer of the American government to support the independence and liberty of each of Her Majesty's Canadian Dominions, with the clear understanding that has already been negotiated between our Minister of State and Speaker Ming that at such time as we request our American friends to depart that they will do so as expeditiously as possible, given the potential need to assist the sick and injured, extinguish fires, and support the detention of foreign prisoners of war pending their fair trials and prompt executions. Potential needs were in fact discussed at some length. We are quite sure that the British Empire and the American Republic are in complete agreement on the notion of potential needs and expeditious withdrawal. Also, Her Majesty's government views the independence and security of other nations in the Americas to be a critical matter for the security of the British Empire. There is no possibility that Her Majesty's government would consider being responsible for the consequences if the independence or security of any of these nations were to be infringed upon. The longstanding alliance between Her Majesty's Realm and the Empire of the Brazilians is viewed as particularly sacrosanct. Having said that, I believe that Ambassador Davout had signaled a desire to speak, mayhaps even before I did, but he graciously offered to allow me to speak first." Featherstonehaugh passed the Speaking Stone to Davout.

"On behalf of his Most Placid and Serene Majesty, the Sixth Napoleon, may His House endure until the end of time, I must most emphatically state that the French Empire categorically and completely rejects the suggestion that foreign powers are entitled to besmirch the name of the Empire and the honor of the Legion of Glory by claiming a right to enter our territory and attack our citizens, as though we were unable to protect ourselves." Davout closed the case from which he had read his short remarks. The Legion of Glory, Buncombe thought, was the French Military Persona Host. The French Empire covered a lot of terrain. Davout's country, including its not-protectorates from the Caribbean to the Eastern Mediterranean, was nonetheless an eminently civilized place in which an American could consider living. Napoleon might style himself Emperor, but its local governments including the Greek and Spanish Kingdoms and Venetian Republic had an independence that only Frenchmen and Americans found entirely reasonable.

Holmgren, fearing what was about to happen, nonetheless was obliged to recognize Ambassador Smoking Frog. "The Living Sun, The First Speaker," Smoking Frog said, "has anticipated the outrageous statements of the American Ambassador and his foreign toadies." Featherstonehaugh and Davout looked at each other and rolled their eyes. "The right of the League of Nations to take possession of the Namestone is beyond question or doubt. It is totally forbidden and contrary to the League Charter, the votes of this body, and the votes of the World Council for any nation to take any other stand. Furthermore, it is the privilege and duty of the persona leagues and military forces of every nation of the world to enforce these votes anywhere on the planet without begging leave of local governments or local persona leagues, all of which are entirely subordinate to the League of Nations and therefore must be brought to heel if they fail to obey the League's righteous edicts. The people of the world may be assured that so soon as the Bearer is located, the Jaguar Knights and the Eagle Legions will descend upon her, strip her of the Namestone, and prepare her to be fed to the Gods, or such other form of painful death as this body may choose to specify."

Holmgren steeled himself for what would undoubtedly be the extended remarks of most of the remaining ambassadors, some saying that their countries were entitled to pursue the Namestone wherever it was found, and others saying that there was no such entitlement. On one hand, he considered, only a minority of Great Powers would claim their right of intervention. On the other hand, Manjukuo and the IncoAztecan Empire would both claim that alleged right. Alas, they were probably the two most populous nations in the world. Both of them were vigorous about seeking out and training persona talents wherever found. Holmgren told himself that he had wisely packed several large flasks in his vest and suitcoat pockets, and suspected that very soon he would be managing to drain them of their fine beverages, all of which had begun their lives as grain and potatoes, variously American, Scots, and Russian in extraction.

At long last, the argument over foreign intervention ran out of steam. "What do we tell our citizens?" Lars Holmgren finally responded prayerfully after finishing another sip at his American flask.

"Mayhaps," Buncombe said, "you could tell the people of the world that you eventually reached this meeting's agenda." It wasn't always necessary to lead Holmgren by the nose, he thought, but it seemed to be necessary more and more often. Mayhaps that reflected Holmgren's decision to fortify himself.

"Ah, yes, the original agenda. Eclipse and how she escaped. Is there an issue here?" The Ambassadors glowered. "Valkyria," Holmgren asked, "Can you add anything to what happened afterward?"

"Rolf," she answered, her use of the first name reminding her audience of the ill-kept secret that she was also Holmgren's mistress, or mayhaps the other way around, "there is a written report with video support, which hopefully all of you have had time to study." Buncombe nodded in agreement. Nonetheless, he knew, Valkyria would insist on giving her report, or at least a precis of it, rather than asking for questions. "Let me," she continued, "note that the broadcast video of my conversation with the Bearer does not completely agree with what I remember her saying. The actual events appeared to be a scenario that we'd examined very thoroughly, namely the 'politely declines to cooperate' option. The plan was not perfect. I believe one of Markgraf Moeller's excellent volumes on tactics treats plan failure." She smiled in Moeller's direction. He glowered. "The first failure was that the Bearer does not look at all like the drawings we are distributing. She's considerably shorter than I am, enough that at first I thought she was not the Bearer, and could not imagine who she was. It did not help that the Maze was doing time distortion, so that my teleport to St. Brendan's Isle took some hours to complete. Based on Eclipse's actions in the Maze, we thought we had a good estimate of her gifts, namely close to none. We appeared on Atlanticea with what should have been overwhelming strength. The ancient American aphorism is 'If a company seems enough, send in a division. That way no one gets hurt.' It's a fine aphorism. We put it into place. We've had time to do a complete reconstruction. Eclipse was a solid target, not an illusion. Most attacks on Eclipse found their target. All six of my team drains drew at full capacity. Lady Sylph is emphatically certain: The Screaming Skull hit Eclipse with his death command. I hit her with the Katana of Justice. All that, and Eclipse's defenses did not go down." Buncombe stared at one of the walls in seeming boredom. Part of Valkyria's remarks had not been in the written report, namely that Eclipse did not resemble her wanted posters. That was going to raise certain challenges for anyone trying to capture her.

"She used the Namestone?" Elizaveta Romanoff asked. The Russian Ambassador's interruption was only almost a question.

"The *Copper Book of Harvest Stars* is completely clear," Valkyria answered calmly. "The Wizard of Mars agrees, or so he is said to have told the Grand Tradesmaster. The Bearer needs several days to mesh with Namestone's powers. Until then, Namestone supplies a few cosmetic tricks, no more. Observe that Eclipse's garb was immaculate, and her face was unmarred. That was all the Namestone did for her. No, Eclipse stood up to us using her own shields. If she had a team backing her, they did a darn fine job of remaining invisible the whole time, not to mention fooling six Drains and a Seer. I am less bothered that we didn't take her down, and more bothered that the Screaming Skull didn't appear to have discomfited her. Mayhaps I should also be bothered that she did not give the Martyr her private persona name. The *Copper Book* says that that is a requirement for being given the Namestone. Somehow she managed to dodge answering the Martyr's question."

"Someone who stands up to the Skull? Is there such a person?" Legate Hong asked. "But which appearance is false? Which image was falsified? The one you saw or the one the world saw? Or both?"

Valkyria rested her chin on her fingertips. "Who else? Other Lords of Eternity. A few personas from ancient history. Ambassador Featherstonehaugh's illustrious ancestor, Morgan Le Fay. The Goetic Knights wore enchanted armor, armor superior to mine. The Marik Master of Parades supposedly wore the Invincible Sigil of the Eternal Procession. This Eclipse person is none of the above. However, manifestly, there is such a person, because I hit her square on with the Katana of Justice, and during the explosion her force field did not waver. Having said that, while her mindscreens were also quite solid, a few of her thoughts leaked very slightly out to where they could be read. She was clearly operating a Medico rules engine. When the Katana of Justice struck her, she was at the edge of taking lethal damage. We also got the slightest impression of her emotions. She was utterly focused on something, too focused to consider that she ought to be scared out of her wits. I infer she was focused on summoning power levels. Or gifts. Though if you told me she is a descendant of the legendary Girl Without Fear, I could believe you."

"If I may?" Prince Shi, ambassador of the Celestial Republic of the Han, rarely spoke. "We are not, Valkyria excepted, masters of the art of battle strategy. We should give those who are masters of battle our thoughts, and let them tell us the answers, not spend time chatting about tactics as the amateurs we are. However, I believe I see why we missed the range of her gifts. She neglected to use them. She did not quite attain the ultimate feat of brilliancy 'defeat your enemy without doing anything', but she was parsimonious in her choice of methods. While in the Maze, she never teleported, mostly showed human resistance to heat and cold, played City of Steel well but not brilliantly. Except for that one move, of course. Until we attempted to kill her, she could have been a very well-trained ungifted woman. Twenties mayhaps sounds young. She might have a touch of the gift of agelessness. Mayhaps Valkyria can explain what I am missing."

"The *Copper Book* explains this," Valkyria answered. "The Lesser Maze tests determination, purity of thought, cleverness, strength of mind, and physical and mental training, not enormity of power." Unless, Valkyria thought, you cheat by presenting the Maze with an artificial construct that has no mental weaknesses. Alas, the construct had not been quite ready to enter the Maze before this Eclipse showed up. "Thus Cortez and Fisher, the latter's fleet being infinitely more powerful than the former's, could come equally close to victory. Your description, Prince Shi, may explain how Eclipse escaped. The capture strategy, in the few hours tactical support teams in

Europe had to insert fine detail, inferred her gifts from her acts in the Maze. We hit her vastly harder than should have been needed, given the gifts she had shown. If there were an error in the tactical analysis, we would appreciate it being pointed out to us. After all, everyone who has ever tried to walk the Maze, whether those two chess grandmasters or any of the World-Class personas who tried and failed, has while in the Maze used all of their talents to their uttermost limits. She didn't."

"She cheated!" Lord Featherstonehaugh interjected.

"A different answer." Saigo Shigetoshi, Buncombe considered, was Legate of the Satsuma Daimyo, so he did not officially represent his country. The Shogun's Court could deny responsibility for what he said. The legal fiction that Shigetoshi only represented the Satsuma Daimyo rather than speaking for the Emperor and the Shogun was one of the quaint aspects of doing business with the Japanese. It was almost as quaint as the fiction that Shigetoshi's wife merely liked a bit of gossip, rather than being the Imperial Spymaster for Europe. "Do not fear. At the end, as foretold by the *Harvest Stars*, Eclipse had a choice. She could reach out and take the Namestone. Or she could ask, and be given it if she was worthy. I am totally confident. She asked. She received the Namestone freely."

"Asked? When she could have taken it? She shows she is weak!" Markgraf Moeller grumbled.

"Then I must humbly pray that we never have to contend with a strong persona bearing the Namestone," Legate Hong whispered. It was a shame, Buncombe considered, that the Manjukuoan Empire could never forgive America for buying Alaska for a few dollars. Hong was a remarkably intelligent conversationalist, but, if he ever chatted with Buncombe, Hong would likely be ordered to commit suicide, probably after being compelled to murder all of his descendants.

"Thus," Saigo continued, "she is as worthy as the Martyr, who read her soul before granting her the stone, so she is no danger to anyone. However, she may defend herself. Such acts might have less than ideal consequences to nearby places, for example the neighboring continents. Accordingly, the Satsuma Domain will not find it entirely convenient at this time to participate in attempting her capture."

"We must mobilize the people of the world," Holmgren said, "to turn their united talents to capturing this person. Wherever she is – yes, I agree the very limited evidence suggests somewhere in Europe – we must find her. In particular, we must capture this Eclipse person and free the Namestone before it falls into truly wrong hands. Can you imagine what the League of Terran Justice would do with it?" The League of Terror and Injustice was a permanent thorn in Holmgren's side. Buncombe perched his chin on his hands. The League of Terran Justice clearly had secret objectives, objectives that no one had yet divined. Those were the objectives that drove its disciplined yet incomprehensible behavior.

"All the power of all the world's investigatory agencies, from the Okhrana to the fabled Pinkertons, is hot in her pursuit," Elizaveta Romanoff said. "There can be no doubt. We shall find her. Of course, what we do then is another question."

"Should you not have some plan for dealing with her before you find her?" American Ambassador Buncombe allowed that it was time to remind foreigners of the practical nature of all Americans. "Lest you find yourself like the miniature poodle that treed the pride of lions? How do you plan to match the Namestone's power? Not to mention, of course, that a person who can stand up to that range of attacks without flinching is no mere milquetoast, no little girl pretending to be her older brother. This Eclipse is a persona of no slight power. The most obvious demonstration of this is the dog that did not bark." Hopefully, Buncombe thought, these people or their political masters will recognize that attacking the Bearer may prove to be less than safe.

"Ahh, the Great English Detective Helmesham," Legate Saigo said.

"Precisely," Buncombe said. "This person was attacked by our League's most powerful Strike Team, not to mention a Lord of Eternity. What did she do? Nothing. Not a thing. Most people, seeing what was about to happen to them, would at least try shooting back, piously hoping that they might possibly fire a silver arrow. Eclipse just stood there. Of course, you could claim that she has no combat gifts, just a sharp knife, but having no combat gifts is an exceedingly odd match to at least twelfth-level screens, not to mention effective second-order defenses. You could also propose she was so slow-witted that she did not recognize what was about to happen to her, but someone so dull could never have solved the Maze. No, this Eclipse person was confident that her gifts would shield her from the League and the Skull. A list of known personae who are that confident about their gifts is very short." Indeed, he considered, he should ask the State Department to generate that list for him.

"Yes," Singh said, "As she is clearly not a Lord of Eternity, there is one obvious possibility. While she is shorter than history books report, it is possible that the Namestone is now in the hands of the Silver General." Looks of horror criss-crossed the room. "Some would feel surprise that the Supreme Mistress of Terror and Treachery was found worthy."

"Mercifully," Featherstonehaugh responded, "I can rule out that inspired and sensible inference. The Silver General appeared regularly in London in Queen Victoria's declining years. My great-grandfather, who was something of a lady's man, became, how shall I put it, her very close friend, and noted in his diary that they were of a height, that height being five feet, ten inches, much taller than the Bearer who Valkyria encountered."

"Mayhaps we should ask those who have so-far remained silent if they had anything useful to add?" Elizaveta Romanoff made her grandmotherly smile, knowing the Special Peace Executive would hear effusive promises of support, promises that she knew to be of dubious reliability. It was possible, she thought, that some of the Great Powers did not plan to keep secret their capture of the Namestone, at least until they had used the Namestone to conquer the world. She hoped that no one would press her to name a Great Power that was so strangely run. It seemed implausible that any Power would voluntarily hand the Namestone over to dear Lars. Nonetheless, the promises would be extensive, time-consuming, pointless, and last until an appropriate hour for recess had been reached.

Chapter Twelve

The Invisible Fortress
Morning

Unfortunately, yesterday evening was when the healing matrix decided that I should start ramping down my mind control systematically, meaning I would feel a bit more pain, so the matrix would know exactly what it had to fix. I did what I was told, but I certainly can't claim I was comfortable afterward. I allowed that if I lay in my bed I was actually falling asleep a reasonable part of the time, even though I was very aware of the interminable minutes when I was too uncomfortable to sleep.

Someplace in the middle, I had a waking dream, asking myself why Mum had tossed me out of our home. I can't understand not being told. I suppose she could've gotten involved in something really dangerous, and wanted to make sure that I stayed out of it. But she knew perfectly well that if she told me not to do something, I wouldn't have done it. What had I done?

I remembered one thing I had done. I snuck off to New York to watch a play by the second-greatest Elizabethan playwright, Shakespeare. Alone at age eleven was way safer for me than for an ungifted. Mum didn't say a word. Yes, I did pay for the ticket, even though I had to sneak-teleport into the theater and hide in the loft to watch. King Lear is said to depict acts so wicked that no small child like me should be allowed to see it. It's like the films and plays in which you have people carrying on with each other, on camera. I did watch King Lear, the whole thing, but it seemed to me that it was terribly sad, not wicked at all. Of course, many children my age would have had a very different perspective on what was happening.

But I'd made mistakes before, and all Mum asked me to do when I made a mistake was to go through my thought processes and see where I might have done something different. Certainly, after I had - not by plan - seen the entrance to the Lesser Maze, and at first didn't say why I was upset, Mum thought I might have been carrying on with a boy, even though I was way too young for that to be possible. She hadn't been at all worried that I had been.

Then my dream carried me back to what surely had to be the worst thing I'd ever done, no matter that Mum said afterwards that I'd done the right thing and she was proud of me. At least it only almost left me dead. It was a year and a half ago. I'd gone to Boston, to the Carnegie Library, to read some of their serious history books on the Summer War of 1908. By standing up to a couple of bullies, I'd gotten into a serious fight, one that might easily have killed me, despite all of Mum's training. Fortunately I'd carefully done all the things Mum had told me to do, if it appeared there was going to be violence and I couldn't readily cut and run. She wouldn't have complained if I ran. She is not a Gowist, but she does repeat the line that a coward may avoid a thousand deaths. She also refers to brave honorable warriors as tin-plated idiots who are routinely slaughtered by competent soldiers.

Oh, yes, Boston. I was finally old enough that Mum trusted me to use a library by myself. I was entirely well-behaved. My gifts were still developing, but were more than adequate to deal with a few street thugs. I had a telepathic null link, something where I could call for help, and Mum would hear it, no matter where on earth I was, without there being any tracing. A telepathic null-link is even better than a radio telephone. No one can tell you are using it. Besides, I would be using the Carnegie Library in Boston, the City of Good Sense, where the Stars Over Boston persona league keeps a firm thumb on criminalistical elements.

Mum wanted me to read recent history, how a Prussian Kaiser's pointless bragging as amplified by an English journal correspondent turned into the Summer War of 1908. This is modern history, history that deals in actual facts, not ancient history, filled with morally edifying tales. You would think that a descendant of Marlborough would have more political eptness, but not so, unless you believe that Winston maneuvered Wilhelm into launching his war with Bavaria. Surely Churchill knew what the Kaiser should have noticed, namely that Austria and France had both lost territory to Prussia and would cooperate to get all of it back, and then some. Mum had a list of particularly good historians to read. I found a very isolated, quiet corner of the library, one where I was unlikely to be noticed, and sat there with book, pad of paper, and mechanical pencil. Yes, I do have a photographic memory, sort of, but that's not useful for this sort of studying.

Most of the room was given over to books on games: Chess, Stones, City of Steel, Territories, and more. Books on the history of real wars were a modest section of the collection of books on games about warfare. Soon I had company, two girls close to my age. The older one wore a crisply tailored, recently-ironed orange pantsuit, something that worked well with her bright-red hair. She was working through what looked to be a school textbook. The younger one was studying, very intently, a book on City of Steel. I wouldn't have called her dress scruffy, but her girl's blue jeans and long-sleeve white polo shirt were rumpled. Every so often the younger girl made a note on her own pad of paper. She looked to be astonishingly focused.

After a couple of hours, I had made fair progress into Weaver's history. Weaver was remarkably clear, but I'd never heard of half the people he was talking about. My pad of paper gained a longer and longer list of names I had to research. Weaver took no sides on the historical issues. A bit of noise marked the two girls getting up to leave. I went back to my reading.

Not three minutes later, I heard a strangled cry for help. No, not a cry. The call was telepathic. There was an image. It was the two girls. Rather, the older one was jumping back and forth, dodging three thugs trying to grab her. The younger one cowered behind her. The girls couldn't just run for it. One of the thugs had put up an opaque force wall trapping them. Where? I called back. Mayhaps I should have bit my tongue, but none of them could see who or where I was. The returned image, hard to see, was the back alley from the library to the subway station, a very pretty brick walk seldom used, or so it appeared.

Mum really disliked persona who picked on children. One of the thugs was a persona, but he looked to be well within the range of power levels I could handle. OK, mayhaps I was a bit overconfident. No, probably I was way overconfident. I triggered the null link, showed Mum what was happening and what I was proposing to do. If she wanted to disagree, she had all the time in the world to speak up. Drop pad and pencil into shoulder bag. Step into little boy's room, meanwhile calling my gifts. Boy's? Yes, that was my disguise. I was dressed as a boy. I'd already checked with a flash of ultravision. The room was empty. Rule One for combat: If you have a choice, go as slack as possible. Call your levels as far down as you can, don't tap all of them, and be free to be pushed into even deeper levels.

The one room I could be sure did not have a video scanner was empty. Rule Two: Surprise is good. Defenses are better. OK. Force field to max, well, as much max as I had at age ten. Flight on and hover. My mentalic attacks were not great, but try them first--there is a library here, armored walls or not. I teleported right next to the younger girl. Her sister was now on the ground, out cold.

"Way cool!" the youngest punk shouted. "Now we've got three of them. Fun time!" I hit him as hard as I could with a levin bolt. His eyeballs rolled up into their sockets as he dropped.

<*Not so fast, little girl! Try me for size!*> That was another punk, from the sound a good mentalist. Mum had given me a firm warning. I was not to go mano a mano with a real mentalist, not until I was a bit better at blocking counterstrikes down through my levin bolts. For the first guy, the one on the ground, I had had surprise, but now I didn't.

"You should live so long," I answered. I started to shift over to flash and plasma attacks. When I was younger, shifting took me a bit of time, during which their mentalist tried several not very good levin bolts of his own. OK, he didn't accomplish anything, but if I'd opened myself by attacking him mentalically, his bolts would have been way more damaging. I make it sound as though I was completely calm, but I was starting to get a bit frightened. I'd expected one guy with a force wall, and some punks with no gifts. Now I was up against several personas whose gifts I did not know. I engaged the next null link. Mum still hadn't said anything. OK, she wanted me to handle this myself. Now their mentalist was trying to drive little icepicks into my mindscreens to crack them open. I was holding him, but not without putting backbone into it.

I flashed the lot of them. I couldn't tell which of them I might have blinded. It wasn't my best attack, but flash is safe in close quarters, and might make them back off. Either I missed hitting their mentalist, or their mentalist didn't need sight to target me. He kept picking away on my mentalic defenses.

Now was very definitely the time to run, and take the two girls with me. Oops. One of their guys was a teleporter. He had a tangle mesh out. If I teleported, I'd take the thugs with me. I could try straight up, say a hundred miles, but I had no idea if the girls needed to breathe. I'd practiced 'Breathe for Someone Else'. Once. For one other person. Mum would simply smash the tangle field, but I was very definitely not strong enough to do that. Not at age ten. Teleport tangle meshes are tough. OK, Mum had me memorize a bunch of Boston terrain features, one being a deserted island in the outer harbor. I could take us all there, and take the gloves off. I could have jumped to someplace near the Stars Over Boston Headquarters, and let them come to my rescue, but the Stars were on Mum's emphatic stay-away list.

We jumped. Rather, I jumped and hauled the lot of them with me. There was a chill breeze off the early summer bay, a breeze that smelled of sea salt and iodine and seaweed washed up on the shore. The sensible city keeps its harbor scrupulously clean -- well, drinking the water by the glassful is a bit optimistic even if it weren't salty -- so the smell was close to open ocean.

Annoying! I'd dragged the two girls along. I thought I'd only be dragging the thugs, but their teleporter had snagged the two girls, not just me and their mob, in his weave. My first plasma blast took the fellow in the rear, the one not doing anything. He reflected it back at me! It bounced off my force field, hit their barrier, and bounced again. They had a tough wall around us.

I called my gifts as deeply as seemed safe. Slack! went the lesson. Keep slack! If you call absolutely everything you've got, your screens become brittle. They hold, or they don't, but they don't have reserve power to grab. Then I hit their force wall with a plasma torch. Hard! Very rapidly, it frayed and developed holes. Behind me, the younger of the two girls was dragging her sister over an edge of the dune.

"Cut this nonsense," one of them shouted. "Take him down. Now! For good." Suddenly I had two attacks coming my way, different sorts of radiation that cut into my screens, and more and more levin bolts. Yes, slack mattered, because now I was drawing hard on my levels to keep up my defenses. What had started as a couple of bullies had blown up into a high-power battle. Only later did I learn it ended as the highest-power combat in New England since Crittenden's War. I would have been delighted to teleport out, but I couldn't. Their teleporter still had his tangle field up. I could teleport, but I'd just drag them along. Flying away was not a choice, either. One of them still had a force wall trapping the three of us in place. Either I won, by myself, or …the old Goetic line is Victory or Death. I triggered my third null link. Nothing happened. I really wished Mum was less interested in making this a learning experience for me, because at this point I was frightened.

There are ways to draw more deeply on your gifts, ways that open up additional channels into each level. Mum had little warnings on each of them, warnings like "Quite painful" and "You will be sick afterward". I ignored the warnings, and opened them up. Now I had some slack.

"Harder. Link powers." The fellow shouting had to be their boss. I reached really deeply into my gifts and hit him as hard as I could with a plasma blast. He dropped, unconscious or dead. Now they had linked, and I needed every bit of strength to block their efforts to kill me. Yes, even back then I had good shields, but holding up shields demands power. I was already as deep into my gifts as I had ever been. Lack of slack is still not good. The next set of ways to reach into power were behind neat tied knots, knots that Mum had vigorously warned me not to untie until I was older, or I would be in real trouble. With her. I untied all the knots. The power I reached echoed all around me like sharp little daggers. Little stars of light crawled across my visual field. If I drew on those resources, and Mum complained, I could always answer 'I'll move out of our house. You can pretend I died.' That was a bit of bravado, when I was that much younger. Living on deserted tropical islands sounds fun, unless you need to do it when you are short on money. Besides, there just aren't many deserted tropical islands, not in a world full of people who can fly or teleport.

I opened the knots, barely in time. Their number two man shot me with a pistol, a weapon I'd never seen before. My shields shuddered and cracked. I dropped through level after level, through The Sun, through The Fall of Crystal, very briefly seeing a level I had only read about, The Tomb. I saw its metaphor, a snow-covered barrow with a girl dressed all in black sitting on its top. She looked up and smiled at me. Dropping through levels was like having my head forced under water, deep into a glacial-cold lake. My heart pounded. I was about to die. I did what I should, drawing as hard as I could on everything I had. Number two had forced me deeper than I'd ever been into my gifts. His weapon had the blinding intensity of the starcore. My shields frayed but stayed up. The brightness vanished. His pistol had to recharge, and I didn't give him a chance to shoot me again. The phrase is 'cut them off at their knees', in this case through a really tough force field coming from his bracelet. That's what I did. Quite literally. I cut him in two at his knees. He fell over, unconscious. He'd driven me way deep into my gifts, and I was still into them when his pistol ran out of steam.

I really did not want them chasing us. I knew which of them was their teleporter. I hit him again, making sure that he was quite dead. Mum eventually pointed out that I might have killed the only one of them who knew where their safe house was hidden. She also reminded me that if I had actually killed their teleporter, his tangle field had gone down, so at this point I could simply have escaped, taking the girls along. I forgot. Then I disarmed their number two man. Yes, disarmed. I incinerated both arms. Modern medicine and a good healer could have grown them back, except I'd killed him first.

To their credit, the Stars Over Boston were finally showing up. A half-dozen of them teleported in, out over the water. I later learned that the younger girl had been screaming for help, mentalically, enough that the Stars knew exactly where to look for us. The Stars' one combat tactic is 'Leap before You Look' and that's what they had done. They were still very fast off the mark to get to me.

Then another persona appeared, not quite between me and the kidnappers. I'd never met Sunssword before. She looked to me to be a young woman, wearing a white laboratory coat over sweater and blue jeans. Very briefly, we had mental contact. I had a sense of great power, greater age, and patient sadness. The younger girl -- I still didn't know her name -- sent Sunssword, lightning-fast, a description of the fight. I didn't let her finish. I did exactly what Mum had ordered, if I looked to be getting into trouble, and teleported the three of us out. I remembered to grab the funny gun and the force field bracer with my teleport field. I suppose I make the fight sound long and drawn out. Not at all. The bit on the island had lasted a couple minutes.

First we were someplace in northern Canada, a few thousand feet above the ground. My flight field held all three of us. The younger girl -- and finally I had a persona name, Aurora -- gave me a solid location near her home, someplace we almost for sure would not be seen when we appeared. I did a soft jump to get there, a bit wearing, but for sure we would appear above, not under, the ground.

I was not quite sure where I was, other than 'secluded point in local park system'. If the muggers showed up in pursuit I was in real trouble. I'd pushed myself way deeper than I was ready to go. Little stars, blinding bright, sparkled inside my head. I was bone-achingly cold. I told myself that happened when you go too deep into your levels. The world wavered around me. I was just too tired to stand. I dropped to sit a stone wall and leaned forward, my head in my hands. If the muggers actually showed up, I would give my 100% to stop them again. I just doubted that would be enough. In retrospect, I should have realized that the muggers were not showing up, because they were all incapacitated or seriously dead, namely I had totally wrecked them up including killing several of them. Stars Over Boston would have done the rest.

I looked at the two girls I had rescued. The older was lying on her face. The younger looked paralyzed with fear. First aid, I thought. What do I do? I fell forward, crawled over, got my arms under the older girl, and rolled her sideways. "Help me," I mumbled. The younger girl, given something to do, leaped to it. Moving a limp body is hard. Now that the older girl was on her back, I could see that she was breathing. Her fingernails were pink. I remembered to pull her knees up to her chest.

"Trisha?" the little girl called. "Wake up!" The younger girl tried shaking her sister. Nothing happened. Then there was a burst of telepathy from the younger girl. She was a strong telepath. The erstwhile kidnappers must have had a heavy-duty telepathy block going, strong enough that in the library I only heard her weakly. I wasn't sure what the little girl was doing, but it didn't seem to help. OK, my turn. I reached out to the null links and reset them. I had seen Mum do that, once and again, but she made it look effortless. It made me dizzy. Then I triggered all three of them at the same time.

Mum was there almost instantly. <*What?*> came her thought. That was not an annoyed what?; it was a very concerned question.

<*Triage!*> I answered, pointing at the other two girls. <*I'm not dying. I think.*> For a while I was shut out of a mental conversation. At the end, the older girl was awake, and the younger girl seemed to have set aside everything that had terrified her.

<*What happened?*> Mum asked. It was a mark of how much she trusted me that she didn't accuse me right off of doing something wrong.

<*I had to reset my null links,*> I thought. <*I triggered them one at a time, didn't hear anything from you, thought silence was approval.*> It is really rarely that I manage to surprise Mum, telling her something she didn't know. I could tell. She was surprised. She had not heard the null links trigger. She later worked out why. The bad guys had had, an aid for kidnapping people, a scheme for blocking them. I sent her my memories, what I had done, and how hard it was to reset the links. <*The guys trying to beat up on these two were way tougher than a couple of punks with knives. If they'd been thugs with pointy things I would have flattened them from one breath to the next.*>

<*He saved us.*> That was the little girl, entering the conversation. <*You saved us, I mean. And you're shivering.*>

"Cold," I answered. "Cold. So cold. And if those guys show up again…"

<*I'm right here.*> That was Mum again. Except now she was really close. <*If they appear, I'll take care of them.*> The undertone to 'take care of' was one of utter finality. But what did happen? I let the younger girl answer, a blur of images mostly faster than I could follow. She was a really good telepath, way better than I am. I can do mentalics, but mostly I am good at wrecking things. Deliberately, but I wreck things. I finally followed with my memories, not hiding that I'd done those things with my gifts that Mum had told me not to do.

<*You did the right thing,*> Mum interrupted. <*Slack is always right. That goes for you, too, Aurora.*> When that name was mentioned the younger girl looked at me and smiled shyly. Then Mum sent to me: <*But your shields shouldn't have*

overloaded, dear, not against a few street thugs.> I dropped in the image of the strange pistol. Now Mum was seriously surprised. <*I should get the three of you home,*> Mum continued. <*And then I need a few words with the people who tried to kidnap you two. I'll be there as soon as I slip into a different persona.*> I think I hid from Aurora what Mum was going to do to the thugs to learn all their secrets. The method has several names, mindrape being the most polite, and an outcome: The targets do not have working minds afterward. They also have absolutely no secrets left.

I was too busy shivering uncontrollably to say anything. The two girls sat down on each side of me, hugging me, close enough that I started to warm up. If someone had come along, it would have been a bit of a scandal, me being disguised as a boy and hugging two girls at the same time, at our ages, but no one else was there. I took the moment to introduce myself to Aurora and the older girl. Aurora's sister was Comet. Comet mostly just flew, but her memories... she'd flown around the world in a few minutes. Yes, she sounded to have all the gifts you needed to do that. Comet and Aurora were their persona names. I didn't ask their other names. Aurora had used her sister's name, but that was my secret now. In this disguise, I was Joe. Aurora was very polite, and tried to hide her curiosity.

Mum appeared in a few minutes. Her disguises are always excellent. She couldn't hide her height, but anyone who looked at her would think she was much older, well, older than she usually looks. She disguised herself as some sort of a businesswoman with attache case.

<*Dear, I really think I should get these two home first,*> Mum said. <*Someone snapped a photo of Comet and Aurora on the island, enough that their parents have figured out that their children were kidnapped*>. Aurora looked horrified. Her sister had, of course, slept through almost the whole thing, and had no idea what happened.

<*I'll be OK,*> I answered. <*Just so they don't show up again.*> As I said, I wasn't thinking clearly. The thugs were showing up no place, except mayhaps an operating theater in the local jail. Mum, Aurora, and Comet vanished, disappearing like a light going out. Mum's teleports are really inconspicuous. Here one moment, gone the next, and no special effect worth mentioning. I made myself stand up and walk back and forth. Then Mum was back.

She took one look at the pistol I had recovered. "Crash drop! Shields!" she shouted. "Absolute maximum power." I had no idea why, but I didn't hesitate. I did a crash drop, something I'd actually never done except in practice, calling my gifts as deeply as I could, mayhaps as deep as I'd gone when the thug shot me. I didn't black out, but I couldn't hold my shields up that high for long. I sank to my knees. Mum's shields, way stronger than mine, had gone up, too. She also had a wall around both of us. She was looking very carefully at the pistol and bracer. <*OK,*> she said. <*You can ease off. There's a particularly nasty trap involving one of those things, but it wasn't there. You relieved the villains of these?*>

<*Yes.*> My shields faded to zero. Now I was really dizzy. Either that or the lawn had suddenly tilted to vertical.

<*Then they're yours. By the way, I was wrong. That is not an Atlanticean disruptor pistol. That's a genuine Krell weapon, worth a large fortune. It runs off an internal charge rotator. It converts matter into antimatter. The power level is way higher. The trap uses the charge rotator; it creates large amounts of antimatter so fast you can't teleport away. The only protection is really strong shields. Like yours were.*>

<*Mum, could we go home? Please?*> I didn't usually complain, but I'd pushed well beyond my limits, well, what I'd thought my limits were.

<*May I carry you?*> she asked. She was very good about that. I was a bit sensitive about not being a baby any more. I could do things for myself. She was always polite about asking rather than just yanking me off my feet.

<*Please?*> and three jumps later we were at home. I then spent several days in bed recovering.

My stay in Boston Harbor had been way more violent than a couple of thugs with knives. My individual attacks would easily have leveled a major skyscraper, and the other side's were much the same power. That last attack? Very briefly I had had a glimpse of a starcore. It almost reduced me to ashes, but not quite. Shields, of course, shunt absorbed power to someplace not in our world, or the scattering would have wrecked up Boston. My counter? I sometimes remembered to use a plasma sword, not the showier plasma torch, so after carving a hole in my opponents my attack went off into foamspace. If I'd used the plasma torch and missed, I'd've boiled a chunk of Boston Harbor. Yes, Bostonians always boast about their municipal lightning screen, but they tend to be too slow about turning it on when it is needed. Comet and Aurora had lived through the event because I'd dropped a wall around them, and managed to hold it up. I hadn't even noticed doing it. That was Mum's very rigorous training.

When I next saw Aurora, she asked the obvious question: If a ten-year-old namely me gets into fights this high power all the time, and grownups are for sure stronger, why are there any cities left in the world? The simple answer is that fights like this don't happen all the time. In fact, the attempted kidnapping was the highest-power shootout Massachusetts had seen in the past two centuries. Yes, the list of other boys my age – I never did tell her I'm not a boy -- who could have held their own in a fight like that is real short. Not zero, but real short.

I snapped back to the present. I was still lying in bed, still trying to understand what I had done that was so terrible that Mum had thrown me out of our home. That bit with kidnappers was surely the worst mistake I'd ever made. I hadn't needed to do it. I'd been way overconfident. Those thugs really could've killed me, but that was all years ago. The few times Mum had mentioned it since, she'd always said how proud she was of me.

I finally got up and pulled all of my curtains tightly closed, so I would sleep through the sunrise into the next day. I did wake up in time for more stretching and bending exercises, hot shower and getting dressed, and finding that it was very definitely time for a late breakfast. Chopped onions, chopped green pepper, chopped portabella mushrooms, chopped sausage, all sautéed in olive oil with garlic and a nice dose of curry powder, followed by two eggs whipped up with a bit of milk, and I had a nice omelet. The supply of multigrain toasted sunflower bread was unfortunately starting to go downhill, but I was very definitely not up to assuming my old lady disguise to go shopping. Mayhaps I would have to start baking scones. They're nice and simple. Even I can make them well. And I had a quite adequate supply of components for the frosting.

I went out to the barn to check on ponies and cats. I was happy to learn that the ponies and cats thought outdoors was just fine at the moment, so I had no barn work, I still visited my ponies, hugged and curry-combed them, checked their hooves, and spent a while petting two cats. Then it was back to *Liouville's Butterflies.*

I can't claim I've had a lot of experience dealing with people who lie out of habit. Mum gave me some abstract lessons. Yes, I'm a persona. I've met a few criminals. Most of them were dead afterwards. Some were less lucky. When I skimmed the later parts of the book, it was really obvious that the people who did not want to believe the Liouville-Gibbs theorem were prepared to say almost anything in order to discredit it. I don't know if they were lying out of habit, but they were certainly working hard at lying, for no particularly obvious reason. Indeed, one of the later chapters, one that I much enjoyed reading carefully, spent its time going through the arguments against the Liouville-Gibbs theorem, and explaining exactly how the authors of the arguments had cheated in making their cases. Learning how people cheat in arguments is good.

The book really wasn't all that long, a couple-three hundred pages. The 30 pages of theorem had been really demanding. That's assuming 'really demanding' is a synonym for 'mostly incomprehensible'. I was going to have to learn a fair piece to understand them. The 250 following pages were much, much easier. No one tried to prove the math was wrong. They just argued about what the math meant. Well, except for the strange chapter on the Dagger of Time. The Dagger is not the same as time travel, but it somehow ignores cause and effect because it lives sideways to the flow of time. The chapter was imprecise about whether the Dagger was an artifact or a person, or both. On the other hand, the chapter was very clear on why the Dagger appeared. It existed to correct side effects when people used time travel. How could it be both an artifact and a person? The chapter was very obscure. It also didn't seem to have anything to do with the rest of the book. The chapter author claimed to be a Prioress of the Goetic Knights, an office that ceased to exist thousands of years before the book was written. She said she had used time travel to make what appeared to be tiny changes that actually had the desired effects. The Dagger of Time cleaned up the minor issues the

Prioress had left behind. Time travel requires enormous amounts of power. It was only on rereading an obscure sentence that I realized that the Prioress appeared to have used the Ring of Fate.

OK, now I sort of understood what the book said. For sure I hadn't understood the math parts. There were a bunch of places, like almost all of them, where I had to take the word of the author that the math actually did what she said it did. It was still a marvelously strange result. One world starts out like ours, and ends up very different, but there's a matching world that starts out very different and ends up very much like ours. People living now on a very different world would see that totally different starting points could lead to almost the same present, the one they lived in. Those people are not in a special place, so our world has the same property. Some nearly-the-same presents, present times very much like ours, had very different pasts. Once I told myself that, I decided that the book's conclusions actually were kind of obvious, even if I might never have thought of them myself. The "Ambassador of the United States of America" could then have been a cross-time traveler, except cross-time travel is impossible.

That left another riddle. Why was this book on mum's forbidden list? After all, there really is only one world, two if you count Otherearth, so this image of a huge number of different worlds doesn't match anything that really exists. The book had been a big effort to read, but I can't say that I learned very much from reading it. The book matches up against the proof that I read before I accepted the Martyr's challenge, another forbidden book, the proof that you can't build a sideways time machine. The reason you can't is that the number of alternate universes is infinitely more than how many numbers there are, so to reach all the universes you would need an infinite number of dimensions into which a sideways time machine could travel, and an infinite number of control knobs to set the destination, all at the same time. I'm not sure I understand the infinite real number part. I do understand "There are as many integers as there are fractions", though I had a flash of joy when I finally saw how obvious the proof was. It was as good as understanding acceleration. There can't be an infinite number of control knobs, I think, so there must not be any, so therefore a sideways time machine can't let you cross from time line to time line, watching the universe gradually change through your window.

With that I had dinner. I finished off the cold chicken I had remembered to debone, and made fresh-boiled lima beans, spaghetti aglio e olio, and a nice pile of hand-shredded romaine with Venetian garlic dressing. That prepared me for an evening at the lessoncomp. I had dozed off a couple of times during the afternoon, no matter how interesting the reading was, but by now I was pretty much awake. There were people I would've liked to see, but it would be hard to explain how I managed to break my ribs. At least three of the people were astute enough to notice that my injuries were remarkably similar to the injuries Eclipse plausibly suffered in the Maze, and must have happened at about the same time. Also, while I could go deep into my gifts if I needed to, for example if I were jumped by a persona team, I certainly didn't want to do that if I could avoid it.

I did spend an hour in front of the video. The advantage of watching a satellite broadcast is that no one can tell which channel you are watching at least if your receiver is set to pick up a lot of different channels all the time and drop most of the signals into shielded grounds. Up came the Persona Network News, and on came the Vera Durand Hour of Power. Durand's garb was a bit silly, but her coverage of persona news was top line. I would have been just as happy if most of her reporting was not centered on plans to capture me. She had worked vigorously to secure interviews with Great Power Ambassadors to the League of Nations. That would be a future program. Most of them knew things. Some were up to reading the speeches their governments had sent them. Computer reconstructions of my physical appearance were evolving. They were getting worse. Now the computers had concluded that I was an improbably well-endowed woman in her late 20s. Good. It was now less likely than ever that someone would look at me and think I resemble the Eclipse they had not really seen on video.

Durand turned to coverage of Medford, Massachusetts. Medford? Up on the screen came photos of Janie, Trisha, Brian, and their parents. The Wells family refused to be interviewed. Why did anyone care about Janie? It was my City of Steel move. Janie had created the original move, and showed me some of the good variants. I used one of them in the Maze. It turns out that the move was better than I thought. The move was Janie's super-secret spring-at-the-nationals surprise move, and I'd given it away. She was furious. OK, my fault. I didn't know the move was that good. The Russians had somehow decided that Janie knows Eclipse. Of course, Janie actually does know Eclipse, but she doesn't know that. I for sure didn't tell her that game-opponent Joe and Namestone-bearer Eclipse are both me. She thinks Joe is a boy. Now the Russians had threatened to kidnap Janie.

The situation was absolutely terrible. It was my fault that Janie was in danger. I couldn't do anything to help her. I knew there were books of recorded games. I'd studied some. I didn't know the Russians could find Janie's games on the datanet and, worse, trace them back to her personally.

When the gamesmasters came to Medford to talk to her, Janie had had a persona champion. Durand explained how champions worked, in case someone in the audience didn't know. Then she interviewed the champion. The champion was Morgana Lafayette, Sunssword in her public persona. She was on my 'avoid at all costs' list. She knows what Joe, the kid who rescued Janie, looks like. She'd realize that Janie's game opponent was the same Joe. She'd want to ask me a few questions, like where I live and how to contact my mom. One question would lead to another. Then I started to wonder: Why hadn't Janie's parents asked those questions? They'd been happy to meet another Janie game opponent, but hadn't been at all curious about where I live or who my mother is. They were less curious than is reasonable. I should have noticed. If I hadn't been so busy prepping for the Maze, well, that's an excuse.

It was a standard video interview…very short. Lafayette was very good at not answering questions, in a way that sounded as though the questions had been answered. Durand was very good at noticing that she still needed an answer. Lafayette gave away nothing about Janie's persona identity. She stayed with the official position. Janie has been questioned. She never used my move in competition play. She plays with friends, but none of them is Eclipse. For starters, none of them is a tall woman in her late twenties.

Chapter Thirteen

Secure Chamber Alpha
The Palace of Peace
Geneva, Switzerland
Early Morning

Ambassadors of the Thirteen Great Powers sank into their ruby-red velvet seats, Chancellor Holmgren and Brigade Leader Valkyria at their head. At least, Holmgren though, with four elevators and three kilometers of rock between us and the surface, everyone is here at the same time. If we have not had much breakfast, the pastries from embassy kitchens, not to mention coffee and that Japanese rice tea, are sufficient to feed a small army. Holmgren wrapped his gavel twice, the sounds reverberating through the nearly empty room. The walls were the finest marble from Thasos, deep-carved in images from a dozen cultures, all symbolizing peace and plenty. The images were warmly comforting, but today the stone echoed his call to order. Mayhaps heavy ruby-red drapes to match the ruby seat cushions, the curtains to be drawn when only the Fourteen met, were needed. Often each ambassador would have four or five staff members in support, all absorbing sound, but today the discussion would be between the fourteen of them and the Brigade Leader.

"May we have order, please," Holmgren asked. "I regret to note that General von und zu Dreikirch, after 60 hours on his feet, collapsed and has been hospitalized. If we did not already have enough problems with the Namestone, the League of Terran Justice has published another manifesto, and staged yet more attacks to advertise its presence. Matters in the Argentine are attracting public attention. Where shall we begin?" He looked around the room. Fortunately, lots had been drawn to fix the order of speaking. "Other than thanking the IncoAztecan Ambassador for his orange juice." The Speaker for the First Speaker nodded. Holmgren passed the speaking stone to the German Ambassador.

"The Almighty Warlord of All the Germans is most concerned as to progress in recovering the Namestone," Heinrich Moeller announced. "If the League produces no progress, it cannot be complained if individual member states work to bring the needed result." The German Ambassador lived up to his country's aggressive attitudes, attitudes that had been little tempered by the Summer War and its rearrangements of the German borders. He passed the Speaking Stone.

"The First Speaker, the Living Sun, most emphatically shares these sentiments," the IncoAztecan Ambassador agreed. Buncombe wondered which of the Ambassadors even knew that the Ambassador was in fact Lord Smoking Frog. His papers named him, in Classic Mayan, as The Speaker for the First Speaker. "Also, the First Speaker, the Living Sun, is concerned that adequate progress has not yet been made on prescribing the form of execution to which the Bearer is to be subject. The Assembly of the Tlatoani and the Council of the Realm are concerned that if the punishment is inadequate, then the workers and peasants will become disorderly."

Count Ferencz shook his head, his massive mane of pure white hair sweeping from shoulder to shoulder. "The Emperor-King Franz-Joseph, the fourth of his name, and the United Parliaments of Austria, Hungary, the Slavic States, Czechia, and Silesia, are unanimous in taking the opposite position. It has always been our position that the terms offered by the Martyr are to be supported, in particular that the Namestone is the property of the person to whom the Martyr gives the Namestone. We hear no reason for change. His Imperial Majesty understands, however, that we are in a minority on this question."

The Russian Ambassador produced and opened a substantial box. "Petit-fours," Elizaveta Romanoff announced. "Hungarian petit-fours. Fresh one hour ago. As fine as Belgian cooking," she nodded at Ambassador Davout, "but even richer. And more likely to provide agreement than a long discussion as to the agenda. We all know that all three topics must be discussed. I propose that we draw lots to choose topic order."

"If we agree, we get to sample Hungarian petit-fours?" Ambassador Mascarenhas da Silva was next in speaking order. "In that case, I urge that we yield to … ummh …your rational argumentation." Ambassadors smiled. The box began its circulation around the room.

"I find that the first lot is for the new manifesto from the League of Terran Justice," Holmgren said.

"Must we consider their ravings?" Moeller asked. The IncoAztecan Ambassador nodded in agreement, then passed the talking stone to Count Ferencz.

"The new manifesto is very different," Ferencz observed. "It is a book, not a broadsheet. It appeared nearly at the same time all around the world, in multiple translations. The number of copies sent out here and there is quite large. These features bespeak a much larger and better-organized League than some people had suspected. Also, the document is either uniquely coherent, or uniquely incoherent. I will read from it, only a few short excerpts:

We describe what should be in the world. It is the empty place between all thoughts, the full-lit shadow. It is the shape between the words that are not the shape. Imagine a rainbow. If there were no word for green, we could still say 'the color between yellow and blue'. If there were no word for orange, we could still say "the color between yellow and red'. We, the League of Terran Justice, can imagine the political rainbow. We know the colors that cannot be named, the thoughts that can have no name. We call for the political colors that can have no name.

We march for the thoughts that cannot be named, the thoughts that are not the void, the thoughts that are captive without form or substance.

The Emperor is to Imperial decree as the people are to X. The Emperor says Go Forth! The people say Go Forth!

Between "the king is to the workers" and "the workers are to the king" is "how the people should be to each other. What is the 'should be'?"

"This goes on for over a hundred pages, filled with what seem to be analogies with missing words that you are to fill in for yourself. But there is no way to fill the gaps in. They do not make sense." Ferencz shrugged and passed the talking stone to Saigo Shigetoshi, Legate for the Satsuma Daimyo. To Buncombe's ears, Ferencz appeared to have been speaking from a carefully memorized script. No one else seemed to have noticed.

"Interesting," Saigo said. "I see mayhaps a step toward understanding the meaning of this book. Rather, my dear wife saw the step, and I was finally able to understand her. We are reminded of an aspect of Japanese philosophy. Ideas are like water- smoothed rocks. If you pile them nicely together, there are gaps between the rocks. The gaps have shapes that are not the spheroids of the rocks. They are the inverse. We cannot see the shape, because it is where there is nothing, but we know that it is a shape. We know that the shape is there. The shape is defined by where the rocks are not. We ponder the shape by pondering the absence of presence. From the absence of presence, we may learn. But I do not understand where my thought is leading me, other than to say that the words in the books are the stones in the puzzle, and the words the author could not say are the gaps in the stones. What are the words in the gaps? Why could the author not say them? This I do not know, except it seems we can't say them, either."

The speaking stone worked its way around the circle and back to Chancellor Holmgren. "With respect to pursuing the Bearer, we did manage with the aid of Baron Supreme Gamesman Kamensky to track down Miss Wells, who introduced the City of Steel move seen in that part of the competition. Miss Wells is Highly Regarded by the Lords of the Games. Miss Wells notes that Eclipse used a variation on the move she introduced, because the Namestone took a response that High Grandmaster Kurchatoff did not. I understand that Miss Wells was more than a bit annoyed with this outcome. No. I gather that she was positively incandescent. She had wanted to introduce that variant herself. Apparently it is even more catastrophic for the opponent than the move she used. She did supply a list of all net discussions of her move. None anticipated the play used by Eclipse. I note for the record that Miss Wells' mindscreens are mayhaps as good as this

Eclipse person's, so we know what Miss Wells elected to tell us, and not one word more. However, American mentalist Krystal North confirmed that everything Miss Wells said matched what she was thinking, and was believed by Miss Wells to be true.

"I understand that, in addition, that when the Lords of the Games interviewed Miss Wells, Miss Wells had a champion, the private persona of the Boston public persona Sunssword. Apparently there was some friction between the Americans and the Russians. The Supreme Gamesman proposed to have Miss Wells kidnapped and subject to rigorous interrogation. Miss Wells' champion did not approve. Kamensky did not carry out his proposal, which might have led to a significant altercation. Ambassador Romanoff? Did you wish to speak?"

"I wish to emphasize," Elizaveta Petrovna said calmly, "that his Imperial Majesty the Tsar of all the Russias was most displeased to learn of this threat of violence against Miss Wells, and remonstrated vigorously with the Supreme Gamesman and certain court officers when he learned of the threat. The lot of them have been informed that they are not to appear in the Imperial Court or for that matter in the Moscow Oblast until they are summoned back, an act not expected to occur in the near future."

Holmgren nodded at the American Ambassador. Thaddeus Buncombe cleared his throat. "To point out what is well known, Professor Morgana Lafayette is the private persona of the public persona Sunssword. She is a biochemist at Rogers' Technological Institution, and is, I am told, widely esteemed as being one of my country's leading scientists. I am advised by the Captain-General of the American Persona League -- that's Krystal North; most of you have met her -- that Morgana Lafayette is an absolutely top-line persona, one who is not to be trifled with. Krystal, Miss North, opined that any attempt to kidnap Miss Wells would have been a suicidal act, but only on the part of the kidnappers. Having said that, I can report that Speaker Ming views the actions of the Tsar, including the personal letters of apology to Miss Wells and to each of her parents, to be entirely appropriate as a correction, and hopes that the matter between our two ancient nations can be put to rest."

Most of the other ambassadors looked relieved. "What sort of young woman," Moeller mumbled, "conceivably is an obstacle to a Russian Elite Strike Group?" Buncombe decided that he was surprised that Moeller had asked an intelligent question. It was such an unusual phenomenon. He really should ask Washington for a clarification with respect to Lafayette. Why was this woman supposed to be an obstacle to the Russians? Also, he wondered, how did Moeller know who Kamensky had as backups?

"Where are we," Holmgren ask, "with respect to the Argentine border issue? Madame Ambassador Mascarenhas da Silva?"

"Tragically," she said, "there has been a fresh attack, this time within the Brazilian Empire. Mayhaps a thousand men, women, and children have gone to their graves…or wherever. There are very few bodies. We are attempting to collect information. It does not appear that any local residents had the presence of mind shown by that fine young Argentine man, a few days ago, who was able to collect good photographs. Indeed, the Emperor Pedro, the Sixth of his name, noting the young man continued to take photographs while he was dodging the claws of the unknown, has asked the President of the Argentine Republic for permission to contribute to the upkeep and education of the young man's family, as a tribute to his heroism. However, through other routes we may yet be in possession of a detailed record of events." She passed the speaking stone back to Holmgren.

Holmgren nodded at Ambassador Buncombe and passed the speaking stone. "It is my understanding," Buncombe said, "that there were sounds of gunfire from across the border, strange lights, and as daylight approached a stream of refugees, alas, a small stream, many hideously wounded, who tried to cross the border. It is my understanding that the refugees were admitted, personae with healing gifts were summoned to the scene, and after not long no more refugees died. The refugees told an extremely confused set of stories, which the Argentine authorities are trying to record as swiftly and accurately as possible, despite the language barrier. While it appears that messages are passing each other in the ether, the Argentine government is happy to have the Brazilian government send people to listen to the refugees, many of whom are really not up to travel even via teleportation. The American government hopes that this tragic event will somehow lead to a relaxation of unfortunate tensions between our good friends the Argentine Republic and the Brazilian Empire, not to mention the arrest of the responsible criminal elements."

"Is there more?" Holmgren asked. "In that case, we should return to the pursuit of the Bearer. There are fifteen reports from major police agencies,…"

~~~~~

Much later in the morning, Thaddeus Buncombe emerged from the elevators leading down to Secure Chamber Alpha. The elevator atrium featured the same architectural features as the Chamber far below: white marble, intricately carved and gilded, depicting each of the thirteen great powers and their contributions to world civilization. There was mutual consent that each of the Great Powers would choose its own contributions, and the other Great Powers would not complain. For many of the powers, bringing peace through superior firepower seemed to have played an important role in advancing the civilized world. The American contributions featured inventors, scientists, law-givers, authors, and a range of more-or-less average Americans farming, working in the kitchen, chopping down trees, building skyscrapers, healing the sick, teaching the young, and many of the other workaday tasks that actually made America a civilized and pleasant place to live. Waiting for Buncombe was one of his new administrative assistants,
~~~~~

Cyrus Hawthorne, a young man who was always eager to please, though not always equally good at identifying what Buncombe really wanted.

"Mister Ambassador, I'm afraid that Vera Durand is waiting for you at the Embassy front door. Apparently she has some questions about the previous meeting, in particular what appeared to be new pieces of American foreign policy," Hawthorne said.

"Oh, joy," Buncombe said. "At least I can be reasonably sure I know what her motives are. It's just that I was really looking forward to a legitimate breakfast. Mayhaps she would suffer through a breakfast interview."

"I'll put that through to the embassy, sir," Hawthorne said.

"Remind them that she will insist on paying, and they should take her money." Buncombe smiled. "There's nothing like a good meal to put people in a better mood."

~~~~~

Not that much later, Buncombe looked over the table in one of the embassy's small dining rooms at his reportorial opponent. She had been polite enough to make small talk when he explained that he had not yet had anything legitimate to eat as a morning meal. However, his second helpings of corned beef hash and mushroom omelet had disappeared, and he had poured himself his third cup of coffee, so the time had come for some serious questioning.

"So, Mister Ambassador," Durand asked, "What was your perception of this morning's meeting?"

"As the ambassador of the American Republic, it is my duty to counsel for amicable relations between all nations," he answered. "When there are amicable relations, there are favorable opportunities for trade. Also, when one has amicable relations, then one may invest wisely in ways that benefit the public rather than investing poorly in instruments of war and terror. It is also my duty to observe that if we do not have amicable relations with a foreign power, there may be consequences for those who are lacking in amity. Having said that, my unofficial opinion is that the last few days' meetings reminded me of several ancient American aphorisms involving slow-motion train wrecks. Without faulting any other Great Power, it must surely have been obvious to all concerned that the stated policies of the Great Powers are so thoroughly contradictory that it will be difficult to avoid incidents of violence."

"Are you sure you don't mean that war is necessarily going to result, mayhaps without the restraint that was seen in 1908?" she asked. When, Buncombe thought, only a moderate number of European cities were burned to the ground.

"The Joint Committee on Foreign Relations and Speaker Ming emphasized to me," Buncombe said, "that the American Republic has not and does not currently plan to threaten war. They were extremely emphatic in saying that under no conditions should I suggest that the Republic is
~~~~~

contemplating an outbreak of warfare with us as a participant. Alas, it takes only one power to start a war. Realistically and unofficially speaking, if the persona leagues and military of some foreign nation were to appear in the Republic and refuse to lay down their arms and submit to arrest, it might be difficult for an outside observer to tell the difference between what would ensue and open warfare."

"Your remarks this morning disclosed a surprising intent, mayhaps you would prefer to say possible intent, to move American armed forces overseas to Canada, the Argentine, or other nearby countries." Durand put on her best serious face. "This seems to be a radical change in American foreign policy. There is already considerable public controversy on this issue. Am I correct in saying that there must have been approval from the Federal District for your remarks`?"

"Oh, absolutely," Buncombe answered. "I'm merely the American ambassador. Any real decision is made in Washington by the Joint Committee on Foreign Relations and Speaker Ming. There is, of course, also some limited input from the White House and the President. Given the number of years I have been here, I am trusted with interpreting our policy to the extent of attempting to clarify to foreigners what they have just been told, except in the clarifications I use simple, straightforward, short, declarative sentences. Fortunately, my fellow ambassadors are persons of high quality and good sense, so I seldom have to do anything of that sort. In any event, the policies I discussed this morning are actually not very radical changes. We have always had friendly relations with the various countries of South America, other than the IncoAztecan Empire, and in some past historical cases when one or another of them was threatened by neighbors to the west it was in fact the case that there were significant American forces relocated to South America or our own southern borders to discourage irrational adventuristic acts. Similarly, it is not that well-kept a secret that we would find it totally unacceptable for our neighbor to the south to occupy any of the Dominions of Canada. Lord Smoking Frog as Speaker for the First Speaker undoubtedly knows this as well as I do."

"How do you expect the differences over pursuit of the Bearer into foreign lands to be settled?" Durand asked.

"Naturally," Buncombe said, "it is the firm position of the American Republic that peace is to be preferred to war, the destruction created by the heat of battle being almost sure to outweigh any possible profit to the victors or the vanquished. It is our pious hope that foreign powers listen to each other's ambassadors and therefore will not carry out any irrational or intemperate acts that might lead to unnecessary violence. Realistically speaking, in my personal opinion, the positions outlined in recent meetings are in a number of cases totally contradictory to each other, so that I do not see how they could be rationally resolved, unless, of course, Eclipse disappears forever without a trace. Certainly, if Great Power A sends its persona teams and army into the territory of Great Power B, against the objections of the latter power, it is difficult to see how there could be a pacific resolution of the circumstances that would arise. That's even before Great Power C comes to the defense of the Bearer, not that she is likely to need any defense. We may always hope that the Great Powers will forbear from invading each other's territory, no matter how likely it appears that such an invasion would lead to the capture of the Holy Namestone. America is rich because we have always rejected the path of war. Other nations are less fortunate, because they have followed the path of war."

"What is your evaluation of the pursuit of the Bearer?" Durand leaped at her next question.

Buncombe shrugged. "She seems to be rather good at hiding. The search so far appears to be challenging. We do not even have agreement on what she looks like. The person that Valkyria thought she met coming up the stairs does not vaguely resemble, beyond gender, the person who was seen engaging in combat within the Maze. Which of those images was the real Eclipse? Is she a shape-changer? Were we fooled once or mayhaps twice as to her appearance? When you get to the point 'she could be anyone' the search appears to become a bit challenging."

"Don't you mean that the search becomes hopeless?" Durand asked. "If she could be anyone, she could be one of us."

"The official position of the American Republic is that there is an ongoing search and that it is highly likely that the search will be successful, eventually," Buncombe said. "I do not have instructions as to how long it will take us to reach *eventually*. Nor do I have instructions as to how likely *highly likely* is. With respect to your final remark, I suspect that history would find it hysterically funny if it turned out that the Bearer was one of the Great Power ambassadors to the Peace Executive."

"On the same line, there are rumors that the Bearer is negotiating with some power, not necessarily a Great Power, about handing the Namestone over to them. Comments?" Durand asked.

"I believe I am in complete agreement with the entire Peace Executive in hoping that this rumor is false. The rumor may be enough by itself to start a general war. No Power will risk having another Power in control of the Namestone. That negotiation, when it is ferreted out and becomes public, leads to most Great Powers, and more than a few Middling Powers, attacking the place that is getting the Namestone. Such a – hypothetical -- negotiation is national suicide for the country participating in it. I have heard no such rumor from a credible source," Buncombe answered.

"Your thoughts on other world problems?" Durand asked.

"I have nothing terribly original to add," he said. "We are naturally extremely concerned about the issue in the Argentine, now tragically spread to Brazil, but the perpetrators remain unidentified. The new event in Brazil is tragic. However, mayhaps it averted a major war. The League of Terran

Justice and the Lords of Death continue their depredations. I see, however, that my clock is ticking, and I have other obligations to which I must attend."

"Thank you for your time, Mister Ambassador," Durand said.

"My pleasure, Vera. And my duty, you being the American pool reporter for the Peace Executive. We should do this more often."

Chapter Fourteen

The Invisible Fortress
Mid-day

I did wish that Medico and the healing matrix would be a bit faster about what they were doing, but I had to be realistic. My injuries would have put an ungifted person in the hospital for weeks, or six feet under for rather longer. Thinking back, I'm not quite sure how I managed to walk the final corridor to reach the Martyr, let alone climb the Stairs. I must be tougher than I thought. I let Medico go about its business, assure me that I am not about to die, and tell me when to exercise, how much to eat, and when to sleep. OK, I cheat a tiny bit on going to sleep if I'm reading something interesting. That's almost every night. I am slowly catching up on studying and homework, relative to my lesson plans. I tell myself I am three months behind, so I should not be upset if I don't catch up in three weeks. The weather has been good, so the ponies don't need me mucking out their stalls every day. I still go out to feed and comb them and cuddle the barn cats.

World news is terrible. None of the great powers have started shooting at each other yet, but the talking heads think it is only a matter of time. Some of those Great Powers will attack me instantly, wherever and whenever found. Others view uninvited foreign armies on their soil as declarations of war. At least one will come to my aid, including invading foreign countries. The Federal Congress has done a partial mobilization of the Army, not putting people into uniform but making sure everything is ready to go on a few hours' notice, including moving weapons to people's homes. Across America, second and third line personae are practicing timed combined attacks, those being way more deadly than they sound. In other news, Brazil and the Argentine are still glowering at each other. They've halfway figured out the sky octopus is someone else's, but popular sentiment is lagging behind. That kid who took all the photos is a real hero, but each reconstruction of the creature is more outre than the last. I thought it was quadridimensional, but six dimensions? Please! Really?

I do miss seeing my friends, but travel is just out at the moment. I especially wish I could commiserate with poor Teranike. She's trapped here. The gate between our worlds has been closed. Her country is what we call

Antarctica, except on her world Antarctica is Polaria, a cold temperate rainforest, thanks to really different ocean currents, an extra continent in the Pacific, and a land bridge between Antarctica and South America. In any event, Polaria has been invaded by most of the rest of the world, their air defenses were betrayed by their Minister of the Skies, and they are fighting back gallantly if not very successfully, Apparently the Air Minister had been promised that after the world won he would rule Polaria as the colonial potentate, took the offer, and got caught. The Polarian legal doctrine is 'treason is a hereditary disease', so they executed his children and grandchildren, too, but they are still losing.

I do track the Persona News Network. My computer scoops up the PNN general feed. I worry about my friends. I just can't do anything to help them, not at the moment. They would get suspicious that I just happened to get beaten into the ground, right at the same time Eclipse did. I really don't want them figuring out who my other identities are. Today, however, Persona Network News also had Vera Durand doing extended interviews of several League of Nations ambassadors. Durand is one person I very much want to avoid, she being on the very short list of people who actually know what I look like.

Durand's video studio is calculated to bring out the splendor of persona garb. The walls are bone white; a long-strand white shag carpet covers the floor. Her chairs are polished aluminum thrones, mounted on central pedestals so they can rotate, with backs soaring well above guests' heads toward an unseen ceiling. Famously, she interviews each guest for exactly the same time, with large timers counting down the seconds. This evening she's wearing a brilliant scarlet ankle-length gown and high-necked long cape. Her first guest comes on screen. His persona bodyguards must be off camera. They shake hands. She sits. She knows exactly how to fluff her cape so she is free to move once seated.

"Our first guest this evening is Her Britannic Majesty's ambassador to the League of Nations, Lord Reginald Featherstonehaugh," Durand said. Featherstonehaugh nodded. "Our time is short, so let us move to the point. What is your government's current position on the search for the Namestone?"

"Of course," he answered, "Her Majesty's government is primarily concerned that the Key to Heaven should not fall into the hands of persons whose interests do not align with ours. I am inclined to believe that each of my fellow Ambassadors, if not constrained by their government to answer elsewise, would say the same thing. Officially, the Namestone must be handed over to the League, where its powers will be used to benefit all mankind. Unofficially, each Great Power would settle for having possession of the Namestone for itself. However, every Great Power has its friends, and knows of powers that are not quite so friendly. In some cases, if power A gained the Namestone, there would be powers B that would move most extremely vigorously to take it away. It would be tactless of me to list powers A and B, but any student of politics would have no trouble doing so."

"Is progress being made toward finding the Namestone, or its Bearer?" Durand asked.

"Of course," he answered, "I am an Ambassador, not a spymaster. Nonetheless, I am confident that Her Majesty's Government is carrying out with the utmost vigor searches for this Eclipse person, and for the Namestone itself. These objectives may at this point be quite separate. The world is a large place, and we have no particular notion as to where to commence the search, but it can scarcely be imagined that the search will in the final instance be other than successful."

"There were suggestions that Eclipse is English," Durand said.

"Quite. Of course, it would be a great matter of national honor, and totally appropriate, if the Namestone had been recovered by an Englishwoman." Featherstonehaugh nodded firmly. "However, and here I shall tip my hat to your next guest and his country's linguists, it soon became apparent that people in different parts of the world heard Eclipse speak with different accents, indeed in some cases in different languages. The Maze let each of us see and hear what it chose, as a result of which we really have no idea what Eclipse looks like, or what language she actually spoke. Many believe that Eclipse is tall, golden-haired, and well-endowed. Englishmen as often believe that Eclipse is fair-haired, not too tall, slimly proportioned, and fluent in English. The latter is not much of a clue, as most cultured people around the world speak English, the one true international language of trade, commerce, art, and culture."

"There is concern that if Eclipse is found on the territory of one nation, other nations may send forces to the scene to capture her," Durand remarked.

"There should very much be concern that the lessons of the Summer War have been forgotten," Featherstonehaugh agreed. "The world is far fuller of personae than it was a century ago. The armamentarium of explosives, incendiaries, toxic gasses, and lethal rays is enormously greater. The expansion of manufacturing has ensured that far more of these implements of destruction have been produced and distributed. Fortunately, the Murray fission suppressor ensures that transmutation bombs are unlikely to be used on a large scale, or mayhaps not at all. In the last war, the United Kingdom was largely spared devastation, but we seem to remember the terrible events of 1908 far more clearly than do some other parties."

"There are rumors that Her Majesty's Government has entered extended negotiations with the American Republic," Durand observed.

"Would that this were true," Featherstonehaugh said. "The Republic has an Ambassador to the Court of Saint James's, but he is rarely seen outside his embassy. His staff is largely equally reclusive, except as they perform their liaison duties as prescribed by the Truce of 1785. As is well known, Speaker Ming is happy to say privately that most people who fought in King George's

War are dead, their children and grandchildren are dead, the grudges that one of his predecessors had stuffed and mounted have decayed to pieces, and therefore mayhaps those memories should be left to the history books. However, there are no negotiations. We have – it's in the Truce – discussed the possibility that a third power would invade North America."

"I fear that the clock has advanced," Durand announced.

"Seeing that my time is almost expired, I shall end by complimenting the Prussian Kaiser on his construction of Museums of the Horrors of War, a wise decision that may cool the blood of impetuous youth."

"Indeed, time is expired, so we must advance to our next guest," Durand answered. She rose. Featherstonehaugh exited, to be replaced by Markgraf Moeller. Moeller marched across the carpet, clicked his heels, took Durand's hand, bowed, and kissed the air above her fingertips.

"It is of course my great honor to meet again with such a sagacious and beautiful host," he announced. "Shall we sit?"

Durand smiled and sat. "Your Excellency, we are of course most grateful that you could make time in your schedule for me."

"It is nothing. It is for you. Besides my master, the His Almighty Majesty, Supreme Warlord of All the Germans, emphasized that he wished me to appear here," Moeller replied.

"I imagine you can speak to your government's position on the Namestone," she said.

"But of course. The Namestone belongs to the League of Nations. There can be absolutely no disputing of this most fundamental and obvious of facts that no one can conceivably deny. It is merely a matter of deploying the forces of all the nations of the world to take the Namestone and prepare Miss Eclipse for her execution and trial. It is also undisputed that the key step in advancing in this direction is to give the League's Persona Team proper, competent, and therefore Prussian leadership. There are many historical examples showing the correctness of this view…"

And at that point I started to fall asleep. The remaining guests, from more doctrinaire states, were simply going to repeat the lines they had already spoken to the League Special Peace Executive. The one bit I had learned from Durand's interview was bad news. People in England had guessed that I don't look like the Eclipse on the wanted posters. Worse, they had a new educated guess as to what I look like, a guess that was much more accurate than I liked.

Chapter Fifteen

Benjamin Franklin Technical Junior High School
Joseph Henry Boulevard
Medford, Massachusetts

"Students, there will be an in-class exam this Friday. The test is through Lesson 60; be sure to review. Everyone has passed that mark already, so no need to worry." Mrs. Gostak looked around her Editing English class. "You should all have your next lesson coming up on your computer screens. Anyone who doesn't, please speak up." Three hands went up. "James, William, you want to restart the lesson, not begin from where you left off? Just a moment, I can key that. Trisha, I'll be with you in a moment." Trisha smiled and lowered her hand.

A few moments later, Mrs. Gostak was at Trisha's side. Trisha pointed at her computer screen. "I can't go farther unless I do those two tests," she said. "I have to do them in-class not at home. It won't let me do them."

Mrs. Gostak poked at the touch screen. "I'll release the first one for you. You have to do it all in-class this hour."

"Got it," Trisha said. "So if I'm done by three, I can do the other one?"

"The rule is one a day," Mrs. Gostak said. "Unless your score on the first one is absolutely perfect."

Trisha grimaced. 'Perfect' was challenging, not something she did all the time. "I'll try," she answered. Her math and biology teachers had been much more agreeable. Editing was sort of easy, but it was real easy to make mistakes or miss things.

~~~~~

Trisha skipped out of editing class. Her first exam had not been perfect, no matter how simple it had seemed, but she'd persuaded Mrs. Gostak to over-ride the block so she'd have something to do for the rest of the hour. However, that was only an in-class over-ride. At home she could prepare for the next two tests, but not go any farther.

"Trisha!" Ingrid Fairhaven waved hello to her friend and competitor, Trisha Wells. "Has Mr. Przemysl said anything to you?"

"No news," Trisha answered. "But don't worry. You," she pointed at Ingrid, "have the lead singer spot. I'm dropping out. I told him before
~~~~~

classes this morning."

"You're what?" Ingrid said in amazement.

"Dropping music club. Quitting singing. Going away. I finally got to hear the recordings of the two of us, and your voice is way better than mine, so I don't see why I'm competing for lead voice," Trisha said. "Other than my Mom pushing me and him."

Ingrid wrinkled her eyes. "But Mr. Przemysl keeps saying how good you are."

"Helicopter mom. Agreeable teacher. Cute trick to motivate you. Besides, I'm totally grounded like forever, so I can't travel with the club. You know, like I can't travel to concerts." Trisha said. Well, she thought, that is what Dad said. Home, school, in between. That's no trips. I don't have to tell him what he said, in case he didn't understand himself. I just have to obey what I clearly heard him say.

"You? Grounded? Why? What did you do?" Ingrid asked. "You don't have to say."

"I don't know," Trisha answered. "Nothing that makes sense. I didn't leak Janie's super-extra-special City move, no matter what the stupid Boston Post said."

"Ooo. Weird. Sympathies." Ingrid shook her head. "That means also no birthday party for Kaylee? My little sister will miss seeing you. Other question. Where did you get the pantsuit you were wearing yesterday? My mom saw it—she does fashion design—and said it had to be four digits in the price."

"I wouldn't dare go to the party. I wouldn't dare ask. Can I slip you my present for Kaylee?" Trisha asked. She looked pleadingly at Ingrid. Ingrid nodded. "The pantsuit I sewed myself. Would you like one? Similar, not the same. But you choose the colors. Maybe blue, and darker blue trim? You look really good in blue. And you need to get me the fabric and measurements. Fabric gets expensive. I'll go with your mom's call on fabrics. We can't meet for fittings; I can sew it loose and your mom can mayhaps pin it so I can tighten it up?"

"I'm sure she can. That's super generous of you. You're always so nice to everyone," Ingrid said.

"You were a lot of help when I was trying to sing better. I owe you. But I have to get going. New club today," Trisha announced.

"Which?" Ingrid asked.

"Fitness," Trisha answered. "Weights. Running. Things I can't do at home while I'm grounded."

"They're real tough. My older brother is in it. And a lot of boys," Ingrid said.

"The girls' sports teams are in it," Trisha said. "Except girls' lacrosse. They think it's way too soft. They're crazy. I have a brother. And he's a base ball nines jock. I can cope. Really got to run."

"Sads on grounding," Ingrid said. "You need any help, things you need, tell me." She stared at Trisha's back while Trisha headed down the stairs. Grounded? she wondered. And does not know why? What's the point of that? It made no sense. What was the point of grounding someone, and not telling them why?

~~~~~

Trisha knocked on the gym teacher's door. "Mister Mahoney?" she asked. Mahoney was an older man, somewhat heavy-set. Not in the waistline, she thought; he must do a lot of training himself.

"Indeed. And you are? And you want?" he asked.

"I'm Trisha Wells. I'd like to join the Fitness Club. I have machines at home, but can't use them at the moment, but this," she waved a bitstick, "shows where I am in training. Well, that's what the manual says."

"Come in. Have a seat." He took the bitstick and inserted it in his computer. "Mercury Track machines. We have Silverplates, about the same." He waited for his computer to interpret her file. "Hmmh, very good. Very good indeed. I want to watch you go through each of these before I let you loose on the machines by yourself. There's a running group first, indoor track. By the time you've done your mile-plus I'll have time to check you out on the weights. You want credit for this as your activity?"

"Switching over from music," she said.

"This is a six day a week activity," he said. "You get one miss a week, unless you're sick." He entered a few lines of data into his computer. "I have to check with Mr. Przemysl on continuity. That should be a formality. Any reason you are changing?"

"My singing voice is someplace between 'badly-played bagpipe' and 'cat having its tail pulled'," she said, "and I wasn't getting better, so I'd rather do something I enjoy than something my mom thinks I enjoy because she is a really good singer."

"Your call. Change in the girls' locker room, be out in five minutes," he said. "It's the boys base ball nines club running first. See if you can keep up with them." Trisha had a grin on her face. Brian had told her about them being proud about how fast they were around the track.
~~~~~

Chapter Sixteen

Secure Chamber Alpha
The Palace of Peace
Geneva, Switzerland
Morning

"Once again, we are in order," League Chancellor Holmgren announced. "It is ten in the morning, local time, everyone has had time for a pleasant breakfast, so now we are in our meeting. I have received multiple complaints that there has not been adequate progress in finding the bearer. I have received complaints that plans for capturing the Bearer, once found, are inadequate. I gather that events along the border between Brazil and the Argentine are continuing. Mindful that the complaints about the Bearer have all been circulated, and that you have all had more than adequate time to read them, I propose unless there is objection to advance to General von und zu Dreikirch, now that he has recovered, and his report on the search."

The Ambassadors all looked around the table. Experience had shown that discussing the agenda at best accomplished nothing. In the time needed to argue which agenda item should appear first, the entire agenda could be handled. After a few moments, Holmgren saw nothing except nods and smiles.

"In that case," Holmgren said, "I pass the floor to General von und zu Dreikirch. General?"

"There are many reports that Eclipse has been seen," Dreikirch said. "Few of these reports are accompanied by evidence. Not even VideoBell photographs, except obviously fake ones, are being reported. It is as though Eclipse has vanished from the face of the earth. There was a large-scale effort to reconstruct Eclipse's original language and accent. After all, we have all these recordings of Eclipse capturing the Holy Namestone, may its name be praised unto eternity. The reconstruction team has concluded that Eclipse was actually speaking in Modern English, her words in other languages being a synthesis by the Maze.

"The League Peace Police are receiving vast numbers of reports from police and intelligence agencies around the world. Collating this information is an ongoing project. However, I have had to call to League Chancellor

Holmgren's attention that some parts of the world have been far more forthcoming with reports than have others. The American Republic is especially noteworthy for the paucity of information it has forwarded to us in Geneva. Mayhaps Ambassador Buncombe would care to suggest a reason? Or mayhaps he would need to consult with his government first?"

'Quite unnecessary," Buncombe said. "On one hand, most Americans agree that Eclipse is the proper owner of the Namestone. Those Americans are not about to assist the Peace Police – nothing personal is meant here, General; even Senator Bullmunk has said that you are to be praised for the diligence with which you are performing your duties – in what they see as obvious efforts to steal the Namestone from its rightful owner. On the other hand, some attention is being given in my country to filtering out wrong and obviously absurd reports that Eclipse has been seen in one place or another. The Americans who believe that the League is the proper owner of the Namestone also believe that we should not waste the time and resources of the League Peace Police with nonsense reports that cannot possibly be true. As a result, the few reports that you are receiving from the American Republic and its citizens have some modest level of credibility. Instead of complaining, you should be wishing that the people of other nations were as discerning about the accuracy of the reports you are receiving. For example, the series of reports that Eclipse is a fifty foot tall woman – that appears to be a media bubble – possibly did not need to be sent on to Geneva. Or anywhere else. You are over-worked, and your friends in the American Republic – yes, you have more than a few friends in America -- try not to make life worse for you.

"Having said that," Buncombe continued, "I am in agreement with your conclusion, General, that Eclipse has vanished from the face of the Earth. There are several obvious alternative interpretations here. The simplest is that she is a known persona and has retired to her secret base. Another is that she was mortally wounded in the Maze, retreated to someplace, and has died, making it impossible to locate her mentalically because she no longer has a mind. There is also the possibility, implicit in the Ode to the Sacred Namestone, that Eclipse, like the Martyr, is from another world, so that she came to Earth to recover the Namestone for her people, and that having done so she has ascended into the heavens. In all these cases, the search for the bearer approaches being futile. Would you care to comment, General, before I continue?"

"I find the American attitude on supporting the search to be entirely unacceptable," Dreikirch announced. "In this time of crisis, there is a positive and absolute moral duty on every person in the world to lend vigorous and enthusiastic support to the search for the Bearer. We cannot be in the position that large numbers of world citizens are ignoring or obstructing our resolute effort to recover the Holy Namestone, the Sacred Key to the Gates of Paradise. There should be legal repercussions against these people."

"There are no world citizens," Buncombe said. 'There are only citizens of individual nation-states. Also, no one is obstructing your silly search. They are simply ignoring it."

"Hear! Hear!" Featherstonehaugh agreed.

"You are wrong," Holmgren announced. "Dreikirch is right. All people are world citizens. Those who do not support the World Government, namely us, in our search for the Holy Namestone are subject to arrest by the League Peace Police and trial for treason against humanity. I shall be directing this point to the Popular Assembly for their definitive final ruling." The Popular Assembly, Buncombe thought, was a fiction of the League Political Office, League Chancellor Holmgren in particular. It was a nonexistent organization in which all nations, not only the Great Powers, were claimed to vote, each nation having as many votes as it had citizens.

"There is no Popular Assembly," Featherstonehaugh said. "Your bureaucrats cannot create a new branch of League governance out of whole cloth."

"Bravo!" Buncombe answered. There were agreeing nods from the Nipponese, French, and Austro-Hungarian ambassadors. Other Ambassadors shook their heads.

Elizaveta Romanoff covered her eyes with her palms. "Surely most of us need to discuss this issue with our governments? However, the Chancellor's proposed path appears to be unwise, not to mention nearly certain to fail."

"The moment seems inauspicious for this step," Saigo Shigetoshi whispered.

"Ambassador Smoking Frog," Holmgren said.

"As Speaker for the First Speaker, the Living Sun, I move that the League Peace Executive endorse this initiative of the League Chancellor," Lord Smoking Frog said. It was obvious to Buncombe that the charade had been planned out in advance.

"Point of Order! Notice!" Marshall Davout was very fast indeed off the mark to object. The motion had not had adequate notice.

"Denied!" Holmgren said.

"Appeal!" Davout said.

Buncombe could count noses in advance. The American, British, French, Austro-Hungarian, Russian and Japanese ambassadors would vote to sustain the appeal. The IncoAztecan, Brazilian, Prussian, Han, Manjukuoan, Ottoman, and Sikh Ambassadors would vote against the appeal. Holmgren's ruling would be sustained. Lord Smoking Frog's motion would be passed. Another giant step away from world peace would be taken.

"Might I inquire," Buncombe said, "Precisely what point are we being asked to vote to have you take to your mythical Popular Assembly?"

"It is no myth!" Holmgren shrieked. "The Popular Assembly is the logical outcome of the entirety of treaties founding…"

"Nonetheless, I endorse this question," Lord Smoking Frog said.

Holmgren's mouth snapped shut. The IncoAztecans never agreed with the Americans. "It seems to me to be an entirely reasonable inquiry, which I anticipate will be asked by the First Speaker, the Living Sun, as to precisely what motion you are taking to our most fundamental legislative body, the Popular Assembly."

"I will need a day to prepare an exact answer," Holmgren answered.

"In that case, I move to recess until tomorrow evening," Lord Smoking Frog said.

"Second!" Ambassador Featherstonehaugh called out. He stared at Lord Smoking Frog, who stared back. The two men nodded at each other, then turned to Buncombe. Buncombe wondered how many of his fellow ambassadors were thinking 'most unlikely political combination of all time'.

"I was actually about to recognize Ambassadrix Mascarenhas da Silva," Holmgren said. "You do need recognition to make a motion."

"I was about to invoke the consultation rule," she announced. "I believe at least four of us wish to consult our governments." Under the rule, a request for consultations was good for a day's postponement.

Holmgren tried to hide his frustration. He looked around the room. No one moved. "Without objection, we have voted to recess, and the consultation rule has been invoked. In some order," he announced. The Ambassadors rose and headed for the elevators.

~~~~~

The Large Dining Room at the Japanese consulate could comfortably seat 50. For the late lunch, it seated a half-dozen. Buncombe sat at one end of the table, as far as possible from host Saigo Shigetoshi. Shigetoshi was accompanied by his wife Saigo Nene. Her presence was demanded by her role as hostess. Besides, it was well known though never stated that she ran the Satsuma Domain's espionage operations in Europe, meaning she was better informed about events than anyone else in the room. Between the two of them were Reginald Featherstonehaugh, Karl-Michael Ferencz, Bernard-Christian Davout, and Elizaveta Petrovna Romanoff.

"Suleiman Pasha sends his regards," Saigo Nene said. "It appears he was aware in advance of the Popular Assembly step, counselled his Emperor not to get involved, and was overruled via court politics in Istanbul. Also, it seems that this afternoon the Brazilian Prime Minister is facing a vote of no confidence, one that he may or may not survive, and until this question is resolved Amanda Rafaela is not sure which side of any question she should be supporting." Buncombe smiled at his hostess. Sometimes he wondered if his Federal District superiors were aware that Brazil had a Prime Minister, let alone that Brazilian politics were unstable. Certainly they had not advised him that he should try to delay Holmgren for another day or two. Now Buncombe had new material for his next report. His past reports were being confirmed by Nipponese intelligence.

"Alas," Elizaveta said, "Holmgren will get his vote. The positions of those
~~~~~

powers on this Assembly may well change, but Holmgren can charge forward without restraint." She paused to sip Shigetoshi's latest wine. A Moscato was a bit sweet for this early in the meal, but then until recently Nipponese had had no words for acid or acrid as descriptions of wines. Many of her countrymen, she thought, drank with vigorous approval any of several even sweeter Japanese vintages to which ample amounts of honey were added after fermentation was complete.

"I noticed Lord Smoking Frog said something to you after the meeting, Reginald," Karl-Michael said. "Surely his boss isn't trying to revive his 'North America is divided into two parts, mine and yours' scheme?" His chopsticks gathered up a few more noodles.

"Hardly," Featherstonehaugh answered. "It seems that it has occurred to First Speaker Golden Buzzard that the rest of the world does not agree that he is the Supreme Being's avatar, and that Holmgren may use the Popular Assembly to eliminate theocracy as a legitimate form of government. In particular, eliminate the legitimacy of the First Speaker's government." He stabbed with his fork, transfixing another segment of octopus.

"I am reminded of historical events," Buncombe said. His fellow ambassadors paused their eating to look down the table. "My ancestors, four and six generations back, held American governmental posts just before the Summer War and Crittenden's War. Afterward they each wrote books about their experiences. They emphasize how rapidly matters slipped from peace and calm to outright conflict, with each player behaving like an actor in some ancient Greek or Atlanticean tragedy. No amount of reasoning could convince any of the players that the dominoes were toppling, one after the next, with conflagration as the inevitable consequence, until cities went up in pillars of fire."

"Holmgren wants his Popular Assembly," Elizaveta said. "He wants it so badly he does not care what else happens, so long as he gets his Assembly."

"Holmgren is almost as brilliant as Napoleon, the third of his name," Davout said. "As he was losing his second war, Napoleon the Third at least had the sense to abdicate in favor of his son, without whom France might be ruled by a Bourbon or, may God have mercy on the land of the hexagon, a President."

"Austria-Hungary enjoys peace," Karl-Michael said, "because we have made the needed balancing agreements, and because the half-dozen figures at the top all view civic tranquility as their primary objective. Holmgren's Popular Assembly could well overturn all that. I spent the last hour counting noses, and listening to the advice of our hostess. It appears to me that Holmgren's appeal to the Popular Assembly, no matter how it is phrased, is highly likely to pass for a long list of wrong reasons. If the British and French colonies in Africa were still counted as parts of Britain and France, matters would be different. Mayhaps the Queen-Empress and the Emperor could claim that they are to be counted. That would at least create some confusion and obscure the validity of the vote. I will circulate my nose count."

"But does anyone here see a way to undo what Holmgren is doing?" Saigo Shigetoshi asked. "The situation is not as favorable as could have been hoped. He has the votes he needs on the Peace Executive, and once he goes to his phony Popular Assembly he will have his bit firmly between his teeth. Mayhaps a sufficient number of nations can be persuaded that they will not like the consequences of voting for Holmgren's motion, so that he loses in the Popular Assembly."

"Assign his negotiations to expert bureaucrats, with vigorous orders to procrastinate," Davout said. "Holmgren is term-limited, after all. Drag things out enough, and he does not get his way."

"Tell him to bugger off," Featherstonehaugh said. "He has backers for different reasons, but most of them don't want a war. Too many casualties, theirs not his. However, if we show up and vote we are conceding that his phony Assembly is legitimate."

"There is another path here," Saigo Nene said. "He is threatening to use the League Peace Police against us. His Peace Police have some excellent personae, but there aren't very many of them. Few governments will agree to lend them people from their National Persona Teams to the Peace Police, unless their neighbors do the same. Oddly, the neighbors are never agreeable. It would of course be highly unfortunate, and something we would of course all work to avoid, if his League Peace Police were to blunder into situations in which their numbers became depleted. After all, we all prefer world peace, and all recognize the great positive contribution of the League Peace Police in support of this preference."

"Of course," Elizaveta Petrovna said blandly.

Chapter Seventeen

Food Court
Benjamin Franklin Technical Junior High School
Joseph Henry Boulevard
Medford, Massachusetts

"Brian! Brian Wells!" Archie McDonald pointed at cashier's podium, where Brian Wells was emerging tray in hand. Archie waved and gestured 'come hither'. Brian nodded and headed for MacDonald's table. Archie was captain of the Franklin Tech boys' base ball nines team. Once a week, in season, his team would play Brian's pick-up team in a scrimmage, a game the school team would often win, but only if they worked hard. Archie pointed at a vacant chair, smiled, and nodded.

"Brian, are you guys and gals going to be ready to play us this spring?" Archie asked. "We need tough opponents to practice against, or we start losing. In particular, that Joe guy wherever he's from. That was a super-incredible-unbelievable throw he made at the end of our last game, even if it did cost us the game. But my sister the spotter was sitting there watching and was sure none of you were persona, well, none of you were using your gifts during the game."

"We'll be there," Brian said. "I don't know about Joe. He was around because he was playing Janie in City of Steel, and then he disappeared."

"He was playing your sister? He must really like losing," Archie said.

"He never did win. But Janie said he kept getting better." Brian looked around for his younger sister, who was nowhere in sight.

"At least your big sister can't hit the ball," Archie said. "She showed up in fitness club yesterday. We did the mile and a half. We took off as a team at a good pace. We let her start first. Hey, she's a girl. She was almost sprinting. She never slowed down. She would've lapped us, except we started sprinting, too. At the end, she was puffing hard, and we were gasping for breath. If she could ever hit the ball, and ran like that, she'd be getting extra bases all the time. She doesn't have some sort of gift, does she?" Archie took a bite of fried chicken thigh.

Brian glared at Archie. "Not a polite question. But she wouldn't cheat. She just wouldn't. Besides, it's Janie and I who have gifts, which we wouldn't have told anyone about. Except that idiot Emperor Roxbury showed up with his stupid giant robots. Why did Roxbury have to show up here? Now I have the principal, the guidance counselors, the school psychiatrist, and half my teachers wanting to be real sure Janie and I don't lose our tempers. I don't. After all, Janie and I had gifts since years ago. No one ever suspected anything. Mayhaps some gamers. Janie plays under an Overton cage."

"That was just Trisha? Running fast?" Archie nodded. "She's for sure fast. Maybe she should join the girls' cross-country team."

"Out of the question. Please don't ask her. I mean it. Just don't ask her. It's complicated. But she wouldn't want to say no. She just can't say yes," Brian said.

"OK! And Joe?" Archie asked, pausing to take another bite of salad.

"He disappeared," Brian answered. He drank half of his glass of milk. "That's been a super-pain-in-the-neck. There were all these people who think Eclipse learned her City of Steel move from Janie. But she's never met Eclipse. We don't even know what Eclipse looks like. So there are all these crazy people. They think Joe taught Eclipse. No one knows how to find Joe. You saw the papers. We had the National Team and a bunch of people from the Federal District on our doorsteps. I met Speaker Ming! And Krystal North! And Janie met three Grandmasters. It was totally frigid!"

~~~~~

Janie sat in a quiet corner, munching on her sandwich and reading a book on Territories. Most days, she had friends to sit and talk with, but her schedule today was a bit complicated. She really did not want to talk to anyone at the moment. There were already people who knew about Trisha being grounded. Most of them would be nice. Or sympathetic. She also knew a couple of meanies, people who didn't like her because she had her Highly Respected ranking, and would take it out on Trisha.

There, she thought, came Ingrid Fairhaven. Ingrid was a nice person. That's why she got along so well with Trisha. They were both just nice people. She was even nice to Trisha's younger sister, even though Janie was a whole grade level lower. A lot of eighth-graders looked down their noses at seventh graders, as though seventh graders were some sort of half-evolved insect. Ingrid waved. Janie waved back.

Ingrid sat down at the end of the table, looked around to see no one was in earshot, and leaned over to Janie. "I promise I won't call you out of your book," Ingrid said. "You're the best Five Games player this school ever had. But I saw your picture in the paper. You and those Grandmasters. And the Speaker of the House. That was really frigid. Are you all right?"

"I'm just great," Janie said. "They were all nice to me. I had a champion, a persona who protects me. They grilled me on my move for two hours. Girl, but they gave away a lot of good ways to think about moves. I was real tired afterwards. Yesterday I won two correspondence games!"

"I'm more-or-less your sister's best friend. I won't pry," Ingrid said. "I
~~~~~

want to help. If I can. Suddenly she dropped out of the music club. She told me that she was grounded, and that she didn't know why. If you can think of anything I can do to help her, just let me know."

Janie frowned pensively. "Please don't tell anyone else."

"Not in a million years," Ingrid said.

"If I said something to you, could you repeat it to her?" Janie said. Ingrid nodded. "Mom and Dad said that Brian and I can't talk to her unless they're in the room listening. But there's something I'd like to say to her, and I can't, because I don't want my parents to find out I talked to her."

"That is totally weird," Ingrid said. "Of course I will. And I won't tell anyone else what the message was."

"Please tell her. Brian and I both love her. And neither of us can figure out why mom and dad are mad at her. We just can't. It doesn't make any sense."

"Will do. Wait. Did they cut off her allowance, too?" Ingrid asked.

"That was this morning. She only gets lunch money. But I think she's dipping into her piggy bank to get enough to eat at lunch. She's a real jock, and eats a lot just to keep up her weight." Janie shook her head. It was all so crazy.

"I won't tell anyone. That's beyond strange. But we can't have her going around hungry," Ingrid said. "I just don't know what I can do."

"Brian and I will sneak money from our allowances to be sure she doesn't starve," Janie said. "But we will get into super deep trouble with our parents when they find out. We'll do it anyways." Janie remembered Sunssword explaining about the life support gift. Janie knew that she and her two siblings could get along without eating, just by calling on their gifts, but that wasn't healthy while you were growing up. She didn't want Trisha to do that.

"I'll see if I can find something," Ingrid said. "Mayhaps my mom knows the answer. Besides, I owe Trisha a ton for dropping out of music club. I was sure I was going to lose the lead singer spot to her." The two girls smiled at each other.

~~~~~

Trisha opened the house's side door and slipped in, closing it very carefully so it would make next to no noise. Her parents complained about everything. They'd complain if she slammed the door, even if she didn't. She kicked off her shoes, carefully untied the shoelaces, and stacked them properly at the door entrance.

"I'm home," she called. She did that every day. Hopefully they wouldn't complain that she was doing the same thing she always did. "I'm going upstairs to my room."

"Trisha, dear," her mother's voice was loud and clear, "don't you have chores to do?"

"Mom, today is Wednesday. That's me cleaning up my room. So I will. And I'll start the dishwasher after dinner so we can hear ourselves talk while
~~~~~

we eat." She wondered what her mother was going to complain about now. There had to be something.

"That's very good, dear," Abigail said. "Call me when you're done and I'll inspect your work."

"Yes, mother, of course I will," Trisha said. Mother hadn't done that in years. OK, a good year and a half, anyhow. Now she was going to have to have the room absolutely perfect in every respect, or she'd never hear the end of it. "And you're always so good about showing me what I missed."

"Trisha, dear? Wasn't there something else you wanted to say to me?" Abigail asked.

"Ummh, well, no, mother. There wasn't," Trisha said. "Oh, wait, do you have any more chores for me on top of cleaning my room completely? And starting the new year's cleaning of the kitchen?"

"Just go to your room, dear," Abigail said. "I will be up to see that it's properly cleaned."

Trisha dashed up the stairs, using just enough of her flight gift that she made no sound on the stairs. All the cleaning supplies she needed were in the closet next to her bathtub. Thank you for being lazy, and having all supplies up here, she told herself; that way you don't have to go down to the kitchen again. Even more fortunately, she didn't have any carpets, because she couldn't use superspeed to accelerate the vacuum cleaner. She didn't quite understand why, but if she tried that she would blow the circuit breaker in the basement every time. It was something to do with how much power the vacuum cleaner was drawing.

So she would start at the top, oil the walnut wall panels in the fourth floor room, clean the windows, dust the valences and the chandelier, clean the desk and shelves, make sure everything in the drawers was very neatly arranged, make sure the books on the bookshelves were all at the front of the shelf the way her mother liked them not the back the way she liked them, dry mop the floor, repeat in her third floor bedroom, clean under the bed, be sure her bed sheets and blankets passed the quarter test, check all the places where she had clothing to see everything was straightened up and properly stacked, completely clean her bathroom including the walls and ceiling, realize she had better clean all the slats in all of the blinds, use flight to pick up the bed mattress and clean the edges of the bed, make sure her plants were all watered, realize she had better dust the top of her books and the bookshelves behind the books, stack her CDs in the lower compartment under the window seat so they completely hid where the secret compartments were, refold the blanket in the upper compartment in the window seat, and double check everything. Mom and Dad had never learned about the secret compartments, and she wasn't about to tell them. At this point she was seriously tired. A glance at the wall clock said she'd needed 10 minutes to do everything. That translated to almost 10 hours real-time, except somehow with superspeed it didn't quite feel that way. She was still tired. She would wash up, take a nap, and tighten the sheets again afterwards before she called mother to inspect.

Her mother, dutifully summoned, carefully looked over absolutely everything, down to picking up the mattress and looking underneath. She appeared to be even more annoyed than she had been before. She could find nothing to complain about.

"When do I come down for dinner?" Trisha asked. Mayhaps Mom had forgotten yesterday. Mayhaps she'd been mean. Trisha decided she didn't care what the answer was. But she'd make Mom say 'you are going to bed without your supper', if that was what it was.

"6:30 sharp," her mother answered. "And you still aren't going to tell me why else I'm doing this?"

"I think I already did, mother," Trisha said. "And you think there's another reason. If I ever come up with it, I could tell you." And I might not, she thought. You do not get to enjoy what I'm not enjoying. Mother was even better at slamming the door behind her than Dad had been. Twenty minutes later, after a shower and change to her formal dinner clothing, she set the timer for 6:28 and sat down with her biology book.

There had been some good things today. She'd dumped music. She'd made the boys base ball nines team sprint until they were gasping for breath just so she wouldn't lap them. Next time she'd really sprint. They'd die. But they were boys. They'd get what they deserved. She had done just fine on the in-class exams, enough to keep her A and A-plus grades in place. Editing English was going to be a pain. Mrs. Gostak was really nice, but carefully obeyed the rules as written. Most other teachers would let her take in-class exams and let her move beyond that stupid limit. The Engineering teacher, Mister Allan, was being really nice about letting her switch to doing her own projects, so long as she was grounded. Her project partners had groaned loudly when she announced she had to split with them, but so long as she couldn't go over to their houses to work on projects, there wasn't a lot of choice.

Hopefully Dad and Mom wouldn't complain when she had to use the basement shop for her projects.

Trisha reminded herself: She'd have to find a solution to the lunch money problem. Dad knew exactly what lunch cost, and with her allowance stopped she was not getting another dime. Janie spent all of her allowance money on books. Brian made his models, brought in way more money by selling them than Dad seemed to have noticed, bought Janie even more books, all sorts of model-building tools for himself, some of her gym equipment, and gave her fabric to sew things like their garb. He'd always say he traded for things at one of the second hand tech stores, fixed things and traded just like Dad had taught him, and Dad just smiled and nodded. At least, Trisha thought, she'd always saved her allowance money. That would keep her going for a few months.

~~~~~

Brian sat at his desk, trying to concentrate on studying for tomorrow's exams. He wasn't being very successful. Dinner had been a nightmare. Everything had gone fine for the first five minutes. Then Trisha announced she'd dropped music for fitness club. She'd even tried to be nice about it, saying she'd watched the videotape of Mom singing in Worcester's Engineer's Hall and realized that her singing was not in the same league. Mom had completely blown her top. Fortunately Dad had been willing to agree you couldn't be a good singer unless you wanted to do the work, and Trisha didn't. Brian had repeated what Archie MacDonald had said to him about Trisha's running. Making Trisha look good should have been the right thing to do. Instead, Mom went after him for undercutting her. Trisha hadn't quite been sent to her room without eating, but as soon as she was finished she'd been sent upstairs. Without asking, he'd cleared the table, cleaned the countertops, and put the dishes into the dishwasher. Janie fled to her library. The whole thing was so crazy.

Janie sat at her computer keyboard. She'd just finished notifying the people in her correspondence games 'family emergency, three day delay', an excuse which the rules let her use once. Unless things got better, in three days she'd have to resign her correspondence games. That would be terrible for her rankings, but these things happened. She couldn't concentrate enough to play; she didn't think anything was about to get better. It was a lot easier to be the girl with the spine of steel over the game board than it was when things came after you in real life. No, games were real life; family life was a problem. She'd just have to work harder someday to get her rankings back. Worse, if things got bad enough here to mess up her grades at school, all sorts of terrible things would happen at home. Grades had to stay good; that was Mom's requirement if she wanted to study games. She had a whole pile of homework due tomorrow. She'd already done some. She'd just have to slog through the rest of it.

Trisha stood in her Tower Room. Today she'd made mistakes in Editing English. Those mistakes held her back. She wouldn't let that happen again. She always felt terrible after finding she'd made a mistake. Today was worse. Those mistakes meant she would plod along for another day. Dinner hadn't been so bad. You just had to focus on not caring about the people talking at you, so that it didn't matter what they were saying. You listened carefully and smiled, but you stayed completely outside the conversation until someone demanded you say something. Then you said something true, not that it mattered. On the English test, she had a 98. That was good, relative to keeping her A-plus record in place; it was a complete disaster in terms of being able to advance early to the next level in the online system, at least before tomorrow. The online class had multiple versions of the same lecture. This time she'd work through all of them, just to be sure. For a moment she grinned. She'd remembered a classmate who'd said she'd worked the same
~~~~~

homework problem five times, not five different problems, and couldn't understand why the teacher was not impressed. Poor Brian had tried to be helpful at dinner, quoting Archie saying nice things about her, but he'd just made things worse. Mom had clearly hoped that she would stick her head into fitness class, be unable to compete, and flee back into music. That wasn't happening. Brian had told Mom the opposite, namely his sister's performance had been excellent, and Mom had not wanted to hear it.

Chapter Eighteen

The Invisible Fortress
Morning

There finally came the day on which I did not feel sick. The change happened all at once. Yesterday I'd been exhausted. Today I felt fine. The bruises had gone away. Medico swore up and down that the broken ribs had been re-knitted as good as new. My shoulder gave me a twinge of pain if I picked up something really heavy, but Medico said everything was actually all right, except I would have to live with discomfort for a few months. That was going to be interesting tomorrow, when I go back to weight training.

I ate, switched to riding clothes, and went out to the barn. Snapdragon and Daffodil had been neglected for long enough. My riding clothes aren't fancy, not like some English Lord hunting his foxes, but after a good ride they tend to smell of horse. That I can do without, so the clothes are only worn for riding. The horses had largely been outside, so cleanup of the barn was not a major chore. The barn cats were not in sight. The very slightest touch of telepathy found them in the orchard, stalking squirrels that had come to feast on the fallen apples, not to mention the chestnuts.

Daffodil and Snapdragon were in the lower pasture, grazing. I gave a whistle; they came at a good canter. They both wanted to be cuddled—I'm a bit light to do that to both of them at once. They each liked a cranberry cookie. I combed each of them, carefully, found they were happy to have me put a halter in place, and dropped blankets over their backs. Some purists would complain this is not bareback riding. Sorry, but horsehair tends to scratch after a bit. They did not complain that I stayed with light blanket and halter rather than saddling them up. They complained even less afterward when I gave them each an extra apple and another cherry-berry cookie. Only very rarely do I give them maple sugar. It's not good for their teeth, inoculations or not.

I vaulted onto Daffodil's back. It was her turn, no matter how disappointed Snapdragon looked, and we were off, first at a walk, until they warmed up, then at a trot, and finally at a gallop. Daffodil was not at all tired, but after half an hour at one pace or another I switched over to Snapdragon. For all that they are the same breed, the two horses have very different personalities. Daffodil will jump a low fence if vigorously encouraged. Snapdragon loves jumping, the higher the better, though I am quite careful not to give her any obstacles that might be too high for her. Jumping is fine exercise for me, too. You hang on very tightly, or you go flying. I have presets on my force field, not to mention that, after all, I can fly, so that sort of accident is entirely safe for me. A stranger seeing me on Snapdragon might still get very upset that I do not bother with a helmet. If I were some other twelve-year-old, she'd even be right.

I put on my running gear and did a jog around the pastures. I forced myself to my normal pace. I did a sprint around the lower field, as fast as I could, being very careful not to draw on my gifts to help me along. By the end, my heart was pounding, my lungs hurt, and my breath came in gasps. I'd pushed as hard as I could, and now paid for it. Mum was right: Medico does keep you from getting seriously out of shape. Note I said "seriously"; my lungs were reminding me that I had not done this in two weeks. My final dash took me out to my mail box. I emptied the hopper and ran back to the house. If I'd heard a car, I'd have dropped into the tall grass next to my driveway, out of sight until the visitor went away.

A fast shower and change of clothes brought me to my mail. There were the sports magazines the mythical male adult resident supposedly reads, and the homemaking and horse magazines the mythical adult female resident shares with me. I had one important letter, the attorney for my alfalfa supplier. There had been a death, there was a settlement in some sort of court, my claim on the alfalfa had been recognized, and the alfalfa would be delivered with only a fractional charge against the delivery fee. There was a promise that the firm was being reorganized, and I would be welcome to order alfalfa again next year.

I stared my list of things that needed doing and considered throwing up my hands. Houses are just a great deal of work. I began by mounting my bookshelves and putting my library on them. Mum had scrupulously packed absolutely all my books, including all of her more advanced books that I had sampled. I used the same shelving arrangement I used back at home, but now I have way more shelves. No, right here is home. It's home for me, now and forever.

That took much of the morning. Catching up on housework got me into the afternoon. There was a certain slant of light in the winter air. What I needed was a long walk, and some time to think. My house was at the dead end of a secluded road, with large fields and woods before you reached the next house. Even so, I might be seen, but it was well late enough that no one would think I had dodged going to school. My ride this morning had been in the lower pasture, out of sight of everything, and my run had taken advantage of cover. This time I would walk the perimeter fence, just in case something had happened to it. I donned outdoor shoes and a padded coat, and stepped out into a chill late afternoon.

After a while my walk took me well into the woods. I was careful where I walked to avoid doing anything massively stupid, like tripping, falling, and breaking an ankle. Yes, my presets are supposed to protect me from hurting myself, but presets are like the safety switch in the coffee bean grinder. You have a safety switch, but unless you are a complete and total idiot you still unplug the grinder before you clean out the inside. So far, the fence had been in perfect shape. I was going to have to do this walk again, carrying a hedge clipper, lopper, and hand saw, just to discourage things from overrunning the wire, but the wire itself was intact.

When you get down to it, I've had months of living by myself, during most of which I've been too busy to think about what Mum did. Now finally I had the chance to think, and I didn't like it at all. One of Mum's important lessons came to mind: You're only responsible for your own choices. I really couldn't think of anything that I had done that was that wrong. Not close. I can't remember misusing my gifts. I think she would've complained, or told me off, but she had said nothing.

If what Mum did wasn't my fault, mayhaps it was something with her. She was in these very deep games with the Lords of Eternity. One of those games might have turned too dangerous for someone my age. In that case, I think she would've warned me that I really needed to dig a very deep hole, hide at the bottom, and pull the hole shut above me. Walking off with the Namestone was about as far from hiding as it's possible to get. It was also as dangerous as getting into a fight with a Lord of Eternity. Of course, I'd done that, too. OK, I liked my life the way it was, the way it was before, but I don't see any way to get back there. To go back, I'd have to find Mum. Trying to find Mum when she doesn't want to be found is straight out impossible. If you don't believe me, ask Solara or Lars Holmgren.

As I walked, the bright sun came full out. It was late in the afternoon. The sky was blue as a beryl. Sunlight sparkled off tree branches waiting for the return of spring. It hadn't rained in a week. December's snow had melted. Dead leaves crunched and crackled under foot. My spring-fed pond was so clear I could see all the way to its surprisingly deep bottom. I walked, and the message *you're only responsible for your own choices* echoed again and again through my mind. For a while I'd been too busy to see that one part of my life had come to an end. I actually had already started on a new part of my life, one where I made all the decisions, which was mostly good. I also had no one covering my back, which was not good at all. *You have to take the bad with the good* was another lesson, one that came very much true, but *bright cheer will always win out over dark despair. Be the bright cheer, and all will do well.*

Today was certainly a day where I had in the end found bright cheer. I picked up my pace. There was not much of a breeze. I was still cold. Not shivering cold, but cold enough that I felt the cold all the way in. Yes, I could've used my gifts to avoid that, but that would've frustrated the whole point of the walk, now wouldn't it? I'd managed to skip lunch, and now my stomach was vigorously reminding me of the error of my ways. Skipping lunch had been my choice, so I was responsible for the outcome.

There are people whose attitude on the world is that something that has happened is over and done with, so they just forget it. Their memories fade. My memories stay as sharp as ever, and will apparently stay as sharp as ever until the day I die. Walking away from something is not simple for me. I couldn't forget what had happened, but I could tell myself that I was going to live with my new life.

I kept my meal very simple. Whole-grain bread with sunflower seeds. Nice slices of Swiss cheese, lettuce, and a bit of butter. Reheated lentil soup. A 2nd sandwich, this time sliced ham, Muenster cheese, a teeny bit of mustard, and more lettuce. Finally, a couple of apples. Okay, that is really a lot, but I had skipped lunch, had had a long walk and a longer run, and was careful to eat slowly.

I took a large glass of orange juice with me up to my den. OK, I call it my den, but it had been the family room for a family, close to 500 square feet. Just before I encountered the Martyr again I had repainted it from a hideous avocado green to bright white. It had a pure white vinyl floor. Even at night, it was bright and cheery.

What had I been doing this morning? I went back to unpacking my books. That was way better than hunting though boxes, but I couldn't have unpacked until the shelves were done, which meant the entire room had to be painted...several coats...which meant...and there was a line of things that needed doing before I could get to the thing I wanted to do. Sometimes that list seemed to go on forever. What was the math phrase? Infinite regression. Now the list was getting shorter again. When I finished unpacking my books, I could go to the next item on the list.

I sat down at my lessoncomp, stared at the list of things I hadn't been doing, and pulled up math. Mum kept saying that math was difficult, but when you finally understood things it was an absolutely glorious feeling. I do still remember when suddenly I understood how the definition of acceleration worked. Further back, there was the moment when I understood, as opposed to being able to parrot the rule, what the zero actually did. The most recent stop was trying to understand how the geometric proofs worked for the sine and cosine and tangent of the sum of two angles. I stayed with one of the proofs. When I finally understood what was going on, I would do the others for myself. There were just all these parts, and if you'd used all of them it worked. But what were the parts doing?

I must've been thinking for a while, because my glass of orange juice had mysteriously emptied itself. Suddenly I saw how the proof worked. It really was a fantastic feeling. I'd worked hard, and now I had the reward. Understanding that bit of plane geometry was indeed the happy moment in a very trying day. I laid out a sketch of how to do the other two proofs. I would fill in the blanks tomorrow. That was a real challenge I had managed to overcome. I'd already made a rule for myself. If at some point if I didn't get it, I would just make a note that I had to come back to this, and try something else. Mayhaps the something else would give me a clue. Even so, I really hate to quit and try something else.

I leaned back in my chair and looked to the far end of the desk. There sat a wooden bowl, lid firmly in place. It was cherry, polished but uncarved, with a single copper band marking the line between top and bottom halves. Inside, behind a quarter inch of impervium, waited the Namestone. Even through the impervium shielding, I could hear the Namestone calling out to me, its owner and mistress. Suddenly I felt absolutely fantastic. For thousands of years, heroes, armies, fleets, and Lords of the Hexagon had taken the challenge of the Maze. The Namestone was the prize. They all failed. I succeeded. I did what no one else in world history had been able to do. If I'd gotten a bit beaten up along the way, in the end it had all been worth it.

The last bit of light had faded from the sky. If I went out over the Pacific, fairly far out if I went south, there'd be pillars of cumulus, rising high into the air, soaring towers tinged gold and orange and salmon by the sinking sun. This was definitely a moment to go cloud diving. The weather map showed where to go. I did remember to check what I was wearing, go very deeply slack into my gifts, and teleport the long way. Now, below me, were the slow swells of the Pacific Ocean. Above me, for thousands and thousands of feet, were spires of cloud. This was not a sport that wanted spectators, let alone jet airliners interrupting my dive. I reached out with my sense of perception. Nothing.

I teleported to 40,000 feet, found a cliff edge, and killed my flight field. I was falling free, the wind whipping through my hair, my body screen keeping me from getting too cold. It's seventy degrees below zero up here. Cumuli sailed by, faster and faster, a brilliant mix of pastels. I reached the base of the clouds, cued my flight field, and made a sharp vertical turn, hard enough that I could feel the gees leaking through the field. Yes, that sort of maneuver is good exercise for your gifts, but a thirty gee turn is also a heck of a lot of fun. Now I was headed vertically up, going supersonic in the first second, peaking at Mach Six, finally turning head over heels to brake to a stop, a bit above the cloud tops. Mum always thought I was being an exhibitionist. After all, she pointed out, I could perfectly well have teleported back to the top.

I did a half-dozen dives. They were a splendid few minutes, minutes that I'd forgotten in the months since my life changed. Yes, the dives were fun. For once I was at peace with myself. There were no looming deadlines, no sense that I was living in an infinite backward progression where each step demanded I do something else first. I had a few things I had to do, soon, but not this instant. I was really happy. Now, though, the sun had very definitely set, leaving clouds lit by the twilight's last gleaming.

On the last climb, I pulled deeply into my gifts, pushing into my limit, the limit on how much power I could draw without hurting myself. It was like the sprint I pulled for my last run around the lower field. That last bit of effort, demanding everything you can do, is good for you. That last bit of effort is what builds strength and endurance and willingness to accept discomfort in a good cause. It was time to watch the inverse sunset, the solar disc rising in the west as I climbed hundreds of miles up out of the earth's shadow. Here comes the sun!

With that I teleported, again the long way around, until I was standing in my bedroom, hovering a few feet off the floor. I felt absolutely great! It was very definitely time to catch a solid night's sleep.

Chapter Nineteen

The High Chamber
The House That Is Forever

"Once again, we are assembled," Prince Mong-ku said. In this century everything that went wrong would be his fault. Someone had to see that things went right, and it was his turn to do so. It was very much one of those centuries, he thought, in which nothing went well. The Plan was not advancing properly. "Our list of difficulties is not decreasing. Worse, the Runes indicate that those who may not be named are changing their trajectories through the heavens. The runes are not yet precise on the direction of the change. The Great Powers would fall into war over this Eclipse person, except they can't find her. Then there's the League book. As usual, Vera Durand wants to speak to us. Where shall we start?"

"Eclipse," the Screaming Skull muttered. "Find her!"

"You do have a point," Plasmatrix agreed. As amazing as that may seem, she thought to herself, the Screaming Skull had actually had an intelligent idea.

"Find her. Find the little whore, so I can crush her like the insect she is!" The Screaming Skull did not quite shout.

""Find her, find the Namestone, and matters calm down," Plasmatrix said. Mayhaps, she thought, the Screaming Skull had had his bright idea for totally wrong reasons.

"Well said, old chap," Starsmasher echoed. "For all that we know nothing of her moral habits or income streams."

"Find her, so I can kill her," the Screaming Skull said. "Slowly."

Colonel Pi glared at the Screaming Skull. "The last time you got yourself in a snit like this," he observed, "Morgan handed you your hat, and I had to waste a year putting you back together to the point your healing matrix could repair you. And, it seems to me, except I forget who it was, you had company in the emergency ward, didn't you?" Starsmasher looked abashedly at the floor.

"Eclipse is hardly Morgan," Solara said.

"Yes," Plasmatrix answered. "Absolutely. Of course. Anyone can see that. Except, please remind me, which one of them did the Maze to hold the Namestone?"

"Let us be polite," Prince Mong-Ku interrupted. "Let us be polite to each other, or I shall forcibly adjourn the meeting. No matter the Terran Justice Book."

"Please," Archivist Green interrupted. "I also have a critical issue to treat. Let us not adjourn the meeting."

"There seems to be a lot of interest in Wells' City of Steel move," Solara said. "This Wells family keeps having things happen around them. First they were attacked by the perverts. Then that idiot and his big robots attacked two of their children. Now a City move. Are they playing a deeper game? Dark Shadow, this might be your expertise."

"I have already investigated," he announced. "That simple study was a royal nuisance. For starters, the Americans interviewed Janie. She had a champion on site. Our dear friend Morgan. Morgan plastered the family with null links, has a casting on their house, and Goddess knows what else." The room became so still that not even breathing could be heard. "So far as I can tell, Professor Wells knows Morgan as Professor Lafayette. Janie asked the Professor, who she mayhaps knows to be Sunssword, to be her champion for the interview. Not one person in her family recognized the little piece of jewelry...you know, the ruby the size of a hen's egg...that Morgan was wearing. Krystal North undoubtedly did, but said nothing. However, I prowled about. The parents are ungifted. The three children are highly gifted. Morgan is coaching them. None of the children used their gifts while I was watching, so I can't say much more. Janie is a mentalist. Brian sees the order of things...oh, and he has a plasma torch and force field. The older daughter apparently flies, when she is not being seriously depressed over some difficulty she has with her parents. She's also the brightest of the three.

"Eclipse somehow got her hands on a move Janie had invented but never used, but Janie is absolutely positive she has never played Eclipse. I could not reach Janie's mind, but reaching Grandmaster Hornpiper was trivial. Janie said that she mostly plays local friends and a boy her own age, but no one resembling Eclipse. The Supreme Gamesman, that Russian, more or less threatened to kidnap Janie to interrogate her, and Morgan did not quite threaten to show him and his country what ultraviolence is. Kamensky does not know who he tried to bully. In conclusion, there is this move, but no one knows how it got from Janie to Eclipse."

"Could Eclipse have invented it herself?" Plasmatrix asked. "I agree it requires a truly warped perspective to see in advance. Like White winning in chess by moving her queen back to the 1 file."

"Sure. Reading Janie's mind without her noticing would be problematic," Dark Shadow answered. "She's competent, has Morgan training her, and has a null link backing her own defenses."

"Let's not bother Morgan," Starsmasher said, "by attacking one of her proteges. She might get annoyed. Talking to Morgan is the wiser course. That's someone else talking to Morgan. I think she is still upset with me."

"Think?" Plasmatrix asked. "You have any doubt? I have a simple path to speaking with Miss Wells. I'll take it. It costs a bit of my time."

"I'll talk to Morgan," Solara said. "What's this about a League of Terran Justice book?"

"There is a book," Prince Mong-Ku announced. "In fourteen languages. It is full of sentences. Every so often, there is a blank where there should be a word. You could say it's a puzzle book." He produced a stack of books from under the table. "This book."

"This is terror?" Plasmatrix asked. "I like puzzles."

"Not these puzzles," Mong-Ku answered. "The blank words. Their memes lie sleeping in Radthninu Tower. Somehow, someone has found a way to define the suppressed memes by showing where there are no words. I did test…the tower is still totally solid."

"I'll ask Morgan," Solara said. "After all, how many people know what lies sleeping silently until silence itself is stilled? And, no, I don't think the Silver General is involved. For starters, I think we managed to trap her memories of these words."

"I'll speak to Durand," Starsmasher said.

"There is also an important book matter." Archivist Greene was short and dark-haired. Contrary to his persona name, he routinely wore trousers, shirt, coat, and opera cape in various shades of brown and yellow. He rarely spoke, much to the relief of his fellow Lords. The matters he thought were important were seldom interesting to any of them, even when he did not explain them in four times as much detail as seemed necessary. "Someone is buying books."

"Many people buy books," Solara said resignedly. "I buy books."

"Not these books," Archivist Green said. "Someone has a list of the valid volumes of the *Arcana Goetica*, the *Physica Goetica*, the *Histories of Gow All-Fleeing*, the *Atlanticean Gnosis*, and, worst of all, asked about buying a copy of the *Presentia*. Actually, their book purchase list runs to four pages of small type. The writer used one of the five standard computer fonts, so the list cannot be traced. Some of those books, *Liouville's Butterflies* for example, are fairly mundane, but other books on the list are quite sophisticated. In particular, there is close to a shelf of books on history. Not classical Whig history on great heroes, but serious studies on the path of Deep Time, all from our maximum suppression list."

"We know this how?" Starsmasher asked.

"We maintain an antique book chain," Green answered. "It's partly to find books I have overlooked, but it also keeps an ear to the ground. At some point in the last few months, a want list went to the extreme-high-end book mongers, including us. Whoever composed it seems to view money as no object. She also speaks Goetic entirely fluently. The person circulating the list did emphasize to the buyer that he would not be buying or selling a copy of the *Presentia*, and neither would any other book monger in his right mind."

"The valid volumes of the *Arcana*? Is the list at all accurate?" Colonel Pi asked. "That's fairly unusual knowledge."

"I have searched the Archives," Archivist Greene answered. "There are vast numbers of studies of the *Arcana*, at least the volumes most readily found. This list is better than any of them. Worse, the list includes every volume on our Closely Held list, and names two other volumes that I knew existed but have never seen. However, the purchaser apparently said that she had seen all the books that she wants to buy."

"Speaking good Goetic is also unusual," Solara remarked, "as opposed to Virgil's pigeon-Goetic. Is the source reliable?"

"The source," Greene answered, "is Monsieur Poulenc of Poulenc et Filles, arguably the world's greatest book monger, even if his collections do focus on acts of improper behavior. His command of Goetic is flawless, and so was the command of the person who wanted to buy the books."

"Do we know who this person is?" Solara asked.

"Monsieur Poulenc respects the privacy of his clients," Greene said. "By inserting a book into the purchase chain, a book that was carefully scanned and teleported by the mystery client, leaving all three tracers behind, no I do not know where the other two tracers came from, and a bit of other legerdemain, I have ascertained that the purchaser was probably an Emily Tattersall, who affects to be an Englishwoman of quite young age, young enough that some of Poulenc's more exotic clients found her interesting--for improper reasons."

"Probably?" Solara asked.

"Tattersall may be a pawn. I had to cheat a bit in questioning one of Poulenc's daughters, so that she did not know she was being questioned. However, the rules on potential purchasers of the *Presentia* are quite clear," Greene said.

"Did Poulenc tell us that there is a potential purchaser?" Prince Mong-Ku asked. Greene shook his head. "In that case, as Poulenc surely does know the rules, I believe that the usual sanction needs to be imposed. Is there disagreement?" The Prince waited. "Very well. Dark Shadow, I believe that this calls for your expertise? Is there any other business? In that case, breakfast awaits."

Chapter Twenty

January 25, 2018
Eclipse
Poulenc et Filles, Livres Anciens
Paris, the French Empire

It was early morning for them and early evening for me. I'd spent half the day at a Beverly Hills supermarket, wearing my granny disguise, complete with blue hair, veiled hat, three pounds of pearl necklace, and fur coat. Only once in all the times I used the disguise had someone suspected I was not what I appeared to be. He'd followed me out to a teleport pad, waited for my shopping carts to be unloaded, and tried to strike up a conversation. For some reason he thought I was a guy in my twenties, in disguise, and wondered if I'd be interested in a really wild party. He had the disguise part right. The rest, not so much. 'Young man,' I answered, 'when I was a quarter my age, I'd've been flattered. Except, as you can plainly see, I am in fact an elderly woman'. He beat a hasty retreat.

The modest sign in the door in front of me read Poulenc et Filles, Livres Anciens, 42 Avenir Chemin de Fer. That's Poulenc and Daughters, Old Books, 42 Steam Engine Avenue. When you are the largest used book store in Paris, you can afford to be modest. It was early morning. My Emily Tattersall identity was the only customer in line. Waiting for the doors to open, I let my memories take me back to my first visit.

The first time I had been here, I'd been a bit intimidated, Mum's rules engine on applied intimidation notwithstanding. Poulenc's was also Paris's largest seller of explicit romance literature, illustrated and otherwise. Carefully chosen clothing or not, I looked younger than Poulenc's usual clientele. Well, most of their clientele. Some of his clientele had looked at me hopefully. Very hopefully. This was Europe, after all.

I'd appeared in late afternoon. Finding a teleport arrival point that was entirely out of the way had been slightly tricky, but that's what back alleys are for. Completely innocently, I'd marched through the alley around to the front of the building and in the main entrance. I noted a glare from two salesmen, people who thought I was young enough to be an inappropriate customer. There was another clerk, busy putting books up on shelves. She was dressed entirely in black, ginger hair in a tight bob, a sharp jaw below eyes that darted back and forth. The rules engine said 'ideal target'.

"Pardon me," I said to her. "I'm here to see Monsieur Poulenc, himself. I have an order to pick up." After it was too late, it occurred to me that she might not speak English, or might in accord with ancient custom refuse to hear a foreign language being spoken.

"Ah, yes," she answered. "An order. This way." She gestured. We walked between beautiful dark oak bookcases, carefully but very lightly oiled, brass fittings gleaming in the late afternoon sun, though several large bays not quite crowded with customers. The overhead lights were banks of sun-white fluorescents. The shop was anything but dark. Monsieur Poulenc's office rose three stairs above his shop. It had huge glass panels, letting him survey the first floor of his bibliographic empire while seated at a truly magnificent desk.

My escort pointed at me, tapped her brow, and withdrew. "Bonjour," I managed.

"Good afternoon," he said in flawless English. American English. He'd read my accent perfectly.

"I'm Emily Tattersall," I announced. "Sunflowers. The *Arcana Goetica*. And the *Physica Goetica*." We'd communicated via the dark interlink. Even before I recovered the Namestone, I was very careful about masking myself. But I knew his code. I gave the transaction password, and named the books I was buying.

"Ah, yes," he said. "Four thousand livres." Once upon a time, that had been a lot of gold, but the price of gold has soared in recent centuries. I almost became annoyed when he misquoted the price, but remembered the procedure.

"Three thousand four hundred seventeen livres," I corrected, "and forty-two sous." It was a bizarre price, which no impostor could know. "And here it is." I began counting gold Great Thalers from my purse. He didn't bat an eyelash, though it was a substantial amount of money for a girl my apparent age -- however much I'd dressed to look older -- to be carrying. "Any luck on volumes three and four of the *Arcana*?"

"I am searching. They are rare and expensive," he answered. "Though not vaguely as expensive as the *Physica*."

"Strange. The Emperor had them printed as sets of four."

"However, I confirmed. The first two volumes have both the original Low Goetic, and Virgil's brilliant Latin translation." The translation was almost totally worthless, and Low Goetic was a pidgin between Goetic and Ancient English. "The other volumes are facsimiles of four books written entirely in High Goetic. *Who has the speaking of the ancient knights?* Those volumes were for almost all people totally useless, a tribute to the emperor's ego, so usually they were discarded so soon as the First Empire ended."

That was impressive. Without an instant's hesitation he'd switched from flawless English to quite good High Goetic and back again. "*Glorious were the deeds of the mighty ancient heroes, and deep the thoughts of their scientist-wizards.*" I answered in High Goetic. Mum had not taught me many foreign languages, but I can manage four, at least if you count Ancient and Modern English as being different.

"*I shall search diligently,*" he said.

"*You are most kind. I hope we can come to a reasonable settlement on a fair price.*" I answered. He might have thought I had simply memorized a stock of epigrams. Now he knew elsewise. Mum always said my accent was flawless.

"Most certainly. Except...*you have no accent at all. Are you a living daughter of the ancient knights?*"

"Hardly," I answered. Best not too many people notice what language we had been speaking. "I'm no older than your oldest grand-daughter." Actually, I am not vaguely that old. Talking about myself was bad. Having someone thinking I was an immortal might attract far more attention, and not good attention either.

He looked at me carefully. "An excellent disguise. Monsieur Pamplemousse could do little better. Had you not told me, I would have thought you were Jean-Marie's age -- my youngest daughter, she who brought you here -- if a bit less tall. Your secrets are safe with us. It will be my pleasure to serve you, or mayhaps you and your house. Did you bring your shopping list?" He winked. He thought I was simply the front for another buyer.

I handed him four typed pages. "I have a master list, though I've marked items I've already purchased. If you can suggest related works?" Solar satellite repair meant that money was no obstacle.

"Jean-Marie," he called, "make me a copy of this, please? I may have some of these available, say in a week. You said you had actually seen all of these, and wanted to buy your own set. I recognize several titles, auctioned through Padgett's; the last sale of a copy of the *Atlanticean Gnosis* went for ten million guineas. I have heard that a publisher is making a facsimile edition. There is a rumor, one I do not care to test, that people who buy or sell copies of the *Principia Praesentia Presentia* soon thereafter receive a visit from Solara, herself, a visit with fatal and highly destructive consequences that always leave a witness behind. I would not care to determine if the rumors are true." He smiled. That was my first visit. There had been more since.

A rattle of locks turning brought me back to the present. The panels looked like innocent glass, but were undoubtedly the Order of Gow's finest battle crystal. The locks looked equally innocent, but hidden clockwork was surely retracting massive titanium or mayhaps even impervium-plated rods into the floor and ceiling. It was very early. I was at the moment the only customer, though that would surely soon change.

"Good morning, Emily," was the welcoming voice from inside.

"Bonjour, Jean-Marie," I answered. I dutifully shook hands, my elegant gloves masking the solid force field underneath. I had spent enough money on very expensive books that I was now a well-known customer.

"My father should be in his office momentarily," she said.

"You're very busy opening the shop. I know the way. Don't let me impose on you." I slipped around her onto the floor. By now I attracted only very polite nods from clerks.

There was a chain across the foot of the stairs to Jules Poulenc's private domain. I took a place on the couch, a scrupulously clean love seat whose fabric might have been more recent than a few of Poulenc's books. Actually, I could see his desk. The corner where I expected to see the six volumes of the *Higher Arcana* was quite empty. In fact, his entire desk was vacant; no letters, no packing slips, no anything. Spring housecleaning? Something triggered my alertness. I didn't do a panic crash drop, but I settled even deeper into my gifts. Jean Marie brushed by me, removed the chain, and opened the door panel -- more transparent Gowist battle crystal.

And here was Monsieur Poulenc himself stepping out of his private elevator. He and his wife lived eight stories up in their 'attic garret', which by report was two stories of elegant apartment, complete with a gourmet-class huge kitchen. Something poked at my memories. His walk was very slightly off: His limp was missing. I dropped even deeper into my gifts.

"Good morning, Miss Tattersall," he called. "Please come up." There was nothing wrong with his voice. With her usual efficiency, Jean-Marie had produced a silver tray, coffee, cups, and fresh pastries. She set them on the very low table between the chairs, the table so low that there was absolutely no hazard that the coffee would be spilled in any unfortunate direction. I was quite sure Jean-Marie had looked at the desk, and not expected what she saw. Monsieur Poulenc was undisturbed. He gestured at the waiting chair. I worried only a bit about being poisoned. On one hand it's really difficult to poison a persona. On the other hand, I had extra protections. Besides, I was really positive that no one here suspected who I might be. Of course, that didn't protect me from being poisoned for a completely wrong reason, for example because someone thought I was the missing daughter of Napoleon VI.

Suddenly Jules stiffened. He gasped. His head jerked back. He managed a stifled gasp.

"Papa?" Jean-Marie realized that something was wrong. Something I had never seen before in my life appeared in the space between Poulenc and me. It looked like a giant silver orb-spider web, every thread blinding-bright, the outermost radiants spreading out yet attached to nothing. The radiants thrust out and withdrew, again and again, looking vaguely like a spider with an impossibly large number of legs.

Jean-Marie screamed at the top of her lungs. I wasn't quite sure what to do. Running away from every potential threat would have me living in my bedroom, hiding under my bed. Doing anything dramatic was likely to give away that Emily Tattersall was someone else. Yes, my force fields had automatically cranked up as far as they would go without becoming visible. High-power battle inside one of the world's finest collections of old books seemed to be a really poor idea. What was the thing?

Jules fell to his knees and sank on his side, his skin turning gray. Jean-Marie had produced from her cloak some sort of pistol. She started shooting. It might have looked like a 0.22, but it was unmistakably a disruptor, ancient hi-tech rather than an Atlanticean or Krell model. From the chromatic disturbances when she hit the Gowist windows, someone had boosted its power level through the ceiling. The windows naturally absorbed the disruptor beam, but not without visible effect. At a guess, Jean-Marie's pistol would readily have disabled a large warship, but it was having absolutely no effect on the spider.

"Emily! Run for your life!" Jean-Marie shouted. Before I could've run, no matter that I was not inclined to do so, the thing was on me. Its attacks were entirely mentalic. It was trying to shred my defenses and cut my mind into little pieces. It was not succeeding. Ultravision – I was going to have a headache again – showed that the creature had no material component at all. It was purely a construction of mentalic forces. Even ignoring the close and delicate quarters, most of my possible attacks would have absolutely no effect on it. Yes, I can hit something with a high-power levin bolt, but anything close that has a mind is likely to suffer minor collateral damage, like insanity or death. Anything close, like two Poulencs.

The very front of the store was vacant. I did a flash attack – blinding light – on that part of the store, made a very fast combat teleport to the storefront, and waited a half second for the creature to follow me. A second flash and combat teleport – very short jump – took me back to my starting location. With any luck at all, anyone looking at toward the front of the store would have been blinded by the flash, so that they would not have seen Emily Tattersall hovering in midair above the shop counters. Now the creature was not close to any innocent bystanders. I hit the construct absolutely as hard as I could with rapid-fire levin bolts. Its structure flared, burned, and dissipated.

"Papa!" That was Jean-Marie again. Her pistol had disappeared. Jules Poulenc lay motionless on the floor of his office. Medico was clearly the needed rules engine. Mentalics was a close second. My healing matrix was moderately cooperative about scanning Monsieur Poulenc, with me kneeling at his side. His heart had stopped. His breathing had stopped. All the things the nervous system did to manage the body had stopped. His mind – there was nothing there. But I could hear the small traces of his thinking. I widened my search. The creature, whatever it was, had shoved him out-of-body. His mind was still in the room, but it wasn't attached anything. That's dangerous, even if you are a persona, which Jules was not. I found him mentally. He was confused and disoriented. Already at the edges his thoughts were trying to fray away and disappear. I lent him my strength and tried to reassure him. Medico was very precise about the next steps. It's a light duty version of mind control. You take control of the patient's body and force it to do the things it needs to do in order to recover. In this case that was restart his heart, restart his breathing, restart and control all of the automatic things that his brain was supposed to be doing, and then ask how I was going to re-embody him. I knew how to put myself back together, but that wasn't the problem at the moment.

"Jean-Marie," I said, "I don't have time to explain. Paris must have experts in mentalic surgery. We need one here immediately. Get one on the phone, and I'll explain to him the problem." She grabbed the telephone. The store was extremely quiet. A glance revealed that the clerks had run out the front and fire doors and not stopped to watch.

After the 1908 war, Europe had acquired extremely efficient emergency services. It seemed like a long time, but it was only a couple of minutes later that Jean-Marie handed me the telephone. "Monsieur Poulenc has been disembodied," I explained. "I'm keeping him and his body alive, but he needs to be put back into his body. Can you possibly come here?" Teleporting someone while you are trying to maintain mentalic contact with them is tricky. I wasn't sure I could teleport a disembodied mind. I didn't remember ever having heard of such a thing. Mind you, what I know about gifts is really extremely limited, but I for sure couldn't say 'I know how to do that.'

"This could be arranged," the voice on the phone said. "Please give me back to the person who called me." Jean-Marie took the phone and started talking very quickly in French. Only a couple of minutes later Professor Cadoudal was at my side. His teleporter had brought him first to the street outside, where a crowd was now being held back by several policemen, and then to the other side of the now closed and locked front doors.

At this point I was really nervous. Privacy screens or not, and Mum had drilled me on those, to pull this off I had to be in close telepathic contact with a really good mentalist.

"We have here the patient," he said to me. "What issues did you see?"

<*Here,*> I answered, mind to mind. <*I'm keeping his heart and lungs and everything working.*> That included persuading the nerve cells in the brain to fire occasionally so that they would not die, but Medico was very clear on how to do this. <*And I am keeping his mind energized.*>

Professor Cadoudal followed my links. "Forgive me, I must speak privately with the patient." I got out of the way. For a bit the Professor was very quiet. "You did the right things," he announced. "And this has to be fixed instantly. But, but, I am afraid Poulenc's mind is too large for me, or anyone else in Paris."

"Large?" I asked. I was entirely outside my depth here.

"Spend a lifetime reading and your mind expands. The re-embodiment procedure stays the same, no matter how big the mind, but the power I must supply -- it's beyond me."

"Together?" I asked. Jules was at this point a friend, not to mention someone had almost killed him to get at me.

Cadoudal's answer was a very clear image, what he would supply and how hard I would need to push. "That is a great deal of power," he observed. "I'm not sure where to find someone who can do it."

"That's within limits," I said. "It's less than what I used to kill the thing that attacked Jules. The precision is the challenge." I was going to have a really bad headache tonight. "I need a moment to focus," I said. He rearranged the image slightly so I only had to push at two points. "Give me a three count?" I asked. He nodded.

"One, two, three, push!" I ramped up smoothly. Very briefly, we were cross-connected at the autonomous nervous level, OK, at the superstructure over that level. There was no doubt that he was a healthy not-quite-middle-aged man, and a very competent mentalist. He was going to know how old I am, physically, and rather more besides. "Enough! Stop!" he said. I stopped. I could hear Jules think. He was back in his body. Cadoudal stared at me. Well, I had tried not to give away who I was, but he was a really first-rate mentalist. "You are not a woman, are you?"

OK, Jules had said my disguise was almost even with the mythical detective Pamplemousse. I'd not considered that my disguise might be completely effective, only that it hid who I am. At that level of contact, though, there is a certain awareness of the other person's body. He'd clearly figured out that I was much younger than I appeared.

"I don't think we discussed my age," I answered. "We were both a bit busy."

"My God, if I had known how young you are, I would never have dreamed of asking you for support," he said.

"Fortunately," I answered, now hiding behind the hardest mentalic screens I could drive, "Fortunately for Monsieur Poulenc, you didn't know. Convincing you that my help was no big deal might have been…inconvenient."

"Inconvenient?" He brushed my screens, discovered they were rock solid, and withdrew. "But I have no time. Monsieur Poulenc, you need a few days in the hospital. Henri?" That was Cadoudal's teleporter. "The Queen Joan the Great emergency entrance!" Poulenc, Cadoudal, and his teleporter vanished. I leaned on the desk and pulled myself to my feet. I was going to want a long nap this afternoon.

"My father?" Jean-Marie asked.

"He's back together. The Doctor saved him. The Doctor left his card," I pointed at the desk.

All this time, someone had been tapping at the door. The sound became more insistent. "Miss Tattersall," Jean-Marie said, "The men in grey. That's the State Secret Police, not the Paris Metro Police. Mayhaps you should leave."

"Mayhaps I should stay. That way they do not blame you. If they ask what books I've ever bought from you, just tell them. I believe you never read my full shopping list. By the way, where is my package for today?" I said.

"It's gone," she announced. "I saw while you were saving Papa. I know exactly where it was, and it is not there. And the other books are gone, too."

"Now, that's annoying. But not your fault. You'd better let them in, I think," I said.

She waved cheerily at the men outside, blew the fellow in front a kiss, and headed for the door. Kiss? This was Europe, after all. And the men in grey were suddenly much calmer.

Jean-Marie unlocked the doors. I hadn't caught when Jean-Marie had locked them, but she clearly had. The Secret Police swarmed in. I really do not speak French. Their rapid-fire exchange was completely beyond me. One of them established we could speak in English, and asked me to please stay where I was standing. I seemed to be in the middle of a recent criminal event, and they did not want me to step on any evidence. I waited politely, hands clasped, while they questioned Jean-Marie. That gave me time to dismiss Medico and call the Mentalics rules engine.

I had a very sharp set of memories of that thing. If I were lucky, the Mentalics rules engine could tell me what I had been facing. Rules engines aren't very good at leaps of intuition, but they plod a step at a time very quickly. After a bit, I found the answer. The thing had been a Marik march-daemon, something sent out to slay those who did not hear the beat of the silent drummer. There was no more silent drummer. It perished when the Great Parade of All Marik made its column-left-by-contingents into the waters of the Pacific and neglected to return. Under modern conditions, a march-daemon will kill everything in its path until someone really good gets in its way. Me, for example.

I had no idea what it was doing here. It was certainly nasty and powerful, enough to kill many personae, let alone Monsieur Poulenc's ungifted customers. That raised an interesting minor question--how had Jean-Marie been able to see it? It was not made of matter. She must have at least some minor gifts of her own. Was it after me? It seemed unlikely that anyone had penetrated my disguise. But why would someone want to kill poor Emily Tattersall, an innocent young woman with absolutely no past? If everyone in the store died, the likely outcome if I had not been here, no one could tell that my books had been stolen. Mayhaps someone had spotted my book-buying and wanted to shut down my line of curiosity by shutting down me.

The preliminary questioning of Jean-Marie was actually impressively competent. Several other senior-looking people arrived while Captain Victor-Maurice du Blois was listening to Jean-Marie. They kept quiet and listened, rather than interrupting. One of the Captain's assistants was recording Jean-Marie as she talked. Finally the Captain turned Jean-Marie over to his superiors, and came to me, an assistant with recorder in tow.

"Good morning," he said. "Miss Tattersall? I am Captain du Blois. I am told you only speak English. Is this correct?"

"I speak English," I answered. I added a few words in French. "Alas, my French is not very good."

"For a very young lady indeed, your command of my language at least has no accent," he said. My disguise did not fool him at all. "Thank you for standing here. We'll have the floor swept in a few minutes so you can move. Why don't you tell me what you saw, and we can go from there?" he asked.

OK, I thought, Cadoudal mayhaps told him how old I am, meaning du Blois has his own telepath in tow. "I arrived to pay for and pick up a purchase. Several old books. I waited for Monsieur Poulenc to descend from his garret. When he arrived, he appeared not quite right. His limp was missing," I said. Captain du Blois looked at me rather sharply. Okay, I do pay careful attention to my surroundings. "I am not a detective, but some things are easy to notice if you are awake. You would have noticed far more. Then the creature Jean-Marie may have described appeared, midway between us. Jules fell to the ground. The creature was a Marik march-daemon."

"Oh?" he asked. "Marik? Why do you believe this? Have Marikites not been dead for some time now?" Several thousand years, if I remember correctly.

"No material component. Colorless mentalic glow. Oscillating radiants. If you have an artist who is not afraid of receiving an image mentalically, well, I will leave a bad headache, I can share the image. Jean-Marie's…" I hesitated. I have no idea what weapons Frenchpeople can legally own."…response had absolutely no effect on it. Then it attacked me."

"I see. You seem to be alive and well. Where is it?" du Blois, suddenly concerned, looked around the room, not that he would have been able to see it if it were there.

"I killed it. March-daemons swallow mentalic energy, but toast if fed too much. So I toasted it. It fell to pieces." I described what-all else had happened. du Blois stared at me. I didn't dare read his mind, not when he had his own mentalists in the vicinity, but he clearly did not believe me. If you did not know about the rules engines, I would appear to be impossibly precocious, showing a vast number of different technically-challenging gifts. Mum had vigorously drilled me in stretching the limits of my gifts, and how to use rules engines in support, but when I had saved Jules that was the rules engines telling me what to do, not something I could have done by myself.

"I'm afraid that I must ask you to accompany to me to the Bureau Nine Headquarters," he finally said. "Your claims are, let us say, in need of further verification."

"Regretfully, that will not be possible," I said politely.

"I am sorry, but I am a Captain of the State Police. It is in my legal authority to detain you, Miss Tattersall, even though you are an

Englishwoman," he said. Apparently my accent was good enough to fool him, though it had not fooled Jules.

"Regretfully, that will truly not be possible," I said. I cued my aura and theme music. My feet floated off the floor. The blue glow and brilliant brass tune fading into woodwinds are uniquely mine. The Captain's jaw dropped slightly. Two of his men reached toward their disruptor pistols, stopping when du Blois gestured at them. The third had very ostentatiously moved his hands away from his weapons, palms out toward me, and grinned. At him I smiled and winked. He winked back.

"Mademoiselle Eclipse, I presume?" du Blois asked.

"Precisely, mon Capitain," I answered. Captain du Blois tipped his kepi. "Here to buy a few books. Books that apparently were stolen before I arrived. From a bookseller who thinks I am 'Emily Tattersall', a nom de guerre for reasons you surely recognize." I smiled.

"Ah, yes, of course. Your disguise is superb. But why here?" he asked.

"I am buying old books. From a dealer in old books. To buy old books, how could I consider anywhere in the whole world other than Paris?" I'm sure he recognized my appeal to Gallic pride, but what I was saying was indeed true. "And now these criminals have torn away my mask. Worse, they appear to have stolen the books I was about to purchase, namely the six volumes of Ptolemy's *Higher Arcana*."

"You were here to buy Ptolemy?" he asked. "Not Casanova or Ovid or Henfrere?" Poulenc included in his collections a remarkable number of books about people carrying on with each other. I grinned. Many girls my age would have been very interested in getting their hands on a copy of Henfrere. Their parents might have had different opinions on the matter.

"Jean-Marie, who did not know who I am, can tell you what I have purchased. Underclad handsome young men do not play a part, well, ignoring the Da Vinci volume on curative gifts," I answered. "In any event, I have truthfully told you everything useful. Whoever did this almost killed a good friend of mine, for no apparent reason, meaning that I am personally very annoyed with them. If you find out who they were, please tell Jean-Marie or one of her sisters, so that I may lecture the miscreants on the error of their ways."

"Lecture? You will tell them they were bad boys?" He seemed unconvinced.

"I promise I will not turn the Hexagon to a puddle of molten glass. I won't even do collateral damage. But I will find out what they were up to, and you will get a full report," I said. "They interrupted my book buying. I am highly annoyed."

He tipped his kepi again. "I will be most grateful. Surely the woman who solved the Maze is also a great detective. I will ensure that Jean-Marie Poulenc is kept apprised of the details of the investigation. I agree you are not detained. And I do not need to know which books you had on order."

I smiled. "Many thanks. I will try to help, though you are surely the better detective. You saw through my disguise immediately. But I must be on my way." I faded into a blue-white snowstorm, the jangling of sleigh bells all around me. This was a great nuisance. Emily Tattersall had been a very convenient additional persona, someone who could innocently visit bookstores, bakeries, even have lunch in one of Paris's inexpensive but first-rate cafes. She had her own wardrobe, not stored in my home. That wardrobe now needed to be turned to plasma. Worse, my book-buying efforts would become far more complicated. Very soon, the Captain's promise notwithstanding, the entire planet would know which books I had on my shopping list. Anyone ordering one of them in a rare book store would attract a great deal of unwelcome attention, like the bachelor who the day before Halloween buys three dozen apples and three dozen razor blades, not to mention that the buyer would likely discover that a half-dozen homing beacons had been planted in his new purchase. When I caught up with the people who had done all this, I was going to be very angry indeed.

Chapter Twenty-One

Legation of the Satsuma Daimyo
The Diplomatic Quarter
Geneva, Switzerland
Afternoon

The garden gate to the Satsuma Legation was a pair of moon doors, pivoting in, their wood inlaid in copper with the circle-plus Satsuma *mon*. Thaddeus Buncombe paused to admire the newest door-knocker. It was the head of a woman, if you skipped over the fox-ears and slitted pupils. The knocker itself hung from her neck as a pendant. Buncombe dutifully rapped the knocker three times, then stood politely back. After a few moments, the moon doors swung open. Centered behind them stood Saigo Shigetoshi's daughter Saigo no Teishi. She was slightly shorter than her parents. Her solid black hair plunged like a waterfall much of the length of her back. Teishi wore a richly colored formal *junihitoe*, though Buncombe noted the layering had been slightly simplified in the modern style. The Satsuma legate had to view this as an extremely important meeting. She bowed politely, a fan half-hiding her face. Buncombe wondered if any of his fellow ambassadors would recognize that she was holding a *tessen*, and was surely trained in its use. The two young men holding the doors open, men who were never introduced, were doubtless even more accomplished at multiple forms of violence. The doors they were holding might be wood veneered, but under the veneer was surely face-hardened steel armor.

"I greet you, Lord Ambassador," Teishi said.

"And I greet you, Ojo-sama," Buncombe answered. He hoped he had the address right; Teishi, so far as he knew, was not a court official, so the formal 'Miss' was appropriate.

"You do me too much honor, Lord Ambassador," she answered, bowing slightly. "My Father the Satsuma Legate was delighted to have learned that you accepted his invitation. He and my Lady Mother wait in the Small Dining Pavilion."

"I hope I have not kept them waiting," Buncombe said. He was sure he had the time right.

"Not at all. Your timing was as always perfect, Lord Ambassador.

However, my Lord Father said that this is an informal gathering among friends, so names rather than titles will be appropriate between the three of you. If you would be so kind as to allow me to lead you?" Buncombe followed Teishi down a string of short corridors paneled in bamboo. She opened a final sliding panel, her fan waving him forward. Buncombe nodded, smiled, and advanced.

~~~~~

The Small Dining Pavilion was paneled in lovingly polished mixed hardwoods, openings filled with large glass panels giving views of a formal garden of small white pebbles. The floorboards were a mixture of blond and dark grains. Century-bleached Brazilian bloodwood, Buncombe realized. The windows were undoubtedly acoustically opaque. Extended eaves and a garden wall blocked all lines of sight to the outer world. "Welcome again," Saigo Shigetoshi said to his American counterpart. "And if you do not mind, we are joined by my wife, who in addition to being a superb cook is a master of small and seemingly irrelevant details."

"I certainly cannot mind," Buncombe said. Small and irrelevant details indeed, he thought. She would know exactly which details signified most strongly. Several polite bows later Buncombe found himself facing the first of many courses, to be spaced out over a glorious afternoon, this first appetizer being a red raspberry on an orange slice on a sautéed yellow pepper on a circle of spinach with garlic on a blue-green seaweed disc on something blue that Buncombe did not recognize on mashed purple carrots, the entire collation being less than two inches across. "Shall we postpone business until after dessert?" Buncombe asked. "Or shall we intersperse the delightful meal with thoughtful conversation? I am the humble guest here."

"Alas," Saigo Nene said, "we have a great deal to discuss, however much my simple dishes and our chef's recipes will extend our time." Her husband nodded agreement.

"In that case, Nene-Tono, let us converse. Just so long as I get to taste the magnificent food," Buncombe answered.

"You give me undeserved honor, Thaddeus-Tono, with your most kind honorific, though we are all of ambassadorial rank here," she answered.

"However, as the host, I shall note that we are in remote and exotic Europe, and propose we follow strange European customs. Is this not wise, Thaddeus, Nene?" Shigetoshi asked.

"Yes, Shigetoshi, it is indeed wise," Buncombe answered. This exchange, repeated at the start of every meal he had had here, meant a great deal to the Japanese, so he would politely agree, just as he had every other time he had eaten here.

"Surely, husband, you are always right?" Nene asked.

"Me? Right? That will be a first. I am always careful to listen to you and do as you say," Shigetoshi said. "Therefore, Thaddeus, as you are the guest, I should allow you to sample the first taste. The wines, by the way are a mix of
~~~~~

American and northern Honshu varietals." Buncombe delicately sliced a wedge from his serving, being sure to capture some of each of the layers. The combination was as flavorsome as he had expected. He smiled and bowed from the waist toward Saigo Nene. "Truly excellent," he announced.

"Mayhaps even as excellent as my gossip," she said. "As it is meaty gossip, it should appear with the next course."

"Oh, Nene," Saigo said. "Punning already?"

"Only once. I promise," she answered.

"I am too old to imagine a response," Buncombe said.

"Better to imagine our next course," Shigetoshi smiled. "So soon as we finish this course. Mentioning imagining surprises, did you hear what happened in Paris this morning?"

"It must have been interesting, as you wonder if I had heard of it," Buncombe said. "Alas, there is little I hear until well after everyone else does. I am sure the news will reach me, mayhaps in another few weeks."

"There is a book monger in Paris," Shigetoshi said. "A Monsieur Poulenc. He has a huge book store, the largest in the world. He deals in old books. A customer arrived. She and Poulenc were attacked by, it seems, a Marik Marcher-Demon."

"Aren't Marikites and their creatures extinct?" Buncombe asked. "Apparently not."

"The customer rescued Poulenc. She also killed the demon. It turned out the customer was Eclipse, herself, in a good disguise," Nene said, "or so the French State Police said. Her theme music and aura are quite unique. Apparently she is shorter and younger than otherwise reported. Curiously, the French did not save any photographs or voice recordings of her. After all, she did save the life of Monsieur Poulenc, a member of Napoleon's High Court of Savants. They also did not try to stop her when she chose to leave."

"The last is indeed fortunate, since Geneva shares a continent with Paris," Shigetoshi said. "But I see the second appetizer is arriving." The second appetizer proved to be a thin slice of sautéed chicken thigh stuffed with truffle and quail eggs, the eggs being stuffed in turn with caviar, garnished with tiny slices of radish, cucumber and a tarragon mayonnaise.

"Do we know which books Eclipse is buying?" Buncombe asked. "That might tell us something about her. It occurs to me that Poulenc is well-known for his collection of romantic literature."

"His collections on the dreaming world are beyond compare," Nene said. "Her interest, it seems, lies in occult works of past historic cycles. *The Arcana Goetica*, for example. There is a rumor with no source that she offered to buy a copy of the *Presentia*. Buying the *Presentia* is said to be inauspicious. Then there are rumors that someone is making very small third and fourth order castings near Poulenc's building,"

"In some circles, it is believed that a book monger in Edo was once so ill-advised as to have offered a copy of the *Presentia* for sale, at a reasonable price." Shigetoshi contemplated another quail egg, this one stuffed with beluga caviar. "Solara's chastisement was said to be the Great Kanto Earthquake. The All-Conquering Generalissimo and the Bakufu have since decreed that anyone offering that book for sale is to be executed immediately, along with their entire family, all of their employees, and all of the families of their employees, following which their establishment and all of their homes are to be incinerated."

"Inauspicious. I see," Buncombe said. He did not recognize that explanation for the earthquake. Unfortunately, it certainly could be true.

"However, Monsieur Poulenc circulated to a few quality book mongers a want list. Saigo Eldest Daughter will have a copy for you when you leave. Parts of it are quite strange," Nene observed. "For example, books not known to exist, even by the Great Library."

"Before you leave, though, surely there will be at least the third appetizer," Shigetoshi answered. "Four hard pastry shells, each containing a different cold soup." Buncombe smiled. "And then three sorts of noodle."

"Mayhaps we might advance to another serious matter," Buncombe said. "We have managed to persuade the Argentines and the Brazilians that neither of them is attacking the other. Without this success there would have been a war. Now they both demand to know from where the sky octopi and their strange soldiers come. They expect America to solve this problem immediately. After all, we are the wealthiest country in the world, so we must know everything. Alas, the answer that would satisfy most Americans, 'accursed foreigners always fight each other', will not suffice here."

"A continental war would be inconvenient," Shigetoshi observed, "especially if the American Republic were to be defeated. We now have to our east two Great Powers with whom we have good relations. If the IncoAztecans were to replace you, an extremely sad outcome that we hope can be avoided, we would face hostile nations in most directions."

"I must heartily agree, especially about the defeat," Buncombe said. If the IncoAztecans were to occupy the Republic, he considered, large parts of America's population would soon be fed to Huitzilopochtli and his fellow gods. "However, our efforts at finding a solution have not been effective. America has excellent computers and competent mathematicians. Efforts to reconstruct a plausible shape for the sky octopus in fewer than five dimensions have so far been unsuccessful. If the creature has a simple shape, it must be six-dimensional. How is this possible? I am authorized to report that for one of the previous incursions we were able to teleport to the scene several top-line spotters. We do not report this because all the powers involved, including our nominal allies, are extremely sensitive about the presence of American Persona League forces on their territory, even when the people who are present see and report, but do not do. Officially, these persons are just tourists who happened to be in an interesting place at an interesting time. In any event, so far as our spotters could tell, the peculiarly-attired soldiers were using no gifts. It's just that they could be seen moving from place to place without passing through the points in between, setting things on fire by waving their sword...but no gifts were employed. I am not aware of any gift that can be used to cloak the use of teleportation, while someone is teleporting, but so far as our observers could tell the invaders were giftless." And now we see, Buncombe thought, if putting a few cards on the table will encourage my Japanese counterparts to do the same. Those were the instructions from the Federal District, and now they have been carried out.

"Interesting," Nene said. "It is a curious fact that a century ago the All-Conquering Generalissimo and the Emperor of Brazil came to an agreement on certain trade relationships, as a result of which Brazil now has a modest number of citizens of the Emperor living in its midst. Unsurprisingly, because Brazil is a beautiful country, these long-time visitors occasionally receive relatives as tourists. Of course, some of these visitors have a few limited gifts, which naturally they use to benefit the people they are visiting. As a result, I can report that by some accident there happened to be a spotter of the Shinobi Corps in a position to observe one of these attacks. He is a person of unusual perspicacity. Nonetheless, he agreed with the American tourists that no use of gifts was evident. One of his friends was a camera otaku who had technology never seen in humble commercial establishments such as All-Nippon Video. There was some delay in returning his equipment to Japan, but we have now recovered all of his images; Saigo Elder Daughter will present you with a copy. We hope the images will assist with your reconstruction efforts, and hope that we will see the outcomes."

"I am confident matters will be arranged," Buncombe said.

"But there is also a less fortunate issue," Shigetoshi said. "Mayhaps after the next round of dishes?" Buncombe nodded. It had been a fine afternoon so far.

Much later, dishes cleared, Buncombe smiled at his hosts. "There had been another issue you wished to discuss?" he said.

"Yes. I am in a difficult position," Shigetoshi said. "However, the Satsuma Daimyo herself has explicitly instructed me that I should, with all the grace I can muster, raise this issue with you and the American Republic. I can assure you that I mean no insult. We are trying to give friendly advice to a friendly foreign power." He folded his hands and waited for an answer.

"We are friends, Shigetoshi. Our countries enjoy peaceful relations. If no insult is intended, then none should be taken," Buncombe said.

"Nonetheless, given American customs, I shall not be offended if you find my advice to be difficult to consider," Shigetoshi said.

"You are always very patient with me, Shigetoshi, even when I have not earned that level of patience, so I shall try to listen carefully to what you are going to say, which I am sure is meant with the best of intentions, and strive mightily not to be offended," Buncombe answered.

"There are reasons to suppose that there is a new alliance," Shigetoshi said. "Unfortunately, it would not be convenient to explain what those reasons are. However, there are extremely sound reasons. The Inco-Aztecans, the Prussians, and the Manjukuoans have formed a Triple Alliance. The Sikhs and the Ottomans are mayhaps also members. They wish to rearrange the world balance in their favor, which they conclude requires removing from existence the American Republic and the British Dominions of Canada. America may not participate directly in world events, as witness the 1908 Summer War, but, by selling arms and equipment to the British Empire, the French, the Austro-Hungarians, the Russians, and on occasion the Celestial Republic, America plays a large role in containing Prussian adventurism. If the Alliance wins, with American and Canadian factories producing for their new Incan and Prussian masters, and Alaskan and Canadian resources being transported to Manjukuo, the position of these powers would be greatly enhanced. Also, they conclude that their attack would have odds better than three-to-one in their favor, which gives them a reasonable chance of success. We gather the plan is to force a large-scale battle between Incan and American persona forces, have the Prussians and the Manjukuoans enter after your forces are fully committed, allow American conventional forces to roll south without persona support for Inco-Aztecan defenders, and then after winning the persona battle turn on the conventional forces. The Daimyo and her advisors agree that American forces are very good, but that these odds may prove difficult to overcome."

"This is unfortunate news," Buncombe said. The American Republic had always assumed, he considered, that noninvolvement in foreign affairs was the safest course. The result was that America had a relatively small standing military backed by very large and well-equipped state militias, and persona forces that emphasized extreme personal initiative. That combination was supposed to make America far too expensive for another Great Power to attack. The notion that several Great Powers might combine against America was surely irrational, but here that threat was being said to be real.

"In any event, now that we have passed through several fine dessert wines, I must offer my Daimyo's advice, which I humbly request that you forward to your Federal District. It appears like that you will need, whether you want it or not, a new set of foreign policies. The Powers in the Triple Alliance have their own natural enemies, with whom you might usefully combine. We can both recite all of the reasons not to take this advice. However, your own Speaker Ming has now observed publicly that your traditional foreign policies are more than a bit dated. This is mayhaps an exaggeration for effect, as they are only nine centuries old. I happen to have here an extended sealed document, which the Satsuma Daimyo hopes you will forward to your Speaker. However, it is now late in the day, so I fear that it is time to bid our farewells..."

~~~~~
~~~~~

Buncombe, a mysterious large envelope clutched firmly in his hands, strode through the American Embassy's gates. He nodded politely in acknowledgement of the Marine guard's salute. Chief aide Marjorie Whitcomb waited beyond the embassy's doors.

"How was lunch, sir?" she asked cheerily.

"Contact Washington. I need an immediate one-step teleport back to FD, and an urgent meeting with the Secretary and Speaker Ming!" Buncombe answered. "Oh, yes, the food was superb, every moment of it!"

"On it, Sir," Whitcomb answered. She scurried for her office. Buncombe ran for his private elevator and the Ambassadors' quarters. His eighth-floor dwelling had walls of glass, affording a magnificent view, precisely the same view enjoyed by the ambassadors of each of the other Great Powers, of Lac Leman. His objective was his winter coat. The sensible Swiss had their capital under a weather screen. The lack of weather screens over the Federal District was viewed by all patriots as a demonstration of American fortitude and thrift. Here was perpetual spring. There was deep winter.

Chapter Twenty-Two

Kniaz Kang's Marco Polo
North Cosmopolis, Washington

"Hello?" The question to Kniaz Kang came from across the counter. "Are you open yet, sir? I had met Jim, and will meet his other friends who are girls."

"We are open. We open at six A.M. Today the young women are in the South Greenhouse. I have not seen Jim in some time. You wish to order?" Kang asked, turning around to face his new customer. The girl in front of him was dressed all in white: boots, trousers, light but opaque blouse, and open, short-sleeved vest. Despite the blizzard outside, she wore neither coat nor gloves, not even a sweater. Emblazoned on her vest were four polychrome sigils. Kang stared at them, needing a moment to translate. Then he contemplated fleeing for his life.

"I'm a bit short of cash. Will this cover a glass of milk, and one of your butterscotch chip cookies?" she asked, setting a stack of change on the counter as she flashed a bright smile. "I'm here to meet Jim, except he'll be too late."

"And a glass of orange juice," Kang answered. "And a bit more. Surely you are the persona who cleared my parking lot?" The girl nodded. "If Jim asks for you, what name will he know? Mayhaps not the one you wear? Can you read those kennings?" And why does she think he'll be late, if she's already met him? Kang wondered.

"*I am indeed Time's Dagger*," she answered in flawless High Atlanticean. "*But Jim will know me when he has met me as Spindrift. And he will deny that I am his new friend who is a girl.*"

Kang made a shallow bow. "I have not seen Jim in some days. A shame. Do not worry about his denials, Spindrift. Young men often deny the obvious." Her laughter was the ringing of tiny silver bells.

"Nonetheless, I will be his girl friend," Spindrift answered.

"The South Greenhouse," Kang said, "The north corner." He pointed the way, quietly thanking the gods when Spindrift disappeared from sight.

~~~~~

"Pardon me? Dorothy? Teranike?" The two women looked up, seeing a
~~~~~

round-faced, amber-haired girl whose clothing was as white as the snowstorm outside. "I'm Spindrift. I will be Jim's new girlfriend. I'm supposed to meet him here, except he will not be here until after I had left," she said.

"Hello," Dorothy managed. "Jim's girlfriend? He forgot to tell us! Let alone tell us that you were coming!"

"Great to see you again," Teranike said. "Have a seat. You ordered?" Spindrift nodded. "After all, you did shovel the parking lot for me, the geniuses with their plows not having arrived. I should be paying for your breakfast." Spindrift grinned and shook her head.

"You? Shovel? The parking lot?" Dorothy asked. "You must be exhausted. Kang is hiring people your age?"

"Hire? I will not have been hired. It was a favor. And afterward I climbed the Arborday Tower to watch the sun rise," Spindrift announced. Teranike's brows wrinkled for an instant.

"How could Jim not tell us he had a girlfriend?" Dorothy asked. "At least he invited you to breakfast, your parents I assume permitting? Especially a girlfriend who knows Atlanticean…You can read the runes you are wearing, can't you?"

"*I am who they say I am*," Spindrift answered in Atlanticean. "*I am Time's Dagger. And I am Jim's friend who is a girl, until the end of days.*"

Dorothy wished Jim were here, now, to translate for sure what his girlfriend had just said. She was reasonably sure she understood what Spindrift meant, but Jim's Atlanticean was flawless. She would do her best to translate for Teranike, who was from a world where there had never been a Gaea Atlanticea. "Teranike, Spindrift said the sigils on her vest say who she is, and that she will be Jim's girlfriend forever."

"Spindrift," Teranike said, "that's very nice, but I hope I am not sounding too, ummh, motherly, if I say that forever is a long time, especially at your age."

Dorothy suddenly remembered a turn of phrase. In Atlanticean '…end of days…' meant '…the end of your days', and was only used if your end was on the horizon and swift approaching. Teranike's advice was good, if it didn't hurt Spindrift's feelings. Surely for both of them it had to be first girlfriend and first boyfriend? "I think my translation wasn't that good," Dorothy said quickly, "I didn't mean to say you might have, ummh, unrealistic ideas."

"She approaches on swift and silent wings. No offense will be intended or taken," Spindrift said. "Sage advice, well meant." Dorothy wished she did not remember what approached Atlanticea on swift, silent wings. The Crone Incarnate came with terrifying images. 'The sun was a blood-red penny. Ashes fell from the heavens. Waves rose higher and higher. The winds blasted from the mountain tops, tearing the trees from their roots. The screaming of the accursed souls trapped above the sky drowned out all other sound.

Whatever words Spindrift might have said next were interrupted by Wang delivering orange juice, three butterscotch cookies, a plate of hash, and a mug of hot caramel milk.

"Master Kang saw you in the parking lot," he announced. "You must be hungry. He cannot pay you, but your breakfast tomorrow is free."

Spindrift smiled. "Thank you," she choked. "I really didn't expect it."

You are a persona, Dorothy told herself. You beat the giant lizard, even if you can't remember your boyfriend who helped. You did stop the League terrorist by yourself, when you were not at all sure your force field was bulletproof. You are not afraid because you are listening to a girl barely two-thirds your age, even if she does speak an extinct language, so far as you can tell flawlessly, telling you that she is about to die.

"So when is Jim showing up?" Dorothy asked. "Have you ever dated him before?" And how will you two each get to school? she wondered, though it was really clear that Jim could teleport.

"No," Spindrift answered. "The first time together is yet to come."

"And he's late?" Teranike said. "These things happen. Don't be too mad at him."

"I knew he would not be here before I depart," Spindrift answered, her breakfast rapidly disappearing. "Do not blame him, either. He is a nice person, kind and thoughtful and self-sacrificing and absolutely gifttrue. And cute."

"How did you meet?" Dorothy asked. Spindrift, she thought, seemed to have really fallen for Jim. "Do you go to the same school? Maybe I should ask, since I am supposed to be studying Atlanticean, how to dissect the kennings in your sigils." Formal written Atlanticean was based on kennings, infolding puns, so that wheatfield started as waves of gold, except waves were shore's call and gold was banker's blood, so wheatfield became fields of sand calling for banker's blood, and matters became more complicated from there, even before references to Atlanticean theology were inserted. She passed Spindrift a notebook and pen, on which Spindrift rapidly sketched symbols and translations, finally infolding to The Dagger of Time.

"I'm sorry," Dorothy said to Teranike, "We must be boring you to tears."

"Not at all. It's an interesting bit of your world's history," Teranike answered. "Besides, the Avatar's Elder Tongue uses different symbols, but the same general riddle and reduction schema. But what is Time's Dagger?"

"I can't tell you," Spindrift said, rapidly finishing the last bit of her breakfast. "Not 'may', 'can't' It's like the Dark Lights of the Starry Void, the *Chelesh N'drageu* and the time before the infinite past. Can't tell. And now I must go." She slipped coins under her plate and dissolved into points of light that swiftly blinked out.

"Teleport," Dorothy said. "But 'Dark Lights of the Starry Void'? And what was the last thing she said?"

"She slipped into my language. *Chelesh N'drageu* is Polarian. With no accent," Teranike said. "No accent at all. I have never met a foreigner, and I am a High Officer of the Lake of Silver Fire, who did not have an accent. The Dark Lights? In both our universes, though in ours the Northern Barbarians want it to be a military secret, there are cosmic dust clouds that have evolved intelligence. In your universe, they stay well away from Earth. In ours, one visited twice, once 70 years ago, almost causing an ice age by accident, and again recently, staying on the far side of the sun and neglecting to mention that it sent androids to Earth, to speak with a few people still alive that it had met on its prior visit. They, the Chelesh N'drageu, live in interstellar space, passing by stars to feed on the sunlight. They have questions -- how the universe that has lasted forever came to be -- whose answers cannot be spoken, because the act of speaking the answers causes the universe to delete the speaker. And its answer. That was why I was here, to see if anything is known of the deletion. An effect that causes the mass of a large planet to vanish, in a single instant, with absolutely no trace left behind, might possibly have a few weapons applications."

"Boys and their toys," Dorothy said.

"Daughters and their spears," Teranike said, "is our version. Mentioning boys, here comes Jim, just too late."

Chapter Twenty-Three

The Lords of Eternity
The High Chamber
The House That Is Forever

Prince Mong-Ku again sat at the head of the Great Table, waiting for his fellow Lords to be ready to meet. For once he was here early to compose his thoughts. The Hall was nearly white, the paint having the slightest golden tinge. Sunlight trapped by giant light pipes and diffusors brought out the Table's rich inlay. The ornate wainscoting and chair rails were dark-finished mahogany, carefully dusted and oiled over the centuries since they had first been installed. Cornices held pieces of blown and pressed glass, illumined from below, each a different brilliant color. The faintest gleam marked the battlecrystal windows shielding them from accident. Soft ticks came from a pair of grandmother clocks veneered in a dozen different woods. Their gleaming dials and hands marked seconds and hours and days and months, the positions of the moon and the eleven planets, and the calendar year. The last detail, Mong-ku thought, meant that any mortal who penetrated to this chamber had to be killed immediately, his memories being fully exfoliated and recorded, but that was a small price to pay for the clocks' magnificence. Alas, he then remembered, in not so many years it would be necessary, once again, to replace the clocks' hardened beryllium-bronze gears, for all that does not heal itself must in the end wear away to nothing.

The flower arrangements were his own. Blood-red irises with white picotee and veining, brilliant white and pitch-black roses, and flawless Great Sky daylilies, luminous blue with a dozen flowers on a single scape, marched along the centerline of the table. The hard part, he considered, was positioning the vases so that each Lord of Eternity had a clear line of sight on each of his fellow Lords, but vast amounts of practice let him solve that constraint in almost no time.

Now he would join the other Lords in the antechamber. In a ritual older than most mortals could imagine, they would then advance together to the sweet tones of the Number Three March, each reaching his chair at the same moment.

~~~~~
~~~~~

Precisely as the clocks struck two, the Lords of Eternity took their seats. This would not, Mong-Ku thought, be the happiest meeting he could imagine chairing. Why couldn't the rotation have fallen to him in one of those quiet centuries when absolutely nothing of any concern took place?

"We have an update on the person trying to purchase a copy of the *Presentia.* Unfortunately," Prince Mong-Ku said, "it is not a favorable update. Worse, it is sufficiently serious as an issue that I decided that we really had to meet at least briefly. My apologies for interrupting all of you. There is also the small matter of the Namestone, which mayhaps is the same as the *Presentia* issue. I call on Dark Shadow to tell us what is going on."

Dark Shadow shifted uncomfortably in his chair. "I did what was specified in our previous meeting. I implanted a Marik Marcher-Guardian in Monsieur Poulenc, tagged the Guardian to trigger when confronted with Emily Tattersall, and ensured that when it attacked Tattersall it would at the same time disembody Poulenc. There is surely no more ghastly death than the disembodiment that Poulenc richly deserved. I also lifted all the books on Poulenc's desk, to confirm that none of them was a copy of the *Presentia* in disguise. The books not meant for Tattersall have gone to their legal owners. However, the outcome of our trap was less favorable than we might have preferred."

"What could go wrong?" Plasmatrix asked. "Rather, what went wrong, since I see where this discussion is heading." She quietly wished that other Lords would get to the point rather than going on forever and a day.

"Everything," Dark Shadow said. "Poulenc is alive. After being disembodied, he was rescued. Tattersall is alive and well. The Marcher-Guardian was destroyed. Those constructs are very difficult to replace. The volumes Poulenc was selling Tattersall, the day she was to perish, are reasonably well known. Seizing those volumes will not hinder Tattersall substantially."

"Her backers, you mean?" Solara said. "This wisp of a girl surely can't be reading all these things."

"Let me try again," Plasmatrix said. "How did any of these things go wrong? Why is Poulenc alive?" Marcher-Demons were highly lethal mentalic constructs. Only rarely did one target the wrong victim before it returned to its nest.

"Monsieur Poulenc was disembodied," Dark Shadow answered. "Unfortunately, Paris has first-rate medical emergency services. Within a few minutes a competent mentalic surgeon, a Doctor Cadoudal of the Polytechnique, was brought to the scene. With assistance, he was able to re-embody Poulenc. As to how Monsieur Poulenc survived several minutes of disembodiment, it appears that Miss Tattersall among other things is a powerful mentalist. She first killed the Marcher-Guardian via the classical overload method, and then kept Poulenc's body and mind functional until a mentalic surgeon could arrive."

"For our records," Archivist Green asked, "have you been able to determine who else the hypothetical Miss Tattersall is? We see that she is a persona. I did do a thorough library search on this name. There does not appear to be such a person, except as connected with these events. Mentalists strong enough to kill a Marcher-Guardian rapidly are uncommon."

"As I said," Dark Shadow answered, "almost everything went wrong. Tattersall was then almost arrested by the French State Police, by a Captain du Blois. She declined to be arrested. I gather that she is extremely angry with whoever tried to kill her favorite book dealer. I am not sure whether she simply failed to notice that she was the target of the attack, or whether she viewed our attempt to be so feeble as not to be worthy of notice, but she was primarily annoyed that her book-buying efforts would be interrupted."

"What happened to the arrest attempt?" Solara asked.

"It appears that Tattersall cooperated completely with Police questioning," Dark Shadow answered, "until du Blois asked that she accompany him to the State Police offices. She declined. At some point, she manifested as Eclipse: Cerulean aura. Hover above ground. She has her own persona tune, quite distinct. Alternatively, she pretended to be the Bearer, and fooled du Blois. In either case, du Blois withdrew his demand that she submit to arrest."

"We think Tattersall is telling the truth about being Eclipse? Why?" Plasmatrix asked. "As opposed to being an extremely good bluffer?"

"I was able to question Monsieur Poulenc privately," Dark Shadow answered. "He does not remember or know that he was being questioned. Disguised as a reporter, I was able to question his daughter verbally…she also has good screens. Miss Tattersall has exactly the same aura and theme music as the aura and music of the Bearer. She also killed a Marcher-Demon, something no fleaweight could do. The challenge is that Miss Tattersall does not resemble any of the images anyone has seen of the Bearer. She is a half foot or more too short, must be considerably too light, must have been wearing a truly uncomfortable set of corsets to disguise her figure, and seems to be shyer than the real Eclipse. I used the Art to invade Doctor Cadoudal's dreams. Cadoudal had deleted his extraneous memories, but failed to mask his impression that Tattersall is not as old as she appeared to be. Indeed, while dream-walking is imprecise, he thought she was much younger than might have been anticipated. He confirmed that she is a very powerful mentalist, though not very skillful. Unfortunately, he is a highly ethical mentalic surgeon, and systematically deleted from his memories all facts he learned from Miss Eclipse outside of a proper physician-patient relationship."

Prince Mong-Ku looked up at the ceiling. What had appeared to be a simple assassination was going rapidly downhill. Assassinations could usually be relied upon to be effective solutions, but this time matters were becoming unfortunate. So far no terrorist organization likely to claim responsibility had been dragged into the event.

"As an alternative, it seems that the Bearer has another gift," Archivist

Green said. "From the descriptions and mentalic recordings, it appears that Eclipse can change her shape. That's actually quite unusual. Assuredly the actual Bearer is a woman of Lady Solara's height and build. This Emily Tattersall is much different. Short. Slimly structured. Of course, one could imagine that Emily Tattersall is a persona of relatively limited gifts, and the real Bearer lent Tattersall (or, worse, engifted Tattersall) with the gifts that Tattersall displayed."

"Very elaborate set of hypotheses," Colonel Pi said. "Isn't there something simpler? If she's a mentalist, couldn't she simply have convinced everyone that she was this young lady, when she's someone else? Mentalics against the electronic cameras would be more challenging, but not impossible. Mayhaps she has invisibility and optical projection, so no one actually saw her. People only saw a projected image."

"I think it's kind of obvious," Starsmasher said, "who has the gifts to pull this off. The Silver General. If she's this Eclipse person, then she has her hands on the Namestone. Except why would she be looking for a copy of the *Presentia*? She must have a copy. For that matter, why would the Silver General want or be allowed by the Martyr to take the Namestone? The Martyr disapproves of people like her."

"The Namestone doesn't add anything useful to the Silver General's powers," Plasmatrix said. "She is optoelectronic, and still has no way to stand up to a photonic quantum teleport attack. If she gets in our way, we can jam most of her brain. In point of fact, she has in recent millennia stayed almost entirely out of our way -- sorry about Featherstonehaugh, Solara. I don't like any of these explanations, but can't say that I have better one."

"Dark Shadow," Prince Mong-ku asked, "When will another assassination attempt be made?"

"When?" Dark Shadow asked. "When someone finds her for me. How will we do this? She is now on her guard. The Emily Tattersall persona will assuredly never be seen again. We did get her reading list. She may be reduced to stealing rather than buying copies of the books she wants. Poulenc had a respectable set of teleport screens, which she went over rather than through when she said good-by to du Blois, but many rare book collections are less well protected than Poulenc's. Alternatively, she does some mentalic trick, and some book monger has no idea that Eclipse appeared and bought the books that she did." Plasmatrix shifted uncomfortably in her chair. It would be nice if someday Dark Shadow's attitude would become 'when we find her' and not 'when you find her for me', but that change might need more decamillennia yet.

"And assassinating Poulenc?" Mong-ku asked.

"Our usual custom has been that book mongers who only failed to tell us about a customer and who then connive to survive an assassination attempt—that's actually happened a few times—are assumed to have been adequately warned," Dark Shadow answered. "Are you proposing to change the rules?"

"No. Mayhaps we should advance to the second topic, which is now the same as the first topic. There is a search for the Bearer," Prince Mong-Ku said.

"You guys did stick me with this job," Starsmasher said. He shifted in his chair, pausing to shake out the loose folds and ruffles of his pale yellow silk shirt. "Though my talents will only be significant if we manage to find this Eclipse person, and need to persuade her through rational means also known as megaviolence to hand over the stone. So where is she? More important, where is it? These is the amusing possibility that she gave it away, dropped it into a volcano, or something even more imaginative. Nonetheless, someone must have the Namestone. If so, where are they keeping it? A reconstitutor scan failed to find it. There are ways to hide things from such a search, mostly by being somewhere else, but the search found nothing."

"I have inquired of the Holy Order of Gow," Archivist Green said. "Across Earth and the eleven planets, they have by far the most extensive set of masked repositories. They're usually quite secretive, to put it mildly, but they agreed to make a careful search to see if this Eclipse had abused their hospitality by hiding something, namely the Namestone, in one of the Great Libraries."

"Aren't we relying on the League to handle the search?" Plasmatrix asked. "I thought we'd agreed on that last time."

"In that case," Prince Mong-Ku said, "there has been no progress. It's not they aren't trying, well, some of them are trying, but they have no idea where to look."

"Only some are trying?" Colonel Pi asked.

"Most. America and Austria-Hungary think the Namestone belongs to the bearer, and are not cooperating," Solara said. "The Satsuma Domain, which appears to mean the entire Japanese Empire, thinks catching the Bearer is too dangerous. The envoys of the Tibetan Lamanate were happy to recommend that we should cast off our attachments to mere material property in favor of meditation. How this lets us deal with those who may not be named remains unclear to me. Many countries are vigorously looking, with the obvious intent of keeping the Namestone for themselves. However, there are huge rewards, so there are vast private efforts to find Miss Eclipse."

"Private takes a while to get off the ground," Colonel Pi said. "We are the world's leading experts on patience. There is a third matter."

"Yes?" Prince Mong-Ku asked. It would have been so convenient to be told in advance, just once, about another agenda item. Given the source, that was almost certainly some highly unpleasant agenda item.

"Something has been probing the Leviorkianu towers," Colonel Pi said. "All of them. Whatever it was, it was too delicate for our burglar alarm systems. I only detected the traces well after the fact. And then something happened, once, to the Radthninu tower." Around the table, interest became focused. "I didn't figure all this out until just before this meeting, or I would have told you earlier. It's as though whatever was done ended before it started. The traces suggest someone took an inventory of contents, and before then tried to teleport out an inventoried ideon."

"Teleport an ideon?" Dark Shadow asked. "I've never heard such a thing, and I should know." He looked down at the table, lost in thought.

"If that's what it was, it failed completely. The traces were only outside the tower walls," Colonel Pi said.

"Should we blame the League of Terran Justice?" Starsmasher wondered aloud. "Their recent book? They are getting close to what we have hidden away. If it escapes, our plans for this historical cycle implode."

"The plans only become uncertain," Prince Mong-Ku corrected. "If the return is soon, the trap is still in working order, and gone forever will be its target." Plasmatrix frowned but bit her tongue. "You disapprove?" Mong-Ku asked her.

"These are nice people. They are often good people. It will be a shame when we sweep them all away, so once again a civilization is faded into the depths of time, its cities and achievements turned to the underment of a palimpsest on which we by and by inscribe a new world culture," Plasmatrix answered. "I agree I see no alternative to sweeping away at the golden moment this billion people and all their proud towers. The Silver General? She thinks we should all be executed for crimes against history. But there's no sign she knows what the Radthninu Tower is."

"It's unfortunate," Mong-Ku said, "that the current world civilization will, incidentally, be obliterated, but that destruction is for the greater good. Besides, a few more repetitions of cultural obliteration and we will at long last be finished. Just in time for the next Polar Conjunction, precisely as was anticipated strange eons ago, after which we may summon and open the Radthninu tower."

"I can think of one person," Solara said, "who might know how to open the lock without a key. I should chat Morgan up."

This was such a beautiful day, Prince Mong-Ku thought. Absolutely everything was doing poorly. Morgan Le Fay was very good at minding her own business, staying out of our way, and assisting the Holy Order. Did we really need to have Solara rile her up? A riled Morgan Le Fay was definitely not a person he wanted to meet. No, a riled Morgan Le Fay was not someone world civilization wanted to meet, not that they would be doing so for very long other than from the afterlife. Mayhaps it was time to move to Otherearth, for all that they were having a planetary war. Otherearth had no almost personas, almost no access to foamspace, and all sides had good fission suppressors, so their war would be far less destructive than a war here.

"You should do this," Prince Mong-Ku said. "But in my opinion it would be much better to enhance the protective systems around the Towers. Is there disagreement?"

Chapter Twenty-Four

Kniaz Kang's Marco Polo
North Cosmopolis, Washington

I was more than a bit shaken up by what happened in Paris. If someone had seen through one of my disguises, how many other disguises had they seen through? But if I followed that out to the end, I would spend all my time hiding under my bed. It was very much time to re-appear at Kniaz Kang's for breakfast and have pleasant conversations with normal people.

The weather report for North Cosmopolis, which through some historical peculiarity is well inland and north of the great port city of Cosmopolis, said heavy snow had ended. I carefully checked my Jim disguise and slipped into a long winter coat and insulated gloves. It was a bit hard to hide that Jim teleports, not unless he always walked in to Kniaz Kang's from the woods at the edge of town, but his other gifts could perfectly well stay hidden. I wouldn't be cold, but Jim pretended that he needed a winter outfit. To make life more complicated, I also had my very separate Joe Cartwright disguise, for use on the other side of the continent, my Emily disguise, my Granny Agatha disguise, and several more, each kept in its own closet.

A complicated loop of teleport jumps brought me to line of sight behind the restaurant and its registered teleport landing pads. The pads were circles of pavement, each three yards across, laid out like giant flowers on each side of a spinal walk. They had thoughtfully all been shoveled already. I'd have to thank Teranike, who did a remarkable amount of heavy lifting for a somewhat minimal salary. Of course, when you are a Polarian, and a decade older than I am, you view shoveling many cubic yards of snow to be light physical training.

My laser pointer was at hand. I tagged the rearmost pad, saw the green light come up on the adjoining service post, and teleported the last hundred yards. Yes, I could have skipped tagging, but then someone else might have teleported to the same landing point at the same time, with unpleasant results, at least for them, me being one hundred per cent at fault. This way, any reasonable person would check the interweb, find the point was momentarily in use, and wait until it was free.

I was halfway down the walk when the scarlet warning lights came up on all six pads. Not five seconds later, what had to be half the Washington State

Persona League appeared all around me. I froze, about to panic. Fight or flight both sounded really bad, when all I wanted was someone else's cooking. Then I realized that none of them had force fields up.

"Hi!" That was Lady Barbara, their lead mentalist, her garb the traditional mentalist dark green trim on cream. "Sorry if we startled you. We're just here for an early breakfast."

"Hi," I mumbled. "Not a problem." I moved very quickly down the walk, conscious that a stack of heavy-duty personae were a few paces behind me. OK, I had seen them eating here before. We were far enough from Seattle that there was a shortage of tourist gawkers. Kniaz Kang did not allow reporters on his premises. He'd sued one large New York newspaper into bankruptcy over that point. Other newspapers had taken the hint.

I pulled the side door open and held it for the Washington League. It's just what a polite twelve year old boy would do for a group of adults. I had also lined them up in front of me in case things got violent. If their conversation was staged, it was really well rehearsed. Half of the guys were discussing the Seattle Base Ball Nines team and its perennial contest with one of the Boston teams, the Boston Doves. Most of the women were tightly focused on Tacoma's Amazon League professional lacrosse team, the Starhawks. That's women's lacrosse, not the much less vigorous men's game. Women's lacrosse is technically not a blood sport. Optimistically speaking. Being charitable. The rules say so. Honest. They really do. I looked. The Washington Team must've all ordered in advance, because they cut through to their private dining room.

I reached the head of the line. Kniaz Kang nodded at me. "You are too late to see her, Jim. She left already," Kang announced. "But Dorothy and Teranike are still in the South Greenhouse, part way through their meals."

"Her?" I asked.

"Her," Kang announced with a not-quite-joking frown. "Your new girlfriend. Your height? Copper hair? Really pretty? Enough of a persona that she wore light trousers and a lighter blouse and vest, no coat at all, despite the weather? Paid for very little breakfast in good coin? After she cleaned my parking lot? And asked where she should sit, you being her boyfriend?"

"Oh," I managed. "Her. My girlfriend. We must have been on different schedules." In particular, my girlfriend schedule is for obvious reasons extremely blank, likely to stay that way for some years yet, and so far as I can tell at the moment going to stay blank forever. Girlfriend? What was going on here? "Now I'd better make up to her, right?"

"That would indeed be very wise," Kang said. "She is clearly a powerful persona, not someone you want angry with you, especially when you are not carrying your slingshot."

"Thank you. My usual, please?" I asked. I had forgotten the slingshot. That was very careless of me. "And an extra side of sausage? Is she really powerful? I can't tell."

"You should eat more," Kang announced. "You are looking thin. But your parents are happy with my cooking." He had a handwritten note, claiming to be from my mother, approving of my having breakfast here. It was a very complimentary note in its discussion of Kang's cooking. I should know. I wrote it myself. "You can't read the runes on her garb?" he asked. "Don't all children study High Atlanticean anymore?"

"I don't think so, sir," I answered. "And an extra side of mushroom hash?" I added. His hash is perfect. And I mayhaps distracted him from a line of questioning I did not want to face. He smiled approvingly.

"A few minutes," Kang said. "Don't let the two girls nag you too much about missing your girlfriend. I hope the runes on her vest exaggerate. You should ask her if they are true. Politely. During a warmly romantic moment. When you are sure she will want to stay."

I fled to the South Greenhouse. Dorothy and Teranike both smiled when they saw me. They were usually really interesting to chat with. I was lucky they both put up with me. Being able to read High Atlanticean helped. Dorothy was studying it in school, but had only limited sources for the kennings. Mine were much better. Mum was not exactly a native speaker, but she had lived in Atlanticea for decades. Of course, Dorothy couldn't remember I'd lent her the two interesting devices, so I couldn't collect on that favor.

"Teranike," I opened, "thanks a lot for shoveling the teleport pads." She nodded primly.

"It is my duty, Jim" she answered. "And I had help."

"We missed seeing you, Jim," Dorothy said. "How is Silk supposed to save North Cosmopolis without her trusty sidekick?"

"I was sick, Dorothy," I answered. That was true. Being beaten almost to death, among the other things that had happened to me, does count as 'sick'.

"You didn't tell us that you had a girlfriend," Teranike sipped her coffee. "You really didn't. And she is very pretty. Should we be jealous?" She folded her hands under her chin and grinned at me.

"Spindrift is a real doll," Dorothy agreed, "and very sharp. She knew a stock of Atlanticean kennings I've never heard. I only found a few of them on the interweb after I knew the answer."

"She must really like you," Teranike observed. "She wasn't the least upset that you were so late that you missed her. In fact, she sounded like she knew when you were going to be here, and knew that your schedules didn't overlap."

"If one of my boyfriends missed a date," Dorothy said, "he would apologize. Abjectly. While on his knees. Groveling. Or I would have words. Pointed words."

"I didn't know she was going to be here," I answered. "I really didn't." That was totally true. After all, I didn't know Spindrift existed. In fact, I still didn't know that she existed. This had to be a deep practical joke.

"Have you worked up the nerve to kiss her yet?" Dorothy asked. "Or are you just holding hands?"

"For sure, no," I answered. Actually No!No!No!No!No!No! Especially not if this alleged person is a girl. I'm fairly sure that when I grow up I'll find that I'm not inclined that way, though it's way too early to tell for sure, and I might be wrong. I rapidly considered making a safe escape, say to someplace far outside the moon's orbit in one teleport jump. "Guys?" I continued, "Was she really a persona?"

"You really haven't kissed her?" Dorothy asked. I shook my head. "Or were you doing other things? She's your height. And you have nice curly hair for her to hang onto."

"Hang on to?" I tried playing dumb. Other? What did she think we had been doing? It sounded ...alarming. Apparently my disguise works. Dorothy really does think I'm a boy. I considered alternatives. Just because no one has ever teleported out of the galaxy before, in one jump, doesn't mean that I shouldn't try to become the first.

"She is a persona," Dorothy said. "She teleports. I think it was a teleport."

"Surely, she is a persona," Teranike said. "I was shoveling the front walk. She appeared out of nowhere a safe height above the parking lot. I was shoveling while the blizzard -- well, that feeble breeze that Americans call a blizzard -- was still blowing. She was wearing much lighter clothing than you are now, Jim, with sigils I am told are in Atlanticean on her vest, and was obviously not cold when she stopped to talk. She turned into a cloud of lights, floated across the parking lot, and when she was done the pavement was clear. She was even polite enough to leave me the walks for my slight exercise."

"Oh," I managed. "I've never seen her in garb before." True. In fact, I've never seen her at all. "What did the sigils say?" I asked, trying to steer the conversation onto safer ground.

"She is The Dagger of Time," Teranike answered, "whatever that is. She explained the kennings for Dorothy. I didn't get to ask her to explain the reference; she left first." So much for safer ground. The Dagger of Time? That was really seriously alarming, if unlikely, but it matched what Kniaz Kang had said to me. Then Dorothy showed me a page in her notebook, all in this person's handwriting. Yes, those were the kennings for Time's Dagger.

"You're sure she's not your girlfriend? You aren't just being shy about it? What were you two doing? When you two were alone, I mean," Dorothy asked. Hiding under the table sounded unlikely to help at this point. "We talked for a while. She seemed to be absolutely everything a boy your age would want." I decided I could be too cowardly to think about what Dorothy was including in 'everything', let alone 'doing' or 'want'. "And she very much likes you." I began to wonder if Medico had gone astray, so that I was running a really high fever and hallucinating the conversation. Becoming delusional made more sense than the other alternatives.

Wang arrived with my breakfast. The orange juice was always absolutely fresh. Also, I did not have to talk while my mouth was full.

"Jim," Dorothy asked, "What am I missing? She seemed to be such a nice person. Is something wrong with her?"

"It's just that, ummh," I thought for a moment, "I don't know who she is. I'm sure I've never met her."

"Huh?" Dorothy said.

"Never met her. I don't know who she is," I explained.

"She knew who you are." Dorothy was quite emphatic.

"In that case, when I meet her, I should ask her out on a date." I took a bite of the all-grain toast. Kang made his own bread. It was excellent. "I could take her out to breakfast…but I don't know what sort of food she likes."

"To judge from the way she finished her meal, she must be quite hungry." Teranike was very matter of fact.

"Or mayhaps I could ask her to see an Edison picture…but I have no idea which Edisons she's seen." Now I had boxed myself in. My knowledge of local teenage tastes in Edison films was a bit limited. A western? A comedy?

"Might be a problem," Dorothy said, "if you choose something and she doesn't like it. That would be a very dragging two hours. Besides, something where you can talk might be better."

"Wait, you said she flies. And teleports." I needed to propose something harmless. Of course, I had no idea how strong her gifts were, though ignoring the weather was impressive. Flying over the parking lot and clearing it was significantly impressive.

"You might wish, Jim, to choose a destination from which you can leave without her," Teranike said, "Depending on her for transportation might be hazardous, if she is annoyed and dumps you wherever."

"Good point," I said politely. OK, if you are a military officer you plan for the bad outcomes.

"Jim," Dorothy asked, "am I supposed to pretend that I have not figured out that you can teleport? And fly?"

That approached being impolite, but she was trying to be helpful. "Was that obvious?"

"Coming in from the forest side? Thanking Teranike for shoveling the teleport pads? Sometimes not leaving footprints in the snow?" Dorothy shrugged.

"Yes to both." She was observant. Besides, plenty of people, like the whole State Team, had seen me on the teleport walkway.

"So you could take her to an exotic destination for breakfast. Seattle. Cosmopolis. Boston." Teranike nodded. Teranike had tried to sound encouraging.

"I know," I said. "Someplace we can talk. No money involved." I'm rich, but Joe pretends he has to watch his pennies. "I don't know what altitude she can handle. But for sure we can go cloud-diving."

"Cloud-what?" Teranike sounded baffled.

"What! Jim! What are you thinking? No, never mind, I'm afraid I can guess what you're thinking, and you've never met her yet." Dorothy was not quite angry, but close.

Now it was my turn to be baffled.

"Why did that come across wrong?" I stared at Dorothy. "Did you want to go diving with me?" Dorothy gave me an indignant look. "Teranike, in cloud diving you find tall clouds, just at dawn or twilight, when they are full of color. You fly or teleport up to the top, or as high as you can go safely. You kill your flight field and fall through gold and pink toward the ground—or ocean; that's safer. You cue your flight field before you hit the ground. It's a lot of fun."

"It sounds like free-fall parachuting," Teranike said. "You fall, and close to the ground you trigger your parachute. Except, Jim, you can just fly back to the top and do it again, while I must put on a new parachute, climb into an airplane and wait to reach altitude again. But why, Dorothy, are you so upset? Surely you aren't afraid of heights. You showed me your photos of North Cosmopolis, the ones you took from so high the sky is black. Like the sky atop the Black Spire."

Dorothy mumbled something under her breath. "Jim, I suppose I have to ask. Have you ever had your talks with your parents, the ones about carrying on with girls?"

"Yes," I answered. Of course, in my case the main emphasis had been carrying on with boys, but that was a minor technical detail. "But what does that have to do with cloud-diving?"

"Ummh, have you ever heard anything about cloud diving?" Dorothy asked.

"Good flying practice. Fun. Is there an issue?" To my ears, this conversation was getting a bit strange.

"Cloud-diving," she blurted out. "If you went cloud-diving with a girl, suddenly carrying on with her would become incredibly tempting. It just would."

"Is this supposed to be undesirable?" Teranike asked.

"Of course it is!" Dorothy stammered.

"American mating customs are very strange," Teranike commented bemusedly. "By Polarian standards, anyway. I listened to a discussion of your mating customs, while I was visiting Boston. The speaker seemed displeased with the world."

"That's Boston." Dorothy snorted. "They remember Leviorkianu propriety, just the way it was when Boston was founded two thousand years ago, and haven't changed since. If they could get away with it, they'd make girls wear dresses. Dresses that hid their ankles. And only speak to boys when they had two chaperones. Preferably armed chaperones. They're impossible prudes."

Of course, realistically speaking, I am too young for this issue to be even vaguely interesting, but Mum hadn't said anything about cloud-diving with boys.

"Ummh. No." I finally managed to break into the conversation. "That's weird. I've never heard anything like that. So if you went cloud diving with your boyfriend, you might..."

"Jim, don't change the topic." She was blushing. Suddenly I remembered the guy she'd been bringing to breakfast regularly last fall, the one who was reasonably bright, quite fit, and to my eyes obviously had flight as a gift.

"Sorry," I said. I wasn't sure she was speaking from experience. It sounded like an excuse for something that the cloud-divers were going to do anyway. "But if the girl has the gifts to cloud-dive, her gifts mean she can't get into trouble that way."

"If you ask Spindrift to go cloud diving, you might be misunderstood. So don't." She was very firm again. "Let's say, only go if there are a bunch of people, to keep you on your best behavior."

"OK. I won't." That had to be the strangest claim I had ever heard about using a gift. "Whoever she is. You aren't teasing me about cloud-diving, are you?"

"No!" Dorothy was very emphatic.

"There's something going on here," I said. "You really met someone who said they were my girlfriend? Really? Word of honor?"

Dorothy looked baffled.

"Yes," Teranike answered, "Though she spoke strangely, as though Modern English was not her normal language. I pledge this by the Lake of Silver Fire". That settled that. She was a good Polarian, and had just invoked the Goddess-Empress Herself as her bond.

"Thank you," I said. "Teranike, I apologize if I sounded like I was doubting you."

"I know your figures of speech," Teranike answered. "No insult was meant or received. But that explains the verb tenses," Teranike observed. "Sometimes when she spoke of you, Jim, it was 'I will be his girl friend'. 'He will have met me.' Future tense. Your universe allows time travel, doesn't it?"

"Isn't time travel impossible?" Dorothy asked. "You need too much power."

"Don't both universes allow time travel?" I said. I really should have bit my tongue. I ate another slice of sausage, made with a little tempura sauce in the recipe.

"Mine does not," Teranike answered. "The complicated answer is that we have an equation with a zero in it, in a place where you have a number. The accurate answer is that the Goddess-Empress ordered the laws of nature to forbid time travel, so it is forbidden." Dorothy looked politely doubtful about the second explanation. Most Americans find it difficult to believe that

Polarians all think that their Empress is a goddess. I wondered if Teranike's claim was true. I was not about to tell her that there is a way -- which I do not know in detail -- to reprogram the Planck volume computers that determine all natural laws. Usually they get rebooted very quickly by the rest of the universe. If you are very clever, you hack the Planck computers, and they stay hacked over a small region, so locally you have changed the laws of nature. The number of people who know about hacking Planck computers is really small. Mum was not happy that I had found out that you could do it, even though I promised not to tell anyone that I knew.

"Did she say when we will have met?" I asked. Two thousand years from now sounded like a really good alternative. Two million years sounded even better.

"She said today and meeting were a few days apart," Dorothy said. "Except we also talked about other things. She really knew a lot. But she had this odd way of speaking. She'd say two events were four days apart, this was the Namestone being taken and that was a League Peace Executive meeting, but was confused about which thing happened first. If you did lots of time travel, you might be confused about that."

"She said she went up to Arborday tower to watch the sunrise," Teranike said, "after helping me shovel. Except I was up at sunrise, the clouds closing in. The snow started falling after a really pretty dawn, so she had before and after reversed."

"OK", I said, "Mayhaps I have a girl friend, and she does time travel. Mayhaps she teaches me how. I wait five years. Then I can come back here and date both of you." OK, I had a chance to firm up the 'boy' aspect of the disguise.

"Personas don't date their sidekicks!" Dorothy blurted. "Well, it sounds better than 'I already have too many guys chasing me'. Even though I think you'll grow up to be better than most all of them. Not that I don't like you, and I really appreciate all the help you've been with Atlanticean, mentioning which I'd better finish eating and get to class on time, but dating someone who is twelve and seventeen at the same time sounds confusing."

"I really do appreciate the thought," Teranike said, "truly it was well meant, but you're the same age as my youngest son."

Now I had really put my foot in my mouth. "I'm sorry, Teranike, I apologize," I managed. "You never said you had children or were married or whatever it is that Polarians do."

"This was supposed to be a very short trip to your world," she said, "completely safe. So now I very much miss my children, they must miss me, and with the OtherEarth War I'll be here for a long time. Or until we win. If I ever get back, and they haven't died in the fighting, my children may be almost strangers. If you want to come back when you're my age, Jim, you will need to wait forty years and then travel forty years back in time." I'd been figuring her to be in her early twenties. She was actually over fifty, and showed almost none of it.

"Jim," Dorothy said, "I have to run, classes, but the girl, she said she would be your girlfriend *until the end of days* and *she approaches on swift and silent wings*. She was talking about her, not you."

"Thank you," I managed. Dorothy had slipped two phrases in High Atlanticean into her answer. We both understood those phrases. At least, I did, and Dorothy sounded as though she did, too. If true, they were terrible words, at least if the girl friend I have never met knew what those words mean.

"Have to go," Dorothy said, slipping a tip under her plate. She looked embarrassed and headed for the door. She must not have known how old Teranike is, either, let alone that she had a family. Either that, or Dorothy thought she actually did like Jim, except he's a bit too young, and was afraid she might have hurt his, well, my, feelings. I didn't know about Teranike, so why should Dorothy?

"I really didn't know," I said. "I thought you were only a bit older than Dorothy."

"There is no issue," she answered, setting her hands on the table. "It's just, I am here, and they are there."

"I'm truly sorry." I reached out and took her hand in mine. I'm not sure how Polarian customs would treat that, but it seemed the right thing to do. We held hands, just for two moments, and then she leaned back in her chair.

Her eyes sparkled. "Once upon a time, from young men not much older than you are, Jim, saying you thought I was almost Dorothy's age would have been warm praise. That's important to remember. You say nice things about people, that aren't too exaggerated, and they like it. Half of my seeming age is absolutely rigorous physical conditioning. My women of the Silver Legion do their morning run, and their weight training, and as their Captain I lead them. The other half is why Polaria has a war with the rest of the world. Some of us live a long time. The world wants our secrets."

"You don't just share?" I asked. "I don't know much about Otherearth." I did, however, recognize the phrase 'Silver Legion'. If Teranike was telling the truth, and I was very sure that she was, Teranike was not some random Polarian soldier, she was the commander of their Goddess-Empress's personal guards.

"Share antiagathics? It's like your world's Namestone. And now you will hear how a Polarian thinks. I hope I won't hurt your feelings," she said.

"Otherearth is not like us," I said. "The English King, once upon a time, ordered the tide not to come in, but it came in anyway. Your Empress…Goddess-Empress…you just said she can tell laws of nature what to do."

"King Canute," she said. "He said afterward that he should have asked Morgan Le Fay to stop the tides. He knew that would have worked. He was right. Unless she turned him into a turnip instead. In any event, so far as we can tell, the Namestone does mind control. It also does other things, like transmutation and atomic rearrangement, but it does mind control. That would work poorly on Otherearth. Mentalics don't travel any distance. But a mind control machine, to our eyes, is an abomination, something so evil it must be destroyed. See, I said you would not like my point of view."

"Actually," I answered, "I agree with you completely about mind control machines." I was not quite up to telling her I had a mind control machine on my desk. To be precise, I had on my desk the mind control abomination she was describing.

"Once upon a time, the Lake of Silver Fire, the Goddess's Avatar Herself, asked if we could send volunteers to Atlantis, to Gaea Atlanticea, to thread the Maze, take the Namestone, and destroy it." Teranike now sounded like someone's mom. "This was while Gaea Atlanticea was still a country. We were surprised that the Lake of Silver Fire would ask us to start a war. There were volunteers to risk the Maze. The answer, though, was that we knew no way to destroy the Namestone if we happened to capture it. We could not guard it as well as the Martyr did. We had to leave the Namestone with the Martyr. Sharing long life is like taking the Namestone. It's enormously dangerous to the recipient. So we refuse to share our secret."

"To destroy the Namestone, you take it to the core of the sun, and wait for it to overheat," I answered. Mayhaps I should not have revealed what I knew.

"And you need the actual starcore, not a feeble transmutation bomb," Teranike remarked. "Our aircraft…flying to the core of the sun would be outside their flight envelopes."

"Flying to the starcore is dangerous. Wait," I said. "Spindrift? All in white? Paneled vest with Atlanticean runes? Dorothy would have recognized them? I have heard of her. Top-line persona, appeared from nowhere a few months ago, seen all along the Pacific Rim. Except no one ever described the sigils. If it's the same person and not a spin-off."

"Spin-off?" Teranike asked. "Another custom we do not have."

"People who are not a famous persona, but have similar gifts," I said. "Usually much weaker. So they take the same persona name, and make similar garb. And then there are the cosplayers, who take the garb but have none of the gifts." I went back to my breakfast. The hash was almost perfect, but better if I ate it before it cooled. The scrambled eggs with onions and little bits of ham and mushroom were perfect. They always are.

"Oh," she said, "like all the Eclipses?" She paused to take another swallow of coffee. "I wondered why there were so many. Thank you for explaining."

I did not quite fall out of my Jim persona, but it was close. "All the Eclipses?" I choked. "Isn't there only one?"

"There were like twenty," she answered. "Before the Namestone vanished. Now there are hundreds. Hadn't you heard?"

"I was really sick," I answered. "I'm well now, but I missed all this."

She pulled her RadioBell from its holster, did something, and set it where I could see it. Then she thumbed through a string of photos. I could tell. It was going to be very easy to disguise myself so that no one recognized me. All the Eclipses looked nothing like me, not at all. The photos were gold-blonde women, a decade older than me, most of them not so athletic. The gold-blonde hair was very gold. Their garb made them look, how shall I put it, top-heavy in front. Especially the ones who were wearing garb that was so tight that it looked like it was painted on. I hoped the wearers were weatherproof, or in the tropics, because otherwise for many of them frostbite of the navel was going to be an issue.

"As you said, Teranike, all the Eclipses. Every one," I answered.

"Those were the conservatively dressed ones. The ones wearing clothing rather than the Eclipse sigil as body paint or a tattoo," she said. I considered where the tattoo would go, shuddered, and decided I could very definitely do without. "Some boys your age would find those Eclipses to be truly fascinating."

"I hope the real Eclipse is not jealous," I said, finishing another piece of rye toast. "She could get really angry." Well, she could, except she would be too busy laughing her head off.

~~~~~

When I returned home, my outside-facing computer reported that I had received a message from Jean-Marie Poulenc, heavily encoded and passed through the dark web. I say 'heavily encoded', but in fact anyone who broke the code would find a completely innocent books-for-sale message, complete with several illustrations from Henfrere. There was a second coded message inside the first, very short, and buried in the digitization noise in the Henfrere illustrations. Jean-Marie had books for me, and proposed meeting me on a hill outside Paris. She would be affecting to be meeting her boyfriend for a picnic, but he would arrive later. The timing was tight. I had to leave almost immediately.

Not without some trepidation, I teleported to the hill described in Mme. Poulenc's message. I first reconnoitered it from a distance. I saw nothing out of place, but ambushes are supposed to be like that. You see nothing out of place until it is too late. However, I was in France, a country that wants to negotiate with me about getting their hands on the Namestone, so my arrival should be relatively safe.

There was Jean-Marie Poulenc, dressed in the mid-thigh ruffled dress proper Frenchwomen wear on formal picnics. It was the purest of whites, safe for someone who, while picnicking, would only be sitting in a proper chair on top of a carpet. Indeed, there were two chairs, the table, a carpet, and a large picnic basket. I wore the last of my Emily Tattersall dresses, which was soon to be reduced to ashes. I appeared a few feet off the ground, waved, and landed next to her.

"Mademoiselle Poulenc," I managed.
~~~~~

"Mademoiselle Tattersall," Jean-Marie said, "as you style yourself. My father is profoundly grateful to you. After all, you saved his life. He wishes he could cook for you one of his famous dinners, but realizes that he is now watched. Not by Frenchmen, because we are a civilized country, but by other people. Prussians, for example. If he were to cook for you, scarcely would have you begin with a slice of stilton on one of his home baked crackers than foreign persona would be coming through every window, and not to share his cooking, either. He cannot even search for the books you want, not without everyone in the world learning what you want to read. The last makes him truly sad.

"However, my father has a gift," Jean-Maria continued. "Not a large gift, but a useful gift. Except only rarely does it do anything."

"A gift?" I asked.

"Every so often, he simply knows which book a customer needs," she explained. "Not the book the customer says she wants, the book that actually suits her. And so my father has given me two books to give to you. He has done this before. For once I argued with him that it was the wrong book, that you might take offense or your feelings would be hurt or…mayhaps you are the wrong age." That was not a gift I knew. How could it possibly work?

"Jean-Marie," I said, "I'm delighted to have the books, in the spirit in which the gift was meant. He's thanking me for doing what I was taught to do. That's all that matters."

"In that case," Jean-Marie said, "I have here the books. They are by tradition given as a pair." She pulled from her picnic basket two books, neatly tied together, a copy each of the *Evangeline* and the *Phillipe*. "We think they have not been given tracking implants, but we are mere book mongers, not the State Secret Police."

I managed a warm smile. "Thank you! Please thank your father for me." I paused. "And he is right. These are something that no one else would think to give me." True. Mum had disappeared first. "After all, I may have solved the Maze, but I am also a woman." That was a slight exaggeration. I am not vaguely that old yet. "But I have ways of seeing inside, ways of seeing if anything has been added." I skipped that I was using ultravision. When I looked, I did not quite drop the books in surprise.

The *Evangeline* and the *Phillipe* are the actually-not-mythical books that French parents are said to give their teen-or-so-age children on relations with the other sex. Actually, it's more complicated than just 'other'. They are not the unpleasant, at least in part, discussions of clinical medical issues, but discussions on carrying on. As I keep saying, I am in Europe. Mum and I had had those woman-to-woman discussions, even if a fair part of it was Mum reminding me that people with really deep gifts grow up late, when they are years older than other people. Mum was worried that I'd see girlfriends growing up, while I wasn't yet, and get upset. After the fifth or sixth time she said it, I began to get bored with the message. There were certain ways in which Mum really didn't understand me. I don't care how someone else is. I like being me, just the way I am right now. Even if I don't see how to stay that way. Jean-Marie looked slightly concerned. Now I needed a face-saving line. What I had actually seen was quite different from what she would have expected. "I can see inside. Can boys actually do that?" I asked innocently. Well, sort of innocently.

She giggled. "When I was much younger, John-Michael and I tried successfully every…"

"Say no more." I interrupted. "Please say to your father exactly that 'I am truly grateful, because there are some presents you can only give, not sell.' But I must seem ungrateful and depart, before vast numbers of personae descend on us with hostile intent."

"Good-by, Emily. Be safe."

"Good-by also, Jean-Marie, and my best also to your boyfriend." With that I teleported away.

I was not going to give Jean-Marie the least clue that what she had given me was anything other than an *Evangeline* and a *Phillipe.* Some snoop would read her mind and find out, putting her life at grave risk. Ummh, no, ensuring her imminent death was more like it. However, under the covers and glued-together-at-the margins exterior of the books was a hollowed-out interior, inside which was a box made of very thin steel, inside of which was what very much appeared to be a copy of the *Presentia.* As I had said, it was indeed a gift you cannot sell. Not unless you want Solara to slag down the local county to send a message to your fellow book mongers. As to how Jules Poulenc hid his ownership of the volume, I can't imagine. Mayhaps he had another gift that he never mentioned, not even to his daughters. However, I now had a very interesting bit of reading material, as if I did not have enough already.

Chapter Twenty-Five

The Lafayette Laboratory
Compere Biological Sciences Building
Rogers Technological Institution
Late morning

There came a gentle tap of fingernails against the door. "Pardon me."

Graham Wilkinson looked up from his lab desk, to see a remarkably attractive young woman towering over him. "Yes? Can I help you?" he asked politely.

"I'm looking for the office of Professor Lafayette. The new room number I was given would put it between this lab and the next lab up the hall." The young lady had a slightly exotic accent with sharply crisp consonants. Graham didn't recognize it.

"Oh, that. The Professor keeps reminding Physical Plant that their room numbering wasn't fixed when the lab was rebuilt last Summer, so the room numbers aren't in order. Her office used to be here. She keeps saying that some things have never changed. However, her office is a couple doors further down," Graham said. He walked towards the door, realizing as he did that the young lady was his own substantial height and tending to block the doorway. If this is a guest of the Professor, he considered, I had best be scrupulously polite. He made gentle shooing motions with his hands. She gracefully backed so he had room to point down the corridor. "On the other side, the third door. Shall I take you?"

"No need. I see it now." The young lady smiled and turned away. Wilkinson backed towards his desk, realizing as he did that that new graduate student Michael Poniatowski was still outside the lab, staring down the corridor after the woman.

"Oh, man," Michael said quietly. "Who was that? Just between the two of us, she was hot enough to play Solara on the NBS Fall of Atlantis series."

"Michael?" Senior postdoctoral fellow Allison Moreland asked from her desk. "Hasn't anyone told you anything about this research group?"

"Dr. Moreland, ma'am, I just joined the group yesterday," Michael answered. His skin had turned distinct tinge of red. He very certainly had not expected any of the women in the research group to have overheard his whispered comment.

"Michael, dear, we need to have a little heart-to-heart talk. Chair." She pointed. He sat down, preparing for the deserved harsh words. "The reason the not-at-all-young lady looks like Solara is that she is Solara. Fortunately, since she undoubtedly heard every word of your remarks, not to mention whatever you were thinking, not that telepathy was needed to guess, she is still amused by her effect on young and impressionable men. However, I've met her before several times in the last five years, so when she knocked, I waved hello, and she waved me off and pointed at Graham. You wouldn't have heard the telepathic message, her saying that she might as well meet the new people in the lab. And, by the way, you should be at least try not to be surprised if another Lord of Eternity, an occasional member of the American Persona League, or a couple of Nobel laureates show up. That happens here all the time. Though the one time Plasmatrix knocked at the door, she lacked the courtesy to wear normal clothing, so I had to chew her out: This room is full of flammable solvents."

"What sort of research group is this? I thought this was just the best biochemistry group in the American Republic," Michael mumbled.

"It's that, too. But no one told you about Professor Lafayette? Her being the persona Sunssword?" Allison looked prayerfully up at the ceiling. Goddess, she considered, but new grad students are amazingly dumb.

"The Professor is a persona?" Michael asked innocently. "She can, I don't know, bake perfect brownies?"

"Ayup. Heavy duty combat type, and bunches of other things." Allison said. She considered tearing her hair out. Poniatowski seemed to be totally unaware of anything in the laboratory he was joining other than biochemistry. "Now having said all that, I gave you a list of papers to read and summarize, and I see from your emailed report that you actually read three of them, which is meritorious for one day, especially since your report made notes where you had to look things up and hadn't had time to do so yet. However, returning to the first paper, did you consider…"

~~~~~

Morgana Lafayette opened her office door, leaving Solara's about-to-knock hand in mid-air. "Always good to see you," Morgana said, her smile not passing above her lips. "Won't you please come in?"

"And good to see you also," Solara answered, not bothering to smile. Morgana pointed at a chair. Solara glanced around the office, then stepped very carefully around Morgana's beautiful center carpet, finally settling into a soft-padded arm chair.

"I allow that there is some reason for this visit," Morgana said.

"Indeed," Solara answered, "Assuming that we can manage to speak to each other civilly."

"I think we have always been polite to each other," Morgana answered. "So I shall affect that the Screaming Skull and Starsmasher took it into their
~~~~~

own heads to try to kill me, without the approval of The House That Is Forever."

"That was, well, you know how many years ago as well as I do," Solara answered.

"It was uncalled for. Even if they did fail completely." Morgana's smile vanished. "Though I see the Skull has finally recovered, as did your other housemates who tried similar things." And someday, she thought, except I am not interested in risking my life to start the fight, I am going to have to have it out with your Lordships, all of you, in what you hopefully will not recognize until it is too late for you is the fight to your deaths.

"Those were foolish errors. We're willing to let bygones be bygones. We'd even be happy to add you to the High Council, if you would only support our plans," Solara answered.

"Your plans are an abomination," Morgana snapped, "a crime against history, albeit one I have not found a way to prevent. So I'm working on changes that will survive what you are about to do, namely terminating the latest world civilization, not to mention the next several world civilizations. What actually brings you here?" No way to prevent it, she thought, without likely getting myself killed while failing. A shame that combat has never been my strong point.

Solara laced her fingers together. "A few matters of common interest," she said. "Someone in Greater Cambridge is doing things with fourth-order gifts. It's unheard of." She gestured. Above her fingertips appeared a map covered by a whirl of colored lines.

"Some days ago? From your map, in Medford?" Morgana asked. Solara nodded. Morgana looked more carefully at the map and time. "That was me, so you have no concern. I was unmaking what someone else had made, several years before." Solara's eyelids rose. "Someone, presumably not one of your people since you don't have a clue about it, put a minor but extremely powerful geas on a neighborhood. A completely pointless geas, telling people not to pry into someone's private -- I think -- persona."

"You think?" Solara sounded dubious. "It wasn't obvious?"

"There is a particular person. He has a persona. But I don't know if he counts the persona formally as his public or his private persona, or if he just has one persona. It appears to be his public persona. He used it in combat. But his garb was what boys that age typically wear: corduroys, hunting shirt, sneakers. Mayhaps he didn't have time to switch from private to public garb. That's why I said 'I think'. The geas made people incurious about him. They didn't wonder where he lived or how he could be contacted. He appeared to be using the same persona as his public and private personas, so you could recognize him on the street if you saw him, except for the geas."

"But people saw him, could recognize him…that's not very private," Solara said.

"As private as most of my research students," Morgana answered. "I don't see the point of the geas, which was very narrowly focused, very high-power, borderline fifth order, and held several buried traps. The traps were powerful, not subtle. I take it you don't know anything about this?"

"No," Solara answered. "It's hardly a secret; the House That Is Forever stays well away from that approach to getting our way. Find and smite works better than fourth order trickery. The geas wasn't your work?"

"No. Nor did I recognize the casting style," Morgana answered. Find and smite, indeed, she thought, but only if I ignore your meme thievery, not to mention the SkyVoice.

"Do I know the persona being protected?" Solara asked.

"Highly unlikely," Morgana answered. "Do you know any ten-year-olds whose shields will stand up to a Krell disruptor?"

"Ten?" Solara asked. "Any?" Solara shook her head.

"There are a few. His did." Morgana folded her hands prayerfully. "And the restrictions that the geas imposed? They were a very odd choice of protections, almost in the range 'why bother?' The one time he did anything with his gifts, that I know of, he nearly got himself killed by being very much for virtue and against vice. However, to answer your original question, the working you should have had no trouble identifying was assuredly mine."

"There is a second question," Solara said.

"Hopefully even less challenging that the first," Morgana said. How had Solara not recognized the casting as mine, she wondered? And what are the faint traces, the other castings that are not mine?

"The League of Terror and Injustice has published a book outlining its program," Solara said, "A book that should make no sense to normal readers."

"I'm absolutely astonished. A political group that issues political tracts. And they make no sense. What will we see next?" Morgana observed. "A politician who is not scrupulously honest?"

"Not like this one. The book is full of sentences with missing words. The missing words are the memes we have silenced. In each chapter are a series of sentences, gradually approaching a silent meme, and then there is a sentence with a blank where no word can exist," Solara said. "Here, look." She passed Morgana a piece of paper.

Morgana scanned the paper for a few seconds. "That's very clever. Someone is trying to sabotage your SkyVoice. Do you know who did it? Is it someone who knows, and is trying to subvert your little plot, or did someone actually deduce by this path what the forbidden thoughts are, even if they cannot think them?" Morgana was puzzled. Whoever did this was truly clever, and worth meeting if only he could be found.

"We were hoping you could tell us," Solara answered.

"I had not heard about this before. I'll have to buy a copy of the book." Morgana smiled.

"But I have a related final question." Solara ignored what Morgana had just said.

"Yes?" Morgana asked impatiently.

"Someone tried to teleport an ideon out of the Radthninu tower," Solara said. "I said 'tried'. You haven't heard of the League of Terror trying things like this, have you? They'd be way beyond their depth, but that doesn't meant they wouldn't try."

"Teleport a meme?" Morgana's eyebrows rose. "That's truly precious. Memes don't even have physical locations, your tower trap notwithstanding. First I've heard of this. The only encounter I've has with the League was one of their mouthpieces who showed up because he didn't like some of my research. He huffed and puffed, and went away," Morgana said.

"I take it that it wasn't you?" Solara asked.

"There are easy ways to remove the memes from the tower, if you don't mind dying." Morgana's voice dripped sarcasm with every syllable. "Taking fear, terror, and pain into yourself will do that. All you have to do is to go to the place where memes are solid material objects. There are quite enough people who think they have the needed access to transfinite power."

"Of course."

"It's all explained in the *Presentia*, that book you are afraid someone else will read." Morgana felt a distinct temptation to kill Solara here and now, and damn the consequences.

"Else? Read that abomination? Thank you, we tasked Plasmatrix with doing the reading." Solara grunted in disgust. "Did you go there?"

"Not I. Unless you have something else you want to ask, I have useful work waiting for me. Putting my sock drawer in order comes immediately to mind," Morgana said. Anything is better than dealing with their Lordships. It's a shame they keep such close contact with each other. Eradicating them one at a time would be a fine idea, if I could get away with it. Solara politely bowed her way out of the office. Morgana went back to work.

Twilight had come and gone. The sky was dark. Soon enough, Morgana thought, it would be time for dinner, and then back to writing. Her telephone rang, once and again. She passed a hand over its parastatic screen. "Good evening. Lafayette here," she said.

"Ah, Morgana." She had no trouble recognizing Patrick Wells' voice. Their paths certainly crossed often enough, though she was extremely careful to make sure that no one outside of his family noticed how often. Without those precautions, suspicions would rise and tongues would wag. She very definitely did not want anyone to think she was having an affair with the chair of the Institution Tenure Committee. With his classic Cantabridgian mindset, he would find the idea inconceivable, meaning he would not be careful about avoiding leaving the impression that such a thing was occurring. She had to cover for him.

"Good evening, Professor Wells," she answered. "How may I be of assistance this evening?"

"If I might pass by your office," he said. "There is a certain question I would prefer to discuss, entirely privately, and your office is more secure than mine."

"I'll be here all evening. Unless you want me to appear at your home as I did last week, blizzard notwithstanding?" Morgana's brows wrinkled. Surely his home was more private than an RTI office?

"I'll be over in a few minutes," he said. "All will see I'm on my way home, via the Edward Square U station."

A few minutes later, there came a knock at her door. "Unlocked," she called.

Patrick Wells, winter coat and brief case under one arm, swept through the door and closed it behind himself. She pointed at the coatrack and chair. "What may I do for you, Patrick?"

He sat and grimaced, as though he had bitten into a particularly sour lemon. "It's about my daughter. Jessamine Trishaset." He waited for her to ask what the issue was. Morgana waited for Patrick to continue. "I want to be clear," he said, "that I don't blame you for what happened. I asked you to use your best judgement in training my children how to use their gifts. You reasonably assumed that they were well-brought-up examples of Cantabridgian moral rectitude, the rectitude that has served the Greater Cantabridgian community well since our foundation two thousand years ago. Am I right to say that?"

"Patrick, I know your children very well." She spent a few milliseconds considering several conversations she'd had with Patrick and Abigail. Hopefully they would remember what had been said. "The training I've given them, which has been incredibly successful, had to have with your and their consent my mentalic support."

"I remember you telling me that," he said.

"So I know the three of them better than, well, anyone else alive, including you and your wife." She hoped he wouldn't go off in a huff, but that truth had to be established. "That's the way this sort of mentalic contact works. Without breaking confidences, I know very well anyone I train. Your children are all fine examples of moral young people."

"Alas, this is not true of Jessamine Trishaset. I don't blame you, since you clearly did not recognize what would happen, but there has been an unfortunate outcome of your training. Jessamine Trishaset went cloud diving. With a boy. A boy her own age." Patrick clenched his fists.

Morgana, near-instant responses or not, was taken aback. "Cloud diving? I must be missing your point. It's a standard training technique for people with the flight gift. Who was the boy?"

"Morgana. Cloud-diving. Really!" He realized she was staring intently at him. "It's inescapable. It's…he must have tampered with her. There's no alternative."

"My lips are sealed, Patrick," she answered. "I'm sorry you are facing this challenge." Whatever it is, she thought. What does cloud-diving have to do with it? He wants to speak, not to listen, so I should listen. "Patrick, when I removed the geases, two weeks ago, I checked all five of you, very carefully, for occult mental influences. You're fine. Trisha was fine. There was no sign of mental interference."

"What if there are consequences?" Patrick lapsed toward despair. "Our family name would be ruined! Ruined! Completely ruined. I'd have to resign my position and take us to someplace far, far away."

"That seems excessive, Patrick. You are not your daughter. Her faults are not your faults." It occurred to her what he might mean by 'tampered'. "I don't see how cloud-diving comes into this. Trisha is a top-line persona. You may have noticed your children almost never catch the flu, never had any of those childhood diseases, heal very rapidly from cuts and bruises? Trisha is medically completely safe from those sorts of things."

"What if my neighbors find out what she must have done with him?" He shook his head. "There hardly has to be physical evidence. I've taken the necessary precautions to guarantee she never has a chance to make that mistake again. She has always been a very difficult child, not at all like her brother and sister, but I've always made sure she had the best possible upbringing. And now she's done this. She shows no sign of understanding how she's let down our family name."

"Who was the boy, Patrick? The one she went flying with? I could discuss matters with him." She suspected that approach was doomed to fail, but the offer might make Patrick feel better.

"Joe. The boy who saved her. The boy she invited into our house, supposedly to play City of Steel with dear Janie." He stared at the carpet.

I am quite sure, Morgana thought, that it was Abigail who invited this Joe fellow into their house, but reminding Patrick of this minor detail sounded unlikely to help matters. "The fellow no one can find. That is a challenge."

"What if she does it again? And again?" Patrick looked prayerfully at the ceiling. "I've think I've made absolutely sure matters cannot repeat, but parents can fail. It's still a horrible thing that has happened. Please do not speak of this, either to her or to anyone else."

Where is he getting his ideas about cloud-diving? she asked herself. He seemed to be absolutely certain about what had happened. Of course, she allowed, he could be right, boys and girls being boys and girls, but young teenagers hardly needed cloud-diving as an excuse. , She had had far more years of practice than Patrick would credit at recognizing covert thoughts; Trisha very definitely did not have thoughts in that direction. What did he mean Trisha had been a difficult child? Trisha seemed to be an absolutely ideal daughter, the sort that any parent should be proud to have raised.

"If there is anything you want me to do about the training you asked me to do, just let me know." She forced a smile in his direction.

"Thank you for listening. I want you to stop the training. Not your fault, but you have already done more than enough damage to my family." He rose and grabbed for coat and briefcase. "The Underground waits for no man."

Chapter Twenty-Six

Medford, Massachusetts
Morning

If Speaker Ming himself had appeared on her doorstep, I had gotten Janie into trouble with various authorities, and needed to see what I could do to fix it. Walking the Maze, I had made a mess in all sorts of ways, so now it was my duty to clean things up. Several weeks too late, I saw the obvious. There were indeed two things I could do for Janie and siblings. All I needed was a few private minutes with the three of them. Fortunately, her parents kept Janie on a very strict schedule, so I could easily find her and siblings walking to school. I'd have the needed ten minute or so window to talk. I teleported into Frog Pond Park, appearing in the depression between the Tory Tower and the pond, out of sight of the street. I had no real trouble finding Janie's mind from a modest distance.

<*Janie,*> I called.

<*Joe?*> she answered surprisedly. <*Where have you been?*>

<*I was really sick,*> I answered. <*But I saw the news reports. I wanted to be sure you're safe.*>

<*I'm fine,*> Janie answered. <*But everyone is looking for you. Be careful. The Tsarists want to kidnap you. Krystal North wants to talk to you. And it's not safe to come near my house. Just don't!*>

<*You had all those guests, even Speaker Ming? How did that turn out?*> I asked. I lay down, sinking into the deep snow. The falling snow was respectably heavy. I'd be completely out of sight if this conversation went on for a bit.

<*Wow! I had all these grandmasters in my house asking me about my move.*> Janie stopped to look both ways before crossing the next street. <*Speaker Ming must play well. He spotted something they didn't. The start and end were a little nervous. Krystal North was there. She said I was telling the truth, that I didn't know Eclipse. At the end it got heated. Lucky I had a champion, Professor Lafayette.*> I caught a fragment of her memories. She knew Lafayette was Sunssword, someone I really did not want to meet. Sunssword would recognize me as Joe from two years ago, and might want to know what I'd done with the Krell disruptor pistol, not to mention wondering who had killed her prisoners. <*She's really neat. Even Krystal North knew who she was.*> Janie dropped in memories of

standing in their garage, with North backing up when she saw Lafayette. Janie's memory showed Professor Lafayette, wearing only a thin cotton blouse above her blue jeans, ignoring blizzard winds coming into the garage. OK, Lafayette is a persona. Janie and her siblings, gifts called, would be equally unimpressed by the weather. However, Lafayette had been wearing a necklace, an image I should recognize but didn't. Intuition said I was missing a clue.

<*Janie,*> I asked, <*Did you ever get a good look at Professor Lafayette's necklace?*>

<*It's sort of silly,*> Janie answered, <*She always wears it, but you never get to see it, and that big piece of glass must be heavy enough to be uncomfortable. Wait, I got a good look at it in our breakfast room.*>

I could feel her searching around through stacks of old memories. <*Here is is.*> Janie has an eidetic memory. She found a very clear image. I didn't recognize it. <*She's a very nice person. She even took the geas off our house, the one involving you.*> Janie followed with another image, a large fiery pentacle hovering above their breakfast room table, with lines of light and letters passing between Lafayette's fingers, followed by details of what the geas had done. That had to have been Mum's work, protecting me when I visited Janie, Brian, Trisha and their friends. Janie must not have recognized the High Goetic. I could read what was there, more-or-less, the image being imprecise.

<*Do you happen to know the Professor's first name,*> I asked.

<*Morgana. Why?*>

<*I thought I might have met her. I haven't. How did your meeting with the Grandmasters go?*> I had met Sunssword, not Professor Lafayette. Janie was happy to flood me with details, most beyond my comprehension, of their discussion of City of Steel and her secret move. I caught the exchange at the end between Lafayette and Kamensky. Kamensky threatened Lafayette. He appeared to have no clue how dangerous he had made the situation for him and his country. He could have started a war with the American Republic. <*I owe you an apology. I didn't realize that move was supposed to be a deep secret.*>

<*OK, I didn't tell you that. I didn't know you have Eclipse as another playing partner,*> she answered.

<*It's a little complicated,*> I answered. <*But I'm pretty sure I can fix things so everyone knows it's actually your idea.*>

<*Don't worry about it. When those grandmasters questioned me, I found a much better move, and that only happened because Eclipse used my old move.*> Janie was really happy about finding her new move. She carefully did not tell me what the move was. <*Then Plasmatrix showed up. She paid me a lot of money to play City against me. She's incredibly good. We didn't tell anyone except my family she was in our house.*>

<*Is everything else OK now?*> I asked.

<*No. It's terrible. And it makes no sense. Dad and Mom think Trisha did something horrible, and won't say what. It's something you two did – Dad said he'll kill*

you if he ever gets his hands on you –but none of us know what it was.> Janie followed with a slew of memories, some hers, some that Trisha had passed on from the three of them talking mentalically in the middle of the night. Her father sounded to be serious about trying to kill me. <*Oh, don't try telepathy in our house. Dad and Professor Lafayette have a whole bunch of traps installed, some to protect me, some to get you.*> What was happening? Somehow all of Trisha's parents' buttons had been pushed, as though they'd been turned into different people, and they were taking something I'd done out on poor Trisha.

<*I'd better speak to Trisha,*> I said.

<*Please speak to Dad and Mom? Please? Tell them you didn't do it? This is tearing poor Trisha apart. Even Brian has figured that out, and he's a boy.*> Janie was not quite begging, but I could feel the desperation in her thoughts.

<*I'll try,*> I promised. <*First I have to figure out what I did.*> Telling Trisha's Mom and Dad I hadn't done something would work better if I had some idea what it was. <*I need to speak to Trisha privately.*> Janie broke the mentalic link between us.

I'd have to be really careful. When I'd talked with Janie, she'd provided most of the link. She's a good mentalist. I'm more the bull in the china shop; I have to be very careful not to hurt people I'm linking into.

<*Trisha?*> I tried to be very gentle. <*Joe here. I'll go away if you want.*>

<*Joe!*> She wasn't upset at all to hear my mind-to-mind contact. <*Where have you been? Are you all right?*> I was slow to understand her tone. She was really fond of me, no matter what her parents said about me.

<*I'm fine. What's going on with you?*> I had to move the conversation to safer ground. If I gave away I'd been sick, she might wonder what I was sick with, and work out that I'm actually Eclipse. She is much sharper than I am.

<*I don't understand. It makes no sense.*> She was caught being very brave and wanting to start crying. <*My parents…*> and I was swamped with her memories of what had happened. I don't remember linking before to someone with superspeed—Mum's thinking was very different – so I was drinking from a fire hose.

<*I have to think about it,*> I said. <*I don't get it either. Are you safe?*>

<*Sure,*> she answered. <*Dipping into allowance savings to buy more lunch. Dad and Mom are just being mean, cut off my allowance, and won't say why.*> At that point she lost herself so far into her thoughts that she tripped. She would've fallen on her face, except a bit of superspeed and flight let her recover.

A mentalic hug is not a substitute for the real thing, but I did my best. For a moment, mentally, she was hanging on to me for dear life. She was terrified by what was happening to her.

<*I'll try to help,*> I announced. What could I do? This was not a 'find opponent. Smite opponent.' scenario. I saw one thing. <*Do the windows in your study open?*> I asked.

<*The ones with window screens,*> she answered. Her answer had a sharp image of the windows in question.

<*Tomorrow morning. Look outside on their outer ledges.*> I said. There was one thing I could fix. <*It's complicated, but there were huge rewards for those people two years ago, even if I couldn't collect all of them.*> Actually, I'd been able to collect none of them, but now she had an explanation that made sense. <*Think of it as them making up for what they did to you.*>

<*I'll be sure they're clear of snow,*> she answered. She wasn't sure what I was going to do. <*Should I let you in, so we can talk face to face?*> she asked hopefully. That sounded like it could create new, unrelated complications. Mum might not have been bothered if she'd found a boy in my bedroom, but that was Mum. Also, Trisha's house sounded to be booby-trapped.

<*First I need to find out what upset your parents,*> I answered. That was even true, though it was more true that I wanted to stay as far as possible from Professor Lafayette. <*I have one other thing I can do.*>

<*Please?*> she said, a touch of desperation in her voice.

<*Just a second. Janie?*> I tried to reach her sister again.

<*Bye!*> Trisha responded.

"Janie," Bryan asked. "You've been awfully quiet. Who are you talking to?"

I answered. <*Hi, Brian. I've made a bit of a mess here for your sisters. I'll try to clean it up. Can the three of you hear me?*> I felt three nods in response. <*OK. Something so I know if you are in trouble. Something to keep people from kidnapping you. Well, make it harder. Are you good with that?*>

<*Please?*> Janie asked. Her brother and sister agreed.

<*Stop walking for a moment?*> I stood up. First Trisha and then Brian saw me. They waved. I waved back. OK, I gave my ponies null links, and my cats null links, and now I'll give them to my friends. I hadn't expected that they already had a set of null links, but everything fit together. The teleport blocks were a little more complicated. The three of them had to be able to turn the block off, if they wanted to. One of my rules engines told me what to do.

<*Janie's going to kill you over that move, if you gave it away,*> Brian warned. <*More important! Archie MacDonald wants to know if you can show up in his scrimmages, after that catch you made last Fall.*>

<*Ask Janie. She has a new move,*> I answered. <*Showing up to play might not be a good idea. Sorry.*>

<*I'll recruit Gold Knight and Silver Knight,*> he announced. After they'd wrecked two of Emperor Roxbury's giant robots, the brother and sister in question had given up trying to hide they were persona. <*They're both ace players. And none of their gifts let them cheat.*>

I smiled. <*They won't be bothered when Archie complains you have girls on your team?*>

<*He gave up on that,*> Brian said. <*Something about Trisha lapping his team every day in the mile and a half run.*>

<*OK. You're getting close to school, and I have things to do myself,*> I said.

Chapter Twenty-Seven

Over the Pacific Ocean

The *Presentia* is actually quite short, the opposite of the *Goetica Physica*, which goes on through many volumes. Monsieur Poulenc said my Goetic was flawless. He was mayhaps optimistic. Mum gave it to me mind-to-mind, meaning I can read it as easily as I can read English, but while I'm reading it I'm thinking in Goetic, so sometimes I have trouble understanding in English what I'm reading. Understanding the *Presentia* was still a challenge.

The *Presentia* claims to have been written by Morgan Le Fay, directed to novice personas who want to realize the full scope of their powers. For all that Le Fay is absurdly powerful, she's also very good at writing so clearly that novices can understand her. I may be good at breaking things, but for sure I qualify as 'novice'. The introduction promised I would finally read about a circle that does not curve, a rainbow that you can touch, and a hole in the ground that goes down forever, those all being Goetic phrases I can't translate right. I finally decided against writing out a translation. My translation could be wrong and mislead me.

At the end of a long day, beginning with meeting Janie, Brian, and Trisha, and interrupted by cooking, weight lifting, a good run, housework, and riding Daffodil and Snapdragon, I decided I had had enough reading. It was after dark at my home. I teleported out over the Pacific to the sunset band, where clouds rose in towering pillars of pink-orange flame. I wasn't near any airline routes, but I was still careful. I arrived low, well below altitudes used by trans-Pacific flights. Perception reached out, finding cloud and sky above and waves far below. Perception is very much one of my weaker gifts, but airliners are large, heavy, and hard to miss. I checked again where I was going to start...There was someone there. There hadn't been moments ago. I hadn't felt any teleport distortion. Nonetheless, someone was hovering, up in the cloud-tops.

Modest caution was in order. I sank deeper into my levels. My shields ramped well up. I teleported above the clouds, a few hundred yards away from the stranger, and waved. The stranger waved back, then darted across the cloud tops toward me.

The stranger was a girl. We were of a height, though she looked to be a couple years older than I am. Her hair was as fluffy as mine, bright red rather than platinum blond. Of course, I was in my Jim disguise; she saw me as a boy and my hair as black. Her garb was bone white, with four polychrome sigils in a square on the two panes of her vest. The sigils were Atlanticean. Normally I'd have had to think to work out what each one meant. This time I knew instantly. Time's Dagger has a remarkably complex kenning but is totally unambiguous.

"Hi, Glory," she said. "I'm Spindrift, to have been your friend who is a girl, until the end of time." Her Atlanticean was better than mine. I did not quite lose control of my flight field and start falling, but I was so startled that it was for sure close. Absolutely no one other than Mum knows my real name, even in its nickname form.

"Hi, Spindrift," I managed to say. "Dorothy and Teranike said they'd met you. I'm, in this persona, I'm Jim. I'm the person you claimed was your boyfriend. Or would have you as your girl friend. Or something like that. Even though we'd never met, which is pretty fast even for speed dating. At least, that's what Dorothy and Teranike told me. They seemed confused about the two of us. You didn't actually tell them we'd been carrying on, did you? Dorothy seemed to think that we had been." OK, that wasn't the best possible start to a conversation with someone you've never met before, but I was a bit annoyed by the ribbing I'd received at Dorothy's hands.

Spindrift giggled. "Carrying on? That was Dorothy's idea. She was teasing you. Or encouraging you, you being a boy, well, your persona that she can see is a boy, even though you aren't, not to be so shy," Spindrift said. OK, she also sees through my disguise, enough to tell that I'm not the boy I'm pretending to be at the moment. "But we both came here to go cloud-diving, so we should start…though on the way up I can't climb as fast as you do."

"I'll let you lead," I said. "Until we discover that I can't keep up with you. Drop on three?" She nodded. I gestured one, two, and on three her gesture matched mine. We dropped, falling faster and faster toward the ocean. "Do we have long?" I asked. "Will your parents worry that you are out late?"

"No more than your Mum does," she answered.

OK, not only did she know my nickname, she knows the name I used for my mother. "You're sure?" I said, ignoring the bait. "I don't want to get you in trouble. Or did my mother send you? But mayhaps I should ask you what you know about the Dark Lights." She'd invoked their real name to Dorothy and Teranike. Mum had taken me to meet one. I had been very polite, even when it took me into its mindspace. How could I not be polite to someone who has lived literally forever? The funny part was that it seemed to like me, while it was only strictly polite to Mum.

"I've never met one," she answered, "and never will, not before the end of time. And I've never met your mother, nor did she send me. Coming up on cloud bottoms." She pulled a vertical loop, me following. Her loop was not as tight as mine could be, and her climb was slower than mine could have been. OK, when I did cloud-diving with Comet I lagged way behind. Comet is amazing. I took a while to notice. Spindrift had no flight field. She was just flying, with nothing holding her up. How was she doing it?

"*..end of time*," I repeated. "That, I was taught, has an exact meaning. So does *she approaches on swift and silent wings*."

"I know," Now she sounded very sad. "You know those meanings aright. I know exactly when she will come for me, a few months hence, just as I know when I will -- sorry, but I am Time's Dagger; I do not live in linear time -- be born, a few months ago."

"You're a few months old?" I asked. This was getting stranger and stranger. "And your parents let you out by yourself?"

"I can't tell you all, Glory. I can tell you the part I'm allowed to tell you. Not 'mom won't like it allowed'. Not allowed by the Ring of Fate," she said. "Just as I'm not allowed to know what you will do with the Namestone, even though you did show it to me, a couple of months from now. The allowed is 'Law of Nature allowed', the allowed found by the Dark Lights of the Starry Void. They solve some question about the universe, but if they speak the answer, the universe excises the speaker from the span of creation. Or it eats them. Or it creates a brand new universe, just for the Dark Light who answered the question." Mum said it was 'new universe'. She never told me how she could know that. And I'd heard of the Ring of Fate. It was a third-order construct. I am very much not up to going near third-order stuff. We reached the cloud-bottoms and looped skyward again. Spindrift's loop might not be as tight as mine could be, but she was no slouch in the flying department.

"I am my parents," she continued. "I called myself into existence, to be born from the fog on a wave-swept beach, born from sand and sea foam and kelp, from the chill breeze off the water and the boom of breaking waves. When I was born, I was this age, the age I'll always be. So I have no parents, no place to call home, no money except what I find in the sands, which leaves me more than a bit hungry. And to that place where I was born I will return to die, all too soon, on a cold beach beneath a twilit sky, alone..., or with a single friend who will have stood at my back when none else could have. Sorry, I can't foresee all that had happened, because you all have free will." I was not reading her mind, not really, but I could feel deep sadness. She was painfully sad, except while we were diving. Then she was wrapped in a bubble of delighted joy.

"You have no place to live," I said, "and I was thrown out of my own house, and had to find a place to live," I answered. I'm never sure if 'we've felt the same pain' is a good answer or not, but it seemed worthwhile to try. Though if she was telling the truth, her pain was infinitely more than mine. For a while we simply dived, enjoying each other's company, making small talk, not that I didn't have my presets peaked up in case this was some sort of a trap.

"I'm three months old," she finally said. "But I don't go through time the same way you do. I'm already partly in the future, the future I won't live to see, and partly in the past, so I've lived those three months many times, so I've lived through much more time than you have. I'm also an echo of another persona. You'll meet PeaceStar after she's done using the Ring.

Suddenly she was not there. She hadn't teleported. I would have seen that. She wasn't invisible. She simply was not there anymore. Then I realized the obvious. Her very strange gifts--they were all third-order schemas masking as first order gifts. How delightful. She knew who I was, knew I had the Namestone, and if she came after me to take it I would be in well over my head. Lords of Eternity don't have third-order attacks, and I am not a Lord of Eternity. Spindrift also had casually mentioned that another persona, one I've never heard of, was using the Ring of Fate.

On one hand, what she had just told me sounded completely crazy. Except for one minor detail: I'd heard part of her story before. It had been in *Liouville's Butterflies.* The Dagger of Time lives outside of linear time. For the Dagger, Past, Present, and Future are all mixed up. Before that, I had met a Dark Light. It gave me a dream, a dream that matched Spindrift's description of coming into existence, of waves breaking and being born out of nothingness. I'd never told Mum about it. She would have chided me for being foolish, for taking dreams seriously. When I had the dream, I couldn't quite imagine that a Dark Light had ever spent time watching waves break in the foggy twilight, one after the next, to know what the sound would be. For starters, Dark Lights are astronomical units across, and seem unlikely to fit inside a planetary atmosphere. However, it had given me a dream of breaking waves.

While I had been hovering, thinking, the sun had moved toward setting. There were no more clouds to the west. I did one last dive and returned home. I wasn't frightened, not exactly, nor depressed, but that encounter had been strange. A persona who did time travel could leave now, get to the Maze before me, and know how to capture the Namestone. Better yet, she could have set me up, know exactly what to prepare me to do so I would capture the Namestone, at no risk to her neck, and then steal it when I came out of the tunnels. I absolutely had to take control of the Namestone, so soon as possible, confirm I knew how to destroy it, and end its existence. Destroying the Namestone required that I finish recovering from doing the Maze, a process I could not hurry. The situation was a bit frustrating.

Chapter Twenty-Eight

Kniaz Kang's Marco Polo
North Cosmopolis, Washington

A few days later I returned to the Marco Polo for breakfast. "Ah, Master Jim," Kniaz Kang said. "It is good to see you. Your new girlfriend is waiting in the South Greenhouse with your regular company. She said you were paying for her breakfast. Sorry, but we are a bit full today." He pointed around the room at crowded tables, with waiters I did not usually see scurrying back and forth.

"My new?" It took me a moment to connect. "Oh, right. And I promised I'd pay for her breakfast." That wasn't quite true. This morning, well before sunrise, I left Trisha a sack of cartwheels for her lunch. I could do that again for Spindrift, even though I was sure I hadn't said that I would. If Spindrift's story about herself was true, she had no income and almost no money, meaning she was going hungry. And if she was the Dagger of Time, mayhaps I had promised tomorrow that I would buy her breakfast.

"So she said," Kang answered. He continued in High Atlanticean. "*And her High Atlanticean is absolutely flawless. The kennings on her garb? Are they real*?"

I took a moment to get back into character. I had not guessed Kang could speak Atlanticean, but his past was secrets hidden within secrets within secrets. "So she says." Kang nodded. I stayed in Modern English, but I had sort-of given away I know Atlanticean. Of course, Dorothy could have told him that already. "However, you keep secrets. She has no money. These will cover her tab for some time to come." With that, I reached into my pocket, scooped out a few coins, and reached toward Kang. His sleight of hand was amazing. That had been four Great Thalers, and he made them vanish without a trace of movement that I could see.

"You can afford that?" Kang asked. I just smiled. "Master Jim, you too have unseen depths. Or are too much taken with a very pretty young lady." I did not quite roll my eyes.

I checked the list of specials. "My usual," I said. "The same for her if she did not order."

"She did. She ordered your usual. I told her you had to pay first. But I see a line of other customers coming up the stairs, so this conversation will soon be overheard. Your girlfriends all await," Kang answered. He thought Dorothy and Teranike also counted as more of my girlfriends.

"Yes, sir! Of course! I wouldn't dare disappoint my three girlfriends." It occurred to me that he might well not know how old Teranike is. I can't see auras myself, but supposedly Otherearth people have unreadable body auras, so you can't tell how old they are using normal gifts.

I found the three of them far in the back of the greenhouse. In mid-winter it tended to be quite cold, which surely would not bother three of us. Teranike wore a heavy sweater and clutched a large coffee mug.

"Hi, gang," I said.

"Jim! Thank you for paying for my breakfast! You will have promised, won't you?" Spindrift said. I nodded in agreement.

"Good to see you!" Dorothy said. "Don't worry; we'll leave you two plenty of completely private time."

"I miss out on two of my girlfriends?" I asked. "That's what Kang said about you." I looked over Dorothy's shoulder at Teranike and shook my head.

"*The Peace of the Goddess be with you*," was Teranike's greeting.

"*And her light illumine you all of your days*." I dropped into Polarian, making a serious dent in my Polarian vocabulary.

"Hmm?" Dorothy mumbled.

"The traditional Polarian greeting," Teranike answered. "I said 'The Peace of the Goddess be with you', and Jim correctly responded 'And her light illumine you all of your days'. With no accent. Very good, Jim. But surely Atlanticean and Ancient English are enough languages for you, Dorothy, with all your other courses?"

"Oh, yes," Dorothy answered. "At least Calc is fairly easy, if you think about things carefully. And I dodged *Genre Fiction* in eighth grade, so now I have to take *Advanced Genre Fiction*. Ancient English is so hard because it's halfway to English, but with different rules. They split infinitives! An Ancient English Star Trek would have opened 'To boldly go where no one went yet'."

"Man," I corrected.

Dorothy gave me a palm-up five fingers high salute. "I missed that! Thanks!"

"Surely," Teranike asked, "nine thousand years ago there was no television?"

My ears perked up at her question. Nine thousand years ago referred to dates before any of the ancient civilizations existed. Why did she use that date for the existence of Ancient English? The standard line is that Polarian history is a pile of lies meant to glorify their Empress. Everything I knew about Teranike said she was rigidly honest. Someday soon I had to ask her about Polarian history. Dorothy looked puzzled. Spindrift had two fingers holding her lips shut. Questions were interrupted by the appearance of Wang with breakfasts.

"It's called deep history," I explained. "Teranike, if you ever get a Sunday off, mayhaps Silk can give you a tour of the Columbia river ruins."

"Be happy to!" Dorothy said. "Especially if I can take my Dad along. He loves ancient history."

"But what is Jammer Fiction?" Teranike looked puzzled. "Fiction about jazz musicians?"

"Genre, not jammer," Dorothy said between bites of pancake and maple syrup. "That word is Ancient English. Means a type of fiction. Detective tales. Sailing ships. Pirates. Space Opera. Even 'romance novels'." At the last she made a face.

"I have heard of these," Teranike said. "Space opera works better if you don't have space ships or decent telescopes. Decent telescopes mean you can see Proxima Centauri's eleven worlds to know to travel there to claim them for the Avatar. What is wrong with romance novels? When Meyer fled Gaia Atlanticea, she came through the World Gate to Polaria, and -- we knew her books—was made the Novelist Court Laureate."

"This is modern genre fiction." Dorothy wrinkled her nose. "It's full of people carrying on with each other. Half the novels on the reading list are illegal to sell in New England. Fortunately there's a secret reading list. It tells you which ones are tea and biscuits and mayhaps a chaste kiss after the couple goes cloud diving."

"Polaria is very different," Teranike said.

We finished eating. Dorothy looked around. "I must have knocked my tip on the floor. I don't see it."

"Tell your trusty sidekick to find it," Spindrift announced. "He's a persona. He must have…ultravision." Dorothy looked at the ceiling. She viewed 'my sidekick' as a joke. Spindrift's question had to be a setup. I didn't know Spindrift that well, but for sure if she did things she had reasons. Giving away one of my gifts was still annoying.

"If you two don't mind?" I asked. Spindrift and Teranike shook their heads. After it was too late I wondered if Teranike understood what I had asked. I looked very gently. "Dorothy, it's under your left shoe," I announced. How had it reached there? At a guess, another Spindrift third-order trick. I was certainly not going to mention how many hideout weapons Teranike was carrying. Before the Polarian War started, Otherearth agents had carried out several assassinations of Polarian visitors to our world. Teranike's weapons were just sensible precautions, even the two that I did not recognize. I was absolutely certainly not going to mention that Spindrift was not made of chemical matter. She'd just found a clever way for me to learn that.

"Thanks," Dorothy said. She scooped the coins off the floor. "How did you two meet?" she asked.

"We went cloud-diving," Spindrift answered. "Beautiful, incredibly long dives."

"You should join us, Dorothy," I said. "Or the two of us could go."

Dorothy blanched. "I have a class," she announced. "Cloud-diving? Not with my sidekick. Never!" She scrambled to stand up, scoop up her purse and satchel, and be on her way.

"Did I say something wrong?" I asked.

"It will be true. You are kind and generous. There will be no fault," Spindrift answered. Once again she was scrambling past, present, and future. "I'll be back in a minute." She vanished. Her teleports are traceless.

"What was this about ultravision?" Teranike asked. She took another bite of her scrambled eggs.

Today was not starting well. "I thought you knew, when I asked," I answered. "I apologize."

"There is nothing to be sorry about," Teranike said. "I trust Dorothy's judgement."

"Ultravision is like X-ray or NMR," I said. "You see a 3-D solid image of the world around you, and what is inside what. You also see – fake colors – what is made of what. Good manners is you don't use it to see through other people's clothing or into their purses or houses. That's why I asked permission."

"So you saw what is under clothing." She finished the last of her scrambled eggs.

"That's why I asked." This was not a good outcome. "I thought you understood what I was asking."

"That would bother you Americans, some of you. Most Polarians are indifferent," she said. "The Polarian sea is too cold for comfortable swimming, but we have swimming pools. I have never owned a…I believe you call them swimming suits. But I am a very good swimmer. It is required for the Silver Legion."

"And I certainly won't tell anyone what gadgets you have under your clothing." 'A small arsenal' came immediately to mind. "Even the ones I don't recognize." She smiled and nodded.

"You recognized some of them?" she asked.

"Most, not all. Dorothy and I both like target shooting. She doesn't know that. But I said something that hurt Dorothy's feelings." I shrugged.

"I will find out. She is sensitive about cloud-diving. Did you intend to say something that would annoy her?" Teranike asked. She took another deep sip of coffee.

"No. I mean, everyone knows she's Silk, and flies great, even high up. There's no reason we couldn't go out to tall clouds someplace, kill our flight fields, and drop though them as the sun was setting. That's when they're the prettiest. Maybe I should have taken what she said, last time, more seriously. I could take you, except you might get nervous, not being able to fly."

"Tall cloud tops are at 40,000 feet," she said. "I would black out."

"You'd be inside my body field," I said. "Like sitting here, only warmer."

"That's all you do in cloud diving? Nothing else?" Teranike asked curiously.

"Nothing at all," I answered.

"I must finish my coffee and get back to work," she said. "And your girlfriend is surely soon returning. Or is here for the first time, wondering how her meal ate itself." Teranike smiled at me and headed away.

I managed two more bites of the smoked pork hash before Spindrift returned. She smiled at me, shyly, and laid into her breakfast. For all that she was mostly not made of chemical matter, she was certainly hungry. I slipped one of my butterscotch chip cookies onto her cookie stack. She grinned.

"This is the moment," I said, "if we were boy and girl friend, I would whisper romantic words at you."

"We aren't." Spindrift was matter of fact. "But since you are who you are, I should finish answering the questions you would have asked. Would have, if you knew in advance where the most interesting answers are hiding."

"Finish?" I raised my eyebrows quizzically. "That's the not-in-linear-time speaking, isn't it?"

Spindrift looked puzzled. "What did I say," she asked. "No, I haven't said that yet." She seemed to be talking to someone else, someone who wasn't at the table with us. That was non-linear time again. Or she was talking to me, just not now.

"Why are you here?" I asked. "How did you call yourself out of nothing?"

"I can only answer some of your questions, Glory," she answered. There was my actual name again. "But I can tell you what matters."

"Yes?" The presets on my defenses were peaked. If she used a third order attack on me, they wouldn't help much.

"When I came into existence, I knew we would meet. That's part of the 'willed myself into existence'. I'm here because of the Leviorkianu Towers. All along the Pacific Rim are the ruined towers of ancient Leaviork. They're like frost-shattered tulips. Only stems and sometimes a few petals remain. A half-dozen lost civilizations tried to understand them, not even learning what they are made of."

"Frozen time," I responded, "says the *Physica Goetica*." I knew that because I'd read a popular summary. The *Physica* and *Arcana* volumes on Mum's forbidden list were way more sophisticated than anything I could understand. Yet. I was still buying them when I could find them. "Except the *Goetica Arcana* says they're made of magic matter."

"Neither," she answered. "They're made of frozen ideas."

"They're made with mind control devices?" I asked.

"No. Something much more sophisticated. And I'm at the edge of what I can tell you about how the world works." She shrugged. "Except the Radthninu tower. It's a prison. Inside it lie memes, locked away so none can think them." She paused. "Yes, that's possible. There are ideas you can't think, despite your rock-solid mentalic defenses, because the ideas were stolen and locked up."

The universe is indeed a strange place, but the place she was describing sounds even stranger. Or Spindrift was seriously not right in the head.

"I'm here to rescue them. That's my whole purpose in life, the reason the Ring of Fate let me find myself. PeaceStar is using the Ring – most people don't know that – so I get to smooth over the rough edges from her time travel adventures. You'll meet her. You'll like her. She is a nice person. She gave up everything beyond her body, her gifts, and the garb she was wearing, to save her family. Please tell her I think she did the right things. They worked. She should not blame herself for my fate. I chose my fate.

"I came into existence out of nothing. A few months from now, I get to die, the same way as I was born, or I fail. Except my end will be hideously painful, and I need to be awake and alert the whole time. When the moon is the narrowest of silver spikes, piercing the line twixt sea and sky, I must summon the true Radthninu tower, become the key without a lock to open the room without a door, and free the prisoners. You're the only person I can tell about this, and you're not supposed to understand what I mean. Not yet. But I only succeed if you stand at my back, when it matters, and I can't tell you when, where, or how. I can only tell you it will be far more challenging than anything else you have done in your life. If I tell you where or when, the answer changes. That's time travel—telling you is a self-defeating prophecy. Except what I do and what you do about something else are somehow tied together. If I fail, you fail in another time and place, and die, incidentally dooming the world. But I don't know why. That's the Ring of Fate. Time travel mixes everything up. And you have free will and choices and outcomes."

"You have free will, too," I countered.

"No. I don't. I have the one path I chose when I was born, the path that saves the world. And I have so many things I must do before then. I never have a choice. Except once, not yet, I get to decide whether to die to save the world, or whether to fade back into the sand, the salt air, and the roar of breaking waves."

With that, she vanished, leaving behind her empty dishes. I leaned back in my chair and stared at the ceiling. For someone preparing to die, she was awfully calm about it. She didn't sound to be trying to avoid her death. That was really strange. But solving the Maze took absolutely everything I could deliver. She wanted more? Anything more was beyond me, but that's what she said she wanted.

Time travel? End of the world? Was she making things up? That chapter in *Liouville's Butterflies,* the one claiming to be about her, had sounded convincing. Was it a fake? I was now beyond my depth. It wasn't I could trust anyone else to give me advice. Mayhaps I should solve my current problems first. I put a tip covering both of us under my plate and headed for an exit.

Chapter Twenty-Nine

Liberty Square
Philadelphia, Pennsylvania

The Great Bell of the Republic, brilliantly gilded, hovered majestically within the pillars of Liberty Hall. To each side of the entrance arch rose cenotaphs commemorating America's Founding Parents. "Here in the Year 17," the inscriptions began, "in Baltimore, Maryland, the Founders of the American Republic gathered together, resolved their differences, and agreed that after two centuries of squabbling that Unity will henceforth be the strength of the American Republic. The Founders, and their years of life upon this Earth, are…" There followed a list of names, their years of birth, and the dates of their deaths. Only the final two names differed. *The Immortal Morgan Le Fay* and *The Immortal Silver General* had only revealed their public personas after the Convention was over. Until then they had appeared to be a pair of quiet delegates representing the few surviving Grand Marshals and Parade Masters of lost Marik.

The spring sun was bright, but the air still bore a wintry chill. This early in the day only a few tourists loitered to take photographs. Beyond the cenotaphs, a quarter-mile triangle of public lawn stretched down to a low, ornate wrought-iron fence separating the grass from the water. Down at the water's edge, a shimmer of light marked a teleport pad in use. Appearing on it was a tall young woman, gold-blonde, statuesque, wearing tight-fitting white trousers, a tighter pure white blouse, and a knee-length white cape. She stepped off the pad and paused to straighten her gloves. An alert tourist standing near her noted the sigil tooled on each glove, an open circle superposed on a sun in glory, rapidly snapped VideoBell closeups of the young lady and one of her gloves, pressed *Transmit* on his very high-speed, very expensive VideoBell, and winked at the young lady, but did not bother to step to the teleport pad before disappearing. Noting the vigorous complaints of Colonel-General von und zu Dreikirch, an alert member of the American Persona League immediately forwarded the images from the Federal District to Geneva.

The young lady turned to face the water. If the tourist had remained, he would have had no difficulty discerning the iridescent shimmer of the young lady's heavily-driven force field. She shook out the folds of her cape, revealing as a sigil the moon and sun pattern seen on her gloves. Another tourist, who just happened to be taking photographs down the length of the lawn with a truly fine telephoto lens, managed to capture her image, the cape's sigil boldly displayed, and patriotically forwarded the image to the Federal district and the League of Nations. The image capture was hardly surprising. After all, Baltimore was usually shoulder-to-shoulder with tourists and their masses of camera equipment. A second image followed the first. The young lady held one hand at head level, palm up. Above her fingers floated a sky-blue flame. Her other hand pointed at the fence, seemingly transformed from wrought iron to polished gold.

She then vanished. If a third tourist, one having the rare gift that allowed her to recognize teleport destinations, had identified the small island in Chesapeake Bay to which the young woman had just teleported, and promptly reported the destination to the Peace Police, she would only receive the gratitude of the League of Nations. At least, she would have received their gratitude, if her claimed identity on her message to the League had had any real existence.

Across the Atlantic, pandemonium ruled. At this hour, the Ulm Cantonment of the League Peace Police was on highest alert, persona in their combat armor, gifts fully called, weapons at the ready, ammunition pouches fully loaded, with everyone ready to advance at a moment's notice. Alarm sirens sounded. Persona and commandos dashed from their ready rooms. As they ran, telepaths in Geneva forwarded to Ulm the American images. Map coordinates were provided. Senior officers compared what information they had with their attack plans.

Brigade Leader Johannes Reichenbach checked again his computer display. Every squad was ready to deploy. Three squads had had reserve teleporters and fliers slotted in. That was sub-optimal, but the extra mobility was too useful to reject. There was actually no evidence that Eclipse could fly, but it was well to be prepared.

A terrain map appeared on the wall screen. The Peace Police had managed to deploy to Baltimore a teleporter, who confirmed that Eclipse was still standing on the small island, seemingly watching the sea birds dip and recover above the waves. The island was largely open terrain. It was peacetime. The Maryland state teleport dampers were powered down. Reichenbach's men and women could deploy in open order, every persona having a clear line of sight on the Bearer. None of his personas were individually as strong as members of the Elite Strike Force, the people who had failed to capture Eclipse on Atlanticea, but his Brigade had far more people in it. On arrival in the island, the simultaneous attacks of more than a hundred personas and a multitude of gifts were certainly enough to crush any plausible estimate of Eclipse's defenses. The needed combat formation was a simple wedge. He would stand at the apex. Eclipse, until she was disabled or killed, would be at the center of the wedge's base. Attacks would be directed at her from both sides of the wedge, directed so that misses would go out over the water. Behind the wedge would stand his elite teleport blockers, all striving to keep Eclipse from teleporting away from the battlefield. Two flying squads would engage her if she sought to escape through the air.

"All ready," Adjutant Heinrich Mueller soon reported.

Reichenbach's personal teleporter and mentalist stood at his shoulders. "Teleport at zero," Reichenbach said, Mentalist-Sergeant Adam Eichel forwarding the Brigade Leader's thoughts to the Brigade. "Four, three, two, one, zero!" At zero, the combat elements of the Brigade teleported across the Atlantic to Chesapeake Bay.

To Reichenbach's eyes, the sun shifted in an instant from afternoon to early morning. He stood on a sandy dune, breaking waves close behind him. Eclipse was clearly visible near the water. Lining the two sides of the combat wedge, conservatively dressed in navy-blue garb, were his men and women. Annoyingly, some components of his Brigade were missing. They had failed to teleport, or something had blocked them. "On zero!" he called. "Three. Two." At two, Eclipse looked over her shoulder. She was clearly visible in his magnifying monocular. She saw Reichenbach's men, but showed no surprise. "One. Zero! Fire! Fire! Fire!" he ordered.

Lines of sun-bright plasma blazed across the sand. Incandescent violet ball lightning spheres rained from the heavens. The air wavered under the impact of hammers of telekinetic force. Reichenbach's mentalist gestured in the air, surrounding the two of them with a massive thought screen. The air glowed incandescently as beams of X-rays, neutrons, N-rays, and partons streaked above the grass. The ground shook as graviton blasts struck Eclipse's force fields.

It took some moments for Reichenbach to notice that not only was Eclipse unharmed, but the grass near her feet was not even slightly scorched. "Maximum effort!" he shouted. "Maximum effort!" What was wrong with his men? Their attacks were having no effect. Whenever one of Eclipse's force fields flared and began to collapse, another appeared at the same location.

The attacks on Eclipse gradually wormed their way through her defenses. She was slower and slower to replace her force fields when they collapsed. Replacement force fields appeared closer and closer to her clothing. Very soon, she would have to surrender, or die fighting a pointless battle.

The glare of large-scale teleports, all at a correct distance behind his two lines, interrupted his thoughts. Reinforcements! he thought. Excellent! The Cuzco Peace Police Cantonment must have moved very quickly indeed to come to his aid. The afterimages of the brilliant light faded from his eyes. The uniforms and garbs of the new arrivals were all wrong. They wore not conservative League of Nations navy blue but a garish mixture of colors and styles of clothing. Americans? They had nonetheless come to his aid. That was not what Ambassador Buncombe had threatened. The American Ambassador in Geneva was a bigoted blowhard idiot. It was good to learn that Americans appreciated the inevitability of World Truth.

He got no farther in his thoughts before the Americans began chanting. "You are under arrest. Cease to attack! Lower your defenses! Lower your defenses, or you will be attacked." Eclipse ignored the demands. Without warning, American persona unleashed their gifts on Reichenbach's men.

"No, you idiots!" Reichenbach screamed. Americans were even dumber than his English friends had warned him. "You are targeting the wrong people. Eclipse is that woman down at the river! We're here to…" Blinding pain between his ears silenced him.

For moments the Peace Police lost all coordination. Adjutant Heinrich Mueller realized that his Brigade Leader was incapacitated. Meanwhile, the Americans were neutralizing his force, one Peace Policeman after the next. What did they think they were doing? After a moment, the answer was obvious. "Formation!" He glared at Mentalist-Sergeant Hertha Pfeiffer, who strained to forward his orders through loud interference. "About face! Attack the Americans! The Americans are traitors to World Truth! Kill them!" Reichenbach vaguely heard the orders, decided in his confusion that they were of no importance, and sank into unconsciousness.

Mueller tried to make sense of his position. He had surrounded Eclipse, but was surrounded in turn. "Fall back! Close ranks!" His ranks already had gaping holes through which American persona fond of hand-to-hand combat were running. And Eclipse? Her force field had returned to full strength. It reflected the attacks directed against her. The position was impossible. "Teleporters! Return us to Ulm!" he shouted. Three of his dozen squads disappeared. Why only three? he wondered. He looked around. Lying on the ground were his other teleporters, dead or unconscious.

The Americans, Mueller noticed, had actually deployed in depth, the teleport flares on their arrivals being very bright to mask the small number of persona landing directly behind his lines. He could try to break out through their formation by advancing at ground level in some direction, but the outcome would resemble swatting at a cloud of enraged bees. You might kill a few insects, but the remainder of the swarm would circle about you so that your arm was still in its middle.

To make life more interesting, some number of ungifted troops had taken up positions in nearby treetops. They were shooting at his men. Individual rounds from heavy rifles were a nuisance, but some Americas were apparently armed with disruptors. Those Americans were a further complication for any retreat at ground level. Besides, he told himself, we are the League of Nations Peace Police. It is our opponents who retreat. We only pursue. The corollary was that he could not remember a single discussion on how to conduct a retreat in the face of the enemy. After all, the Peace Police never retreated, so there was no need to consider how to conduct a retreat, because one would never be needed. Besides, he was the Adjutant, and such exotic military topics as retreating would lie purely in the jurisdiction of the Brigade Leader. What should he do?

He pulled his communicator from its chest pouch, tapped the power stud, and gave it a two-count to open a satellite commchannel to Geneva and Colonel-General Dreikirch's Supreme Headquarters. "Emergency," he said, "Emergency! I am Brigade-Adjutant Mueller, Acting Commander of the Ulm Brigade. Brigade is surrounded and taking heavy casualties. I need massive reinforcements immediately. Contact the American FedCorps. It is their duty to support us. Instantly!" The Comm display flickered, then read 'Message not acknowledged'.

"Transport-specialist Jones?" Mueller turned to the woman at his side. "When are our teleporters coming back? We need an advance to prior positions."

"They aren't," Jones answered. "Not until you neutralize the American teleport blockers. We are now pinned in place, just like Eclipse is."

One obvious option remained. "Flight advance!" he shouted. "Across the water!" At that command, fliers in each squad were supposed to entangle their non-flying squadmates in their flight fields, the Brigade then flying in formation out of the combat zone. Here and there, Peace Police did take to the air, each carrying a half-dozen of their fellows. They were immediately mobbed by Americans flying well above the waves. One group did manage to cross the bay and reach Baltimore, not that reaching the city did them any good. Other fliers had followed the Brigade's teleporters into unconsciousness.

We have to break out, Mueller thought. We're pinned here and getting taken down, one man after the next. Worse, the Americans know exactly where we are, and are bringing up reinforcements. "Brigade! To the east! Reflex fire! Forward at fast walk. Take down the Americans. We are breaking out!"

The surviving Peace Police advanced toward the Americans, leaving behind a trail of bodies, the majority in navy blue. Mueller made a rapid count. He had fewer than 60 effectives remaining, meaning he had taken two-thirds casualties. Most of his casualties were clearly dead.

The Americans continued their chant. "Cease to fire. Raise your hands. Surrender!"

Now he was down to fifty effectives. This was one for the diplomats, Mueller decided. "Attention! Attention! Cease to attack. Hold your fire. Do not attack. Stop walking. Raise your hands! Keep defenses up!" He pulled a handkerchief from his shirt pocket and waved it in the air. After a few moments Mueller's Brigade ceased to fire. American fire slackened and then stopped. Mueller walked forward, stopping when several Americans in front of his held up a hand.

The Americans spoke. Mueller answered in proper Hochdeutsch. Clearly a translator would be needed. Mueller regretted that he did not happen to read or speak English, but after all there were so many foreign languages and only so much time to study any of them. To demand Eclipse's surrender, only a few phrases needed memorization. By reputation, almost no Americans spoke any foreign language.

A short wait brought three Americans to the scene. The older man in forest-green garb was a senior officer with the Maryland persona corps. A tall, heavyset gentleman in three-piece suit and opera cape proved to be a local university professor who spoke understandable High German. The young lady in bright orange trousers, shirt, and winter-weight coat was a County Bailiff.

"I am Colonel Heinrich Mueller, Acting Commander, Ulm Brigade, League of Nations Peace Police," Mueller announced. "We are here under the authority of the League of Nations to arrest Eclipse, the young lady down at the river, for crimes against civilization. I demand that you come to our assistance, and further demand that you place under arrest, for crimes against peace, all the persona who attacked my Brigade."

"You're the League Peace Police," the older man said, "and I am the Emperor of Antarctica. No, you are a bunch of criminals who illegally entered the American Republic and attempted to kidnap this young lady." He gestured at the statuesque blond now approaching Mueller, "This young lady is one of Baltimore's leading cosplayers. So you can now surrender, in which case you will all be arrested by this other young lady, the one in orange, and be given fair trials in American courts, or you may choose not to surrender, in which case, given the number of my people you have already injured and killed, I will be delighted to order Kill them! Kill them all! No quarter." He smiled. "Your call."

"My injured will be properly treated?" Mueller asked.

"Absolutely. After all, for a change you are in a civilized country." To Mueller's ears, the older man sounded completely calm. Mueller decided not to take umbrage at the inference that the Prussian Empire, the most civilized place in the world, was not a civilized land.

"In that case, I will order my people to put down their weapons, cease to use their gifts, agree that they will not attempt to escape, and surrender." Mueller shrugged. Sooner or later his people would be sent back to Europe. Sooner than these Americans expected, though not soon enough for him, these Americans would be punished for their arrogance.

"Very good." The young lady smiled, but her eyes were cold as helium ice. "On behalf of Kent County, I am taking you into custody. You are all under arrest. Charges will undoubtedly include rioting, attempted kidnapping, attempted murder, and assault with deadly gifts. "

Chapter Thirty

The Invisible Fortress
Late Morning

The next morning I overslept. To my annoyance, I noticed one of my presets had triggered, reporting that someone was on the property, without waking me up. Had I slept through it? No, it reached me in one of my dreams. I saw a deliveryman, taking his truck down the paved barn road. Oh, alfalfa. Everything was fine

Everything was fine until I got up and looked out my balcony window. There was my alfalfa shipment, neatly tied in fifty pound bales, looking as though it had been dropped off the rear of a dump truck. Mayhaps several trucks. There were a lot of bales. They were very definitely not under cover. I was facing a large, irregular pile of bales out in the open, not several neat stacks already moved by fork lift into the shelter. For once I very definitely used a whole bunch of those words that Mum did not like.

I had paid extra for the small bales, because I had to be able to move them. A hundred pound bale would weigh what I do. Yes, I can move something that heavy, with forethought and attention to leverage. If you are careful, almost always you are only moving half the bale's weight. I've seen videos of people slinging bales onto a flat-bed. Those people were way heavier than I am, in an exercise where strength and weight really matter. Last fall I tried that. Once. I slung the bale. It went one way. I went the other way and ended up sitting down. Now I needed to move a truckload of bales, enough for a year for two horses, from where they had been dumped, into my large if not very tall aluminum shed.

At that point I completely lost my temper. The Attorney in that letter had said 'minimum delivery support', and I was looking at the minimum. Yes, I had helped friends in Medford move firewood, but there was no way they could return the favor, not without my giving away where I lived. On the bright side, the weather report yesterday said I had several days of dry weather ahead of me, so I did not absolutely need to move all of it this morning. Still, 250 bales were going to take a long day or more to store, with a lot of nibbling of climbing trail mix to keep me moving. I did remember to check the bale weight of a few bales to be sure I was not being short-changed. No such luck. There were 60–plus pound bales, even more fun to get on top of each other. It would be enormously demanding exercise, exactly what I needed.

A very long day later I had moved a fair fraction of the bales. It was getting dark, and Medico was warning me about long muscle exhaustion. I'd have to finish tomorrow. Yes, there are folks whose competitive race is based on distance run in 24 hours, but I'm not one of them. There were, after all, seven and a half tons of bales. The carry was gently downhill, each bale being centered on my hand truck so that I was not trying to support its weight, but for most bales after reaching the shelter I had to do several lifts to stack. Prop one side against a lower-level bale, grab, and lift with your legs helps. With care I almost never had to handle the full weight of a bale, but there were still a lot of them. All the work gave me plenty of time to think about what I'd been doing over the past few weeks.

I spent the evening reading bits of the *Presentia.* The first half seemed very clear. It was all things I had learned from Mum. Was I missing something? The second half of the book rapidly became opaque. I told myself that Le Fay was a really good writer. I'd worked through the first half very carefully, did all the exercises, and made sure I had Le Fay's way of saying things down pat. With all sorts of interruptions, housework, breakfast at Kniaz Kang, occasionally cloud-diving with Spindrift, I'd had several interesting weeks, and now I understood much of the book. I'd heard it all before. I still hit a wall at the Straight Circle. I could do all the steps Morgana described for summoning the Circle, the Solid Rainbow, and the Well of Infinity, but nothing happened. OK, some people cannot develop some gifts.

I'd taken a break from trying to understand the *Presentia.* I'd spent some time researching the Radthninu Tower, sneaking into small libraries at odd hours. There are very good pictures of all the Leviorkianu towers. Every tourist guide of the Pacific Coast Highway has them. After a bit, I generated the illusion that my mythical family is planning a Summer road trip, the length of the Pacific Coast Highway, and started ordering high-grade maps, tourist guides, coast motel guides. I prowled used book stores for books on sea stacks, ancient ruins, and coffee table books on the towers. None of the books mentioned a Radthninu tower. Spindrift said she couldn't tell me where it was. I could tell she was happy that I asked.

My web search, at a small-town library I'd never used before, got a delay on the search. I felt incoming teleports all around me, and jumped out. Fortunately I'd already been deep into my gifts. The incoming people were Lords of Eternity. They'd thrown a strong teleport block at the library. I barely escaped, then spent several hours dodging their pursuit.

I finally created a map of all the towers, and all the names that I could find. If there weren't too many nameless towers, I'd determined where the Radthninu tower wasn't. That took some days, but in the end I was missing only a few names. On my map, those half-dozen unlabeled dots probably included the Radthninu Tower.

Two days later, the alfalfa safely stowed, my house computers started firing alerts. Lots of them. I turned on the Eagle news channel. It took only a moment to figure out what was going on. It seemed that the highly unpleasant Lords of Death had appeared over Cambridge. They had scanned Janie's house, found she was not there, scanned Benjamin Franklin Tech, found she was not there, and were now demanding that Janie surrender to them, or they would make Greater Cambridge flat.

The National League might eventually come to the rescue. From the point of view of the Lords of Death, Greater Cambridge had a good feature. The Boston city team had a top-line reputation, so people elsewhere would assume that the Stars Over Boston would deal with matters. No one else needed to help the Stars. The Lords knew that the Stars didn't deserve their reputation.

OK, it was my fault that Janie was in danger. It was time to ride to her rescue. I was already wearing boy-style clothing. Without even thinking about it, I started dropping through levels. I pulled on my padded coat, pulled a wool cap over my hair and ears, caught my breath, took the time needed to fold in on myself until I was completely slack, and teleported. I appeared over Boston Harbor, several thousand feet up, so I could see what was happening before I got involved. 'Preliminary Reconnaissance-The Right Decision' Mum always said.

There was Boston Harbor beneath me, with the Carolus Fluvius winding inland between Boston and Cambridge. Colored bursts of light were second and third line personae trying to stop the Lords of Death. If enough second-rankers had some coordination, they might well have pulled it off. Three or six dozen relatively weak attacks can be much more effective than one strong attack. Against a big attack, your defenses tune to that exact attack. Against a bunch of weak attacks, no matter what you do some of the attacks will find chinks and weaknesses in your defenses. You have to be stronger than all of the attacks at every point. Mum promised me that being stronger worked perfectly. After all, it worked for her. She sort of skipped over how I was going to reach that deep into my gifts. At least, she skipped over the answer, until the answer was glaringly obvious.

All I really had to do was delay the Lords until the National Team arrived. Flattening the Lords would be just fine, but I didn't need to do that. I just had to delay them. The moment National showed up, I would be very much is someplace else. I prepared to do a tactical teleport, right on top of the Lords, and start slugging. I didn't get the chance. They must've had a really good spotter, because all at once they were right on top of me, not where I was looking. I was hit from behind by heavy-duty energy blasts, mediocre levin bolts, an impressive illusion of the entire Legion of Evil Overlords, and a flash burst. Bright, but not starcore bright.

I could feel my shields bend - 'rigid is brittle' Mum would say. Time to fire back. However, the Lords were right behind me, meaning aim was a challenge. I did a tactical teleport, very short, just to turn around. Yes, I could aim using ultravision, but I did not need a sharp headache at the moment. I was still almost on top of them when I opened fire. Flash, plasma torch, ball lightning stream, levin bolts, all at once. Their defenses were rock solid. Their mentalist parried my levin bolts. They had two gals putting force bubbles around their group, enough to stop my ball lightning. I was still dropping deeper into my gifts. In a bit I'd be hitting them way harder. I'd guesstimated how long to wait before I jumped to Boston. I should have been more patient. Deeper I'd have to go. Drilling deeper, when you're in active combat, is a pain, no matter how much Mum had trained me how to do it, but that's what I had to do.

The Lords teleported to vacate my line of fire. The teleport was to right behind me. I got hit really hard, more than once. My shields wavered. These people were living up to their reputation, 'as tough as a Lord of Eternity". Teleport was a game that two could play. I jumped behind them, tripling the distance between us. They jumped at the same time, expecting to be behind me. They didn't jump far enough, so I was behind them. They teleported in place. rotating 180 degrees, so we were facing each other. I repeated the move, again increasing the range. This time they were there before I was. Their teleporter was very fast on his toes, faster than I am. I looked left, teleported forward and right, while they jumped straight back. They'd expected me to jump where I had looked, so they were looking the wrong direction. I teleported to Cambridge, directly above the Piazza Leprecano, did a flash burst way above me to attract attention, and switched my attacks to plasma spheres. They're more powerful an attack, but only good at longer ranges.

I had a couple of moments to see where I was. Slack? I eased off a bit on the plasma spheres. Shields? No matter how much power I dumped into them, they were starting to fray. Levels? I was dropping though them; indeed I was down as far as I'd ever gone, enough that I felt uncalled gifts crackling in the air around me. I wasn't in pain yet. The exercises in the *Presentia* actually worked. Tactics? Time to jump. I jumped before they arrived. Their spotter had no trouble finding me, but their spotter and their teleporter were different people, so the spotter had to find me, tell the teleporter where to jump, and then wait for the teleporter to charge up and jump. I'm not a spotter, but these guys and their flame corona were impossible to miss.

I had a mayhaps-bad idea. Everyone wouldn't hear broadcast telepathy, but enough might. <*Cantabridgians! Joint attack on the Lords. On three!*> The Lords appeared in front of me. This time I had to stay in place, or the Lords might follow me. They might also figure out what I was doing, no matter that my broadcast was focused down. <*One! Two! Three!*> On three I hit them as hard as I could with my plasma torch. They responded in kind. The folks on the ground chimed in. More attacks than I could count blazed through the air around me. Most hit the Lords, more or less simultaneously. Some of them hit me. The Lord's force fields didn't budge. Somehow they had an absurd amount of power backing them.

I finally figured out that the Lords were thinking two-dimensionally. They always appeared at my altitude. I'd been making the same mistake. We played flashdance, teleporting, ducking, and weaving to keep the other side from getting solid hits. I was getting in more hits than they were, and mine were harder. Their shields still weren't fraying. I did a double jump. The Lords followed my first move, but I was already above them, firing into the top of their force bubble. Once and again, someone in Boston coordinated an attack on the Lords. Those attacks were getting stronger.

Supreme Lord Death Ray started screaming at me. "You! You! Give it up, give me Wells, or I torch the city!" That's what Death Ray said. Actually he put a bunch of adverbs and adjectives between his other words. Mum would not have approved of his adjectives, let alone his adverbs.

"You and which army?" I asked. While I was talking, I hit them several more times. They had two good shield projectors, who kept shields around the lot of them. I could see their shields were now starting to fray a bit at the edges.

Five of them started firing at Cambridge. The Massachusetts Institution for Theology Bridge and its gilded statues of John Harvard, Founder, dropped into the water. I was pretty sure Death Ray hit the bridge pilings, so that no one on the bridge was killed immediately. Roofs on several blocks of apartment buildings burst into flames. Their mentalist started setting really twisted large area lunacy attacks. I put up a force wall, horizontal, to cover the city.

Death Ray would point to where his people should appear next. I followed his lead. I was screening Boston from being wrecked. Screening a whole city takes a lot of power. I'd ramped down farther than I'd ever been, far enough that Medico was firing warnings that I was doing bad things to myself. I could shield Boston and keep battering at them. I had to keep in mind the little consideration that I wanted to fry the Lords of Death without setting the entire city on fire. I had to be careful. They felt no such constraints.

Someone finally raised the Greater Cambridge lightning screen. Thank you, Benjamin Franklin, for your contributions to world civilization. Death Ray and friends teleported. I followed. When I teleported, my wall flickered. For a moment, the Lords of Death had a clear shot at the Rogers' Long Bridge. The lightning screen dispersed the attack, enough that the bridge was still standing.

Now I had company. Sunssword was one of Boston's high-power personae. I didn't want to meet her, even in my Joe disguise. She let loose with truly high-brisance starbursts, firing way faster than I can, each starburst being separately targeted and tuned to hit some flaw in their shields. She was amazing, almost as good as Mum. OK, mayhaps better.

<*I'm Sunssword,*> she said, introducing herself. Except she pronounced it Sun's Sword.

<*Joe,*> I answered. <*Just Joe. Persona name.*>

<*Coordinate attacks?*> She asked. <*I shatter shields, you blast?*>

<*Good,*> I answered. Their shields were slowly going down. Mine weren't in completely good shape either. <*Teleport with me?*> I asked. <*Stay together?*> She was a teleporter, too, though her tactical range looked to be short.

<*Let's try,*> Sunssword answered. I forgot to ask which of us would do the teleporting. For a few seconds we both were. That didn't help our aims, but the other side quit hitting us.

<*I'll do the porting,*> I announced. <*You shatter them.*> Their shields were showing cavities into which I happily concentrated my plasma torch.

<*I need some recharge time,*> Sunssword finally announced. Through the mentalic link I could feel the load on her power reserves. Her reserves were huge, but she couldn't keep her attacks up indefinitely. Indeed, her attacks had faded a bit.

<*I distract, you fade away?*> I asked. She nodded. <*On three?*> I asked. I did something I couldn't keep up for long. For a few moments, the villains were surrounded by a continuous flash and an all-around plasma attack. Sunssword vanished. I dropped my attack. The Lords of Death guys were really good, and reinforcements were taking their own sweet time about arriving. I reminded myself that I just had to distract them, not take them out.

I did not expect Spindrift to show up more or less on top of me. Whatever she did next, it was rough on their shields. Their leader switched their heavy-duty energy attacks over to her. Her force field flared red-orange-yellow-blue-ultraviolet. It was real obvious that her force field might be good, but it wasn't vaguely good enough. Very quickly she would be going down.

I teleported more or less directly between her and the Lords. My screens would cover her. This turned out to be a bad mistake, one that almost got me killed. I teleported. Spindrift hit everything in front of her with a different attack. A drain. I've been hit by drains before. The clowns who accompanied Valkyria to the Tomb of the Martyr were supposed to be the six best drains in Europe. Believe me, I knew they were there. I'd just gone deep enough that they couldn't budge me. Spindrift's drain was a third-order attack, and way more powerful. I felt all my gifts starting to fade. The counter to any drain is 'Dive the Waterfall'. You let the drain push you deeper and deeper into your levels. I dove.

It took me a moment to realize that Spindrift was draining the Lords of Death, not just me. They took it much more poorly than I did. I made myself dig in even deeper, no matter how much it hurt, and hit their shield projectors and their teleporter absolutely as hard as I could.

Death Ray produced a palm-size glassy sphere from his cape. I should have recognized it, but I didn't. He cupped it in both hands and waved it in my direction. For a few moments the world was simply impossibly bright. I crash dropped. I saw the impossible circle. Felt the warm caress of the solid rainbow. Fell feet first into a cerulean well that goes down beyond forever. Medico glyphs burned blue and flickered violet. DeathLord's attack was killing me through my screens. My wall above Boston was about to fail. If I dropped it, several million people would die. Grimly, a process that actually took no time, I dove far deeper into the Well of Infinity. I had impossible glimpses of concepts turning into solid objects. Determination was a marble statue. Duty, heavier than worlds, was this Japanese gentleman saluting me with his sword. Medico switched to flashing a different set of glyphs, all bright violet, the ones telling me the power I was handling would destroy me.

The impossible attack stopped. The sky above Boston, above my wall, was a huge incandescent fireball, rising beyond the stratosphere. I have seen a transmutation bomb detonate. This fireball was much larger. Sunssword was back, recharged. She did something outside my experience. The fireball vanished, replaced by normal air. Their leader stared at me. He clearly hadn't expected me to survive.

I was still impossibly deep into my levels. I ignored the Medico warning to pull out of the Well of Infinity and hit the Lords again with my plasma torch. Their shields collapsed. Their teleporter had some really feeble personal defenses, which I blew apart. I was like a large rocket engine hitting a layer of skim ice on a New England pond in late November. I am not sure if their teleporter realized what was about to happen to him. I really don't care. I had heard about these people, and all the terrible things they had done all around the world. I came back out of the well.

Their shield projectors and flier lasted very little longer. I left those three sort of alive. Their flier was surely the least dangerous. His idea of attacking me was shooting at me with a pistol. OK, he was an incredibly good shot. We were both flying and dodging. He hit the force field in front of my left eye every time. Big deal. Mom had always taught me to play for keeps, and that was what I did.

Not hesitating, Sunssword went one-on-one on their prime plasma combatant. Sunssword's targeting was way better than mine. Her rate of fire was even higher than it had been before. This time she was for sure not tiring. He went down in a hurry. Spindrift knocked out their mentalist.

Meanwhile, I faced off with their leader. It seemed that he could hover, but not fly very well. I put an extra wall under Death Ray, just to be sure I was protecting Boston, and hit him with all the strength I could muster. I was back out of the well, saw the Straight Circle and the Rainbow Connection way below me, but I was still deep into my power levels. My attacks hadn't penetrated his shields last time. That was before Spindrift drove me deep into my gifts. He hit me back. For a moment, it wasn't clear which of us was going to be the stronger. I'm way stronger, all told, but I was shielding

Boston and he was only shielding himself. His shields failed. I even pulled my attack fast enough that I didn't quite kill him.

The characters flying up from Beacon Hill had to be Stars Over Boston. They were finally organized enough to enter the battle, now that the battle was completely over. They were polite about relieving me of Death Thinker, Supreme Lord Death Ray, and company. I'd completely forgotten what the Lords' flier's name was, assuming I'd ever known it. Angel of Death is so original. Not. Two of the Stars made snide comments about Sunssword. The comments were completely undeserved. Her attacks had wrecked up the Lords of Death enough that I could shield Boston, and beat on the Lords at the same time. She could have taken the Lords herself, I think, but mayhaps not shielded Boston while she was killing them.

<*You're really good to do that,*> Sunssword said to me. I could hear what lurked behind her words. She was not just being polite. Lurking in her words were undertones, languages no longer spoken, patterns of numbers calling out to each other. She was computing how much power I had used, which levels I had called. I really wished she had not been able to do that. Accurately. I pretended not to hear the undertones.

<*I had a lot of help,*> I answered. <*You and Spindrift, in particular. And the nice people in Cambridge. Please thank them for me.*>

<*Wait. How far did you overpower yourself? Are you sure you can recover?*> Sunssword asked.

<*I'll be fine,*> I answered. I was even telling the truth, assuming Medico was reading my health correctly. < *Not as bad as the time someone pulled a Krell pistol on me. This time it helped to have read the* **Presentia**. *You should do that.*>

She broke into laughter. I hadn't said anything funny. Why was she laughing? Stress release? <*Wait! You're Joe, aren't you, the Joe who rescued Janie and Trisha Wells, aren't you? And played City of Steel with Janie, too? We really need to talk. Later?*> she asked. <*Saturday? Ten days out? Is that enough time for you to recover? Tip top of the Adams monument, six in the evening? Bring dinners?*>

<*Complete secret that we're meeting?*> I caught her rigid mental agreement. <*Absolutely! Go someplace more private? I have a place. Promise not to tell anyone else?*> I asked.

I got a sharp nod and mentalic <*Word of honor.*> in response.

<*But where did that girl go? The redhead? I'd like to meet her, too.*> Sunssword meant Spindrift.

<*She's wicked shy,*> I answered. <*I'll try to get her to join us.*> Either Spindrift was not available, or she already remembered our picnic.

Then Stars Over Boston wanted to talk to me. One of them, I think Mighty Mind, had been eyeing Spindrift until she vanished. Mighty Mind was a famous womanizer. His eyes would get him no place. Yes, Spindrift is older than I am, but not that much older. I think. Except for the time travel part. It's not as though Mighty Mind, the living Adonis, is short of girlfriends. Mind you, as far as I can tell, he's a jackass that looks like a man, but…Spindrift is too young for his attentions. I saw no reason to talk. I teleported out to someplace over the Indian Ocean, followed by the Lunar L-2 point, someplace well above Antarctica, a couple of closed loops, and finally to the island where I'd promised to meet Spindrift if we ever needed to get together.

I found her there. She was sitting on a large piece of driftwood, bent over, crying her heart out. I landed by her side. "I almost killed you," she managed to say.

"You didn't," I answered. That was even true, if you took a very narrow view of 'almost'. I knelt on the sand and put an arm over her shoulder. By this time I felt absolutely ghastly. I'd pushed way deep, and gone one on seven against really-top-league opponents. They'd practiced fighting together. Spindrift and I hadn't. Medico was flashing red. My healing matrix was doing chemical-level repairs. A few times, my shields had started to leak radiation. That's why the matrix was there, after all, to keep me going when I needed it.

I was starting to feel colder and colder, the serious side effect of overloading my gifts. "You didn't. We never practiced combat together - actually, I didn't know you did high-power combat." OK, I hadn't asked, and she hadn't said. "Yes, you almost took me down, but that was my fault," I continued, "I should've thrown a wall, not jumped into the line of fire." That was a bit optimistic. I had already been shielding Cambridge, their lightning screen really not being up to the job. For me to throw another wall at the same time would have been really demanding.

"I, I'm stuck on this path, and if I fall off it, everything awful happens," she said. "If I keep going, I keep doing things like that to you. Or worse. And you're my only friend, ever." I hugged her. What else could I do? She'd explained to me what was going to happen to her in the end, her end of days. I was the only friend she would ever have. The sun was on my back, a slight counter to the bitter cold inside me. I'd really gone deep into my gifts. They were reminding me that those depths are not safe.

Spindrift stopped crying. "Eclipse?" she said, "This is one of those moments I knew in advance. I'm going to lose faith in what I'm doing. Or not. But I need to face it by myself, or I'll just fold up and fail. Could you please…?"

I was torn three ways. I wanted to stay with her and support her. I didn't want to risk her life, what was left of it, by staying with her. And I really wanted to go home and to bed. I hugged her once and stepped back. She solved my quandary. She winked out like a light, here one moment and gone the next, with absolutely no gap in between. And with that I did my own teleport sequence, finally reaching my bedroom. By now I was shivering. I dumped my clothing on the floor, set the shower as hot as I could stand, and stood under it. I cheated to dry off. I did a very short teleport, leaving the water behind. On the bright side, I realized, I had now seen the three impossible objects of the *Presentia.* They would now be there whenever I wanted. I hoped that 'whenever' would be very rarely indeed. Staggering, I crawled under my quilt and sheet, rolled up into a ball, and fell into deep sleep.

Chapter Thirty-One

The Lafayette Laboratory
Compere Biological Sciences Building
Rogers Technological Institution
Cambridge, Massachusetts

Michael Poniatowski looked up from his desk. He'd heard footsteps, and now there was a visitor at the door. "Hello, Captain-General," he managed.

"Ah, Michael." Krystal North smiled. "Where is your boss hiding? I knocked on her office door; she is not there."

"She's meeting with the Tenure Committee," Michael explained. "By rumor, she politely told them she had unsolicited job offers from TechCal, Hill University, and Berkeley. Full Professor. With Tenure. They all knew her house is on the west coast. She hasn't said a word about it."

"She wouldn't." Krystal nodded. "Her work here is hers. I'm not a biochemist. My expert knowledge on the topic is that no past civilization knew the biomedicine that we do."

"There's coffee and cookies if you'd like some," Michael said. "I have no idea how long she'll be."

"Coffee is always good. Whose cookies?" Krystal asked.

"Mine. Snickerdoodles." Michael smiled. They walked to the seminar room. "Improved recipe," he announced. He passed her a large bowl.

"Improved?" Krystal asked.

"Cinnamon and vanilla in the dough. Double the sugar content. A pound of butterscotch chips into the dough," he explained.

Krystal took a bit. "Improved!" she said enthusiastically. Keeping up your weight is a challenge, she told herself, but here is a bit of a solution. "And I'll want the recipe."

The office began filling with people. "Boss sent a mentalic 'all appear' message," Allison Moreland explained. "Michael, you were here and busy."

A few minutes later, the room was crowded. Morgana came through the door. "Hi, Krystal. In a few moments. First, folks, I had a really unpleasant meeting with the Tenure Committee. They told me where to go. Impolitely. Their chair, Professor Wells, was especially emphatic. Don't sign leases for next year. It looks like we're moving. Hill University on Half Moon Bay had by lots the best offer, if not the closest to my home. We have to negotiate yet."

"Have cookies. I'll be back in a bit. Guest first. Oh, the large container next to the cookies, the one that just appeared, is my home-made maple cinnamon ice cream." Morgana pointed. From nowhere two dishes appeared in her hands, followed by two spoons and two large helpings of ice cream. "Cookie in my dish, please, Michael? Yours are really good."

Moments later, Morgana and Krystal were sitting in her office.

"You seemed perturbed," Krystal said to Morgana.

"I had spontaneous outside offers of faculty positions. By custom, I tell the tenure committee. They make a counteroffer. Instead, they were really unhappy with me, Patrick Wells in particular. His attitude was close to 'you had better accept one of them because you are not staying here'. He also sent me a note that I am to cease tutoring his children in using their gifts."

Krystal wrinkled her eyebrows. "That's very strange. Does he know who you really are?"

"Yes, though he can't tell anyone not on the tenure committee. He is unhappy with something involving his oldest daughter, the really smart one. I don't know what." Morgana shrugged. "Moving to Central California will still be good. But that's not why you are here, I think."

"True. Notwithstanding General Dreikirch and his fulminations and secret reports against the English and the French, claiming they are hiding Eclipse, there is a reasonably likelihood that Eclipse lives here in America. If she's found, the Prussians and the Aztecans descend on us with their persona teams, my people and hopefully the State Defense Forces ride to the rescue, and very quickly things get really ugly for us. We're outnumbered. My question to you is whether or not I can ask you for support, you as your primary persona. I can't conscript you, I can't give you orders, but that combination is alarming."

"It is especially alarming because the Eight Banners of Manjukuo will show up at the same time," Morgana said. Krystal swallowed. "There should be concern that the Lords of Eternity are behind this as one of their master schemes, at the level of the destruction of Atlanticea, Marik, and Leaviork, among others. But this time they may have the America Republic as the target. If that's the case, America is most likely doomed. I say 'likely' because the Bearer may actually be an American, and might turn the power of the Namestone against the Eternal Lords. My best suggestion is that isolationism may have worked for the past millennia, but a radical change in American foreign policy is now needed. The anti-invasion powers, England, France, Austria-Hungary, Russia, China, Brazil, may well be served by a mutual defense alliance."

"Change our foreign policy? That's…unthinkable," Krystal said.

"I have heard unthinkable before." Morgana's voice turned cold as ice. The smile vanished from her face. "From the Grand Tradesmaster of Sarnath.

The Poet Supreme of Gaea Atlanticea. The Goetic Grand Sorcerer. They refused to think. They refused to change. They met their dooms. Refuse to think, and eventually you will be unable to think, because you will be dead, the ashes of your cities scattered to the six winds, your names reduced to myth and soon-lost memories. You know who I truly am. You will arrange for me an audience with Speaker Ming, President Pro Tem Gompers, and President Webster. If they are uncooperative, remind them that I do have the right, thanks to Thomas Jefferson and Benjamin Franklin, to address Congress, even though I have never used it."

"As you request. For your aid, we are most grateful," Krystal North bowed from the waist.

"Unfortunately, there is another issue," Morgana said. "There are stray copies of the *Presentia*. Recently, someone worked through all the exercises up to the Straight Circle. I'll skip the fine details, but that deed is easy to sense from a distance. Very recently, that someone achieved breakthrough into the Well."

"Who escorted him?" Krystal asked. Another persona, she thought, who had passed that barrier was unfortunate.

"No one. It was the crash drop route," Morgana answered. "On the bright side, the person is an American. On the other side, he survived the experience."

"One of the Lords of Eternity?" Krystal asked.

"Didn't do it, and very likely don't know it happened." Morgana shook her head. "Would you like more ice cream? I have to get back to my research group, which by now is likely about to be researching applejack ice cream, skip the ice and cream."

"I need to be back to my office, meaning I need to walk back to the Institution's teleport pads," Krystal said.

"No need. Is that your office?" Morgana gestured. A door appeared in the air, through which Krystal's vacant office was clearly visible.

"How?" Krystal stared. "Our teleport dampers?"

"That's a fourth order working. Go ahead. Just walk through." Morgana winked.

"Thank you!" A grateful Krystal stood and passed the door, which promptly closed.

Chapter Thirty-Two

The Invisible Fortress

When I got down to it, summoning the Namestone was even more frightening than entering the Maze. Walking the Maze was something I had to do, a matter of duty. Summoning the Namestone was something I wanted to do. The Namestone's power was hideously seductive. It might be tricking me into summoning it. I'd spent the needed days to recover from the Lords. I had no more excuses for postponement.

For a moment my memories carried me back to my first encounter with the Namestone. Rather, I was carried back to coming home, being more than a bit upset, and Mum asking me what had happened. On one hand, she was very protective of me. On the other hand, she expected me to stand up for myself, knowing that my gifts could get me out of all sorts of predicaments.

"You don't have to tell me if you don't want to," she had said, "unless you did something seriously wrong."

"No, Mum, nothing like that. I didn't kill anyone, or wreck anything, or even let people see that I'm a persona. But it was…I'm not sure I should say. It might be embarrassing or something, or cause all sorts of trouble."

She gave me a look. "Is it a boy?" she asked. "Your gifts will protect you."

"A boy?" It took me a moment to understand what she meant. Then I realized: She thought I'd been carrying on. OK, she was telling the truth. We'd had those talks, so I knew about getting pregnant, or the truly rare diseases that spread that way. And my gifts protect against foreign DNA, RNA, whatever, which for sure guaranteed nothing like that would happen to me. However, back then I was way too young to be carrying on. I still am.

"No!" I said. "No! You said I had to grow up more first." I had a fit of giggles. "No. I was coming home. I made a stop above Atlantis. Supposedly on a really calm day if the sun is just right you can see the Hill of the Orators under the waves."

"Sort of," she said. "It takes a truly perfect day. Did you see it?" She sounded enthusiastic.

"Couldn't possibly," I answered. "The Tomb of the Martyr rose while I watched. The whole thing."

"Some poor fool is trying… You didn't try to rescue someone, did you?"

Now she was legitimately concerned.

"That never works. You told me that." I paused. She bit her tongue. "No. The Tomb rose, and there was the illusion of the Martyr holding the Namestone." OK, I should tell her. "He looked right at me. No one else was there. He asked me if I had come to try the Maze. And he waved the Namestone at me, and said 'behold the prize that awaits you'. I managed 'Sorry, I came to look for Atlantis.' I thought that was being polite. He smiled, said 'Then I shall wait', and vanished. The Tomb sank. I actually saw Orators Hill. I think he must have tampered with the waves and the water. For a few moments, the ocean was absolutely still and clear as glass." That was the only time in my life that I've ever seen Mum look seriously frightened by something that I did.

Then I went off to a library and read *The Copper Book of Harvest Stars*. The section on its mind control powers was frightening. No, it was so terrifying that I had nightmares about it. Mind control is horrific. It was totally obvious the Namestone had to be destroyed. At the time, I just didn't see how I could do it.

Standing here wasn't going to put this behind me. I unscrewed the lid on my impervium jar, tipped the jar on its side, and let Namestone's weightless presence roll into my hand. I gestured with wrist and palm. The Namestone floated obediently above my skin.

One last check. All my shields, all my presets, were at hair-trigger sensitivity. My gifts were called as deep as I can go without hurting myself. Yes, I can go way deeper. You can always go deeper if you don't mind dying.

"Namestone, I invoke thee." That was the Copper Book's phrase. "Be one with me." I was still standing on the floor of my den. The Namestone hovered over my hand. We merged. We were inside each other. I stood in the Hall of Blue Flame, the hidden space within the Namestone. Inside the Hall, the Namestone rests on an ivory pedestal. I counted slowly to forty-three. I had complete control of Namestone's power. I think.

I could feel its gifts all around me. Mind control. Material summoning. The list of gifts went on and on. I had a specific task to complete. Shillyshallying around made it all the more likely that I would fail to complete it.

"I summon *The True Copper Book of the Eternal Harvest Stars*," I announced. *The True Copper Book* appeared before me, hovering in mid-air. The me inside the Namestone took the book in both hands. The book was heavy as all get-out, as much weight as I can handle. Yes, I'm strong, but only as strong as physical work and vigorous weight training make me. My shoulder grumbled. The book joined me, me and it now each being in two places at once. The me in the Hall leaned back, raising the book just enough that the me outside the Namestone could set the book down on my desk. *The True Copper Book* came to rest, taking part of its weight off my shoulders. I pushed forward with my hips, shoving the book ahead until its weight was entirely on my desk. A floorboard creaked.

"Namestone, I release your power." Now I was only standing on the floor of my den. The Namestone floated above my desk.

Shaking, I put the Namestone back in its hiding place. We'd only been one for a few moments, but I could still hear its gifts calling to mine. Even Mum didn't realize I'd picked up true mind control. I had. The Namestone was loaded with mind control, seductive of all the good I could do the world, if only I merged my gifts with its power. I dwelt emphatically on a practical issue. After we merged, I would lose most of my personality, not to mention all of my ethical principles, such as they are. It would be running the world, not necessarily with good intentions.

I checked that the bowl was tight closed, then released my grip on my gifts. One by one, they settled away from me. I'd done enough with my gifts for one day. Besides, my next step was to read *The True Copper Book*. OK, it is in one of the four languages I actually read fluently, but reading it was still going to take a week, that after I finish rereading the *Presentia*.

The next morning I dragged. I was still alert. It seemed to be a fine day to have breakfast and make a start at reading the *True Book* and then finish re-reading the *Presentia*. After demolishing a stack of pancakes, Medico politely applauding, two glasses of orange juice, a glass of milk, and preparing a pot of tea, I went up to my den. The teapot and mug went onto a tea tray, not my desk where they usually went. The book might be indestructible, but it was still owed proper respect.

I began to read. "Underlying all is the true fire, the fire of the One Presence. The Presence is complete, but it is fulfilled by the …there was a word in Goetic that I do not know, and I have a very good reading vocabulary…of Creation and Destruction, and the...the same word…of the Six Quarters." I could tell the mystery word was a plural. I made a note to myself and kept on reading. For all the *True Book* is quite thick and very heavy, it is not so many pages. It is printed on copper plates, the letters being inlaid in black glass. Inlaying meant that the reverse of each page was blank.

Chapter Thirty-Three

Secure Chamber Alpha
The Palace of Peace
Geneva, Switzerland

An exhausted League Chancellor Holmgren rapped his gavel once on its bloodwood sounding block. The tension in the room was unbearable, but he had no choice. "This meeting of the Special Peace Executive, the Council of the Thirteen, will be in order. I humbly thank Elizaveta Romanoff for agreeing to serve as the Secretary. I shall preface the meeting with the observation that we have reached several dread days under the League Constitution. On one hand, despite the obvious threat to peace posed by the Namestone, this Executive is very surely not unified. Worse, the Hall of the People has assembled the votes to force it into an unsummoned meeting, a meeting in which I will be subject to questions by our Parliamentarians. They know the Namestone will bring us to Paradise, and want an explanation of why Paradise has not already been attained. Worse yet, the Popular Assembly has only now agreed by majority vote on its day and time of meeting. Still worse, I have in front of me a list of Serious Threats to Peace, each with the needed attestations." At his mention of the count of votes in the Hall, several Ambassadors snapped sharply alert.

"How is this possible?" Prussian Ambassador Heinrich Moeller mumbled. "Surely the parties of the right are the majority in the Hall?"

"A wise question," Holmgren answered. It was better, he decided, to keep saying nice things to people than to snip back that the representative of the German Emperor had interrupted him. The German Emperor kept Moeller on a very short leash; if Moeller interrupted, he was surely doing as the German Emperor had commanded. Several other Council members looked remarkably unsurprised. They had known it was coming. "However, many parties that support the current order are also parties that respond to their national leaders. Others have differing perspectives as to what order is. Then there is the peculiarity in the Argentine."

A grumble arose across the chamber. "Gentlemen, could we please calm down?" Amanda Rafaela Mascarenhas da Silva was the slim, dark-haired representative of the Brazilian Emperor. Her service on the Council of the

Thirteen extended back through four decades and two dozen international crises. "We only have three kilometers of granite above us. Surely we do not want the reporters on the surface to hear our every word? Good. Elizaveta, be so kind as to put your cookies into circulation. And having said that, I believe we are supposed to start with fixing our agenda, aren't we, Lars, dear?"

"Yes, mother," Lars answered. Ambassador da Silva's grandmotherly presence had more than once brought meetings back to order. "Of course. First we must set the agenda. Then we can start our rational discussions. Having said that, issues for this meeting include Baltimore, the Namestone, a series of small villages near the Argentine-Brazil border, the so-called Lords of Death, and, of course, the Assembly meeting. Did I forget anything? Wasn't that enough? I have your votes for a preferred ordering. There is no consensus. I propose Lords first, because it should be short and happy. Yes?" The Council nodded. "Ambassador Buncombe, your city, your report."

"I have circulated a document. The Lords of Death, a wanted group of highly dangerous international criminals, attacked the city of Medford—that's a Cambridge suburb. Rumors that the Lords of Eternity intervened in the fray appear to be incorrect. The Lords of Death were engaged by local personas, including Sunssword of the Boston organized militia, and two others. The Lords of Death lost. Their survivors are being subject to enhanced judicial inquiry as to their criminal acts, in particular where they hid their loot. In accord with American law, interrogation is being conducted within the American judicial system. We are providing information to local authorities around the globe as it is found. I gather that the League's Elite Strike Team is currently disassembliating their previously secret bases. There's much more in my report, but I don't see anything we need be bothered with," Buncombe said.

"Questions?" Holmgren asked. "Ambassador Romanoff?"

"Thaddeus?" Elizaveta Romanoff was the petite, sharp-witted representative of the Russian Imperial government. "The Lords of Death attacked Moscow. They took out the Moscow garrison, grabbed the Tsar's Easter Eggs, and escaped before the Imperial Host could arrive from Saint Petersburg. The Lords were extremely powerful and effective, but in Boston were stopped by only three people. Are we sure you have the real Lords of Death, not some faux replica?"

"The Judicial Inquiry has already confirmed the guilt of the accused. These are the people who took your Easter Eggs. Alas, we still do not know what they did with them. They hid their loot not in a secret base, but someplace else that they did not think about very often," Buncombe said. "They appear to have been fond of collective mind control on themselves to hide useful facts. As noted in my report, the power levels above Medford were extremely large. If one of the trio protecting our city had not thrown an area shield, Greater Cambridge might well have burned to the ground, despite its lightning screen. I ask that your experts consult our written report, which is a work in progress."

"As this Council owes these three Americans a vote of thanks," Legate Saigo observed, "It is only polite to ask who these three distinguished personages are, that they may be properly thanked. I did not find this in your report."

"As I said," Buncombe, said, "My report is a work in progress. One of the three is the Cambridge persona Sunssword, who is readily reached. Another appears to be the Pacific Shore persona Spindrift, who is very difficult to find except when she chooses to appear. The third is, we think, a boy aged not as much as thirteen. We do not know who he is. We only think that 'he' is appropriate. That picture shows what American boys usually wear; it's not garb."

"Hmm," Saigo said, "A boy with no name. I shall if there is no objection draft an appropriate statement of thanks for our approval. Thaddeus, thank you. Enough on this. Time spirals away like a fall of semiprecious stones, gleaming once and gone forever."

"Might we hear about the Hall?" Moeller asked. "I dislike surprises."

"There are a series of issues," Holmgren answered. "We have not yet caught the Bearer. We are pursuing the Bearer. Baltimore. The Argentine. In any event, the entire American delegation requested a meeting. So did the French. So did many delegates from South America. Count noses. That's well more than enough."

"Was a blocking vote not sought?" Moeller asked. Holmgren looked thoughtful. It was well known that Kaiser Friedrich IV had no interest in popular assemblies, but surely his ambassador should have been paying some attention to what was happening in the Hall of the People?

"I understand that such a vote was sought," Holmgren answered. I should know, he thought. I spent much of the last week on the phone whipping unsuccessfully for one. Apparently the Prussian delegation chose to keep their position secret from you, Moeller, which is at least odd. "Indeed the German, Russian, Brazilian, Manjukuoan, and IncoAztecan delegations were solidly supportive, as were their expected allies. However, the South Asian, Japanese, Austro-Hungarian, Ottoman, and British delegations, and their usual allies, remained neutral, so the needed majority was not obtained for a block. We shall meet in three days."

"I thank the Chancellor for his detailed political reporting on this very surprising event," Moeller said, "and having impolitely interrupted, support the Chancellor's choice for the next topic."

"I propose matters in the Argentine, though I gather it is now the Argentine and the Brazilian Empire," Holmgren said. "I also gather that matters have mayhaps moved away from war. I believe Ambassador Buncombe represents his country's Argentine friends."

"However," said Buncombe, "I have already talked, so I shall defer to

Amanda Rafaela. You are correct. While it is not good news, the mysterious attacks have now clearly struck on both sides of the border between Brazil and the Argentine, including once with Brazilian witnesses, so there is now less finger pointing and more serious concern. Besides, what we are politely calling cookies from Elizaveta are about to reach me, and I wish to avoid starvation," Buncombe said, reaching to touch his lapel. Buncombe's colleagues all recognized the small pin that marked him as a Superior Porker of the Prestigious International Gourmand Society.

"I shall of course thank my illustrious colleague," Ambassador Mascarenhas da Silva said, "for protecting an innocent young woman namely myself from Elizaveta's temptations. After all, I cannot be eating while I am talking. Having said that, there have been a series of tragic events near our national borders. Something appears from the skies, cuts all communications to a small town, butchers its inhabitants, and loots the town. This has happened now thirteen times. In support of the something have been oddly dressed people wielding swords and deploying very strange gifts.

"I have here a map of events up until a few days ago." Her map appeared on the wall screens. "You will notice that the events have gradually moved south and west toward the coast. The numbers are the town populations. Progressively larger towns have been destroyed. The earliest events were near Posadas, leading to odious suggestions that the events were the responsibility of our Empire. I suppose I cannot fault people for declining to believe that Uruguay is behind the attacks. However, recently the events have skipped across the border into my country, so there now appears to be some agreement that these events are not due to some unspecified national force.

"Survivor descriptions are extremely scanty. The only path to surviving is apparently to run away very fast, starting very early in the attack. Only one good set of photographs are extant, for which we may thank this young man." The wall screen showed a glum little boy.

"He escaped, but one of his sisters later died of her injuries. But when his family ran, he grabbed the family camera, pointed it skyward, and held down the trigger button. He captured three images a second through a good telephoto lens, giving pictures like these:" More images appeared on the screen. "These have also been seen on the video news, though at lower resolution. The object in the sky doesn't seem to be a solid object. It moves through itself. More recently, we gained these photographs from Japanese tourists. They are superb images. There's also a video. These are all existing light, but a few were obtained the next morning in daylight. This unknown people are a uniformed force, complete with scarlet capes and ornate hats, waving swords that also create special effects resembling long-range attacks. Whoever they are, they all teleport or have very good cooperation with remote teleporters. We were lucky enough to have a spotter watching one town that was attacked. She maintains that absolutely no gifts were in use, either by these men or by the sky creature."

"I compliment you on these photographs," Ambassador Moeller said, taking advantage of a pause in the presentation, the cookies having reached the Brazilian ambassador, "but how did you manage to obtain them?"

"We deployed a large number of soldiers with very good cameras," Amanda Rafaela answered, "in carefully hidden positions outside of the towns. There were thousands of towns to cover. We deployed five divisions of our army, most of whom watched towns that have not yet been attacked. The photographs and videos you are now seeing were taken yesterday. Our National Police are now preparing a detailed report for this council."

"In a spirit of cooperation," Buncombe said, "the Brazilians shared their plans for observation sites with the Argentines, who have made similar deployments. We must now wait, so to speak, for the fish to take the lure. It is very sad to use towns full of innocent men, women, and children as bait, but that is our current situation. No one appears to have any information that would let us trace this creature or these people back to their lairs."

"Please forgive another question," Moeller asked, "but have there been no local personas to grapple with these criminals?"

"The towns were quite small," Ambassador Mascarenhas da Silva answered. "There would usually be a few people with gifts, but in our part of the world most gifts are not so useful for fighting other people. The attacks occur in the middle of the night. In small agricultural towns, at this hour people are sound asleep. One town had a significant police garrison. From the number of spilled cartridge cases, someone spent a considerable time firing the garrison's heavy machine gun, but there were no signs of casualties on the other side. We have not identified any persona with combat gifts who engaged the invaders; I gather that the Argentines are in a similar boat. Or are they?"

"I can speak to that," Buncombe said. "There are several places in the Argentine in which personae with modest combat gifts lived. No one who engaged the invaders survived the experience. No witnesses to the combat survived. No one knows in any detail what happened. There are signs of damage that appear to have been due to the local personae using their gifts. The invaders do not use normal gifts to damage things. Whatever they are using is quite distinctive in its effects."

"However, as was not true when we jointly requested this item be added to the agenda, the likelihood that these events will create strife between Great Powers has been greatly if tragically reduced. We also agree that these attacks are themselves acts of war. However, "To Whom It May Concern" is just not an appropriate opening for a Declaration of War, and we do not know who the responsible parties might be. Mindful of the League Charter, I report that there is now a Memorandum of Understanding agreeing to joint military action against the perpetrators, when we catch them. The Memorandum is signed by Brazil, the Argentine, Uruguay, and under the Monroe Doctrine the American Republic. That seems to finish this discussion."

Several Ambassadors shifted in their seats. The American Republic prominently did not involve itself in foreign affairs. The James Clerk Monroe doctrine had created a series of bilateral agreements, each stating that the American Republic would on request provide support to nations of Southern America that were attacked by transoceanic powers. Those agreements had never been invoked. Now America was showing signs of applying its substantial wealth and power, if only against a mysterious group of bandits. Saigo Shigetoshi leaned back in his uncomfortable European chair. The shift in American attitudes was a pleasant surprise. Mayhaps his missive from the Emperor and the All-Conquering Generalissimo had been considered favorably by the Speaker of the House. Mayhaps there were facts that Buncombe and Mascarenhas da Silva had neglected to stress.

"What's next?" Holmgren asked. "With respect to the search for the Bearer, I report no progress." The look on Holmgren's face suggested that he had swallowed a particularly sour pickle. "All I shall say is that anyone who can thread the Maze is not a total dunce, anyone who can stand off the League Elite Strike Team and the Screaming Skull himself at the same time is a persona with gifts of some power, and we are only guessing that searching the world is the right answer. There is also the unfortunate matter of the Baltimore Incident. Yes, Ambassador Buncombe?"

"First, I note for the record," Buncombe began, "that I specifically requested that General von und zu Dreikirch should be here to answer questions about the Baltimore Incident. I do not seem to see him."

"As Chancellor, he reports to me, and I directly ordered him not to attend, your request notwithstanding," Holmgren said. "I am the Chancellor, there is a world emergency, and you should show the needed solidarity to support my decision."

"I understand why you ordered him to be absent," Buncombe said, "namely to answer my questions about the League's attack on the American Republic. Second, I am ordered by the American Federal Senate to specify…"

"That will be enough," Holmgren interrupted, "In an emergency, you are not to allowed question the Chancellor's decisions on the deployment of our League persona forces. …"

"…that the Baltimore Attack was an act of war against my Republic…"

"Baltimore was not an attack! It was a legitimate police operation. In times of emergency there is a need for…"

"…and that American Federal Senate categorically and absolutely refuses to be responsible…" Buncombe rolled on without a pause.

"solidarity with the League. Enough, I said!"

"…for the consequences if such an attack is repeated," Buncombe concluded.

"Strike that from the record!" Holmgren shouted.

"You will not," Buncombe said.

"Don't you dare contradict me!" Holmgren snapped. "I am the League Chancellor. I am entitled to make that decision."

"I think not, old chap," Featherstonehaugh said quietly. "Needs a vote. And I much doubt that you have the votes for a deletion." Other Ambassador's jaws dropped. English hatred of the American Republic went back nearly two and a half centuries. King George the Mad had managed to lose the larger part of the royal navy, much of the English Army, various mercenary forces, and a substantial number of English personae during his unsuccessful effort to merge the American Republic into the United Kingdom. He had then had no choice but to concede to the Emperor Napoleon French rule of much of Europe. Only in the next century did the French regret not including Prussia in the French Imperium. If the American Ambassador said the sky was blue, the English Ambassador would be expected to explain that poor, benighted Cousin Jonathan should abandon his superstitious belief in the myth that there is a sky. Suddenly, here was an English Ambassador supporting the Americans.

"We are in a time of emergency, and I simply order that the remarks be stricken," Holmgren said. "Your duty of solidarity requires that you support me."

"Lars, old chap," Featherstonehaugh continued, "You may manage to chuck the rules, but if you do, you chuck all of them, not just the ones you want to chuck. In particular, you would chuck the rule of confidentiality, which some of us might view as a loss. Not me, but some of us."

"Don't you dare suggest…"

"Your call, Lars," Featherstonehaugh said. "If you want something stricken, you must have a vote. If you want to claim that in this emergency you are suspending the rules, you have suspended all the rules, not just some of them. The confidentiality rules, for example."

"Forgive me for the interruption," Prince Shi said, "might we begin with a description of the actual event? So we all understand why there is some lack of cordiality? While reports have been received in the Celestial Republic, they appear confused. Of course, eyewitness reports by virtuous and honest but uneducated and illiterate peasants and craftsmen are often misleading though entirely true, but surely there is a good description of events? We may recall the circumstances of four centuries ago, when peasants on Hainan informed the local District Magistrate that they had seen a dragon, and he correctly informed them that they had in fact seen an airplane. Mayhaps our illustrious Chancellor and most respected American Ambassador would allow someone else to speak to this?" Ambassador Saigo nodded and smiled at the Prince. The nod and smile were returned. The discussion had been going downhill very rapidly. Shi Fang's not-entirely-innocent question might serve to defuse the tension.

The Ambassadors looked around the table, waiting. Featherstonehaugh tentatively raised his hand, but heard no objection. "By what I honestly believe and Her Majesty's government hopes to be coincidence, Her Majesty's battleship *Majestic* had arrived in Baltimore the previous day, bringing new members of the diplomatic staff to our American embassy. The visit had been scheduled a year in advance. My colleagues in London insist we had no prior warning of what happened.

"The *Majestic* was anchored well off-shore, with a good view of the island where much of the combat took place. As is often the case in combat involving personas who fly, some of the combat reached urban Baltimore. Several of our sailors enjoying shore leave were injured rescuing children from a burning school. It is excellent news that the children were unhurt. However, we had a considerably number of witnesses more or less on scene, many of whom recorded events with their VideoBells. There are also videos taken by the *Majestic*. Many other videos are available on the net, from which a reasonably consistent picture can be assembled.

"In any event, there appeared on this island a contingent of the League Peace Police, personae teleported in from someplace. We do not understand why the Peace Police appeared where they did, and must insist on an explanation. They fell upon a young lady, a woman who resembles Eclipse, who turned out to be a persona of substantial defensive gifts. She somehow attracted the attention of the local authorities. Several state militias came to her rescue. In any event, the young lady was uninjured. The Peace Police detachment was arrested, though not until a significant amount of violence had taken place."

"There is no *arrested*," Holmgren snapped. "League Peace Police are not subject to interference by member states. Indeed, the League Interlocutor is now preparing arrest warrants for the Maryland Liberty Guard for their criminal acts."

Count Ferencz raised his hand. He wore the traditional dress of the Austro-Hungarian Diplomatic Corps, a plain dark suit with a scarlet tie bearing the Hapsburg crest. "Please. Must we seek to make matters worse rather than better? Somehow the League managed to assault the wrong woman, who for unclear reasons was believed to be Eclipse, reportedly without first advising her that she was under arrest. The local militia, who had no idea who was trying to kill a local resident, intervened. The Maryland judiciary has blocked the criminal investigatory process, the copying the memories of the arrested and charged people, while the diplomatic and legal issues are sorted out."

"The detachment," Holmgren said, "clearly identified themselves as being from the Peace Police. They were in proper Peace Police uniforms. It is utterly unacceptable that they should be attacked by local riff-raff. Surely this rule is entirely clear?"

"Of course," Moeller said. Several of his colleagues nodded assent.

"If peasants attacked the representatives of the Great Inca, they would be thrown off a cliff," Ambassador Smoking Frog observed, "unless they were personas. Then they would be burned alive." Buncombe wondered, in the present case, which side Ambassador Smoking Frog thought should to be incinerated.

"In America," Buncombe said, "Foreign hooligans who appear from nowhere and assault young women are treated like the hooligans they are. Any man with a few hundred dollars in his pocket can purchase an adequate facsimile of a League uniform, so their costumes did not identify them. It is a mark of traditional American liberality that the hooligans in question were arrested and not hanged on the spot. Those thugs are precisely the opposite of foreign visitors, Her Majesty's sailors, for example, who risked their lives to protect small children. They are being treated like the heroes they are. With respect to the League Peace Police, assuming -- which has not yet been confirmed -- that the arrested persons are Peace Police, 'obeying orders' would be a defense during trial. The Republic has a clear and unambiguous law specifying how requests for extradition of American citizens for acts committed on American soil are to be handled, namely they are to be rejected out of hand."

"As my question has been answered," Prince Shi said, "I should note that foreign dogs who appeared from thin air, assaulted a Chinese citizen, and refused to surrender to the Legion of Perfected Men, pending a proper inquiry, would be liable to being beheaded."

"The American position," Moeller said, "is totally unacceptable. It is entirely correct for the League to insist that the Americans who assaulted and murdered League Peace Police should be arrested and extradited to Switzerland for trial and execution."

"I can assure you, Ambassador Moeller, that no such event will occur," Buncombe said flatly. "Mayhaps, since several of the alleged Peace Police claim to be Prussian nationals, you should be more concerned with whether or not the foreigners in question will be tried and hanged by the Maryland authorities."

"If I may," Suleiman Pasha intruded, "I have a modest question. Princess Elizaveta and I were comparing notes, based on the video reports. There is a riddle. Eclipse, this woman dressed as Eclipse, dressed so indecently as to be wearing not even one veil, first appeared in a Baltimore Park. Images were very rapidly forwarded to Geneva. She then teleported to that island. Its name, by the way, is *Captain Hawley's Smugglers' Bar*. Within a few minutes, the Peace Police arrived. The Commandery of the Faithful, possessor of the largest and best-trained persona force in the world, opines that the Brigade Commander in question did a superb job of deploying his forces swiftly." Holmgren beamed at the praise. "Not more than a few seconds later, several America state militias arrive, already prepared to engage the Peace Police. A few seconds? The implied efficiency is unbelievable. You'd think they had been sharing timing notes with this cosplayer, who I hope was not injured. Can you explain this, Thaddeus?"

"We're Americans. We do things right." Buncombe shook his head. "Suleiman, do not undersell yourself. The efficiency of the Ottoman military is world-famous. Your Empire, when it became needful, would have done as well."

"A minor question," Amanda Rafaela said. She paused, waiting for Holmgren's nod. "Did I follow that there has not yet been a formal extradition request, asking the Americans to turn over these state militia members?"

"Correct," Holmgren said. "It is being prepared."

"And the Americans have not yet received formal documentation letting them identify which of their prisoners are Peace Police?" Amanda Rafaela sounded doubtful. "But for the nonce American authorities are suspending their criminal investigation? Did you know that, Heinrich?"

"You are correct," Heinrich Moeller agreed. "Also, Friedrich, Invincible Kaiser of All the Germans, asked me to specify that American treatment of the surviving members of the Ulm Peace Police Brigade has been rigorously proper, except of course that they are being held prisoner. In particular, they have been allowed access to the Prussian Consul in Washington."

"In that case, mayhaps we should not put the carriage in front of the donkey. We should let all this paperwork transmit one way or the other. I propose we postpone this discussion until papers have had a chance to transmit." Amanda Rafaela looked around the room.

"I agree," Fateh Singh said.

"As do I," Prince Shi said.

"And I," Legate Hong agreed,

"Must we?" Holmgren asked. "Hands if this is the sense of the body? Opposed? There appears to be overwhelming agreement. Postpone for a week? We are agreed."

Chapter Thirty-Four

Thaddeus Buncombe
The Satsuma Legation
Geneva, Switzerland

Standing, admiring a large bouquet, were Saigo Shigetoshi and his wife Saigo Nene. The Small Dining Pavilion was its familiar understated self. Table and chairs were a concession to Buncombe's age and national background.

"Welcome, Lord Ambassador," Saigo said. "We are entirely in private and among friends. Let us not stand on formality. Here I am just Shigetoshi."

"You do me great honor, Shigetoshi-Tono. And it is always most interesting to hear your gossip, Nene-Tono," Buncombe answered.

"My little rumors, Thaddeus-Tono," Saigo Nene answered. "But we are in Europe, and should try European manners. I am Nene," she answered.

"And I am then Thaddeus," Buncombe answered.

"Friend Thaddeus?" the Japanese Legate gestured to his American counterpart.

"Yes, friend Shigetoshi?" Ambassador Buncombe answered.

"A happy end to a tedious morning?" Saigo asked. "My legation's chef has received and been testing the latest book of recipes from the Steel Gastronome. Pates and terrines are much work, but are truly magnificent in their complexity."

"This would be excellent," Nene added. "And you brought only your appetite, as we asked." They turned to their lunch. Several courses later, conversation began.

"In that case, Thaddeus," Saigo said, "mayhaps you could, between bites of the quail eggs, not to mention the turkey egg stuffed with foie gras in that magnificent reduction, explain to us about the combat above Boston. Your barony--state--defense force was largely absent, Sunssword seemed much more effective than rumor had it, and these other two people, well, almost no one has heard of them. Nene tells me that a few people have heard of Spindrift, mayhaps for the past few months."

"No one expects the Lords of Death," Buncombe explained. "Not until they show up. However, the timing appears to have been that they appeared, announced their demand that Jane Caroline Wells surrender to them, and very soon thereafter the very young man appeared. There was already some effort by local unorganized personas to discomfit the Lords, but that takes a while to get going. Why did the Lords attack the young man? The Lords apparently had a good spotter, who immediately identified -- let's call him X -- as a very high power persona. X appears to have been waiting for friends, or mayhaps looking at the situation before he leaped. While he was doing this, the Lords of Death jumped him. They teleported behind and launched multiple mentalic attacks, multiple physical attacks, and mayhaps others. Matters became very violent, very quickly. The Lords' combat style is find and smash. The teleport dodge and weaves? X seems to be very well trained, not to mention being able to use a great deal of power indeed. It is therefore truly interesting we do not know who he is. Yes, there are a vast number of personas all across the world, but not at this level, especially when you start counting how many different gifts X used.

"Apparently the Stars Over Boston expected Sunssword to appear at their Castle Island fortress and move them to the scene of battle. This expectation continued even though some time ago they had more or less ejected Sunssword from their group over some theological issue. In any event, she did show up in Boston, and went after the Lords, expecting to be by herself. She is a very private person, so members of our National Force had to be discrete in interviewing her. The detailed analysis of her back and forth with the Lords is in my report. Her position is that she did a fair amount of damage to their force shields without extending herself, and returned for much more just as Spindrift and X took the Lords out. The National Team added that in talking with Sunssword they were speaking with a young woman who at the same time seemed very old and very tired, as though she has seen all this many times before," Buncombe continued. "I am left with the impression that there are matters I do not understand."

"That last one I believe I can explain," Nene said. "The clue is her name, which is being pronounced Sun-sword, but which is actually Sun's Sword. You obtained an excellent photograph of Sunssword, who is almost never seen in photographs except while masked. For better or worse, I am almost sure I recognize her, namely she is the same person seen here." Nene unrolled a reproduction of a classic Heian period painting. "Sure these two people are the same, down to the enthusiastic unJapanese smile and golden hair. The painting, however, is the Golden Warrior, the Living Sword of the Sun Goddess Amaterasu, sent to earth three thousand years ago. Even the descriptions of the powers match. She is indeed truly old, and not at all fond of combat, for all she is very good at it. It is fortunate that your National Team was polite to her. If they had not been polite, they might have suffered from the error of their ways."

"Very interesting," Buncombe said. "Our American custom is that personae are entitled to their privacy, a custom that our National Team doubtless honored. Apparently, a fact not well hidden, Sun's Sword in a private persona works in Cambridge at the Rogers Technological Institution. Her friends seem to be aware that she is Sun's Sword, or at least Sunsword, but not that she is particularly gifted other than as a teleporter. On the other hand, also not in my report because it does not refer to the powers of the Lords of Death, we have a fairly precise account of how the Lords were rendered unconscious. It appears that Spindrift, in addition to her other gifts, is an extremely powerful drain. While X was in the process of defeating the Lords, who were also losing to Sunssword, Spindrift substantially took down all of the Lords' gifts. The minor detail omitted from my report, because it says nothing about the Lords, is that just as Spindrift was about to drain the Lords, X teleported directly between her and them to shield Spindrift from the Lord's physical attacks, and managed to be the main - say 90 or 95% - target of the drain. X was not neutralized."

"Hmm," Shigetoshi said, "that would make X more powerful than the Seven Lords of Death, put together, by a significant factor. Mayhaps we already knew this, given that he protected Boston from incineration. There are people so powerful, but not many of them."

"Indeed, husband," said Nene, "the list is sufficiently short that I can call their names from memory, and surely X is not any of them. I gather X was not forthcoming while handing the Lords over to the Stars Over Boston?"

"Not at all," Buncombe said. "Indeed, Spindrift and X both faded from sight when the Stars Over Boston and then the National Team arrived. The one tracker who tried to follow Spindrift later made the emphatic assertion that she did not teleport, though I cannot see how this claim could be possible. I can, however, see that the small dumplings in duck broth and the seaweed salad are now upon us, so mayhaps we should give more attention to your most magnificent repast."

"You are most wise, Thaddeus," Shigetoshi said.

"Indeed," Nene said. "Let us return to this when we are settling our digestion prior to the first of the terrines. Yes, the small dumplings are superb. And every one is slightly different."

Several hours later, they reached the final main course. "The Angela's Pillow was amazing," Buncombe said. "As were the three predecessors. Once again, your Chef has shown he is the culinary master of the world."

"Mentioning masters of the world," Nene said, "there was an interesting question here. Your nation is populous. Surely Americans are the richest in the world. But your country has never been interesting in foreign intercourse. Now suddenly there is this joint communique with Brazil. While we could congratulate the Daimyo for his sound advice to your Speaker, on which you have acted, we might wonder if there will be more miracles, or if our humble Province is truly responsible for these changes."

"I am but a humble ambassador," Buncombe answered. "I am not privy to the thinking of the Federal Senate, except as it tells me what to do. You saw that today when the Chancellor tried to interrupt me. However, it is not a secret that our Senate met in closed session and our Congress met in closed session. The latter refers to an arcane feature of our Federal Constitution, never before invoked, that the Immortal Morgan Le Fay as a founder of our Republic is entitled to address our Congress. She did. I gather that she gave an extremely concise and incisive critique of our foreign policy, a critique which was in remarkable agreement with the positions of the Satsuma Daimyo and Speaker Ming on this topic. I am advised that after debate there was overwhelming support for this change. I have been instructed to say that there will be further changes in this direction."

Chapter Thirty-Five

The Blue Hills
and
An uninhabited isle in the Pacific

The John Adams monument is the final tribute of the people of Massachusetts to their father of the Fourth Republic. Strictly speaking, the John Adams Monument is 25 feet shorter than the Jefferson Monument, just as the Jefferson monument is 25 feet shorter than the Washington Monument. However, the Washington Monument rises from tidal Washington, the Jefferson Monument across the Aqua Potomociae starts at the same altitude, but the people of Massachusetts put their monument at the top of Great Blue Hill. The observation deck lets you see out into the Atlantic.

I appeared near the monument, moderately above the Franklin rods. I was a few moments early. Sunssword was exactly on time. <*I brought dinner,*> I announced.

<*So did I,*> Sunssword answered. <*Is your girlfriend joining us?*> She was looking at me very intently when she asked that.

<*We meet her,*> I answered. <*On a remote and deserted tropical isle. Except she isn't my girlfriend. Well, not that sort of girlfriend. She apologizes deeply. I did the cooking for both of us. May I do the teleporting?*> For once I did not try dodge and weave, here to beyond the moon and back. No sense in letting Sunssword see how I avoid being followed. One jump brought us to the island, a hundred feet above the lagoon. The sunrise was absolutely beautiful. Being tropical, it would also be short-lived. Spindrift had set up my pavilion tent, table, and chairs. We landed. Off came Sunssword's helmet and cape. She was, indeed, drop-dead gorgeous, exactly as rumored.

"You're Sunssword," I said. "We didn't have time to introduce before. In this persona, I'm just Joe. And this is Spindrift." We grasped hands in a circle. "My appetizers will get cold if we don't get started." I said, "Let's talk while we eat."

Yes, my openers would get cold. They were fresh-baked hard-crust biscuits, but each piece was stuffed differently. Hot shrimp with a very little molten stilton. Lettuce casing, chopped cucumber, a little sausage, and sweet mustard. Mascarpone cheese with a touch of brown sugar. Fine sliced portabella mushrooms, sauteed in olive oil with a good bit of garlic.

Sunssword looked at the two of us very intently, but sat and opened some of her own dishes. She certainly could cook. Her fish terrine in three colors was to die for.

"I told you," Spindrift said.

"Yes, but for you some of this has already happened. You knew," I answered.

"Yes?" Sunssword wasn't exactly nervous, but she was staring very hard at the glyphs on Spindrift's garb. I'm sure she was staring at the glyphs, not Spindrift's chest.

"One of your gifts, Sunssword, and you never tell anyone, is like Medico," Spindrift said. "Except you can use it on other people to see if they're in good health."

"It's like me looking with my eyes," Sunssword said. "It just happens. I don't control it. But any persona I can name, Joe, your age, who got into a fight like that would be seriously dead. So I was a bit concerned you were hurt. My lips are sealed. But I can hardly not notice," she faced me, "that you are in good health."

"Lips sealed?" I asked. Sunssword shook her head. "Yes," I agreed. "In good health. Among other things. Hard to deny. But when we were linked for combat, Sunssword, I could hear your mind. Not know everything, but hear you thinking carefully."

"Absolutely no one knows that," she answered. She knew what I meant.

"It's easier if you've heard the numbers calling before," I answered.

"You met another survivor?" she asked desperately. "Another person like me?" To be precise, I knew, she was hoping to find another survivor of the long ago place that had had people like her.

"Not another survivor," I said. "I'm told there are some." I could see Sunssword's face sag. Sunssword was an enhanced person, someone with a second, quantum optical brain and other improvements. Enhanced people had not been born in thousands of years. She was hoping to find someone else who'd survived since the last enhanced people were born. That did incidentally mean she was some thousands of years old, so she was very definitely worth cultivating. Sunssword had hoped she knew other people like her, and I'd let her down. "I'm sorry I don't have better news. I was more worried Mighty Mind was interested in me, given that he thinks clothing and people are transparent."

"Actually, Joe, Mighty Mind didn't notice you. He was too busy looking under Spindrift's clothing." Sunssword said.

"He likes girls as young as me?" Spindrift sounded dangerously annoyed. Unlike me, she was on the other side of that certain age.

"Not that way," Sunssword said. "I think. He could see you aren't made of chemical matter. Or you were bits and pieces of matter, interwoven with gifts and powers and aspects. When you get down to it, that's just a bit unusual. The *Presentia* discusses people like you. Albertus Tralfalmadorius lines people like you up with the Invincible Star Demons. Mighty Mind likely also noticed you're a girl, but that's not so interesting to him. After all, he sees everything as somewhat transparent, so whatever he sees, he's seen it before. Though you two have really solid shields. His sense of you, Joe, was at most clothing deep."

"Star Demons? Slight exaggeration," Spindrift said. "If you two hadn't been there, those guys would have taken me out."

"Mentioning taking out," I said, 'there is a bit more of the terrine, and then we can be taking out my stuffed toasted shells … homemade, stuffed with curried chopped egg, or anchovy, or caviar and sour cream…and then we get Sunssword's soup, don't we?" We hadn't actually eaten that much, the appetizers being small, but moving the topic off backgrounds might ease tempers. It might also distract Sunssword from remembering, if her gift did what she said, that I'm a girl. Mind you, Sunssword had just given away that she had read the *Presentia,* which made her a person very much of interest, so abandoning the conversation was not an option.

"Spindrift," Sunssword said, "Next time, drain first. The Lords of Death were terrified of you. But if someone pulls one of those glass balls, get out of the way. They're dangerous. Aren't they, Joe?"

"It wasn't fun." It didn't, I thought, quite kill me. It only tried hard. "But I'm here. The Lord of Death is in prison. What was that thing? Some sort of condenser?"

"It was a *teles*, Joe," Spindrift said. "It stores the thing that powers gifts. Death shorted his out, all stored power in a single blast. And it was very old, so it had been storing power for a very long time. How old? Not allowed to say."

"The Lords of Eternity collect them," Sunssword said. "Solara will be really annoyed that one was toasted. Once toasted, worthless forever."

"Is this going to happen all the time?" I asked. "People show up with arcane weapons to kidnap the Wells kids? I owe Janie. She played City of Steel with me. But it gets tiring."

"Joe!" Sunssword's exasperation showed in her voice. "It's going to get you dead, is what it is! I don't understand how you survived, last week. By rights you should be dead. The Lords should've killed you."

"They didn't," I answered, calmly.

"You're what? Twelve?" Sunssword was a bit exercised about this. "You should leave these things to grownups. Go back to base ball nines! Or models! Or wishing for a pony! Or whatever!"

OK, she doesn't know who I am or how many ponies I already have. I suppose that's good. This was still supposed to be a friendly picnic.

"If I'd done that, Janie would have been kidnapped," I answered.

"What would your parents say?" she asked.

Of course, Mum was nowhere to be found. "Mum always taught me to follow my conscience," I answered.

"What about your father?" Sunssword asked.

"Mum long ago said I was making the right decisions." That seemed to answer matters.

"I asked about your father."

"I just answered that." This conversation was getting a bit odd.

"Sunssword, he can't hear you," Spindrift said. 'He' had to be me, but what was Spindrift talking about? This had to be one of those conversations where Spindrift was in two places and times at once. Sunssword and Spindrift stared at each other.

"Never mind," Sunssword said. "Sorry. You did answer me. I'm being opaque."

"Sunssword?" Spindrift intruded. "I did the damage to Joe. My drain mostly hit him, not the Lords. You were the only grownup there on our side. Without me, the two of you would have captured them. Without Joe delaying them, the Lords would have kidnapped Janie Wells and killed most of her family. Besides, I remember parts of the future. Joe did things much more dangerous. Soon. And succeeded. Or the world dies."

Sunssword looked at Spindrift, then back at me. "In that case, Joe, do whatever you have to do. And win. You have so far. Having said that, my roast baby boar is going to get cold."

We went back to eating. There was something very strange about the last bit of the conversation, as though Sunssword was not hearing what I said. I allowed that I could think about it later. Spindrift's promise that I would soon be doing even more dangerous things was less encouraging.

Chapter Thirty-Six

The Wells Residence
Arbalest Street
Medford, Massachusetts

At precisely 6:29 PM, the three Wells children filed down from their rooms to have dinner. Janie had already set the table. Brian's contribution to dinner, the soup, was warming on the stove. Janie came first, with Trisha right behind her. Trisha had worked the order out. Neither parent could accuse her of being early without Janie being earlier. Brian was right behind her. Neither parent could accuse her of being late without Brian being later. Trisha couldn't tell if she was annoying her parents, but it was easier on her than having Dad berate her, and mayhaps sending her back upstairs without her supper. Ingrid Fairhaven had been willing to pay her in survival rations as well as cash. Most of the rations hid in the secret compartment under her window seat. Brian had hidden the rest in the secret compartment behind his workbench. The supply of rations was being depleted, but Ingrid's sister Kaylee wanted fancy clothing, too, which Trisha would soon be sewing. Their mom's charity project would be even better, but that only happened a few times a year.

"Ah, children," Patrick Wells said, "exactly on time, I see. Timeliness is such an important virtue. It shows thoughtfulness, determination, attention to detail, all the virtues that have made the American Republic great for the last twenty centuries. Indeed, let us sit down and consider your schoolwork."

"Yes, indeed, shall we?" Abigail Wells repeated.

"Yes, Father," Janie said "We also need to talk to you about a couple things." . The three children sat.

"Oh, good, but grades first. Unless you have something you want to say, Trisha?" Wells glared at his older daughter.

She bit her lips for a moment. "No, sir."

"In any event, Janie, I see your grades had a bit of a hiccup but have recovered. Was there a reason for that?"

"I just had to work harder, Dad, the way you always say," she answered. "There were a couple of weeks when I was just tired. Some correspondence games did badly. I did what I'm supposed to…I told some opponents that they had checkmate in three or five or once nine, so I was resigning. They were good opponents. I thanked them a lot." Janie told herself not to point out that the hiccup started right after Trisha got into trouble with Dad and Mom.

"And, Brian, your math, science, and engineering grades have sagged a bit. And you don't seem to have been working on your models as much. Any particular reason?"

"No, Sir," Brian answered. "Something isn't quite right with the George Washington model, so I let it sit so I could come back to it fresh. My grades were better when I could ask Trisha to ask me questions."

Patrick Wells frowned. "You had Trisha do your homework for you?"

"No!" Brian raised his voice. "I'd hit a point where something didn't make sense, and she'd ask me what something meant. Except some of her questions were dummies, that didn't help, but I didn't know which ones, so I had to think. Could we please do that again?"

"I'll think about it." Patrick nodded sagely. "And you, Trisha. What are these weird grades supposed to mean?" He waved a sheet of paper wildly in the air.

I could read that, Trisha thought, only because I am using superspeed and telescopic vision. "E is Exemplary. It's above an A+." If he doesn't know, she thought, that E is based on total points earned, not average grade, I'm not telling him. Not that the average grade is not an A+. "And Q isn't a grade. It means I went up a grade level, so I'm in the next grade."

"How can you have two Qs?" he asked, his voice harsh.

Trisha started to wilt. "I worked hard. The levels are set so that real dummies who can barely finish high school get to pass on to the next grade, so I passed the absolute minimum I needed to be in the next grade, but my real grades are good, except there's a placement exam next weekend."

"Yes?" Patrick asked.

"It gets complicated except the Guidance Counsellor told me what to do, so I show up next Saturday and Sunday and take all-day exams; it's one of these things that's in the rules someplace but only applies if your grades are really good."

"I see. I need to drive you there on Sunday?" he asked resignedly.

"No need. I turn invisible here, fly there, go into the gym locker room where there are for sure no cameras and turn visible when no one is there," she explained.

"Why didn't I know about this?" he asked.

"I just found out," she answered. "That's why our guidance counsellors are so good, they tell us about things no one ever hears about, but it must be someplace in all the school paperwork we were sent from last fall, I think."

"Very well." Patrick took another spoonful of soup. "Do well. For once, be a credit to the family."

Trisha peaked her speed, letting her wait until the pain faded. "Yes, sir," she answered sadly.

"Dad, Mom," Janie said. "There's something we need to talk about. I got a letter from the Wizard of Mars. We used to visit him, back when Trisha could take us there."

"I didn't see that letter in the mail," Abigail answered. "And I certainly don't remember reading it."

"Mom," Janie answered, "letters from the Wizard are like quarters from the tooth fairy. They appear under your pillow." That way, Janie thought, I at least get to read the letter before Mom does, instead of the letter mayhaps never reaching me. "He really wants me to visit him, two weeks from now. He says the world ends if we don't. I have the letter here." She passed the letter to her father, tilting it enough that Trisha could read the whole thing while she was passing it.

"Do many people get invitations like this?" Patrick asked.

Janie stammered, faked a cough, and started again. "I read someplace that these are really rare. And always mean what they say," she answered. She shuddered. She'd almost mentioned Professor Lafayette. Speaking that name would throw Dad into paroxysms of rage, almost as bad as mentioning her City ex-opponent Joe.

"How can the world be ending?" Abigail asked. "What's supposed to happen? It sounds silly to me."

"Mom, the Wizard of Mars does not make jokes," Brian said. "At least he never did last winter when we were having tea with him."

"Dad," Janie said, "All I have to do is fly there, listen to him, and we'll know what he's talking about. But you said we shouldn't go to Mars again, and you grounded Trisha, so we haven't been going there."

"Do you want to go?" Patrick asked.

"Mayhaps we'd better," she answered.

"You've been waiting to say something, Brian." Patrick turned to his son.

"I got the same letter," Brian said. "Same reason 'otherwise the world will end'."

"Also under your pillow?" Patrick asked.

"Right under the middle," Brian answered.

"Do you want to go?" Patrick asked.

"It's to save the world. I'd better want to go," Brian answered. "Shall I serve the roast?" He took his mother's nod to be an affirmative.

"You two both believe this letter?" Patrick asked.

"It's not a long trip," Janie said. "Wait. If it's real, why did he only tell us? Why not you? Or Krystal North? Someone who can tell us what the answer is?"

"What about you, Trisha? Did you get a letter?" Patrick asked.

"I'd have to look," Trisha answered.

"Didn't you notice a letter?" Patrick asked.

"I need to look," she answered. "Real letters come in the mail. I made my bed early. The letter might still be there."

"How could you not see a big fat letter when you were making your bed?" Abigail asked. "Do you ever pay attention to anything?"

Trisha tensed. "Mayhaps I didn't get one," Trisha answered. "Mayhaps it fell behind the bed while I was asleep. Mayhaps the letter appeared after I got up and made my bed, so it's there waiting. But if it was on the floor, it went in my waste paper basket when I swept my room this morning."

"You didn't look at it?" Abigail asked.

Trisha stared at her mother. "Dad always teaches me to be neat and throw out scrap paper so if it was in an envelope I would have looked at it but if it was just loose paper I'd have wondered how it got there because I always try to be very neat but I'd just drop it in the trash, I mean for some reason I keep finding loose sheets of paper on my dresser of all places and can never figure out how they got there because it's not that my room is drafty but I always pick things up the way you tell me."

"It was a loose sheet of paper," Brian said, not quite talking over his sister.

"I've been putting your mail on your dresser," Abigail snapped. "Don't you ever read your mail?"

"No, mom, there's been no mail on my dresser," Trisha answered. "I'm sure I'd have noticed envelopes with stamps on them."

"Young lady," Abigail said slowly, "I carefully take all your mail, take it out of its envelopes, read it to make sure there's nothing improper in it, and put it on your dresser for you to read."

"You've been reading my mail?" Trisha asked quietly. Which I knew perfectly well you started doing, she thought, but I'm not going to say that. "Oh. That's very kind of you. Well, if you read it, it's your mail, and I wouldn't read your mail, except by mistake if Aunt Petunia absent-mindedly puts my name on an envelope meant for you, which she keeps doing."

"Those letters I kept," Abigail answered. "What about all your letters from your aunts?"

"What letters?" Trisha asked. "I didn't see them."

"All the letters my sisters and your father's sisters have been writing you about how you disgraced our family," Abigail answered.

Trisha took a deep breath, a breath that lasted far longer that her parents thought, because she'd ramped her superspeed up to its absolute maximum. "I'm sorry, mother, I didn't see any letters like that. Mayhaps they blew off the dresser and fell in back. I'll check after dinner."

"How could you not see them? Don't you sweep the floor?" Trisha's mother snapped.

Trisha forced herself to smile. "Yes, mother, and you are always nice to me and check that I swept my room right. But the letters might have snagged someplace on the way down."

"Coming back to the original topic," Patrick said, very firmly, "Trisha, since you are the only child I have who can transport her siblings to Mars, do you believe this letter enough to fly there?"

Trisha shrugged. "Father, you always say not to make hasty decisions, that the American Republic is great because we think carefully about what we're going to do rather than jumping to conclusions, so I'd have to think about it and ask your advice before I said anything; I mean it's not there aren't other personas…"

"Personae," Patrick interrupted. "Form your plurals correctly."

"Personae. Where was I? …other personae who can fly them to Mars and Janie said we should not show up on Mars for weeks yet."

"This is the end of the world," Brian said.

Trisha shrugged again. "Atlanticea ended. All those other places I memorized in seventh grade ended. Why should America be different?"

"America end?" Patrick's eyebrows rose. His face flushed. "That's a totally disgraceful idea. Jessamine Trishaset, it is very definitely time for you to go to your room, even if you haven't finished eating. Now!'

Not saying another word, Trisha stood and left the table.

"Don't either of you," Patrick almost shouted at his children, "ever dare to suggest that the Republic will not last forever or need to change! Is that clear?" His children dutifully nodded their agreement. "Now, young people should always be keeping track of national and world affairs. What did you read in the evening newspaper?"

"Eclipse appeared over North Dakota," Brian said. "You could tell she was the real Eclipse because she wore one of the Niederhof garbs, bright white and lots of gold trim, her sigil on her cape and her chest. She was carrying the Namestone. There's a bunch of orphanage-ranches there. She turned several schoolhouses to solid gold, with diamond windows. She appeared over North Illinois. A whole bunch, they're still counting, of judges left notes confessing they'd taken bribes. Then they killed themselves. That's good. She saved Illinois the hangman's fees. The newspaper claimed Eclipse used mind control on them. She vanished."

"She teleports," Janie added. "Congress met in closed session. That happened a while back. But today it came out why. Morgan Le Fay appeared and talked at them. She gets to do that. It's in the Constitution. It's never happened before. No one is saying why. Oh, Governor Miller mobilized our State Militia. All of it. People are supposed to show up at armories and collect their laser rifles and disruptors."

"The stock market fell again," Brian said. "A lot. Oh, the Sera Lama announced a truce, so he could speak to Eclipse. China and South Asia are both backing it."

"Fortunately, I sold out when Eclipse grabbed the Namestone," Patrick said. "There was sure to be a panic. At some point we buy back in. Soon someone will kill her and move the Namestone back into the Maze; that will be the right moment."

Chapter Thirty-Seven

Eclipse
The Sera Lama's Truce Tent
Far Western Tibet

I accepted the Sera Lama's Truce offer. He announced security precautions. We promised each other's safety. Supposedly, the *Arcana Goetica* claimed, the Tibetans had a secret, an alternative way to destroy the Namestone. Large parts of the Arcana were incomprehensible, but that section I could understand. I think. The claim had been written thousands of years ago. The Tibetans might well have misplaced the method in the centuries since. It was still worth a try.

I arrived by teleport. My next-to-last teleport brought me to Far Western Tibet. I was looking down at the tallest land mass in the world, a place where the air was scarcely dense enough to breathe. Not quite below me was the tent described in the truce announcement. Ten miles out I could see flashes of color. That was the Tibetan Flying Host guarding the location. I'd also promised to protect their Lama. Ultravision showed the Sera Lama himself sitting near the center of the tent, as promised.

I teleported into the tent, to stand next to the second chair, facing the monk. "I greet you, Illustrious Sera Lama," I said. I'd looked up the appropriate English language title to use.

He rose. "And I greet you, Mighty Bearer of the Holy Namestone," he answered. I was not bearing at the moment. The Namestone was safe in its jar. "I hope you've read my proposal?"

Indeed, I had read it. It got to the point. I would gift him the Namestone, which I could do, and he would use the Namestone to convince everyone in the world to abandon material goods in favor of simple agriculture and meditation. He could do it, too, if he got full control of the Namestone. The Namestone let bearers do truly awful things; he was offering to do one of them.

"Yes, I have," I answered.

"Do you see the magnificent dream, how simplicity will elevate all souls to higher planes of existence?" He tried to sound convincing.

"If the bearer stays honest," I answered. "That never happens. Not for long."

"You sound very sure of yourself," he said.

"*The True Copper Book of the Eternal Harvest Stars* has plenty of historical summaries," I answered. Those were truly weird entries to put in the Namestone's operating manual. Whoever had written the book had done his best to tell readers not to use the Namestone.

"You have read *The True Copper Book*?" he asked. "And understood it all?"

I almost said that I had, but that wasn't quite correct. "The first few chapters have an occasional word I can't read. 'Underlying all is the true fire, the something of the One Presence. The Presence is complete, but it is fulfilled by the somethings of Creation and Destruction, and the somethings of the Six Quarters.' What is this something? I don't know. The chapters on the Namestone's deeds are all too understandable."

"Something? The Goetic scientist-wizards had part of a clue as to how the world works. That clue is not important, because it will not help you to purify your soul. But the deeds chapter, you understood those?"

"Those chapters were very clear. Death. Destruction. Terror. The Bearer goes off her rocker and does terrible things," I answered.

"I am saddened to hear this. But I can see you are saying the truth." The Lama was downcast.

"I have a different path. I will end the Namestone. Supposedly Tibet has a secret means to do this." I smiled at him.

"There are ancient scrolls that speak of this method. The method is lost. To destroy the Namestone, you must take it to the heart of the sun," he answered. "And who can do that?"

I smiled. "The *Copper Book* says what to do. I was hoping you had another way..." Suddenly the two of us were surrounded by a silver mirror, a perfectly reflective wall. "As I was saying," I managed. My presets had triggered me into a deep crash drop, a dozen levels in literally no time. The levels were called, but the draw on them had ramped up very steeply. I was a bit faint. Tomorrow I was very much going to pay for making that deep a crash drop in no time at all.

"What is this?" The Sera Lama was shocked. "You promised my safety."

"As it happens, that mirror is me keeping my promise." I called teleport. Blue sparkles and harp strings filled the space around us. The load on my force wall dropped nearly to zero. I waited a bit, remembered that we were in a small force bubble so I now had to breathe for my host, and slowly lowered the wall to transparent. I'd done a hundred-thousand-mile jump, enough that the earth was a giant blue beach ball below us. "Sorry, but by the time I'd said anything first, we'd've been dead."

"Oh?" His eyes sparkled with curiosity.

"Somehow, someone managed to detonate a half-dozen big transmutation bombs within a few feet of us. There must have been a teleporter. He must have pre-memorized the exact coordinates of the hall. There was no delay.

The bombs went off just as he arrived," I explained.

"You will forgive me, but I had not expected to be surrounded by stars while I am temporarily absent from Tibet awaiting reincarnation. We are dead, aren't we?" the Sera Lama asked. "Starcore bombs at ten feet surely killed us."

"You are alive, well, and in as good health as ever," I said. Temporarily absent? Oh, right. If you believe in reincarnation, you are not dead, you are only momentarily hard to reach. "I don't know where you go when you're dead, ummh, temporarily absent, but this is just outer space. Honest. I've been here before. Now we'll return. Someplace in Lhasa. When we arrive, please ask the Tibetan Flying Host not to shoot at me."

"Of course. But I am disgraced. Someone tried to kill you while we had a truce," he said.

"For me, it comes with the job," I answered, actually not cynically. Then I saw the obvious. "Someone tried to kill one of us. You, for example. They could strike you, and no one would ever suspect I was not the target."

He took a moment to consider what I had said. "That is very…subtle of you. I must consider this," he said. He truly did smile at me.

We teleported. "And now you are almost home. I'm happy to talk with you, some other time, but someone just dropped a half-dozen starcore bombs on your country. You must be distracted."

"I, oh, dear, I forgot," he said. "We were in the middle, the explosions all around us. Outside the hall, to be ten miles away, was my deputation. They could have been killed. But I am being rude. You saved my life. For this I am most grateful." And with that I left the Sera Lama on the stairs of the Potala Palace.

I really wanted to go straight home, but that was a bad idea. There was a good reason I wore a pantsuit rather than garb -- I could cheaply dump it in case someone had managed to teleport a tracker onto it. My body field protects me from trackers, but clothing is more susceptible. Out over the Pacific I stripped and reduced my clothing to an incandescent cloud of gas. Then I did a long string of teleports, twice with hour gaps in between, several times multiple jumps as fast as I could manage them. Finally, having reached my bedroom, I crawled under the quilt.

I wish I could say I had deep and dreamless sleep, but my sleep was anything but deep or dreamless. First I was too hot. Then I was too cold. I had nightmare after nightmare. I was speaking with the Sera Lama, and when the attack came my gifts would not quite call. My force wall would glow, and come down, and…I have a vivid imagination, so I dreamed of being burned to death. Then I was back in the Maze, confronting the Solid Shadows, the creatures that dredge up every nightmare. In my case the dreams were dreams of failing, being stupid, being lazy and caught, and much more. In the Maze I had a defense. It failed in my dreams. In the Maze I had my mother's list of terrors of crazy people, starting with the insects that live under the skin and burrow along the blood vessels, and the cannibal mice eating down the optic nerves into the brain. I gave the Shadows a full and vigorous dose of their own poison. They fled in terror. In my dreams, everything I used to scare the shadows just made them more real.

The stranger dreams were voices from the sky. I could hear them, but could only remember traces of what they had said. The echoes I could remember were very strange. 'Do what you are told.' "Leaders lead.' 'Keep in your proper place.' "Might makes right. Follow the might.' If someone told me the voices were Prussian and IncoAztecan propaganda broadcasts, I would have no trouble believing them.

Finally I woke up. Nightmares about failing were all too familiar. The voices from the sky were new? Or were they? It seemed to me that I had heard them before in my dreams, if much more softly, over the past few months. I checked, as well as I could, my mentalic defenses. They seemed to be better than ever. When I tried listening mentalically, I didn't hear anything. If I listened very carefully, I heard my ponies sleeping in their barn, my barn cats cuddled together in their nest, field mice raiding the fallen apples, further away slumbering bears, mountain lions, and a herd of big-horn sheep. The two homes closest up the road from me were summer retreats, places used on weekends when the weather was sure not to snow. They were vacant now.

Finally I got out of bed, slipped into my down bathrobe and moose-skin slippers, and stumbled to my den. The flash-heater would have a cup of rooibos tea in a few minutes. The cookies I baked were in the tin. I took out two. Where had I been, last time I was in here? Oh, yes, trying to understand another paragraph of *Goetica Arcana*, a treatise on gifts even less clear for being in a mixture of Ancient English and Low Goetic. I'm fluent in both of them, thank you, because Mum insisted, but that doesn't help much if the guy writing the volume only knew them only eclectically. At three in the morning, the *Arcana* suddenly seemed clear, paragraph after paragraph, on which I took careful notes.

Suddenly I realized I was slumped head first on my desk, with bright morning sunshine coming through the windows. I remembered to look at the notes. Surely they'd been a dream, one more pleasant than the earlier nightmares. No, the notes were in my schoolgirl-sharp notehand, and seemed to make complete sense, all but the very last. I must have been writing that one as I fell asleep.

Chapter Thirty-Eight

A Sidewalk
Frog Pond Park
Medford, Massachusetts

The sun had set. Walking in a tight triangle, Janie, Brian, and Trisha headed home from school. Even opposite Frog Pond Park, the streets were respectably well lighted. As in any community in the American Republic, the sidewalks had been properly shoveled of snow. They were dry as a bone. Trisha let Janie and Brian lead, so they could talk and not appear to be talking to her. Janie was thinking about a chess position. Brian was carefully carrying a box with something heavy he'd made using the school's machine shop. He had a superb set of machine tools at home, all paid for with his models, but for large pieces it really helped to have a full-size lathe. Apparently he'd shown the two metal shop teachers some of the things he'd built. They let him use the shop if he helped do the serious cleanup. Trisha wished that the world was different. Dad had been very emphatic that Trisha was not allowed to talk to her two siblings except over the dinner table, so she didn't. Of course, she couldn't help but hear what Brian and Janie were saying. The two of them were very good at discussing things she liked to hear about. Dad could hardly have ordered her not to talk to people at school, not when she was supposed to be doing homework and classwork, so he hadn't.

Dad had briefly discussed the idea that they should wait at school and have him drive them home, because it might be safer that way. Brian had tried to be polite about explaining that if nothing violent happened, they could use the exercise, and if something violent happened, Dad would be in the way. Patrick Wells very rarely lost an argument with his children, even when he was wrong, but for once he looked at the three of them, nodded, and said "Brian, you're right. But you're only right if you have your gifts right at the surface of being called. You should be doing it anyhow all the time, outside the house." Janie, Brian, and Trisha had nodded agreeably.

Brian was a bit frustrated. If he called his force field where it belonged, everyone would see it. If he called it at the surface of his skin, it would work just fine, especially after it finished reducing his clothing to incandescent gas. Worse, once he called his force field, he could protect himself and Janie, but that was the largest volume he could shield. Protecting Trisha at the same time was beyond him. His force field had to be held ready, not quite called. Morgana had shown him how to use a preset. A sniper might try shooting him, but his force field would feel the incoming round and trigger to full power before the round reached him.

Trisha kept her superspeed ramped up all the way. To her, the walk home seemed to take hours and hours, not minutes, but her father had told her what to do, so she was doing it. Trisha saw as sharply in the dark as she would in a bright summer afternoon. How did that help, she asked herself? What was she looking for? She wished that Morgana's efforts to teach her about combat awareness had done any good. If anything unpleasant happened, for sure Janie and Brian would fix things while she was the target dummy.

Suddenly, the ground shook. "Earthquake," Trisha started to say. Then she remembered. She was at full speed, so her voice pitched way above the frequencies Brian or Janie could hear. The ground shook again, harder, a single sharp motion to one side. That wasn't like the other earthquake I was in, she thought, remembering a trip to California. There the ground swayed back and forth. Here the ground wasn't swaying. All around her, leafless tree branches sat stationary in the cold winter air.

Across the continent, Eclipse found herself lying face-down on the floor of her library. What just happened, she asked herself? Something had dropped on her, crushing her to the ground like a thousand pounds of feather pillows. No, one of her presets had triggered, and she gone into a crash drop, deep enough to see the Straight Circle, feel the warm caress of the Rainbow Connection, look down into the blue of the Well of Infinity.

What had the trigger been? Her force field was powered up, driven toward its ultimate defensive limits. She shook her head, trying to clear her thoughts. The actual trigger was the teleport block she'd put on Janie and siblings. Someone had tried to kidnap them, twice, with an enormous amount of power backing a remote teleport. Blocking a remote teleport remained way easier than projecting the teleport. Without that differential, the kidnap attempt would have succeeded. A vast number of teleporters had tried to grab the Medford trio, all in one coordinated effort. If they'd teleported themselves to Medford and then grabbed Janie, they'd've gotten away with it.

She made herself stand. Whoever tried this stunt might be about to move to their Plan B. She knew much more effective counters to being teleported, but she had to be on scene for them to work.

To Trisha's eyes, Brian and Janie were taking forever and ever to respond to what had just happened. Slowing down to warn them was the wrong answer. If she dropped out of superspeed, she'd be practically defenseless. She might be strong, but she was a thirteen-year-old girl, not a FedCorps commando.

All at once a dozen men appeared from nowhere. The men were in a circle. She was in the middle. Teleport! She thought. The two closest to Brian and Janie had large medical injectors. They thrust their devices at her brother and sister's arms. From her perspective, the men moved as slowly as if they were submerged in molasses.

Someone behind her started to grab her by the shoulders. A man to her left was about to stab her with a syringe. She cut on her flight field and flipped her feet to the left, legs drawn up in a tuck well off the ground. As hard as she could, she first kicked the syringe, and then kicked its bearer in the stomach. The syringe shattered. Now her foot really hurt; the fellow she kicked had body armor under his clothing. He was still sailing into a snow bank. The man behind her tightened his grip. He moved way faster than the rest of them. She flipped again. Much more gently, she kicked Brian and Janie in their posteriors. They started to fall forward, meaning they were no longer where the two syringe bearers had expected.

The fellow behind her clamped down hard and reached for a chokehold. Her elbows shoved back, doing absolutely nothing against a heavy, tall man determined to hang onto her. She engaged her flight field, full power, straight up. Morgana had measured her maximum power climb at close to one hundred gravities. Inside the field, she felt none of them. Neither did anyone she was carrying, including the fellow hanging on to her. In tenths of a second they were headed straight up at close to Mach One. She collapsed her flight field inward, so tight that it barely grasped her clothing, and accelerated straight down, going in the same instant into a sharp roll. The fellow hanging on to her was very fast and very strong, but not that fast or that strong. He lost his grip and flew off, still going almost straight up. Unless he can fly, she thought, he's stuck in midair for a while.

She looked at the ground. One syringe needle had bent against Brian's force field. Brian was taking his time about doing anything else. Morgana had warned him that sometimes he was a bit too placid. This was going to be one of the times. Trisha accelerated straight down, feet first. The timing was going to be really difficult. She wanted high-speed when she hit the guy facing Brian, her feet into his shoulders, but she also wanted to stop before she tried to put a hole in the pavement.

One of the fellows in front was bringing up a pistol of some sort, not a conventional firearm, preparing to point it in her direction. She turned invisible and jinked sideways. A glance upward confirmed that the fellow she'd sent flying was still on his ballistic trajectory upward. There was a peculiar hum. Brian's force field flickered, but came up, bathing him in brilliant light. The two fellows in front of Janie went limp, falling ever-so-slowly to Trisha's eyes toward the ground. Trisha hit one of Brian's assailants, kicking him firmly in the skull, and pulled away upward. Brian's plasma torch cut on. The fellow with the gun was bathed in flame. Two more attackers crumpled toward the ground. That had to be Janie, Trisha thought. The people she chose to kill all died immediately. Brian pivoted right, looking for more targets.

<*Trisha?*> Krystal North's mind came through sharply clear. <*I have people covering you. Where are you? I don't see you. Fly up!*>

<*Invisible,*> she answered, recognizing that it was really bad that Krystal now knew she could turn invisible. Invisibility wasn't that useful if people knew you could do it. <*Going up! Not grabbing the guy above me.*>

Trisha looked down. Another dozen personas appeared on the scene, people she did not know, all in FedCorps uniform. Janie and Brian were back-to back, surrounded by a ring of bodies. The FedCorps people were in another ring, half facing in, half facing out, just beyond the bodies. A really large number of people appeared, their formation a wedge stretching up from Frog Pond and pointed at Brian. Their garb was strange, she though, making them look like animals, tigers and birds.

She realized she still heard Krystal's mind-voice. <*Trisha, you're going too high. You'll run out of air*!> For a moment, Trisha was deeply hurt. Krystal was just another adult who didn't trust her judgement. No, Trisha realized, Krystal assumes I need air, and is trying to protect me.

<*No air, no problem,*> Trisha answered, She accompanied her words with an image, the majestic seven-fold spiral of the Milky Way galaxy, as seen from 600,000 light years to the galactic South. <*Been there, seen that myself.*>

Trisha felt Krystal's startlement. <*Oh! Frigid! Keep going.*> Krystal turned her attention to the remainder of the battle.

Blindingly brilliant light flared across the landscape. Trisha's vision filtered the glare from bright to dim, but nothing could be seen behind it. Were those Brian's attacks? Something the FedCorps agents were doing? Or were those the newest set of people, trying to kill the FedCorps people? She couldn't tell. Now she had pulled well above the stratosphere, up where the sky was black.

<*Trisha?*> A different voice, one so loud it hurt. <?>

<*Yes. Joe?!*> she answered. <*Are you OK?*>.

<*Yes. A bit busy helping Janie and Brian. Stay up there.*> Trisha felt from Joe a moment of intense concentration. <*OK, that's half of them.*>

<*Joe, thanks!*> Janie broke into the conversation.

<*Wait!*> Krystal dropped into the conversation. <*Joe, we really need to talk*!>

<*No, we don't. You're busy enough with these Jaguar Knights! The ones I haven't killed already.*> Joe, Trisha decided, must have nerves of ice to stay so totally calm in the middle of a battlefield.

<*Jag...*?> Krystal's answer was tinged with surprise.

<*The ones I just killed. They remembered leaving from that Plaza with the big volcano in the distance. Just a second.*> Trisha felt gentle pressure against Joe's shields. Joe concentrated again. <*That's the other big lump of them. Well, it was. I left some for prisoners*>

<*Hang on,*> Krystal said.

Morgana Lafayette, still wearing her lab coat, appeared over Frog Pond.

Suddenly, the four surviving villains were all standing in a line, Morgana hovering above them. Trisha heard the conversation through Janie's ears.

"You attacked three of my proteges,"

Morgana said, her voice cold as ice. "Who gave you those interesting weapons?"

"We will say nothing," one of the men said. That was the fellow, Trisha thought, to whom she had given a flying lesson. He had somehow reached the ground. "We demand you contact the Prussian Embassy and secure legal representation for us." Janie had heard that Prussians were sometimes arrogant, but this fellow was completely astonishing.

"That will not happen," Morgana said deliberately. "You are going to tell me exactly who sent you and why. And why you think in Aztecan and can't speak German."

"This is America. We have legal rights!" The ringleader did not quite bellow.

Now one of the FedCorps people spoke up. "You four are under arrest," he announced. "You're coming with us to the Federal District."

"No, I'm taking them." Morgana sounded entirely sure of herself.

"We're FedCorps," another man spoke up. "Don't you dare try to walk off with them."

"Do not bother telling me," Morgana said quietly, "what you think I would not dare. There is absolutely nothing in this world that I would not dare to do if I chose to do so." Suddenly, the streetlights turned blood red. Snow, or something like snow but heavier, started to fall from the sky. Janie could hear above her, very faintly, incomprehensible high-pitched screaming.

The FedCorps agents all looked slightly to their right. They were in a telepathic conversation with someone. "Sorry, ma'am, and apologies." Their leader sounded frightened. "Krystal North says they're yours."

"Very good." The street lights turned white again. Morgana's smile did not reach to her lips. "As for you four, to exert your American rights, first you would have to be captured by an American. You were not. Now I am going to learn everything you know. Does the word 'exfoliate' mean anything to you?"

"You would not dare! The Kaiser would retaliate!" The ringleader sounded very sure of himself. Morgana laughed in his face. Suddenly she vanished, taking the four men with her.

<*Krystal?*> Tricia said, hoping the older woman was still listening, <*Please tell Janie I'll be back in a minute and take the three of us home.*>

<*Please give me a moment; I'm setting up medevac on a few of my people. And you'll have two of my people with you in a moment. Please persuade Joe to stay.*> Krystal's attention moved elsewhere.

<*Joe?*> Trisha called. Her sense of his presence in her mind had vanished.

<*Trisha?*> Krystal called. <*Please pause when you're at a stop.*>

<*I will. Are Brian and Janie safe?*> she asked. She inverted her flight field to

reverse her head-long race into the deeps of space.

<*We're OK. Just scared. Please come back now,*> Janie answered.

Trisha looked around. In most directions were her friends, the silent stars, the stars that never put her down. The Sun was a disk of incandescent fire. Below her, now thousands of miles away, New England was filled by the glow of streetlights.

Two figures in environmental suits appeared from nowhere, mayhaps twenty feet from her. One of them gesticulated wildly in her direction. "What?" she mouthed. It would have been really convenient to be a telepath. The other pulled from a pocket an assembly of wires and held them out in her direction, tapping first a lump at one end of a wire and then the side of his head. A few moments later, they could hear each other speak.

"You're in outer space! We have to get you down before you asphyxiate!" The first man shouted. "We're going to teleport you!"

"You can't!" Trisha answered. For a moment the stars shimmered. "Stop! You can't!"

"Of course we can!" The stars shimmered again.

"I have a teleport block! And I don't need to breathe!" Trisha wondered if the fellow was paying any attention to her.

"Take it down! Now!" the first man ordered.

"I'll fly us back," she said.

The first man grabbed her by the shirt collar. "You will do what I say, little girl!" He shook her vigorously.

"Bill, calm down," the second man said.

"Take it down now!" This time he slapped her. She was too startled to try fighting back.

"Bill, really!" the second man asked.

"I am an adult. I am in uniform. When I give a child an order, there should be instant obedience. When she does not obey me, she deserves to be punished! Immediately!" The first man was screaming at the top of his lungs.

<*Let go of her. Now!*> Trisha needed a few instants to recognize the mind shouting in her ear.

"Joe?" she said. Bill let go and drifted back, arms waving flaccidly.

Joe appeared between her and the two men. She grabbed and hugged him, holding on as tightly as possible.

<*You're safe, now, Trisha,*> Joe said. Trisha realized she was hugging a boy, in public, with an audience. Dad was going to be furious.

<*Can you two get home by yourselves?*> Joe politely asked the FedCorps men. <*Or does Trisha have to rescue you?*>

<*Joe? Trisha? Krystal here. Apologies I am late intervening. And apologies to you, Trisha, for what just happened. As for you, Mister Murrow, when you are back there are a few things we need to discuss.*>

<*Like restoring discipline in our young people?*> Murrow answered. <*Those Californians are ruining our country!*> Without warning the two men vanished.

<*Late? You were busy keeping people from dying,*> Joe answered Krystal.

<*Joe, we really do need to talk,*> Krystal said.

<*That would be a* really *bad idea,*> Joe answered, <*before next week. I'll explain then.*>

<*OK.*> Krystal answered.

Trisha saw the stars shimmer. She and Joe were standing on the surface of the moon, the Earth a huge ball near the horizon. <*I can work around my own block,*> Joe explained.

<*It was terrible,*> Trisha said. <*Terrible. And those people who were supposed to rescue me? I didn't need 'rescue'. No one trusts me to do anything.*> She realized that she was at the edge of tears. <*Home is terrible and life is terrible and everyone is blaming me for something I had nothing to do with.*> She dropped into Joe's memories all the things that had happened with her parents.

Now Joe hugged her. <*Trisha,*> he said calmly, <*I can't make it so that it didn't happen, but I can make it so you aren't upset about it. Like what happened to you after those kidnappers, two years ago. I have to think about your parents.*>

<*What your Mom did for us?*> Trisha asked through her tears.

<*You weren't supposed to know who did it,*> Joe answered. <*I can't do it myself, but I have a script for doing it. It just takes a few moments. You might get a headache afterward. Then we'll teleport back to Frog Pond.*>

Trisha nodded. Her thoughts tickled. She had no other way to describe the sensation. And then those memories of the terrible people in the strange masks, and the other two terrible people, the ones from FedCorps, faded into the distance. She still remembered them clearly, but she didn't get upset when she thought about them.

A few minutes later, Trisha returned to Janie and Brian. "I don't care what dad says." Trisha adopted her best older sister to younger siblings tone. "I'm flying us home, all of us invisible. I'll take whatever punishment I get." There had been rows of bodies on the ground. They were gone. Janie and Brian were leaning on each other. They had, Trisha thought, to be terrified. She would have been terrified, too, if Joe hadn't fixed her memories for her. He was such a nice boy, she thought, coming to her rescue again and again. She dropped to the ground, grabbed Janie and Brian in her flight field, swaddled them in invisibility, and took off.

"Trisha," Janie finally said, "Krystal North says she has us covered, so please don't go supersonic at low altitude." Janie paused. "Wait, I was actually saying that to you, Brian. Get that right, or dad will kill me."

"Oh, no," Brian said, "You never said a word to our wonderful sister who just took out three of those baddies and saved both of us. And I never said a word about how supergrateful I am that she was right behind us covering our backs."

Trisha giggled. She was aware of another mind, very gently in contact with her own. Not Janie. Someone older. <*Hi?*> Trisha managed.

<*Hi, also.*> Krystal again. <*Those were fabulous take-downs, guys! Your friend Joe*

really came to your rescue when you needed it. His teleport blocker. That's why we were so slow to show up.>

<*Teleport blocker?*> Trisha asked.

Krystal North's answers came fast as thought. <*They tried to kidnap you by teleporting you someplace else, and couldn't.*>

Trisha wished she understood what was going on. <*And when I get home, Dad is going to kill me.*>

<*Joe is an interesting person.*> Morgana Lafayette's thoughts were laser-cut sharp. <*The depth and range of his gifts is quite respectable.*>

<*I greet thee, Morgan.*> Krystal's thoughts had a patina of deep respect.

<*And thee also, younger sister,*> Morgana responded.

<*Dad wants to kill Joe. For real. And I don't know why.*> Trisha wished she would escape the nightmare she was been living in.

<*Girl,*> Krystal asked, <*What is wrong with you? Why does your father want to kill this Joe person? He's saved your life. He saved Greater Cambridge from incineration.*> Her private message to Lafayette was sharper. <*Morgana, do you have this covered? What is wrong with the young lady?*>

<*There is a family disciplinary matter,*> Morgana said coldly, being careful that Trisha heard not even a fragment of her answer. <*Trisha's parents do not approve of some aspect of her behavior. I do not interfere in these. Indeed, I do not even understand this one.*>

<*What's wrong, Krystal?*> Trisha broke into tears. <*Everything. My parents hate me. I'm totally grounded and they won't say why.*> All in a scramble, she dropped into her mentalic link with Krystal her memories of the last few months. <*I couldn't give away Janie's move. I don't know what it was. And no one believes me. Dad keeps talking about me cloud diving with Joe. I'm not even allowed to talk to Janie or Brian. Only at breakfast or dinner. It's all crazy. Sometimes I just want to fly away, straight up into forever! I can do that. Wait. Krystal. Never mind me. Can you do for Brian and Janie, what Joe did for me? He made me not get upset about everything that just happened. Not 'forget', but 'not upset'.*> She waited, listening to quiet.

<*Covered,*> Morgan said. <*Trisha. I'll do it. I'll be cheating with the flow of time. Your flight speed may feel strange for a moment. Don't be afraid.*>

<*I'm not afraid,*> she answered. <*It's for Janie and Brian.*> For a moment, her mind tickled again.

<*Joe did a fine job on you. Are you sure he's your age?*> Morgana asked. <*All right, I took care of Brian and Janie.*>

<*Yes. Well, I was about to ask him out on a date. As soon as I'm not grounded any more.*> Now that it was too late, Trisha wondered if she should have told Morgana that. <*And he said he had a script for whatever he did.*>

<*Script! Date Joe? Don't tell your parents,*> Morgana said. <*Not a word to your parents on that. And there's a complication we need to discuss. First. Before you ask Joe out on a date. Please? It's really important.*>

<*OK. I promise. Does he have another girlfriend already?*> Trisha asked.

<*Way more complicated than that. Not at the moment.*> Morgana's mindvoice blinked out.

Chapter Thirty-Nine

Secure Chamber Alpha
The Palace of Peace
Geneva, Switzerland

Chancellor Holmgren contemplated the shambles that the Namestone and that cursed woman Eclipse had made of world tranquility. At this point, he was prepared to disapprove of the IncoAztecan execution proposals, but only because they were too humane. The English and the Americans were perpetual obstacles to WorldTruth. They were not alone, but without their leadership opposition to WorldTruth would fall apart. He rapped his gavel once.

"Let us be in order," he said. "There is an American complaint of a serious threat to peace. However, under the rules alliance and military force declarations come first." They come first, he thought, until all military forces come under League control.

"Ambassador Featherstonehaugh?" Holmgren called on the first of many ambassadors who had asked to speak.

"Mister Chancellor. Delegates. First, as specified by the treaties establishing this body, I report a change in the treaty arrangements of the British Empire. Her Majesty's government has concluded a mutual defense agreement (details are being elaborated) with the government of the American Republic. Under this treaty, an attack on the American Republic, its ships and aircraft, or its citizens abroad will be treated as an attack on the Empire. In particular, in the event that there is an attack on the Republic, the Empire, or our allied states, we will immediately come to each other's defense. Furthermore, in light of yesterday's attack by foreign elements on the American city of Medford, Massachusetts, Her Majesty and Her Ministers have ordered a mobilization of our armed forces and personas."

"Ambassador Singh?" Holmgren wondered where this was going.

"Mister Chancellor," Singh said, "the South Asian states have approved new mutual defense treaties with Manjukuo, the Osmanli padislahari, Prussia, and the Empire of the Mexica and the Inca. We also note a threat to peace, namely the continuing Celestial Republic claims of suzerainty over the Lamanate of Tibet."

"Ambassador Davout?" Holmgren took another swallow from his hip flask, whose contents had started life in an American rye field.

"His Imperial Majesty, Napoleon the Sixth, noting the bellicose threats of one of our neighbors, has ordered total mobilization of the Imperial Armed Forces and the Legion of Glory." Bernard-Christian Davout plowed ahead, ignoring the looks from his neighbors. "This mobilization commenced last night, thirteen hours ago. While these precautions are purely defensive in nature, in the event that the Empire or its allies are attacked we will respond with the full weight of our military. Also, His Imperial Majesty would view an attack on any of the pacific Great Powers by a coalition of Great Powers as a threat to the French Empire, and would take the matter of an appropriate military response under advisement. Finally, the Emperor has approved mutual defense treaties with the British Empire and the American Republic."

"Ambassador Ferencz?" Holmgren wished he could be someplace else. This was a complete disaster, and it was happening under his watch.

"The Emperor-King Joseph III, noting issues arising around the world, has ordered a mobilization of the Common Army, the Austrian Army, the Honved, the Czech and Slovak Armies, and their associated Air and Persona forces, and the full occupation of all fortresses." Ferencz seemed completely calm. "Also, noting our long and friendly relations with foreign powers, His Imperial Majesty has agreed in principle to mutual defense agreements with the Celestial Republic of the Han and with the American Republic."

At Ferencz's mention of the American Republic the room became noisier. The Americans never signed mutual defense agreements. Holmgren felt slightly puzzled, then remembered that the Austro-Hungarians already had mutual defense agreements with France and Russia. "Who is next?" he asked, fumbling through his notes. "Ah. Apologies. Suleiman Pasha."

"The Osmanli padislahari is most concerned that despite the clear historical record of a century ago that we are lapsing toward war. Accordingly, the Emperor, may he prosper forever, and his Court, may their piety and wisdom be a bright star in the heavens, have withdrawn to the winter capital, Angora. The military of the Ottomans is already the most powerful in the world, so we see no need for further mobilization. However, if we and our allies are attacked, we will defend ourselves and come to their aid."

"The Speaker for the First Speaker?" Holmgren wished his flasks were larger.

"I am the Speaker for the First Speaker, the Living Sun, Lord Silver Lilypad Jaguar." Lord Smoking Frog paused in his remarks, hoping his fellow ambassadors would notice that there was a new First Speaker. "Mindful that the American Republic has begun a large-scale mobilization, the Council of the Realm has ordered a purely defensive mobilization of the armed forces of the Empire.

"In addition, we note that the elite persona forces and the sky creature of the American barbarians and their South-American puppets, previously used against those puppets' peasants in a pathetic effort to hide the creature's true origin, have now been used to devastate isolated villages of the southern Empire. The Living Sun, Lord Silver Lilypad Jaguar, and his ministers categorically and totally refuse to be responsible for the consequences if the American Republic does not immediately cease its attacks on the Empire and, as a token of good faith, hand over the perpetrators and their families so that they may be executed and given trials."

"Scholar Shi Fang? For the Celestial Republic of the Han?" Holmgren realized that the situation was going very rapidly to pieces. If the IncoAztecan Empire announced no treaties, there was an ugly rumor that they had treaty agreements not just for defense with Prussia, the Turks, the South Asians, and the Manchurians.

"We continue to counsel that peace is better than war. We continue to support the independence of Tibet, Siam, Vietnam, Cambodia, and other Buddhist states of south Asia. We are saddened that our positions do not meet with universal support. The Emperor of the Han has therefore summoned to the colors the Reserve Host of the League of Perfected Men. Purely as a precautionary measure, reservists have been called out to fill gaps in the Imperial Military. Also, we have concluded mutual defense agreements with the Satsuma Daimyo and the American Republic."

"Ambassador Saigo? Do you wish to add anything?" Holmgren asked himself if there were anything that could make matters worse.

"I speak for the Emperor and the All-Conquering Generalissimo." Saigo Shigetoshi let those words sink in. He was now speaking for the Empire, not just the Satsuma Daimyo. Holmgren took a deep sip from one of his flasks. "The Two Leading Men and the Imperial Diet have approved mutual defense treaties with the Celestial Republic and the American Republic. All samurai and members of the Shinobi Corps are always ready at a moment's notice to smite our enemies without mercy, so no mobilization of the Imperial Armed Forces is necessary."

The Shinobi Corps, Holmgren recalled, was the secretive Japanese persona group. "Legate Hong, you raised several issues?"

"Thank you, Chancellor. First, the Emperor stands resolutely in support of your position on the Baltimore issue. Second, when the Namestone was first captured by Enemy of All Civilization Eclipse, the Emperor ordered: Men and Women of the Horde! To your horses!, so we are already totally mobilized. Third, we have no idea who dropped all the transmutation bombs on far western Tibet, and were gratified to learn that the Chief Lama escaped injury. Fourth, we continue to believe that the American Janie Wells actually does know how to find Eclipse, and believe that the correct solution is for this body to declare her a Threat to Peace, have her arrested, and transport her to Geneva to have her memories exfoliated. Finally, we note the roles that the American Speaker Ming and his coterie have played in delaying the search for Eclipse, and believe that they should be hanged as the war criminals they are."

There followed loud thunks as Objection pyramids appeared before multiple ambassadors, followed by more thunks as several scarlet Threat to Peace pyramids were placed on desks.

"Under the rules, I am obliged to finish the first round of remarks before I can recognize the objections. "Ambassadrix Romanoff?" Holmgren took another swallow from one of his flasks.

"His Imperial Majesty, Tsar of All the Russias, His Court, and his Duma are in complete agreement that the world situation has become unfortunate." Ambassadrix Romanoff paused to put into circulation a large box of chocolates. "I hope that I have here something on which we can all agree. While few now alive remember the horrors of the Summer War of 1908, all people around the world should be grateful to the German Kaiser for funding his museums on the horrors of war. Warfare is indeed horrible. Some of us remember how rapidly the peaceful world of 1908 fell into general war. We should learn from that lesson. Having said that, the Tsar has ordered a purely defensive mobilization of the entire Imperial Army, Fleet, and Host of the Air, and has asked the Duma to approve of a substantial increase in the size of those forces."

"Ambassadrix Amanda Rafaela Mascarenhas da Silva?" Holmgren managed a smile in her direction.

"Brazil urges the great powers to sheathe, not draw, their swords." Amanda Rafaela leaned back in her chair. "I concede we and our neighbors have mobilized forces, but those are land forces fronting on the Atlantic, not deployed in places where we can invade our neighbors. With respect to the just complaint of Lord Silver Lilypad Jaguar about the peculiar sky creature and its minions, we deny that they are ours. Less formally, we suggest that the Living Sun consider the alternative, namely that the creature belongs to a third party, one who would benefit if our empires went to war. Lemuria comes immediately to mind." Ambassador Smoking Frog nodded thoughtfully.

"Having finished with declarations," Holmgren began. At this point Thaddeus Buncombe loudly cleared his throat. "My humble apologies, Ambassador Buncombe."

"The American Republic has traditionally eschewed foreign entanglements," Buncombe said in his best ambassadorial voice. "However, traditions can sometimes be brought to an end. On one hand my government was disappointed to learn of several conspiracies to conquer the world, one Great Power at a time, conspiracies on whose menus we were to be the appetizer. On the other hand, after our Congress was lectured very firmly by one of the Eternal Powers, and Speaker Ming was lectured, privately, by another Eternal Power, Congress agreed that it would be better to change those customs. Accordingly, we have entered into mutual defense agreements with the British Empire, the Celestial Republic of the Han, the French Empire, the Austro-Hungarian Empire, the Russian Empire, the Satsuma Daimyo, and have declared interests in South America. Congress has just appropriated effectively unlimited sums for the manufacture of additional modern weapons, not that the American Republic is currently undersupplied with them, which will be made available to our allies at cost. Warning orders have been sent to all of our military reserves. It is the hope of the American people that with these sensible precautions the world's diplomats and great captains will see that peace, not war, is the preferred option for the future."

"Having said that," Buncombe continued, "the American people are very seriously concerned about several foreign incursions into our territory in past weeks. There was the Baltimore incident. Now there has been a kidnapping attempt in scenic Medford, Massachusetts, by a crew of Jaguar Knights, the attempt targeting a twelve-year-old girl. This act on the part of the IncoAztecan Empire is entirely unacceptable, and will surely lead to war if there is no clarification of the situation."

"If I may?" Lord Smoking Frog asked. Buncombe nodded. "Why does your Republic believe that these persons are Jaguar Knights? And where are they, anyhow? If they are prisoners of war, they should be in contact with the Red Cross."

"As it happens," Buncombe said, "there are two groups of them. Approximately four dozen of them are dead. That includes the six the intended victim killed, at least two her brother killed, and several dozen apparently killed by a friend of the family. The remaining four eventually ended up in the hands of the immortal Morgan Le Fay. They had their memories exfoliated, the memory recordings proving beyond any doubt that they were personally sent by Lord Golden Buzzard. Would you care to respond, Lord Smoking Frog?"

"As it happens, I am happy to do so," Lord Smoking Frog said. "Your claims are correct. The Council of the Realm was most concerned by certain unauthorized actions of the former First Speaker, Lord Golden Buzzard. After a rational discussion of differences, Lord Golden Buzzard and his family agreed that they had erred and would best serve the state by feeding the gods. They have now been offered up in a glorious totally voluntary act to feed the Mighty Lord Huitzilopochtli. The Council of the Realm has offered to pay a large donative, in gold, as weregeld for damages done by former First Speaker Golden Buzzard within the American Republic. Ten tons of gold, two tons for each member of the Wells family, are proposed to be a reasonable weregeld, and another ten tons to your Republic. We also agree that we will immediately notify the American authorities if the Ears of the First Speaker or any of our other citizens become aware of additional attempts on any member of the Wells family by any party."

"Mister Chancellor," Buncombe said, "the American Republic finds these terms to be acceptable." Their kidnapping attempt was a total failure, he thought, and they want to avoid an unscheduled war. The American Republic had no interest in a war on any schedule. Mentalics had guaranteed the kids won't be too upset, and two tons of gold left each of them wealthy for life. The IncoAztecans had lost an elite platoon of Jaguar Knights. Apparently something had done significant damage to their teleport network. It seemed they had tried a remote teleport kidnapping, a feat wisely left to second-rate spy novels, and it failed in a way that generated a severe backlash. Finally, Lord Golden Buzzard had been an egomaniacal idiot the world was better off without. The disadvantage of his having had his heart cut out was that his successor might not be an idiot.

"I believe it would be in the interests of Peace," Holmgren said, "since I do not believe that all governments were equally aware of the newly revealed treaty interests and force changes, if we were to recess for two days and take up the objection pyramids at that time. I will briefly note that we have no other interesting news on Eclipse. League forces in American hands continue to be well-treated. Is there objection? Seeing none, we are adjourned."

Chapter Forty

Eclipse
The Invisible Fortress

There was a great fuss on the video channels. Notwithstanding diplomatic protestations, part of the League Elite Strike Team had jumped into Santa Monica, California, and tried to drag someone off as the Bearer of the Namestone. After the Baltimore Incident, I would have thought the Europeans would be more cautious, but no such luck. The person they attacked was not me. I think they managed to jump Mum. The height, build, and walk were right. The hair color wasn't, but Mum taught me a great deal about disguise. Valkyria wasn't there, but Thorsson -- the Prussian armored oaf -- was, along with a stack of drains, mentalists, and a bunch of energy people. They must have had a really good spotter, or someone reported a convincing Eclipse sighting. Mayhaps Mum teleported into a point that was not quite as hidden as she thought, and someone phoned Europe to collect the prize. Mayhaps she reported herself to them, and hoped they would take the bait. She does look a lot like the Martyr's broadcast images of me.

The person the Prussians attacked was seriously annoyed. The Europeans were fighting way above their weight, if not for very long. Why do I think it was Mum? She made a point of killing each of the Europeans, including combat teleporting right in front of their lead mentalist and punching the mentalist's heart out. It's a very dramatic use of extreme strength: Your fist goes all the way through the person you are punching, starting with their force shield. For sure, I can't do that. I'm in good shape for a girl my age, but no more. This person, whoever she was, delivered a 'goes through battleship armor like soft butter' punch. Thorsson got cut in half with a plasma sword, an attack much like mine. The drains were turned to charcoal.

Considering the depth of levels involved, collateral damage was really minor. Most bystanders resorted to the best known protective device against persona combat: track shoes. Nearby eucalyptus trees became pillars of flame. Several houses had their paint scorched. After the very brief fight was over, the not-Eclipse person did something and put out all the fires with a wave of her hands.

On due consideration, Mum ambushed them. For sure they did not surprise her. She had a lot of levels called and was ready to go when the curtain went up. I'm not nearly as clever about breaking things as she is. I still stand where she does. I can call all the same levels she can, not to mention the levels in the *Presentia*, except I get sick afterwards. She went way deeper way faster than I could, unless I prepare first or find out if this time a crash drop really does kill me. Sooner or later, that's what crash drops do to any persona. Crash drops turn you to incandescent gas.

The Santa Monica Emergency Response Group did a good job of moving spectators out of the way. They also remembered to carry cameras and drones on their way in, cameras and drones that they left behind when they teleported bystanders back out. Persona Network News gave the Santa Monica event an excruciatingly detailed analysis. Mixed in with analysts talking about the persona combat were people bewailing the League's failure. As soon as the Namestone was recovered, we would have Heaven on Earth. Poverty and disease would be abolished. Everyone would love each other. Cities would be architectural marvels, all spotlessly clean. Tigers would lie down with sheep.

That evening Vera Durand and her Hour of Power talked about politics. Her guests were Secretary of State Humperdinck, House Foreign Relations Committee Chair Smith, and President Pro Tem of the Senate Gompers. After introductions, Durand tried to begin with the Santa Monica incident.

"Starting with Santa Monica," Durand said, "did Washington ever receive notice that half the European Elite Team was in Santa Monica?"

"Not a word," Smith said. "Not a word. I do have a casualty report. The Elite group went into Santa Monica, but none of them came out again. Whoever they attacked was extremely efficient at terminating people. So soon as she finished terminating the lot of them, she disappeared."

"Has there been a League protest yet?" Durand asked. "Do we know who this mystery persona was?"

"The League protests everything, down to the capital doors being closed or open, but no complaint yet about this event, which just cost them half of their really top-line personas. At least the IncoAztecans and the Manjukuoans understand that in America we have Congressional supremacy, so they send missives to me. League and Prussian complaints go to the Senate, the State Department, and a few times even the White House. I'm sure that woman wasn't a Lord of Eternity, and there aren't that many other people who are that powerful. That woman may well have been the real Eclipse."

"Has the Baltimore Incident calmed down? Are we still waiting for their documents?" Durand wondered.

"Still waiting," Gompers said. "Not clear it matters. The arrest is under Maryland law, these people are not diplomats, and the Governor of Maryland recently said 'If Holmgren shows up here, I'll punch him in the nose.' "

Humperdinck then dropped his first bomb. "Vera, you make it sound as though the Baltimore incident was unique. In the last two days, there were similar incidents in Edo, Hiroshima…that's a beautiful, completely obscure city in southern Japan, Chichester, England, Yekaterinburg, Smolensk, Besancon, and Capurso, Italy. Each time, someone thought they saw Eclipse and notified Geneva. Each time, a League Peace Force Brigade teleported to the scene and immediately attacked Eclipse. Each time, there was a local, provincial, or the like response, with both sides taking heavy casualties."

"I seem to have missed these." Durand said. "My staff reported riots in Edo and Chichester, no more."

"If I may?" Smith said. "Without naming places or details, the Russian and French Empires advised us that they had had additional repeats of Baltimore, beyond these, but were still clarifying the situation…except that, like us, they have all these Peace Police Prisoners."

"Worse, this afternoon there was the Sandpoint event," Gompers said. "I heard just as my car was pulling up here. Your competitor somehow got the story."

"Tip of the hat to the Continental News Network," Durand said. "This afternoon yet another false Eclipse was spotted. She was jumped by people dressed as Peace Police, stunned, and teleported out. She's been identified as Marjorie Holmes of Sandpoint, a woman with no known gifts."

"It gets much worse," Humperdinck said. "Someone stunned one of the kidnappers. For kidnappings of minors – Holmes was fifteen -- North Idaho Courts are very fast indeed. The kidnapper cooperated with a mind scan. The choice was memory exfoliation. The North Idaho Procurator has already issued arrest warrants for his alleged accomplices."

"That's very good," Durand said.

"Not when one of them is League Chancellor Holmgren," Humperdinck answered. "However, according to the memory scan, Holmgren himself gave the orders to the kidnapping team."

"There have been a flurry of reports of kidnapping by teleportation," Gompers added. In most cases, the victim was a young woman alleged to resemble Eclipse."

"But why so many kidnappees?" Durand asked. "Surely no one can think that all these people are Eclipse. At worst, a mind scan by the kidnappers would have shown that the victim was innocent and should be returned."

"Alas," Smith said, "Our diplomatic contact with the IncoAztecans—who emphatically deny they are involved, indeed saying they have lost several young women—indicates that Holmgren has gotten into his head the idea that Eclipse has the Dispersal gift."

"And you get the year prize," Durand said, "naming a gift I've never heard of."

"That's because it's generally believe to be a fairy tale," Smith said. "The IncoAztecan Ambassador and I actually agree on this point. Allegedly, when the public persona changes into the private persona, she splits into a considerable number of people. To capture her private persona, you need to capture all these people."

"That's absurd," Humperdinck said.

"By report, Lord Smoking Frog tried to convince Holmgren that there is no such gift, but failed," Smith said.

"Mentioning the Chancellor, how are Holmgren and allies taking the wholesale demolition of his Peace Police, in what seem to be a remarkable series of coincidences?" Durand asked.

"Extremely poorly." Gompers shook his head. "I do see European newspapers. World news takes a while to percolate from central Europe, but it does get here. Not to mention that all these Peace Police who did not live long enough to surrender had relatives, mostly in Europe, so the news gets out. The Prussians are convinced we help Eclipse escape. My great-grandfather watched the Summer War launch. The world went from peace to war almost overnight. What I now here from abroad sounds very similar to what he described."

"On the bright side," Gompers said, "my office is swamped with mail from fellow Americans. They're all delighted that the Marylanders whipped the Peace Police, who've been way too arrogant for way too long. Newspaper editorials are running thirty-to-one in the same direction."

"There are also more thoughtful commentators," Humperdinck said. "No complaints that we protected an American. They have concern that Europeans are taking the event poorly. The Peace Executive is due to meet again. It may prove entertaining. Ambassador Buncombe has been ordered to object to any proposal to close the meeting, and to walk out if the meeting is closed."

"With respect to the Argentine-Brazilian border events..." Durand began. At this point, I yawned and turned off the video broadcast.

Chapter Forty-One

Eclipse
The Invisible Fortress
and
White Bluffs, Washington

The westering sun began to shine through my den windows. I paused studying to lower the blinds. As I did so, my computer tracking newsfeeds started chattering out alerts. It wasn't a very good computer program. The news feeds were also not that great. The combination was considerably better than random chance. If computer alerts were triggered, something was extremely wrong someplace. Whatever it was, it might be important.

Where was White Bluffs? I'd never heard of it. Side panel on screens says town of some thousands, near the Columbia River. And, oh dear, it was being attacked by the giant sky octopus and its minions. Or mayhaps they were its keepers.

There was local news coverage. The Washington Persona League and its reserves were in Alaska on classified exercises. The West Oregon, North and South Idaho, and Western Montana Persona Leagues had been notified. Governor Molnar had called the State Militia to active duty. Efforts to telephone people in White Bluffs and nearby Hanford were unsuccessful. The Richland Police Force had sent two cruisers toward Hanford. Radio contact was lost when they approached the town.

Three of the Walla Walla video stations sent video trucks into the area. One met people fleeing the scene and started collecting if it bleeds it leads interviews. Another had advanced via unpaved trails, parked on a hill for good signals, and sent a camera crew ahead on foot. Spokane video stations had sent news helicopters. This sounded to me like a really bad idea. The lead helicopter was eaten by the sky octopus. There were strange video images from the lead helicopter, seemingly from inside the octopus's stomach. They didn't last long. The helicopter that stayed back broadcast footage of the lead helicopter. Then it sent nap of earth images while it was dodging and outrunning the sky octopus.

The Richland Militia commander called on unarmed civilians to leave the area. He rattled off a list of towns from which people should flee.

Apparently Richland had sent a few State Militia men and a pair of light fighting vehicles off toward White Bluffs, on different roads. One encountered refugees on foot, some wounded, and stopped to provide first aid. The other was someplace in the wild. The troops had dismounted and were advancing on foot.

The Militia unit in Othello, a town I also didn't know, had been very fast to move. They were across the Columbia River, shooting at the sky octopus, not to great effect. They mostly had really old projectile rifles, some with armor-piercing rounds, but the sky creature was not armored. It was somewhat insubstantial. The militiamen had VideoBells and were sending back images.

Someone there had a super telephoto lens and tripod. With his camera, he picked up details of the strange people on the ground. Their clothing was entirely scarlet, even their pointy hats and long dress capes. They appeared to be armed with swords. The videographer caught a sequence in which one of the redcapes pointed his sword at two Hanforders, there was a burst of light, and all that was left of the Hanforders was a pair of skeletons. That had to be some sort of gift, but I've never heard of a gift that turns people to skeletons.

The camera tipped up, giving a real closeup of parts of the sky octopus. The image was such a closeup because the sky octopus was coming across the river at the Othello militia unit. Their commanding officer must have realized it was time for his men to fall back. Most of the militia men ran for the hills. They may have lived. Others stood at the river bank, firing wildly. The camera was facing sideways. It gave an excellent view of the sky octopus floating closer while redcapes teleported across the river to engage militiamen. Someone opened up on a redcape at full auto, using tracer rounds. The rounds didn't bounce. They meandered away ever more slowly without hitting anything. It was almost completely a massacre. The only militiaman to do anything effective tried to bayonet a redcape, who jumped backward after being touched and reduced the militiaman to a skeleton.

Eventually the Air Militia showed up with a fighter plane. It fired rockets and machine guns to no effect. The missiles went right through the sky octopus without slowing down. The pilot then tried flying through the octopus. Mayhaps he thought the exhaust flames from his rocket engines would do something. His aircraft broke up in midair, all seen on live video. It was really strange. The wings and tail and fuselage flew apart. They seemed to get smaller and smaller but they also appeared to be moving closer together. If the parts started moving away from the video camera, faster and faster, the image might make sense.

Someone had a new camera angle from the far side of the town. You could see residents walking out of town, seemingly under their own power, walking up to a redcape, and placing their hands behind their backs, seemingly voluntarily. How was that possible? Mind control? One redcape did something that tied the victim's hands together. A second tapped the resident with a sword or pole or the like. The resident turned transparent and disappeared. Were these people Aztecans? If so, the residents were being hauled off to south of the border for a god feeding ceremony, or any of several even worse alternatives. Meanwhile, the announcer was discussing how long it would take to get a good persona team here. The answer appeared to be hours, not minutes.

I could just mind my business. I don't live near White Bluffs. The people of Washington don't expect to be attacked, so they didn't take adequate precautions. Not one of these towns had a municipal force field. On the other hand, it might be better to discourage the redcapes before they showed up in my neighborhood, so the collateral damage would be on someone else's property. I started dropping through levels. I was in boy clothing, but I might want to pass for an ungifted. I pulled on long heavy socks, a heavy padded jacket, warm gloves, and a wool stocking cap. For once I was going to be sure I had enough slack for my defenses. These people and their creature looked to be truly nasty, even before you considered what appeared to be mind control tricks.

Reconnaissance was very definitely in order. My good maps of the state said that there was a local rise, peaking around a thousand feet above sea level, mayhaps four miles from the town. That sounded like a good start. I'd then teleport closer to town, a modest distance at a time, until I was as close as I wanted to be. I could just jump into the middle of town, but that sounded like a good way to get myself killed.

I was as ready as I was going to be. To the sound of a majestic gong, I dropped into the blue of an ice cavern. Here I was, three hundred feet in the air, facing a humpback hill. White Bluffs was on the far side. Another teleport hop and skitter up the slope, not quite flying, brought me to a lookout point. The sky octopus was big, mayhaps a mile across, but thin from top to bottom, seemingly a hundred feet.

I watched though my monocular as the redcapes led docile civilians out of town. The distance was a bit much, but it was straight line of sight, and there weren't a lot of other people around. I tried reading the mind of one of the townsfolk. There didn't seem to be anything there, as though the person was sound asleep. Another pair of townsfolk were the same way. Then I tried reading the mind of a redcape. The experience was very strange. I reached out for the redcape's mind. It was as though I had hit an invisible wall in the air. I couldn't feel a mindscreen. My probe simply stopped before reaching its target. The redcape whose mind I was trying to read looked in my direction and thrust his sword toward me. I did a flash teleport to the other rise in the humpback. Down at the town, there was a flash of light, something created a wall of dust partway from town to my former position, and then all was still. To judge from the dust cloud, whatever he'd done had a range of about a mile.

I'd try this again from much closer to town, being very sure I teleported away so soon as my attack had gone home. This time I tried levin bolts, one for each of the three redcapes. From a fraction of a mile out, as seen through my monocular, their swords seemed to flicker. They didn't appear to be inconvenienced. I teleported back to the hill before they countered. With a crash like steel pipes falling on each other, the rock I'd been hiding behind before I teleported turned into a column of dust. I tried reading the mind of the sky octopus. Animal minds tend to be really shallow. This one was remote. In some sense, it was very far away, not at all close to the creature's body. How could that be? OK, I'm not very good at mentalics. The mentalic attacks were worth a try, something that would reduce collateral damage, but for me they weren't very effective.

I teleported again, this time to another side of town. This time I'd try ball lightning, both on one of the keepers and on the creature itself. I launched the lightning spheres and teleported to the side, where I got a brief look at the spheres zipping across the ground. Two hit the sky creature. They detonated, expanded, but faded very rapidly as they spread out. The ones targeting the redcapes reached the men and detonated. Once again, their swords seemed to flicker just before the ball lightning detonated, though not in the same way as it did against a levin bolt. I was too far away to say more.

This time a half dozen of them appeared close to where I had launched the ball lightning. I let first the sky octopus and then them have it with plasma torch. The torch went into the creature and spread, as though the creature was much larger inside than it was outside. Each redcape answered the plasma blast differently. Some had shields that cancelled it. Two bounced my plasma blast back at me, not very effectively. I was too slow on my next move. Three of them appeared within a dozen feet of me.

I tried flash, to blind them, at the same moment that tried their skeleton rays. My shields did not like their skeleton rays, but I was still there. Flash appeared to have done nothing. My next attack, for reasons lost in the dawn of time, is called 'ground zero fireball'. I did not stint on how much power I put into it. In the same instant, I teleported. One of them had a teleport tangle on me. I hung on to his tangle field, something I am really bad at doing. Unfortunately for him, the good evasion is straight up, up several hundred miles, up to where the sky is pitch black and stars shine in the day sky. He panicked, and tried first his very strange teleport and then a skeleton ray attack. Both failed. Death by vacuum is not vaguely as gross in real life as it is in some horror flicks, but he was rapidly unconscious. I teleported to someplace over Richland, spotted the flashing lights of a dozen State Police cars, and teleported into their midst.

The redcape dropped flat. I kicked his sword away from him and shouted 'Artifact! Danger!" Then I kicked him in the head. Hard. "He's a sky octopus keeper!" I shouted.

By this time five of the State Police had drawn their laser pistols. Four were pointed at the keeper. One, impolitely, was pointed at me. The senior fellow bellowed "Hold your fire! Hold your fire!" Four of them got it right. One of them shot me. Five times.

The laser pistol did not impress my force field. "No harm, no foul," I said calmly. "He breathed vacuum, about ten seconds." I pointed at the redcape. "That sword thing is his weapon."

To his great credit the fellow who had shot me reached behind his back into his car trunk, grabbed an oxygen cylinder without looking, and started supported breathing on the keeper. I took the moment to try reading the keeper's mind. I wasn't seriously dizzy afterwards, but I did lean back on the car behind me. "It's not vaguely human," I announced. "And it's super-incredibly like Lord of Eternity old."

"From another world?" the senior man asked. "Oh, and I'm Bill McMorris."

"Hi, I'm Joe," I pointed at myself. "Just Joe. And him? Another universe. He knows the world is flat and infinite. His memories were weird. Except he strongly thinks of us as being cattle. Poorly bred cattle." I read his mind again, incidentally making sure he would stay asleep. "The sword – his word is *treldiar*—only works if he's holding it."

Now I had a good look at the sword. It looked to be made of glass, filled with different glowing channels. I counted four colors of glow. I'd seen them before. For once, photographic memory was useful. Each time they used a gift, one set of channels lit up. The fellow I'd captured had bounced my attack, used his skeleton ray, and set up the teleport tangle, all at the same time. Three of his channels had lit up. The other fellows had blocked my flash and attacked me. Only two groups of their channels lit up, the same two in each *treldiar*. That should have been a clue, but I didn't see it quite yet.

"You were the person out at White Bluffs, weren't you?" McMorris asked. "The one who made serious gift attacks? There was video coverage."

"Was, and will be," I answered. "On this fellow, please call The House That is Forever. When he thinks of his age, it's huge."

"You kicked him while he was down," McMorris said.

"These guys are seriously dangerous, Lords of Death dangerous," I answered, "And, yes, I am the Joe who captured the Lords." OK, it was a group effort, and I only captured the ones I didn't kill first.

McMorris nodded. "Please wait. I'd like him to stay captured, and his buddies might show up." I smiled. He started speaking into his throat mike, then touched a button on his collar. There was a modest delay. Now we had a speakerphone setup.

"Yes, this is Colonel Pi, himself," was the toneless voice on the speaker phone. "Why do you think he's so old?"

"I'm a telepath," I answered. "Not that good, but his mind space is huge." I almost said 'as large as yours', but then he'd wonder how I could know this.

"Please wait. Starhome and Dark Shadow will be there in a few moments." Colonel Pi sounded completely calm. All around us, this side of the conversation, people were running in all directions. The State Police officers were doing something intelligent, now that Lords of Eternity were involved. They were backing away from the prisoner. Quickly.

I was more than a bit uncomfortable. Yes, I did live through my one confrontation with an Eternal Lord, but the Screaming Skull is one of their dimmest bulbs. His attacks are really effective, but only if you don't have second order defenses. If you do, they're not very strong.

Starhome and Dark Shadow appeared in the air, twenty feet up, and teleported again, this time to the ground. Dark Shadow is an older man, dark-haired, face an unreadable smileless neutral. "One sky octopus keeper, old," I said, pointing at the fellow on the ground. "His magic sword that works." I pointed at the sword.

Dark Shadow gestured twice. I didn't recognize which mentalic gift he was using. "You are an observant young man," he said to me. "You picked out: He is indeed old. This is indeed a matter for the Forever House. Asher, he and me to Isolation One? The not-sword to Isolation Alpha?"

Asher had to be Starhome. "Agreed," he said. They disappeared, taking keeper and sword with them.

"I'm busy, talk later," I said to McMorris.

"Wait?" McMorris suggested. "Dark Shadow told me – telepathy -- Starsmasher is showing up to deal with the White Bluffs people."

"Starsmasher? Frigid! I've never seen him in action." Mum always said that if you watched really good people you might learn something.

I teleported back to the camelback hill. Some redcapes were still busy taking prisoners. Another group of them were in a line, searching the ground near to where I'd captured their friend. Where was Starsmasher? The redcapes were still marching people out of the town, so hitting the sky octopus again, as hard as I could, would endanger bystanders. Endanger? Actually, it would kill the lot of them.

OK, I'd tried Levin bolts, ball lightning, flash, plasma spheres, and plasma torch. None of them had worked. I hadn't tried flying gravel, but the redcapes were immune to gunfire. Someone would say I hadn't tried hand-to-hand combat, but that's for people with lots of speed and enhanced strength. The only way I can disable a guy the size of a redcape, hand-to-hand, is to stand directly behind him and hit him over the head with a wrecking bar, before he notices that I'm there. I could try teleporting more of them into space, except they now appeared to have teleport blocks up, enough to stop remote teleport. Teleporting something into their midst might be interesting. Tons of rock. A cylinder, top half missing, filled with chlorine trifluoride under high pressure. Nerve gas sounds amusing, if hard to get my hands on. But I can breathe it, so they might be able to, too, ignoring that their minds – well, the mind of the guy I captured – wasn't vaguely human, so their nervous systems might be unbothered.

Those swords? They had four channels. Did that meant they were good for blocking four attacks at the same time, fewer if the user was doing something himself? I could sort of manage five different attacks, all at once. Mayhaps I should see what Starsmasher did, first? He'd for sure show up in a bit.

What about the sky octopus? What was the thing? I had a clear line of sight. I tried ultravision, just for a moment. Its insides were dizzying. When I moved my head, very slightly, the creature's innards looked completely different. I hadn't recognized the tentacles before, but I saw them now, not to mention the serrated beak.

Where was Starsmasher? Mayhaps McMorris had been wrong. Mayhaps Starsmasher was taking his time. Eventually I thought of the obvious. The redcapes had teleport blockers on themselves. Did they have the whole town blocked? It didn't seem so. A mental search found dozens of alien minds, and several hundred human minds. I'd have to use ultravision to find exactly where the people were, see how many people I could grab at once while using a remote teleport, and repeat the process until I rescued everyone who was still there.

The rescue took half an hour, at the end of which I had a nasty headache. Every time I grabbed a group of people, the aliens converged on the place that had hidden the people I grabbed.

Finally Starsmasher showed up. What took so long? The ways of the Eternals are sometimes strange indeed. He promptly attacked the sky octopus. His plasma torch was truly impressive. I'll let someone else get in its way. The octopus seemed not to notice. He also tried to blast several redcapes. It appeared to me that they were shunting the plasma beam to someplace else, where I could not see. He went back to trying to torch the sky octopus, which was busy destroying houses. There was no effect. Meanwhile a half-dozen redcapes moved from wherever they had been to form a circle with him in the middle. The air around them shimmered. His plasma torch became weaker and weaker. The ground shook. Someone had tried to teleport him out, but the redcapes had a remote teleport block up. I'd learned something. The redcapes could block remote teleports that didn't target them personally. They just hadn't done it while I was rescuing the remaining townsfolk. Now Starsmasher fell over. The redcapes were using some sort of drain on him. His shields started to flicker. Once they were down, they could send him off to wherever, or simply cut his throat.

Eternals were notorious for having one strategy...find and smite. Running away was not in their list of possible strategies. Now it was too late for Starsmasher to run. I could simply let him die. He'd certainly earned his place on Darwin's List with his tactics here. He'd also been on the right side, for once. Accidents happen. How was I going to try this? All attacks at once, meaning continuous flash and levin bolt, everything else with as much power behind them as possible, and then teleport him out. His own teleport block was probably still up, too, meaning I'd be trying to move a small battleship when I grabbed him. I couldn't possible hit all six redcapes at the same time. I also didn't want to give them a chance to react. The trick solution was aimed autofire. I'd blast the six of them, one after the next, as fast as my glance moved from one of them to the next. I reached down in my levels, down to where my skin felt as though I was on fire.

Finally I targeted the exact point for my teleport. I'd hit the redcapes at point blank range. I hesitated. Doing this was actually dangerous, several different ways. I teleported.

All at once! Flash! Ball lightning! Plasma balls! Levin bolt! Plasma torch! Hit them! One! Two! Three! Four! Five! Six! The first five had internal explosions as all the water in their bodies turned to steam. Redcape Six got some defense up, enough that he was staggered but alive. I didn't stay to see if I could beat down Redcape Six's defenses. I grabbed Starsmasher and jumped, once, twice, three times, finally ending up high over the Pacific Ocean. My vision blurred. Little stars crept across my visual field. Starsmasher and teleport block were heavy as all get-out, but I had to keep moving him, lest the redcapes catch up with me.

Chapter Forty-Two

Around the World in Forty Seconds

I stared at the man I had just rescued. What was wrong with Starsmasher? He just lay there. He didn't appear to be bleeding. His body screens, not to mention his teleport block, which had the mass of a middling-large battleship, were up and running. The healing rules engine told me what to do, I thought, but working through his body screens was difficult. Sitting still and getting jumped by the characters with swords was a bad idea, so teleport we must. I gritted my teeth and made jump after jump.

Eventually his eyelids fluttered and opened. He was conscious again. I can confirm the scandal-sheet report. He has absolutely gorgeous baby-blue eyes.

"Truce of Randor!" I shouted. We weren't that high up, not so I that I would've had to breathe for him. He couldn't but hear me.

"Truce? Ummh, do I know you?" He was a trifle confused. "OK, Solara is telling me you pulled my chestnuts out of the fire for me, so I should agree to a truce. Not that we remember having a quarrel with you. For starters, we don't know who you are. OK. Agreed. Me and all my friends, you and all your friends," Starsmasher said. "Whoever they are. We have a Truce of Randor. What happened?"

"Truce agreed. Could you please drop your teleport block? Hauling it every few seconds is a lot of work," I asked. He had confirmed the rumor that the Lords of Eternity were more-or-less always in telepathic contact.

"The Scarlet Mandarin is reminding me that if you wanted to kill me by teleporting me someplace unpleasant, you'd've done it while I was out cold, not to mention that if you had wanted me dead you could simply have officially missed and blown off my head and not the other fellow's. So, done. My teleport block is off," he announced. "But why all these teleports? You're making it a real pain for Starhome to track me."

There had to be some trick inside his question. I mean, the tactic I was using is really simpleminded. "The other side teleports? So it's hard for them to track us, too? But the guys with swords don't fly. OK, I didn't see them flying. So we're in mid-air, not where the sky jellyfish is. We're dodging until I choose my battlefield. But I'll feed you the jumps so Starhome can track."

Starsmasher looked a bit puzzled. I suppose if you are a Lord of Eternity, dodging opponents is not your most natural response to a battlefield situation. Lords of Eternity tend to view tactics as 'Find opponent. Smite opponent. Cheer for collateral damage.' That tactic almost killed Starsmasher. If I hadn't been there, he'd now be a really dead Lord of Eternity.

"But why did you ask for a truce?" he asked. "What did you do? Rob a candy store?" That was impolite, but I let it pass. Besides, he was looking at me. No, not at my face. He was doing what Mum described as undressing you with his eyes. Of course, I'd dropped into Hanford in corduroys and long-sleeved, padded wool coat, standard boy's garb, the coat being warmly heavy but not loose. But I am not that old, not old enough to have an interesting figure. If he'd belonged there, Mum would have put him on the short list of perverts powerful enough to be dangerous. He wasn't. He was just trying to figure out who I was.

I crossed my arms across my chest. "I'm just as happy you don't know me. You might feel tempted to break the truce."

"Not us," he said. For a moment he looked offended. "Truce of Randor is way too useful. But you might be wise to be cautious. The truce rules make clear that we each learn who the other is, so my friends know who to kill if you break the truce."

I had to think about that one. He had dropped his teleport block, making life way simpler. Yes, Mum had mentioned that rule. "OK," I said. "Though most of my friends are likely not up to winning a fight with you guys, if you break the truce." He smiled. "I said most. And I've already lived through one of your friends trying to kill me." For half a second he gave me this quizzical baffled look. He stared into my eyes. Suddenly he had a flash of recognition. I suppose there are not that many people with silver-grey eyes who a Lord of Eternity has recently failed to kill.

"Eclipse?" he asked.

"I'm Eclipse. Alive and well. Despite the Screaming Skull's best effort."

"You're Eclipse? Aren't you supposed to be ten years older?" he asked. "And a girl?"

I smiled. The disguise actually worked. "Am I that obvious?" I asked. "That you recognize me?"

"Eyes. Posture," he answered. "Very definitely not age." OK, it was really inconvenient that all this started just before I recolored my hair. I hadn't expected to be seen, let alone have a conversation with an Eternal. "Not to mention we usually kill people when we try. Starhome thanks you for feeding me the teleport jumps. He says it would be really good if I went back to the House That Is Forever for medical attention. He says what you're doing is good, but I have some really serious injuries." I must have looked doubtful. There are places I absolutely do not want to go, because getting out again might not happen. The House That Is Forever was one of them. "The Scarlet

Mandarin offers himself in my place."

I was beyond my depth here. I asked for the truce only so he and friends wouldn't turn this into another battle. I'd had enough of those for one evening. Replace the person with whom I had the truce? Was that OK if I agreed? Rectitude was not the Mandarin's middle name, but you could surely trust him 100%. "He promises that's by the rules?" I asked.

<*Absolutely. After all, I did write them.*> The mentalic voice passed to me via Starsmasher. Yes, supposedly he did write them. The Truce Rules do say that you aren't allowed to deceive about the contents of the rules.

"I accept," I said. I extended my flight field, floating Starsmasher a distance out.

"Thanks for the save," he said. I assume the kiss he blew me was meant the right way. He vanished; instants later a Manjukuoan gentleman in the scarlet robes of his persona name was hovering in the same place.

"Madam Eclipse?" he said, bowing gracefully.

"Indeed," I answered. "Pleased to meet you, Scarlet Mandarin." I bowed, but kept my eyes on him.

"And I also. The Maze was a great puzzle of many ages, and I stand before the woman who solved it. Besides, you saved the life of a long-time friend of mine." The Scarlet Mandarin bowed again. Then he leaned back and sat down on the air. In mid-air, I'm most comfortable if I stand while hovering. I dropped a bit so our eyes were at the same height. "I endorse your regular teleport jumps as a sensible precaution," he continued, "and will not resist if you continue to teleport both of us."

"Done," I said. "And you're inside my weather screen, too." He nodded thanks.

"This is not the usual state of affairs," the Scarlet Mandarin announced, as if I did not already know. "It is customary for we immortals to rescue mortals, and for you mortals to grovel and praise us as we so obviously deserve. Instead, you rescued one of us, but asked only for a truce, a truce we shall surely honor." He looked at me very closely. I had all my defenses up. So far as I could tell, he wasn't trying to get around them. "Mayhaps we should instead ask how you killed the strange people. We? You have nearly the entire attention of the Lords of Eternity, all of us. After all, the strange people have become an annoyance. Like the bugs they are, they must be crushed, for which purpose it is easier to advance if the effective method of crushing is established. That's assuming they reappear. Soon after you rescued Starmasher, the aliens and their creature all disappeared. With luck, they will seek other hunting grounds. We had noted you fighting them. Indeed, Starsmasher asked that one of us pursue you to determine who you were and what you had learned about the strange people. Why didn't you quit when your attacks failed? What was your remarkably effective attack?"

"Not one attack." I shook my head. "Those swords they carry, they counter in an instant any one attack, or even four. I hit them with five attacks, all in the same instant. They died."

"So if several of us attack at once?" the Scarlet Mandarin asked.

"Timing will be really tough. I had to get it just right, and I've practiced making multiple attacks." I tried to be honest. "That creature of theirs. It's weird. It's bigger inside than outside. My attacks went in, and faded way too fast when they spread out. I hit it really hard. Nothing much happened."

"Without the masters, the servant creature will flee into the outer darkness." The Scarlet Mandarin nodded confidently. I was not going to remind him that Starsmasher had been even more confident just before he had it out with the Sky Octopus People. They'd handed him his hat. "Of course, within the Truce, we wonder what you will do with the Namestone."

"Nothing." He looked at me very strangely. "Nothing. The schoolhouse in East Dakota and the judges were parts of how you gain control of it."

"That is a surprising answer. Why do nothing with it? Is it not the Gate to Paradise?" I do not want to play whist against this man. His face betrays nothing.

"You do realize that the Namestone is a mindlock amplifier, don't you?" He nodded. "Aren't you bothered by how it's been used, described in the *True Copper Book*?"

"Only you have read that book. Is it so bad?" he countered.

"Worse. You should call the Namestone *The Supreme Quintessence of Evil*." Quintessence was such a fine word to get to use. How had he not read the book?

"Really? Wait. Plasmatrix is saying that she has read the *True Copper Book*, and heartily endorses your description of the Namestone. She compliments you on your judgement." He didn't know that already? Mayhaps the Lords of Eternity were not good at talking to each other. That would explain why they hadn't rescued Starsmasher.

"So I am going to destroy it. Sorry if you had plans for it, but it is way too dangerous." In particular I thought, a good mentalist could use it to mind control me, something I am not about to put up with.

"Young lady, we agree with your direction, but you can't destroy it." He sounded very certain of himself. "And you can't leave it lying around. It is too dangerous. Would you let small children play catch with a live hand grenade? You should give it to us."

"Destroy is the working plan," I answered. He recoiled.

"You can't. To destroy it, you must fly it to the core of the Sun. You did know that, didn't you?" he asked.

"Everyone knows that," I answered. The Mandarin was starting to sound like one of these adults who prides himself on how good he is at talking down to children. I would not let him get under my skin.

"Fly it to the core of the Sun? Child, you cannot do that," the Mandarin explained.

I shrugged, casually. "Been there. Done that," I answered. "So I'll do it again, one more time."

"You will fly to the core of the Sun, and back again? By yourself?" he challenged.

"Destroy only requires me flying to the core," I explained. "Flying back is a bonus move."

"You will do this soon?" he asked.

"The *True Copper Book* says there are timing requirements," I answered. "The Namestone must finish submitting to my will. Then I destroy it."

"Plasmatrix tells me you need some weeks yet, and that there is no choice in this matter." The Mandarin nodded firmly. I decided that these people really don't talk to each other very much.

"Three weeks is more than enough," I answered. "I must go at the full moon, and, no, the Book does not say why."

"We will give you a month's truce. After then we insist on taking possession." He paused. "In that case, we wish you well and hope you succeed. The Namestone is indeed an abomination."

He vanished. I hesitated a fraction of a second and teleported way far away. I'm not sure exactly when the truce ends, but I don't want them to locate me when it does. That was the moment at which I looked at the moon, the moon so very nearly new that it barely hinted at a crescent. Then I remembered Spindrift's words. Spindrift, I realized, was about to die, with or without me. She'd told me I'd forget to be with her until it was almost too late. She was right. Now was the moment at which I had to find her. I had to hope that Radthninu was one of the unnamed Leviorkianu towers.

Chapter Forty-Three

The Radthninu Tower
The Pacific Shore

I found Spindrift on a lonely North Pacific beach, waiting for the rising tide to take her. She wasn't far from my home, the home she had never seen. Out in the waves were six Leviorkianu towers, of which I could name five. The sixth, nameless, tower was the one that mattered, but I still didn't know why. The towers gleamed in the late twilight, like frost-shattered frozen tulips formed from stained glass. The sun was below the horizon. Still slightly above the horizon was the newest of new moons, a pale bar of silver light not yet showing a curve.

"There's one last thing I have to do,' she said. She was exerting an absolute maximum of self-control, but there were still tears beneath her eyelids. "I must free the Radthninu Tower."

Every Leviorkianu Tower has a name. Finding this one by process of elimination had been remarkably challenging. "What do you mean, free it?"

"The towers are frozen ideas," she said. "The ideas lie sleeping where I must now go. Level Minus Infinity, where ideas become matter. But I'm, I'm not strong enough. I'm just not."

That was really bad news. Whatever she was about to do, either she succeeded or – she claimed -- the world ended. Fortunately I was deep into my gifts already. I knew perfectly well that she was a drain, an incredibly powerful one. "Draw on me," I said. "Take what you need."

"But…" she started to object.

"There is no fear," I answered. "You earned it, sacrificing your life." She didn't argue. Her drain was a whirl of butterfly wings, intricately and impossibly veined. The load on my gifts was absolutely incredible. I saw flickers of incomprehensible images. A circle that did not curve. A rainbow that you could touch. It felt like warm glass. A well, cerulean blue, that went to down forever, into which Spindrift fell, using me as her lifeline. Then I realized. These were the three Great Steps from the *Presentia*. The Straight Circle. The Rainbow Connection. The Well of Infinity. I was seeing them the way she saw them. To me they looked very different. Spindrift dropped like a stone into the well. The call on my gifts crashed deeper and deeper.

Medico glyphs flared deep violet.

I was on the beach, but I was with her, too, down beneath every level I had ever heard named, down to levels where matter and energy were pale dreams, where ideas took solid shape. She was Spindrift, who knew her death when she chose to be born. She was Courage, incarnate. She was bubbly happiness, and undying dread of the future. Gold: Hair. Glyph. Jewelry. Sunset. Her body was dissolving, replacing its skin and bones with ideas transformed to matter. She was…and I was supplying the power she needed.

"I am the key,' she whispered, "the key for the lock to the room without a door. And you will be the next keyholder." We were on the beach, and someplace beyond reality, and inside the Radthninu tower, all at the same time. She did something, something I couldn't understand, using every fragment of her gifts, cleaving the tower's crystal, releasing that which lay trapped inside. She provided the aim, and I gave her the strength she needed. Traces of her gifts blew away like fallen leaves in a strong wind. Handling that much power was burning her up, fragmenting the weave of gifts that was her true nature. She knew she was dying, but she did not hesitate to strike.

The tallest of the Leviorkianu towers shimmered. Suddenly it was all there, as perfect as the instant it was formed. It was a vertical column with a huge tulip-flower dome on top, more beautiful than Leviorkianu poets promised. It stood unmoving, then exploded into a chromatic fantasy. Colors. Lights. Words. Ideas. Old ideas. New ideas. Ideas not yet born. Ideas that would never be. In a moment all was over. The tower was gone, leaving a stone foundation and breaking waves.

"That's it," Spindrift announced. "All done. Except…I'm done. I did what I chose to do. I did all of it. And now I'm afraid. So afraid. And so tired." Her hands gripped mine. She rose above her fears. "All the things I never did. I never flew to the moon. Never watched the stars come out. Never played…anything. There was just no time at all. Every instant I had to do something, so I could do something else. I was trapped in that path, trapped from the beginning. But I knew that. I knew that would happen, I knew that, the moment before I called myself together from the sand, the salt air, the roar of the breaking waves, the kelp and the sea foam. I knew what would happen to me, and I made my choice. I chose to be born, so I could die, now, here, on this beach facing the breaking waves. I named the unnamable in the tower, and someday you will do the same for all the world. And now, oh, it hurts. It hurts everywhere. So cold."

She gripped my hands. Hard. "But I never… never slept in the Ice Hotel. Never climbed a mountain, not calling on my gifts. For all our picnics, every one necessary, I never swam in the lagoon of a Pacific island. Never. I'm cold, colder than Antarctic ice, darker than the deeps between the stars, fainter…" There was absolutely nothing I could do to save her. I couldn't even share her pain, so I would feel some of it for her. She had to die, exactly this way, or truly terrible things would happen. From the moment before she had willed herself into existence, she had known her fate, dying on a deserted beach, mayhaps dying alone, mayhaps with one friend for company, She accepted from the beginning the price she would pay for her moments of life.

All I could do was cradle her shoulder against mine, hold her hands, and hug her gently. She died in my arms, in incredible pain, talking alertly about things she wished she had done, things that she had always known she would never have the time to do. At the very end, just as the crescent moon kissed the line twixt sea and sky, she gasped, said words I heard but did not then understand, and vanished. In that instant I was holding sea foam and kelp and sand, ephemeral traces that blew away into the dying twilight.

Her weight had left almost no depression in the sand. There was a sharp gust of wind. The depression was gone. Now even the sand had lost her memory. Only I remembered her. With that I rolled on my back, dead unconscious. Her drain hadn't quite killed me, but it had come way close.

I'm not sure how long I was out, except when I came to the sky was black. The stars were blurred behind the faintest trace of fog. I tried to stand. The world swirled around me. Carefully, I sat up, folding up my legs so I could lean my head forward and look over my knees. Quilted jacket or not, I was really cold, but I needed to gather my wits before I tried going home.

I was going to have to walk, too, at least for a while. I was in a pocket in the dunes, a dark hollow surrounded by sea grass, where I could look out at the surf but almost nowhere else. All around, I could hear motors, helicopters, sirens, voices. The waves sparkled where headlights and searchlights played across them. I could see a good dozen personae hovering, a hundred yards out to sea. These people must have taken a while to arrive.

This was getting silly. Leviorkianu towers don't just disappear, after all. Especially not in a large explosion. Those people ought to have spread out to look for clues, in particular look for clues hiding where I was lying unconscious. Surely some of the personae out there could see in the infrared, where I would glow like a lamp. A motionless body in the dunes, right near where a tower had disintegrated, ought to have been interesting to someone. Someone might at least have had the courtesy to wonder if I'd been injured and needed an ambulance.

I looked harder at the folks hovering in midair, and thought a considerable number of words that Mum would not have approved. She would have understood, but not approved. The fliers were not the local water rescue team. I was looking at a half-dozen Lords of Eternity, and a couple of top people from the national team. Someone had put an incredibly strong teleport block up. I probably couldn't break it, not with the damage I'd taken standing at Spindrift's back, but if I did I would be noticed. A lot. Then I would get to play hide and seek, with a dozen highly motivated personae, the most powerful personae in the world, hot on my tail. Even if I were in tip-top shape, which I was not, dodging that mob would be next to impossible. As it was, I was thoroughly worn down. This was very definitely not the moment to be in Rome and therefore be a Roman candle. It was the moment for me to play the role of a shy field mouse and sneak away into the darkness.

Stop and think. Why had no one noticed me? Should I just sit here and wait? They'd surely be here until daylight. I could hardly hide then. Of course, I was in my boy disguise, but when I was found someone would insist on taking me to my parents. Bluffing out of that would be tricky. Why was I hidden now? Several of them had a clear line of sight on me. It had to be some trick, something making me invisible even to top-line personae. It had to be…it had to be a parting present from Spindrift, something she'd done before she died. I squeezed my eyes shut, forcing back tears. Being with her when she died, even knowing in advance it would happen, really hurt inside.

Her present was valuable. I'd better not waste it. If I kept down, I could scuttle through patches of seagrass, all taller than me, away from the lights and sounds. That worked until I got to the coastal highway. It was flat, straight, and wide open. Cars zipped by on a regular basis. I was on some sort of access road. Across the highway was a road up into the coastal hills. I found a high point where I could see what was coming without readily being seen. I'd have to wait until there was a gap in traffic. I'd dash along some sort of access driveway, across the main highway, and up the road opposite. Finally, there were no cars. I had my chance, and broke into a sprint. Yes, it was pitch dark, but roads are flat, and I remembered to pick up my feet.

I was half way across the road when someone pulled out of the parking area opposite the towers. Their headlights swept sideways. Their tires screeched as they floored their accelerator. I was at my fastest run. The lights almost touched me. I dove off the road into the ditch, hoping I didn't land on anything really hard. I did, and would have bruises where I usually sit. If the driver stopped to look, because he thought he saw a motion, I would be in trouble. I pressed myself flat into the ground, not moving at all. I heard the roar of a car engine, the driver pulling from a dead stop up to 85 in a few instants.

Time to go. No cars were coming. I dashed up the side road. I'd have to slow in a bit, but I wanted more space between me and the highway first. If a car appeared behind or in front of me, I'd drop off into the drainage ditch. It was deep enough that I could lie there unseen by a passerby in an automobile. At the sound of brakes and flash of green-gold police lights behind me, I looked over my shoulder. Three police vans. Several dozen guys spread themselves across the road and up the sides of the canyon. At least two were in each drainage ditch.

"Listen up!" Someone had a bullhorn. "Our friends say there's a very recent track across the highway. It stops before it reaches Athenai Canyon Road here. But it doesn't go anywhere else." Yes, I thought, it stops. I'd done my running jump and rolled. 'Obscure tracks' is a line in a story, not something that I know how to do. Having not obscured my tracks, I had returned to the highway and started my climb on paved road. The fellow with the bullhorn continued. "Whoever it was went up the road. We're going to catch them. Guys in the ditch keep very alert. Gals on the flanks, it rained in the afternoon; tracks of someone splitting off from the road should be easy to see in the sand. OK, quick time! Forward!"

Following the searchers, not far back, were the police vans. Each had raised a scaffolding above its roof. The scaffolds held really powerful searchlights. Two swept back and forth covering the ground close in front of the searcher's line. The third swept randomly well ahead. Drat! If they saw me moving…I was in dark clothing, not an invisibility cloak…they would know they were on the right track. I ran up the hill. It was a very long way to the top, a couple of miles. If I didn't want to call on my gifts to escape, I had to keep ahead of them. Their very fast walk was slower than my run. All those hours of vigorous exercise now paid off. Breathe deeply from the start. Pace yourself. That was harder to do when the spotlight fell close behind me. Near-sprint it had to be. My legs hurt. My lungs burned. My heart pounded. Swinging your arms really does help with climbing hills, but now my arms hurt. For the longest time, the top of the hill seemed to fade away into the distance, retreating faster than I could advance. Twice I found a pothole the hard way. I spun, bounced from side to side, managed to keep one foot or the other under me, and regained my balance. The second time, my ankle started complaining. It took my weight, but it complained.

Back in the direction of the beach flashes of strange light came and went like exotic flashbulbs. I glanced over should, saw the lights, saw the flow of High Goetic letters between the lights, and went from seriously afraid to utterly terrified. Someone was doing a fourth-order casting, against which my force fields and mentalic screens are almost worthless. If I was the target, I would soon be seriously dead. Or worse. Having my conscious mind deleted came to mind as a possibility. I would have been happy to say that fear spurred me to greater speed, but I was already at full sprint. I had no more reserves to call upon. Either I got out of the way in time, or very bad things would happen.

Finally I passed the hill's military crest, passed the real top, and swung downhill. The road was flanked by light woods. Don't stop! I reminded myself. The people behind you are still coming. You just can't see them. I still had to slow down and force myself to breathe more evenly. Here was a cross road. Neither "Processional of the Great March" nor "Coastal Heights Drive" sounded promising. Oh, yes, 'turn immediately' is the instinctive bad step. A few more minutes brought me to the next crossroad. There were lights in the distance in all three directions. I listened mentally. Right and straight had dogs; the preferred left did not. Left? The natural turn is, of course, right. I headed down the left turn, 'The Byway of the Elder Ones'. By and by I reached out mentalically, ever so gently, and tweaked the dogs' awareness. They all started barking, growling, and other good doggish things. I was slightly sorry that I woke them up. I would have been more sorry to have been shot. Soon there were more lights and shouts, back at the intersection. The lights and shouts faded behind me. They were headed for the dogs. At the next intersection I turned inland. My steps were coming more and more slowly. In a bit I'd catch my second wind.

I had a hike in front of me. Someplace out there was the edge of the teleport damping field. I didn't have every lane memorized, but the Governor who claimed his state owned the entire coastline had also claimed that he could require every rural intersection to have a street sign tagged with east and north directions. With a little attention I could always tell close enough that I was going the right way. Under the trees I could risk calling a light, enough that I would not fall on my face. Over the coastal ridge I should be able to stay on a road, keeping very alert for late-evening traffic.

Once again I swam up toward consciousness. Once again I felt absolutely awful, as if all my reserves of strength had been drained dry. That had happened tonight when I covered Spindrift's back. Now it had happened again. It was still pitch dark, I was cold as all get-out, and I was not lying in bed. I was lying on one side, my shoulder both bruised where I had landed on it and half-asleep where I had been lying on it, and I had no idea where I was. I managed a cautious roll onto my back and looked up. I was seeing stars. Real stars, not concussion stars, and after a bit a shooting star, too.

Where was I? It took a bit to remember. I was in a field someplace. I'd decided to cut across a field to the next road. Something happened. I'd been walking, and then I was knocked flat. None of my presets or defenses had done anything. Suddenly it was much later. At least I hadn't cracked my skull on anything when I went down. I must have been stunned while I was still standing, because I could not remember falling. I had been walking, and now I was here.

I can't really see in the dark, wasn't up to using ultravision… a bad idea in any event, as it would readily get me noticed…but I did not hear anyone near me. Ever so slowly, I sat up. Clearly the time I had spent, putting on a proper jacket and wool pullover hat, had paid off. All my gifts had been knocked to zero. Without the jacket I would have added hypothermia to my other complaints. As it was I had been lying still for too long. My leg muscles complained vigorously when I started walking again.

It was not quite dawn when I reached the edge of the damping field. I gave myself another half hour of fast walking, two miles along an empty road, called my gifts, and teleported. I went around the world, saw the dark side of the moon, made several escape loops and two stops until teleport traces faded completely, and at long last reached my house. I was totally exhausted. I'd also missed dinner and breakfast, not to mention having made a long forced march. Oh, yes, I'd used my gifts a bit, too, enough that I now understood clearly the lines in the *Presentia* about the Straight Circle, the Rainbow Connection, and the Well of Infinity. I very much understood why Solara would not be pleased to learn that I understood that part of the *Presentia*.

Now I was home. I moved very quickly indeed to get a solid meal in place.

I was so sleepy that I hurt from exhaustion, enough I had trouble falling asleep. My out-of-body defenses politely waited until I woke up, late in the evening, the last bits of sunset a golden glow on my porch, before I did my mental check. Everything appeared to be where it should, except I had these weird memories of crossing the field while also hovering in midair above me, an adult and someone else I couldn't quite see at my shoulder, and then waking up. Two places at once. That must have been an intense dream whose meaning I might eventually uncover. The next day-and-a-half of sleeping got me on schedule again. I cooked a great deal, napped a lot, rode my ponies, and finally was back in shape.

The *Presentia* talked about the Straight Circle. Now that I'd seen it, those sections made more sense. I spent the evening re-reading what I had read before, except now I understood it. But when I reached the end of the section, I realized that the last sheet of page was split in two, with a thin envelope crammed inside.

That was impossible. How could I have missed the envelope? Ever so carefully, I used a pair of tweezers to pull the envelope from its holder. It was from Spindrift! It was addressed to me! Her and my names were brilliantly colored, turned into miniature paintings, hers of breaking waves, mine of the starry mid-day sky with the moon centered on the sun.

The envelope was not sealed.

"Dear Eclipse," it opened. OK, I haven't received many letters from dead people. I had to catch my breath before I could continue reading.

"I owe you the most profound of apologies for using you the way I did. I could easily have killed you. I had no choice, not if our world is to live. The alternative was that all world civilization would be swept away, so that America and IncoAzteca and all the rest will be one with Marik and Sarnath and the Arch of Infinity. Monsieur Poulenc had this copy of the *Presentia* because I planted it with him, knowing in advance he would give it to you, thinking he was giving you an *Evangeline* and a *Phillipe*. He did not know he had a copy of the *Presentia*. There was still a risk, but he did owe you his life. He has now repaid that debt in full.

"You didn't understand all of the *Presentia* when you first read it, but it taught you what you needed, enough that I could drag you through the Straight Circle, the Rainbow Connection, and finally the Well of Infinity. No, 'drag' is unfair; I anticipate that you came entirely willingly. You have been there twice. The gates to the deep levels are yours forever. I can see, very distantly, that you will need them once and again, though I can't tell why, or if those deep levels will be enough to save you.

"By the time you find this note, because while I lived the note was masked with a fourth-order spell, I will be dead. I promise you that I went willingly, knowing exactly what would happen to me while I lay dying. I have returned to sand and kelp and sea foam and the chill salt air, to be once again a part of the roar of the surf and the breaking waves. I solved a piece of the Great Puzzle. The rest of the solution is on your, much stronger than my, shoulders. The only advice I can safely give you is an aphorism you already know.

"Life, lighter than atoms.

"Duty, heavier than worlds.

"When it matters, you'll know what to do. You will be the key without a lock to the room without a door. You will name the unnamable.

"I can't see exactly what happens after I die. You will meet my avatar...she's a nice person, who has no idea that when she used the Ring of Fate she let me call myself into existence. That's 'let', not 'forced'. I chose to live, knowing in advance how and when I would die. PeaceStar is very strong, deeply gift-true, sacrificed her entire past, every bit of it, to use the Ring, and will insist on learning all about me. Tell her. Tell her ***I*** made the choice to live and to die, knowing before I was born how I would go to my death. She will still blame herself, but she will get over it.

"Please also tell Sunssword what happened to me. Tell her about you, too. Just tell the complete truth, even about the Namestone and the *Presentia*, and everything turns out right.

"And don't blame yourself for helping me. Yes, I did die by overload, calling levels so deep that my body could not survive. Without you I would have died anyway. This way, we did save the world...as you'll learn in the end. I promise.

"Love,

"Spindrift"

For a while I just sat there looking out my window over fields and woods.

I've never heard of PeaceStar. The Dagger of Time remembered some of the future. If she said we'd meet, we would meet.

Chapter Forty-Four

A Deserted Pacific Isle

I used the dark internet to send Morgana an obscure message giving a time and date. At the appointed time I teleported to the deserted island. I had to wait a very little while before Sunssword appeared. "Joe," she said, "I got your message. Sorry I was a bit late. My lab is moving to California. I was supervising packing."

"Spindrift asked me to speak to you," I said.

"I was hoping to see Spindrift again," Sunssword said. "She is always cheery, almost bubbly, no matter what lurked deeper in her mind. She is really nice, but awfully lonely. Way more lonely than anyone else I know. Even us two."

"Can't," I managed to get out before I choked. I hadn't realized how much those memories hurt. I'd hid them away, but now they were back. Then I broke into helpless tears. There were just so many burdens I was carrying, and for a moment I just couldn't handle all of them.

"Joe, what's wrong?" Sunssword asked.

"It's," I gasped through my tears. "I, I'm sorry. You can't. She's dead. She died in my arms, and there was nothing to be done about it, so I had to be with her…"

"Oh, no. She was so alive. Couldn't you get help? What happened?" Sunssword spoke a mile a minute.

I really didn't want to face this conversation, but what else could I do? Spindrift asked me to tell Sunssword, and I had promised. "I, I think I'd better start at the beginning," I said. "Spindrift wasn't what she seemed to be." Once I started talking, the tears faded.

"I knew that," Sunssword answered. "All those powers that weren't powers. After all, we linked mentally over Boston, and things leak a bit. Even when someone is as careful as you."

"You're careful, too," I answered. "I try to be. But I'm, ummh, not quite what I appear to be, either. Or did I hide that, too?"

"I don't pry in your private persona," she said, "and you never asked me about mine. So if you want me to keep pretending you're a boy, I will not object."

I think I blushed. "It was supposed to be a good disguise," I answered. "Though I meant something else. And I won't ask you why you're so tired of things, like you were really old." She looked at the sky for a moment. "But I promised Spindrift that I would tell you about her. Fortunately, you told me you're one of those people who has read the *Presentia*, so it's simpler than it might be. Spindrift is in there. And she's in the book on Liouville's butterflies."

Sunssword nodded.

"She was The Dagger of Time," I explained. "She was here because someone got the final use out of the Ring of Fate. She called herself into existence, knowing that in the end she would die, die a terrible death."

"Oh, dear me," Sunssword managed. "*The Future Chronicles of Gow All-Fleeing* warned about that."

"In the end, she did something, something I can't explain, and destroyed the Radthninu tower." I had to pause for a moment. "I was the person who stood at her back. She wasn't strong enough by herself, so she drained me -- I told her to -- for the power she needed. At the end of her life, she had to die, and make the tower perfect so it could die, too. We summoned the Straight Circle, the Rainbow Connection, and then she dropped to the bottom of the Well of Infinity. I was there with her, and outside the Well at the same time. That's what killed her. I could give her the strength she needed, but not a way to survive using it."

"Joe, who are you?" Sunssword asked. "Really?"

"Trade questions?" I asked. She nodded. "Maybe you understand the *Presentia* better than I do. Is there a way to destroy the Namestone, another way other than the one in *The True Copper Book?*

"No. The Namestone can only be ended in one way," Sunssword said. "It was created in the heart of a galaxy. It can only be destroyed by a starcore. But I did not just read the *Presentia.* I wrote it. Yes, I am Sunssword. But before that, for far longer than you would believe, I was and am the immortal Morgan Le Fay," Sunssword said.

This was one of those...this is really bad...moments. Morgan Le Fay was by all reports the most powerful persona in the world, bar none. She had destroyed the hosts of William the Totally Defeated and the Spanish Armada, been the Divine Wind that smashed the navies of King George the Mad and the Manjukuoan Grand Fleet, and trashed several Lords of Eternity.

"I agreed we'd trade questions. You're honest with me, and I'll be honest with you. Besides, Spindrift told me I should be completely honest to you, and everything would turn out right," I said. "Being a boy is just to confuse people. They see what they expect to see. No, I'm really someone else."

With that I took a half step back, raised my hand, palm up, and summoned the Namestone. My aura and theme music came up at the same moment. "I am Joe. But I'm also Eclipse." I was taking a real chance, except that I had seen farther inside Morgana's mind than she suspected. She was a good person, a young person bubbly and full of vitality, and at the same time someone who was very old and very tired.

Whatever she had been expecting, it was not coming face to face with the Bearer. She took a half-step backward. "You're actually Eclipse!"

"In the flesh," I answered.

"Eclipse, what will you do with the Namestone?" she asked.

"It's the most dangerous artifact in the world. It's an abomination. It's a mind control amplifier, and much worse," I said. "I took it, so I could destroy it."

Her smile was radiant. "Yes," she said. "Yes. Wonderful! Except so far as I know there really is only one way to end its existence."

"Then that's what has to be done," I said. "Fly it to the starcore."

"I may be the sending of Amaterasu, the Goddess of the Sun, or so the Japanese thought, but I cannot reach her heart." She looked puzzled.

"I should have said," I answered, "Fly to the starcore again. I've been there before. Would you like to come along?"

"That's outside the range of my powers," she answered resignedly. "My shields are not that strong. I might survive to reach the core, but I'd never make it out again."

"I'm supposed to finish what Spindrift started, when we destroyed the tower," I said. "She said I will also be the key without a lock to the room without a door. I am supposed to name the unnamable, and I have no idea what that means." Morgana looked puzzled. "And at some point I get to read about real ancient history."

"You may have an answer that will only make sense when it needs to," Morgana said. "There are some very dangerous traps involving deep time. Eclipse? If you can destroy the Namestone, please? Do that first? End one menace, before you start another one?"

Chapter Forty-Five

The Great Chamber of Wisdom
The House That Is Forever

Keeping perfect time with each other, the two grandmother clocks of the Great Chamber of Wisdom struck the hour. It was six in the morning, the stars still spangling the heavens. Seated around the long table were most of the Lords of Eternity, Plasmatrix at its head.

"I see we are all here," Plasmatrix said. "All who will be here. In accord with Disaster Plan Sixteen, Solara and Corinne are elsewhere. Prince Mong-ku reports that he is busy with further tests on the remains of the Radthninu tower, but until they are complete he has nothing to tell us."

"Are we sure," the Screaming Skull asked, "that the Tower is gone? Could this be some trick?"

"I can speak to that," Dark Shadow answered. "And to my conversation with our dear friend Morgana." Plasmatrix nodded her approval. "I've had no trouble detecting examples of the formerly trapped memes, wandering about in the open air," Dark Shadow continued. "They remain isolated from their names, so they aren't directly dangerous, but someone can now name the unnamable and succeed." Frowns crissed and crossed the table. "Whether the tower was literally destroyed no longer signifies. It ceased to function as a cage, so that which was within is loose on the world."

"A total disaster," Starsmasher mouthed. "Can we at least kill the guilty parties? That Morgan person?"

"Now there's a fine idea," the Screaming Skull agreed.

"I discussed matters with Morgana," Dark Shadow answered. "She was surprised to learn that we had not guarded the Tower adequately, not that such a thing is possible. She is busy moving her laboratory, and was demonstrably elsewhere with lots of witnesses, some of whose minds I have checked carefully, while the Tower was destroyed. She did recognize the fourth-order working seen over the Tower foundation. It is a null operation with attached fireworks. It runs in a circle in a very complicated way, but it does absolutely nothing other than create some bright lights. When I questioned this, she took me out over the Pacific, generated the working, and showed that it did what she said. She also claimed that the destruction was by itself harmless, because the memes are inert until they are linked with their true names."

"Colonel Pi," Plasmatrix asked, "were there any traces of the guilty party to be found anywhere?"

"Very few," Colonel Pi answered. "I found a place where someone had been sleeping in the dunes, quite close to the shoreline. That's the person who got chased up Athenai Canyon and then disappeared. The very slight echoes I located of the destruction method suggested that the guilty party perished in flagrante delicto, namely they took the locks into themselves to shatter the Tower, and then expired from the malignant evil of the locks."

"Wasn't there a search, last night, for witnesses?" Starhome asked. "How did we miss this person asleep in the dunes?"

"An interesting question," Colonel Pi answered. "He should have been in line of sight of people in the sky over the tower. He wasn't. Also, he left an exit trail but no arrival trail, so either he was there for a very long time, or he arrived by teleport or flight after we'd scanned the area. Flight seems unlikely. His escape seems to have used nothing more complicated than 'run uphill fast'. The pursuit was only at a fast walk. The pursuers were more concerned with checking that he did not escape sideways from the road than with catching up with him. The State Police did get a roadblock in place at the first intersection, but it must have been too late. Remember that the locals were view the event as a petty act of large-scale vandalism, the sort of act for which the usually juvenile perpetrators are routinely caught because they cannot keep their mouths shut."

"The escapee was a juvenile?" Starhome asked. "You have been saying 'he'?"

"There were footprints in the sand," Colonel Pi answered. "The tread pattern is a well-known line of boy's sneakers. There can be no doubt that the person was a boy. The perpetrator did a jump into the sand at the far edge of the highway, left part of a body impression, found a pool of water the hard way, and got his sneakers wet enough to leave several more foot prints. The shoe size and gait says he is a few inches over five feet tall. Must be a conditioning fanatic to get up that hill so quickly."

"Not a persona?" Starhome asked.

"We had detection for people using gifts, seven ways from Saturday, all the way to the top of the hill" Colonel Pi said, "and a teleport block out for several miles. Nothing was found."

"But the person did run away," Starhome said. "This suggests guilt."

"If I were a young man," Plasmatrix said, "and had gone to a deserted section of beach for an assignation with a young woman, and managed to fall asleep while waiting for the event that did not occur, until it was very late, then discovered that I could not teleport back home because of our block, I might very well choose to run home as though all the hounds of Hell were pursuing me, not daring to get caught, lest my parents find out what I had been doing. That also explains how he disappeared. He reached his house and snuck through his bedroom window."

"Perhaps this young person also saw something of interest?" Starsmasher asked.

"Perhaps," Plasmatrix said. "Though if I had watched a large explosion I might well not have been able to sleep. At a guess, the tower exploded; then he teleported in before we put the block up. Meanwhile, his paramour was a little late, and discovered she could not teleport to the beach to meet him."

"Alternatively," the Screaming Skull said, "while waiting he entertained himself by blowing up the tower, in which case we need to chase him down and torture him to death. Slowly."

"That would not have worked," Colonel Pi said. "In order to release the memes, you needed to start by summoning the perfectly intact tower, which as it happens requires a near-infinite amount of power."

"Perhaps we should be more concerned," Starsmasher said, "about what this does to the current cycle of the Great Plan, which requires that those memes stay carefully locked away until the unnamed one appears, becomes entrapped in this world, and perishes when we eliminate this historical cycle from existence. That calculation is in Prince Mong-Ku's bailiwick. Perhaps we ramp up the SkyVoice, do the summoning, and eliminate the visitor before matters fall apart. Perhaps we can't do that, in which case we might as well eliminate this historical cycle now, and start all over again, one more time."

"Perhaps we should consider," the usually-silent Librarian Greene observed, "that a large number of recent events have matched our desires poorly. Someone tried to buy a *Presentia.* This sky octopus matches nothing we had intended. No one should have recovered the Namestone. The well-ordered states -- the IncoAztecans, the Manjukuoans, Prussia, South Asia, are showing unexpected signs of instability, when perfect stability was expected. We need those nations in place, as rigidly hierarchically organized as possible, if the trap is to bite. One might propose that we are facing some extremely subtle but far-reaching and well-organized conspiracy against us, one much like the conspiracy of the League of Terror and Injustice."

"An interesting thought," Plasmatrix said. "I believe we need Prince Mong-Ku back with his report before we can decide if the report is true. I therefore propose adjournment. Are there objections? Seeing none, we have adjourned."

Chapter Forty-Six

Near Modesto, California

Once again, studying was interrupted by my radio sounding a National Defense Alert. I had the radio turned almost all the way down, so that I really couldn't hear it, but Defense Alerts use separate circuits. I could simply have turned it off, but I hadn't.

I went down to the kitchen and turned on the video. Eagle News was up and covering events. It took a while to figure out what was happening. The IncoAztecans had found a serious gap in the country's teleport defenses, and were marching an army through a teleport gate into central California. Setting up gates is difficult, but breaking them is nearly impossible. On one hand, the commentator claimed, their objective was relatively transparent. They threatened to march on San Francisco and Silicon Valley, the attack point being about as close as they were likely to get to the California coast. They could also advance south toward Los Angeles and San Diego, finally to take our border defenses in the rear. They had to advance a significant distance, but there wasn't much in their way. Finally, they could cut off most of the water supply of South California.

I was somewhat puzzled. Hadn't they just apologized for trying to kidnap Janie? They had handed over the gold they promised. Someone casually mentioned that the First Speaker was Lord Jade Ocelot. Apparently they had yet another coup. There was no mention of the prior First Speaker.

At this point the American Elite Team appeared, the Grizzly Persona Guards teleported in from Sacramento, and a seemingly endless number of IncoAztecan Jaguar Knights marched through the tunnel, Eagle Knights providing overhead cover. American state and local leagues persona were slower off the mark, but started arriving in force. No one invited anyone else to surrender. They just started shooting.

"Krystal North has ordered Plan Hoffman," the commentator announced. "I say again: Plan Hoffman. Plan Hoffman." That must have meant something to people on the ground, but I didn't know what. Mum always said there was a competition between keeping your plans secret from the enemy, and accidentally keeping your plans secret from your own people. Some plans didn't need to be kept secret from the enemy. 'Kill the enemy teleporters first' is a good example. The other side could tell very quickly what you were trying to do, but if they wanted teleporters in their combat groups the teleporters had to be available as your targets.

I had vaguely hoped to see Krystal North face off against Lord Popocatepetl, the Living Volcano, but that didn't seem to be in the cards. She was overseeing the battlefield, not fighting herself. From the remote drone images, the battlefield was more than a bit chaotic. Popocatepetl was there, but the Americans facing him refused to go toe-to-toe. He would do some damage, and then whomever he'd been blasting would be switched out for someone else. The invasion force had a fair number of really strong combatants, each looking for a one on one against the strongest Americans. Low-level Jaguar Knights covered the sides and back of the Aztecan top line personas, without wearing themselves out by attacking the Americans facing them. Once and again the commentator spotted a top-line American, always seen taking down a bottom-line Jaguar or Eagle Knight. The Aztecans were taking a lot of casualties, but then they had a huge number of personae, with more arriving on the scene every moment.

The video slipped to a split screen, the other half being the Texan-Aztecan border. By some accounts, this is the most heavily fortified border in the world, with masses of artillery, particle beam batteries, and combat aircraft on 24 hour alert. The Texas Ranger commanders, to the great surprise of the commentator, had bothered to confirm with the California Grizzly Guard that real Jaguar Knights were in California before they started to shoot. The Texans opened fire with a very great deal of artillery. Some clever reporter managed to get video of a titanium tsunami battery doing a full barrage. Each firing tube contains a stack of rocket shells which rapidly shoot, one after the next. They were firing at high elevation, so rounds went into the stratosphere before going their rocket assisted drops back to preplanned targets. The battery while firing looks like a forest of fire. Yes, those warheads won't stop a high-power persona, but against conventional fortifications and municipal teams the artillery was truly devastating. The Arizona and New Mexico borders were quieter. The border between California and Baja California was confused. Aztecans made weak attacks, perhaps to distract the California State militia in San Diego from what was happening in their rear. From the sound of things there had been a Grizzly Guards plan to move south to shield San Diego, some people were instead headed north, and there was much confusion.

I could feel a very slight tingle in my skin. That had to be someone ramping the continental fission suppressors up to maximum power. Video reported around the country. Cities were bringing up their municipal force fields and teleport dampers. Most of that stuff is ineffective against high power personae, but there aren't that many of us. My shopping expedition for the day looked to be cancelled. I could still teleport, but someone would for some reason suspect that I am not granny who needs a cane to walk.

Unfortunately, the IncoAztecans had opened their teleport gate before the California screens came up, and were fast-marching Jaguar Knights and Eagle Legionnaires through the hole in the air. It appeared that very rapidly we were moving from local unpleasantness to a general war.

I had some thought that Mum would demonstrate what a truly first line persona can do, for example by wiping out the people invading America, but she seemed to have vanished. Yes, I did feel a modest temptation to crank my levels truly all the way down, summon the Namestone, and use it to deal with the matter. It would have worked, too. I rejected that temptation. Firmly. The Namestone is way too dangerous, especially when we were not losing.

To make life more interesting, the Manjukuoan Grand Fleet had now been located in the North Pacific. To be precise, they were in the eastern North Pacific. There was some question about how they had avoided reconnaissance satellites. They were clearly preparing to visit Cosmopolis, or mayhaps Coos Bay. Either of these was getting more than a bit close to my home.

In the rest of the world, South Asia had invaded Tibet. Manjukuo had invaded Han Sinkiang. The Celestial Republic responded. The Ottoman Empire was clarifying its border in the Sahara, clarification meaning they were advancing south into former British and French colonies. It appeared that the German Kaiser looked at the Russian, French, Austro-Hungarian, Bavarian, and British forces facing him, and decided to pound the table for peace. Prussia was likely stronger than any two of those other countries, but there were five of them. I wondered what was happening with my friends in North Cosmopolis.

~~~~~

"Kniaz Kang," Wang said, "there is something odd about the sky. It looks dark. And the sun looks orange."

"Tend the register for a few minutes," Kang answered. "I shall see for myself."

Kang stepped onto the front porch of Kniaz Kang's Marco Polo. There were no clouds, but the afternoon sun was dim. The sky indeed looked gray. The solar disk was a ruddy orange. The air had been still, but now a breeze blew dead leaves clattering across the parking lot. In the trees, higher branches shimmered. Kang closed his eyes, listened very carefully, and ran into the restaurant.

"Wang!" he shouted. "Close the blast shutters! Call all staff in from outside!" Kang stepped to the maitre de's podium and turned on the microphone. "All guests," he announced. "All guests. This is Kniaz Kang, himself. A great storm approaches from the east. You have not time to go anywhere. You will be safer if you take the stairs down two flights to the shelters." He turned to Teranike. "Please fetch your interesting equipment from your apartment. All of it. Then guard the basement stairs. That which approaches often has followers prone to violence. Smite them without
~~~~~

mercy!" She nodded and ran up the stairs to the third floor.

Kang walked to his office, picked up his phone, and typed in a set of numbers he almost never used. A handsome young man eventually answered the phone. "Hello, Office of the Governor. Smythe speaking. We're a bit busy at the moment. The Aztecs have invaded."

"It is I, Kniaz Kang himself," Kang announced. "The coded message to the Governor is 'the black dragon eats the sun'. Hopefully we are not the ones who have given offense."

"I may need some time to interrupt..."

"Death herself approaches. Can you not hear the chanting of the accursed souls, the doomed men trapped above the sky? You hear approaching the Crone, the Living Death!" Wang said.

"Morgan Le Fay?" Smythe asked.

Kang nodded. "Fully manifested." The young man paled and ran from his desk. Kang hung up and dialed another number.

"North Cosmopolis Disaster Center, Van Horst speaking." The voice on the phone was calm and professional.

"It is I, Kniaz Kang. Do you see the sky, the sun?"

"We have two people on the roof watching. Is there a forest fire?" Van Horst asked. "The Sun has turned blood red. The snowfall is gray."

"Those are ashes," Kang said, "and powdered bone. Sound the municipal disaster alarm. Everyone should go to the deepest available shelter. And get your people off the roof. They face Death Incarnate herself." He hung up.

There was a gentle knock at the door. Teranike, now wearing battle armor and a range of weapons, stuck her head in. "Someone's being rowdy," she announced, "chanting, but I can't find them to tell them to hush up."

"What are they saying?" Kang asked.

" 'Death to life! Death to life!' It seems a bit far-reaching," she answered.

"You hear the voices?" Kang asked. "That is surprising. You are a Polarian. They should not speak to you. Mayhaps you spend too much time around very powerful persona. You don't have a boyfriend you haven't mentioned, do you? No, apologies, you said you were married. You should be quite safe from the Avatar, except for the storm winds that may level the local town."

"Yes, but what sort of a chant is 'Death to Life! Death to Life!'?" she asked.

"It is the Crone, herself, the Avatar, the Living Death. She announces her impending arrival. Indeed, I must now go to the front portico to greet her," Kang announced. "After all, she is a very long-time friend. Now it is time for you to go down to the shelter. Take all your weapons along. Do not hesitate to use them."

"Yes, Sir." Teranike hesitated. "Sir? Did you say 'a long-time friend'?"

"Longer than you – well, mayhaps not you, Polarians knowing more history than Americans – would believe possible." Kang nodded gravely. "I should introduce the two of you someday. I'm sure you two would like each other. But at the moment she must be in a really bad mood. So, off to the shelter."

Kang stepped out to the front porch. Something was a bit puzzling. Teranike could hear the Avatar. She must have absorbed enough of the Presence to activate one of her gifts, a gift that would have lain latent while she was on OtherEarth. But she worked in back, out of sight, not where she would meet any of his clientele. Silk was more powerful than she thought she was, but not that powerful. Jim obviously had a few minor gifts and a crush on one or another of the young ladies. Where was Teranike getting regular exposure to someone at the very top end of the power range? The answer was not obvious.

~~~~~

I could have turned off the video and gone back to studying. I was well above expectations for my age. Full year classes do that. You don't forget what you learned, and you don't forget how to study. I could still tell. I was lagging. Mayhaps I can't reach my standards for myself. That's no reason not to have them. I stayed downstairs and watched the video.

The IncoAztecan top-level personae were visibly frustrated. FedCorps had trained vigorously in team combat. Their elite did not go up against ours. Their elite each faced a team of well-trained second-rank persona whose job it was to keep them busy. Their second-rank people each faced American third-rank people with the same mission. We didn't even try to kill their elite people. That would anyway have been difficult. Each of their elite was covered by a large group of bottom-rank Jaguar and Eagle Knights, whose job it was to block, neutralize, and disperse attacks directed against one of their elite. Their strategy made perfect sense, once the commentator explained that their elite were each fighting for personal rank and glory, rank and glory being based on how many top-rank prisoners they each sent home to feed their gods.

Meanwhile, our top people and our lower-tier people all went after their Knights, their bottom level people. A Knight targeted by a group of people or someone like Krystal North almost certainly dies very quickly. If he doesn't, she jumps to another target. Of course, they have a huge number of Jaguar, Eagle, Ocelot, and Shark Knights, but even at a run marching through a teleport tunnel takes time.

The area the Aztecans controlled kept expanding. We didn't have enough people on the ground in front of them to hold them back. After not long, that area was well larger than the targeting error of modern rocket artillery. If you fired a rocket shell at the Aztecan-controlled area, it would come down someplace inside that area. The fixed fortifications covering Modesto, Madera and Morgan Hill first fired ranging shots and then started shelling the IncoAztecan occupied zone. Yes, the Eagle Knights were quite effective at stopping artillery rounds, most of which therefore got nowhere near their
~~~~~

targets. Some did make it. Blocking all those artillery rounds still kept a large number of Eagle Knights busy.

California also has a State Guard, ungifted people with good weapons. Many of those people still had to reach their armories, be given their weapons and supplies, and head off overland to the battle field. The Eagle News commentator kept repeating that we did not know if we were seeing the major IncoAztecan attack, or if California was meant to draw our forces out of position.

At some point, my conscience began to bother me. All the wars now starting around the world traced back to me recovering the Namestone. Everyone expected that if a war did start the League of Nations Peace Police would appear on the scene to force each national army back into its own country. The League had been chasing false Eclipses. None of the people they tried to arrest had been me. Almost every time they appeared on the scene, locals took exception to what they were doing and zapped them. This had happened often enough that most Peace Police brigades weren't up to fighting anyone at the moment. What did that mean? The Peace Police were not about to ride to America's rescue, or anyone else's rescue, either.

Now there was another split screen. Unmistakably, Morgan Le Fay had appeared over central and then western Washington. The sun turned red. Gale-force winds shook the trees. Ashes fell from the sky. Screams could be heard coming from far overhead. Historically, she disliked countries invading each other. Eagle News put pretty lines on their map. Soon Morgan Le Fay would reach the Manjukuoan invasion fleet. She was supposedly the most powerful persona in the world, but there was only one of her, while surely there were a lot of Manjukuoan personas with their fleet.

Eagle News had a really short video, what appeared to be a group of farmers and shopkeepers on the outskirts of a small town, facing off against Jaguar Knights. They were all really old men and women. They'd sent off the children and grandchildren, and stayed behind to fight for their country. They had heavy duty rifles, elephant guns and single-shot 0.80" pieces. There were only a few of them; the place was more a crossroads than a small town. There were a lot of Jaguar Knights. The townsfolk did not try to maneuver. They just sat in their foxholes and shot at the enemy. After not long at all, there were Jaguar Knight bodies on the ground. The town's defenders were dead. When you are fed to the gods, you are not anaesthetized. The last few defenders shot themselves or blew themselves up to avoid being captured.

The Aztecans did not have Eagle Knights doing air support. The announcer had said something about that. We had better fliers, an Air Force with good air-to-air missiles, antiaircraft missiles, particle beam weapons…The Eagle Knights stayed very close to the ground near the main IncoAztecan force, where they had plenty of cover.

I really did not want to use the Namestone to end this. For starters, its powers don't line up well with battlefields or persona alert to mental attack.

Weak mindscreens are enough, over the short term, to silence its bitter tunes. It did help me to find the corrupt judges, people who were abominations upon the face of the earth, and inflict on them the punishment they deserved. Sacrificing them was one of the things I had to do to take complete control of the Namestone. That was subtle mind control. Subtle mind control wouldn't work with persona combat.

OK, this mess really was my fault. I'd thought people had read the *Copper Book*, the book you could have read two thousand years ago, and realized what a terrible thing the Namestone actually was. It should have occurred to me that all these people risking their lives to get their hands on the Namestone weren't doing that in order to destroy it. No, they actually wanted the Namestone because they believed its phony promises.

I am good at breaking things. I could show up in California and help. The danger is that I'd manage to get myself killed, in which case the Namestone would go back into the Maze. Or would it? It was behind a quarter-inch of impervium, after all. If I died, Kniaz Kang would not be pleased to learn he had just become the Bearer. I'd have to be very careful. I should go.

I started dropping through levels. Even here in my home I had a reasonable number of them called, with crash drops giving me access to the rest. Crash drops kill. I would not take that chance. My hair was dyed. I'd go in my boy disguise, complete with heavy felted jacket and woolen stocking cap. A knapsack was a good idea. I started packing the things that a boy my age, not too heavily gifted, would want. A bunch of ration bars. Trail mix, high-cal version. Two quart water containers. Spare heavy socks. A change of underwear. The waterproof ultralight thermal blanket. The waterproof underpad. Compass. A combat knife, borazon edged. Cuts anything, in particular you if you are careless. The Ruggels 0.70 pistol with APDS ammunition was possible, but heavy and unlikely to be useful. Mess kit. Light folding shovel? Clipped to the outside. Toilet paper, sealed packets. Tubed soap. Pocket comb. Toothbrush. Sewing kit. No, most kids my age wouldn't think of that. Adjustable magnification monocular. Perception is good, but it's not high-resolution. Most kids my age would have a RadioBell. That's a good way to get yourself tagged and tracked, a really bad outcome for me. My house has a Bell line.

Now I was way down in my levels. Where should I go? The announcer had made a point about rocket artillery from the heavy defense batteries around Merced being blocked by IncoAztecan antirocket battalions, personas specifically trained to shoot down rocket artillery shells. There were good maps of the current front lines. One group of IncoAztecans was causing most of the problems for the artillery. They were as good a place to start as any. I did my usual teleport string, ending up on the ground a couple of miles back from the fighting, almost due south of the Aztecan zone. The crash of artillery rockets exploding, way up in the air, was almost continuous. I did a mind scan. The low rise in front of me had a line of people on it. Several of them had the assurance that comes with command authority. I couldn't see most of them. Then there was a gap with very few people, and, beyond that, large groups of people moving slowly this way. I teleported almost up to the line. I do not have hearing as a gift, but I could hear a Lieutenant talking with a sergeant. Loudly. At least, those were the titles used. That was a good place to start. Two fast teleport jumps put me next to the sergeant.

They continued shouting at each other.

"Sergeant, I am tired of your insolence. I want your men to pack up, advance to the next rise, and attack! That's an order!" The Lieutenant was tall, built like a football player, and had a superb command voice which he was using, to little effect.

"Lieutenant, you are Regular Army. We are California State Militia, not even State Guard. We are so much not in your chain of command. And I am not sending my boys charging forward to get themselves killed." The Sergeant, no, I could not read his rank, but there were a lot of chevrons on his sleeve, was not impressed.

"And who are you?" The Lieutenant pointed at me. He put a bunch of impolite words after who. Mum always said you should never use those words on a battlefield. They slowed down giving clear orders. "Kid, there is a war on. Go home! This is no place for someone your age!"

"Begging the Lieutenant's pardon," and now the Sergeant turned, enough that I could see his name ribbon. 'Davis' it read. "The young man here has a force field up, which is more than I can say for you. Young man?"

"Yes, Sergeant Davis?" I answered. It was clear which of these people had some sense.

"I see the field," Davis said. "Can you reach out and touch the enemy, say, set a fire on the next rise?"

I did a fast mind scan on the next rise. "At least four people on it," I said. "I'd be doing green on green fire."

David did a double take. "How? You're right."

"Mind scan," I announced. "Same way I found you." Meanwhile, the Lieutenant was turning beet read. "But around that ruined barn there's no one." I pointed off to the left.

David nodded. "Show us. Then our Lieutenant may have a few words for you."

I let the barn and neighboring field have it, using plasma balls. A series of loud crashes shook the ground. Debris flew into the air, hit the wall I'd put around the target, and fell back to earth.

"You can do that again?" Davis asked.

"All day. And more violent things, but we're too close," I answered.

"Lieutenant, thank you for finding us our antitank weapon. Aren't you supposed to go back to your HQ now to tell your superiors we have the weapons we need, and, no, you may not use one of my men as your messenger?"

"Kid, go home! Now! That is not a suggestion. That is an order!" the Lieutenant screamed. Now I saw his name tag. Piton.

"Lieutenant Piton, my mother taught me you should never give an order that won't be obeyed." I said.

"And you think your mother knows something about war? That's absurd!" He screamed.

Given who my mother is, it is hard to imagine how he could be more wrong. "Yes, and you can't make me." Lieutenant Piton stormed off, cursing under his breath.

"West Point graduate," Davis said. "Recent. Not under the wing of a good Staff Sergeant. What were his mistakes?" Davis asked.

I thought for a moment. "Not using a resource, me. All those bad words. They use time that you could be using to think. Not remembering chain of command. Giving orders that aren't followed. Oh, ordering your two squads to attack what must be five hundred Jaguar Knights beyond the rise. Is that enough?"

"You learned all that from your mom and dad?" he asked. "I should make you a Sergeant, put you in charge of the Lieutenant. But that battalion is shooting down our rocket artillery shells. They've got a screen of folks in front of them, dug in; if they didn't, attacking the battalion would be almost worth it."

"Put me in charge of Piton? Against idiots, the gods themselves lose." I quoted.

"What do you propose to do?" he asked.

"Teleport ahead. Take out Jaguar Knights." I paused. "Can you tell which ones are sergeants and officers?"

"No Sergeants," Davis answered. "Feathered fools don't use NCOs. Every officer has a pink shoulder patch."

"Got it. This may take a bit," I said.

"You just said ordering an attack on them was a mistake," Davis said.

"Ordering you. I'm not you." I answered.

"You ever see persona combat?" he asked. "You have some idea what you're getting into?"

"I'm Joe. From Medford. You ever watch PNN? That was me and the Death Lords," I said. His mouth made a wide 'O'. "You have someone on the next rise?".

"You see the big tree, two rises out, with the bushes in front? There's someone underneath it, out of sight. He found a hole in their screen. Join him. Your password is 'password'. His response is 'atomic mouse'."

"Password. Got it." I teleported, coming in parallel to the ground just behind the peak of the rise. "Password password" I said quietly.

"Atomic mouse." The fellow had a really good camouflage suit. I barely saw him. "And you are here to?" he asked.

"I'm your heavy duty persona support. I'm here to kill bad guys," I explained.

"Plenty of targets. Come up here to see," he answered.

I did a low crawl, slowly, around the far side of the bushes, and peered around the side. A distance out were a large group of Jaguar Knights. Their force fields were visible. They were shielding this side of the Aztecan position from rocket artillery and aircraft. I took out my monocular, affixed the sun cover, and looked carefully. The men were in small groups, each mayhaps a dozen people. The men in each group stood in a horseshoe pattern. The open end of each horseshoe faced away from me. In the middle of each horseshoe were two taller men with pink blurs on their shoulders. I began tuning a preset to trigger on the shoulder flashing.

"You going to do something?" the fellow I could now not see at all asked.

"In a moment," I said. "I'm prepping something complicated. Concentration needed; quiet would help."

"Sorry," he said.

Tuning the preset took a bit of time, and two failed trials. Then I had it. "You may want to run," I said. "There'll be counterfire." I reached very deeply into my gifts, putting everything I could find into my plasma torch. "Leave slack" I reminded myself. "When I do this, they'll know exactly where we are."

"Give me a minute," he asked. He rolled over the military crest of the hill, and fast-crawled over the top. I could hear his run. He was way faster a runner than I am. I gave him two minutes.

Aimed automatic fire is really impressive if you don't know how it's done. The preset triggered my plasma burst every time I saw one of the pink spots in my monocular. I didn't have to identify the spot consciously. The preset did that. And I could sweep the monocular really fast. I did. I almost forgot to start sweeping at the back of their formation. If I'd started at the front, the dust from the explosions would have blocked my visibility.

Toward the end I had to slow down. The more alert officers realized where I was, and had their troops move their group force field to my direction and shoot back at me. That meant reinforcing my shields and hitting theirs harder, without doing a crash drop. The flicker before my eyes was the circle that forgets to curve. I stayed away from it.

I was done. I teleported back to Sergeant Davis and his men.

"You get a few of them?" he asked.

"Officers," I answered. "Most of them."

"Sergeant?" An older woman at a video screen spoke up.

"Yes, Corporal Parker?" Sergeant Davis said.

"Still reviewing the slow-mo on our way-right camera. But it looks like all of them," Parker said. "And bunches of their troops got thrown about and are lying there."

"Should have asked sooner," I said. "Didn't these guys have anyone on the ridge? I should have taken them, too."

"They did, an hour ago." It was the fellow in the camou suit. "I'm Leavey."

"He's Joe." David pointed at me.

"Those people," Leavey use impolite synonyms for 'people', "had guys on this side of that hill, just like you said, Sergeant. Idiots had no one covering their rear, the side toward their friends. I came up behind them. With all that noise, it was like slaughtering rabbits."

"That's real good," I said. "Thanks."

"My job. My pleasure. I was clearing an opening for friends of mine not yet here. Sergeant, those folks from way south may come visiting soon," Leavey said.

"Like the thirty of us are going to stop a thousand of them," Davis said. "We'll need to be ready to bug out."

"No rush yet," Parker said. "Their troops, except the ones still shooting at the same hill location, are just standing around doing nothing."

"Moses?" Leavey said.

"Yes, Ahab," Davis answered.

"Aztecans." Leavey said. "Almost zero initiative. The private who tries to give an order, he's poaching an officer position. He's god-food."

"Lunch?" Parker asked. "We've some moments."

"We're still short ration packs," Davis said. He said a few more things about that.

"How many?" I asked.

"Eight." Davis answered.

"In my pack," I answered. "I've got more than that." I slipped my pack off my shoulders and started taking things out, enough I could reach the rations.

"Everything except a Ruggels," Leavey said.

"I left the ought-seventy at home," I answered. "Heavy. Food sounded more useful."

"You don't mind?" Davis asked.

"I have some left," I answered.

"Wait," Leavey said. "We need to strip the serial numbers from Joe's packs. Protect his privacy. Does someone have a sharp knife? Mine snapped, last Aztecan I killed."

I passed him mine, handle first. He looked at it lovingly, and careful snipped a tag off each pack, finally returning me the knife and the tags. I held the tags in one hand and reduced them to ashes.

"Sergeant Davis," Parker said, "The Colonel is on the phone."

Davis took the headset mike pair. At that point I noticed the wire going back toward the road. "Davis here. Hello, Colonel…No, we didn't. The young man standing with me did all that. Killed their officers. Do it again? Joe, you feel up to it later today?"

"Now is good," I said. "I've also done high power work."

"That wasn't?" Leavey asked. I shook my head.

"Yes, Colonel," Davis said. "He says he's good to go. Teleporter. Where? Morgan Hill point 7. Got it. Yes, Sir. Out."

Parker was already typing something. "We're here. That's Morgan Hill Point Seven." I looked carefully at the map.

"Has someone been there?" I asked.

Leavey waved at me. "And I teleport, like twice a day, a few feet. I'll go with you. I'm envisioning the point." With a flare of light, a cloudless sky, we teleported. The air was a bit cooler; the sky was the same.

"Welcome to Morgan Hill," Leavey announced. We jogged off the teleport pad.

"Captain!" The Marine standing guard on the pad saluted. "Car is waiting."

The State Militia Headquarters was camouflaged and guarded. The guards obviously knew Leavey. A few of them glared in my direction. "He's with me," Leavey announced. One finally said "Map Room B." Leavey led the way.

Indeed, there was a modest room with large wall screens displaying maps. One showed central California, an ugly red blob indicating the Aztecan positions. Every so often it reset. Each time it reset, the red area was a bit larger. Another showed the north Pacific and coast. "What's the flashing blue circle?" I asked.

The man sitting at the display terminal answered. "Impossible storm," he said. "Tesdri says four hundred knot winds, and three hundred foot waves, which is impossible. That's where the Manjukuoans are. Must be radar jamming."

"Divine wind," I said.

"Morgan Le Fay." The woman making the announcement was behind me, standing in the doorway. "We have that from Prince Kong. The Manjukuoans may not be dead yet, but they will be soon enough."

Leavey and I turned around. "Krystal," he said.

"Ahab, always good to see you. I gather you cleared their outposts from Pegram's Ridge, just before this young man showed up."

"This is Joe," Captain Leavey said.

Krystal looked at me. "You're *that* Joe."

"Yes, ma'am," I managed to answer. "You said we needed to talk."

<*I really want to know who you actually are,*> she said. <*You somehow got Trisha Wells into serious trouble with her parents.*>

<*I know,*> I answered. <*I don't understand how, don't see how to help.*>

"Has to wait. Are you up to repeating what you did? You wrecked up a piece of their antimissile defenses. Repeat might be dangerous. Eventually you run into Popocatepetl," she said.

"Meeting Popo is death," Leavey warned me.

"I'll send his widow a card," I answered.

"Widows," Leavey corrected. He smiled and rolled his eyes.

"What do you want me to do?" I asked.

"Show me how you did it. So I can share it. And we'll do it again," Krystal North said.

"Let me think for a moment." None of my rules engines were being helpful. But Mum had done that for me. There was the memory I needed. "I've given someone a preset. No, that won't work. OK, I see what to do. But I have to put something in your mind, and I'm clumsy at that sort of mentalics. You'll get a headache."

"People are dying in hideous agony! Do it!" She wasn't quite angry.

"Easy, Krystal," Leavey said.

"Yes, Ahab," she agreed.

"OK, I have to set something up." That went slower than it might have, but I don't like stress when I'm doing something complicated. "I'll put a mind screen around us both. You'll need to drop yours, meaning you'll want a chaperone."

"No. Wait. You're moving a *structure*?" she asked. The last word was in Goetic, but I knew what it meant.

"Yes."

"I've been here before." She put a mind screen around both of us. Ever so gently I passed the mentalic structure over. It's like handing a baby to someone else, which Mum had taught me how to do, not that I've ever done it. I mean, yuck. Babies leak in every direction. "Got it." She held up a hand, spent a while thinking. "OK, I have the whole thing in place."

"It wants a lot of levels. You may want to scan slower than I did," I warned.

"Noted," she answered primly. I was quite sure she didn't quite believe me. "I have a list of people to reach with this. I'll be a few minutes."

Late that evening, I had taken down five more Aztecan air defense battalions. I left some of them alive, but without officers they were not effective. I also met Popocatepetl. He was seriously over-rated. What was Mum's word for it? Glass jaw. All offense, weak defense. My shields were good enough. His weren't. I owe a card to his wives.

The State Militia from across California had converged on the Aztecan invasion site, charging down interstates at 100 miles an hour, with weapons perfectly adequate to take out bottom-tier personas. Aztecan formations that lost their commanding officers were prime targets.

America is still the greatest industrial nation in the world, meaning our rocket artillery batteries were not short of ammunition. Freight teleporters moved it to where it was needed. The Aztecan bridgehead had been shorn of its antirocket defenses, mostly not by me, though I did a part. Now the rockets were getting though. The Aztecans were still expanding the area they controlled, but their casualties were steep and getting steeper. However, they'd pushed an army of personas and their equipment and supplies through their teleport gate, enough that it was touch and go whether they'd be contained or whether they'd break out and take Silicon Valley. The fighting fronts got close to Modesto and Morgan Hill. Across the continent, the Texans had crossed the Rio Grande and advanced into the Empire, carefully staying in range of the fixed Texan rocket artillery and particle beam batteries.

Captain Leavey gave me a Grizzly Guard brassard, enough that anyone who saw me would assume I had a few gifts and was doing something helpful but not dangerous. The brassard meant I could go into an ice cream bar, late at night, and no one asked where my parents were. I was working on my second caramel sundae when two older women sat at the bar a few chairs down. From their clothing, they were doctors with healing gifts, taking a break from treating the wounded. I smiled politely in their direction. They went back to talking.

"I saw on the video," the older one said. "Someone killed Popocatepetl."

"He's dead?" I asked. I was fairly sure.

"Oh, yes," she gushed. "We watched him die. Everyone cheered. But Krystal North's strategy is terrible. We don't even try to kill their lead personas. We're shooting up their peons, people with only a couple gifts. There's sure to be a Congressional inquiry."

"We wrecked their anti-rocket defenses," I said. "That means all that artillery is getting through. And, I've heard, our good people aren't dying, too, are they?"

"I thought I'd be healing National League heroes," the younger woman said. "I've been saving the lives of militiamen who have no gifts at all."

"They're still our people," I remarked.

"That young woman who killed Popocatepetl," the older woman said. "She'll be a national hero. Have to fight off young men all the time."

I stiffened slightly. How had someone penetrated my disguise?

The younger woman looked around, checking who could hear her. "She was really flat-chested, though. But maybe you'll be the one to be chasing her." She pointed at me. I grinned. OK, no one got a good look at me, but I'm not six foot three, I am not two hundred pounds of muscle, and I do not have a dashing mustache. Not now, not ever would women be falling for me. "She's still a national hero."

For some reason I suspected that what I was going to do at full moon would cancel that.

"Me? I just do what any American would do, given the chance." I went back to my sundae.

<*Joe?*> That was Krystal North again.

<*Just finishing another sundae. Shall I bring you one?*> I answered.

<*Thanks, but just finished a ration pack. I was checking on you.*> She sounded concerned.

<*I'm fine. When do you need me back?*> I'd been urged to get something to eat and had done so.

<*We're good for the moment. The Brits are here. Lafayette has returned, this time*

with the Legion of Glory. That's much of three national teams, and their state team equivalents. Army, Militia, and Grizzly Guards are here in force. Aztecans are regrouping. Did you know Popocatepetl was their commander?> Krystal North asked.

<That's crazy. What was he doing on their front lines? Was he a total idiot?> I did not use any of Mum's deprecated – another fine adjective – words, but the tone likely crept through.

<Their top people fight for personal glory. He did.> She sounded to agree with me.

<If he were Norwegian I'd say he's gone to Valhalla. I was happy to run with your strategy, but I don't understand it. They can lose an awful lot of low-level peons, and their core persona force is still effective.> I'd killed a bunch of those peons myself. Actually, I lost count of how many. *<I have to think about more about your strategy.>*

<Can't talk about it. Secret. Can you sleep? That was very violent.> Krystal North sounded worried.

<I'm fine,> I answered. *<Killing your enemies is good.>* Mum's training had been very clear on this point. *<OK, I really do need some sleep.>*

<Yes! Alert is life-saving. That's your life. Don't be back before ten tomorrow. Show up here when you do,> she answered. *<Oh, Captain Leavey said we'd be grateful for your mom's strategic thoughts if she wants to give them. He emphatically said I get to figure out your parents' names for myself.>* I'd have to ask him who he thought my mom is. Hopefully he had it wrong. It would be safer to let her forget the conversation. Sleep still sounded good. Medico had already been running sleep regeneration, enough I could supposedly keep going indefinitely. The key word there is "supposedly". With that I finished my sundae, put a generous tip under the dish, and teleported.

Chapter Forty-Seven

The Invisible Fortress

The sun was well above the horizon. Yesterday, the third day since the Aztecans invaded, I'd returned home before sunset, gone straight to bed, and slept the long night through. Several days of persona combat had been good training, but it was still physically draining, especially when you get knocked back through a reinforced concrete wall or two. Popocatepetl had a glass jaw, but he and friends also had solid graviton blasts. I'd been away from home most of the time for three days. Three times, I'd had a top-line Aztecan persona appear more or less in front of me. The Aztecans were now down three top-line people.

I finally figured out Krystal North's strategic plan. It was brilliant. In large-scale persona combat, the traditional approach is that people at each power level take on their more-or-less equals, so there is something of a draw. Weaker personas fill gaps in defense lines, suppress teleports into the enemy rear, and the like. In Plan Hoffman, the American Republic's top-line people were helping our bottom tier people to wreck up the Aztecan bottom-tier people. The Aztecans were actually taking very heavy casualties, but for the most part these were not their elite persona. They were the peons barely noticed by the Aztecan elite. These peons were also the persona deployed to keep the Aztecan ungifted under the boot heels—OK, the sandals and god-feeding knives—of the ruling classes. The Empire didn't need their political police to be very gifted personas, but they did need a lot of them.

The Aztecan plan was to flood their persona host through their teleport tunnel into California, sweep to the ocean, and then roll south to San Diego. They had a large teleport tunnel. They moved really large numbers of personas, and a fair piece of their army, through the gap in very little time. They'd counted on their Eagle Knights to shield their attack force from American artillery, which is the best in the world. That hadn't worked well for them.

The Aztecans had pushed through Morgan Hill toward San Jose. In the western half of the central valley, they rapidly advanced south. Their drives to take Modesto and move north were blocked. Destruction as they advanced was total. The Kaiser's antiwar museums would have vast new exhibits. The intended main Aztecan advance was into Silicon Valley, so those forces got all the reinforcements and supplies. That advance would cripple American industrial production, but only if it succeeded. Of course, the Aztecans were advancing into an urban area loaded with reinforced concrete buildings, strongpoints that had to be taken down one at a time. By day three estimates of how many people the Aztecans had pushed through their teleport tunnel were huge.

Krystal North had concentrated her best people in the California central valley, east of the Aztecan-occupied zone, centered on Merced. The Aztecans viewed this as a relatively inactive front. They could have advanced due east, finally reaching the Rocky Mountains, but that area was all beautiful farmland, not major industrial centers. Aztecan east-flank commanders apparently kept begging for reinforcements, but were turned down. They were the quiet front. Obviously the Americans would have their best personas in San Jose.

Somewhat before noon on the third day, Krystal's plan worked. Aztecan lines near Merced collapsed. There were some perfectly good top-level Aztecan personas in the east, but so many of their bottom-tier people had been taken out that the Aztecan top-level people were swarmed, attacked from all sides, and taken off the map. I made a modest contribution. The French Legion of Glory was the fist that punched through the Aztecan rear area and captured the Aztecan teleport zone. We were now dropping artillery shells through their teleport tunnel. Lots of artillery shells. Suddenly the tunnel popped shut. We must have hit its generators.

The French rolled toward San Jose, successively capturing lower and lower Aztecan headquarters. Attacked from the rear, their people made disorganized counterattacks, or panicked and ran. Their best people fought bravely. They'd already been concentrating on moving people, not supplies, to the front, and were now cut off. The general announcement that Morgan Le Fay had annihilated the Manjukuoan Grand Fleet and its large invasion force, the cream of the Manjukuoan Army, did not help Aztecan morale. Overnight the Aztecan positions collapsed.

The full moon was a week off. I now had a more important mission than helping to turn the battle into a massacre. I went to zero and then started increasing the draw on my gifts. Meanwhile my lesson computer glared at me. I'd obviously taken another vacation when I should be studying. I was clearly, as far as the computer was concerned, a bad person

Three days later, the Aztecan pocket in central California had completely broken up. Between fighting for personal glory and the French attack, they'd lost their command structure. Combat was reduced to dealing with isolated groups of survivors. There were a lot of them, but the issue was not in doubt. More and more often, an isolated Aztecan battalion would conclude that their position was hopeless. The battalion high priest would then give everyone in the battalion the opportunity to serve the state by feeding the gods.

Commentators asked how the Empire of the Inca and the Aztecs would hold together now that their army had been wrecked. The peasants were overtaxed. They were regularly volunteered to serve as food for the gods. Peasant riots were frequent. The American border was rolling south. The peasants loved us. We gave them news that infants and young men would no longer be taken off to Tenochtitlan to feed Tlaloc. Few people have ever lived in Baja California. It was annexed to the American Republic.

The League Peace Executive finally got around to meeting. God forbid they should try meeting while there was an actual war going on. They might feel obliged to try doing something. I decided to watch the opening minutes, meaning I saw the interesting parts.

As seen on video, the representatives of the 13 Great Powers sat around the Omega Table, League Chancellor Holmgren at the top.

Holmgren rapped his gavel twice against its sounding block. "If we may have order, please," he said. "Seating has been rearranged so that delegates from nations at war with each other are not sitting shoulder to shoulder. I hope that this precaution is not needed, and that here we may conduct ourselves in a positive and polite manner. Having said that, as we have wars, not threats to peace, ongoing, we begin with those. The luck of the draw—I used playing cards-- is that wars involving the America Republic come first. In alphabetical order, I believe the Manjukuoan ambassador is first. Legate Hong Sangui?"

"Manjukuo believes we should follow the wise advice of the Prussian Kaiser and turn our backs on war. Our navy has been conducting peaceful exercises in the North Pacific. Efforts to order it to return to its home ports have been hindered by American radio jamming. We have failed in our efforts to contact the Grand Fleet and its support vessels. I am confident that our sailors look forward to returning home. We ask that the Americans cease to jam our fleet's radio network."

"And now the representative of the IncoAztecan Empire, the Speaker for the First Speaker."

Lord Smoking Frog nodded politely. "I speak for the First Speaker, Lord Honeybee Sloth. The former First Speaker, having been found to have conducted national affairs in an undesirable manner, successfully petitioned the Council of the Realm for permission to resign his posts and offer himself to the Gods. The Empire agrees that our invasion of the American Republic was ill-advised, unnecessary, and should not have occurred. We propose to return to the status quo ante bellum, with the specification that the Americans will return to us their prisoners of war, our persona host, and the territory they have now occupied."

"It is my understanding that the Queen Empress Victoria and the Emperor Napoleon have deferred to the American Republic with respect to war issues in the American Republic." Holmgren took another drink from the flask standing on the table in front of him. "Am I correct? In that case, I should ask the Ambassador Buncombe for the American response to these

Manjukuoan and Aztecan peace proposals."

"Chancellor Holmgren!" Buncombe paused to polish one lens of his spectacles. "I take note of these proposals to which the word 'peace' has somehow mysteriously been attached. No matter. My honorable colleagues may call their proposals whatever they want. I am not offended. The American people may be led to question their good sense, but we are not offended by foreign words.

"With respect to the Manjukuoan Grand Fleet, neither America nor, so far as we know, any other nation is attempting to interfere with Manjukuoan radio communications. However, several days ago She Who Is, the Crone's Avatar, the Living Death, the Immortal Morgan Le Fay summoned the Divine Wind."

"Kamikaze," Saigo Shigetoshi whispered.

"The Manjukuoan Grand Fleet encountered five hundred knot winds and three hundred foot tall waves. It was obliterated, removed from existence. It had no survivors. For this reason, it is difficult for Hsinking and Ulan Bator to establish radio contact with their former navy.

"With respect to the Aztecan requests, I note the well-known fact that it is impossible to take personae as prisoners of war, because they cannot be disarmed. Therefore, neither the American Republic nor any of our allies attempt to take personae as prisoners. There is no practical way to do it. I can disarm an ungifted soldier. I cannot strip a persona of his powers. The persons to whom Lord Smoking Frog is referring are therefore dead, have offered themselves as food for the gods, or are being hunted down as the murderers and pirates they are. Unlike some foreign states, we do not desecrate people being executed, but we do kill them. In the absence of a legitimate peace offer by the Aztecan Empire, we will continue our liberation of Mexico, which we expect by and by will become an independent Republic under Mexican rule, save that Baja California, which was stolen from our Republic during the 1436 War, will be returned to the American Republic. Finally, with respect to the specific request elsewhere that we return Lord Popocatepetl, the 'Living Volcano' as he styled himself, the Living Volcano engaged in single combat with an American, a stripling youth of mayhaps thirteen years. The American smote him mightily and struck him dead."

"Having said that, I have here an important document for the Council, to be inserted later in the Agenda. It is from North Idaho. It is an arrest warrant and request for extradition, the charge being child molestation. The accused is Chancellor Lars Holmgren." Buncombe smiled at the Chancellor.

"Don't be ridiculous," Holmgren responded. "Nonetheless, it goes into the Agenda, so in due course we may reject it. With respect to the dispute over Tibet..." Chancellor Holmgren continued. At this point I turned off the video and returned to computer classes. I missed the Ambassadors from Manjukuo, Azteca, the Ottoman Empire, South Asia, and Prussia storming out the meeting. That was only five of the thirteen great Powers, but they did command a near-majority of the world's people

Chapter Forty-Eight

The Great Chamber of Wisdom
The House That Is Forever

Deep twilight, trapped by a dozen light pipes, illumined the Great Chamber of Wisdom. Prince Mong-ku glared at his fellow immortals. The weather outside might be pleasant, but the interior of the chamber was frigid. Several thousand years planning appeared to have gone down the drain in a few hours. The IncoAztecan, Manjukuoan, and Prussian hosts were supposed to be world conquerors, but they were not conquering anything.

"Let us be in order," Mong-ku said. "It appears that reviving the Great Plan is going to be taking much more of our time and energy." His remarks were met with grumbles. "We had expected the forces of order to dominate the globe, so every person knew his proper place, precisely as that entity would want and enjoy. The SkyVoice was to ensure that even the disorderly states were well ordered. Now the IncoAztecans have lost much of their Army and their persona forces. Worse, the American concentrated on eliminating the hordes of low-grade personae, the folks the IncoAztecan hierarchy relied upon to keep the peasants properly subservient. Without them, their police state will surely fall apart. The Manjukuoans are about as badly off, their fleet and the troops it was carrying having gone to the bottom. The Prussians were on so much of an ego trip that they united all of their neighbors. Against them. The Ottomans are emphatic about protecting African Islamites from African Christians, and no more. In short, our planned political developments appear foredoomed."

"Surely the Americans must have some hidden very powerful personae?" the Screaming Skull said. "To win, you must be more powerful than the other guy. That is the one and only thing that matters in persona combat."

That's the only thing, Plasmatrix thought, that matters if one is dumb as a rock, perhaps even dumber than the Screaming Skull, assuming that is possible. "The Americans appear to have won through superior strategy," she said, "with the aid of several European friends. They would have won anyhow, but it would have taken much longer. They won while outnumbered, their supply of artillery ammunition being a major equalizer."

"Americans? Strategy?" The Screaming Skull laughed. "They had no strategy. They didn't even try to pair their most powerful combatants against their IncoAztecan opposites. Krystal North against Popocatepetl? Now that would have been a contest worth watching. Instead, the noble Popo was left trying to swat a dozen second-raters, none of whom would even try to stand and fight. It was a farce."

"The Americans won," Starhome said. "That victory was definitely not in our plans. As a sacrifice to lure the unnamed one, the American Republic should have been the first course."

"By the way," Plasmatrix asked, "whatever did happen to Popocatepetl? He was actually decently powerful, for a transient person."

"He fought in his front lines," Colonel Pi said, "thus showing his virtue while at the same time being supreme commander of the Aztecan Host. He met an American of superior strength, someone who just walked off the streets and into combat, who killed him."

"He was running the whole show?" Plasmatrix said in astonishment. "And he was in the front lines, not concentrating on doing leaderly things like an intelligent military commander would do?"

"He was doing leaderly things," the Screaming Skull answered. "He deployed himself to slaughter his enemies like the sheep they undoubtedly were. That is the path of a warrior, not the path of a useless coward."

"In the end, his thinking got his army slaughtered like sheep, which seems not to explain what killed him." Plasmatrix tried to return the conversation to her question. "He ought to have been more or less even against Krystal North, if they met man-to-man."

"He encountered the person who was busily wrecking the IncoAztecan antirocket battalions," Dark Shadow said. "This person with no name that I could find beat him into the ground. However, his defenses were poor. He relied on crushing his opponents before they could shoot back, a tactic that failed here."

"David and Goliath," Dark Shadow said.

"Returning to our main topic? Please?" Prince Mong-ku shook his head. "We may be able to stabilize the IncoAztecans with surreptitious intervention. That will keep us all completely tied up until the end of the cycle, but that end surely cannot be all that many centuries away."

Plasmatrix and Starsmasher looked at each other and shook their heads. "No way," Plasmatrix said. "Ignoring that they are truly unfortunate people in their societal structure, the Empire was stable because close to one hundred percent of their personas were combat trained, all of them were brainwashed into serving their state, and the ruling class was happy to commit atrocities to keep people in their place. After all, the IncoAztecans believe that atrocities feed the gods. We can't be in a million places at once to keep things under control, not to mention the American and Brazilian invasion forces are showing no signs of slowing down."

"But we have no choice! We have to!" Mong-ku said. "If we don't, the

Great Plan for this cycle is likely to be a failure."

"On one hand, we seem to have lost the Radthninu tower already," Plasmatrix said firmly. "The Terran League seems to have a path to finding those memes. On the other hand, the ordered states we expected to be the core of the trap are in the process of failing. At some point, you have to reconsider your entire strategic plan. Perhaps we can still reconfigure the winning side into being the core of the trap. The winning side has its own weaknesses that could be enhanced into an order trap, say by amplifying legalistic arguments and parliamentary rules of procedure. Alternatively, if we engift well enough people, we can probably beat the unnamed by direct means."

"We need to think about this," Starsmasher said. "I propose we put things off for a week and see what happens."

"No! No!" Prince Mong-ku shouted.

"And I ask for a vote," Starsmasher said. "That's a big majority." He stood and left the room.

Chapter Forty-Nine

The Invisible Fortress
and
The Core of the Sun

I'd spent a week slowly increasing my draw on my gifts. The air around me hummed with energy. The Straight Circle, the Rainbow Connection, and the Well of Infinity were right at the edge of being called. I'd had a solid breakfast, done a walkaround of my land, fixing it sharply in my memories, and fed my pets the maple sugar treats and powdered catnip that is really not good for them.

I had no more excuses. It was time for my trip to the sun. For today's trip I broke out my working garb, gray with my sigil embroidered in darker gray. Even with the cape and low boots, it was by far the lightest of my garbs. Six months ago, it had been exactly the right size for me; it was still exactly the right size. Massive healing does age you backwards, so I had not grown any taller. If I'd thought that the weight of the fabric were going to matter, I could perfectly well have left all my clothing behind. No one was going to see me in the core of the sun. However, clothing does make the girl. The sure knowledge that you are immaculately dressed for an occasion bolsters your confidence.

Once again, I had a good chance of dying. Solo flights to the core of the sun are not safe. Most people who try one don't come back. So long as I die after and not before destroying the Namestone, I will be content. I'll have done what I set out to do. I'd set five email messages for time delay transmission. If I wasn't back in a week, the messages would transmit. Four were to Janie, Brian, Trisha, and Silk, asking them to have Silk rescue Snapdragon, Daffodil, Bluebell, and Columbine. She was welcome to keep them. The fifth was to Kniaz Kang, making him my heir, with instructions on sharing the money in my basement with Silk, Teranike, and the three Wells children. His lectures had been that valuable to me. My pets should be all right here forever, the pastures and orchards being that large, self-seeding, and full of squirrels and chipmunks, but the four of them would miss human company.

For the last time, I recovered the Namestone from its hiding place. With face to the sun, I teleported. Easy quarter-million-mile jumps, once a second, took me in a few minutes to the Sun's surface. Now came the hard part. I drew as deeply as I could on my gifts, putting all that power into my force fields, and took my first teleport step into the star in front of me. Five more steps, the load on my force fields increasing with every step, took me to the starcore.

I gestured with one arm, and waited for the Namestone to reveal itself. That's when the sun went totally bats. Yes, I was in the core of the sun, local temperature not quite 30 million degrees, surrounded by a hot gas, density a hundred times that of water, with at a pressure of, oh, 300 billion atmospheres. The outside view is bright and featureless. I've been here before. It was warm last time, too. All mum's comments about solitary solar core visitors vanishing without a trace were very active in my mind.

I was not going to stay around. I was drawing very deeply indeed on my gifts, with my force field reminding me that if I dozed off I would be dead in no time at all. But, usually, the deep core of the sun is reasonably quiet. After all, the power production of the sun, watts per cubic yard, is about the same as the power output of a good compost heap. It's just that the sun has a lot of cubic meters, and good insulation to keep the core toasty warm. Now there were wild flares of power, larger and larger with every instant. There had been a fair chance that I would not make it back out. At the moment 'not' was looming larger and larger.

The *True Copper Book* was very clear on the timing. I had to park here and wait for the Namestone to show itself. Summoning it was right out. It had to reveal itself, which might take a while. I forced myself to stay calm and used ultravision to look around me. Perhaps I was in an unexpected local hot spot.

Oh, my. The deep structures were anything but stationary. They were whirling wildly, passing through starcore liquid as though it was not there. They were moving, too. They were moving fast. They were moving straight at me, even from halfway across the sun.

Solve one problem at a time. Here was the Namestone, appearing at last, parked right on the other side of my force field, exposed to the solar fires...which it simply ignored. Supposedly it was not even getting hot. I was about to find out the hard way if that was true, though an extra layer of force field should protect me from anything worse than serious burns on my dominant hand. The pain block had better keep me from going into shock. If it failed, my force fields would at least hiccup, following which I would be incandescent plasma.

"Namestone," I said. "Thy locks I open. Thy puzzles I release." The moments I needed to wait seemed to stretch out toward eternity. The starcore all around me went off the charts, temperature and pressure soaring without limit. That's not what's supposed to happen. The sun's core is supposed to be stable. Medico's glyphs all flared bright violet. The space around me was a killing field. The draw on my gifts was way outside what I could handle safely.

I had to draw ever more deeply on my gifts to hold my force field up. I saw the Straight Circle, felt the caress of the Rainbow Connection, and found myself entering the mouth of the Infinite Well. If I hadn't read the *Presentia*, and hadn't had Spindrift show me what the *Presentia* meant, I would now be dead. I could go on about how painful dropping into the Well was, but complaining that deep calls on your gifts are unpleasant, well, eventually whining gets boring. Actually, whining gets boring incredibly quickly. Besides, I'd completely pulled the limit stops. I might feel on fire, every atom of my body burning, but I could take the load, for the seconds I needed. Probably. The alternative was very bad, though I'd miss seeing it. Being dead is like that.

"Namestone, I take thee fully." The sun outside my force field went totally berserk. My chances of escaping were about to disappear. I could teleport out now, or hang on long enough to destroy the Namestone. Very certainly I could not do both. That was a very easy choice. Life, lighter than atoms. Duty, heavier than worlds. If I hadn't wanted to risk dying, I would have left the Namestone in the Tomb.

"Namestone," I said, "I am thy mistress. Thy powers I deny. Thy existence I end." Now I had to wait for the response from the Namestone. There it was. Namestone changed color from brilliant cerulean to pale robin's egg blue.

I clamped my hand down, hard as I could. Namestone, but not the solar core fluid around it, came inside my force field. Weight lifting and barn maintenance and combat training have not left me with a weak grip. Namestone crushed, shattering like a Christmas tree ornament. I felt a few tiny shards drive into my palm. The rest vanished.

Suddenly, the load on my force field dropped to zero. Being in the starcore was like sitting in my subbasement, every surface painted bright white, bright lights all on, and nothing in sight.

That made no sense at all. This was, after all, the core of the sun. I was supposed to be surrounded by an incredibly hot, insanely pressurized liquid. Was I dead? Ummh, temporarily absent, as the Sera Lama would have put it?

I was not going to stay around to find out what happened. Teleport took me a hundred thousand miles out. Yes, I can go farther in free space, but I had to push hard to make an opening at the far end. Another half dozen steps and the sun was a wall of light below my feet.

<*We thank you.*> That mentalic voice came from directly below. Startlement overtook me. Had I had company the whole time?

<*Hello?*> I managed. <*I somehow missed seeing you.*>

<*You were pre-occupied. Besides, you did see us, though you did not understand.*> Those words came with an image. Oh, my. I was talking with the solar deep structures, the mystery that had baffled the scientists of ten civilizations. It seems that they are alive. <*We are the Timeless Ones. We have suppressed the minor*

disturbances we created in your star core, thus averting the imminent supernova that we were summoning. We believed you were going to take full control of the Ancient Evil, not that you were going to destroy it. We therefore, a regrettable error, prepared to destroy you first.>

<*No harm, no foul,*> I answered. If I weren't down to my last reserves of strength, this would have been a fascinating conversation. I wasn't going to emphasize that they would have *tried* to destroy me. They might decide to *try* again. <*What is going on?*> I asked.

I was touched by a pattern of thoughts, the actual answer, but the pattern was so huge, so complicated, that I understood only a few fragments. The Timeless Ones hadn't really been aware of my presence until I summoned the Namestone. Once they saw the Namestone they didn't have time, from their perspective, to ask me what I was going to do with it. I had to be destroyed before I used the Namestone to do something truly evil. Most of their answer was way beyond me. I would remember large pieces, but understanding them would need years. I did learn one thing, assuming I believed whoever was talking to me. The Namestone had all the bad features I thought it did, and lots more besides. I was part of a conversation that went on forever, or mayhaps next to no time at all.

<*When you are older, we will explain more clearly,*> the voice answered. <*You will be welcome to visit us. But we are now going home, and are not offended if you do the same.*> I had a clear image showing where home was for the Timeless Ones, someplace in the deep structures of a quasar. The environment was highly energetic, even ignoring the black holes. They were the islands of relative calm. Mayhaps it would be safer if I knocked on the door and asked if anyone wanted to come out and play. Some environments are simply beyond what my screens can handle reliably.

I took the hint. In space I can do a third of a million miles in a jump, twice a second, especially with my gifts pushed so deep. That would take me to earth in a few minutes. I had company, something all around me, majestic clouds of sparks. Ultravision said that the clouds contained no chemical matter. The Goetic Knights would have called those sparks photinos, whatever they are. I have this long list of 'odd things you can see with ultravision and what they look like'. Photinos are on the list. All around me, I saw giant birds, vaster than worlds, full of wings, lighter than gossamer, more brilliantly colored than all the peacocks and parrots that ever lived. They were absolutely gorgeous, but all too soon left me far behind. Okay, mayhaps I had learned what the solar deep structures used to be, and watched them go home, their long watch over the Tomb having come to an end. I'll let someone else visit the core of the Sun, thank you, to see if the structures are actually gone.

Suddenly I was cold, colder than the starlit peaks of Pluto and distant Proserpine. The heat of the Sun behind me left me as chill as ever. I was cold inside, cold where I had drawn into levels far deeper than I'd ever gone before. Now I was about to pay, mayhaps with my gifts shutting down while

I was still in the interplanetary void. I pushed my jumps as hard and fast as I could. Rapidly, I lost control of my gifts to the cold within me. My vision reddened. For a few moments, I couldn't find the teleport key. Then my body screens started to leak air. I don't actually breathe in outer space, except as a courtesy for people around me, but no air pressure has some awful consequences. The Earth loomed ahead, a giant blue-green-white disk. For once my dodges and evasions to hide my teleport path were unavailable. I dared not take them. I had to be on the ground now, before my fraying contact with my teleport gift snapped. Flight…I could still fly, but that was way too slow for what I needed.

I was standing in a field of oats, my house a few hundred yards away. The house might as well have been on the other side of the galaxy. I dropped to my knees, then managed to roll on my side. Where it peeped through the wall of oat stalks, the sky was gray. A stiff breeze blew off the Pacific, filling the clouds with a promise of rain. The natural windbreak of the oat field shielded me from the wind, but would not protect me from the rain once it started falling.

I must have passed out, because it was much later in the day when I woke up. The cloud had turned to drizzle. My clothing was not quite soaked. I was being vigorously prodded by two ponies, both sniffing at my garb in the vain hope that they would find an apple or even better some cookies hiding in one of my pockets. They were out of luck. My pockets were empty. I managed to get an arm over Snapdragon's neck. She straightened, dragging me to my feet. Daffodil pushed on the other side, so for a few minutes I was sandwiched and warmed by two overfriendly ponies. They eventually realized there were no treats to be had, snorted, shook their heads, and walked away, leaving me to stagger home. I crawled upstairs, rolled under my quilt, and dropped into deep sleep.

The next day I found I had left a trail of discarded clothing from the kitchen door up the stairs and into my bedroom. I couldn't remember anything between closing the back door and waking up in the morning. It was painfully clear that one-girl expeditions to the heart of the solar furnace are a way to die, especially when the local residents are trying to kill you. It would have been a novel way to die. No one has ever died before by being in the middle of the Sun when it blew up. Death could readily have been my one-girl-expedition's terminal destination. No matter. I had won. The Namestone was destroyed, gone forever. I'd saved the world. And I'd made some new, albeit very strange, friends.

Chapter Fifty

The Great Chamber of Wisdom
The House That Is Forever

Colonel Pi's laboratory was filled with glowing tubes of colored gas, large panels covered with meters, switches, and dials, computer monitors displaying numbers, plots, and arcane symbols, and in the center a desk littered with papers, technical journals, opened books, and coffee mugs. The Colonel sat in a stiff wooden chair pointing at a computer screen. Plasmatrix and Starsmasher sat to his left and right.

"So what happened," the Colonel explained, "was that someone did mass manipulation of quantum probabilities, across the entire sun. We've seen persona who can do that, for example changing the decay rate of a radioisotope or choosing precisely which atoms of radon gas in a container will choose to decay. However, that's on a few-atom scale.

"This was an entire star, being manipulated to have its entire mass not-quite simultaneously fuse to iron, forming a spherical shaped-charge targeted at squashing something in the middle. The manipulation was effective down to choosing, every time a photon collided with an electron, which way each photon in the entire sun should scatter to maximize the squash effect.. I am quite sure that a set of rules were being applied, as opposed to someone doing a separate microscopic calculation and then manipulating each scattering event. And suddenly at the end everything was turned around. All the hydrogen that had fused to iron was turned back into hydrogen, the regions that were heated to totally absurd temperatures cooled off, and the sun was back to being its normal self. I gather, Plasmatrix, you have an explanation."

"One I will be giving the world in an hour when I crash Vera Durand's TV show," Plasmatrix answered. "The part I will not mention is that we just watched Eclipse keep her promise and destroy the Namestone. That's her secret to tell. The sun doing these things was the Solar Deep Structures trying to stop her, then figuring out she was on their side."

"The structures have sides?" Starsmasher asked. "As if they were people?"

"They are people." Plasmatrix smiled. "I've known them since, well, since I was actually a young woman and visited the outer layers of the sun to see what was there. They Deep Structures – they call themselves the Timeless Ones—are actually quite friendly. After yesterday, they were happy to be able to abandon their long watch and go home, which they have now done. They were a bit unclear on what happened to Eclipse. She did get back out of the sun, but they were unsure if she made it home alive."

"Too bad if she didn't," Starsmasher said. "She seemed to be a nice kid in really deep water, and we certainly owed her one for saving my neck. She could have asked for help on this. Perhaps she thought the Namestone was too tempting a target if anyone knew where it was."

"And you will tell the world, Plasmatrix?" Colonel Pi asked.

"One time event," Plasmatrix answered. "The cause was visitors from another galaxy, friends of mine, preventing something extremely unfortunate. What they prevented I shall not say. They succeeded excellently and are now on their way home. I won't mention they left me a so-to-speak phone number so that I can call for help if the sun becomes cranky again, an outcome they do not expect."

Chapter Fifty-One

The Invisible Fortress
and
Frog Pond Park

All of my null links to the Medford group triggered at once. That was the "end of the world" warning. The hard part was I just listened to the morning news at Kniaz Kang's, and I for sure did not remember any reference to the world ending. Not even a hint that something was unusually wrong. Well, if you ignore the enormous Eclipse hunt, the creatures in Argentina, a stock market crash in Germany, and rioting across IncoAzteca, nothing was unusually wrong. I leaned back in my chair, closed my eyes, and brought up my reflective force field, so that there would be absolutely no hint of what was around me. Then I focused very carefully on Aurora's exact mental frequencies.

<*Yes?*> I asked.

<*Joe! Emergency! Please! Come Here! In Park by Pond! Emergency!*> Janie was in a state of total panic.

<*Combat status?*> I asked. <*Am I teleporting into a battle?*> I listened very carefully for clues that something was wrong. Suddenly I was seeing through Janie's eyes. Her brother and sister were sitting next to her. The other two kids were Gold Knight and Silver Knight. I'd met them a few times in base ball nines games. They'd carefully never said their private persona names, though the other kids in their school knew. They all looked completely calm.

<*In a minute,*> I answered. I broke the mental link and dashed to my bedroom. Joe had a color scheme for his shirts and cowboy jackets, not the color scheme I was wearing. At least I was wearing corduroys, and the right sort of sneakers. I stripped, pulled a Joe shirt from my dresser, pulled it on, pulled on a cowboy jacket, and spent 30 seconds in front of my big mirrors making sure that everything looked right. Meanwhile, I was dropping through levels absolutely as fast as I could without a crash drop.

I even remembered to turn off the stove. OK, I was way down in my gifts, I'd ramped up all of my screens, so I levitated and ran a fast teleport loop sequence via the L2 point ending up in Frog Pond Park. The five of them stared and waved as I floated over the pond. Meanwhile, I was following Mum's advice and doing a fast search of everything around me. I landed facing the pond, meaning I could now look at the directions I hadn't been able to see before. "What gives?" I asked.

"Brian and I had tea," Janie said calmly, "with the Wizard of Mars." I tried to keep a whist face. I won't say that that tea with the Wizard was a lot more dangerous than taking the Maze, but for sure I wasn't about to drink that tea if I could help it. "Trisha took us there. Dad let the three of us go. The Wizard told us the world is about to end. We can stop it. We go on a really long trip and do something. The Wizard said if we fail then eight billion people will die. The trip has to be three of us, and one more. Gold and Silver Knight get to stay here. The Wizard will talk to our parents, so they understand the other choice is everyone dies. The trip is for the four of us. Except, Joe, we have to find our fourth, and it's not you. I finally got out of the Wizard who we have to find. He wouldn't tell me at first because he has absolutely no idea how we find her. He doesn't like admitting there is anything he does not know."

"Where are you going?" Silver Knight asked. "How long a trip? Do you need to pack? How will your mom and dad be convinced?" Thank you, Silver Knight, I thought, for asking good questions.

Trisha answered all in a blind rush. "The Wizard said I have to fly us all from here to the Gates of Infinity and back again twice and that's actually a long way all the way to the center of the universe so it'll take me at least eight or ten hours each way hauling all four of us and we should expect to be gone a week and should each pack a big duffel bag to match but there is no problem with mom or dad because when we come back through the Gates of Infinity we will come out like ten hours before we went in and when I get us back here it will be only four minutes later. But first we all stop to say hello to him."

We certainly weren't about to do things by halves. Yes, I do have deep space navigation. I could do that flight myself, but not in anything as short as ten hours. It would be a truly grueling trip even using sleep suppression, gifts to replace the needs to eat and drink, and mind control to stay focused on flying fast. It would be seriously hard on Trisha, even though she is incredibly faster than I am. It took me a while, but eventually I noticed what Trisha had just said. "Did I hear you say that we're doing time travel? Well, the three of you, while I hold the fort, I mean. Time travel is seriously dangerous."

"The end of the world is real dangerous, too, Joe," Trisha answered. "And holding the fort might be important; for starters, if I heard it right, when we spoke with him, there was the warning we might not come back at all, because we might lose, in which case the world will end, anyhow, unless someone else saves it and he didn't think that anyone could."

It's nice to hear that the Wizard has absolutely no confidence in the Lords of Eternity to do something about saving the world. Or are we going to be attacked by the mythical giant whale that lives in foamspace and eats universes as though they were krill? "Janie," I said, "there was this little detail you left out. Exactly who is this fourth? Other than 'not me' and 'she'?"

Janie looked puzzled for a moment. She must have forgotten I am not invited to tea with the Wizard of Mars, not that I would do other than to decline his invitation. "Oh. Right," she said. "We have to pull off what the League of Nations can't." Yes, I thought, and that is? "We have to find Eclipse and persuade her to go with us."

"Is that all?" I asked, mostly sarcastically. "OK. You want Eclipse to come along. You are joking, aren't you? As a starter, you need to promise her the Truce of Randor, from right now until you have come back and go your separate ways. That means no one learns she is going with you until it's all over. Or is it too late for that?"

"It's not a joke, Joe," Trisha said. "Really. Please believe me?"

I looked at her. "I always believe you, Trisha, whether anyone else does or not, but the Wizard has a strange sense of humor."

"Who's Randor?" Brian asked.

"I know," Janie answered. I have no idea where Janie picked that up. "Faster mentalically," she added. Very quickly, we heard her explanation. She had everything right, too. The nice bit about mentalic transfer is that you get the understanding, not just the words.

"Yes, we have to agree to that Truce," Brian said. "Save the world is good. Do we all agree?" The five of them agreed. They all stared at me.

Then I realized the obvious. "Yes, I agree, too. What exactly are you guys doing when you get wherever you are going?" The Wizard had given Aurora a presentation, a presentation she now replayed mentalically. His lecture was, no surprise, completely convincing. After all, he knows what happens in the future, including what happens when people listen to him, so he changes his words around until they work perfectly. He would give Trisha a starcompass. I took a moment to see why she needed that, when she has deep space navigation. She didn't know where we are going. We would win, said the Wizard, or eight billion people would die. When there are only one billion people in the world, it is not clear how eight billion of them could become deceased. The Wizard was very explicit on the number. He was talking about people like us. There were enough scattered images that we clearly weren't talking about Martians or whatever dying. We were talking about Americans. The deaths were truly appalling, too, the sort of thing associated with Corinne and Invincible Star Demons. Unfortunately, the Wizard had neglected to tell the Wells kids what we would find, wherever we were going, or what we had to do before we came back.

Couldn't Corinne handle the Star Demons again? No, Mum had warned me. Last time, Corinne had had the advantage of total surprise, most of the Star Demons had gone on their way, and the Star Demons still almost won. Next time they would be forewarned and forearmed. I suppose I should take this seriously. "OK,' I said. "I'll find Eclipse by tomorrow at four. And extract a Truce of Randor oath from her. I won't promise she agrees to go with you. You get to persuade her. You'll meet here? You three and her will then be on your way?"

"We'll be here," Janie announced. "Then we go to my house. My parents need to meet Eclipse, and Professor Lafayette will be there to manifest the Wizard. He gets to convince them it's OK for us to go."

"Joe," Brian said, "Mayhaps you don't want to show up at our house after you find Eclipse? My dad wants to kill you, and he's serious about it."

"Why?" I asked. I was sure I'd always been a polite house guest.

"He won't tell me." Trisha launched onto a full speed complaint. "He won't tell me, and he's treating me terribly and so is Mom so I don't get an allowance and I'm totally grounded and Janie and Brian aren't even allowed to talk to me except at breakfast and dinner and in school except he said if the Wizard of Mars summons us I'm allowed to go but it's terrible and I completely hate it and I can't do anything about it or even escape until I finish High School."

There was one more problem I'd created by solving the Maze. Trisha's parents were blaming her for something, being terribly mean to her, and I had no idea why or how to fix things for her.

<*Joe?*> That was Janie. <*Please do not ask Trisha about her Atomic Tech entrance exams. She completely aced them, got admission to their all-year program with all tuition and costs covered, and when she told Dad and Mom the good news they went berserk and told her she wasn't going no matter what she said. I don't know why.*>

Sometimes there is a moment that just clicks in your mind that something really good or bad has happened, even though you do not consciously know why. I had just had one of those moments.

As an outcome, this one was really bad. I was still recovering from destroying the Namestone, not to mention beating up on the Lords of Death, a stack of Aztecans, not to mention standing at Spindrift's back. Several trips across the universe were not something to look forward to, not for me, not now. However, the Wizard of Mars really did not play games. If he said 'or the world will end', he meant the world would end. Worse, he could foresee the future enough to know how his words would be interpreted. His words are never misunderstood. He'd always phrase things to get the right message across. Still, I really did not want to go on this trip. What I wanted to do was to go home, go to bed, and sleep for a week. Mayhaps two weeks.

"You're going to find her?" Gold Knight asked me. "When no one else can? In a day?"

"Don't worry, Gold Knight," Brian announced, "It'll be easy, won't it, Joe?" He looked right at me. He sounded unreasonably confident that I could find Eclipse for them. His two sisters began giving him that look, the one suggesting that they thought their brother was being willfully stupid, and needed to be beaten up again.

"Oh, sure. I'd better find her, hadn't I?" I answered. "Unless I want the world to end. Therefore I will find her. I'm absolutely positive I will. I promise."

"How can you say that?" Silver Knight asked. "The whole world is looking for Eclipse, and hasn't seen a sign of her. You just promised you'll do it, by yourself, in two days."

"Joe's thinking of the payoff," Gold Knight announced. "He finds her, and he'll be so incredibly frigid that people will give him whole candy stores. Mayhaps even candy factories. He'll even have girls asking him out on dates. Dates? No, that last one is totally silly. Why would you possibly want that, Joe, anyhow?" Janie and Brian looked at each other, baffled. Neither of them noticed Comet and Silver Knight giving Gold Knight ominous looks. He'd obviously said something unfortunate, but what? And with that I teleported out.

"He will," Brian finally announced. "I'm absolutely positive Joe will find her. I'll even make a bet on it. How about a pound of candy?"

Chapter Fifty-Two

Captain-General's Office
Grand Headquarters
American Persona League
Washington, Federal District

Krystal North glared at her desk. The working surface was a magnificent "U" more than fifteen feet long. Her staff occasionally grumbled that it was an imitation-wood plastic, not the solid teak to which she was undoubtedly entitled. Her response was to remind them that she had a working desk in a working office. It was a complete accident that the League tower had an irregular shape, giving her office three walls of glass on the next-to-top floor of the building.

There was a knock at the door behind her. Secretary Mindy Evans had been given emphatic instructions that she was not to be disturbed, except for another war or the end of the world. "Enter", she called, turning and standing as she did.

The door swung open. "Sorry to bother you, Krystal." Standing in the doorway was Morgan Le Fay in her formal garb, a not-quite-tight white bodysuit and white waist-length cape with high collar. The trim lines were blood-red. The Orb of Merlin draped from her neck and spread across her chest.

"I greet thee, Morgan," Krystal said.

"And I greet thee also, younger sister," Morgan answered. "I see you are buried in paperwork."

"My staff does most of it, but no one expected we would need to fight a major war," Krystal said defensively. "Please come in. Tea?"

"Thank you," Morgan answered. She took one of the comfortable padded chairs near the desk. "No one expects a war, except people who plan to start one. Those people are often surprised when the war actually starts."

"I'm always happy to see you, but what brings you here?" Krystal asked. "Something important, I suppose."

"Does the end of the world count?" Morgan said

"End of the world?" Krystal's brow wrinkled.

"Which is why I need to have a few words with Speaker Ming," Morgan said. "He is polite not to intrude on me, so I would rather not simply appear in his office. I need to take him out of Washington for an afternoon, the day after tomorrow. I brought for you a token of my appreciation." She set a large box of scones on one corner of Krystal's desk.

"Oh, my. He's swamped." Krystal shook her head. "Fortunately Secretary of War Stevenson is actually very competent, but there are still issues the Speaker has to resolve. And at the moment – not widely known, please? – the Speaker is trapped in DC by the Vespasian Act."

"That's why I need him, too," Morgan said. "I have a head of state, so to speak, coming to Massachusetts the day after tomorrow. He has to be there. The Vespasian Act says so."

"You, Morgan, can remember when the Emperor Vespasian visited the American Republic. The rest of us don't. Was it really the complete disaster the history books say?"

"Yes. Those accounts are decently accurate. I was there." Morgan smiled. "And so we have a law: A head of state arrives in America. The Speaker must be there for the negotiations. Which is why America mostly doesn't let foreign leaders into the country. Who is he seeing today? I didn't know anyone was here."

Krystal stared at the floor. "Chancellor Holmgren. Mayhaps that's ex-Chancellor Holmgren. He wants political asylum."

"Holmgren? He who would be world dictator? Here? I hadn't heard of this." Morgan looked puzzled. "Why is he here?"

"You didn't hear what happened?" Krystal asked.

"I've been busy moving my lab. Please do not get me started on Wells the father." Morgan rolled her eyes.

"Holmgren discovered who would support his crackpot Political Assembly." Krystal shook her head. "Yes, he had the votes. Azteca, the Ottomans, Persia, South Asia, Manjukuo, Africa south of the Sahara as far south as there are Islamites, Prussia and its African colonies, and the Celestial Republic have a lot of people. The Celestial Republic was offered Indochina and the Malay Peninsula, while the Sikh Empire and Manjukuo promised not to attack the Celestial Republic any more – they already got handed their hats. Russia formally abstained. The Tsar is not a strong-willed man, and being threatened by Prussia, the Ottomans, Persia, and Manjukuo was more than he wanted to face. That's enough votes in the Popular Assembly."

"Doesn't the Peace Executive have to approve League Constitution amendments?" Morgan asked.

"The Popular Assembly claimed they had expelled France, Britain, the American Republic, and Satsuma from the Peace Executive. They recognized the Incan east border as the Atlantic, meaning Brazil does not exist, and agreed that Austria-Hungary is in fact a Prussian protectorate, so the Prussians cast the Austro-Hungarian vote. That let them pass their amendments. They then tried to arrest Ambassador Buncombe and the ambassadors of our friends. At this point Ambassador Davout revealed that the French knew about Holmgren's plot, the Legion of Glory was lined up on the nearby French border, and if Holmgren made any effort to keep the allied ambassadors from leaving, the Legion would come calling. With a guillotine for Holmgren. Holmgren retreated to Ulan Bator, where the Popular Assembly was meeting. The Popular Assembly eliminated the other league Legislative branches, assigning all power to the Chancellor."

"That imbecile Holmgren is now dictator of two-thirds the world?" Morgana asked.

"He had a few moments to enjoy his victory. He had walked into a trap. The Assembly impeached him for not finding the Namestone, removed him from office, and elected Hong Sangui as the new Chancellor. Hong is anything but stupid." Krystal shook her head.

"Oh, dear," Morgana said.

"So now the Speaker is trying to explain to Holmgren that there is an Idaho warrant for his arrest for child molestation…the woman who was kidnapped…which in Idaho is a death penalty offense, so he really wants to take his political asylum request someplace else. I suggested the Palmer Peninsula. It is legally a country, after all." Krystal opened the cookie jar.

"I see," Morgana said.

"Who are you bringing to America?" Krystal asked. She took another sip of her tea. "The Great Khan of Manjukuo? You did wreck his fleet, after all."

"The Wizard of Mars. To explain the world is doomed, unless certain things are done." Morgana leaned back in her chair.

"The Wizard?" Krystal choked on her tea. "On Earth? Isn't that impossible?" Krystal began to worry.

"It's magic," Morgana said calmly "The Wizard contacted me. In short, the Wizard, who can sometimes see the future and mostly sees the present, says that we need to send a team of persona on a voyage across the cosmos, or the world ends. They have to leave the day after tomorrow. First we have to persuade them to go. Wizard says there is an invisible obstacle, and we may fail to persuade them. Oh, yes, in addition to the three unreasonably young people who have already been told about the oncoming disaster, we have to find one more of them. He declined to tell me who the fourth is. You see, the four personas who must go are the three Wells children (you've met them) and someone else who they and their friends must find…"

Chapter Fifty-Three

Office of Vera Durand
Persona News Network Tower
Buffalo, North York

Vera Durand sat in her corner office, The view was north across the city of Buffalo. The Persona News Network tower was not the tallest building in the city, but she was still 100 stories above ice-covered Lake Erie. Constellations of street lamps, fluorescent advertising signs, and the pastel ribbons of personas flying over the city far outshone the stars and waning Moon in the night sky above. The constellation of ground lights rolled off into the distance, coming to a sharp stop far, far to the north at the waters of Lake Ontario. On her video screen, the last credits were rolling on the Vera Durand Hour of Power. It was a masterful show, it had astronomical rankings, but it was exhausting to record, even on its Monday-Wednesday-Friday-Sunday Morning schedule. The network's pay was munificent, but at some point she was going to decide she had enough millions socked away and retire.

<*Durand!*> The imperious voice was painfully loud in Durand's mind. You have mindscreens, she thought, not the world's greatest, but mindscreens. The building is supposed to have top-line mindscreens. The voice didn't seem to have noticed them as an obstacle.

"Yes," she answered sotto voce.

<*I am Eclipse, the one and only. Your guests went on about the Solar Event and the search for the Namestone.*> The voice was accompanied by an image, the top of the stairs out of the Maze. Valkyria in her golden armor was straight ahead, the Screaming Skull was to the viewer's right, and on the viewer's left parked within the faintest of hazes were Vera Durand and her cameraman. Durand hardly needed several decades of experience as a video reporter to realize that only one person could have seen that image: Eclipse herself. <*How would you like an interview with me?*>

"How many Lords of Eternity do I have to kill?" Durand asked.

<*None.*> The faintest of laughters echoed behind the voice. <*You will be by yourself. No cameraman. You will need your camera equipment. I will not be in the image. Your viewers will have to believe your claim that you are interviewing me. The*

interview will be on the surface of the Moon. That should be enough for many people to believe you. However, the interview must be now.>

Durand was already standing and moving toward the closet that held her own personal video system. A touch confirmed the battery in the camera was charged, the spare battery packs were charged, and the extra bitsticks were ready to go. She shrugged into her dress cape. "How will we hear each other on the Moon?" she asked.

<*We will be in an air bubble. I will maintain it. You have to trust me on that. If I wanted to kill you, I'd do something way more simple than popping the bubble.*> Eclipse answered. <*And I'll check the fall on your cape for you.*>

"I'm ready to go," she answered. She heard the faintest sound of little bells.

"I'm right behind you," Eclipse said. A startled Durand looked over her shoulder. Hovering behind her so that their eye levels matched, a few yards away across her office, was the young woman she had seen at the Maze. Her garb was a brilliant white, with ornate gold lace at collar, wrists, ankles, and cape fringes. Eclipse's hair, Durand noted, was now platinum blonde.

"Welcome to Buffalo," Durand managed.

"And now we are on the Moon," Eclipse announced. There was a brilliant flare of blue-green light. Durand had the sensation of falling, a sensation contradicted by the stationary gray rock surface on which she stood. Low gravity, Durand realized. And some sort of carpet, so I'm not actually standing on the moon rock, which is either way too hot or way too cold. "I didn't try snatching one of your fancy chairs," Eclipse said. "You'll have to stand during the interview. Oh, yes, how do I prove I'm the real Eclipse? You should recognize my garb, and under the cape is the very-hard-to-duplicate Niederhof label." Eclipse spread her cape, letting Durand examine the label.

"I didn't need that," Durand said, "but I'll get an image of it." She wondered how many personas could teleport to the moon in one step. Few indeed. Durand set up her camera equipment, checked the automatic camera focus, and walked out to the taped position marked on the carpet. "Testing Testing one, two, three, four," she said. "Please say something so I can tune the camera volume."

"The quick brown fox jumped over the lazy red dog" Eclipse said."Prekrasnivaitse, prekrasnivaitse, odin, dva, tri, chetiri."

Durand's ears perked up. Was Eclipse actually a Tsarist? She checked the readouts on her camera hand control, made a small adjustment, and nodded at Eclipse. "Good to go," she announced. Eclipse smiled and nodded back.

"This is Vera Durand, broadcasting from the surface of the moon. I have with me today, at her insistence off-camera, the world's most famous persona, the one and only Eclipse, Bearer of the Holy Namestone. But first, a tiny demonstration that I am in fact on the moon and not in PNN studios in Buffalo." She pulled a pen from her blouse pocket, held it up so that was clear to the camera, and dropped it. Every schoolchild had seen things being dropped in Lunar gravity. Now they would see one more. Eclipse's smile reached to her eyes.

"I understand that you probably won't tell me," Durand said, "but I have to ask, no matter how unlikely it is that you will answer. Where is the Namestone now? When will you use it to bring the world to utopia?"

"I will answer those questions," Eclipse said. "After all, that's why I wanted this interview. Nowhere. It's nowhere."

"Nowhere?" Durand echoed.

"Nowhere. I destroyed it."

"You…That's impossible! The Namestone is indestructible," Durand countered.

"Well, no. In fact, the *Copper Book of Harvest Stars* tells you how to destroy the Namestone. 'Brought at birth from the fire of a star. Returned to the fire of a star to meet its death.'," Eclipse quoted. "The instructions in *The True Copper Book* are much more specific and useful. I'll show you my memories of the event."

Durand stood stock-still as images of the star-core, the Namestone shattering, and the Solar Deep Structures cascaded through her. "You destroyed it. You really did. And you almost destroyed the Sun."

"I did not disturb the sun," Eclipse countered. "The Solar Transient was launched by the Solar Deep Structures, the photino birds. They call themselves *The Timeless Ones*. They're actually people, and nice ones at that. They invited me to visit them someday. They were going to turn the Sun into a block of iron... very hot iron…to save the rest of the universe. From me." I didn't say the photino birds would have succeeded. "Then they learned why I was in the core of the sun. They cancelled the transient."

"Why did you destroy the Namestone?" a horrified Durand managed to ask.

"The Namestone gives you nothing good you could not earn with your own two hands. And that's what any good American will do. Make himself wealthy with his own hands. The Namestone is a mind control generator. Someone with mentalics could make himself world dictator. *The True Copper Book* describes some of the ways it was used. Massacres. Atrocities. Whole worlds gone mad. If I'd used it, that insanity would have happened here. Go back to the *Ode to the Glorious Namestone*. It's all there."

"So you made yourself judge and jury and executioner of *The Gate to Heaven?*" Durand raised her voice in horror.

"Correct," I answered. "I saw what was right. I did what was right."

"You're how old?" Durand said. "And you made a decision that affects the whole world? Who do you think you are?"

"I'm Eclipse. Yes, I made that decision. Because it was the right decision."

"How can you hope to escape justice?" Durand asked. "All across the world, people will be howling for your head."

"Some of them are smart," I said confidently. "They'll remember I flew to the Starcore. I survived lithium transmutation bombs being dropped on my head. Picking a fight with me is a bad idea, especially when it can't possibly do any good. No matter what you do or say to me, the Namestone is destroyed, gone forever."

"Suppose I agree with you about mind control being a bad thing," Durand said. "I do, by the way. What's your reward out of all this?"

If I recalled correctly, Durand had been controlled by the Mad Mind just before Krystal North vaporized him. That was not much of a hypothetical.

"I just want peace and quiet," I said. "That's all for tonight."

"Thank you for the interview," Durand managed to answer.

Two days later, I tuned in to Durand's show. She had had a guest list already. "Good evening from Buffalo. This is Vera Durand and the Vera Durand Hour of Power. Our first guest will be on in a moment. But first, a short clip from our program this Sunday. It's something I have never done before. Recorded, from the moon, it's Vera Durand." Durand pointed at an off-screen technician. The image of her studio was replaced by an image of Vera Durand, standing on the surface of the moon. The image spoke.

"This is Vera Durand, broadcasting from the surface of the moon. I have with me today, at her insistence off-camera, the world's most famous persona, the one and only Eclipse, Bearer of the Namestone. But first, a tiny demonstration that I am in fact on the moon and not in PNN studios in Buffalo." She pulled a pen from her blouse pocket, held it up so that was clear to the camera, and dropped it. It fell all so slowly groundward.

The image vanished, to be replaced by Durand in her studio. "Yes, that was indeed me on the surface of the moon, and my first guest this Sunday is the one and only Eclipse. I shall not reveal what you will hear on Sunday, but I can guarantee it is the most earth-shattering news of this or the last three millennia. For the full interview, tune in this Sunday to the Vera Durand Hour of Power.

"And now, our first guest today, the former American Republic Ambassador to the League of Nations Peace Executive, Thaddeus Buncombe from North Maine. Ambassador Buncombe, I'm sure you will find our forthcoming interview with Eclipse to be entrancing, especially as it puts a radical new light on the search for the Namestone. However, you have your own story to tell, a story just as important and just as interesting as Eclipse's. So, tell us, how should the American people react to the threat of war by the League of Nations' new Peace Executive?"

"Vera, that is an excellent question. Mayhaps the League should rename their disaster zone the *War Executive*. It is also only the *League of Some Nations*. That's what it's become, after all, an Executive for making war on the civilized world." At that point I turned off the video. I had heard quite enough about stupid foreign wars, even ones that were my fault. I'd made my contribution to destroying the IncoAztecan Invasion. At first I hadn't understand Krystal North's strategy, but I'd certainly done my share of carrying it out. Once people found out they couldn't have their shiny bauble, those wars would become pointless and stop. After all, politicians aren't stupid.

Chapter Fifty-Four

Frog Pond Park
Medford, Massachusetts

The Medford Five were already at the park, all in persona garb. Gold Knight and Silver Knight wore long-sleeved jumpsuits in the gold and silver hues of their names. Brian's jumpsuit was bright orange with a yellow star across his chest. The fabric was loose, but draped gracefully over his arms and legs. Janie's clothing was cut to the same pattern, in a midnight black fabric intricately laced with silver thread. Her sigil ran from neck to waist;

it was a slight modification of the dollar's pyramid, eye, and radiants. Trisha's garb was Kelly-green spandex, tight enough that there was no doubt that she exercised very vigorously. The gold-embroidered comet of her public persona name wrapped around her body. The comet's head rose almost to her neckline, while the tail swept down across her chest, wrapped around her back and waist, the last bits of the tail wrapping each of her legs.

"It's almost four," Gold Knight announced. "There's no Eclipse, and no Joe either. That guy was just bragging himself up when he promised to find her."

"Want to bet?" Brian asked.

"It's not quite four," Silver Knight said. "Joe can still find her. At least the Wizard of Mars showed us sort of what she looks like. Not like all those pictures, or the imitators. But how can you search for her? Legally, I mean." The Medford Five looked back and forth. For that question there was no good answer.

At that moment I materialized behind the Old Tower, out of their line of sight. Janie suddenly looked around. "Where are you, Joe? I hear your mind, but I don't see you."

"I'm right here," I called, using my Joe voice. Janie fed me mentalically her memories of the conversation they'd just had.

"That's great," Gold Knight said. "But where is Eclipse? We need her right this instant!"

"She's right there," Brian announced. "I bet. I bet a candy store." I don't think Brian can see through walls, but he sounded awfully confident. "Make that two candy stores!" He upped his bet, not that anyone was taking it.

I cleared my throat and switched to my normal voice.

"You're right, Brian, I'm right here," I answered. I stepped out from behind the tower. My dress garb shone brilliant white in the afternoon sun. Niederhof's was very proud of all the gold lace trim. My garb's sigil, a golden sun in glory with partly-superposed jet-black lunar disk, stretched across my ribcage. The Medford Five froze.

"What did you do to Joe?" Janie asked. That was not quite a question. "His mind vanished."

I dropped to his voice. "He's right here." I switched back to my normal voice. "Did my disguise actually fool you guys, enough you couldn't tell Joe is a girl?"

Silver Knight and Trisha pointed at me, slack-mouthed. Janie and Gold Knight stared. Brian had his hand over his mouth, trying not to laugh. I could tell. He had somehow figured me out.

"Oh! No! I was about to ask you out on a date," Trisha blurted. She looked horribly embarrassed. "I mean, I was about to ask Joe out on a date. Well, ignoring that I am completely totally grounded. I mean, Joe is cute, and intelligent, and friendly, and nice, and good-looking, and comfortable to be around, and flies really well. But he's a boy!"

"Oh, no," said Silver Knight. "So was I. Except Joe isn't, ummh, you aren't, I mean, a boy. Oh, no, I mean." Her voice trailed off. OK, I had them fooled, not that I had had any idea what inclinations Trisha or Silver Knight had. Well, I hadn't until now.

"I'd have told you I already had a girlfriend," I answered, which was literally true, if you skipped the detail that my friend who was a girl had died in my arms, "and we had agreed to be together until the end of time." That was also literally true, at least in High Atlanticean if not in English. It had been the end of Spindrift's time, as she had known from her beginning, when she summoned herself into existence…I broke that train of thought. "So I would have said no, and wouldn't have hurt any feelings."

"Your 'boy' was perfect," Silver Knight said. "Except he figured you out," she continued, pointing at Brian.

"And he didn't tell us." Janie was actually not, it sounded, mad at her brother. Respecting private personas is as gifttrue as you can get.

"There are, like, how many personae our age who are as strong as seven Lords of Death?" Brian asked. "None? One? Joe. Eclipse. Besides, Joe was way too confident he could find Eclipse." I was quite sure my disguise had some other flaw. I would need to ask Brian what it was.

"Except I said you had to convince me to go along with you. Let's hear it," I reminded them.

"First," Trisha said, 'we're doing our public personas. Janie is Aurora. Brian is Star. You've met Gold Knight and Silver Knight. And I'm Comet."

"Aurora. Star. Gold and Silver Knights. Comet," I repeated.

They looked back and forth at each other. They hadn't expected me to tell them that they had to convince me to go with them. Now they had to do it. They were skipping school, or their parents had covered for them.

"Who's using ultravision?" Aurora asked. "Someone's focus really peaked, just a moment ago."

We all shook our heads at each other.

'Now it's getting way more intense," Aurora announced.

"When did it start?" Gold Knight asked.

"It's been there all along," Aurora answered. I considered tearing my hair out. Aurora could have warned us.

"Stand! Form a circle! Call your gifts!" I shouted. I put a force wall around the group. To her credit, Comet turned invisible immediately. The rest of them took their time about doing anything. If we'd been ungifteds, I might have suggested taking cover, but that's kind of useless when the cover is unlikely to offer any protection.

<*Trisha, Janie,*> I thought, <*Breathe for vacuum! What we're there, Trisha, you both run for it.*>

<*I'm good! But I can't do anything.*> I could hear Trisha's frustration. In persona combat, she had no shields, and no attacks better than a good kick to the stomach or knee. Admittedly, with her speed no one could possibly karate-block her, but the kick would be no harder than what a strong girl her age could deliver. Mentally, I sent them a plan. <*Breathing for both of us,*> Trisha added.

<*Ready.*> Janie nodded assent.

We teleported. The Dark Side of the Moon is a truly forbidding place, one you cannot see from Earth. Trisha grabbed Janie in her flight and invisibility fields and took off, not quite directly away from Earth, at her maximum acceleration. Janie wrapped them both in a mindscreen. Whoever was preparing to grab Janie—my best guess—couldn't see her, couldn't catch up with her, and had no idea where to look for her. I teleported back.

"Where'd you go?" Gold Knight asked.

"I put them someplace safe," I answered.

"What's that?" Silver Knight pointed skyward. She'd been spinning on one toe, not too fast, looking for surprises. For all that she had no combat training, she'd picked up very quickly indeed on paying attention to your surroundings.

'That' was an expanding sphere of feathers. Ultravision said no feathers were there, just air. It was a strange special effect, one rapidly replaced by a tall, heavyset man in feather cloak and headdress. Classic Aztecan nobility, I thought.

"Clever disguise, 'Joe'," he shouted. "You can pretend to be a girl, but you cannot fool the Eye of Quetzalcoatl. Go ahead, cry like a girl and beg for mercy, but I will give you none. You destroyed my Empire, however much the fools on the Council of the Realm deny the obvious, but I shall destroy you! And then I shall offer up your beating heart to Indiwiwi." I didn't recognize that last name.

"Meet me in the sky!" I shouted. I dropped my duffel bag. "The three of you, stay out of this." He was probably very good, too good to be safe for the three of them to tackle.

"Agreed!" he answered. "A mile up, I propose?"

"A fine distance," I answered.

"I have notified the lightning screen," he said. "I am here to kill you, not incinerate your beautiful city!"

He wanted a formal Aztecan duel. We both teleported to five thousand feet. I got there first and waited politely.

"I knew you would return to the scene of your crime!" he shouted. "You slaughtered three dozen Eagle Knights. Not only are you such a coward as to disguise yourself as a girl, you pretend to be the arch-enemy of civilization, Eclipse! You can't frighten me with your disguise! Prepare to die!"

"I am a girl," I answered. "More important, I am the real Eclipse. And after I kill you, I will send cards of sympathy to your wives." For a moment he hesitated. Then he began screaming at me. It seems he blamed me personally for wrecking his country's invasion of America, a defeat he described in great detail. I take no credit for their second military disaster. The commander of their hosts in Mexico ordered a general northern advance against our people, promising the crushing victory their first attack had missed, ignoring the minor detail that our people were still in range of all our border defense artillery, particle beams, and force shield projectors. The outcome was a total massacre with few American casualties. He also blamed me for creating general social disorder and the successful Brazilian and Argentine invasions in South America. I credit Krystal North's Plan Hoffman and foreign allies for our victory. Yes, I had helped a bit. Killing Popocatepetl mattered. The two sides had been evenly matched in strength, but our tactics were far superior.

With that we had at each other. After not long at all, his force fields collapsed and he was transformed to an expanding cloud of fire. I will not brag myself up by claiming I beat a superior opponent. He was good, but I'm better. To his great credit, he had agreed to move the duel to someplace where there would be no collateral damage. I teleported back to the ground. For me, the duel had been a good warming-up exercise. It took a few more minutes to recover Trisha and Janie from deep space.

"Where were we?" Gold Knight wondered.

"Convincing Eclipse to join us," Star answered. "Eclipse, would you believe the Wizard of Mars, if you spoke to him?"

"He always tells the truth," I answered, "and you never misunderstand him. But fly to Mars, to his castle, and ask him questions? Thanks, but I only do safe things. Thread the Maze. Beat up on the Lords of Death. Fly to the core of the Sun. Safe things." I decided not to bring up Spindrift.

"You flew into the sun?" Comet asked. I nodded. She hadn't heard that bit of news yet. Vera Durand's program broadcasts tomorrow morning. "But you don't have to ask him any questions because we can do the asking and you just have to listen and you don't have to fly to Mars because Professor Lafayette is going to bring him, a projection, into our living room to talk to our Mom and Dad and Speaker Ming so you don't have to do something dangerous, except we have to stop at his castle so I can pick up a starcompass from him." Comet's sentences did rush together a bit, I thought, when she was worried.

"The Wizard?" I asked. "Here? And you do the all the talking?"

"Are you all packed and ready to go?" Comet asked. I hefted my duffel bag. "Gold Knight, Silver Knight, you'll keep a watch on Medford until we're back?" Comet asked again.

"Four minutes," Silver Knight said. "How much can go wrong in four minutes?"

"Unless it's forever," Brian added. "We fail, we die, then the world dies." Sometimes he could be just so optimistic.

"Right. Exactly. We'd better get back to the house," Comet said.

"Your back yard?" I asked. "All good with a teleport?" I waited for agreement. Silver Knight and Gold Knight waved us good-by. There was a blue lightning flash, a single chime stilled at once, and we were all in the Wells' back yard.

Chapter Fifty-Five

The Wells Residence
Medford, Massachusetts

For a few moments we stood there. Trisha, dressed as Comet, took the lead, taking us up the back stairs through a large breakfast room and well-appointed kitchen. I stayed in the rear of the column. The whole front of the house was a big living room. Sitting across one wall were Patrick and Abigail Wells, Krystal North, and -- it took me a moment to recognize him -- Speaker of the House Ming. Morgana Lafayette was in her other garb, her Morgan Le Fay garb. I could see what she was wearing, including the Orb of Merlin, but Patrick and Abigail Wells didn't seem to notice that the Living Crone was sitting next to them. Like any good American, I made a proper bow in the direction of the Speaker.

Abigail Wells surveyed her four new guests and gestured at the couch. "Joe found you, Eclipse?" she asked, "And then didn't come along to be thanked?"

"He didn't come along," Patrick Wells shouted, "so I can kill him for tampering with my daughter!" He used several very harsh words other than 'him'.

Suddenly I understood why Trisha's parents were so upset. They thought Joe had been carrying on with Trisha. They assumed she knew what a terrible thing she had done, so they refused to say it out loud. They were even more ashamed that she refused to confess that she had done such a thing. Real Americans always stand behind their deeds. I blushed slightly. Joe had been a convenient alternative persona, but sometimes other things were more important than continuing its pretended existence.

"That would be kind of impossible," I answered. "You only get one of us at a time. Joe and I, we're the same person. He's just a good disguise. For me. And I'm a girl. For sure 'Joe' did not carry on with Trisha."

"But I spoke with him," Abigail said.

I dropped into my Joe voice. "You spoke with me. Didn't she, Aurora?" Janie nodded.

"What was wrong with my daughter that she didn't deny it? That's beyond disgraceful!" Patrick shouted. Trisha looked at the carpet. I really wished Trisha's parents would have some faith in her, but they didn't. No matter what she did, it was wrong. Even when she was about to go off, possibly to her death, they were saying how little they trusted her.

"But the appointed hour approaches," Morgana announced. A large piece of paper, mayhaps three feet across, appeared in the center of the room. That had to be Morgana's doing, I thought, but I hadn't felt the least trace of any gifts in action. "Eclipse, you've read my book, so you need to be the second pole on this casting. Don't worry; all I need you to do is summon the sight of the Straight Circle, which only the two of us will see. Just stand there." I moved to where Morgana was pointing.

The space above the paper filled with a spherical latticework of light, tiny blue flames being linked by lines along which passed traceries of High Goetic letters. That had to be Morgana's working. She must have set it in advance. This was not the moment to tell Morgana that I could read the words as they passed between the flames.

"The circle, please," she asked. I reached down through all the levels I had already summoned. For once, the Straight Circle came effortlessly, almost as though it wanted to be called. Morgana smiled at me and nodded approvingly. "Nin amner Morgoth," she said. "Nin amner Calirath." I had to concentrate to hold the Straight Circle in place.

The casting worked. Standing on the paper was the Wizard of Mars, or an optical projection. The Wizard looks sort of like a man, but the bodily proportions are not quite right. His neck is a little too long. His head is a little too large. His skin is ruddy; an ungifted man with a touch of sunburn might look like that. He wore classic wizard's robes, the fabric being a deep blue within which clouds of stars swam. The stars appeared to be well behind the fabric. It was certainly an impressive bit of artistry.

"We meet again, Sorceress Supreme," the Wizard said, bowing slightly to Morgana.

"We meet by your request, Ancient Prince" she answered, her bow being precisely as deep.

The Wizard turned to Ming. "Mister Speaker, you are here as your laws require. I am saddened that you are taken from your work, but if I were not here your world would surely be doomed."

"Lord Wizard, please be welcome to America. May your visit be fruitful for all concerned." Ming's greeting was, if I remembered correctly, fixed by law.

"I greet thee, Bearer of the Namestone," the Wizard said, bowing in my direction. So much for rumors that the Wizard is omniscient. Fortunately, I had put gentle mind control on me, so I could not speak without thinking about it carefully first.

"I greet you, Mighty Lord of the Scarlet Castle," I answered. "I stand here asking no questions, no matter my words or tone." A fair amount of time, this past day, had been looking up his titles. The last bit was the legal formula I'd learned from Mum.

"And these are the parents," he said, the sweep of his hand taking in Patrick and Abigail Wells. "They must permit their children to travel or their mission will fail." Now he was pointing at me. "And you? Whose permission do you need?"

What should I say? "My own permission. I haven't given it yet. Emancipated minor," I said. "Emancipated as a matter of fact. And Heinlein certificate. Me asking for the usual court ruling would be…inconvenient."

"Just a bit," Speaker Ming mouthed.

"Wisely and correctly said," the Wizard agreed. He was giving me an odd look. "But I am here to speak to the parents, not to you. And I will charge them nothing to answer their questions, though I may decline to reply." Interesting, I thought. He knew I was telling the truth about emancipation, or didn't care, but he'd never been able to find me.

"I have heard my daughter and son," Patrick said, "tell me what they thought they heard you tell them, but I would prefer to hear it from your own lips, so to speak. What is the challenge, and what are you asking them to do about it?"

"There is the great challenge and the lesser challenge. The great challenge is the doom of the world. It approaches from far away, but very quickly. Either it is stopped now, or everyone in your world will die. The path to stopping it is narrow. It is these four who must go, and no others, to stop the doom, or your world will die. The lesser challenge is the doom of your civilization. Again, either it is stopped now, or everyone in your world will die or be turned to a mindless slave. These four must leave soon. They will return in four minutes, whichever of them lives, or they will die and not return here ever."

"Brian or Janie might die?" a horrified Abigail asked.

"If they do not all go, they will surely all die, as will the rest of you." The Wizard's oratory filled the room. "If they do go, some of them may die, but at least some perhaps all will live. I cannot predict which of the four may die, and which will surely live."

"Can't we ask for volunteers, to send someone in their place? Patrick asked. "Professor Lafayette here, for example?"

"Gee, thanks, Patrick," Lafayette said. To me, she did not sound to be grateful.

"If you attempt this, the mission will fail, and all will die," the Wizard answered. "I should emphasize, though this number does not match with your knowledge of the world, that eight billion people will die, not only the tenth of a billion Americans."

"Professor Lafayette," Brian asked, "can I trust his answers?"

"I am aware of no case, looking back into the farthest depths of human history, in which the Wizard has misled a questioner," Morgana said. "Of course, there are crazy people who are told that the sky is blue, but are so sure that the sky is green that that's the answer they hear. None of you are crazy that way." She stared at the Wizard.

"True," the Wizard answered. "And all here correctly understood what you said, for their own interpretation of 'farthest depth'." My intuition told me to remember very carefully that qualification.

"The world will die?" Brian asked. "Soon?"

"Another wise question." The Wizard smiled. "Not as much as three months."

"Dad," Brian said, "I think we'd better go. It's the least bad choice."

"City of Steel," Janie said. "If all else fails, mass desperation attacks are better than surrendering without trying them."

"Your logic is impeccable," Patrick said. "Please come back alive." He glared at Trisha. "Don't you dare think you get out of being grounded afterward, after what you did!" I asked myself what poor Trisha had done, other than revealing that her father was a fool. He seemed to have ignored what I just told him about Joe.

"The four of them have agreed. We now have four slightly tense minutes," Patrick announced.

"No. Stop!" Comet stood up. "You're government agents." She pointed at Krystal and Speaker Ming. "And you," she pointed at Morgana, "I looked up your necklace. You're a government all by yourself, aren't you, Avatar?"

Morgana broke into a broad smile. "You figured it out. Yes." Patrick Wells' face was turning ruddier and ruddier.

"Eclipse, I need a champion. Now! Please?" Comet was half way between belligerent anger and terror. I jumped to my feet and teleported next to her, putting a force wall around the two of us.

"Trisha," I said, "To do champion right, I sort of need to know what is going on." She took me by the shoulder. The world outside my force field stopped. She was calling superspeed, with me inside her speed zone.

"No time," Trisha said. "You need to read my mind, no matter how much it hurts me." I started reading. Her grip clamped down, hard, but I could tell. She wanted me to keep reading her memories. It took a while to digest, but ten seconds outside was a quarter of an hour for the two of us. Trisha had everything laid out in her mind, what she had gone through, what she had tried to do, and how her father had reacted. Several of my rules engines actually made useful suggestions. She took a deep breath, shook her head to clear her mind, and returned us to normal time.

"No!" Trisha shouted. "No! You didn't even ask me if I want to go! Why should I care what happens?" She looked at the Wizard of Mars. "Wizard, you've always been nice to me. You helped Janie and Brian. I'm not mad at you."

"I know," the Wizard said. "But if you want a good outcome from this, you yourself must now find the path to it."

"Someone has my two tons of gold," Trisha said. "I want it. No one challenged Eclipse when she said she was an emancipated minor. Isn't that true, Mister Speaker?"

"Indeed." Speaker Ming answered. "Emancipated de facto, and I gather Heinlein Act qualified. Though I fear it was somewhat less than two tons delivered, but still enough that you can live a comfortable life. " He looked at Krystal North. They were exchanging thoughts about something.

"You want me to go on this trip. I might die. I want something in exchange." Trisha stared at the Speaker. At this point I figured out where she was going. She's smarter than I am, and saw in a few moments what would have taken me a week.

"Within reason." Speaker Ming looked thoughtful. "Actually, based on the experiences of several past Speakers over two millennia with the Wizard, the future of America is at stake, so very much is reasonable. What do you want?"

"Full-year student status at Atomic Tech Half Moon Bay." Trisha was very clear on what she wanted. "I can pay, once you get me my gold. A trust account for most of it is OK. A place to live, someplace out there. It doesn't have to be as nice as my rooms upstairs."

"So you can carry on with boys again, whenever you want? You..." Abigail Wells' further language was decidedly to the point.

"The Heinlein Act. I want out." Trisha was now entirely calm. Heinlein had been a Navy Admiral turned divorce attorney and later Nobel laureate writer. It would be unusual for a girl as young as Trisha to divorce her parents, but it had been done.

"Good," Patrick said. "Then our family is no longer shamed." His wife nodded agreement. Everyone else in the room was shocked.

"You're sure, Trisha?" Morgan asked. "It's very final."

"Yes." Trisha stood up, backbone ramrod straight. I felt in her the determination of the founders of Massachusetts, people not much older than Trisha, the people who two millennia ago crossed the continent from Washington to Massachusetts on horseback to create America.

"So be it," Morgan answered.

Speaker Ming turned to Krystal North. "Captain-General, will you please do the mentalic validation?"

"Under the Heinlein Act," Krystal said, "Mentalic validation of the state of affairs is required. Any party may decline, but the worst possible interpretation is then placed on their claims and positions. Trisha, Patrick, Abigail, I need your permission to read your minds."

"I am an innocent and virtuous man," Patrick Wells said. "Read away."

"I agree," Abigail said.

"Please?" Trisha said.

<*Eclipse,*> Krystal said to me, <*As champion, you get to watch over Trisha, represent her side, and validate my mentalic report.*> I nodded.

Krystal was a very good mentalist. Little time was required for her to extract the information that was legally required. Unlike my ham-handed memory scans, Krystal was very gentle.

"Mister Speaker," Krystal said, "I find that all parties understand correctly the legal issues at stake, that the conditions of the Act are entirely well-satisfied, and therefore that you may properly grant what is requested." She followed with a mentalic report that only Speaker Ming and I heard. Heinlein divorces might routinely be done by filing paperwork, the way I did, or with a judge's decree with dueling attorneys, but the Speaker is also the Supreme Magistrate of the Republic, for all that Speakers of the House almost never used that authority.

"As Trisha's Champion, I endorse Captain-General North's finding," I said. Some people would complain that I was way too young to be standing up as Trisha's champion, but Trisha knew exactly what she wanted, and the facts of the matter were dismayingly clear. I thought I had bad relations with Mum, but that was only at the very end. Trisha was much worse off. I couldn't understand why, but I didn't have to.

"As First Speaker of the Republic, I hereby grant this request of Jessamine Trishaset no-longer-to-be-Wells, including possession of all her personal-use property." Speaker Ming was said to be extremely decisive; I'd just seen that in action.

"Trisha," Morgan said, "I have a house a bit south of Half Moon Bay, on the beach, that should fit your needs. It's vacant, and needs some inside work, but you can be moved there when you return."

"There may be some legal odds and ends," Speaker Ming said, "but Congress will clear them up today."

"Wisely done, all of you." The Wizard of Mars turned to me. "And you, Eclipse?" the Wizard asked. "You seem not to have been asked about your choice."

Surely I'd done enough for one month? But the Wizard does not deceive. My glimpse of the deepest depth of the Well of Infinity came to me. I could see the Nipponese gentleman saluting me. Trisha's divorce meant that I'd cleared up the last of the disasters I'd created when I solved the Maze, that being Trisha and her parents. Trisha had just made an enormous sacrifice. Could I do less?

"Life, lighter than atoms. Duty, heavier than worlds," I answered. "I'll go."

The Wizard of Mars bowed to me, a bow I returned. "About ten minutes," he announced, "and you four and I shall depart on separate paths. I see all four of you are already packed."

A faint sheen of sweat covered Morgana's face. "This is the highest power sending most of you will ever see," she said, "Not to mention being dangerous, if only to the caster."

For an instant Trisha was not there. She returned with ice cream cones. "White chocolate," she announced. "Brian's best." The first two she gave to her father and mother, as any dutiful American daughter would do. The cone she gave Morgana was considerably larger than the rest. Trisha remembered an ice cream cone for the Wizard. I had not expected him to be able to take it, but he did. However he had come to be in front of me, he was not a simple optical projection. Then she handed Speaker Ming and Krystal North theirs. Finally the four potential travellers were fed.

Cones finished, I looked at the three Wells kids. OK, one of them was no long a kid, and no longer a Wells. "It might be faster if I teleport us a ways up," I said. Comet nodded. "Are you all set for vacuum?" They'd all done interplanetary flight. Every so often, someone forgets to call on their gifts when needed and does something inadvisable, like flying straight down into the ground at Mach ten. This was not the moment for such a mistake.

"Ready." "Good to go." "Breathing for all of us." The last was Star. He was covering for the whole crew, if anyone made a mistake. I gave him a smile and thumbs up. Thumbs up is of course a boy gesture, just like an open palm fingers high is the matching girl gesture. He responded in in kind, then smiled and gave me an open palm back. We dropped into the heart of a Great Sky daylily, a harpsichord in its highest register playing around us.

I did not do my absolute maximum jump. No sense in showing exactly how good I am, not that Comet and Aurora hadn't already seen that. The earth floated in front of us, a blue-green-white disk four times the size of the full moon.

<*Next stop Mars*>, Comet announced, her sister providing telepathic links so we could all hear each other. I felt a deep pit in my stomach. For once in my recent life I was deeply frightened. Crash dropping toward negative infinity was dangerous. Flying to the Starcore was more dangerous. Doing the Maze was incredibly dangerous. Asking the Wizard of Mars questions was suicidal. I had the verbal formula which supposedly cut you out of any meeting with him, so he would neither answer your questions nor make you pay their prices. I had to hope it would work.

<*Joe? Eclipse, I mean? Strictly private line now?*> Aurora paused.

<*Yes?*> I answered.

<*Do you really have a girlfriend? Gifttruth says you must, since you said you did,*> she continued.

<*Everything I said was true. At least, it was true in High Atlanticean, the language in which she and I talked.* >

<*?*> Aurora waited for me to explain.

<*She was my friend who was a girl,*> I explained. <*And she was, until the end of time. Well, her time, at least. That's what end of time means in Atlanticean. It's when you die.*> That last memory really hurt, and bits of her death leaked out of my thoughts.

<*She died? In your arms?*> Aurora was horrified.

<*I did for her what she needed. I stood at her back when no one else could. It gets real complicated, but I did what had to be done. And I was with her at her end, so she didn't die alone,*> I answered. I wasn't quite crying, but my memory of the moon, a

silver nail touching the sea, just as she vanished, brought tears to my eyes. It took a while for me to realize that Aurora was hugging me.

<*What was that about?*> Star finally asked. Aurora had been hugging, not carrying on with me, but it was still unexpected.

<*I had a friend,*> I answered. <*A friend who was a girl. Like your sisters. And she reached the end of time. Her time. She died in my arms.*> Star and Comet saw the same memories that Aurora had. From Star there came a dead silence. I changed topics. <*OK, Star, one question. How did you figure out I'm me?*>

<*Our last base ball nines game. Bart made that deep hit, and you got to the ball just after it hit the ground. I mean, that would have been an impossible catch, but you came real close, and you caught it on the way up. Then you made the throw, all the way back to Trisha at home plate.*> Star winked at me.

<*No gifts involved. Honest,*> I said.

<*I know. It was an honest throw. But you throw like a girl. OK, you are a girl. Wrist. Arm. Pivot. Really fast. Straight at home plate. Like a girl who plays hard ball nines. Not like a boy playing slow-pitch soft ball.*>

<*Oops.*> He was right. Mum had taught me how to throw. You never knew when you might need to kill a grizzly bear by throwing rocks at its head. Mum worried about an awful lot of improbable contingencies.

<*Once I figured out you were a girl in disguise, everything else came together.*> Star smiled at me. He was really good at fitting things together.

<*Great work. Have you told your sisters yet that you're actually* Ronald Helmesham *in disguise? That was really sharp of you.*> I meant every word of my compliments.

<*Trisha?*> I asked, focusing our contact so we only heard each other. <*Speak up if you want to be spelled on flying. Or talk about what you did.*>

<*I'm good for now,*> she answered. <*I'd rather not talk about that other thing, not now. I just don't want to. It was too much. Talk? Mayhaps later. I need to know how to keep up a house. But all the thanks in the world for being my champion.*> I could tell she knew: She'd done something very brave, and was wondering if she'd made the wrong choice.

<*OK. I have your back whenever you want it.*> I broke the mentalic link between us.

And now we were on our way to Mars.

The End

for *The Girl Who Saved The World*

In Book Two, *Airy Castles All Ablaze*, we learn how Eclipse and friends deal with the dooms of the world.

In Book Three, *Of Breaking Waves*, Eclipse must complete what Spindrift began, and become The Key Without a Lock to the Room Without a Door.

Glossary

action: An Action is a planned use of violent gifts. A Regular Action is a constabulary operation, in which the miscreants are presumed to be criminals subject to arrest, fair trial, and swift execution. A Full Action is open warfare, with no constraints on levels, gifts, or instant consequences for the enemies of all humanity.

Aurora: Public persona of Jane Caroline Wells, twelve-year-old resident of Arlington, Massachusetts. Her public gifts include telepathy, clairvoyance, clairaudience, and other mentalic techniques. In private life, she aspires to the rank of Mistress of Games, based on attaining the rank of Grandmaster in chess and the equivalent rank in four other games. Her games include chess, go, territories, and City of Steel, the last being a prehistoric game of elaborate rules played on a hexagonal grid map which, to a vivid imagination, loosely resembles the westernmost reaches of the Russian Empire.

Atlanticean: Any of several languages of Atlantis (or Atlanticea), an ancient civilization that flourished in the eastern Atlantic several millennia ago.

Comet: Public persona of Jessamine Trishaset (formerly Wells), a twelve-year-old resident of Arlington, Massachusetts. Her most noted gifts are flight, fast conscious response, and sensitivity of vision. Her private persona seeks to imitate her father, one of the world's great physicists. Her siblings Jane Caroline and Brian Sean also have public personae.

Corinne: Daughter of Solara. Appears to be sixteen. Her date of birth lies in prehistory. At some date in the depths of time she took up the Ambihelicon of Geyer against a foe poetically described as ``invincible star demons''. She won, but was reduced to a near-comatose state from which she emerges for a few days in each generation.

Eclipse: By vote of the League of Nations, the Supreme Enemy of All Mankind. A female persona, age twelve. Her private persona name is known only to a few. She solved the Lesser Maze, liberating and keeping for her own use the Most Glorious Namestone. For refusing to yield up the Namestone, the League declared her guilty of crimes against the future. The League ordered that she be captured and given a fair trial and a slow execution. The price on her head includes a hundred tons of Manjukuoan gold, life loan of the Mona Lisa, and a Roman castle.

Edison theater: A dramatic establishment in which actors and scenery are replaced by their pre-recorded optical images, using a technical scheme based on the Edison patents.

engift: To grant another the use of a gift. Engifting, turning an ungifted into a persona, is generally believed to be solely a power of the Lords of Eternity.

FedCorps: The Federal Corps of Volunteer Personae. FedCorps, composed of persona volunteers and ungifted support staff, is stationed primarily in the area of the Federal Capital. Unlike the Armed Forces, who are sworn to the Constitution with the Secretary of War as their Commander-in-Chief, or the State Militias, who are sworn to the Constitutions of the Republic and of their respective states with their state governor or state president as their Commander-in-Chief, FedCorps is formally the Sergeants-at-Arms of the Congress, sworn to the Constitution with the Speaker of the House and the President Pro Tempore of the Senate as their joint Commanders-in-Chief.

garb: A costume, brilliantly colorful, often including a domino (mask) and decorated with a sigil. Garbs are typically worn by a public persona. The custom of wearing garb has transmitted itself to public life: would the Senate of the Republic be nearly so imposing if the Senators wore morning suits or opera capes rather than violet togas? Would the officers of the Army Air Corps be nearly so impressive without their feather capes? How would university students recognize their professors if the faculty did not routinely dress in robe and mortarboard, cape and stole and staff?

gift: Gifts are the powers that let one fly, become invisible, or read another's mind. Most people have at least some very feeble gifts. The true physical source of gifts is unknown. There is no evidence that they are hereditary or a result of mutation, training, or surgical intervention. Pasteur's hypothesis that gifts are contagious has statistical confirmation, but no causative agent has been identified. Gifts have always existed, though typical gifts have varied from epoch to epoch.

gifttrue: A persona is gifttrue if he uses his gifts morally, in the service of his chosen community. Gifttruth is itself a gift.

Glorious Shield of Sarnath chess opening: The Sicilian.

Goetic Knights: A globe-spanning secret society and sometimes-dominant governing structure, dedicated to the belief that the best government is government of, by, and for the deeply gifted. Some thousands of years ago, they apparently ruled a fair part of the world. They have since faded from sight. High Goetic remains a standard language of mathematics and science.

Greater Maze: A structure, traversal of which allegedly gives one the opportunity to reweave the fabric of time.

Holmgren, Lars: Chancellor of the League of Nations, Defender of the Peace of Mankind, Lawful Holder of the Heavensgate, the Most Glorious Namestone, and several paragraphs of additional titles. Recently seen arguing that the Supreme Enemy should be flayed and burned alive, as opposed to being crucified, as had been recommended by the Special League Subcommittee for the Resolution of the Mode Question.

Horns of Hattin chess opening: a4, h4, Ra3, Rh3, Rad3, Rhe3. The variant with PxB, PxB when needed should be noted. The author has actually played a game against this opening. Readers will doubtless be shocked to learn that the outcome was negative for white.

Krystal North: FedCorps' premier mentalist. Captain-General of the National Persona League

league: A collective voluntary organization of personae who agree to support each other and work to common objectives. Aurora, Comet, Silver Knight, Gold Knight, and Star are the Greater Medford Persona League.

League of Nations Special Peace Executive -- composed of the Thirteen Great Powers

World Council – All notions are represented

Hall of the People all nations are represented by elected persons

Political Assembly – only the popular mass is represented.

League Chancellor Lars Holmgren

League Secret Political Police-General Wilhelm von und zu Dreikirch

League Elite Persona Brigade Leader Valkyria

The American Republic, Ambassador Thaddeus Buncombe

Austria -Hungary, Count Karl-Michael Ferencz

Brazil, Ambassador Amanda Rafaela Mascarenhas da Silva

British Empire, Lord Reginald Featherstonehaugh

Celestial Republic of the Han, Prince Shi Fang

French Empire, Marshall Bernard-Christian Davout

Prussia, Markgraf Heinrich Moeller

Empire of the Mexica and the Azteca, The Speaker for the First Speaker, Lord Smoking Frog

Indian Ocean States, The Sikh Empire, Ambassador Fateh Singh

Japan, Saigo Shigetoshi, Legate of the Satsuma Daimyo; Saigo Nene (wife, spymaster)

Manjukuo, The Celestial Kingdom, Legate Hong Sangui

Russia, Princess Elizaveta Petrovna Romanoff

The Empire of the Ottomans, Grand Vizier Suleiman Pasha

League of Terran Justice (League of Terror and Injustice): A globe-spanning conspiracy of terrorists, bandits, and political malcontents, allegedly dedicated to world government for, by, and of the deeply gifted. They are rigid egalitarians. The League's secret purpose is only known to their innermost circle.

Leaviork: A civilization of several millennia ago, its focus being individual achievement and the enjoyment of beauty. ``Better a small frog in a smaller pond" characterizes its worldly attitude. Leaviorkianu technology was advanced but oddly focused. Its boats had gold fittings while its homes used synthetic diamond and emerald windows. It is said that no Leaviorkianu ever voluntarily travelled more than fifty miles from the homeland, the continental Pacific Rim.

Lemuria: Any of several militaristic cultures believed to exist under the Pacific and Indian oceans. Lemurian incursions onto the land continents provoke regular and bloody wars. Some authorities believe that Lemuria actually exists elsewhere, with the gates to elsewhere existing under the oceans. The Lemurian language, which uses four different syllabic and hieroglyphic alphabets simultaneously, is said to be the most difficult in the world to learn.

Lesser Maze: A puzzle palace on St. Brendan's Isle, the last fragment of Gaea Atlanticea, hiding and protecting the Namestone and the Tomb of the Bearer. The Lesser Maze and its defenders are the Namestone's creation. The Defenders are keyed so that they are always just weak enough that they can in principle be defeated by their opponents, if only the opponents use sufficient wit and dedication as well as brute force. The Lesser Maze creates a world-wide eclipse during serious attempts to traverse its obstacles. The eclipse became Stellar as well as Solar when the Lesser Maze was solved by Eclipse. Descriptions of failed attempts to traverse the Lesser Maze are widely distributed by unseen methods, so that all may know and fear the Lesser Maze.

Levels: The Sky, The Breaking Wave, The Sea of Grass, The Temple, The Sun, the Matrix, The Fall of Crystal, the Tomb, the Hall of the Lidless Eye,... are paths to drawing power from the source of all power for gifts. One gains more power by calling deeper levels, or by calling a given level more broadly or more than once.

Lords of Eternity: A group of immortal personae of great age (most are said to predate all recorded civilizations) and power, supposedly including the ability to engift normal mortals. The Lords do not ordinarily concern themselves with issues of concern to mortals. Well-known Lords include Solara, Prince Mong-Ku, the Screaming Skull, Dark Shadow, Colonel Pi, Starsmasher, Corinne, and Plasmatrix-the-Desolation-of-the-Goddess.

Manjukuo: One of the great powers of the modern world, ranking in importance with the Russia Empire, Austria-Hungary, France, Prussia, and the American Republic. Its borders extend west through Mongolia, north to the Arctic Sea, east to the Pacific Ocean, and south to the Celestial Republic of the Han.

Marik: A technically advanced civilization of several millennia ago, located notably in the western Americas. Marik was given over entirely to public spectacle. Its most eminent government officials were Parademasters and Grand Marshals. Virtually its entire population supposedly perished in the space of half an hour by marching en masse into the Pacific Ocean.

Master of Airships: An eccentric public persona who plotted to make the rigid airship the dominant form of air travel. To accomplish this end, he planned to transmute much of the Indian Ocean to krypton gas, thereby increasing ten-fold the density of air, eliminate both polar caps by changing oceanic currents and deleting the Tibetan plateau, so as to eliminate major storms and severe seasonal weather, and infect all living things with a series of plagues to protect them from the biological consequences of the Earth's new atmosphere. Efforts to render him deceased are believed to have been successful.

mind: A non-physical construct corresponding to the ability to process information. Telepathic testimony shows that minds are possessed by essentially all animals, and by the more complex calculating machines. It is not agreed whether the mentalic memories of the deep rocks --- the Currents of the Earth --- are symptomatic of a planetary mentation.

Mind control: A forbidden gift, possession of which is punishable in many civilized lands by death, that allows one to dominate the mental processes of another being.

Modern English: The dialect of English spoken by our heroine, to be distinguished from Ancient English as spoken in Leaviork, and Standard Edited English as spoken by the reader, and drawing more heavily on German than does Standard Edited English. Modern English has such constructions as mayhaps, for sure, and gifttrue.

Namestone: The Most Glorious Namestone, the Gate of Heaven or Key to Utopia, is an artifact of great age and supernal power. In addition to enhancing the gifts of the persona who wields it, the Namestone has intrinsic abilities of its own, notably Rationalization and Material Transmutation. By use of Rationalization, a persona may supposedly purge men's hearts of fear, evil, and all other disorder. The power of Material Transmutation allows the wielder to transform arbitrary objects into other objects. Moving the Namestone to the possession of a qualified user, thereby transforming the world into the kingdom of heaven on earth, has been a primary goal of most human cultures for thousands of years. The Namestone was brought to this Earth by the Bearer, as described in the Atlanticean Sacred Ode to the Most Glorious Namestone, the translation of Tennyson being authoritative, however much Tennyson apologized for the meter and structure of his translation.

persona: (pl. personae, personas) The identity assumed by a person. Public personae are usually persons with gifts, using their gifts to public or private benefit, often while brilliantly dressed. Many public personae also have a private persona with orthodox dress and occupation but no sign of gifts. An open persona is a gifted person whose public and private personae are the same.

Plasmatrix, or Plasmatrix-the-Desolation-of-the-Goddess: A Lord of Eternity, whose somewhat scanty garb appears to be composed entirely of incandescent gas. Her gifts lie in the field of material obliteration. Supposedly she is among the most intelligent of the Lords of Eternity.

Prince Mong-Ku: A Lord of Eternity, a being whose existence predates recorded civilization. While some would see him as the personification of a European interpretation of 18th century Manjukuoan culture, the relative ages of Mong-ku and Manjukuo imply that he shaped Manjukuo in his image, not vice versa. Certainly, without his influence the Empire would not have forestalled Russian expansion into Mongolia and Siberia by seizing the territories first.

privileged bands: In the structuralist unified theory of physics, each point or quantized volume in the universe has associated with it a list of attributes that determine what objects and fields are present (at least in part) at that point. The privileged bands are claimed to communicate directly with the attribute list of each point, allowing one, e.g., to create matter out of nothing by redefining the attribute list in a region from ``vacuum" to ``solid gold", or, e.g., to change the structure of space to alter the laws of arithmetic.

Rationalism: The discredited Rationalist School of history asserted that human motives and behaviors in distant cultures were basically the same as our own, so that if one understood what a culture valued one could understand the behavior of the culture's members. Irrational behavior of members of foreign cultures was interpreted by the rationalists as a rational striving for a differently ordered set of goals. Efforts to apply Rationalism to the ancient historical record are a total failure. Most modern historians instead understand that ancient men are fundamentally incomprehensible, so that the primary purpose of history is the presentation of morally educatory tales, such as Leonidas and the Three Hundred. The Temporal Rationalists propose to eliminate certain inconsistencies encountered by the rationalist school by claiming that, contrary to the physicists, time is not well-ordered, so that different observers need not agree on the order in which historical events occurred.

RTI: Roger's Technological Institution. A scientific school located in Cambridge, Massachusetts on the northern bank of the Carolus Fluvius. Its sister school along the banks of the Carolus is the Massachusetts Institution for Theology, John Harvard, founder.

RadioBell: A personal communications device

Sarnath: A world-spanning technically advanced trading empire of several millennia ago, its culture being given over entirely to trade, commerce, and personal enrichment. The causes of its disappearance are unknown. It is difficult for moderns to credit the traveler's tale that a single Sarnathi speculator managed to corner the entire food supply of the country, then allowed the population to starve to death in an unsuccessful effort to maximize his profits.

The Screaming Skull: A Lord of Eternity, a being whose existence predates recorded civilization. The Skull is urbane, witty, and polite, but fond of keeping grudges; he dresses entirely in black. His primary gift is the ability to order people to drop dead.

sigil: An ornamental pattern or mark, identifying a public persona, featured on garb or other clothing. Sigils seen here include: Comet: a comet, Star: a four-point rayed star, Aurora: the radiant eye and pyramid, and Eclipse: the new moon triumphant over a sun in glory.

Silver General: Not a Lord of Eternity, though of similar age and power. The cycle of rise and fall of each civilization is said to follow from a struggle between the Silver General and Solara.

Solara: A Lord of Eternity, whose existence predates modern civilization. Her garb features a golden sun mask, eyesockets bejeweled. Scholars infer that she is primus inter pares among the Lords of Eternity.

Star: Public persona of Brian Sean Wells, twelve-year old brother of Comet and Aurora. His most notable gifts are an effective body screen and an extremely potent energy attack. A first-rate student, he is more interested in traditional boyish pursuits: base ball nines, grass hockey, and model building. He knows that his sisters will solve puzzles before he does, but becomes bored while waiting for them to do so.

StarCompass: A quadridimensional set of metal sheaves, programmed to lead the holder to predetermined objectives. A loan to Comet from the Wizard of Mars.

Supreme Illusionist: A public prankster and rogue persona, whose masterwork was the transformation of John Harvard's Square into the Piazza Leprecano. His urban reconstruction of central Cambridge has been left intact, except that the fifty-foot tall statue of John Harvard no longer glows green.

tesdri: Tesla Detection, Ranging, and Identification; radar.

transient person: The Lords of Eternity view normal mortals to be scarcely longer lived than mayflies, their lives being transient shadows (hence transient persons) on the great warp and weave of history.

transitivity: (Einstein's Theory of Transitivity). In 1922 Solara appeared to Einstein, transporting him in the space of hours to AutumnLost. Based on his observations of certain peculiar phenomena seen at exceeding large velocities, Einstein replaced Special and General Relativity with Transitivity, of which Relativity is a limiting case. Transitivity explains faster-than-light travel, and indicates conditions under which travel through time is possible, the concept of causality being generalized via replacement of the familiar time t with three time dimensions: t, u, and v. According to Transitivity, one may use time travel to proceed to the past, alter past events, and return to a present not resembling the present that one remembers.

Wizard of Mars: An immortal, seemingly all-knowing, being resident in the Scarlet Castle, a vast structure that was once Mons Olympus. The Wizard is confined to the surface of Mars. It reveals its knowledge to others for a price often too great to pay. The Wizard is neither omnipotent nor omnicompetent: it can be outsmarted.

###

About George Phillies

George Phillies is a retired Professor of Physics. He had previously worked at the Worcester Polytechnic Institute. He had also been a member of WPI's interdisciplinary faculty in Interactive Media and Game Development. He taught in both areas. His lectures on game design, polymer dynamics, and statistical mechanics were all video recorded and may be seen on the GeorgePhillies channel on youtube. Phillies' ongoing scientific research is focused on polymer dynamics.

Books by George Phillies include:

Fiction
This Shining Sea
Nine Gees
Minutegirls
The One World
Mistress of the Waves
Against Three Lands
Eclipse: The Girl Who Saved the World
In preparation: Airy Castles All Ablaze
In preparation: The Lords of the Air
In preparation: The Merchant Adventurers

Game Design
Contemporary Perspectives in Game Design (with Tom Vasel)
Modern Perspectives in Game Design (Second Edition; with Tom Vasel)
Design Elements of Contemporary Strategy Games (with Tom Vasel)
Designing Modern Strategy Games (with Tom Vasel)
Stalingrad for Beginners
Stalingrad Replayed
Designing Wargames - Introduction

Politics
Stand Up for Liberty!
Funding Liberty

Libertarian Renaissance
Surely We Can Do Better?

Physics
Elementary Lectures in Statistical Mechanics (Springer Verlag)
Phenomenology of Polymer Solution Dynamics (Cambridge University Press)
Complete Tables for 'Phenomenology of Polymer Solution Dynamics' (Third Millennium)
In preparation: Theory of Polymer Solution Dynamics
In preparation: New Studies of Polymer Solution Phenomenology

Excerpt from Against Three Lands

Clan MacDonald is surrounded by enemies. Clan Gunn wants its lands. Mysterious pirates assail its shores. The All-Conquering Generalissimo suspects it of treason. Foreign trade is interrupted by barbarian invasions -- or are they blue-skinned demons?

Angus Valentine Macdonald, seventh child of the One MacDonald, must travel to remote Mercia, where he must defeat the treachery of the Lunarian Empire, the corruption of the Langwadooran invaders, and the rapacious greed of the alien Trell to protect his homeland and win the hand of his lady-love.

Authors' aside: Against Three Lands is a tale of geographic alternative fiction, set on a world – The World of a Thousand Isles – broken into vast numbers of moderately large islands. Readers will recognize the extant technology as that found on earth in the early 17th century. There are gunpowder weapons, but they are not yet battle-winners on land. Unlike my novel *The One World,* you will search in vain for the magicians with their spark gap-coherer radios, and the accountants and their Babbage machines. The cultural settings of the Hundred Isles, Mercia, and their foreign visitors, are lifted from settings found on our world. I have quite deliberately interchanged lists of names, so, no, the Hundred Islers are not Scotsmen in disguise, and the Mercians and their Empire of the Stars are certainly not the Spanish Empire on which the sun never set.

Chapter 10

Early morning. Nancy Juliet sat on a piling on the seaside, ostentatiously painting a single seabird. The background was lovely. The aqueduct feeding Puerto Nova came to an end a hundred feet inland. It fed into a narrow stream surrounded by cherry trees, all in bloom, the stream ending by dropping over the sea wall into the harbor. Most of Puerto Nova was filthy, but the little park was scrupulously clean.

This was her third day here. She had wandered the waterfront, affecting to be painting seabirds, of which Mercia had a considerable variety. No one had looked askance that the paintings included careful renderings of the background. One officer had offered her money, a generous amount, for a painting of himself. She was not a hereditary horseman, rusticated to work a farm, but being paid for her hobby was strange. However, accepting his gift made him feel better about the exchange, so she accepted.

She had listened carefully to what Angus said about negotiating with the blue-robes. The things that they viewed as important were not at all like the things that a sensible person would view was important. Apparently they had some religion. They had not quite come to blows when Angus was asked if he would convert to it. Though perhaps they thought he had promised to convert, which he had not done. She had looked carefully for a book monger selling books from Langwadoor. There had been no sign of any. There had been a wine merchant. She paid what she suspected was actually an outrageous amount to sample three different wines, just a touch of each in three small glasses. She had smiled politely at each taste, though the truth of the matter was that all three wines were so awful that you couldn't imagine how anyone could drink them. They were like lemon juice. They smelled like vinegar. There were no words for the tastes. They bit the tongue and jaws. They were certainly not good Hundred Isles plum wine.

Nancy Juliet had asked Angus about obtaining scrolls that would show from where the Langwadoorans came. If they were to invade the Hundred Isles, surely that was a favor that needed returning. Angus had persuaded one of the Langwadooran monks to travel to the MacDonald domain. There he would learn the One Tongue and teach good sons of the MacDonald clan how to be speaking and writing Langwadooran. Apparently the writing was claimed to be very easy to learn, much like the syllabic script taught to small children of the Hundred Isles. So far as Angus could find out, the Langwadoorans did not have an adult script in which single characters represented entire words. They did, however, have fine maps, of which he had been given several copies.

She had already counted the large group of Spicelander troops forming up on the quay next to their newly-docked ship. The Spicelanders were marched off. For all that they were foreigners, if she were challenged she would have to agree that their formation was tightly held, except that they never appeared to have heard of marching in step. She would not have guessed you could cram that many men in a ship that size. Perhaps the voyage was short. Perhaps the draft of the ship was enough that it had more decks than she expected. Now sailors and navvies were offloading things from the second ship. There were horses, large numbers of barrels, and what appeared to be cannon. They appeared to be cannon, if you ignored that they were tiny and mounted on huge wheels. Here were men somewhat differently dressed, in dark gray jackets and black pants, looking carefully at the cannon. There were several men, ornately dressed, waiting while blankets and saddles were thrown over horses so that they could ride off in splendor. She would not have cared to ride a horse that it just had a significant sea voyage. The poor thing was likely not to be in the best possible health. Apparently blue-robes viewed matters differently.

Suddenly there were voices close behind her. Nancy Juliet looked over her shoulder. There was a blue-robe soldier. The other fellow had to be a skirt-man. He wore a white shirt and leather vest above a brilliantly polychrome skirt that failed to reach his knees. The two were actually a fair distance down the quay, but they were speaking quite loudly and giggling. Perhaps they were somewhat drunk. She stood and faced them. They came closer to her and started talking at her in Mercian. Their accents were so bad that she couldn't tell what they were saying. Finally one of them pointed at her and made a series of obscene gestures whose meaning was completely unambiguous. "No," she answered. She was not fluent in Mercian, but some words she knew very well. They started shouting at her. She glared at them. They looked at each other and chattered in some other language. She had heard the blue-robe tongue spoken enough, but this sounded different. They both started to draw their swords. Hers came without summoning to her hands. She moved sideways, giving herself more room to move, and perhaps luring them away from her painting.

They rushed her. Her brilliant Kiai! warcry sent a flock of gulls scattering in all directions. There was a clatter of steel. For all that they were significantly shorter than she was, they were very strong, but their ideas on swordsmanship were pathetic. The blue-robe lost arm and throat to a double cut. The skirt-man's thrust was deflected by her short sword. A downward slice cost the skirt-man his right arm, then his left arm, and after the pivot his head. These two might have been soldiers, but in their worship of the art of the blade they were beneath many street bandits. She swiped her sword clean on one of their coats.

Now there were voices behind her again. Nancy Juliet wheeled, keeping her sword up. Fifteen feet away a blue-robe officer, or something of the like, to judge from his fancy clothing, stood gawking. His companion, a man less well dressed, was clearly also a blue-robe.

The officer put his hands in front of himself, palms up and open. It was a gesture that even dogs and small children recognized, the sign of peaceful intent. He spoke in Mercian. "I named Captain Raoul Bonnet. I speak Mercian," he said slowly. "Do you speak Mercian?"

"I speak a little Mercian. I am Nancy Juliet. I am from the Hundred Isles," she answered. "These two men fought me. They were first to draw. Do you speak the One Tongue?"

"I heard them," the officer answered in Mercian. "I saw them. They attack you. You made me have no trouble of…" He made a throat cutting gesture… "punish them." Nancy Juliet sheathed her swords.

"I am honored to be of service to you," she said. There was a look of bafflement on his face. "I am glad. I helped you." She pressed her hands together, smiled, and bowed. He returned her gesture.

"I see you make paintings. And you are good with sword. Do you teach sword?" he asked.

"I am only a horseman. I am not a sensei to teach. I am not very good with the sword. I had to block the second blow before I chopped him." Nancy Juliet wished that the foreigner spoke the One Tongue decently. Neither of them spoke Mercian very well. The junior officer said something emphatic to the senior officer.

"They have friends," Bonnet said. "Friends will want to hurt you. You should leave Puerto Nova. Soon!"

"Yes," she answered. "I will go now. I am pleased to have talked with you."

"And we are pleased to have seen your swordsmanship. It was magnificent. Have a safe journey," Bonnet saluted.

She rolled her watercolor, folded her easel, dropped her watercolor kit into its bag, and bowed to the two officers. The senior officer's hand gesture was unfamiliar, with fingers pressed to forehead, but appeared to be a token of respect. She made a formal bow, smiled a last time and headed briskly up the street away from the dockyard. This was indeed a time to leave town in a hurry.

~~~~~

Nancy Juliet, moving at a very brisk walk, reached The Inn of Distant Views without further incident. Who would be there? To her relief, Junior Factor Mara Ainslie was sitting under the front portico reading a scroll. James May had wanted someone always to stay at the Inn to keep track of who was going where, and now that would make a difference.
~~~~~

"Mara! We have a problem! Please help me saddle my horse! I must leave town. As rapidly as possible." Nancy Juliet pointed at the stable behind the Inn.

"What's wrong, Nancy? I've never seen you alarmed before. Yes, I can help with the horse. Surely I've done this before." The two women headed for the stable.

"I was down at the docks. I was doing paintings of birds. Well, birds and the soldiers and cannon standing behind them. Two soldiers tried to rape me," Nancy Juliet snapped.

"Oh, this is terrible. We must ask the city governor to have them arrested." Mary helped Nancy center the blanket on the horse. "Should we not brush the horse first?"

"I did that when we arrived. I did that first thing this morning, so that my horse would always be ready to be ridden. That is a horseman custom, not a trader custom. A good horseman is ready to ride to battle at a moment's notice. This is the moment. And I checked the hooves. Now here's the saddle over the top." Nancy passed her plain riding saddle over the horse's back. "I need to leave before the city governor finds out. I said they tried to rape me. They drew swords. So did I. As they were soldiers, I am now entitled to two more silver threads for my longsword, though perhaps I should not claim them. Blue-robes are terrible swordsmen. Surely you are better. If I understood their officer correctly, the two men I killed were troublemakers who he would've executed if I had not killed them first. However, he told me to leave town quickly, so I shall. Please tell James May and Angus Valentine that I do remember how to find the rendezvous point. And now my saddlebags. Yes, the cinch on the saddle is indeed tight enough, especially for a horse as placid as this one." Nancy led the horse out of the stable into the alley behind and vaulted one-handed onto its back. 'I must be cautious until I reach the city gate, but then I will ride like the wind."

"I will offer prayers for you to the Goddess of the Sun and the God of Martial Forms." Mara bowed politely. Nancy Juliet gently prodded her horse's ribs with her heels, setting the creature into motion.

Back at the docks, Captain Bonnet watched helplessly as his troops dissolved from formation into a riotous mob. Two of their comrades had been killed. For sure they would be having revenge against the worthless inhabitants of this even more worthless town, preferably including the Mercians who had ambushed the two soldiers and killed them. He had done his best to convince his men that had been a fair fight, two soldiers on one woman. The woman lived up to all the rumors about the quality of Hundred Isles swordsmanship. He deeply wished he could have this Nancy Juliet as a sparring partner. She was clearly someone from whom you could learn a great deal about how to slaughter your opponents.

In the distance he heard sounds of doors being broken, people screaming, and an occasional shot being fired. The Eighteenth Spice Islands Native

Volunteer Regiment was not yet in its barracks. Assuredly, if there were a riot, they would join in. With some luck, his junior officers and sergeants would manage to beat sense into their men, perhaps before his men managed to burn the city to the ground. What was happening was just too bad for the local Mercian population, but their predicament was their fault: If they had fought back successfully when the Royal Army landed, they would not now be under Langwadocian occupation. They hadn't, so they were. He waited patiently for his troops to remember themselves.

"Captain Bonnet! Captain Bonnet!" A messenger was running toward him. He waved. "The Governor hopes you will avoid excessive violence in quieting this riot. The natives are already perturbed by the undoubtedly virtuous actions of our holy clergy in revealing the truth of our faith, and incidentally justly smiting mercilessly the false-god temples of the Mercians. He believes the natives have already been sufficiently irritated, and wishes to leave them no more disturbed than they are now.

"Of course," Bonnet answered." I promise I will use absolutely no more force than needed to restore order. Actually, I promise I will use considerably less force, because I have nothing like the force I need to restore my troops to a state of discipline. Perhaps after they've burned down a few homes they will realize that they are doing nothing effective." Bonnett scanned the lines of rooftops next to the docks, concluding after a few moments that while there were a few cook fires burning, there were no signs of a major conflagration breaking out. Yet. That woman, he thought was a truly magnificent swordsman, someone who could have qualified as an instructor in the Royal Academy, and with the muscular body – except in certain key places – of a young Royal Guardsman.

Where did that leave him? Apparently in the Hundred Isles gold was so common that it sold at one-to-forty to silver. Louis the Dyer had settled a little high, offering fifty silver for a gold, but now Louis had a customer who knew his products. Perhaps Louis had not recognized the tells that the customer would've been willing to settle for forty to one. She appeared to be an innocent young woman. Taking complete advantage of her might be bad for future business. Louis would be paid at the Governor-General's absurd price for dyes, on paper, but after the exchange would be getting something quite reasonable. The gold could return home, where gold could be exchanged for silver at one hundred twenty-to-one. It had taken him a few moments to see where that led. Then he had sent a runner to bring this Maura Anesley back to the docks so they could chat. Fortunately his manservant Rene had an eye for pretty women, and had had absolutely no problem catching her. And if he had offered sixty to one, that was for ten thousand gold pieces, an Emperor's ransom. Besides, a few exchanges like that and he would be able to hire an army to take back his silver, and everything else the Hundred Island idolaters owned.

Excerpts from Mistress of the Waves Chapter 1

The weather was absolutely gorgeous. The sky was crystal clear, the Five Day Stars sharply visible at the eastern horizon. I'd caught the fish I needed to keep the cook happy. I could catch a few more for the fishmonger. He pays cash. I don't need lots of money, but my clothing was frayed and patched before I bought it, and besides it was getting small again.

The first time I took my boat into the Outer Bay, meaning me by myself against the wind, the waves, and the blue sky, I was more than a bit scared. Yes, I did wear a lifejacket. I did have a life line. *Northstar* is a planked dory with solid deck and flotation compartments, not an overgrown rowboat. It's big enough for the Outer Bay, if you're careful and the weather isn't too rough. I'm not scared of the Outer Bay any more, not more than a sensible sailor should be. Besides, I've grown a bit since then. Dad always said I would grow up to be my mom's daughter, and she'd been even taller than he was. Than he *had been*. How tall was she? I only have a little girl's memories. I can remember her calling me Amanda, but never me saying 'Kira' instead of 'Mommy'.

There, across the bay, were the visitors. The fellow handling their main sail might have travelled from another star, but he wasn't that good at tending his sheet. He kept letting his sail luff. Then I got curious. I'd watched him tack. He wasn't close to going into irons, and he was still fewer points from the wind than I'd ever been. The pennon on his mast made that very clear. Blinding hot pink and a lattice of black lines on his pennon was nothing like the Starlanding Island star, the bottom two feet touching a very stylized island, but his pennon still trailed downwind. How did he do it? I knew the answer I'd get from another sailor. That starfarer uses the Starry Wisdom. If you copy his Starry Wisdom ways, you'll be worse off for it.

Starfarer? Like everyone else in town, last week I'd walked the miles up to the landing field to see the starship. I'd never seen one before. Odds are even that I'll ever see another. The Shire Librarian did his duty and talked to the Starfarers. They didn't want to trade. They only wanted to go sailing.

It took no end of time for them to explain that they went sailing for fun, the way other people read stories or listen through the twilight to a chantey. They went from star to star, so they could say they'd sailed more seas than anyone else. Okay. Some people collect sea shells. They were collecting, well, having done something. I think. At the landing field, I didn't see how they could sail at all, their starship being up on the plateau. Then their...machines...flew their sailboat down to the bay. Now the two of them tacked across the waves.

I carefully did all the things I needed to do to come about, put my tiller over, and made a guess where I might meet them when they came back across the Bay. *Northstar* wasn't as fast as they were, not by a fair piece, but on their return they would come to me. Of course, they'd be heading down wind, but I'd get a good look at their rigging. Perhaps they would say hello. Perhaps they'd even let me board their yacht. A yacht wasn't their starship '*Sorcerie...ex-Veil Worlds Battlecruiser Glorious Hot Pink*'—whatever that meant; it seemed like a long name—but their yacht was still a ship from another world.

I would never have guessed what happened when we closed. I waved. The two of them stood and waved back. No one at their tiller. No one tending the sheets. No one over there thinking, not at all. The wind shifted. Their boom swung. Their yacht heeled, just enough to send one of them into the water. Of course, if he'd been more cautious than standing right against the gunwale, he'd only have fallen onto his deck.

His companion screamed. I knew all the words, but she made no sense. He thrashed, arms pumping desperately, not swimming at all. She finally remembered to put her tiller hard over and drop her sails, something I would have done in half an instant. She had my weather gage. She had at least remembered to turn to windward. Her bare poles would blow her back to him.

By this time I was very close indeed. He paid no attention when I threw him a life ring.

"Help!" she shouted. "Help! Where's the harbor tractor net? Save him! Save him! He can't swim!"

I had no idea what a tractor net was, had no idea why tangling him in a mesh of ropes would help keep him from drowning, and had no idea how anyone could go sailing, not know how to swim, and not wear a life jacket. Dad had drilled into me how to save a drowning man, starting with the marlinspike tucked into my belt. Yes, marlinspike. To knock him out if he grappled me. Release my life line. Then grab a long line, and another life ring. Lucky I had two. Spill my sails; they'd be enough of a sea anchor to keep *Northstar* from escaping.

OK, have to do this the hard way. I kicked off my sandals, dove, stayed under with life ring bobbing across the waves on its tow, came up behind him, grabbed him by the neck so he couldn't turn around and choke me, took in the life ring, and got it around his head. That was a struggle. He couldn't grab me, not in a choke hold, but he was happy to try. He did remember to grab the ring. I got one swallow of water while he thrashed, and coughed it up before I had us back to the side of my dory. I can swim like a fish, but water doesn't fight back. He did. That's blind panic. It makes you stupid. He hung on to *Northstar*'s gunwale for dear life. I swam to the battens and climbed. Yes, I can hoist myself over the edge, but that's a long lift, something I'd only do to show off how strong I am.

His yacht drifted alongside. Machines overhead, machines from his ship, glittered like silver-metal sea eagles. He calmed down, enough hear me. "On Nova Capricornis 4," he declaimed, "I almost drowned." I completely pass on what 'now caper corn is for' means. His companion and I got him into their boat. He flopped on their deck, gasping for breath. I was soaking wet myself. Bright sun or not, the spring breeze was not making me any warmer.

His companion looked at him. She was pretty, in an odd sort of way. They couldn't go sailing very much; she didn't have the tan or the muscle. "Jim, I've called the *Sorcerie*; we'll have you in an autodoc in a couple minutes." She had an accent, every sound cut short. Every so often there were funny sounds from her mouth, sounds where there should have been a word. Not strange words. Funny sounds. Chirps. Whistles. Bird calls. Noises a human being can't make. Well, human beings not from starships. "Where was the harbor tractor net?" she asked.

"The harbor what?" I answered politely.

"The tractor net." She said those three words very firmly. "The harbor computers should have seen Jim was drowning and pulled him out of the water."

I was baffled. "Our computer? She sailed for Westport yesterday." I know the Spencerport computer. She teaches business arithmetic at Stone Academy. I'd waved her good-bye.

"No. The harbor computers." She was more emphatic.

"She's off checking the books of their Readers. She'll be back next week," I said.

"Computer." She looked puzzled. "A machine who thinks."

Were we speaking the same language? Machines are not 'who', and only people think. It seemed a good idea to change topic. "I did pull him out of the water," I said. "That saved him." I sneezed.

I didn't know what she'd been expecting to happen, but it hadn't. "You saved Jim," she said. "And you need an autodoc, too." Suddenly her boat, followed by my dory, rose skyward and moved, impossibly fast, toward the landing field.

~~~~~

And that is all I remember until I awoke. I was in a strange room, dressed in clean clothes, clothes that looked just like my old clothes, except they were my size, and not frayed at all. I had no memory of getting here. I was just…here. I remembered my dory rising into the air, and then my memories stopped. Something must have happened, but I couldn't remember it.

The light came from sun-bright balls, not like any candle or oil lamp. The wall opposite me was glass, a whole wall of glass pitched away at the top. You could see the reflection from the glass, very faint, and beyond the glass was
~~~~~

another room, pitch dark except for this bright blue-green-white thing. The thing's top edge was a circular arc. I stood up and took a few steps. When I walked toward the window, the thing didn't change size. That further room had to be huge.

"Oh, good, you're awake." The voice behind me was the woman from the sailboat.

"Hello," I managed to answer. She was dressed entirely differently than on the sailboat. She wore violet shoes, a green shirt hanging outside her very baggy bright-blue trousers, the shirtwaist cut in long triangles reaching almost to her knees, gold coat—if you wore a short bathrobe open so it came only to your breasts, but this was cut to be worn that way, that would be it. A rose-red scarf. And something was in her hair, coarse copper-orange strings filled with little lights that winked on and off. After I saw the lights in her hair, I realized the glints in her clothes were more lights, barely bright enough to be seen, each flashing on and off in its own tune. Every bit of the clothing was worked with patterns, so the blue was three different shades of color, and the green and yellow were more. I couldn't imagine how much the seamstresses had been paid to embroider it. More than I made in years. Maybe enough to buy a boat.

"I'm Martina Parker," she said. "Jim—my other half—is still in the autodoc, having his lungs cleaned. And you're all back together. Isn't she, autodoc?"

"That is correct, Miss Parker." The voice came from the open air. I didn't see where their doctor was hiding. His voice was a gorgeous baritone. I know some people are shy, but so shy you don't let people see you is a bit much. Otto Doc's voice was still gorgeous. "I have transformed Amanda Kirasdotr to a full state of normal health. All indicators are positive. No more…" I am sure the next sounds were all words, but not ones I know, and I aced my final vocabulary tests. "…will be needed."

"Why, thank you,' I said, "Wherever you are." It took me a moment to wonder. How did he know my name?

"Autodoc. Dismiss. Private." Martina said that in a very different tone of voice. Otto, wherever he was, never said another word. "We're sorry it took so long. The autodoc makes medical decisions here. I spoke to your guardian. He agreed we should take the days needed to care for you. Your ship is protected. Your fish were given to your cook. Arrangements were made to replace the fish you did not catch in your absence. We infer you and your ship should be returned to your harbor, just before first light in good weather. That is in one dekan—sorry, two hours." Was it Martina's accent? Her voice held a trace of exasperation.

"Thank you. That's very kind of you. Did you say…days?" I knew exactly what she had said.

"Oh, yes, not quite three of them. You were asleep. The autodoc was very insistent. But it did everything it should. And it gave you the…." More noises, almost ones a person could speak. I tried to repeat them, pitching the last sounds into a question. Martina paused. She turned her head to the side, her lips moving slightly. It was an invisible conversation, right in front of me, and I heard neither side of it.

"Have you learned how to dream?" she asked. I nodded. I don't think you learn how to dream. You just do it. But she was the host, so I didn't argue. "The…when you go to sleep, take yourself to a classroom. A classroom with the autodoc's voice. It will tell you about being healthy." She spoke every word slowly and carefully. I repeated what she said. It made no sense, but when someone sounds like that, they think it's important, so you should, too, even if you don't know why. And I don't sleepwalk, so walking to a classroom after I nod off is plain impossible.

"But, yes, you were in the autodoc for most of three days. We brought you up to find out how to contact your…your guardian." Three days? Now I found memories from before I woke up, memories I'd lost until this instant. I'd been awake, but I couldn't see anything, I couldn't hear anything, I didn't know what was happening, and I didn't care enough to do anything. I was asked who my parents were, where my guardian was. The questions had somehow gone on forever.

"I see. Cook will be really grateful to you, for covering for me not being there to fish." I didn't understand the part about being made healthy. I'd already been healthy. Time to change the topic of conversation. "But…what is that?" I pointed at the object in the next room. It really was amazingly strange.

"Why, that's Goddard. Go look closer." I walked across the carpet. Even up against the glass, I was no closer to it. I couldn't see anything in the next room other than the patterned circle.

"Goddard? Is it a globe?" Goddard is the world. Was it worthwhile to ask questions? Whenever I did, the answers left me feeling I knew less and less. And I'm not dumb. No, be honest with yourself, you passed citizen test after citizen test way younger than other girls, you passed your competency test, and you're being allowed to park in the orphanage, study or fish until you're old enough to claim your inheritance, what little there is of it.

"Oh, no." Her voice brightened. "That's Goddard. Itself. You do know Goddard is a planet, and round. Don't you?"

"Sure."

"Barlemnon, give Amanda a geo overlay, lowest labeled resolution." She was speaking to someone else.

"As is commanded." Another voice in the air. A spiderweb of scarlet lines appeared in front of the globe, outlining the green areas and putting names next to them. It took me two breaths to recognize those names. Those were two dozen continents, a quarter-way around the world—yes, I am my mother's daughter, I do know a world map when I see it, even if it's upside down. And then I understood.

"That's a window to outside. We're flying! We're up here." No one would ever believe me. But Goddard, from high in the air, so high you could see Damien and Relnovo at the same time, was totally beautiful. The most beautiful thing I'd ever seen, well, except the first fish I caught and gaffed.

Chapter 6

The end of week rolled around. I went fishing by myself. It was an odd day. The wind was gusty and intemperate. The air was warm and muggy, much more than you would expect for this early in the Summer. I looked carefully at the weather flags the Harbormaster was flying. Solid green. The water gauge was high. There was no sign of a storm.

We'd been fishing close to the near edge of the Outer Bay. I decided to go well out. Kalynikos Rock gave a nice wind shadow, so I could stop, chop my bait fish, and then put out the lines. Actually, I decided to eat my bread and cheese before I chopped the fish and got my hands dirty, so it was into the morning before my hooks and lines were ready. The sea beyond the bay was choppier than sometimes, so getting things done took its own good time.

The choppy waves were also loud where they were breaking again the Rock. Still, there was an odd noise in the background, growing slowly louder, but starting so softly that I didn't notice it. I didn't pay attention until I pulled out from the lee, oceanward side of the rock and looked back toward Spencerport.

I allow that Da would not have blamed me for the words I said next.

Looking down the bay toward home, the sky was black halfway from horizon to zenith. The grumbling was continuous thunder. Lightning was continuous. Spencerport could not be seen behind the wall of rain. I was lucky. The bait and hooks were in neat rolls in the bait chest, so I didn't have to decide between pulling them in or cutting the fishing lines and losing the hooks. I grabbed at the sheets, brought jib and mainsail all the way up, and started a tack into the bay. It wasn't the sharpest tack *Northstar* could hold. I was too busy pulling out my foul-weather gear. Checking the ties on my lifeline came next.

Then I looked at how much progress I had made toward shore, and how fast the storm was sweeping up the bay at me. You are being stupid, I thought. You can't possibly reach any shore before it reaches you, and shore in the Outer Bay is lousy as a storm anchorage. Anchoring behind the Rock in its wind shadow is not an option. The Rock goes straight down. The water there is deep, way deeper than I had anchor line.

You have to run before it, I decided. And you have to run out of the bay and east, or you'll be blown into Cameron Land…that was the next big island south, and at Spencerport it was really close. I came about, turning *Northstar* onto her broad reach. The wind was already building up, driving *Northstar* across the waves faster than I've ever taken her before. I had a clear idea of how long I would need to take down and stow her mainsail, which I wanted done well before the storm wall hit. I also wanted to clear Tappan point on Gorath Head, the exit from the Outer Bay. Being driven ashore in a storm the likes of which I'd never seen was a really bad idea, not to mention that I'd lose my boat for sure.

Getting the mainsail down in a high wind is a challenge. The jib in a higher wind was worse. I did carry a storm jib. By the time I had mainsail and jib stowed *Northstar* was being lashed by wind and rain. Setting and hoisting the storm jib was a nightmare. The wind had built to a gale and beyond. Heavy rain beat across my back. I had lashed shut the fishing well. Had I remembered to prime the pump this morning? I seldom needed it. But there was a pump handle at the tiller, and when I gave it a push I could feel water lifting out of the bilges.

Now the storm was overhead. . The clouds were black no longer. The sky turned green, the color of dark-tarnished copper. I'd always thought that line was a proverb, but it was very true. Lightning bolts, fiery serpents from the skies, were everywhere. Clouds burned from inside, salmon and pink and gold, pulsing from the lightnings they had inhaled. The wind shrieked through the rigging. Waves tossed *Northstar* left and right, hard enough that I could barely keep my footing, even clutching the tiller.

The storm went on and on and on. Fast onset, fast over, was not happening today. The waves rose to the height of *Northstar*'s mast. I leaned on the tiller, finding my ship sliding down into a deep trough. I fought the helm to keep my position on the wave. Steering, to the extent I could, was totally demanding on my concentration. I suppose I should have been terrified, but I was too busy. Pushing at the pump, keeping *Northstar* from swamping, demanded more and more of my strength.

A crack of thunder left me half-deaf. A glowing ball of ruby light the size of an apple appeared at the top of the mainmast. It floated down the rigging toward me. My scalp crawled. Then it turned away. For unimaginable minutes it floated back and forth along the mast. Suddenly it blinked out.

Long ago, Da had taught me tricks for staying under water longer and longer. He had also emphatically told me they were extremely dangerous, and I should not use them, unless someone's life was in real danger. Now someone's life was in danger. Mine. Some tricks applied before you were submerged. Some tricks applied when you were under water. Time and again, the water went over my head, driving me into the gunwale. I held my breath. Once and again, and then a third time, I was down so long I started to see black. The last time, my sense of balance insisted that I was upside down, that *Northstar* was recovering from a roll the wrong way. And then I was down so long I had to start to exhale. One bubble, another, a third. I started to cry, unashamedly, because I was sure I had done everything I could, and I was still about to die. *Northstar*'s stern popped high into the air. I gasped for air.

One thing I was not was thirsty. Torrential rain poured from the heavens, soaking me through the all-weather gear. I had but to open my mouth and the spill off my rain hat poured down my throat. I had no idea how long the storm went on. I was totally focused on the now, because the waves this moment could kill me.

Suddenly, the lightning stopped. The wind dropped from unimaginably wild to a gentle breeze. The waves were huge, but no longer wild and wind-tossed. Looking over my shoulder, I could see why it was still dark. The lights in the sky were the northern stars. The pale silver in the great distance must be moonlight. It was after nightfall. I tried to remember what I had done, and memories all blurred into each other. Earlier, for a while all had been totally black, lit only by lightning bolts. Had that been last night?

The clamorous pounding of the thunder faded into the distance. I listened hard. I heard nothing. Any surf would be enormously noisy. I must not be close to a shore. Where was I? Well off the coast, it would appear. Well off some coast, anyhow. I checked my course. I'd been going east of south, and that was still true, though in what was now only a breeze the storm jib—which I could just barely see, what was left of it—would give me little speed indeed. I went back to the pump. *Northstar* didn't appear to be taking water, now that the hull was no longer being worked by the waves.

First the stars were overhead, then visible toward the southern horizon. Finally the moon peeked through the southern clouds. It was last quarter, not that far from setting; I would have dawn soon enough. Then, surely, I would see land, at least from the top of a tall wave.

My stomach reminded me I had not eaten in untold hours. Was it the next day, or the day after? I couldn't tell. Surely not more than that. I was bone tired, but not yet drowsy. Locked in the chest behind the wheel were emergency biscuits, rich with raisins and dried nectarines and honey. Clumsily, I managed to open the chest, pop the storage locker, slip out a pair, and slam everything shut before a wave could soak the rest. I leaned against the wheel and began, hungrily, to nibble. The biscuits were dry and tough, but still sweet beyond belief.

The sky brightened from steel to pink to robin's egg blue. Down at the horizon the sun, a blinding ruby chip, peeped above the horizon, at first when *Northstar* rose a wave crest, then visible more and more often. Those had to be hills, cloud-shrouded, into which the moon was setting. Southwest was the only land in sight.

I lowered the tattered storm jib—I'd be a week sewing its rips, in fact it was more rip than sail—brought out the jib and mainsail, and came about toward land. For sure, it was not Starlanding, so my money would be worthless, but I could rewater and take a nap. I was alive, bruised where I'd been battered into the gunwale by the waves, and so tired I ached when I moved. It took me quite a while to realize that I was sweltering because I was in direct sun, and storm coats do not breathe. At least I was not becalmed.

The storm winds were gone, the waves were dying, and I had a good breeze over my shoulder.

What was the coast on which *Northstar* was closing? I didn't know. Nor did I see any towns. Buildings might be lost in trees, but windmills are easy to spot. At some point I was going to need to rethink my approach; landing in this high a surf would be suicide. South along the shore, though, there seemed to be a break in the coastline. I tacked, the sun now warm on my face, steering a course well out to sea.

A harbor! At least, a broad opening of several miles in the coast line, with waves that clearly were not breaking as they rolled into more protected waters. I dropped the mainsail, proceeding into the calmer waters of the bay under jib alone. I saw no homes, no lighthouses, no buoys, but there were lines that perhaps were unpaved roads. As I passed into the inner bay, I sighted two long stone piers. There were no buildings, just the two piers. I weighted a line and started taking soundings. *Northstar* does not take that much water, but with the sun angle and chop I could not see bottom. The water was plenty deep. As I closed on the piers, out went the bumpers and down came the jib. I'd timed it just right. My speed carried me around the end of the pier, letting me coast along until I reached a mooring point. The stern line went over one bollard, a gust made it a bit tricky to snag the other bollard with the bow line, and then I hauled in and set spring lines.

Grass grew between the cracks in the pier. A layer of windblown sand lay on top of stone pavings. Down near the end of the pier a small tree had taken root in a cranny. There were no buildings, none at all. If my boat blew away, I would be truly stranded. . I put out my bow and stern anchors, both with double line. With some thought I grabbed more biscuits, the nearly empty water cask, my sunhat, and the sandals I'd stowed days earlier. I set out inland.

There were fields, and places where the grass grew thinly. I looked at the lines in the field. It was an outline of a town, roads, buildings, walls, but everything was flat. There were no traces of people. There, however, inland a ways, up a slope, was what was left of the town aqueduct. It was an open channel, ten feet above the ground, ending in broken stone on the ground. The last arches had collapsed. There must once have been a reservoir for the aqueduct to fill, but it was not there any more. By now I had finished the last of the biscuits I'd brought. My clothing was salt-soaked, just starting to dry. I marched up to the end of the aqueduct, and resolutely walked into the fall. I remembered to fill the water cask. I didn't have soap, but rinsing the salt from my hair was delightful. There was no one here, no one had been here in a long time, and it was a brightly sunny day, so I squeeze-washed my clothing and spotted where I could nap. My clothing I spread where it would dry, hanging from tree branches in the sun. I would be a few feet away, resting on equally tall grass in the shade, my sunhat to protect my face. I did remember to check for nettles before I lay down.

I may have awakened slightly, once or twice, to drink more water. When I finally woke up, it was sometime at night. The moon was high in the sky. My clothing was where I had left it. The sun and land breeze had dried it, enough that I could dress without feeling damp.

###

Made in the USA
Las Vegas, NV
13 May 2023

72023166R00256